Cleelok, Book III
The Belegs

by

Sean Nuber

FRITTER AND
BOONDOGGLE

Contents

Chapter 1

Vrric was done with Vatlisi. Or, more accurately, Vatlisi was done with them. All of them. Even Clerin. Oh, Vatlisi had understood how horrible their prince was and that his death was not only sanctioned by Lembin itself, but even ordered by it. Albeit a bit belatedly, Tureyn threw its entire weight behind the regime change. They sent scores of delegations to calm the local royalty, giving several prominent families instant elevations in stature. They sent skilled labor and engineers to rebuild the heavily damaged palace. They showered praise upon Clerin and the Toswin name. Everything to show that this was a top-down decision made by Fluens for the benefit of Fluens. Everyone in the coterie besides Clerin was relegated back to the foreign quarters of the city and were strongly encouraged to keep their heads down and mouths shut. Even Vrric.

This shuffling out of sight seemed to affect Trela much less than Vrric. He was a little annoyed that Clerin did not fight to keep him by her side, though he did understand her predicament. No, Trela looked at the time they got in the background, out of the Fluen public's eye, as a gift. She immediately sent her spies out to track down any of the Cabal's weapons, writings, affiliate members, anything she could think of that might still be in Vatlisi. The Tureyn delegates were happy to hand over everything related to the Cabal that they found in the palace during the restoration. They just wanted to regain the peace and stability, which took regaining the city's trust, which meant letting the foreigners perform any required dirty work— as long as the good citizens of Vatlisi did not get their suspicions aroused. It was a symbiotic relationship of necessity, in which both parties shifted between parasite and host.

Vrric was provided with a nice, but modest, room at the far end of the Luften Quarter. It was in the back of the inn, on the third floor, near the entrance to the attic. It was difficult not to think they were hiding him away. But the meals were good and the innkeeper friendly, truly he had little to complain about. He was vaguely disappointed after sneaking into the attic and finding little but dust and old furniture, but he could not blame anyone for that.

It was the feeling of being trapped that bothered him more than anything. During the day he was stuck in the Luften Quarter at best, stuck in his room at worst. The night was actually not that bad, he was able to travel to other quarters, chat with fellow adventurers, be of some use to Trela. It was the daytime that ate at him. He tried sleeping then, but it was difficult with the light, noise, and stuffy dense air. He meditated a lot and hung out with his fellow trapped Luftens, but they seemed to be able to rest easier than he. It was amidst this heavy boredom that he heard the footsteps.

Someone was walking past his door. The light from under his door, diffused due to the general lightness of his room, darkened almost imperceptibly as a hint of a shadow passed by. The footsteps paused, but then continued. Vrric, no longer willing to be patient for the sake of security or secrecy, jumped up from his bed and ran to his door.

"Aha!" The exclamation pierced the hallway as he threw open his door. There was no one there, however. He heard footsteps around the corner, so he jogged after them. He exclaimed once more as the turned the corner, but there was only the fleeting corner of a cloak. He sped himself up, hoping to catch up before the wearer of the cloak could make the stairs. He was too slow, but whoever it was obviously went up the stairs, not down. That would be their undoing since Vrric knew the attic only had the one entrance. He smiled to himself with the thought that they had trapped themselves but at that same moment wondered if he had left the door to his room wide open. He was concerned about it, but not so concerned that he turned back and let his prey escape. He bounded up the stairs two at a time hoping to close the gap as quickly as possible.

Vrric slowed when he reached the top. Nothing was moving, nothing caught his eye. They could not have gotten far; he had been fairly close behind them. He tried to examine the dust on the floor, but that had been disturbed by his earlier foray in the attic. There were tables and chairs and unrecognizable things all hidden under various discarded bedsheets. He did not want whoever was up there to escape behind him, so he started to pull the sheets off the furniture, one by one. He had barely gotten a quarter of the way into the room when someone short and skinny leapt from underneath a sheet and scurried hurriedly towards the exit. Vrric lunged and half-tackled them. It was a youngish Fluen covered in soot and anger, who kicked and bit at him.

"Let me go, you have no right!" It appeared to be a girl.

"I just wanted to talk to you." Vrric had more to say, but her hand snaked out in claw-like fashion to scratch his face. He barely parried in time, letting her go in the process.

"You can't just chase everyone who walks by." She was somewhat crouched, eyeing the exit behind Vrric.

He knew she was right, that he had been in the wrong to run after her, but it was almost instinctual to chase after one who was fleeing. For his part, he was certainly more intrigued than scared. She did not look either, she just looked angry. Curiosity got the best of him and he kept his body between her and escape.

"I said let me go." Her brows furrowed to a sharp point over her nose.

"This is a Luften inn and you certainly don't work here." He did not want to sound more accusatory than he was, so he followed himself up in the silence. "Who are you here to see?"

There was a pause as she eyed the exit some more, he could see her calculating in her head. She suddenly relaxed and straightened a little. Her arms crossed in front of her instead of out to her sides. Her brows kept their angry furrow, however. "Escha. I am here for the Luften spy, Escha."

"Ha, Escha's not a spy." It came out naturally, just as a truth. That was not her job in the coterie, technically she was a scout not a spy. As the silence extended, he wondered at the statement. If Escha was doing some reconnaissance work for Trela, could it not appear as if she were a spy?

"That's what Thiale told me she was." The girl kept her arms crossed but her brows weakened slightly. "She pays for information is what I hear. That's what a spy does, amongst other things. I need to be paid, so I found some information."

"How about you give me the information?" He stood up straighter, allowing an escape route around him. He kept his muscles ready to pounce, though he was not sure if that would be proper after he was already reprimanded.

"I don't know you."

"You don't know Escha either."

"Yeah, but I know *of* her. I've never heard of you." She looked at him askance, pausing for a moment. "Nope. Not you. My information is only for Escha. I have a description of her and everything."

Vrric thought about offering her more money than Escha, not that he even knew how much she expected to get paid for whatever her information was. What was the point, really? He had already bothered her enough. He was still intrigued, however.

"Fine, I'll take you to her." He smiled at her and though she did not smile back, she did appear to relax a little.

He turned and went back down the stairs, listening to make sure she was following, but not looking back. They were soon in front of Escha and Torpalin's door. He raised a hand to knock, but the girl tapped him on the shoulder, stopping him.

"Escha?" Her voice was powerful but not loud.

"Yes, hello?" There was a tiny commotion heard behind the door.

Vrric turned and raised an eyebrow to the Fluen. "Just making sure," was her reply.

The door opened and there was Escha. Vrric thought he could see Torpalin in the background, sitting on a chair. It took her a brief moment, but Escha's smile found her mouth. "Come in, come in."

Vrric let the Fluen enter first. He followed slowly behind, pulling the door closed behind him. Escha made a shooing motion, getting Torpalin to stand and wander over to the bed to sit down. Vrric sat down next to him. Torpalin grunted quietly when he sat but did not speak. There was still a small miasma around him. He had never fully recovered his gregarious self after the Tlana attack. Vrric wondered if there was some healing regime or something that could be done for him.

"I hear you pay for information." They were at a tiny table with wooden chairs, the Fluen was sitting opposite Escha.

"Intelligence. I'm paying for intelligence, not information." Escha smiled and so did Vrric. It was the same clarification that Trela had used when confronted with Rewista's warpack.

"Well, what if I know where a knife that glows in the dark is? No spells around it whatsoever, no magic of any kind." The smile on her face was a little smug, a little self-assured, but it was certainly something that Trela would be willing to pay for. Which meant that Escha would as well.

Vrric was not quite sure how, but all the coins that went into the coterie seemed to go through Trela before leaving again. Even if they came from a specific source outside of Trela or her direct warriors, such as the money from Tureyn that came through Clerin. No one seemed to care and she was fairly liberal with spreading it around to where it was needed, so he guessed it did not matter much. He had certainly never brought any coins to the group.

"Well now, that is intriguing." Escha nodded slightly to herself. "You know where it is, but were unable to bring it to me?"

For a split second, the girl looked nervous. Then her back straightened and she took a breath. "It is at the bottom of an old cistern. In the basement of an abandoned house. I... I sleep there sometimes. You can see it glowing down there in the distance."

"How do you know it is a knife?" Escha paused and twitched an eyebrow. "I mean, is it so far down that you just see a slash of light, or can you truly make out the object?"

"What color is the glow?" Vrric could not help interjecting.

"Well, it's a slash of green. I know what you are getting at, but we all know it's a knife. Eralyn saw the guard throw it down there." She looked between Escha and Vrric, as if he could somehow corroborate her story.

It was at that moment he realized they did not know the Fluen's name. Escha had not asked when she opened the door, nor when they sat down. He wondered if she assumed he already knew it. They had arrived together after all.

"I think you are going to have to show it to us before you get paid." Escha bowed her head as she quietly rummaged through her pouch. She pulled out a copper crown and slid it across the table. "This should hold you until tonight. Come back here shortly after dusk."

"Thank you, I knew you were the right one to talk to." The Fluen nodded politely to Escha, stood, turned, and left without another word.

Vrric listened to her footsteps as they faded into the distance. After it was quiet for a moment, he looked over at Escha. "Think she'll be back?"

"Oh, yes. I have no idea as to whether or not the knife is what she says it is. I would not even be overly surprised if she attempted to fake the glow. But she will surely be back. She will not be satisfied with one small copper." She tapped the table with her finger a couple of times. "What was her name again?"

"I never said. She, ah, never told me." The heat of embarrassment crept up his face. He wondered why he had not spoken up when he had first realized the omission. The conversation had just happened so fast. Honestly, he had been off his game the entire day.

"No matter. She'll definitely be back." Her eyes darted over to the bed and back again. "Want to grab lunch in a bit? We were thinking of heading down to the common room soon."

"Sure, sounds great." He figured that was his cue to leave.

Vrric walked down the hall, turned a corner, and walked a little more. To his consternation he realized that he *had* left his door open while chasing after the Fluen. He cautiously entered and made sure there were no hidden intruders. Nothing seemed out of place. He shut the door and laid mostly on the bed, letting his legs dangle off the side. He berated himself silently for a little bit. He was certainly not thinking about things very thoroughly. He felt like he was tired a lot, not sleeping during the day and still adventuring at night, but that was a poor excuse. His thoughts were wandering and he must have dozed off for a moment. He awoke to Escha lightly rapping on his door.

They ate and talked quietly on a wide range of safe topics. There were not many others in the common room while they were down there, but it was best to keep good habits. Though Torpalin had gotten quieter over the last several moons, Escha seemed to be opening up a bit more. It was as if she were taking up the slack. Vrric enjoyed it, she was probably the Luften in the coterie that he knew the least about.

Afterwards, they went their separate ways, to their separate rooms. Vrric did his best to get a good nap in. It was going to be several hours before nightfall and he needed to shake some of the cobwebs from his mind.

The nap was so successful that he only woke to the sound of Torpalin's heavy knocking on his door. It took him a moment to get himself oriented and off the bed. It took another couple to get dressed. Finally, he was ready to leave. His apologies met with an open hand and smiling face.

"Escha bade me to wake you a little early, she's not even ready yet. We were hoping you got some rest." Torpalin looked good. Even better than that, he looked happy. Vrric grinned back at him.

"Good, we should definitely harass her while she's finishing getting ready." He wiped the sleepers from his eyes as he shuffled out of the room.

The Fluen was in the room with Escha, both of them sitting and chatting quietly at the tiny round table. They did not look up immediately, but eventually Escha smiled over at Vrric. "Feyazki, meet Altiola. Altiola, meet Feyazki."

"Finally, a formal, non-threatening introduction." Altiola smiled at Vrric. It was a warm smile, one that looked genuinely amused. "Isn't that nice?"

"Yes, yes. It is a pleasure to meet you." He almost yawned as he grinned back at her. He hoped it did not overly distort his face.

They were out on the street fairly quickly, enjoying the low light of the quarter moon. Vrric had imagined there would be more of the coterie joining in, but it was just the three of them. Apparently even Malghain was out busy with other errands for Trela.

They shifted from one city quarter to the next easily since the guards all knew them at this point. It was the regular citizens they were supposed to be avoiding. Of course, that was not always possible. There did not appear to be any Fluens staying home during the afternoon, and nighttime was barely better. Though they seemed to have less organized events, communal events, than the Pyrans did, Fluens definitely enjoyed wandering about in small groups. Especially in the shallow dark of the evening when they were out in droves, sitting at small exterior tables, sipping wine, watching everyone walking by. And those that were walking watched the seated ones. Basically, the typical Fluen evening had made sneaking about quite impossible. Anything hidden had to be done late at night or early morning; any time earlier than that left them conspicuous enough that it may as well be done at a comfortable hour.

The slid from street to street, being watched from bored eyes half-covered with lazy eyelids. The citizens inevitably noticed and some were surely angry at the foreigners, any foreigners, but most did not seem to care, especially as the small group was being led around by a Fluen. It must have seemed an odd procession, unconsciously or not they were lined up by height with Torpalin in the back and Escha in front of Vrric.

It took some time to get to the Fluen Quarter and some more to find the warehouse that held the cistern. It was empty of life, but there was a lingering warmth in the air. Vrric wondered if there were those who made the warehouse their permanent home. There were odd knickknacks in corners and along walls. Nothing largely domestic was visible, no sleeping bags or cots, no cooking fires or pots. There were a couple of torches lit at one end of the warehouse and it appeared that some sections might still be being used by some disparate businesses, but the dim expanse lent an air of dereliction about the building.

Altiola grabbed a torch from a wall sconce and brought them to a lonely corner. There were stairs that spiraled out of view, down into a basement. Even walking down the rickety stairs did not set off any alarms for Vrric. Even the dilapidated basement felt lived in enough to keep it from feeling creepy. It was not until they crossed much of the area down there, back to the other side, and arrived at a sealed cap of a cistern that the hairs on the back of his neck began to lift. The cistern was sunk into the basement floor, with a large hatch that had a wheeled rotating dog lever on it. The hatch covered almost a quarter of the entire cap and the wheel was a larger diameter than Torpalin's chest was wide. They stared at it in silence for a couple of seconds, listening only to the sputtering torch.

"The guard dropped it down there." Altiola pointed in the direction of the hatch with her thumb.

They stood around for another second, not saying anything, before Torpalin finally shrugged and walked over to the wheel. He had to stand on the hatch itself to properly get at the wheel. He had his hands on it for a moment before straightening back out. "This opens outward, right?"

"Yes, of course." She smiled at them all.

Vrric had not thought about the situation being a set-up until that moment. He squinted hard at Altiola for a moment. She appeared the image of innocence.

"Wait. Just in case." Vrric stopped Torpalin as he was beginning to turn the wheel. "Let me give you a featherfall. Mekkinderto!" He stepped back away and turned towards Altiola. "Not that I don't trust you."

"I can assure you that the hatch opens outwards. Who makes a hatch that opens the other way?" Her mild annoyance turned into something a little more appraising. "You're a mage, huh? I was wondering what you actually did."

Torpalin spun the wheel until the dogs were removed from the locks. He stood over the wheel for a moment grinning, then glanced over towards Vrric. "So I can just fly up and pop this thing open?"

"Well, you're not really in control…" It had been while since Torpalin looked that happy, so rather than argue about who was controlling what or whether or not he could shift the featherfall after casting it, Vrric decided to just give it to him. As close to under his breath as he could muster, he cast, "Narkinderarc!" He smiled up at Torpalin and nodded. "Go for it."

Torpalin grinned even wider and gripped one side of the wheel with both hands. Vrric pulled up on Torpalin and Torpalin pulled up on the hatch. It swung open easily, no sticking rust tried to hold it down. Once the hatch was at the halfway point, Torpalin yanked it open the rest of the way. The clanging reverberated throughout the basement. Vrric left Torpalin floating up there while he covered his ears. Escha did the same. Altiola tried, although holding the torch in one hand only allowed her to cover one ear. They were stunned for a moment before Torpalin spoke back up.

"Well, the Fluen was right about one thing. There is definitely something glowing green way down there."

Escha and Vrric shuffled near the large opening. He squinted and peered for a moment before it caught his eye. There certainly was something very small, long and thin, and glowing a little. Looking at the cistern from above, he had not realized just how deep it really was. His instinct was to drop something down in there to see how long it would take before it hit the bottom.

"So, here we are. I've upheld my side of the bargain." It was Altiola's voice that wafted up from behind them.

"Ha! No, we do not know what is down there yet." Vrric interrupted Escha's speech, which was probably quite similar.

"Hey, float me down there." Torpalin was smiling enough that Vrric could not refuse him.

Vrric hopped up to the side of the opening to be able to watch Torpalin descend better. Altiola grumpily tossed her torch over to Torpalin, which he deftly caught. Slowly Vrric began to lower Torpalin into the cistern. He was laying somewhat flat, arms and legs spread out, his face pointed directly at the green glowing object. Vrric had a mischievous thought of pushing him down faster, for just a moment, just to give him a jolt, but quickly thought better of it. Torpalin was about halfway down when he started to speak.

"There is definitely something here. And it does look like a dagger. I think..." Then just screams. Full-throated, chilling screams. There was a fluttering in the dark interior of the cistern, as if by a hundred bats, or a thousand moths. The torchlight was splayed sporadically around as many tiny objects cast their shadows upwards.

Vrric yanked him back up as quickly as he could. As Torpalin was finally crossing the threshold, headfirst as if he were standing on solid ground, Vrric could see the full terror on his face. It was frozen into a scream, eyes screwed shut and mouth wide open. As his legs finally passed the opening, Vrric thought he saw something else. A black gloved hand that was grasping Torpalin's leg let go and slipped back down into the cistern. It happened so fast that Vrric was unsure that he saw it.

"Tlana! There's a Tlana down there!" Torpalin got himself half crouched at the exterior of the cistern. His hands brushed all over himself, as if he were scraping water off of his flesh. "You! You did this to me!" With a great lunge he shot forwards and upright at the same time. His right hand easily scooped up Altiola by the throat. She floated there, eyes bugged out with fear and the inability to breathe, grasping his hand with both of hers, trying to alleviate the pressure.

Suddenly Escha was on his arm as well. She had both of her hands on his, pulling herself up in a vain attempt to loosen his grip. He was still for a long moment, holding both Altiola and Escha up with one arm, face red with rage or fear or something, with several prominent veins shooting up his forehead like an upside-down bolt of lightning. Vrric was unsure if they were there due to the emotion or the exertion, maybe both. Escha was screaming something to Torpalin, he was still screaming about the Tlana and Altiola's perceived betrayal. That was when the rumbling began. It started at the bottom of the cistern, low in register, felt more than heard. Vrric pried his eyes away from the spectacle in front of him to stare at the open cistern hatch. The floor began to shake as the noise increased in intensity. Tendrils of black smoke began to waft their way upwards, spiraling and splitting as they emerged. There were about three, maybe four, that were about the diameter of Clerin's forearm, branching into more smaller ones like a tree growing and blossoming in front of his eyes. A panic rose within him.

"Surdeeleclo!" He cast the biggest spell he thought he could get away with and still stay conscious. He was wrong. The lightning lit up the cistern like it was noon, doing more damage to more enemies than he had planned on, drawing more energy from himself than he had wished. He did his best to cut it off before it drained him completely, but the glow continued down the cistern even as his vision dimmed. Just before he hit the ground and lost consciousness completely, he could hear Escha yelling at Torpalin to close the hatch.

When Vrric awoke he was on a stretcher. He was still in the basement of the warehouse, but he could hear plenty of other derlians around. Even before he opened his eyes, he could hear Ryshial and Serghno. He almost smiled, but then the headache hit him. When he thought too much about the headache, he grew nauseated. Before long he had rolled onto his side and vomited. There was not much in his stomach, so it was more of a dry heave, but it made him feel miserable just the same. Nochiel cast some healing spell on him and he slid back into sleep.

When Vrric awoke again he was back at the inn, in his own room, in his own bed. It was not Nochiel next to him when he finally opened his eyes, but Croy. He smiled and tried to speak, but it came out as a croak. Croy jerked to attention at the sound; he must have been napping or, at the least, not paying any attention. After the healing spells and water, Croy explained what happened after he had passed out.

"There really was a weapon down there, one with a Yaven in it. Ryshial, Serghno and I finished what you had started. Well, it was Ryshial mainly, though Serghno certainly helped." Croy was still modest to the point of self-deprecation, even after all this time. An odd mixture of nostalgia and frustration flooded over Vrric, but he was too tired to chastise Croy for the belittlement. "Torpalin and that Fluen said that they did not notice any other smoke escape, but that can be hard to notice sometimes. Ryshial figured you had stunned whatever you had not destroyed, so we were able to get here in time after Escha had found us. It's hard to know for sure…" Croy trailed off for a second before realizing he had gone quiet. "Well, once we felt the cistern was cleared, we searched around down there and found the knife. We have it stowed with the others now."

"I should talk to Ryshial about that. I'm unsure of how much smoke makes up one Tlana, but I thought I hit it hard enough to rupture one pretty good." Vrric took another small sip of water. He was half propped up on some pillows, but his neck was still bent oddly while he drank. He wondered if there had been more than one Tlana down there in the cistern. It had certainly felt like he had been drained further than he should have. "So—do you think it was all destroyed? In the end? Or do you think it just dissipated?" He was always unsure if any Tlana were actually killed. Maybe they just coalesced somewhere else.

"Well, there were an awful lot of Vijen leaves at the bottom of the cistern, if that makes you feel any better." Croy smiled.

"Yes, actually, it does." Vrric smiled back.

They spoke about Trela's growing pile of Yaven trapped items for a while, naturally shifting to how long it was going to take for them to find everything in Vatlisi. Then they talked about nothing for a while. Finally, the conversation shifted to the Cabal and how long it was going to take to track all the members down. That was mainly up to Arnasta, but Vrric started to wonder if he could be of some use in that area. He was sure Trela would consider him "too wounded" to be wandering around the city at night, so maybe he could help in other ways. At least for a couple of days. For now, however, he felt like he needed more sleep. It did not take Croy much convincing and Vrric was soon alone with his pillow.

When he awoke again it was Clerin who was in the room. She was not hovering about, however. In fact, she did not immediately realize he was awake. She was diligently scratching out a letter onto some parchment by the tiny light of one candle. She had a habit of placing the feather of the quill in her mouth while thinking of the next sentence. It was cute. It took a quiet cough from him to pry her eyes away from her work.

"Ah, you are finally awake." Her eyes went back to her writing as soon as the comment was out of her mouth. Rather than stop her, his awakening merely quickened her up. She furiously scribbled sentence after sentence. She always had amazing handwriting however, so he doubted the addition in speed would diminish it. Even her tiny notes that she left for him appeared to be painstakingly swirled out by a professional scribe.

"Yes, finally, and though I am starving it will take me some time to get myself put together enough to be seen in public. So… take your time." He lay there a moment longer, contemplating how much time he would need once he threw off his covers.

"Not to worry, I only have two more letters to write. I doubt you would beat me getting ready even if you had not been asleep for much of the day." She smiled at him but kept her face focused on the parchment in front of her.

"You writing back to Tureyn? Don't they have a delegation here?" The bed was quite comfortable and he was having a hard time escaping it.

"Of course they do. And I am not writing back to Tureyn, but to their delegation here. As well as writing to the delegation for the Vatlisi palace. We meet every day, we talk every day, we discuss every day. That is not enough for us Fluens, however. Whenever there is something seriously amiss, something that involves delegations, we need everything written down. Someone, somewhere, must approve all of this and they want someone's signature on the requests so they can know who to blame. Unfortunately, both delegations have seen fit to keep the blame on me, so it is my signature they desire." She held up a densely worded page and blew on it for a moment, setting the ink. "I think they see me as a representative of Lembin, which means I am blameless, which means they think they can get more than they should if they can just convince me to formalize their requests. It is terribly circular."

"So, are they taking advantage of you? Or, more precisely, are they taking advantage of each other through you?" Vrric decided to get up and start shuffling around.

"Maybe. There was certainly a lot of damage done to the palace and I certainly have no idea of what it will take to fix it. Tureyn does want it restored as well, and to its full former glory. I think they think the restoration will give them more sway once a new royal is put in place. Luckily I have nothing to do with that decision. We should be long gone by the time those negotiations begin." She started another letter.

"Does Trela have an estimation of that?" He began to get dressed. He would like to bathe at some point, but food was higher up on his priority list.

"Not that I know of." The scratching began anew.

"I was thinking of helping Arnasta after this. She might have a better idea of how much more hunting is required." He wandered about the room a little more, finishing getting dressed.

"That would be nice. I hear she is swamped, even with Ryshial helping out." She did not look up.

Eventually Vrric was dressed and ready. Clerin was still writing, so he lay back on the bed perpendicular to its length, his feet still touching the floor. He stared at the ceiling for a little while, listening to her scribble away. Though the sound was a bit hypnotic, he was fairly sure he did not fall back asleep.

Eating was great. His chat with Clerin was great, as always. The bath afterwards was great. His body craved movement and his mind required stimulation. Clerin eventually had to head back to the palace to mediate between the delegations, so Vrric decided to seek out Arnasta.

The Pyran Quarter was fairly small, so that Trela's coterie had most of the available rooms in the few inns that existed. Though Arnasta and Serghno were not at their inn, Vrric had already explored most of the area and he knew just where to check next. They were dining at one of the few eateries that did not have an inn associated with it, a place clumsily called The Campfire. It was billed as the "best grog in Vatlisi" and he was told the claim was true. Of course, it did not have much competition for that market, so he was never quite sure if the grog was actually great or not. For himself, he preferred mead, though he was getting quite fond of wine. Vatlisi had an enormous selection of wine and Clerin seemed to have no end of knowledge about it. He had hoped to be able to spend more time with her, wandering around the large city, enjoying its myriad flavors, but they never really found the time.

"Sit, please, have some grog." Serghno appeared to be enjoying himself immensely and was quick with the invite. His ready smile made his mustachios twitch a little, moving with his face but following their own complex vibrations.

"And what brings you all the way to the Pyran Quarter?" Arnasta pushed the carafe towards him.

"Boredom mainly." Vrric poured himself something small, just enough to be polite. It was still early.

"You were laid out by a Tlana and now you're bored?" Serghno laughed heartily. "You know it took Ryshial, Croy and I to finish that thing off. It was mightily weakened but still feisty." He lowered his voice conspiratorially. "I think it gained strength during the time it took us to arrive. It certainly seemed to gain some during our fight."

"While you were fighting it?" He had been about to shift the conversation to Arnasta, but he was started to get intrigued by the emphasis Serghno was adding.

"Oh yes. It would be getting beat down and you could see it shift over by the green glowing knife and then, whoosh!, it would come straight for you." He gesticulated wildly with his hands. "I think maybe it was sucking energy out of the trapped Yaven." He nodded to himself a couple of times. "I told Ryshial that as well. Not that I can tell what she thinks about anything, she tends to ignore the likes of me."

"She does not. She respects you Serghno, you know that." Arnasta chided him and gave him a small elbow.

"Not like she respects either of you. I just throw fire. That's typically very useful and I do it well, but I don't think it means the same to her as it does to the warriors." He took a small drink. "And these are certainly atypical times. We're facing atypical enemies."

"Well, if you really think they can draw energy from the trapped Yavens, that is something to be concerned about. Did you tell that to Trela? Or Clerin?" Vrric took his own sip.

"No, not yet. But I'm telling you. Croy agrees with me as well, you should ask him." He glanced at Arnasta before looking back at Vrric. "To be honest, I thought he would have brought it up."

"Well, we did not spend much time together. I've just barely recuperated enough to get bored." They all chuckled.

Vrric helped Arnasta for a while. It seemed to him that the Pyran inn had even smaller rooms than the Luften one. All three of them were sitting around a small wooden table which was jammed near the bed. Serghno would read the descriptions of what they were attempting to track down and both Arnasta and Vrric would cast spells to try to find what or who he was describing. Apparently all of the easy objects or derlians, those that they had some sort of physical tie to, such as a favored item from a missing derlian or the empty sheath for a missing dagger, had already been searched out. Now there was just descriptions of rumors. Vrric began to think Escha's method, that of paying street urchins for information, might have been more effective at that point. Trela popped in from time to time, obviously trying to keep her boredom at bay but also not trying to bother or interrupt. She always seemed to be doing something, or at least planning something. And, if not, she became miserable.

It took about two hours before Arnasta hit on something. Vrric was hoping he would find something first, but this sort of thing was not his specialty. It was the description of a low-level guard who may or may not have died during the fight with the Cabal. According to Arnasta, the scales were tipped towards the guard still being alive but being underground somewhere.

"It smells of mold and mildew. There's a dripping sound that echoes. There's a taste of iron, maybe blood, and the occasional sound of chains. Hmm… Maybe to the southeast from here. Maybe towards the Gaen Quarter." Arnasta had her eyes closed and head down, her hair covering part of her face.

Serghno nodded to Vrric. "We should accompany her as softly as possible. We don't want to break her concentration if she's found a thread." He took the official description of the guard and folded it up while whispering. He put it in his vest while attempting to scoot his chair back quietly. Vrric started to move when Arnasta suddenly looked up.

"Ugh, no it's fine. I've lost it." She stood and moved her own chair into a cramped corner. "We can try again when we are a little closer. I am pretty sure we should head to the Gaen Quarter."

Trela met up with them in the hallway. Vrric wondered if she had heard some tiny movement from two rooms away and scurried out to be able to run into them. It would not have surprised him.

It did not take them long to get to the quarter. Once there, they decided to call upon Croy, figuring the quiet and stillness of a friendly room would help with the tracking. Luckily he was in. Vrric had figured he might be out with Knill or someone.

Croy let them in and let Arnasta get situated. She sat a table and took several deep breaths. Vrric sat on the bed, just trying to be out of her way. Serghno stood near her and carefully reread the description of the guard she was searching for while Trela stood off to one side.

"Narfindersfe!" She cast another tracking spell. Her eyes fluttered closed and her hair fell in front her face as she dipped her head. Her hands were palm down, flat against the wooden table, fingers splayed. After several long moments passed, she spoke back up. "I think I have him. He's... he's somewhat close. Serghno, lead."

She stood slowly and carefully. Serghno swiftly but quietly, without scraping anything across the wooden floor, moved everything out of her way. He sort of led, but he kept looking back at her and kept his shoulders somewhat sideways. With his girth it was almost humorous, but he was quite graceful about it. He was obviously well practiced.

They shuffled out of the inn that way. Serghno crab walking sideways, Arnasta with her face turned towards the ground, Vrric and Trela following, and Croy, lastly, closing everything up behind them. There had been enough weirdness in the city lately that they barely got stared at as they were crossing the common room towards the exit.

Several turns, several streets and a couple of alleyways later, they stopped outside of a modest residence. No one said anything, all of them just waited for Arnasta to guide them. Vrric even tried to only move while she was moving, though he was not positive that helped. After staring at the ground in front of the house for a while, tilting her head and swiveling her waist as if she were seeing through the dirt, she finally spoke again. "Someone knock, we'll have to get permission to enter."

Vrric went past them all to arrive squarely at the door. He knocked three distinctly individual times, slowly and insistently. He glanced back at the others while he was waiting, trying to listen for footsteps. Suddenly, the door opened and there stood an alluringly attractive Fluen. She almost smiled but then stopped. She glanced behind him to the others. Her body appeared to be poised to flee, it was turned inwards slightly, but then she stood her ground.

"You're here for the wounded guard, aren't you?" Her blue eyes flashed with a sudden anger. "He is about to die, you are almost too late. He's downstairs in the basement being interrogated as we speak. You can save him or capture me, but you can't have us both." She ran like a loosed arrow up the stairs. Vrric was stunned for a second while Serghno pushed his way past him. He moved aside as a smaller Arnasta walked towards him. They were headed around the other way, down the stairs. Their eyes were set downwards, and grim. Trela pointed aggressively at Arnasta as she bounded after the Fluen. So he followed the others down, glancing back often enough to make sure they were not being followed.

Serghno shuffled down the stairs quite quickly, if not quietly. There was a door at the bottom landing that Vrric could spy beyond his comrades. He wondered what spell Serghno was going cast once he reached the door. Something to melt the lock or burn through the door or something else spectacular. He did nothing of the sort, however. He flung himself bodily against the door and bashed it open. It swung open with a large boom and struck the perpendicular wall with a loud crack. It was not as if Vrric was listening to any voices before the door opened, but there was an audible silence once it did, one that could only follow after noise. The dense quiet was pierced by a muffled cry. The cry, though muted, was quite energetic and thick with desperation.

All three of them rushed towards the noise. It was not completely like a maze down there, but there were many different rooms and hallways. So many closed doors to run by, so many twists and turns to make. When they arrived at the door most likely to have the Fluen they were looking for behind it, Serghno sallied forth without a pause. He leaned his considerable shoulder into the wood causing a loud creak then crash as the door flung itself inwards.

There were three derlians in the room. One was tied to a chair, naked and covered in blood. Vrric quickly surmised who their opponents were since they both drew their swords. He shot one with an arrow of flame, "Nardepiarc!" Serghno cast a similar spell on the other. Croy ran towards the wounded prisoner and began healing him. It was only afterwards that the idea hit him. What if they should have kept the captors alive for questioning? What if the soldier they were after was one of those that were splayed out on the ground before him and they had been supposed to kill the prisoner? It all happened so quickly.

His fears were soon lifted once he realized how much attention Arnasta was pouring on the young guard. She untied him, removed his gag and cast a healing spell of her own on him, all the while talking to him in a low soothing voice. This was apparently the Fluen she had caught scent of earlier.

Vrric performed a cursory search of the Fluen he had killed. He was hoping that there would be a signet ring, or badge of some sort, that tied the body to the Cabal. Or, even better, some form of paperwork, maybe written orders of some kind. He found absolutely nothing of value, however. Nothing indicative of the dead Fluen's past.

He tried the next body while Serghno wandered off a bit, exploring the large basement more thoroughly. Trela arrived and smiled as she waved her dagger, silently bragging of her success catching the sprinting Fluen. Croy was standing near Arnasta, taking an interest in the young, wounded guard. Vrric did not find anything indicative on the second Fluen either. As Serghno returned he glanced over, hoping to catch a smile that would indicate that Vrric had found anything useful, but no. The young guard had a wide-eyed crazed look that constantly shifted focus between all of them. It was disconcerting to be sure.

"I know you've been through a lot here…" Arnasta looked around at the scene, nodding slightly to herself. "…and recently… But I need you to focus on me, okay? I'm going to ask you some direct questions and I just need you to answer as truthfully as you can. Can you do that for me?" The guard glanced at Vrric before settling back on her.

"Yes, I can do that. I wish to be helpful. You've saved my life." He stretched his jaw around for a moment while he rubbed his wrists.

"Good, good. Now we'll start off simple, okay? Your name is Treynith Wasolein, correct?" Arnasta appeared to be concentrating, though her eyes were still smiling at Treynith. He nodded.

"You have a sister named Mika, yes? An older sister?"

He nodded again, but more hesitantly that second time.

"These warriors who were beating you, who were most likely going to kill you, they worked for someone specific, yes?"

He nodded again, eyes squinting slightly in thought.

"We need you to say who they worked for. Without prompting. Just to make sure we are all thinking the same thing. We don't want to lead you anywhere."

"The Cabal of Lochom, that's who they work for—or, who they worked for. That's who you want me to name. It is the name on everyone's list, the only topic of conversation in the entire town. You could not lead me there if you tried, I'm already there waiting for you." His eyes darted back and forth but the rest of his body appeared completely calm, his hands still absentmindedly rubbing his wrists.

"Well, let me know if you are here as well—your sister works for the Cabal. And not as some simple guard, no. From what we hear, she's much closer to the top of the pyramid than the bottom." Arnasta had seated herself across from him, with her chair spun around backwards, with her chin on her arms on the high wooden back.

"So you've come here and saved my life just so I can betray my sister?" His eyes deadlocked on Arnasta's. "You should've just let me die."

Trela shifted herself into his view, to the side of Arnasta. The young guard's gaze naturally followed her. She settled herself into a stance, her feet shoulder width apart and her arms crossed in front of her.

"Maybe. That's certainly an option. That's certainly still an option. But we are not asking for anything we don't already know, not yet at least." Trela's spine was straight and rigid. "And who knows, maybe you're not betraying her at all. If she gets us the information we are seeking, we may still find an amicable way to part."

"So… why were friends of your sister beating you to death?" Vrric knew that Trela was trying to build up to something, but he could not help himself.

"Even if they were in the same organization—" Treynith turned to look at Trela after the word 'organization' "—which I'm certainly not saying that they were—" he turned back to Vrric "—even if they were, it would not mean that they liked each other. Or even worked well with each other. You see, in an organization that is kept solvent through fear, fear *of* your superiors and to induce *in* your inferiors, there is a precarious balance. Everything is braced off of everything else. Once the top of the pyramid is cut off, all the supporting pillars rush in to fill the position, causing further destabilization. There will be killing until the one strong enough to wrest control emerges from the morass."

"That is excellent news!" Serghno chuckled lightly to himself.

"Except for the smart ones. The patient ones." Trela brought the focus back to her. "There are those who've decided to go to ground rather than fight for control."

"You've got guards at every gate, checking all those who wish to leave against their lists. How many derlians have you even let leave? Fifty a day? There are even merchants who can't get past the shining walls." He shook his head.

"We are not going to leave until it is finished. Understand? We have the full backing of Lembin, which means Tureyn, which means Vatlisi. We cannot allow anything to escape, nothing with knowledge. Not a book, not even one sheet of parchment. Nothing that understands Yavencide, what it is or what it does, certainly nothing that knows the how. Certainly not a mage." Trela stared hard at Treynith.

"How did you know she's a mage?" His eyes got big at that. They darted once or twice quickly between all three of them. He then took in a deep breath and let it out slowly. He was staring at the floor in front of him, looking despondent.

"She had the brains, the skills, the ambition. 'Why not,' she said, 'what is a Yaven anyway? They are like dangerous animals. They feel no remorse when they kill us, why should we feel any for them?' Anyway, it paid more than we had ever dreamed of. It was fun while it lasted. You are warriors, right? Mages? You have all killed plenty?" He looked up and stared at them, his eyes white and gleaming amongst his bloody face. "It is all a cruel business." He paused for a moment before continuing. No one interrupted.

"If you won't give Mika amnesty, give her amnesia. Please. For me. Forget her past and only judge her for her future. She raised me when no one else would. It wasn't easy, I can tell you that!" He chuckled to himself for just a moment. "All right, all right. I suppose you need some information from me now. Whereabouts and all. Thanks for listening to me. And thanks for removing my gag." Treynith smiled for a second, still staring in front of him, when he took another deep breath. "Nardepipri!" Whoosh! He was engulfed in flames.

Vrric instinctively jumped back and shielded his face from the intense heat. He was completely taken by surprise, and it took several moments before he had the presence of mind to cast a healing spell. "Lumliderarc!" He got the flames out, but it was too late. Much too late.

They were all stunned. They stood there, spread apart since they had all leapt backwards, staring at the charred corpse. The stench was horrendous. It took some time before someone finally spoke up.

"I can't believe he got that out so quickly. I just… wasn't expecting that." It was Serghno who ceased the silence.

"I should have realized as well. To be honest, I'm just happy to have jumped back in time." Vrric stepped back a bit farther.

"We'll try to reverse track him, there's certainly enough of him left for that." Arnasta had her hands on her hips, calmly surveying the situation. "Maybe find his home at least."

They were soon all trying to root through his small shack, jostling and bumping into each other. After several minutes of fruitless searching, Vrric decided to wait outside in the light rain. At least it was quieter there. He walked away from the door a bit, not wanting to draw attention. They were in a sea of shacks, however, so he was pretty sure someone was noticing. They were at what was basically a barracks for the palace, inside the outer courtyard, except instead of having a hundred bunks in a large room there was a hundred shacks in a gigantic courtyard. Vrric was amazed that Arnasta had found Treynith's home, he doubted he could have found the courtyard. Though, after thinking about it, it should have been obvious that he had been a guard for both the Prince and the Cabal. It made Vrric wonder how many of the other guards there were part of the Cabal. Should they not just search everything? He kept getting told that there were not that many members and that they had tracked most of them down already, but it did make him wonder. How did Treynith navigate through all these other Fluens on a daily basis without them realizing what he was up to? Or did some know and not care? Should they be discussing the possibility of collaborators and what to do about them? Being outside surrounded by shacks was making him paranoid, he decided to go back inside and help with the search.

They found nothing incriminating, of course. No written missives with instructions, locations, or lists of names. Arnasta cast several spells and found a belt that she hoped was a present from his sister. The buckle was ornate with a carving of a dolphin within its brass. It did not look like it had been worn often, maybe three or four times from the appearance of the leather, and it was found rolled tightly in a silk-covered box. They decided to bring it back to the inn since, to figure out if it was a present from someone besides his sister, Arnasta needed to spend some time examining it exclusively. Vrric felt a little useless, a bit of a hanger-on, while she did all the heavy lifting.

Instead of winnowing down their numbers at the inn, they added several. Estfale insisted on coming along to protect Trela and they brought Jalin, just in case. They would certainly not be able to move about the city unnoticed.

Trela was excited at the prospect. It had been a few days since they found someone higher up in the Cabal hierarchy. They wanted to move as quickly as possible since there was a worry that Mika might try to escape the city. Would she know the Cabal had tortured her brother? Did she know they had found him? Did she know he was dead?

Croy stayed with Arnasta in the room, healing her as she cast her spells. Vrric was down in the common room, surrounded by Pyrans, while they waited. He was not sure where Malghain had ended up, but Trela kept insisting they already had too many warriors. "I know we can't rest much before chasing down Mika, that time is of the essence, but isn't it a bit contradictory to then say we have too many warriors? If you want to find her and crush her, shouldn't we use an overwhelming force?" He was instigating a conversation more to fill the time than for any actual concerns.

"We need swiftness and agility, not strength. Besides, she's a mage, so if we need anyone else with us, it should be Ryshial." Trela smiled at him and sipped her juice. No wine before the fight. "I am quite confident with the force we have assembled, aren't you?" Her smile got bigger, but he did not bite.

It was not long before Arnasta came downstairs indicating that she had a direction. Not a location or anything, but at least a direction. They all stood to leave and slowly shuffled out. Trela was right, in essence; there were already too many derlians to move swiftly.

Vrric wondered what would happen if someone other than his sister had given Treynith the belt as they were shuffling. Would they arrive at the wrong spot, tracking the wrong Fluen? He kind of wanted to ask Arnasta but she was at the head of the line, concentrating heavily. She could probably be able to tell who they were tracking anyway; it would have been rude to suppose otherwise. So he brought up the rear silently, following just behind Jalin. The ubiquitous rain was gaining in intensity.

They walked all the way across town, going slowly and a bit haphazardly. They must have been following a path taken previously by their prey. It had too many turns and jogs to be otherwise. Vrric would pay more attention when they switched directions or turned a corner. He was trying to figure out if Mika had stopped at any of those locations. Would they be stores, friends' houses, ambushes? Nothing jumped out at him and he was never quite sure. Maybe it was just that Arnasta was having a difficult time with the tracking. Finally, after a couple of hours, at the start of dusk, they came to a building. At least Vrric assumed it was the one they were looking for since Arnasta came to a halt in front of it.

It was a large stone building, near the northern docks that jutted out into the Clatsvol Sea. The stone looked rough and gray, the mortar was gone or fading making it appear to be dry stacked, though there was no light visible through the joints. The air coming off the building had a faint musty odor to it, but that may have been the sea breeze that was wafting ashore. They stood for a moment outside, all of them staring at the tall and imposing façade. If anyone was in there, they would surely have noticed the group of derlians gathered at the front door. There was certainly no sneaking up at this point, which made Vrric a bit nervous. There was a wide flight of steps leading up to two large wooden doors that were banded together with black iron. There was no filigree on the iron, just wide straps with large square heads on the lags.

After about half a minute had passed Trela coughed loudly behind Arnasta, but it did not cause her to turn her head. She merely stood there, staring at the same imposing door that they all were. Another half minute passed.

"If we are not to approach the door, we should at least move out of sight. And, if not out of sight, at least out of an archer's reach." Trela spoke quietly but she had an insistent tone to her.

"I think Mika is in there but, if so, she is very deep." Arnasta tore her gaze from the building. "I am having a difficult time sensing her. You are correct, of course. Maybe we should find a nearby spot from which I could probe a little further." They all nodded in agreement.

They quickly found a more secluded location. Then they waited patiently in the lengthening shadows for a little while as Arnasta concentrated on her magic. Some of them more patiently than others.

"We should enter and get closer to whatever Arnasta is sensing. Being this far out is obviously not helping." Trela eventually had Jalin sneak around to the door to get it ready. "Even if she comes back completely sure that this is the wrong place, I've gotten too curious about it. If there are innocent civilians in there we'll surely apologize. Worst case, we might need to have Clerin spread some more of those Tureyn crowns about."

Jalin got back before Arnasta finished. They waited for a few more minutes before she finally reengaged. Her brow was furrowed in frustration. "It's… inconclusive. I am pretty sure Mika is somewhere in that building, probably in whatever basement it has, but I just can't get anything definitive no matter how I try." Arnasta looked a little crestfallen.

"No problem at all. We figure we just need to get you closer. Jalin has already opened it up for us." Trela had a mischievous grin on her face, but it quickly smoothed out into a warm smile. "You've been fantastic Arnasta, you really have. And I don't just mean here, today. You've been the most essential weapon in our arsenal. Without you, we'd still be scouring the palace for rogue guards. Really. Once we get back to Agoge, you can relax for the rest of your days in luxury." Arnasta started to shake her head, but Trela raised her hand to stop her. "Don't argue with your Queen. Besides, there will be plenty of grueling work to perform until then."

They all hugged the wall as they tried to sneak up on the door. Jalin, of course, led the group. She did not make a sound, it was almost eerie. Vrric even had a hard time seeing her and he was watching her intently. Both Trela and Estfale were incredibly quiet as well, but the rest of the group completely ruined whatever secrecy had been started.

The door opened and a mass of light tumbled out. They quickly entered and shut the doors as quietly as possible. They were in a massive entrance hall encircled by torches fitted within black iron scones. A large, empty, hall. It felt like their breath was echoing.

They let Jalin explore for a few moments, standing bunched up at the entrance. Vrric strained his ears while he stood but could not hear a sound beyond the low background noise they themselves were making. "Mekfinderclo!" He said it as quietly as possible. His main concern was calling attention to himself, so he cast something small just to try to sense anyone below them. To get a rough feel of what was down there.

There were several derlians nearby, underneath them. He tried to tap into their communication, to hear their whispers, but he could not quite get the mumbling sounds to coalesce into words. He probably should have cast something more powerful. He then tried to get an idea of rough numbers. How many were down there? He figured that would be the simplest information to get, but still had some difficulties. There were several of them, at least two, maybe up to five. Soon Jalin had snuck back to them, and Vrric let his spell dissolve.

"I saw at least four derlians down in the basement, grouped around some canal or underground river or something." She kept her voice low, barely above a whisper. "I didn't examine anywhere else and certainly did not try to get too close. They were arguing about something rather heatedly, I did understand that."

Trela glanced over at Arnasta. "You are fairly sure that Mika is here, correct." She nodded in response even though her brow was still furrowed. "Then we should go. Quickly. We do not want them moving from their spot. Hopefully they are still arguing and won't notice us at all."

As quickly and quietly as they could, they headed downstairs. Jalin led the way, with Estfale and Trela close behind. As they neared the bottom of the spiraling stairs, still out of sight from the doorway, they paused. Jalin slowly crept forwards. There were several voices that wafted over to the stairwell, their argument was quiet but heated. Vrric was in the back with Croy and sidled up next to him.

"Cast a shield spell." He spoke so softly that he was almost just moving his lips. Croy squinted at him in slight confusion, so he again mouthed the words. This time Croy was paying enough attention to figure it out.

"Narteclufclo!" Croy was almost as silent as Vrric.

The voices paused for a moment just after the spell was cast. Vrric hoped that they had not sensed it. As the voices returned, they were louder and more animated. He could still not quite figure out the individual words being said. He wished he was closer to the front.

It was barely perceptible amongst the rest of the voices. "Go. Go now." Vrric was not positive, but those were the words he thought he heard. He frantically made a shooing motion towards Trela and Estfale, to get them to round the corner, but they had their backs to him. Suddenly Jalin pulled back from peering around the opening. Her eyes were wide and she jerked her thumb towards the arguing derlians in the other room. They all sprang into action.

Trela and Estfale ran around Jalin, past Croy's shield at the entrance, and into the room proper. Serghno followed closely behind. Vrric did his best to jostle pass Croy, Arnasta and Jalin.

Trela and Estfale were screaming and drawing weapons while Serghno was shooting fire from his hands. As Vrric finally entered the room he saw someone leap into a canal. "Nardepiarc!" He decided to throw some fire as well.

Trela reached the third derlian with a thrown dagger and, just like that, it was quiet again. It took a couple of moments before the fires burned down. The third derlian was coughing and sputtering, the dagger had found his throat. Vrric took precious moments peering around the smoky room, anxiously expecting another member of the Cabal to leap out and attack them. When he realized that was not going to happen, he ran to the wounded derlian and attempted to heal him, but it was too late. They would be unable to interrogate anyone.

The entire room was made of tight-fitting gray stone blocks. Each block was shaped differently, hand-carved to fit snug in its one location. The faces were not jagged by any means, they were chiseled somewhat flat, but they were certainly rough with small protuberances throughout. The ceiling was a large span barrel vault which supported the floor above. That, along with the two spiraling stairwells that came down, gave the room a round feel even though the floor and walls were quite flat. Running through the middle of the room, splitting it in half, was a small river confined by a canal. It flowed in from a round hole in the wall whose perimeter was encased with sand-colored brick and out through another of the same construction. The roundness of the hole allowed some breathing room, but Vrric was quite afraid that, if the diameter were to decrease much, it would quickly turn from a canal into a pipe. If that were to happen, there might not be enough time to cast a spell.

"That had to have been Mika. We have to follow her." Trela was shedding her larger sword and other heavy or bulky items. So was Estfale.

"We have to have a waterbreathing spell on all of us who follow her." Vrric spoke his fear, then decided to follow up. "We may not want every single one of us to follow her into the dark, swiftly moving waters.

Trela paused mid-buckle. "Well… I guess I see your point." She frowned while her fingers froze on her leather belt. "I guess you and I. Arnasta for sure. Maybe another mage… Serghno, can you cast waterbreathing?"

"I've never used it beyond recreation. But, yes." He and Arnasta had been talking quietly off to one side, but Trela now had his attention.

"Good. It would be nice to have more but, as you alluded to, we do not want to get trapped down there without a way to breathe." She finished removing her belt that was holding her scabbard.

"My Queen…" Estfale tried to protest but he was quickly interrupted.

"Your Queen needs to track down this Luften as quickly as possible. That leaves you behind protecting the others." She nodded towards Croy and Jalin. "It cannot be helped."

Estfale visibly bit his lip but did not reply. Vrric quickly removed his bulkier outer clothing. Soon they were all ready, clad only in their undergarments.

"I'll cast one for all of us to begin with. If we get inundated with water, cast something on yourself and Arnasta. I'll stick with Trela." Vrric could feel Trela's impatience begin to pierce his back. He took a deep breath. "Eqetecfluclo!"

Trela leapt into the water and swam like a fish. Vrric was unsure where she had learned to swim. He leapt in immediately after her. Rather than hearing it, he felt the vibrations of Serghno and Arnasta entering the water. He swam as hard as he could just trying to keep up. They were soon in pitch blackness. "Mekmorfflurefpi!" A small globe of burning water lit the canal in front of them. Vrric made it heatless, so as to not enter into combat with the surrounding water and extinguish itself. They still had their heads above the water, more from habit than need, so the glow lit them up from underneath, casting eerie shadows. The tunnel they were in was round and made of the same sand-colored brick as the entrance. The water filled about two-thirds of the tunnel at that point.

There was a small current they were able to swim with. Trela was moving fast enough that he had to swim fairly hard to keep her within sight. There was a rumble in the distance that worried him a little. It felt like the current was picking up, almost imperceptibly at first, but then gaining in momentum. The rumbling increased in volume as well. Eventually Trela's head popped up from the surface as she slowed her swimming. He pushed forward for a little longer to get closer. The rumbling was beginning to sound like thunder. Vrric looked back and could barely see the heads of Serghno and Arnasta bobbing along. He turned back to see Trela pointing and gesticulating. He had no idea what she was trying to sign to him, but he could certainly tell what was coming up. In another moment he could see it as well, the end of the tunnel. The sound was deafening now. Whoosh! Trela dropped from view as the water leapt from the tunnel out into the open air. Whoosh! Before he had time to react to Trela's ejection from the tunnel he began his own.

Vrric flew sideways with the water, somewhat skimming the surface. He also plummeted in a shallow parabola towards a pool of water below him. There was not much time to look around, but he did notice the shaft he was in had several other waterfalls, from varying heights and directions, that emptied into the same pool below. When he hit the surface of the water, the air was knocked out of him. He got sucked under with the water he was traveling with and then pounded from the continual cascade of the various waterfalls above him. He was grateful that the waterbreathing spell was working well since he surely would have drowned without it. Though he was not necessarily close to losing consciousness, he was having a difficult time getting his bearings. He was unsure of which direction to swim but knew that Serghno would be coming down on top of him at any moment. He decided to swim downwards, away from the thundering vibrations of the waterfalls. He swam a bit horizontally as well but had no idea if he was heading towards the tunnel he just exited, or away from it, or off to one side. He just swam as hard as he could.

Vrric finally floated up towards the surface. He was near the middle of the shaft, as far away from each individual waterfall as he could be. The sound of all of them combined echoed about the tall room. It was deafening. Soon all four of them were treading water near the center. Trela tried yelling at Arnasta for a while, but it was impossible to hear anything specific. Of course, Arnasta knew what she wanted and shouted her own spell into the roaring room. After a little while, she waved for them to follow her, and she dove under the surface. They swam for a while after her, somewhat circuitously, as she honed in on which tunnel to enter. The entrance was deep in the shaft, near the bottom of the pool. Vrric still had his light spell and he let it float near Arnasta. Part of his mind was trying to sense how long the waterbreathing would last, the other part mindlessly swam along behind Trela.

Arnasta, and the current, was moving slower than Trela had been earlier. When it was obvious that they might spend a lot more time stuck underwater, Vrric began to get their attention. Since he was controlling their light source, it was not too difficult. Once he got them all to stop and congeal together, he recast the waterbreathing. "Eqetecfluclo!"

Did he really need to? Maybe not, but it made him feel much better to have it completely refreshed. They then swam along at a leisurely rate for some time.

Eventually the pipe ended. They popped out into what Vrric assumed was the Clatsvol Sea. He could feel the water getting saltier as they rose towards the surface. He was not exactly sure how, but he felt it on his skin and eyes. They all bobbed to the surface at the same time. They were beyond the shining white walls of Vatlisi proper, those were visible and still imposing even at their distance. They could also see some of the wooden docks protruding out into the sea extending beyond the protective embrace of the walls. There was a wide beach next to them with scrub brush, turning greener fairly quickly beyond.

Vrric heard a cry of alarm coming from the beach. He looked over to see a derlian jump up from where she was resting on the beach and head inland. She had a mane of dirty blonde hair extending out from her face in tight curls. Skinny and lithe, she was certainly a Fluen. She had to be Mika. They all swam as fast as possible to get to land. Trela was in the lead, then Vrric, Serghno and Arnasta. It was difficult to jog as waterlogged as he was. He wondered how long Mika had been able to dry out. He tried to ignore his fatigue as they jogged along, even though it clung to him as surely as his wet clothes. He let Trela decide where they were headed and just did his best to keep up with her.

The brush became greener and larger, which made the trail they were on more of a path. It was getting to the point where a derlian could veer off the path and hide well enough to let them pass by. Vrric was just beginning to worry about that when they came upon a clearing. Suddenly a stream of fire was heading towards them. "Narteclufsfe!" He cast a shield spell just in the nick of time.

"Mekdepiarc!" Serghno ran past the shield and attacked Mika. Vrric assumed he was just feeling her out by casting a lower spell. They were supposed to capture her alive, after all.

Vrric hid behind his invisible shield and took a brief moment to survey the situation while Serghno and Mika traded fire. It looked like her back was to a birch tree. Rather than attack her directly, since she obviously had a shield of her own she was casting through, he decided to hit the tree.

"Eqedeelearc!" The lighting came straight down from above and burst the birch in twain. Mika went flying from the shockwave and crumpled many rods away. They all ran over to her.

Mika was moving slowly but still conscious. Trela had a short sword drawn and held near her throat, though that was probably a lesser worry. Serghno and Vrric flanked Trela, ready to rain immediate destruction down upon her. Mika glared up at them, looking entirely feral with her wild hair and angry blue eyes.

The shock of seeing her stopped Vrric in his tracks. It was Laqual's wife! He instantly recognized her and, by the look in her eye, she instantly recognized them. He stared hard at her lips, waiting for her to cast an illusion.

"You win, you win. You can put your weapons away." Her face suddenly changed from feral to almost charming, though her hair stayed frayed out, framing her head like the mane of a lion. She smiled up at them with bright eyes and shining white teeth.

"Who says we are taking prisoners?" Trela smiled back.

"I do." She coughed for a second and waved her hand at Trela's sword, which was warily retracted. "Because I know where the blind Gaen is headed."

Chapter 2

"Because I know where the blind Gaen is headed." Mika laughed hysterically. The words were a punch in the gut. She was right. If she knew where the Blind One was, or where he was going, they could not kill her. Could they beat the information out of her? Probably. But Trela wanted much more than some vague information. Mika may have been a large part of the Cabal, and for that Gorbanax would not allow her to live for too long, but the Blind One had betrayed them for the Cabal. Trela wanted punishment, she wanted vengeance. She needed to see his downfall, she needed to orchestrate it. For that, she needed Mika's help, her willing assistance. For that, she was willing to let Mika survive longer than any other member of the Cabal. Not only survive, Trela was willing to pamper her. She wanted the utter destruction of the Blind One that badly.

Trela sheathed her sword. The others took a step back, watching for her lead. "If you are lying, your death will be a thousand times more painful than if I kill you now."

"I know, oh how I know. I have met your type before and seen what they are capable of. With my own eyes." Mika sat up in the space left around her. "And I was not sure if I could betray my fellows. Besides the honor of loyalty, they would surely make my death as painful as possible if they knew I was even speaking with you." She stood and brushed herself off. "But I found out something about myself today. Something that I had not known before." She grinned at each of them. "I don't want to die at all. Not even painlessly. So I hope you have more honor than I and at least let me live until we find the Gaen. And, if I have proven my worth, maybe a bit longer?" There was a mischievous look to her grin. As if she were enjoying herself. Trela was not sure what was going on in Mika's head, but she knew that Mika could not be trusted. And that she would make herself incredibly useful for as long as her freedom was dangled in front of her.

"So, where is he headed?" Trela grinned back at her.

"He's heard there is something etched on the wall of a cave at the edge of the Eidyon Peninsula. He is heading there." She nodded to Trela. "I'm assuming I have your assurance of my safety."

Trela nodded back. "Is it there? Whatever he is looking for?"

"No idea. I'm not even sure what he is looking for. I do, however, know the cave system he wants to search. My grandmother is from there." She pointed in the direction of the sea. "I still have family up there."

The words made Trela think of Mika's brother, who had immolated himself rather than betray anyone. She wondered if Mika knew of his death, let alone his sacrifice. She did not get a chance to ponder for long, however.

"The Blind One can travel great distances in the blink of an eye. How do we know he has not already found the cave, the carving, that he is looking for?" Feyazki interrupted her thoughts.

"Because I told him about the wrong caves. He will not find what he is looking for at the outset. He will need to ask the locals about which caves lead where, and the locals do not trust strangers. They do not even trust other Fluens from Tureyn, let alone a blind Gaen. And if he runs into any of my family up there, they have been instructed to stymie him as much as possible and then contact Vatlisi. I have not received word from anyone that he has arrived on the peninsula yet." She seemed quite pleased with herself.

Trela was unsure of what to make of the story. It seemed incredibly convenient. Almost too incredible to be true. She racked her brain trying to think of a question that could prove it either true or false. How would Mika know which caves were the wrong caves? Trela was silent for a while as nothing clever enough came to mind.

"Who was supposed to give you the word? In Vatlisi, I mean." Feyazki was staring hard at her, studying her reaction.

"A friend at the Mages' Guild." Her smile slipped a little as she studied him in return.

"A member of the Cabal?" He cocked an eyebrow. "How do you know that your messenger is still alive?"

"He is alive. Or, at least, he was." Her smile dropped completely. "What are you getting at?"

"Your brother is dead." His voice was deadpan. His face betrayed no emotion.

Trela looked over to Mika. Her face, smileless, also betrayed no emotion. Her eyes stared fixedly on Feyazki with nary a twitch.

"My brother is not much of a mage. He would not have made a very good messenger." The air felt suddenly thick. "I am referring to Hupdor. He is my lover and I suppose you have murdered him as well."

"I thought you were handfasted to Laqual?" Feyazki looked momentarily confused.

"I can have a lover as well. Besides, Laqual died during the battle. You have killed everyone in my life, it seems."

"We did not kill you brother." Trela decided to intervene. "We saved him from the Cabal. He was being tortured by them, you see."

"He killed himself when we asked him about you. He immolated himself. With magic. Woosh!" Feyazki had an odd look on his face.

"Enough!" Trela made a hand gesture to Feyazki, hoping to keep him quiet for a moment at least.

"What? Am I supposed to lie to her?" He glared at Trela for the briefest of moments.

"He is correct. I would rather know." Her eyes were downcast, but she still did not betray her emotions. "That does sound like him. He was fiercely loyal…" Her voice trailed off.

"We really were not planning on killing him. From all accounts he was a low enough member of the Cabal to not know anything of import. Well, anything except for your whereabouts." Feyazki could not seem to stop himself. He crouched down and looked her in the eye. "If you need revenge, now is the time."

Trela searched Mika's face for any indication of anything. Anger, resentment, fear, planning some type of revenge with malice aforethought. But she was impossible to read, her face did not shift emotions. Did not show emotions. Her eyes, no longer downcast but now staring back at Feyazki, did not twitch. Her mouth did not twitch, her teeth were not clenched, her hands were not clenched. It was eerie. It was quiet and tense and the air was still thick. The conversation stayed in remission for what seemed like a very long time.

"Good. I had hoped you didn't need revenge. Again, we were not planning on killing him." Feyazki spread his hands briefly and then straightened. "Remember, I was there. She was there." He jerked his thumb towards Trela. "Most of our friends were not. Assume anyone else you meet was not." And then turned and wandered off back towards the sea.

It was quiet for another moment before Mika finally stood, still completely inscrutable, and brushed herself off. "I suppose I should be sandwiched by mages until I have gained some trust. I suppose I should follow him. Will you be following me?" She jerked her thumb towards Serghno.

"Yes and yes." Trela waved her hand for her to proceed.

They walked back to the beach. It took a lot longer on the return. She had not realized how far they had chased Mika in the heat of the moment.

"Do you wish to have some discussion here? Make a fire? Sit down?" Feyazki cocked an eyebrow to her.

"No. Or yes, but we can't." Trela looked at out the water for a moment. The rain was dying down, but the clouds above the sea were still quite ominous. Dark and brooding. Trela glanced at Mika, attempting to find any readable emotions upon her, but again, to no avail. "We need to head back as quickly as possible, Estfale will be getting worried. And, I fear, we cannot go back the way we came. We'll have to fly."

Feyazki flew them all back up over the white walls. It took less time than Trela had feared. Mika helped them find the building where Estfale and the others were, allowing Trela not to call attention to Arnasta's capabilities. Trela thought it appeared Mika was willing to be helpful even if she was no longer grinning, or maybe especially because of that. The real test would be when they asked her to help find other members of the Cabal. Would she be as willing then, when lives were on the line?

They all eventually made it back to the palace, some inn in the Pyran quarter would not do. Trela needed to feel Mika out. She wanted to be able to leave her unguarded, to pamper her as they tracked down the Cabal and the Blind One, but she could not trust her. Not yet. They assembled in a posh room with tables, couches with pillows, and tapestries covering the walls in vivid hunting scenes. She wanted Mika to be comfortable but did not want her wandering freely amongst the coterie just yet. So her access needed to be restricted. She wanted Mika to meet the coterie slowly, one-by-one.

In the room with the two of them were Feyazki, Serghno, Arnasta, and Ryshial. She would have let Arnasta head back to the inn for some rest but wanted her to be able to verify the veracity of any information they could get out of Mika. Trela decided the new face for Mika to meet should be Ryshial. At first she had wanted Estfale, mostly because she trusted his judgement. But she thought that another mage might be warranted, just to keep Mika compliant.

As an added benefit, Trela had come to highly regard Ryshial's judgement as well.

"We are going to start with some names and some locations to those names. Then, while that list is being confirmed, we'll ask you about yourself. Get to know you, know about your brother, to know how you became a mage, to know why you joined the Cabal, et cetera. Then we can chat about the Cabal itself. This is how we are to build the trust needed to give you some freedom. This conversation may take more than this one evening, which means you may be under constant watch for a couple of days. You will probably always be under some sort of watch, of course, but I do intend to get to know you well enough that I do not need three mages around you at all times. I intend to give you the opportunity to gain my trust. For without that, we will be hard pressed to track down the Blind One. That is what I need. That is why you are sitting here, in front of me, still breathing. You need to understand that my goal here is to track him down and destroy him. This makes you useful enough to me that I am willing to let you live. And, if you have been exceptionally useful, if you have proven yourself to me, then I might let you live beyond his destruction. You need to understand that you died earlier today, we killed you. You are living on borrowed time. You are, if you were a Pyran, my ghulzan." Trela had two of the couches pushed to be facing each other. Mika was alone on her couch while Feyazki and Ryshial shared hers. Arnasta was at a nearby table, quill and ink available at hand. Serghno was sitting with her, just in case she needed anything, with a map of Vatlisi at his hand.

"I have no idea what that word means." Mika looked a little tired, a little exasperated. "But I know what *you* mean. I live at your whim."

"Well, more like 'at your capacity to be useful,' but 'whim' is close enough." Trela tried to smile warmly at her but was unsure of what was really projected. The smile did not feel very comfortable, so she assumed it must not have looked very assuring. "To test your willingness to be useful, we will begin at the top. Who is Hupdor and where might we find him?"

"I did not say he was a member of the Cabal." Mika was leaning back on the couch, somewhat relaxed looking. She was looking more bored than defiant.

"Are you saying now that he is not?" Trela did not like vagueness. She surely did not trust it.

There was a long pause. "No, I am not. I'm just saying that I certainly did not mention that. You are just guessing and accusing."

"Call it a hunch then. I feel that your… what did you call him… lover? Yes. I feel that your lover is a member of the Cabal. Is this correct?"

"Yes." She gave a little sigh. "Though, in his defense, he did not want to be. I talked him into it. It took a bit of effort as well if that makes any difference."

"We will get to that, I am sure. For now, however, we need his location. Where might we find him?" Trela knew that this would define Mika's trustworthiness. If she gave him up and everything checked out, then she could be trusted. Everything else was just a story.

"He could be in one of three places at this point. He used to spend a lot of time at the guild hall itself. Though I doubt he is anywhere near there currently. He could be at his home, he has a little place in the back of the Fluen Quarter. He might be there, but I doubt it. Or he could be in his hiding place. That is in the middle of the Luften Quarter." She slowly got up and walked over to the table. "I suppose you would prefer if I showed you."

Serghno pushed the map over to her. Mika made circles and notations at the three locations. She then walked back over to the couch and flopped back down in almost the exact same position that she had gotten up from.

"Round him up and ask him. He wanted nothing to do with the Cabal until I cajoled him into it. Him and Laqual, both." She stared straight at Feyazki. "You want me to remember who was there when my brother immolated himself and who was not? You should know who was a full-fledged willing member of the Cabal and who was not. My brother enjoyed the money and the camaraderie but, as you said, he was at a low enough level that he did not really know what the Cabal was doing. Not specifically. And Hupdor… He knew what the Cabal was doing and did not care for it. He is… more sensitive than most." She paused for a moment, then turned her gaze to Trela. "Don't kill him without trying to understand him at least. Can I ask that of you?"

"I would like to think that the happier you are, the more willing you will be in helping us track down the Blind One. The more cunning, creative, and enthusiastic you will be." Trela bit her lip a little, trying to think of the right words. "I will not be taken advantage of. You understand that I know you will say anything to save your own skin, to save your lover's life. We will certainly talk to Hupdor and try to understand him, but how can we know what the truth is? The real underlying truth?"

Except that she did know the truth. The truth was that there was no way Gorbanax was going to allow Mika and Hupdor to live. No matter how helpful they were, how nice they were, how honest and trustworthy. They had knowledge that Gorbanax needed destroyed. It was that simple. So, in the end, it was Trela who was lying to Mika so that *she* would trust *her*. She needed to dangle the idea of freedom, of escape, just enough that Mika would perform the duties required of her, but not so low that she actually escaped. The freedom needed to stay illusionary. It felt a bit hypocritical of her, to demand of Mika the ability to convince her of trust, when she was faking that same trust. She tried to put the whole idea from her mind, for if she thought about it too much Mika would surely sense it.

Feyazki and Serghno left to track down Hupdor. Mika readily gave out other names and locations. Trela had Arnasta make sure they could be truthful but did not want her spending too much energy. Mika stopped at five names, stating the others she knew were dead or captured. Trela was not going to press her for any others until they had those rounded up. The only one Mika had hesitated on was Hupdor, which was a good sign.

"How did you become a mage?" Right as Trela spoke the words, she realized she needed a Fluen with her. A Fluen mage would have been perfect but even Clerin would have helped. Trela did not understand enough of how Fluen society worked to know if Mika were outright lying, let alone if she were merely stretching the truth.

"How did you become a mage?" Mika stared straight at Ryshial.

"My family was wealthy enough to get me a tutor once they realized I had some aptitude. I joined the guild as an apprentice and worked my way up through years of hard work." Rather than argue, Ryshial merely answered the question.

"Hmm... Oddly enough, that is similar to how it is typically done around here. I had been brought up on stories of Pyran savagery, that your whole society is based upon constant warfare. In my mind, I had assumed you had survived in the back alleyways of a dirty city, stealing bread and learning magic from anyone who would teach you. Each new trick earned through pain and abasement. Each syllable learned, each new spell understood, had to be wrung from the world like strangling an attacker. How depressing that I am incorrect. I was hoping to commiserate." There was a bit of annoyance in the gleam of her eye. "At any rate, that was how it was for me. I had no tutor, only a little brother to feed and protect. I joined the Cabal while I was still fairly young. They were willing to teach me magic without the same… requirements… as other teachers of mine. All that they asked of me was loyalty. Well, and to help kill some Yavens."

Trela opened her mouth to speak but was quickly interrupted. "I know, I know, the most horrible thing in the world is to kill a Yaven. Trust me though, it did not seem like it at the time. I was able to learn as much as I wanted and earn enough crowns to provide for myself and my brother. I had a roof that kept the rain out and a door that locked. Locked! And I had never met a Yaven before. What were they to me? Do you feel bad killing a deer to eat?" Her eyes suddenly met Trela's. "Do you feel bad slitting a derlian's throat? Anyway, that was how I learned magic. That answers your question, neh?"

"Yes, yes it does." Trela thought for a moment of how best to delve into her past without distressing her. "We are not here to judge what you did to survive, or to thrive. The morality of it all is up to others. I have certainly killed many, some who may have been innocent of everything except for being between my sword and my goal. It is not I who thinks it is the worst thing in the world, though I do find the concept repugnant—it is my understanding that it is more like eternal torture than simply killing something—but it is the Belegs who have decided to destroy everything pertaining to the Cabal. You just happen to be on the losing side of history concerning this. The Belegs created this entire world, and they were willing to destroy it if the practice of Yavencide was allowed to continue. In short, you will not offend me with any of your tales. I am just looking for honesty, a way to trust you enough… How about the upper echelons of the Cabal? What can you tell me about any of them?" Trela wished to avoid the subject of Mika's brother, at least for a little while.

"They're all dead. They really thought they could best you. The main leader of the Cabal that I knew was Hylaxia. She did not have a last name, a familial name, like most Fluens do. We were similar in that regard. She had a saying, 'Not over, not around, but through.' That was her in a nutshell. Always straight through. She did not believe in dodging or hiding. Her abrasiveness made others feel she was not a good negotiator, that there was no talking to her. But I found her style of diplomacy refreshing. It was also straight through, straight to the heart of the matter. What is the discrepancy, the disconnect? Find it, expose it, solve it. She said that it was always what was hidden, what was held back, that really mattered with most derlians. But not with Hylaxia herself." A wistful smile crossed Mika's face.

"She knew you were coming, you know. The details may have been a little foggy, but she knew something was headed her way. Her downfall was her confidence in her own capabilities. She thought that if she gathered everyone, and I mean everyone she had any control over whatsoever, and she swallowed your small group whole, brought you in close, allowed you to see the whites of our eyes, and she unleashed everything at once, hit you with everything she had, that she could strike though you. 'To finish it,' she had told me, 'once and for all.' " Another wistful pause.

"I really don't think she understood what you represented. She did not think the Belegs were sending an army consisting of warriors and mages of each race. She did not think there would be Yavens amongst you. She underestimated you, or overestimated herself, or whatever mix you choose. But she brought all she could bear. She gathered every warrior of skill, every mage of potency, every force at her disposal. I am sure there are some hidden somewhere and, as your tracker can attest, I have given you the names at my disposal. But you have already crushed the Cabal. There really are just tattered rags left."

"You are saying the Blind One did not tell her we had Yavens?" There was so much to the story, but Trela could not wrap her mind around that portion.

"To be honest, I never knew if he talked with Hylaxia. He spoke with the Prince and he spoke with Zipkol. I believe it was Zipkol that knew him well, though I cannot be sure. And even if he did mention them, he certainly did not indicate that one was unsummonable and another would destroy itself and everyone around it. We were not prepared for your onslaught, that is all I was trying to say. We figured the first ambush would cripple you and the second would finish you off."

"So, you were there at the end? You saw Baltuz enter Taglo? How did you survive?"

"I was hiding in the back. I had gone to get reinforcements, my brother amongst them, and when I returned it was almost too late. It was certainly too late for Laqual." Mika was no longer smiling. "I could have rushed into the room and died, like several of the guards I had brought with me did, but I chose to hold my brother back. Once the Yaven immolated everything we ran."

"Well… We'll get back to that. I would like to hear your side of that battle, but I need to understand everything you know about the Blind One. You see, we have been operating on the premise that he was betraying us the entire time. If he only gave partial intelligence to the Cabal, however, that would indicate he was not fully with them."

"Oh, he betrayed you, there is no doubt about that. It is just that he betrayed us as well." And her smile returned.

"Well, if he was not on either of our sides, I wonder if he was just working for personal gain, or what? Riches never seemed to motivate him, not that I know him that well." Trela could not imagine the Blind One just amassing wealth, or even power. He always seemed to have some plan or other. She would have to discuss this with Croy and, maybe, Aedon. "What was he searching for? You mentioned an etching… There has got to be a clue there somewhere."

"Really, I know very little about the cave, but it is supposed to have etchings of names in it. Yaven names." Mika had the decency to look a little sheepish since she had repeatedly said she did not know what he was trying to find.

"And you told him the location of the wrong cave?" Trela gave her a pass on the Yaven names and leaned in a little.

"Yes. He was looking for the oldest of the caves, there are several you see, and I gave him the location of the youngest." She sat back as Trela leaned in. "He will need a guide to find the older caves. They are hidden in a different area."

"Their entrance would be underwater, I presume." Ryshial spoke up. "The older caves."

"Yes, but not just that. They are under a glacier. A specific type of glacier, what we on the peninsula call an ice dam. They have a lake behind them that slowly fills with fresh water and when there is finally enough water back there, it floats the glacier and the water comes gushes out from underneath, sometimes destroying the dam as well. The floods are catastrophic. We do not allow any villages downstream from these since they sometimes give little warning. It can take decades for some of them, the smaller ones, especially if the dam has to refreeze. But this one has not lifted for at least a century." She nodded to herself, looking above them a little. "It is under this glacier ice dam that the entrance to the oldest cave hides. There have been mages so impatient to enter that they drilled through the bottom of the dam, hoping to leave it intact while they explored the cave. Some died in the resulting flood, some died trapped in the cave underneath. Or, at least, that is how the legends go."

"The Blind One does not need to wait for glaciers, and he does not need to drill into them, he can just appear beneath them." Trela could not detect any dishonesty in Mika during her story. It was a little far-fetched, but she made it seem as if she believed it fully.

"Yes, you've said. Do you know how he does that? Would he at least need know where to begin the search? In any case, I have not heard that he has arrived on the peninsula yet. If he has, he is lying low." Mika almost shrugged.

"And Hupdor is supposed to tell you when the Blind One is noticed up there… How did the two of you meet?" Did she really care about that? Not really. But she figured that Mika wanted to keep some information back concerning the cave, as a way of protecting herself. Trela did not mind waiting for the specifics.

They spoke congenially about nothing of import for a while. Trela enjoyed it, but Ryshial appeared to be a little bored. Arnasta was almost asleep at the desk, her head nodding periodically. After some time, Trela came to the realization that the others had not found Hupdor. They should only have been gone for a half hour, an hour tops. Still, it took almost two hours before Trela started to get nervous. Eventually she had Ryshial *whisper* to Feyazki. When that produced no results, she had Ryshial escort Mika to a holding cell while she figured out what was going on. She sent Arnasta to her room at the inn, making it an order when she argued to help find Serghno, and went to find Croy. She was starting to run out of mages.

Trela left with Croy, Estfale, Dartsyle and Jalin. Croy was hesitant at first, arguing that he should be guarding Mika, not Ryshial. But Trela was worried that tracking down Hupdor was a set-up, that Mika was going to attempt an escape, which meant she wanted Ryshial to keep watch over her. Not that Croy was not capable, but more that Ryshial was instinctively more distrusting than he was. Plus, if she had to admit it, Ryshial *was* a more skilled mage. Of course, she did not share these thoughts with Croy, she merely repeated her demands until he acquiesced. He came around fairly quickly.

They headed to where Mika had indicated Hupdor's hiding place was. Trela figured they would start there, then head to his house, then the mage's guild hall. That should have been the same order Feyazki and Serghno had taken. By the time they had gotten going it was quite dark, making the navigation a little harder even though they had a map. She was a little frustrated at herself. She should have just let everyone rest the evening away and started questioning Mika in the morning. She had been concerned about more members of the Cabal escaping, however, Hupdor in particular. And, she had to admit, she was a little trusting of Mika. Maybe too trusting. There was no conclusive evidence that Mika had betrayed them, not yet at least, but that did not lessen her frustration.

They finally arrived at the building. It was a large home in the middle of the Luften Quarter. It was a wooden structure three stories high, had a large porch with a small bench swing, and was covered with wooden scrollwork and filigree. She was sure there would be several accent colors painted on the filigree to bring out various architectural elements, but it was impossible to tell in the dark. Jalin went around to the back to make sure no one made a run for it. There were splashes of flickering light that escaped the interior curtains, occasionally casting shadows out onto the porch. Trela walked up and knocked heavily on the front door, leaving the others down below, off the porch. She did not want to cause alarm to anyone who was not part of the Cabal by sneaking in or breaking down a door or anything. Clerin had asked her repeatedly to be as polite as possible to the typical citizenry of Vatlisi and Trela did her best to oblige. Trela had grown impatient enough to raise her fist for a second knock by the time she heard footsteps. There was a scraping noise as the door opened a crack and a nose became visible from the bright interior.

"Do you know what time it is?" The voice was certainly annoyed, but the tone was held back in a manner of one who was habitually dignified.

"Yes, I realize it is late, but we have come by to check in on some friends who were headed this way. May we enter?" Trela attempted to keep her voice casually dignified as well.

"They left a while ago." An eye peered between the crack.

"I have not described them yet." It was hard to ignore the urge to shove the door open. "May we enter?"

"Two mages, a Luften and a Pyran. Not many Pyrans around here, typically." The eye glared at her. "I feel fairly confident when I state that I know who you mean and that they have already left."

"Then you understand we will need to take a quick look around. It is not that we don't trust you, but we need to make sure for ourselves." Trela showed her empty hands to the eye, thinking that would help somehow. "We mean you no harm as long as you meant our friends no harm."

"You know, this is why your kind is so despised around here. You just cannot leave well enough alone, can you? We are trying to enjoy a quiet evening." The voice stayed completely dignified, but it now sounded pompous and arrogant to Trela. She was unsure if it, itself, had changed, or if it was the way she heard it that had changed. "First it was your friends threatening us and now you."

"Oh, I haven't even begun to threaten you. You'll know when I threaten you!" She could feel her face get hot. She had to consciously remove her hand from the hilt of her short sword. "This will come one more time as a request. May we enter?"

"On whose authority do you threaten me?" The door did not budge.

"While a new prince is being found, Clerin Toswin is the regent. In this moment, I am acting as an agent of the regent." She took a deep breath. "And I have not threatened you."

"Well, I think she is a traitor to her race. There is no other way to say that. We, here in Vatlisi, have been too kind to foreigners for way too long. Tell me, young Pyran, do you have a Fluen quarter in whatever backwater you come from?" The eye glared hard and the voice lost some of its dignity.

"You are not in the Fluen quarter. Are you even a Fluen?" Trela began to wonder if this derlian was here to just stymie them, to keep them busy while something else was going on out of sight.

"That is what I thought. The answer is 'no' or else you would have responded to my question. You cannot tell us what is right, what is proper, especially when your own kind will not extend us the same courtesy." The derlian was going to continue, Trela was sure of it, but a hand came out of nowhere and grabbed the derlian by the forehead. The eye opened wide in surprise and then disappeared.

Trela pushed the door open immediately, more out of concern than opportunity, and stopped short when she saw Jalin holding the derlian with a knife to his throat. His arms flailed wildly for a moment, but not so wild as to get himself cut during the struggle. Dartsyle was behind Jalin. Trela was not sure when he had gone around the building. Estfale was behind Trela, weapons out. Croy was still at the porch.

"Let him go." Trela waived a little dismissively. She was grateful that Jalin had interfered, but did not want to hurt the derlian yet. She had to assume he was innocent, at least as far as Feyazki and Serghno were concerned. At least at the moment.

"This. This is the kind of treatment we get from the savage Pyrans." The Luften raised his voice as if he had an audience.

Trela motioned to Estfale and Jalin to search the house. Dartsyle stood nearby, but not menacingly close. The Luften drew himself up and glanced between the two of them, making Trela try to judge if he was going to run. He was older with big, bushy, white eyebrows which stuck out at odd angles. His hair was similar in color and unruliness. She quickly realized he was not thinking of escaping, just attempting to regather his dignity. Croy came in and closed the door, leaving the night on the outside.

"So, you were visited by our friends. You say they threatened you?" She decided to let him describe the encounter in his own way.

"Oh, yes. Not at first, of course. No, they first asked to enter, polite as can be. Nicer than you. They said they were looking for a Fluen. Someone named Hipcore or some such. So I let them in and told them I had never heard of such a name." His spine was straight and rigid.

"You are saying you do not know Hupdor, that you've never met anyone by that name?" Trela squinted at him. "We have been told, by his supposed lover, that this is where he goes when he needs to go into hiding."

"That is just what they said as well." His eyes got wide, pushing his bushy eyebrows upwards.

"And what did you tell them?"

"The same as I am telling you. I do not know him. I am not sure if I have ever met him. Maybe I have, I meet a lot of derlians, but this is certainly not anyone's hiding place." He pretended to think about it. Maybe that assessment was uncharitable of Trela, maybe he was thinking about it, but he just looked weird whenever he thought about anything, making her mistrust his intent. "No, no. That name does not ring a bell. Who is this lover who keeps implicating me in some nefarious scheme?"

"First off, what is your name?" That came from Dartsyle.

"Oh, my manners, where have they gone?" His eyes rolled in what Trela thought was insincerity. "My name is Wreyvaine. I am a mere merchant far from my native home, though I have lived here long enough to be able to claim a little Fluen heritage as well, if not direct blood. And who might you be?"

"Dartsyle, Pyran warrior. This is my first time in Vatlisi, basically my first time anywhere Fluen."

"Croy, Gaen farmer. My first time as well."

"Trela, Queen of the Pyrans."

"Your Majesty." He gave a quick, deep bow. It was a type of move that typically annoyed Trela, but somehow he seemed genuine when he did it. She could not detect even a hint of sarcasm in his voice.

"So, you were telling us how much you do not know Hupdor." She tried to steer him back on topic.

"You don't really act like a queen." His eyebrows wiggled a little as he talked. "Not that I've met many of them, mind you."

"Must be the different cultures."

"Must be. So… you must have killed Qizern then?" He was staring hard at her, measuring against something unspoken.

"Yes. In single combat." It was her turn to stare at him. "Are you hinting that you met him?"

"No, no, of course not." A smile broke out on his face and his shoulders and stance loosened. "But, unlike the majority of Vatlisi citizens, I have heard of him. I have heard tales of his skills, his prowess. You must be quite the warrior to have bested one with such a solid reputation."

"You were saying about Hupdor?" This came from Dartsyle.

"Yes, of course. Please, let us sit." He started to wander towards a large open room that held several sofas with a myriad of pillows on each. "I will tell you all about the vast nothingness that I know of him."

They followed him. Trela sat on a sofa across from him, while Croy picked one off to the side. Dartsyle remained standing, keeping himself between the front door and the room they were in. There was a small fire burning in a large fireplace.

"When you bested him. What sword was he using?" His eyes got suddenly nonchalant.

It gave Trela an odd sensation. It took her a moment to realize why, but when she did, she did her best to keep her own eyes nonchalant. "He was using his mistress, Strife."

"So, I must apologize if I am prying, but did you get cut at all during your fight? Even a small scratch, even a nick?" He was going for it. She did not think he would. Did he not realize they were killing all the members of the Cabal? Did he not care? She had not realized at first that Qizern had to have gotten Strife through the Cabal, at least not consciously. But of course, he did. Where else could he have gotten such an item? She had decided to confront Wreyvaine with his involvement in the Cabal when Jalin entered the room.

"They are nowhere to be found." She nodded towards Wreyvaine. "He is telling at least that much of the truth."

"You see? Why would I fraternize with…" He was quickly interrupted by Jalin.

"But we did find these." She jerked her thumb behind her and there was Estfale, holding a long, thin, ornately carved wooden box.

Estfale's grin expressed how pleased he was with himself. "I found them. Or… it." He hefted the box a little. "This thing is chock full of letters. You would be amazed."

"Now… those are mine." Wreyvaine immediately stood and took a step towards Estfale. Dartsyle took a step towards him, stopping him in his tracks. "Those are private letters. They have nothing to do with Hupdor."

Trela even let his sudden capability to say Hupdor's name correctly slide, maybe he picked it up from their conversation. But she was certainly not going to let him think she did not know about his involvement with the Cabal. Not after he had been so blatant about it.

"How do you know about Strife?" There was a twinge of fear in his eyes as he turned from Estfale to her. She was unsure if it was because of her words or of what was in Estfale's hands. "How do you know that Qizern had a weapon made by the Cabal? That seems like specialized knowledge to me. How about you?"

"Seems pretty specialized to me." Though Trela was looking at Wreyvaine, it was Dartsyle who answered her. His grin looked almost as pleased as Estfale's.

"Well, I just heard… I mean everyone in Vatlisi knew. It was common knowledge." Wreyvaine's dignity was cracking under the weight of their stares. "Listen. I have friends who were in the Cabal. Almost everyone—well anyone with any power at least—had friends in the Cabal. The Prince himself was a member. I mean…" He stopped himself and took a breath. He let it out, quickly and audibly, and stared hard at Trela. "I knew derlians in the Cabal. I know derlians in the Cabal. I will help you find them, truly. I will help you hunt them down. That is why you are here, yes? That is why you sent the mages to look for Hupdor, yes? I will be a great asset for you." He took another deep breath, never faltering his gaze. "But those letters are mine. They are private and you have no right…"

"We have every right. It is you that have no rights." Trela glared back at him.

He suddenly turned and stepped onto a sofa, leaping over its back. It was astonishing that a derlian of his age was that spry. Estfale looked confused holding his box of treasures, as if unsure if he could just drop it to chase down Wreyvaine. Dartsyle appeared too stunned to move, which would have been more annoying to Trela if she had been able to move. She had not been expecting Wreyvaine to bolt like that. She was unsure of where Croy was, but Jalin immediately leapt over a different sofa in one bound. As Wreyvaine reached the door, she reached him. He screamed profanities as he was tackled and then grappled. As Trela and Dartsyle arrived on the scene, at least a couple of seconds later, he was subdued. Trela had not realized that Jalin knew wrestling, or something akin to wrestling. She was on her back, with his back on top of her front, her arms were folded up behind his head with his own arms uselessly dangling from the crook of her elbows, and her legs were wrapped up and around his, spreading him out in all directions. His head was bent to his chest and his limbs looked like a turtle stuck on its back, stomach baking in the desert sun. It was almost comical. He was sputtering aggressively, but soon stopped his useless struggling.

"You are going to have to teach me that sometime." Estfale had finally come over, still cradling his box. "That was impressive." They all nodded in agreement. Everyone but Wreyvaine, that is.

They let him up and sat him back down on a sofa. The others gathered around as well, though Estfale was a few paces away. Trela did not think Wreyvaine would make another run for it.

"So, you do know Hupdor then." She wanted to get back to the subject at hand.

"He stops by every once in a while, we have a couple of drinks, some laughs, he goes on his way. We are friends in the loosest sense of the word. Whether or not his lover thinks this is a hiding place is beyond the point, since that is just plainly false. I have no idea who she thinks I am." He looked crestfallen, his bushy eyebrows kept still over his downcast eyes.

"If he is not here, then where is he? And, somewhat more importantly, where are our friends?" Trela did not care to argue his specific relationship with Hupdor, nor Mika's interpretation of it. They had a new box of letters to examine and another prisoner who said he knew where other members of the Cabal were hiding. At this point, if she could just find Feyazki and Serghno, even without Hupdor, she would call the day a win.

"I would try his house. Have you checked there yet?" There was a little exasperated sigh at the end. Trela ignored it.

They sent Dartsyle back to the inn with Wreyvaine and the letters. Though she doubted they really needed to, they tied Wreyvaine's hands behind him and gave Dartsyle the other end of the rope. The box of letters was unwieldy enough that she did not want him dropping it if Wreyvaine suddenly decided to become difficult again. At least he did not appear to know magic. They then set out to where Mika had marked Hupdor's house. It was only when they had gotten halfway there that she realized she had forgotten to make Wreyvaine tell her where he thought the house was, just as a confirmation.

They finally arrived at the house. It was now quite late and Trela was getting tired and annoyed. There were flickering shadows cast through the windows of the house. It was obviously occupied and well lit from within. She had Jalin head around to the back again. Estfale and Croy stayed with her. She strode up the wooden steps to the small porch and banged loudly on the front door. There was a quiet commotion before the door swung wide open and the outline of a Fluen stood silhouetted against the interior light.

"Hupdor, I presume?" She braced herself for a fight, or at least a mild argument, but got none of the kind.

"Oh, hey, it's your friends!" He shouted drunkenly behind his shoulder back into the room. He staggered slightly and then caught himself. "Come in, come in. I've heard so much about you."

There, in the main parlor, were Feyazki and Serghno lounging on a deep cushioned sofa. They each had a goblet of wine in their hands. They at least had the decency to look sheepishly embarrassed as she entered. It tempered her annoyance a teensy bit.

"Did you miss a *whisper*?" Trela could not remember who was supposed to communicate so she glared at both of them.

"Oh, that is totally my fault. Please. A thousand apologies." Hupdor made a half bow which induced another stagger.

Estfale made towards one of the other sofas. "Oh no, we are done here. Pack everything up, we are heading back to the inns." She made a swirling motion in the air with her right hand.

Everyone returned to their respective quarters. Trela kept Hupdor separate from Mika but did not truly jail either one. Hupdor was incredibly friendly and likeable, completely gregarious. He talked their whole way back about various adventures. Certainly nothing about the Cabal, everything stayed light, but she knew he had to be thinking about it. He had locked up his house, even shuttering his windows. He knew he was not going to be let back there, certainly not at any time soon and even then, certainly not alone. But his smile did not slip, his stories did not waver. For all intents and purposes, he was having the time of his life. She bunked him with Estfale and found her own room. Knill was there curled up in the warm bed, snoring. It was comforting.

Trela woke late the next morning, Knill had let her sleep in. Even though she had a slow start, she was much better off than some of the others. She had left a note at Feyazki's inn, letting him know he was under orders to show up at her room once he had gotten himself presentable, and it was into the afternoon before he finally arrived. She might have been more annoyed about his tardiness, but Dartsyle had brought over the letters a little earlier and they had been reading through them. They were quite fascinating.

Wreyvaine had obviously been some sort of liaison between the Prince of Vatlisi and someone within the Luften Royal Branch. Though there were some that appeared to have a royal seal and there were even a few that had Queen Vanelia's signature, most of them were signed simply as, "Your Friend." Those letters had similar handwriting, making Trela assume they were from the same derlian. It was quite intriguing. The only thing she knew for certain was that those letters were not from Vanelia.

Some of the letters were quite banal, weather or commerce reports. Some were trivial, *hi, how are yous*, and the like. Most of them were of that style, merely conversational. But some had an odd gait to the language, as if something else was being hinted at. Some were intriguing and some conspiratorial. She wanted to separate them out into more cohesive piles, but they appeared to be in some vague chronological order, and she was hesitant to ruin that. Eventually she might need to get Wreyvaine's explanations or opinions on some of them and she did not want them in a jumbled mess when it came to that.

That was when Feyazki finally arrived. It had just been her and Dartsyle; Knill had left before Dartsyle had arrived, Estfale was guarding Hupdor, and Ryshial was guarding Mika. Feyazki looked a little bored as he closed the door and pulled up a chair, all in silence. He also looked a little hung over, but nothing too excessive.

"You wanted me over here?" He did not even glance at the letters, though she and Dartsyle had barely looked up.

"These are Luften letters, I wanted your opinion." She pushed a small pile of already read correspondence over to him.

"You should have invited Gyllhelon or someone." He dutifully picked up the top of the pile.

His comment made her pause, even though it was tossed out without forethought. She should have. She wondered why she had not thought of that. A quick follow-up thought came to her, *should other Luftens be brought in as well? Malghain always knew more than he let on.* But her thoughts were interrupted.

"Wait a second. Is this Chiavel's handwriting?" Feyazki was squinting down at the letter in his hand.

Chiavel, she thought, *why does that name sound so familiar?* Then it came to her. He was part of the retinue that Vanelia brought to the temple with Hulgert.

"How do you know his handwriting?" She should have eased into her questioning of him, but it just came out.

"He was always writing secret notes. Not that they were very secret, but he loved to keep an aura of conspiracy about him. As if he was privier to what was going on than you were. Even when it was obvious you knew nothing about anything since you were locked away in a tree the vast majority of the time." He glanced up as both Trela and Dartsyle stared at him. "It was just his way of being superior." He waved his hand in the air briefly. "I'm not really sure since it has been so long, but it does look like his writing, and he did sign a lot of stuff with a vague 'Your Friend' or whatever. He never liked putting his name to paper, unless it was some public honor or something."

"Well, it seems as if you've given yourself a job." Trela scooted the pile of letters in front of her across the table towards him. "They should all be kept in order so that when we return them to Wreyvaine, if we have to, he should not be able to tell."

"But he knows we're going through them now. What difference does it make?" Dartsyle lifted an eyebrow, a letter of his own in his hand.

"We should return them as neatly as we found them. If you like, I'll get you a Fluen scribe to copy them all, and number and catalog the copies. That way you won't have to pay as much attention." She patted the table as she got up. "And I'll get you Gyllhelon if you like."

"And Malghain," he yelled at her retreating back.

"And Malghain," she retorted.

It was not that she was completely bored with reading the letters. It was just that it was a little tedious and she had so much other stuff to get caught up on. There were several other guards Mika had mentioned that they needed to round up for one thing. She decided to get Estfale and Jalin together for a little hunting. She ended up with Arnasta and Serghno as well.

Between Mika's directions and Arnasta's skills, they were able to catch the first two together. It was in the Fluen quarter, at the north end, near the docks. It was a large, decrepit house with a giant rowan tree in the front yard at the edge of the cobbled street. The tree had a ring of brick around it, partly demarcating the end of the cobbles and partly separating the tree from the split path that led to the house. Jalin had gone the long way around and, Trela assumed, was at the back of the house by the time she knocked on the front door. No one answered. She knocked again. Still no one answered, but this time the sound of someone rustling inside was unmistakable. She could have kicked herself for not bringing two spies. Of course no one was answering their doors anymore. Word had gotten out that the entire Cabal was to be obliterated and they were reacting accordingly. Trela had tried to let it be known that some of the lower-level guards, if they cooperated, were being let free. But those were often killed by the remaining members of the Cabal, if nothing else but to keep them from cooperating any further. All the low hanging fruit had been captured by this point anyway. Those who were left were typically more dangerous. She pulled her short sword and had Estfale break down the door.

A flash of metal caught her eye as the door banged open. The twirling dagger caught Estfale in the leg. She wished she had a dagger in her hand instead of her sword but could not switch that up in time. She danced around Estfale as he dropped to one knee, and she rushed the fleeing figure. She heard other commotions around her but could not spare her attention. She knew she could not lunge fast enough to catch the fleeing guard's tendon as he ran up the stairs so she just ran as fast as she could. She did fumble a little with her left hand, reaching across to unsheathe her dagger. She was not as good at throwing daggers with her left hand, not by a long shot, but she had certainly practiced and wanted to be ready. The fleeing stranger would reach the top of the stairs soon. Unfortunately, pulling her dagger slowed her about half a second. The stairs spiraled a little, keeping the top out of her view. He was pulling heavily on the handrail in a bid to gain as much speed as possible. She could only chase him with her feet.

When he got to the top he leapt across the threshold, yelling wildly. Trela took another half second to process what was going on. It was another flash of metal coming towards her at lightning speed. There was another figure at the top of the stairs, arm outstretched in an exaggerated throwing motion. Time slowed as she stopped and brought up her sword and dagger crossed in front of her. The thrown knife glanced off her steel barricade, clattering down the stairs behind her. The door slammed shut. She made two more leaps up the stairs and jammed her sword as far under the door as she could. She felt a satisfying thunk and heard a scream as she sliced through someone's leather boot. She tried to wiggle it, hoping to lacerate the foot some more. There was a definite thud as a body hit the floor, but the foot was no longer within her reach. She pulled her weapon back as she screamed behind her.

"Serghno! Quick, Serghno!" It was not much, but all she could get out. She rammed the door with her shoulder, but there was no landing and coming up the stairs at the door slowed her down a little. It did not budge. "Quickly!"

She jammed her sword under the door again but connected with nothing. She rammed the door again, but it still did not budge. She turned to yell for Serghno again, but there he was, lumbering up the stairs towards her. She scooched past him, giving him the room at the top of the stairs that he needed.

"Mekdepiarc!" A burst of flames engulfed the door. She had not really considered the consequences of starting a fire in a wooden building and, by the look on his face, she guessed that he did not either.

"Move!" She ran past him as he did his best to compress himself against the wall. She struck the flaming door with her right shoulder again, she could tell a bruise was coming up. But at least her hair had not gone up in flames. The door burst open and she ran into the attic.

She saw movement in the distance and hurled the dagger from her left hand. There was a Fluen on the floor clutching his wounded foot. Her right hand guided her sword into the prone Fluen's leg without her thinking about it. It was nice that her hand had decided not to kill the Fluen, they needed to take prisoners when they could. She leapt over the wounded guard and ran down a hallway towards the fleeing figure. At first she thought her dagger had missed, but there was some definite blood on the floor from someone. She heard Serghno following but did not hesitate in charging down the hallway. She was having a hard time keeping the guard in her vision.

The door at the end of the hall was slamming shut as she neared it. Without a pause she threw her body against the door, though she probably could not have stopped even if she had wanted to. Luckily her shoulder struck it before it latched. It vibrated oddly however, and she stumbled as she crashed through. A large double-bitted axe sliced the air above her as she tumbled. She swung her sword out wildly, not really aiming at anything. The guard leapt backwards even though he was already out of her range. Trela was able to pull herself into a crouch by the time he was able to reverse himself and lunge in with the axe swinging in a high arc over his head. There was no way to block the axe, anything put in its way would surely shatter. So she did the only thing she could do and rolled out of the way. She ended in another crouch as the axe stuck into the wood floor with a thundering thunk. The guard struggled for a second, trying to dislodge the axe, when Trela sprang forward with all her might. It felt about as graceful as a frog leaping for a fly, but it gave her an enormous amount of momentum. She thrust forth her sword at the end of her leap, catching the guard just under his armpit. The sword jarred heavily in her hand, making it difficult to keep ahold of, but his body crumpled nicely and she was able to stay on her feet as she skittered to a halt.

Jalin came running up another set of stairs behind Trela just as Serghno lumbered into the doorway. Trela sat herself down for a quick moment to catch her breath, then stuck out her heel to get some leverage against the guard's body. It took some yanking, but she was able to finally dislodge her sword. She waved her hand above her head, pointing back down the hallway towards the wounded guard in the other room, rather than saying anything. Jalin immediately jogged down the hallway. Trela sat and panted for a moment before getting back on her feet.

"How's Estfale?" She rolled the guard over to look for her dagger.

"Arnasta's working on him, don't worry." Serghno smiled and wiped a bit of sweat from his brow.

"Well, then we had better work on wounded guard." She walked after Jalin to see how much information they could glean from the surviving guard.

They got another name, another location. Building by building, room by room, derlian by derlian, they scoured Vatlisi. Back and forth through each of the quarters. It was agonizing. Trela knew she had to keep up the pressure, however. There could be no rest. They could only lock down the city for so long. Tureyn would only allow Clerin to run things until a new prince was appointed. The obliteration of the Cabal needed to happen as quickly as possible. But it was incredibly tiring.

At first they had the full cooperation of the city's denizens. There were those who had always had conflict with the Cabal. Even amongst those who were partial to the Cabal, there were those who agreed with whatever Tureyn decided upon. And there were plenty in between. Trela's entire coterie was active at all times, tracing all leads and hints. But things had changed. The city's mood seemed different.

It was not just that foreigners were still roaming the streets, killing neighbors. It was not just the constant questioning and interrogation. It was the lockdown itself. The fact that no one could leave the gleaming walls. They could not go fishing, go trading at another village, go hiking, or even just picnicking. They were not confined to their homes, however. They were allowed to go and wander the streets. Trela would have thought that was enough. Surely some of the denizens rarely left the city. There were Pyrans who had never left Agoge—ever. But now they were not allowed.

That was the bone stuck in the throat. That was the thorn in the side. It was a festering sore, the lockdown. A derlian could not want something at all, could completely hate it, and yet if you told them that they could not have it, it would be all they would want. It was a basic nature of derlian. And this thing, this freedom of movement, it was precious. It was a thing that derlians craved, which made the sore fester even more. It was getting close to gangrenous. Trela needed to be done with Vatlisi, for Vatlisi was surely done with her. She needed to finalize the obliteration of the Cabal and move on. Chase the Blind One down and wreck vengeance. That was where she wanted to turn her attention. But there always seemed to be one more mission.

Then it finally came, though she had not realized it at the time. The last known members of the Cabal hidden in Vatlisi. There were three of them, they were brothers. Strange how many siblings had been caught up within the Cabal's web. She wondered if it had something to do with secret societies in general, or if there was something more specific to the Cabal. If she had known they were the last, she would have brought her entire coterie. Estfale was still wounded, well not exactly wounded, but he still had a small limp and Trela did not want to tax him. She had Feyazki and Dartsyle, Serghno and Arnasta and, of course, Jalin. At that moment in time, Jalin probably knew the layout of Vatlisi better than those who had called it home for their entire lives. She had certainly covered more ground than Trela, who had scoured the city. One of the brothers was a mage, so she felt she had to bring several with her, just to have him outnumbered.

They were in the Fluen Quarter, towards the palace grounds, but not quite within visibility of the gates. It was a nice sturdy home, built of the hard white stone common in Vatlisi. Jalin had already scouted the exterior of the building and given them a verbal description at least. There was one double door in the front and a single one at the back. The front faced the street while the back quickly led to a path between buildings before ducking under a rounded arch to the alleyway proper. There were several shuttered windows scattered on each side of the building, at each of the floors. Jalin had not mentioned a basement, which certainly would not have been visible, and Trela hoped it did not exist. She was tired of crawling through basements, especially those that linked up with the maze of tunnels that spiderwebbed under the city. She hoped this would be a simple mission. She was tired of complications. It had been a long moon, to say the least.

Jalin went around to the back. Trela had told her not to enter but to only capture those attempting to flee. She usually left it up to Jalin, and Jalin usually snuck in, but she figured with at least three Fluens in there, someone was bound to make a run for the back door. More than anything, she did not want to lose anyone in the shuffle. That would just add time to the whole ordeal.

Trela had Serghno and Arnasta hang back at first. They were to come in after the others had fully entered. She knew she had been leaning on Arnasta a lot lately and wanted to give her some rest, to at least leave her outside once they confirmed they had the right house. But she wanted Serghno's help, and if she brought him along, she got Arnasta as well. So they were watching the side of the house, just in case one of the brothers attempted to leave through a window.

Trela, Feyazki and Dartsyle walked up to the front door. She knew it was a bit foolish to announce her presence, but she figured they probably knew who was outside. At first it had been a lot simpler, members of the Cabal would actually open their doors and invite her inside, but that had changed. A while ago.

Bang, bang, bang. She struck the door with the hammer of her hand, making a nice solid sound. They waited with bated breath.

Nothing. Bang, bang, bang. Nothing. She had Feyazki get ready and Dartsyle ram the door. It flung open on his first try. Trela charged in right behind and Feyazki slid in afterwards.

The front foyer was quite tall and echoey, compounded by the cold marble floor. There were carved stairs to her left that wrapped to a landing, then continued to the second floor. There was an open hallway to her right with a nice, rounded arch entrance. There were a pair of large double doors in front of her. They looked to be of a dense wood with iron bandings. They were shut and, Trela assumed, locked. They stood in the foyer for a moment, primed and ready, but strain her ears as she might, she could not hear any commotion in any direction. She popped outside briefly to wave at Serghno. She wanted to check the upper floor before attempting to go through the robust double doors, so she wanted Serghno to guard the front door.

Trela, Feyazki and Dartsyle cautiously went up the stairs. She had a dagger out in her right hand, leaving her left empty. She wanted to be able to fling steel at a moment's provocation. She crept up the stairs until she reached the landing. She paused for a moment, straining her ears further, then continued. The second floor was a fairly open plan, full of hallways and archways, but no doors. They scoured the entire floor before she was satisfied that it was empty. As she creeped around white stone pillars and open archways, she imagined seeing movement in every shadow, but there was nothing. They went back downstairs and regrouped with the others.

"Do you think they're here?" Trela nodded her head towards the doors. She was asking Arnasta but would have accepted anyone's opinion. It was eerily quiet.

"They're here somewhere." Arnasta nodded, then went to cast something in the far corner. But she did not get that far.

There was a scream from the far end of the house. It sounded like Jalin, so Trela immediately took off running towards the noise. She was not sure who was following her, if anyone, but she did not get very far either. As she reached the large, rounded archway, the double doors burst open. Flames shot behind her as she continued in her sprint, the roar was deep, like a lion screaming into a waterfall. Lighting flashed in return making the room flicker with both types of light, the warm red overcome with the cold blue. The thunder drowning out the waterfall. These thoughts tore through Trela as she tried to keep her footing on the marble floor. It felt like she was being buffeted around by the air pressure shock waves, which may not have been entirely true, but she could not pause to examine the feeling. She had to assume that Feyazki and Dartsyle, Serghno and Arnasta, were fully capable of dealing with whatever was coming through those double doors. Her blades could not help them now, she could barely spare a thought for them. She ran headlong down the hallway hoping what was ahead of her was less frightening than what was behind.

There was a turn and then another, back to the same direction. That was when she saw the Fluen in front of Jalin. He was incredibly tall and gaunt. His long blond hair was held back with something, maybe a piece of leather, his left hand held Jalin's throat, pushing her against a wooden door, and his right flung wide as he slashed her stomach. There was a spray of blood that arced into the air in slow motion. Trela's knife left her hand as she charged forward, attempting to outrun it. She pulled her short sword over the next two steps but, without thinking, she leapt into the air shifting her body so that spun in a slow arc until her feet were in front of her. Her body jarred against his just after her knife, her boots placed at the small of his back, and she shoved him into Jalin.

He screamed and dropped his knife. He turned towards the new threat and tossed Jalin aside while doing so. Trela, attempting to get into a half-crouch at least, just started stabbing. She got him at least twice, maybe three times, before he kicked her away. She slid a ways along the marble.

He charged toward her as she slowed, trying to get her feet under her. He appeared to be trying to draw a sword of his own. She slashed at his legs as he got into range and caught his shin as he kicked at her again. Her sword hit bone, jarring free from her hand. He let out a horrendous howl and dropped the sword he had barely gotten free from its sheath. He fell almost on top of her, but with his momentum only his legs were tangled up, his body proper struck the floor beyond her. She scrambled to get free. Luckily only one of his legs was really working, the other flopped around rather uselessly. She was able to clamber up his back as he struggled against the slick marble. As she neared his shoulders, she was able to get her right arm snaked in and wrapped around his neck. His hands began to flail at her, smacking her head, but not with a huge amount of force. She was able to grip her wrist with her left hand, locking her arm against his neck, choking him with all of her might. One of his hands was able to grab a clump of hair and yank it out. The pain was excruciating, but she just kept pulling on his neck. He was able to get up on his knees with her hanging on his back. He tucked and slammed her into a nearby pillar, attempting to dislodge her. He did not strike her head against the stone column, however, just her back. It knocked the wind out of her, but she was able to hold on and keep squeezing. His hands came back, trying to find an eye or something soft to gouge, but she kept her head down, her eyes shut, her teeth gritted, and kept squeezing. He tried to pull out more hair, but he was getting weaker. She knew she was supposed to take prisoners, to leave one alive during every fight, but all she could do was keep squeezing. She was not even sure how long he was dead by the time Dartsyle cautiously approached her.

"It's okay now, you can let go." His voice seemed distant. She slowly opened her eyes and saw that he was crouched a short distance away. Close enough to be comforting, but outside of arm's reach in case she became startled. His eyes were soft and kind. At that moment she thought of poor dead Yarsurle, his lover. She was tired.

They did their best to find others, but they could not get any further information. Either the Cabal in Vatlisi was crushed or they had escaped. Just in case there were some so hidden that they could not be found, Trela was leaving her coterie under the command of Rewista. She would have left it under the command of Clerin, who was running Vatlisi and would be able to glean rumors about any vestiges of the Cabal but, by the same token, had no time for such things. Rewista would keep the coterie under control and out of Clerin's way, unless and until they were needed for something. Trela, for her part, was finally able to focus on a more appetizing hunt. She was going to find the Blind One and wreck vengeance upon him.

So she gathered a contingent of her coterie. She needed magic to defeat the Blind One, and so brought Feyazki, Croy and Serghno. She needed Arnasta to be able to help hunt him down. She needed muscle, and so brought Estfale, Malghain and Haswyxe. She needed Jalin, obviously. She needed someone who understood the Blind One, so she brought Aedon. Then, she needed some Fluens, by all accounts the Eidyon Peninsula was distrustful of foreigners. So she brought the Dylsun twins for muscle, those who had been the

Prince's bodyguards only to betray him in the end, and she brought Iphnora Zinfara as a Fluen mage she could trust. Finally, she brought Mika and Hupdor, because she needed Mika. Was fifteen too much? Yes. But she was unsure of who to get rid of. They would obviously stick out like a sore thumb. They would not be able to hide nor sneak. But would eight have been easier to hide? Would six? If she needed Mika, then she needed a guard for her. If she brought Hupdor to keep Mika happy, she needed mages to guard him. Haswyxe would protect Croy and Malghain would protect Feyazki. Did she really need Croy? In her mind, and she hated to admit this, but Croy would be the perfect bait if they needed to draw the Blind One out. It was all a balance. She knew she had way too many derlians with her, but she was willing to deal with that. Each of them had a reason to be there. They were fully provisioned before they headed out.

Chapter 3

Croy was a little concerned about hunting down the Blind One. He knew they were a large and well-balanced crew. They had warriors and mages galore. They overwhelmingly outnumbered him. They supposedly knew where he was headed and Arnasta could track almost anyone down. They probably even had the element of surprise over him. Croy was still nervous about it, however. There was a niggling voice in the back of his mind, spreading doubt. He had been kidnapped and imprisoned by the Blind One, which surely had an effect his nervousness. And he had seen the Blind One escape situations where he had been completely surrounded by warriors and mages galore. Even with their overwhelming force, Croy was more than a little concerned.

He did not want to stay around Vatlisi for longer than he had to, however. Everything he looked at reminded him of Baltuz. This inn, that restaurant, an alder tree they had kissed under, a street they used to stroll down; everything. He needed to be somewhere she had never been, somewhere he had never been. He needed new surroundings to take his mind off of her, new dangers to keep his mind occupied. Would his tent in the middle of nowhere work? Most of their travels together had involved sleeping in tents, at least when they were not in some mostly abandoned village. Chatting, laughing, loving, all under that hot and muggy beige canvas. He was gambling on it, however. Staying in Vatlisi was certainly not helping.

They set out fairly quickly. One thing to be said about Trela, once she set her mind to something, she did not waste time. Croy did not have many to say goodbye to, Knill and Tumu mostly, so the night before they left was a fairly mild one as far as he was concerned.

They reached the docks quickly the next morning. Fluen porters climbed over everything, shuffling things onto the large ship like a stream of ants. Just staring at the boat made Croy more nervous than when he thought of the Blind One. The concept of boats was one he was comfortable with. He had even been in a couple tiny ones on Lake Serif before, but this was something utterly different. It was massive, taller than a house. It was long, it was wide, it creaked and groaned just sitting there, bobbing listlessly around in the sheltered cove that was the docks. There were three massive masts. The middle one was the tallest, the one in the back the shortest. There was a great tusk that stuck off the front of the boat at a shallow angle which had ropes stretching back to the front mast. The ropes were everywhere, really. It was dizzying.

Underneath the great tusk was the ship's figurehead, which was an ornately carved winged female with her hair stretched back in a non-existent breeze. The lower portion of the boat was black, while the upper sides were a rich brown, almost leathery in appearance. The sails were rolled up on the mast crossbeams, making it difficult to tell their color. They appeared to have been white at one time deep in the past.

The wooden gangplank stuck out at a sharp angle. He watched his horse, Buttercup, walk unsteadily up and vanish. He watched the other horses disappear as well. He watched the other derlians, his companions, in small loose groups, chatting and mingling. Some would break off and flow into another group, shifting pods of flesh and minds, growing and shrinking. Croy should join in, he knew. They were creating comradery. He was nervous, though, and did not feel like chatting. He watched the gigantic boat bob slowly on the water for some time. Finally, it was his time to walk up the plank, he could stall no longer. The ship seemed to move under his feet opposite of how he wanted it to, making it difficult to walk. And they had not even left the dock yet! He hoped to get his "sea legs," as Clerin had called them, as quickly as possible. He did not want to be stumbling around the entire time they were on the boat.

The first thing he saw on deck was that the horses had little frames around them that cradled them in cloth slings. Some of them looked wild-eyed and nervous, but not Buttercup, so he walked on by. There was an upper portion to the ship, with a giant wheel, but he did not head upwards. He was led down, towards the back of the ship, to his quarters. Little did he know that was the last he would feel somewhat normal.

Croy was nauseated. The constant bobbing and rolling roiled his stomach fiercely. He barely left his room the first day. He had thought some fresh air would help, to get him away from the stench of his own stomach, and for a moment it did. But then the ship began to roll again and he lost control again. It was slightly better in the open air, but he felt others staring at him with sad and compassionate eyes. That just made him feel worse, so he staggered back down to his quarters.

Feyazki would come and cast a healing spell on him in the mornings and as long as he kept up on it, Croy could heal himself most of the day, making living bearable. The spells, though helpful, were such a constant drain that it just seemed better to hide in his room and be miserable. He did not want to bother Feyazki or Arnasta every hour. He did not wish to be a burden. So he stayed in his bed, ate as little as possible, and basically muddled through the entire voyage with gritted teeth. He was told many of the sights they passed were quite beautiful.

They traveled straight southwest across the Clatsvol Sea. They arrived at the tip of the Eidyon Peninsula with Johcal Island to the north and slightly to the west. The town was not much more than the docks. A couple of inns and taverns to keep the sailors busy was all. Apparently, there were tiny villages all along the coastline living almost exclusively on the fishing trade. Croy thought about visiting some and talking with the Sea's equivalent of Sie'tin but, more than anything, he just wanted off the boat.

They disembarked and rode out of town quite quickly. Trela had not wanted to stay in the town they disembarked at. They made it far enough out of the town to keep a protected fire invisible and camped for the evening. It was the first night of good rest that Croy had since leaving Vatlisi. He relished the cold hard ground in a way he never thought possible. It took them another day before they found a separate town with a couple of inns. They piled into one of them and rented it out. Trela had been adamant that they not share the inn with anyone besides the proprietors and workers. She had been prepared to buy out any other visitors but, as luck would have it, she was able to find a small inn that had no other patrons.

This insistence on a loose secrecy seemed a little odd to Croy. Whether or not there were other patrons, the citizens of the town would eventually realize that one of their inns had Pyrans staying in it. And not just a race that rarely, if ever, visited the Eidyon Peninsula, but that all the races were represented at one inn. Together. It seemed to Croy that the secret was too big to keep. They could have stayed in the previous unnamed town and had the same effect. They could have stayed in an inn full of strangers and had the same effect. After a full meal and a goblet of wine, he asked her about it.

"We are not gaining secrecy about our existence, I agree with that. No matter where we go on this peninsula, conversation will follow. We are, in my opinion, gaining a little bit of time with this. The speed of the conversation should be slower, as long as we do not make too much of a splash in any one town. That is not the reason, however. The only thing I really want to keep secret is that we just came from Vatlisi. If I had been able to dock at Tureyn, stay there a couple of nights, then take a different ship to the peninsula, I would have. Unfortunately, time is of the essence. If we hope to catch the Blind One before he finds what he is looking for, we must be as quick as possible." Trela smiled around the table. There were a couple of others there, Estfale, Aedon, and Mika. Trela was encouraging conversation and questions, which she did not always do.

"Why Tureyn?" Croy pressed forward before thinking about it. Of course, Tureyn would be the main town that foreigners would come from. He rephrased himself. "Why not Vatlisi? If the Blind One is looking for Pyrans following him, why does it matter where they come from?"

"It is not him that we are overly concerned with. He will recognize us once we get close. Individually, of course, but even as a group at a distance. We must make sure we can catch him unawares before he recognizes us. No, it is more how he will ask about what he seeks. It is more how he will talk about who might be following him. I think, or I assume, that he will discuss being followed to others. He can easily say he is being followed by derlians from Vatlisi. I think, or at least I hope, that he will hesitate to bring race into it. Why would a Gaen be followed by a group including Pyrans? He is seeking something quite delicate. Something that only the Fluens can provide him, way up here away from civilization. No offense." She smiled at Mika who, luckily, smiled back. It appeared that none was taken. "He has to gain trust without explaining too much of what he is looking for. I agree that this secret may not help too much. He might tell everyone within earshot that a Pyran is looking for him. With no way of knowing, with little in my arsenal to assist our tracking of him from a distance, I can only do what I can. I cannot change who we are or that we need to ask questions of the locals to find him. All I can reasonably do is to sow some confusion as to where we came from and hope for the best, hope that we gain a little bit of time with the ruse."

"Just what, may I ask, is the Blind One looking for?" Aedon asked what Croy wanted to know. What they all wanted to know. It was quiet for some time as Trela stared into her goblet.

"He is looking for a cave, or caves." It was Mika who filled the stretching silence. "I have, of course, told him the wrong location."

"Well, if you are going to make me ask, what is in the cave, or caves?" Aedon leaned back and shifted her chair to look upon Mika more directly.

Mika glanced at Trela. It appeared to Croy that Trela gave her a slight nod. "The caves have etchings of names. Yaven names." Mika paused for a moment. "He asked for the most ancient of the caves, I gave him the location of an empty cave and a way to contact my grandmother, Rumhulga. She was supposed to get in contact with Hupdor the moment she ran into your blind Gaen, but we have heard nothing."

"So a mage could summon any Yaven whose name was on the wall?" Estfale cocked an eyebrow. "Do the Yavens get a say in that? Is it a wall of advertisement?"

"Yavens can resist summons if they wish." Mika sounded a little defensive. "Some of them, yes, I believe some of them were proud to have their names displayed thusly. Of course, there were probably others who did not desire that. To be honest, I'm not really sure how the system works. I have never stepped foot in any of the caves."

"How can you say Yavens can resist summons?" Croy felt angry. "Wasn't that the entire point of the Cabal? To summon Yavens without their consent?"

"I think the more important question is, 'What name is he looking for?' If we had any clue as to what type of name he was seeking, it would surely help us figure out the why." Aedon leaned forward, ignoring Croy. "Are there only Fluen Yaven names in those caves, or are there names from all the elements?"

"I believe there are more than Fluen names on those walls." Mika nodded to herself, also ignoring him for a moment. Then she stopped and stared at him. "The Cabal did not use any names from the caves."

"Why not?" Everyone stared at Aedon as she spoke. "What, it is an honest question. It seems like easy pickings, really. Why were none of the names from the caves used?"

"The Cabal did not go after known Yavens, illustrious or glorified or… popular. They went after nobodies." Mika kept her gaze down, away from anyone else's.

"So, just the young and naïve. The easy pickings, as Aedon would say." Croy was not even sure why he was getting caught up in the argument. The whole idea just seemed so callous and cruel.

"Well, not just that." She held up a hand to rebuff any rebuttals. "That is certainly a part of it, I am not shying away from that. Wolves do not take the healthiest and fastest deer, after all. But it is not just that. Taking popular, well known Yavens calls attention to yourself and that was something we did not want. Whether they were known in the Yavens' own realms or in ours made little difference to us. We tried to reach loners and outcasts mostly, which certainly included the young and naïve." She paused for just a moment. "I'm just pointing out that it was not only the weak that we were aiming for, that there were other criteria." Another short pause. "Criteria that meant we left the caves alone."

"And what of your grandmother? She's the one who was supposed to contact Hupdor if the Blind One was noticed sniffing around the area, correct?" Trela picked up the conversation before it had a chance to lapse.

"Well, I should be clear, we are not actually related. I never actually knew my real grandparents." Mika smiled and looked up at Trela, her forehead losing all its wrinkles and worry. "My parents died while I was young, and she helped my brother and I when she could. We had several cycles of relative comfort, here on the peninsula. Poor, to be sure, but safe and loved. We had a little cabin outside of the village and would visit Rumhulga often. She always had some food and would mend our clothes. She really was a great grandmother. After a while, however, Treynith began his… troubling phase. I don't know how else to put it. He stole, well we both stole, he just got caught repeatedly, and then he started getting into fights. He began mugging and… and I don't know what. Rumhulga wouldn't let him into her home anymore, which made my visits awkward and then sparse. So my brother and I left for Vatlisi. I've visited when I can, and she has stayed a great friend. In that sense, I count her as my most trusted ally on the peninsula."

"So, does she guard the caves?" Estfale squinted at her.

"No, of course not. No one guards the caves. They are just hidden and the way to reach them is treacherous." Mika turned from Trela to Estfale. "If it helps to soothe you, she lives quite close to them." She paused for a moment, looking upwards before returning her gaze to Estfale. "She is what is known around here as 'a grandmother of the rain.' She is everywhere, she talks to everyone. She soaks the leaves and percolates through the soil. She lives to gossip and keeps tabs and opinions on everyone in her purview. She is a vivacious busybody, and her purview is vast. Technically, she is an herbalist and minor healer, but in reality she trades in secrets, and no one has ever bested her in haggling. In fact, I would bet that she knows more about the derlians on this edge of the peninsula than any spymaster in Tureyn. I guarantee, *guarantee*, that if there is some strange Gaen looking for the Caves of Names anywhere in this area, she will know about it."

Estfale merely held up his hands in defeat. He did have a smile on his face, however. He looked satisfied with Mika's answer.

"So, how do we get in touch with her? Should we travel to her village, her home?" Trela was also smiling.

"Oh, no. We do not get in touch with her. She will get in touch with us." Mika finished her goblet. "Don't worry, I've already sent out some feelers. It should not be more than a couple of days. As I said, she is a vivacious busybody."

Croy enjoyed the next several days immensely. The main enjoyment came from being on dry land. The ground did not sway underneath his feet, his stomach did not churn, his head did not pound. It was fantastic just to feel like a derlian again. He felt hunger, he felt happiness, he felt normal. It was amazing that feeling normal could make him so ecstatic. His other enjoyment was chatting with the innkeeper. He was not really allowed to wander freely amongst the villagers and, besides, most of them spent all day on their boats catching fish. He was not about to get on another boat and so, in the interest of keeping Trela happy as well, he decided not to leave the inn.

Wystolla Aldrune was the innkeep and the inn was called the Hare and the Lynx. She was tall and blonde, with her hair pulled up and high in a slightly frayed bun held together with several small, sanded sticks. She was a matriarch in every sense of the word. She had seven children in all, and they were all kept busy. One would come and check to see which room to clean next and she would rattle off a number. One would ask what needed to be added to the soup stock and she would go and give it a taste and add the herbs. One would ask about the chickens not laying eggs, or where the grease was to fix a squeaky hinge, or who to contact about the thatch on the roof. She was a whirlwind of activity even though she mainly stood behind the bar. She kept all her children constantly occupied. Her youngest was barely taller than the broom he was using to constantly sweep up the great hall.

Croy had asked her once about how she kept her children so motivated. "Besides the beatings?" was her response. Her eyes sparkled and one half of her mouth lifted when she told something that was supposed to be funny, which helped Croy immensely since her voice rarely changed tones during the joke. Plus, he could imagine her beating a child who was slow to respond. Not hard mind you, but enough to get their attention. She had that steel within her demeanor, she always meant business. "It's always been this way really. My poor dead husband was always out fishing, leaving me alone to care for my family's inn. He'd leave before dawn and get back after dusk. He was a hard worker he was, though maybe not quite as hard of a worker as I. But he had a terrible tenderness that I was never cursed with. He was away from the children for so long that he would dote on them whenever he was home. He never wanted to see them working, even though there was still work to be done. He never wanted to see their dirty faces frowning or pouting. He was always sunshine and smiles, kisses and hugs, gifts and toys. It was fine really, I'm not complaining. But I was always the mean one to the children. They would complain to him about me before he was fully through the door. They stood up straight when I was around. They asked what they could do if I was alone, how to help and whatnot. They may have feared me, but they trusted me as well. I was always here, always looking out for them. So when my poor dead husband's boat sank into the Clatsvol, the children, they stepped up, and rightly so. We no longer had the fish to sell, no. It was only the inn that was feeding them after that, and I can tell you that children do not enjoy starving. An empty belly is the greatest motivator in the world." They both laughed heartily at that. Not so much because it was funny, but because some truths hurt.

Wystolla would not let him do chores, saying it wouldn't be right what with him being a paying customer, her honored guest. So instead he chatted when he could and it helped to while away some hours. Not surprisingly, he was chatting with her when Iphnora brought the news that Mika's grandmother had made contact. He had not really spoken with her much, but she was considered quite a competent mage. Most of the others had gotten to know each other on the boat ride over, a luxury that Croy had not been able to afford.

"So, which was it? Did her grandmother get in touch with Mika, or did she *whisper* to Hupdor as she was originally instructed to do?" He was a little nervous about chasing the Blind One through some foreign realm, even if they did outnumber him, even if the realm was not foreign to all of Croy's allies.

"She contacted her granddaughter, why?" Iphnora raised an eyebrow but the rest of her continued to the empty stool adjacent to Croy without any veering from her original path.

"Just seeing what to expect. If she had contacted Hupdor, it could have been that she did not know we were here yet, that we were settled. Contacting Mika first, however, makes me think that she has probably already been watching us, feeling out our story, seeing to the safety of her progeny." He nodded, mostly to himself. "Do you think the dynamic between Trela and Mika will change? Be tested?"

"Oh, it will definitely be tested. And I would say it is pretty definite that it will change as well, at least for the immediate future. How could it not?" She nodded to Wystolla to provide a glass of wine. "Rumhulga probably has some friends in the area, probably more than enough to overwhelm us in our sleep…"

"I would never let that happen. At least, not to a paying customer." They all laughed. Croy also nodded to Wystolla for a glass, since she was there with the bottle already.

"The real question will be if it can somehow get back to its current dynamic later. That will be a battle of wills between the two of them." Iphnora took a tiny sip. "I do not know her very well, but from what I have heard and witnessed, there are few derlians who can demonstrate a stronger will than Trela. But Mika will be fighting for her life, for Hupdor's life. If she, if Mika, can prove to be indispensable; if she can capture the Blind One, protect us from locals, find this cave, and so on. If she can do all that, then I cannot see how the dynamic does not change."

"So, this dynamic involves the death of Mika?" Wystolla poured her own glass.

Croy's stomach dropped when he realized what was going on, where the conversation had gone. *Had Iphnora done that on purpose?* he thought. *Was she to be trusted?* He stiffened and the pause extended too long; they were both looking at him.

"A thousand apologies, truly. I have intruded where I was not welcome." Wystolla took her glass and made a turn to walk away.

"No, it is not your fault. It is mine." Iphnora looked truly distressed. "I had assumed you two were close. Had already discussed why we were here."

"Not in detail, not with full honesty." Wystolla turned back. "I have been asked curious things by some of the patrons, however. My children have been asked curious things. There are even others around here, locals. They have asked questions about your group as well. I listen. I pay attention." She smiled and made a small nod. "But Croy here has been a pillar of discreteness. He has divulged nothing of your true purpose."

"So… What, may I ask, do you know of our mission?" Croy felt that the damage was already done. Whether or not he could trust Iphnora he was not sure, but at this point they may as well figure out how much the locals knew.

She looked nervously back and forth between them for a brief moment, then took a healthy draught. "Well, I know you came from a recent fight near Vatlisi, though you wish to appear to have come from Tureyn. You are an odd mix of foreigners, with Fluens that may or may not be captives. You are looking for a Gaen, or maybe several Gaens. You have more mages with you than is healthy, almost half your numbers. You are looking for locals, or at least quasi-locals, that do not know you at all. And you have various quasi-locals concerned that you are looking for the Cave of Names. Is that about right?" Before Croy could tell her how close she was, she threw in another sentence. "Oh, and if you are looking for, or are worried about, Rumhulga, she knows you're here. She would know when you landed, I would bet my inn on it. She might have even known while you were still sailing. Nothing, and I mean nothing, slips past Rumhulga. So whatever secrets you think you are keeping from me, you are certainly not keeping them from her."

Iphnora turned from Wystolla back to Croy, peaked her eyebrows at him and nodded, downed her drink, and stood. "Well, let me apologize for speaking out of turn, but do I believe we are not as hidden as we might have thought. Or hoped. We should use allies where we find them, yes?" She turned to Wystolla, who gave her a lopsided smile. "I do assume you are an ally?" Then she left the same way she entered, leaving Croy and Wystolla alone with their wine.

"I didn't know you knew Rumhulga." He gave a shy smile, not knowing what else to say.

"Well, not really. But I know of her. She is a bit of a legend. Everyone has heard a different story about her, but few have met her. I've had her pointed out to me as she has traveled through the village, so she certainly exists." She paused for a moment. "Unless, of course, I was being lied to." She giggled to herself. It did not *sound* as if she thought she had been lied to, but it was difficult for Croy to say at that point.

"So, she has a bad reputation?" He wondered if Rumhulga struck fear into anyone or not.

"Not bad. Not really good either, if you want the truth." She paused again, eyes drifting upward in thought. "She has a solid reputation, yes. She does what she says, whether you would think her capable or not. Does she say good things or bad things? Both. Neither. Who can say?"

"But you would recommend that we stayed on her good side?"

"I would at that, yes. However, it appears a little late for that. You've done whatever you've done. She's done her research and reached out to your captive, Mika. I am not sure if Gaens have this saying, but 'the die is cast.' It is in the air right now and no one has any idea of where it will land except Rumhulga. And, just maybe, Mika. But probably not. From what I hear, Rumhulga does not like variables she cannot control."

It took another two days before the meeting could be arranged. Croy was not sure if he would have felt better being left behind at the Hare and the Lynx, but the decision was not his in any case. They were all going. If it was a trap there would be no rescue. On the other hand, with all of them together they had the best odds of escaping a trap. He tried to breathe slowly, consciously trying not to worry. He was dressed in furs, waiting outside of the inn, standing next to Buttercup. He was warm under the weight of his outer clothing but was assured he would be cold by the time they got to wherever they were going. It was early in the morning and they were to travel all day. He had wanted to argue for them to fly, but Trela preferred that they all be a little tired by the time they got to the meeting rather than her mages being mostly spent.

They did travel much of the day, and it was a little chillier as far up the mountain as they had gotten, but Croy was certainly not cold. They were nowhere near the snow line as of yet. There was a hut in the distance with smoke emanating from its chimney. He assumed, correctly, that their destination was finally in view. There were not any locations for an ambush to be lurking as far as he could tell. It was not completely reassuring, but it was better than nothing. They arrived at the hut at least an hour before nightfall.

The hut was a cold and gray affair. It was comprised of old gray wood, split from the weather. It was not large by any means, but it was not small either. There was a little porch on the front, with a gray baluster surrounding it. The door was open and a lit fireplace was barely visible behind it. But Croy barely had time to register that. There was an old Fluen in a rocking chair on the porch that commanded his attention. She had a long and hooked pipe stuck out of her mouth which puffed out gray smoke periodically as she rocked. The pipe was larger than any he had seen Jalin use, and he wondered if they smoked the same herb. Her gray hair was held back in a long braid that had been tossed over the back of the chair. It swayed as she rocked.

"That's far enough for you and your army." The old lady stood and placed her pipe on the railing. "Kinda seems foolish to bring so many to a simple parley. Kinda like you're scared of an old lady."

Croy felt a rush and almost panicked—he definitely sensed magic. He thought for a moment they were being ambushed, but the rush he felt came from Feyazki. He had cast a spell of some kind. Feyazki whispered to Trela. Trela nodded.

"Which of you holds my granddaughter in bondage? Which one is named Trela?" The old lady leaned forwards and had two hands resting on the rail, propping herself up.

"I am Trela. My warriors fought with and captured Mika. By all rights she should be dead, not in bondage. All her companions were killed during combat." Trela took several steps forward, separating herself from the pack. "And, though we understand that you are quite formidable and fully respect you and your capabilities, it is because of the score or so of warriors you have hidden around us that we are wary, not just you."

"Well, I have found that it is better to be surrounded by friends than enemies. Wouldn't you agree?" She was still slightly stooped, leaning on the rail. Her laugh was dry and quiet. "Before we chat, I want to see my granddaughter. Bring her forward."

Trela nodded and waved back to Estfale, who had been keeping guard over Mika. They both approached. Mika stood to the right of, and just behind, Trela. Estfale stood behind her.

"I am glad to see she is not fettered. I would have thought you would bind her hands at least." The old lady nodded appreciatively.

"While she owes us her life, she is not necessarily our prisoner."

"Then she can come and go as she pleases?"

"No, she cannot. She owes us a mission."

"And what mission is that?"

"A life for a life. We are hunting a Gaen that betrayed us. The reason we did not kill her in combat was that she offered up her assistance in finding him. She assured us she knew where he was going and what he would be looking for there. We felt the mission overshadowed our desire for her death." Trela paused and looked around. "We would like to discuss these types of things quietly. We know we are surrounded by your friends, but cannot be sure that we are not also being watched by our enemies."

The old lady was quiet for some time. Croy was not sure if she was pondering the request or just trying to be dramatic. Try as he might, he could not sense anyone casting anything. That, at least, made him feel more comfortable.

"You can bring five of yours inside, along with Mika. You can keep Hupdor out here with the rest of your army as collateral. I promise that no harm will come to you tonight, at least not from me or mine. And I am a Fluen of my word." She abruptly turned and disappeared through the door. Croy thought it odd that she did not require such a promise from Trela.

Trela brought Feyazki and Estfale, of course. Then she grabbed Malghain and, oddly enough, Croy. Croy was not sure what to think. He had assumed he would be left outside with the others. He tried to think of what his special skills were that he had been invited but could not immediately come up with anything convincing.

They all filed into the cozy interior. There were several Fluen warriors already inside, attempting to look nonchalant. The interior was comprised of one large room. There was the fireplace against the far wall and a large table surrounded by chairs filled up the rest of it. Nice cast iron sconces lined the walls. The torches created more light, in aggregate, than the fireplace did. The front door was left open. Croy supposed it was to make them feel more comfortable about being split up.

The old lady sat down at the far side of the table, motioning to them to take the chairs opposite hers. There were goblets in front of each chair, and a narrow burgundy tablecloth, not more than two hands wide, ran the entire length. Croy sat down off to one side, leaving plenty of room for Trela and her more trusted advisors, but no one else sat down. It was awkwardly silent for a moment.

"What are you waiting for?" Rumhulga sounded impatient.

"I'm waiting for Mika to sit so I can place her guard near her. Then I'll sit." Trela had her arms crossed.

Croy assumed the guard meant Estfale. He was not quite sure why Feyazki did not sit, but he knew that Malghain would not sit before Feyazki. It was like an odd puzzle. Rumhulga turned to stare at Croy. He smiled sheepishly back.

"Please, Mika, sit. You're making everyone nervous." Rumhulga motioned towards the end farthest from Croy. It took a moment, but soon everyone was seated. They were all on one side of the table, their backs to the open door, with Rumhulga centered on the other. None of her non-nonchalant warriors took a seat, leaving the table feeling quite lopsided.

"This is a peaceful gathering, one that I hope will mutually beneficial. There is no reason, in my mind at least, why we cannot be friends." Rumhulga smiled at them all in quick succession, and then waved to one of her guards. He brought over a full pitcher of wine and began filling each goblet that had a derlian in front of it. "Do you wish to switch?"

"What?" Trela cocked an eyebrow at Rumhulga.

"It is customary to allow the guest the opportunity to switch wines during a parley. It is to reduce nervousness. You see, if you choose to switch, you'll drink from my glass and I'll drink from yours. If you choose not to, we'll each just drink from our own. In any case, since I do not know which you would prefer beforehand, it cuts down the odds that anything is poisoned. It is an old Fluen custom more than anything."

"Oh, that makes sense. No, I'll just keep my glass, that seems more trusting. I do want to trust you." Her smile was slightly crooked. Rumhulga responded with a large, warm smile on her somewhat wrinkled face.

Rumhulga lifted her glass. They all lifted their glasses. They all drank at the same time. Not that Croy was a paranoid type of derlian, but he assumed if they were to be ambushed, that was the time to do it. Luckily nothing happened and, to his delight, the wine was delicious.

"So, you lost the battle and were about to be killed and you made yourself useful enough to save your skin in the nick of time, eh?" Rumhulga stared straight at Mika, who merely nodded in acquiescence. "Good girl." She turned to Trela. "If she performs her usefulness… or if I perform it for her to your satisfaction, do you promise her safe return?"

Trela took a long time to speak. Croy could tell that she furiously thinking something, but had no idea of what it could be. He was not sure how much time was passing, but the silence was excruciating.

"We have a problem." Trela and Rumhulga stared at each other intensely. Not in anger or force, but full of intent. Everything about each of them was fully relaxed except for their eyes. "I may not be able to guarantee her safety."

"Even if we provide the Gaen traitor to you?"

"Correct."

"Interesting. Even more interesting is that you did not just lie to me about it. After all, accidents happen, do they not? Yet your word is strong enough you are unable to do that."

"My word is my life."

"Good. You will have to explain yourself to me, however. Currently I am unable to offer any sort of deal."

"I am not the party that demands the obliteration of… all that Mika represents. Or, I should say, represented."

"The other interested party… is more powerful than you? You are a queen where you come from, are you not?"

"The Belegs want me dead, oma." Mika interjected herself into the conversation. Though Croy was not familiar with the word "oma," he understood it to be a term of endearment.

"Shhh, hush dear. Let's not get too specific yet, at least not out loud." Rumhulga turned back to Trela. "This is truly the other interested party?"

"Unfortunately, yes."

"Then you should kill her now. And, of course, you will get no assistance with the traitor."

"Oma!" Rumhulga did not even glance over at Mika's interruption.

"And I assume there are no exceptions?" She kept her eyes trained on Trela.

"It has not been discussed. Our liaisons are unreachable at the moment."

"And I suppose that, your word being your life and all, you would be unable lose Mika in the shuffle. You could have Hupdor..." Mika's eyebrows shot up and her eyes glared angrily, but she did not provide a verbal outburst.

"Even if I were to agree, the lie would be found out eventually. But you are correct in the first instance. I have already made promises."

"So your plans were to betray Mika once you got what you wanted? You gave her no promises?"

"I have been very honest with Mika as to what I can promise or not. Are there things left unsaid? Of course. My plan, my hope, is to plead our case with a liaison once we are all back together again. As long as she is helpful along the way, I will do my best to convince them to let her live, that is all I can promise." Trela paused for a moment, but the only one who drank was Mika. She was really the only one drinking throughout the entire exchange.

"That's not good enough."

"So... we are back to killing her now and not receiving any help?"

"I need to think on it."

"No!" Mika did not quite slam her empty goblet on the tabletop, but it did strike forcefully. "I prefer the chance, oma. She is right, she has never promised my life to me, and I never asked. To be honest, I was afraid to ask. But I need a chance. A sliver of hope. I refuse to let you just kill me tonight."

"You refuse, do you? Do you know what I refuse? I refuse to assist your murderer in anything. I refuse to spend considerable time and effort and still have to watch you die." Rumhulga finally appeared to start getting angry. "In fact, I should just do the deed myself, here and now!"

"I thought you said you needed to think on it." Croy found himself speaking up. "This is a lot of information, there are a lot of emotions. I don't think any decisions should be made until the morning."

It grew quiet again. They all began to take sips of their wine, Croy included. *Where would they sleep? Would Mika try to escape? Would Rumhulga have them attacked during the night?* The thoughts careened around in his head, bouncing off one another.

"So, no one dies tonight, correct?" It was Mika, just making sure.

"Fine." Rumhulga downed her wine and stood. "You all may camp around here. I assume you will keep Mika and Hupdor. We'll speak again after dawn."

The rest of them shuffled around and slowly left the hut. Most of them had their eyes somewhat downcast. It certainly did not go as they had hoped. As they were leaving, Croy thought he could hear Feyazki. "You should have just lied." This was not totally unexpected. What was odd, however, is that he thought he heard Mika chime in as well. "Yes, I agree with the mage."

They gathered their group and decided to make camp just outside of the hut, maybe fifty rods off. Trela's reasoning was that they could not hide from Rumhulga's warriors, so they may as well gain some protection from any outsiders by sleeping in their shadow.

Croy did not have to help with guarding the prisoners and was not asked to join in any strategy sessions, if there were any. So he set up his small tent, ate his iron rations, and snuggled himself into his sleeping roll. He was not looking forward to trying to fall asleep, but was too tired to try anything else. He could only hope that Rumhulga was true to her word and that the night would be uneventful.

She was and it was. He awoke due to the light of dawn, nothing else. As he started to roll around and gain a little clarity, he thought he heard shuffling and voices. When he left his tent, he realized what the noise was. There were at least fifty warriors casually walking around. He would have felt more nervous but as he got up one came up and gave him some breakfast on a pewter plate. Another brought a glass of juice. It seemed to be made of oranges, which was quite a delicacy in the Gaen realm. Another offered to help him with his tent, but he declined. He slowly made his way to a long wooden table that had been set up outside of the hut. It had sturdy plank benches running along each side. Trela and Estfale were already there, eating. It appeared that Serghno and Arnasta were still asleep. Everyone was moving quietly and talking in whispers. It did not seem creepy, however, but more that they did not want to disturb any of Trela's little group. Feyazki joined them just as he sat down next to Trela.

"So… weird, huh?" Feyazki lifted his tray to let everyone know what he thought was weird.

"But tasty!" Estfale appeared to be fully enjoying himself. As soon as he finished his plate another was offered to him.

This happened for another half hour or so as everyone woke up and was served. Croy took the time to pack his tent and sleeping roll, balancing everything on Buttercup just in case they had to leave at a moment's notice. Finally, after they were all back at the table, Rumhulga arrived surrounded by more warriors. She sat down opposite of Trela as everyone else began to shift sides. All her warriors on one side of the table, all of Trela's along the other.

"I have thought long and hard about it. I want your help, Trela. I do not wish to see my granddaughter slaughtered. You need my help. Correct?" Trela nodded back to her. "Then we shall be friends. I will offer you everything at my disposal. Warriors, information, provisions, whatever you need. We will catch this traitor. We will catch him together, you and I." Trela made a motion to speak but Rumhulga waved her off. "Do not tell me again what your limitations are. I know you cannot promise results, I understand this. You, however, can promise me to try. To try your best, as if it were your own granddaughter's life. You swear an oath to me that you will do everything in your power, short only of risking your own life or that of your warriors, to convince the Belegs to spare my Mika, and you may have all that I can give as we track down the Gaen you wish to wreak vengeance upon. All I can do is trust in your oath. You appear to me to be someone who holds their own honor in high regard. I am counting on that." Her voice dropped a little quieter and she held Trela's gaze with her own steely eyes. "I need that."

"I swear a blood oath to you, Rumhulga. I will try my hardest to move the implacable, to convince the Belegs and any Yavens that may be their agents, to have mercy upon Mika." Trela whipped out her dagger and cut the palm of her hand before anyone had time to react. Rumhulga did not reciprocate, so Trela stood on the bench, over the table, squeezing her fist, dripping blood droplets on the center of the table. "You have my word of honor that I will do all I can to bring her safely back to you."

All of Rumhulga's warriors began to beat a slow rhythm on the table. Thud, thud, thud. Those that were standing beat their fists on their chests. It went on just a moment too long for Croy, just long enough for him to begin to look around in anticipation. Anticipation of what, he had no idea. Rumhulga stood on the bench opposite of where Trela was still standing.

"You are Trela's now. You are the Queen of the Pyran's warriors. You will serve her as you have served me. Faithfully, skillfully, and courageously. May you come back victorious. If you fail, however, do not come back at all." The slow thudding continued for another moment too long. Then, finally, silence.

The warrior to Rumhulga's right stood, though not on the bench. Trela had put her arm down, but was still standing. All the others at the table were sitting, all but those three.

"This is Sapryne. He is my most capable warrior. He will lead you to the Cave of Names and lead my warriors when they are not under direct orders from you. I have ultimate trust in him. If he is unable to achieve what you need, then I am of no help at all." The Fluen warrior bowed deeply after Rumhulga spoke. He did not say a word, but kept his gaze on Trela until it was broken by his bow. He paused for a moment, the upper half of his body perfectly horizontal, his face a mere hand from the tabletop, and then he slowly raised himself.

He had longish blond hair, held back with a piece of supple leather that encircled his head. His dress was the same as all the others, covered in a stiff leather shirt, pants and boots. It was dark in color and had wide stitching. He did not smile, but he did look relaxed and comfortable. After some time, he sat down as well.

"You may leave whenever you are ready." It seemed that Rumhulga did not want to sit while Trela was still standing. Croy was not really sure why she was still standing, maybe she was waiting for Rumhulga to sit first.

They did leave fairly soon after that, but they got well provisioned first. Mostly fur clothing and heavier tents for the cold mountains. Plus food enough for at least a moon, which was quite excessive or extravagant, depending on how one looked at it.

✳✳✳

It felt good to be on top of Buttercup again. Swaying along to an unheard rhythm, following a long line of other horses. He did not have to pay attention to anything, he could just be. And yet, even with his mind untethered and wandering, he did not think overly of Baltuz—at least not with too much melancholy. The rhythm kept his mind blank, which was how he liked it. Their small group was in the midst of Rumhulga's warriors, surrounded on all sides. Though he supposed they were Trela's warriors now. They all looked to Sapryne for orders, and he would immediately turn to Trela. It was a strong and unbroken chain of command.

They had been gone for three days of cold, cold travel. Though it was difficult to do so, Croy sought out Sapryne's company when they set up camp. Croy wanted to get to know him, learn about him and, maybe, Rumhulga as well. He was always surrounded by other warriors, however. And, even when Croy was able to ask him a couple of questions, he would usually just stare back with his intense dark blue eyes. He was incredibly taciturn, providing only a grunt or a nod. At best he would say a single word answer to Croy's queries. It was unsatisfying to have his curiosity so roundly rebuffed.

Having such a large force seemed to slow them down a little, but knowing where they were going made it worth it. Besides, would they have actually flown if it was just the coterie? There might have been enough mages when they were just fifteen, but that would have definitely needed to include Mika and Hupdor which, as much as he might consider them to be trustworthy, he doubted that Trela had the same consideration.

He was not sure why, maybe it was Sapryne's minimal communication skills, but at about the fifth day Croy began to wonder about everyone's true loyalties. What was to stop fifty warriors from slaughtering them and rescuing Mika and returning to Rumhulga? Sure, several would die in the process, maybe even many of them, but would that be a deterrent for a loyal warrior? He decided to ride next to Feyazki to see if he shared this new concern.

"Of course, we are concerned about that, but how else are we to find the cave? Estfale or Malghain are within striking distance of Mika at all times. We are constantly aware of where the warriors are. We sleep in shifts. We do all we can to keep ourselves safe and the way to do that is to be able to kill Mika as quickly as possible." Their horses crunched through the snow.

"So… why did no one tell me?"

"Well, you do such a great job of exuding innocence. You keep talking with Sapryne and the other warriors with your earnest questions. That feeling of goodwill and camaraderie extends over to the rest of us. You perform a very important function, Croy. You keep everyone smiling and we are able to forget we may be enemies for a while."

"But I will no longer be able to do that."

"Yes. That is unfortunate. We need to have a good talk with Sapryne anyway. It has taken a long time to get here and we'll need to figure out how much longer it will be. It might be good to have an honest discussion."

Croy paused for a long while, thinking. Now that he was overly concerned, he could not slow his mind down. "So… What if there is no cave? What if there is no Blind One, or at least not here, in the middle of the Fluen realm? What if this entire voyage was predicated only on Mika not wanting to die?"

"Ha! That is exactly what I told Trela." Feyazki chuckled to himself for a short moment. "She feels that the original story is true. There was some corroboration of that back in Vatlisi and so on. I think she feels this part of the story is also true. That Sapryne will take us to the cave, which will lead to the Blind One, and that Rumhulga is satisfied with a mere promise from Trela that she will do her best." He shook his head. "Who protects a derlian from a Beleg? Have you ever heard of such a thing?"

"So you think we are on a fool's errand?"

"I do, that is my opinion. But I have almost as much trust in Trela's instincts as she does. Who would have thought she could find the Luften Temple? Who would have thought she could have confronted Qizern in time, before his warriors destroyed hers, and that she could defeat him? Who would have thought we would find the Cabal and destroy it, or at least most of it? There are so many foolish errands I have performed, that I did not necessarily believe in, at least not fully, and yet here I am. Still alive, still fighting, still getting Clerin where she needs to be. I am fully amazed at the preposterousness of life. Does that mean I don't think what we are doing is absurd? Of course not, none of this makes any sense. However, I keep trusting that it will work out, that Trela's 'destiny' gives her insights that others ignore. That one day, when Clerin and I are old and gray, we will laugh at the absurdity of it all." He nodded to himself. "I keep myself vigilant to the point that I verge on being paranoid, but I do have hope. I guess that is something I gained through Clerin. I did not always have that, or at least not in this manner."

That night Croy did not seek out Sapryne. He had become overly worried and thought he would stammer or something to give away his misgivings. He did not want to appear to be conspiring either, so he just set up his tiny tent on the hard snow and lay down. It took him a little time to warm up his bedroll but once he did, he fell into a deep and dreamless sleep.

He woke up along with everyone else once dawn reached the sides of his tent. There was the typical commotion of food prep and breaking camp. He spent some time folding all his stuff up and burdening Buttercup before he wandered over to the breakfast fire. Before he was able to get anything, however, he was pulled away by Feyazki and Trela. She had decided to have her talk with Sapryne, who had just finished eating, and she wanted him to accompany her. They had to wade through some warriors to get within speaking distance.

"As you might imagine, myself and my Pyran warriors are not accustomed to the freezing temperatures here." She just launched into her spiel, without the niceties of any salutations. "Therefore, while we are certainly willing to endure all of the necessary hardships that are required, we would like to know how close we are to our goal and approximately how long it will take to get there." She almost sounded like Clerin for a moment.

Sapryne sat there quietly for a while, his eyes travelling between the three of them. The left side of his mouth twitched up in what some might describe as a smile. "You are wondering where we are, where we are headed, and how soon we might get there, are you not?" Trela nodded, being the taciturn one for a moment. "And you are also hoping for a little more assurance. Correct? It has been some time since you spoke with Rumhulga and you have been stuck with myself and my Fluen warriors for too long, hoping we are not wandering aimlessly or, even worse, towards some sheer cliff that you may stumble down." He looked around to his warriors and they all nodded. Croy was not exactly sure why. *They* were certainly not concerned about a cliff.

"We are just looking for a timeline." She may have been going to say more, but maybe not. She stopped just before he interrupted.

"We are close. Two days. Full days. Three days at the worst." He nodded back at her, falling back into his customary silence.

"Good, thank you." She turned to walk away.

"And you may rest assured that we have as much honor as you do. Rumhulga made you a promise and we intend to keep it." All the Fluen warriors nodded at them as they were leaving.

The two days were slowed down by drudgery and the cold, but they did finally pass. The group made camp with Sapryne's assurances that they would be able to reach the cave within a couple of hours of waking. It was odd that this made Croy a little nervous. He did not think that they would, but if they were going to attack at night, this would be the night to do it.

Croy awoke to the peaceful cold once again. It seemed that Sapryne was, indeed, honorable. Croy went through the same motions again, packed his gear away, tried to stay warm. He ate the same food again, but since it was always hot food, he rather enjoyed it. It was when they had to eat their iron rations on their horses that he protested. Well, not out loud, but in his head he protested.

After about two hours of travel, they arrived at the mouth of a cave. It was a dark gaping maw against the bright snow. Somehow Croy was able to get more goosebumps.

About ten of Rumhulga's warriors were to stay just outside the entrance to guard the horses and their equipment. Croy hoped they had arrived before the Blind One, but he also hoped that the Blind One was not too far behind. Once they had scouted the cave out and felt comfortable, they would move what equipment they could inside and hide everything else. Croy dismounted and headed towards the mouth. Trela and Sapryne were talking in low tones, so he approached enough to eavesdrop. He was one of several that had the same idea, making a rough but well-distanced semi-circle around the two of them.

"No, this is the youngest cave." Sapryne was standing stiff with his arms crossed.

"Our concern was that our prey was looking for the oldest." Trela was gesturing with her hands, still open for discussion.

"You might be able to get there from here, but there is no other entrance. There's a whole system under here is what I understand. Whether or not they all have names carved in them or whatever, I do not know."

"That's not what was discussed."

"That *is* what was discussed. Trust me, the oldest cave is impossible to get to without magic. At least directly." He paused and squinted. "Listen, I am not a mage. Rumhulga directed me to take you to the Cave of Names and here we are." He swept an arm to encompass the whole entrance, but then it quickly returned to its stubborn location.

"Are there several caves?"

"Yes."

"Then we wish to go to the oldest, not just whichever one is easiest to…" Trela was interrupted, which was just as well since they were getting nowhere.

"Sapryne is correct, there is only one entrance besides the ice dam." Mika left Estfale's side and walked into the argument, making a triangle out of their energy, changing the dynamic. "We can attempt the dam, but we could check this cave first. As he mentioned, it does go fairly deep into the mountain. Maybe there is an easier way to get to the oldest cave. Maybe the Blind One is looking for this one. There are many unknowns. What is known, however, is that arguing about this at the cave entrance is not helpful to anyone."

Trela gave Mika a long hard stare before responding. "Fine, we explore this cave, but if nothing is found then you shall show us the ice dam."

"Of course." Mika nodded and went back to Estfale. Sapryne just stood there with his arms crossed. Trela turned and walked into the cave, as if she could explore it by sheer force of will alone. Croy trotted after her.

"Mektralufreppi!" He cast a light spell as they began to move away from the entrance. They walked for a while in silence. Well, their boots made a fair amount of noise and he could hear the others scramble behind them, but they did not speak for a while.

"Thanks for the light." She was striding briskly and turning corners purposefully, choosing the way to go as if she had spent her whole life in the caves. "I just need… some distance."

After some wandering, they turned a corner into a tall and long hallway. One of the long walls had many deep etchings in them. Huge, long names. Each letter was approximately the size of Croy's head and there must have been twenty names scattered along the wall.

Trela walked down to almost the center of the wall and then stepped back, leaning against the opposite wall, and just stared. Her head was tilted, reading names approximately halfway up the wall, approximately five rods high. There was a small smile on her lips.

The others were fast upon them. They had dawdled out of deference, not because they had been unable to keep up. Rumhulga's warriors were not among them, they were probably setting up a main camp closer to the cave entrance, but all those who had sailed across the Clatsvol were there. Everyone stood and stared at the carved letters in silence. Croy wondered if he should write one down or something.

Feyazki wandered to the end of the hallway and back. He broke the long silence. "It has the word 'Fluen' in the corner over there." He pointed from whence he had come. "Do you think all these names are of Fluen Yavens? Do you think there are other hallways with other races, other elements?"

Mika did not answer him. No one offered their opinion on the subject. Others went to investigate, and all came back nodding. Croy took Feyazki's word for it. That word was carved into the wall. What it meant, however, was still up for interpretation. He assumed they would explore the cave further and find more walls. Once that happened, the different theories could be examined.

"Is there any way to tell if he has been here yet?" Trela turned to Arnasta.

"I can try. It depends upon how he travels here and how he leaves." Arnasta walked back over to the entrance of the hallway, muttering to herself. Serghno followed faithfully.

Croy just stared at the wall. The hallway was so tall that it seemed narrow. The names were spread out and the letters had small shadows cast over them, they were so deeply carved. The derlians around him faded away, growing dimmer and quieter. It was an odd form of mesmerism, the vastness of it. Usually Croy needed to stare at repetitive movement to lose himself, to feel this small, but the wall was perfectly still. It loomed over him. His mind wondered how many cycles those names represented, how many eons of experience they encompassed. It was unfathomable.

"Croy. Croy!" It was Trela; she was waiving her hand in front of him. "Arnasta wants to chat with you." Her serious face relaxed into a smile as his eyes refocused away from the wall. "Pretty mind-boggling, huh? I understand how you feel. Even though I doubt I could describe it." She patted him on the shoulder. He shook his head to clear it and walked over to Arnasta and Serghno.

"I'm having a hard time sensing anything. I don't think he has been around, but it is hard to disprove an emptiness." Arnasta was waving a hand at him, bringing him in closer. "I want you to sit here and get comfortable. Get weightless. Get blank. Then, when I need you to, I want you to think of the Blind One, only of him. Anything that brings emotions, good or bad, it does not matter to me. I just need intensity."

"Okay." What else was there to say?

This type of thing, blankness, always depended on some comfort for Croy. If there was a rock digging into him, or if his legs were crossed too tightly, his mind would get fixated on the annoyance. So he cleared the area, sat down, and did his best to not anticipate what was to come, to just be blank. He slowed his breathing and thought of a neutral gray color. Yes, a gray stone wall that stretched in all directions. Except the wall became peppered with carved letters spelling Yaven names. He shook his head lightly to clear the image. Maybe a different color would be better. He was blank for a moment, but then thought of Ilana. Arnasta did not scold him, was not really paying attention to him, so he let his mind wander a little.

Thinking of Ilana made him think of the School of Larelt, and of when she watched his trances, his dreams. An unconscious smile crept into his lips. Thinking of her watching over him as he slept, her body next to his, the lavender smell of her hair, it was all very relaxing. As his mind wandered, however, it slipped to Rycher, when his dreams were watched by the Blind One. He had never really understood that, why the Blind One would imprison him to watch his dreams. He felt himself getting angry. Angry about the imprisonment, of course, and angry about his capture and that no one had been able to stop it from happening, that Feyazki had been unable to stop it. Mostly, though, his anger was about his dreams being spied upon. It had felt violating, to know that someone could recall your sleeping life more completely than you could yourself. For Croy did not always remember all the detail of his dreams upon waking, even the ones that felt *important*. That was what did it, the anger at another being, the Blind One no less, knowing his inner unconscious visions better than he ever could, that was what triggered his memory.

It was not a dream itself, and certainly no vision. Croy could feel that it was just a memory of a dream. An old memory of an old dream. He was deep in a cave, as usual in his dreams, and surrounded by robed and cloaked figures. The idea of the robed figure was quite usual, but there were many more than typical. They all had their backs to him and formed somewhat of a rough circle around him. He rotated slowly, staring at all of their backs, seeing no details, just the vague notion of "figure." They all had cowls drawn over their heads. Their cloaks and robes were of the same color, making it difficult to distinguish where one started and one ended. They were all so drab and the memory so hazy, that they certainly could have been the same figure, repeated over and over. He had a hard time counting them since he was unsure of where to start and stop. The monotone background was not helping either. He tried holding an arm up, pointing at one of the figures, to get his bearings as he counted, but could only come up with a vague number of approximately twenty-one. Since it did not matter to him much, he abandoned the project soon after he started. That was not the importance of his memory.

He had to strain for the important part. He was certainly not as blank and relaxed as Arnasta had requested, but he could feel the memory being teased out like a complicated knot with one loose string. He picked at it until it was a loop, until he could get an end worked out. He had his eyes scrunched shut, thinking only of his long-forgotten dream.

In his mind, the ground below him began to rumble and shake. He was in the middle of the circle of figures and the ground was bulging up. It knocked him backwards, onto his butt. The ground erupted upwards and became a Yaven, a giant Yaven that pulsated with immense power. It picked him up as it knelt down. He was pulled close to a giant face of stone, like an enormous statue, or maybe that he was a tiny ant crawling around on a regular sized statue. The face was rough-hewn, he could see the chisel marks. There was almost a look of worry on the face, of concern. Then, without warning, he remembered the one message given to him in that dream. "You must stop Clerin Toswin!"

That was a dream that the Blind One had seen? Stolen from his slumbering head. *That* was a message that he could barely remember? It shivered him to his core, his remembrance. But, more than that, it angered him. It welled up and spilled over. How could the Blind One have seen that dream and not told him? How could he have kept Croy's own dream a secret from him? It made Croy wonder why he had not remembered the dream at the time. Why he had not remembered any of his dreams from Rycher, at least none beyond the birds. Could the Blind One have done something to him, suppressed him somehow? The one thing that did not enter Croy's mind was that his memory was false. It felt truer to him than his own name. But did that make it so?

"Yes, perfect! Keep up the intensity Croy, we are almost there." Arnasta's voice pierced the fog. Of course, she did not want the fog pierced, she wanted him to think intently of the Blind One. So he let the anger wash over him. The imprisonment, the feeling of violation, the supposed suppression, all of it. He let it all crush down into one iota of thought. The Blind One. He seethed.

"Yes, I have it, I've found him!" Arnasta was patting him on the back. "He's down below us, incredibly deep!"

Her voice had not seemed incredibly loud, but suddenly there was commotion all around. Warriors were suddenly busy gathering stuff up, Feyazki stopped writing down names from the wall, Trela was telling Sapryne that she had known all along that the Blind One would be in the ancient cave. Croy had not even realized that Sapryne and the others had found them. It was all a bit of controlled chaos.

They were soon on their way, a long sinuous line that followed Arnasta down into the cave system. Croy wondered if she could tell the path to get to the Blind One, or if she could only tell what direction he was in or how far away he was. Then they reached a dead end and he realized it was certainly not the path that she sensed.

Sapryne conferred with his warriors as the rest of them paced. Arnasta was attempting to slowly backtrack, staring below her feet seemingly through the rock. She then began walking with purpose again.

Trela was following, with Mika and Estfale near the front. Then the coterie. Bringing up the rear were Sapryne and his warriors. As they went deeper into the caves, Croy began to feel a wave of nervousness wash over him. If they were to be ambushed, would this not be the perfect place? His only calming thought was that they could have been attacked at any point along the way. Sure, they were *more* trapped now, but at least Mika was separated from the warriors. He, at least, had sincere faith in Arnasta and her abilities. He felt they were truly tracking the Blind One.

They wended their way through the cave system for some time, an hour at least. The Blind One was obviously looking for a Yaven name, but Croy had no idea how long that should take. They had passed some more walls with writing on them on their way down, so the names were certainly scattered about, at least in the younger cave. Arnasta had said they were getting closer, so the Blind One was certainly still in the system. Eventually, after another half hour or so, they arrived at a dead end, capped by a frozen wall that bulged into the room a little. The cavern was quite large, allowing them to spread out so they could each examine the wall better. It was not overly interesting to Croy, it was merely the stopping point.

"How far does it go?" The question was asked by more than one observer. No one had an answer.

"Forever." Mika nodded to herself while staring at the wall of ice.

They pondered and discussed for a while. Serghno had suggested melting a tunnel through it, while Feyazki wanted to shape a tunnel more directly by turning the ice into air. Both options seemed like they would take a while. And, if it were a dam, did that mean there was a giant lake somewhere behind it? He knew they were headed down, but drilling sideways for a while would surely risk a rupture. Though Mika was obviously exaggerating with her response, it was estimated by some that the ice covered the same amount of distance as they had already traversed. Croy thought the idea of estimating the thickness of the ice was a bit ridiculous. How could they really know without probing? Then he got an idea.

"What about Wil? Could we resummon Wil to help us move through this more quickly?" He was speaking to Feyazki, who was still arguing with Serghno and not really listening to Croy, when Trela slapped him on the back rather hard.

"That is a great idea, Croy!" She spoke loudly enough and with enough direct intent focused on Feyazki that he stopped his speech and glanced over. "Croy thinks we should summon Wil, the Fluen Yaven. You still remember his name, don't you Feyazki?"

It took Feyazki a moment to respond. It appeared that he was thinking hard about the name, his face blank and his eyes fluttering upwards. Suddenly he looked over at Croy and smiled.

"That is a good idea." He snapped his fingers and turned to Trela. "I think I had it written down somewhere, just in case, hold on." He removed his backpack and quickly found the book he was looking for. He wandered to a far corner, away from the distracting conversations, as he thumbed through the pages.

Trela quickly became distracted herself, leaving Croy alone for a brief moment. He could still feel the slap on his back as she gotten Feyazki's attention. It felt good.

Everyone was milling about, so he did is well. He started to mill over towards Feyazki when Wil, the Fluen Yaven, suddenly appeared. It flowed up from a fissure in the floor, a small geyser of erupting water. It quickly capped out at derlian height, then filled out into its typical form. The arms were rather stiff and the legs appeared melded together, like the bottom of some robes. The facial features, however, seemed quite well defined. Even more so than usual. It always amazed Croy that though Wil was made of a roiling mass of water, it never seemed to get the ground wet.

"I should not have come." Those were the first words Croy could discern.

"We need you, and quickly." Feyazki was bowing, which made the others in the room bow. This seemed to take Wil aback a bit. It swiveled its torso in a full circle to take in the scene.

"I assumed; I could sense your urgency." It paused in its swivel, facing Feyazki. "Where is Clerin Toswin?"

"She's back at Vatlisi."

"I should not have come."

"Please, Wil, we just need to travel through this glacier. We are trying to track down the last of the Cabal's mages." Trela inserted herself into the conversation. "The Blind One is here, far below us. We must get to him before he escapes."

Wil swiveled around some more, but this time appeared to be examining the surroundings more than the derlians. No one interrupted it. It rounded back on Trela. "The Gaen mage?" She nodded. "We are not sure about that one. That is a murky pond. We doubt the intent is truly aligned with the Cabal... but there is something nefarious there." Another long, uninterrupted pause. "Yes, of course, the chase. I can take three of you definitely, four of you possibly."

"We'll need four." Trela turned to the crowd, snapping her fingers at Croy, then yelling out for Arnasta. "We cannot risk an escape."

Croy was not really sure why he was coming, maybe as bait, but he was especially not sure how helpful Trela would be. It was always just a given that she would participate—how else could she lead? Though they were each crammed into a separate chamber of Wil, he could still feel the others quite intimately. He was uncomfortably close with Arnasta, almost spooning as it were.

Then they were off. Wil leapt into the glacier's wall, and they slid down and around and through. It was a wild ride that Croy kept his eyes screwed shut for the entire time. He even held his breath as much as he was able. Then, as suddenly as it started, they came to a jarring stop. They popped out of another glacier wall within the cave system, this one presumably much lower.

"You must find and confront your prey on your own. I should not influence events. At least, not unduly. At least not more than I already have. Yavens are not supposed to be visiting your realm right now. I will wait here for you, be quick." Wil faded back into the wall. It was a little eerie. Arnasta pointed out the way and they lost no time starting the hunt.

They were almost jogging as they flowed down through the various tunnels. Feyazki had a light spell going, which lit up much of the area, but cast eerie shadows around them as they moved. Croy wondered briefly if he should cast one as well. Then, with little warning from Arnasta, they turned a corner and there, way off in the distance, was the Blind One.

He appeared to be staring up at a wall in the dark, with no perceptible light of his own. The hall was similar to the one Croy saw above, tall with deeply etched names. He seemed to be writing something in a tiny book as he was looking upwards. The only thing that indicated that he was aware of them was that his writing sped up. Trela and Feyazki both burst into a dead run, streaming past Arnasta. Croy decided he may as well join them. His short legs churned underneath him.

"What, did you use, a Yaven?" He sounded surprised at the notion. "You do not understand what is happening."

Trela yelled something unintelligible. Lightning shot from Feyazki's hands an instant later. The Blind One disappeared.

They ran all the way to the end of the hallway, though Croy was unsure why. The Blind One had certainly escaped once again. When they got there, Trela looked around on the ground for a while.

"I must have hit him with my dagger, I can't find it anywhere." She kept searching while talking.

"Good." Feyazki smiled at no one in particular. "To be honest, I wasn't sure if this was to be a prisoner thing, or an execution thing. That kind of slowed me down; I apologize."

"Don't worry about it, I wasn't sure either." Trela had a wry smile on her face.

Chapter 4

Clerin did not necessarily enjoy what she was doing, but she enjoyed where she was doing it from. The running of the day-to-day items for Vatlisi was a bit tedious, but not odious. The repair work on the palace and some parts of the city was actually quite interesting, when it was not also tedious. The main complaint she had of the job was trying to track down the last of the Cabal, though she did not have to do any of that personally. She felt that they had captured or killed most everyone associated with it such that now there were only rumors of rumors of members. Or, even worse, those who were willing to fake evidence or lie about hearsay to settle old grudges with bad neighbors. It seemed that the way to settle a score in Vatlisi at the moment was to get someone marked as a Cabal member, the higher up the echelon the better. Clerin did not enjoy sifting through petty lies and grievances to try to find that one last grain of truth. Still, it was important work, and she was surely not going to shirk any of it, even if it had been quite some time since the last "real" Cabal member was found.

Clerin also collected items that came from the Gaen realm. Gunzgak did whatever Belegs did, and a half wagon full from Hifrim arrived shortly after the Cabal was destroyed. Another smaller wagon arrived from Serif later. At least they did not have to hunt down every Yaven-infused item by themselves. She handed over the wagons to Wesduin, Trela's quartermaster, who was keeping track of all the items. The items themselves were kept secret, even if the desire to hunt them down was not. Handing things over to Wesduin was quite a simple task, and making sure the Gaens who dropped things off were kept comfortable and paid was not too difficult either. They typically left soon after arriving, having their own time schedules to keep.

What Clerin did enjoy, however, was the palace. It was beautiful and wonderful and amazing. It more than made up for any annoyance or tedium she endured during her workday. The view from the various turrets, truly each and every individual view, was spectacular. She spent as much time as she could each day in a different turret. The food was fantastic, the guards courteous, the officials… well the officials were not always perfectly pleasant, especially when you had some from Tureyn and some from Vatlisi in the same room at the same time arguing opposite points, but everything else was great. She knew the Toswin name was too small to attach to a city such as Vatlisi. She knew that this could never be a permanent post, that she was filling in until a new prince or princess could be elevated, but she enjoyed it while she could. She enjoyed it immensely.

She spent her days there while Vrric was out with Trela chasing the Blind One. In truth, time seemed to fly by. Each day was full and busy, but each week passed within the blink of an eye. That was until she received a new contingent from Tureyn. There were several of them, maybe seven, and they were huddled together in a group. They were milling about when she entered the room, talking amongst themselves, not really expecting her. Once she glided in, they began to line up and present themselves. There was one that shocked her, and she ended up ignoring the others. He was a little older than her, clean shaven and strong, with soft brown eyes that were rare amongst the Fluens. It was his smile that she recognized more than anything, though. It beamed through his entire face.

"Olwinn!" His name burst from her unbidden. It had been cycles since she had last seen her magic teacher, when he had summoned Wil that first time, but it felt like an eternity. Somehow his smile got bigger.

"Clerin Toswin, you are the spitting image of Midinarre." He bowed low. She did not like being told she looked like her mother, not typically, but he made it sound like such a compliment that she let the comparison slide. At least he did not say she sounded like her mother or, worse yet, acted like her mother.

"And what brings you to Vatlisi?" As she spoke, she realized she cut off the rest of them from being able to introduce themselves. She would have to rectify that later. Surely Olwinn was not the highest-ranking member of the group.

"We—" he pointed amongst his companions "—have been appointed by the King to help finalize the repairs to the palace and to prepare Vatlisi for Princess Inquella Erintwala's imminent arrival."

"Ah, excellent. We should prepare a feast for you all." Though she had never met the princess, she knew the name Erintwala. They were a prominent and powerful family. It made sense they would be given Vatlisi. "When you say imminent, what exactly do you mean?"

"Not for a couple of days. Probably three." It was one of the other Fluens who answered, probably the one who had been chosen to lead the contingent. She smiled warmly at him.

"Good, good. And your repair discussions? Might they wait until after dinner? It appears that you have traveled far and are probably in need of a little rest before business." It was a strong Fluen custom to allow your guests time to recuperate before discussing serious matters. They would surely want to bathe and dress for the occasion, to be able to put their best foot forward as it were. She had been spending enough time surrounded by Pyrans to second guess herself, however. Maybe they were in a dire hurry to discuss the repairs?

"Thank you, much obliged." He, still unnamed, bowed low to her. "Though we had favorable winds, it *has* been a tiring journey." They all bowed, and they all looked grateful. They were certainly not in a dire hurry to discuss anything.

"Good, I will send for you shortly after the evening bell." She snapped her fingers to one of her guards, who quickly trotted over. She had chosen that guard since hers was the only name she could recall on such short notice. She did not have Trela's gift of memorizing all those who worked for her. Or, at least, she had not exercised it enough to compare. "Yaghan, please show these very important guests to the suites in the south tower, then return to me."

"Of course, Regent." She bowed as well. Yaghan did not always bow, so Clerin assumed it was for the benefit of the guests. What she lacked in protocol, she typically made up in capability. Clerin fully assumed that Yaghan would get the guests' names and some simple information about them for her. Nothing too complicated, but enough to make a smooth transition at dinner. She was not disappointed.

The leader's name was Weitno Catajohl, and though Clerin had not heard of that family, Yaghan impressed upon her that Weitno thought they should be well known in Tureyn, if not Vatlisi. There were other names, Dinara, Jinlulo, and Altinca, that she could remember. There were two or three others. Clerin ordered the chef to make it an impressive dinner, leaving just enough room to maneuver for the true feast required for the Princess's arrival. She was certainly not going to overshadow that. For this contingent, though the food would be extensive, there were only so many guests. The chef was delighted to have several days to prepare for the

Princess. He was already planning the feast, writing notes to himself, while he was talking to Clerin about the upcoming meal.

Clerin had her regular business to attend to, so was unable to do proper research herself. She asked everyone she dealt with if they knew anything about the Catajohl family, but none of the guards, servants, or visitors did. She thought about bothering Olwinn, to try to get an idea of what kind of wine would be enjoyed the most but decided against it. She opted, instead, to have several nice bottles brought up from the cellar for her guests to choose from.

The day flew by and soon the evening bell was rung. Clerin sent out Yaghan to get the others, finished her bit of business, then began the walk to the dining hall. She had invited Rewista, Escha and Torpalin just to add some flavor. She had not really wanted to bring any Fluens from Vatlisi to the dinner. She would wait to mix the new Tureyn group in until tomorrow. At that moment, the only Vatlisi Fluens that officially knew about the Princess's immanent arrival were the chef and a couple of guards. She supposed that the rumor was spreading through the palace fairly quickly but did not intend to assist it in any way.

The dining hall in the south tower was not huge, but not small either. The table was large enough to seat twenty, so they left one end empty. The chandelier was full of candles, all pleasantly lit and flickering even though the sun had not fully disappeared. The table itself was single slab of some hardwood and surrounded by high-backed, armless chairs. The chair cushions were of a light-blue velvet which stood in stark contrast to the dark, thick, and roughly filigreed wood. There were windows along the south wall, showing a bit of city in the distance, letting in a little light and lot of air. There were large tapestries, somewhat faded from time, that adorned the north wall. Majestic landscape scenes and the like. She enjoyed the room and wished she had eaten there more often.

The guests were milling about when she arrived. They bowed when she entered, showing respect for her position even if it was a temporary one. She reciprocated. Quick introductions were had, and they all sat down. The food was good and the wine even better. They laughed and joked and talked of small matters while they ate. The conversation did not turn to more serious matters until after they had finished the food.

"We understand the repairs are running smoothly." Weitno pushed his plate away and brought his glass closer.

"Yes, as much as can be expected." Clerin had pushed her plate away a little bit ago but reached for her glass in commiseration. "It will certainly not be finalized in the next couple of days. Maybe a couple of more weeks."

"Oh, no, that is fine. Just fine. The Princess may wish to make the more decorative repair decisions herself anyway. We hear you have done a fine job. Really, nothing but good words about you." He nodded to himself, which got all of the others nodding and agreeing. "Yes, the Toswin name has grown quite a bit, what with your mother being a favorite of Lembin's and you…" He waved his hand effusively about him, indicating the palace in general. "If Aillel had survived, he might be getting the promotion instead of Inquella."

The mention of her father's name stilled Clerin's heart. And that his death was so casually spoken of. She had not been expecting it. Much to her chagrin, she had not thought about him for some time. Her body froze, her face froze. Luckily, there was a small smile already in place. She wondered what her face would have looked like if it had frozen halfway in-between expressions. With a monumental force of will, she made her arm raise her glass of wine up to her lips. She took a nice long draught before placing the glass gently back on the sturdy table. The small smile did not slip.

"You did know of course, yes?" He still looked relaxed. She wondered what his game was. Maybe he was just used to being a jerk.

She made herself nod to him. She made her smile slightly bigger. She made her arm bring her another draught of wine.

"Good, good. That is another reason we have come here, dear Clerin. Your father was fantastic, liked by everyone. He always thought things through, made sound decisions, even if they were simple. We believe that you may have some of his traits as well. We have been watching you during the repairs." He waved his hand again. "You see, with Aillel gone, and your mother being who she is, we are trying to figure who will best carry the Toswin torch, as it were."

"Well, my sister is older…" She unfroze, more because of the bizarre turn of the conversation than anything else.

"Yes, yes, we understand that. But you, dear Clerin, you, like your mother, have communed with Lembin. Like your father, you have ably traversed the maze of bureaucracy. We see in you a gentle mix of two great Fluens. We see in you the most capable hand to carry the torch."

"Well, I am certainly flattered…" Her cheeks were getting some heat behind them. She glanced around the table and everyone was just staring. They were smiling, to be sure, but all eyes were fixed hard on her. It made her a little uncomfortable.

"The marriage would not be for some time, of course." Weitno was still smiling at her. Clerin froze again. *Marriage?!* "I can tell by the look on your face that this had yet to occur to you. Let me assure you that none of us here would be wooing you." He laughed a bit nervously for a second. "And since you are the keeper-of-the-name, you would get your choice from a list of suitable suitors. A list that would be vetted through Midinarre, of course. We wish, more than anything, to sustain and enhance the name of Toswin."

"You believe in marriage without love?" Escha crossed her arms while squinting at Weitno. "What if she already loved another?"

"What if she loved a foreigner?" Torpalin added his bit. Clerin wished he had not, that they had not. She did not want to be involved in the conversation, and certainly did not want them involved at all. She felt she would scream if someone mentioned Vrric's name.

"What if she loved another female?" Rewista stepped in with some misdirection.

Weitno looked taken aback from their various questioning. He glanced quickly between them, eyes furtive as he decided which to respond to first. He picked the simplest. "Well, no, we are talking Familial Marriage here. This is a marriage that requires progeny. We are combining families. Without children, you see, there is no tie. Marriage amongst your own sex is forbidden in a Familial Marriage. Same gender affairs are encouraged, however. If they must happen. Since then all the children are obviously of the marriage, not of the affair. We do understand the burden of bringing families together, we are not monsters, and, as you are the keeper-of-the-name, you would have greater latitude in these matters."

"That still doesn't seem very fair." Rewista squinted at Weitno with her raptor's eyes.

"This has nothing to do with fair, this is the elevation of one name through the absorption of another. It is an almost-symbiosis scenario and, though each side of the family may argue that they are the most tread upon, it is always the poorer. It is always better to be elevated than to be absorbed. You are in a good position here, Clerin. You have a great opportunity. For your family name, of course, but for you personally as well. Think about it. Seriously. That is all we ask. We are not yet in a rush." He nodded to her, ignoring Rewista. "Oh, I almost forgot, we also bring a message. Lembin wishes to commune with you again. We were told to escort you back to Tureyn at your earliest convenience. Olwinn will fill you in, won't you, Olwinn?"

"What do you think, exactly, would 'earliest convenience' mean, Weitno? Three days' time?" She smiled brightly. It was an effortless smile at this point. It was the smile she used with older Lords, and she had recovered from her earlier shocks.

"To be able to enjoy the extravagant feast with the Princess once she arrives? I believe that would fall squarely into the 'earliest convenience' time window. Nobody would begrudge you that. After all, since you will have to plan that exact extravagant feast, you should be able to share in its indulgence. Besides, we are sure the Princess will wish to speak with you about all you have done and are doing for Vatlisi." He abruptly stood, which made his fellows stand as well. "I wish you a long and insightful evening Clerin, followed by a night of empowering dreams." He patted Olwinn's shoulder as he walked by.

As they left, she made a mental note to do some real research into the Catajohl name. She was going to need more information about them. And if she could dig up anything on Weitno himself in the process, that would be counted as serendipity.

It was quiet for a while as the servants cleared the table. Clerin drank her wine and refilled it. The others were of similar mindset. The impatience welled up in her slowly at first, but then suddenly.

"So, are you going to fill me in?" She stared pointedly at Olwinn.

"Oh, well, I was thinking we could talk in a setting that was a little more private." He glanced over at Rewista, Escha and Torpalin, who were all that were left. His eyebrows arched and he gave a small nod towards them.

"These are my friends. I want them to hear." She gave a small nod as well.

"You don't know what I have to say."

"About Weitno's Familial Marriage proposal? Please, be my guest." She took a gulp of wine down.

"No, not that. You know what that is."

"And they already have my mother's approval, I assume? That is why you are here, to make sure I get back to Tureyn?"

"Yes, I am supposed to get you back to Tureyn."

He threw his hands up defensively as she made to stand.

"Not for that. No, it's nothing like that." He was waving his hands in front of him, as if warding off an attack. "Lembin wishes to commune with you, Clerin. It is that simple, nothing nefarious. And it is *not* a request, that much is clear."

"That doesn't fill me in, now does it?" Her eyebrows arched in turn. "Weitno assumed you could fill something in. That is what I got out of that exchange. Would you agree?" She turned her attention to her friends. They all nodded in return, their eyes heavy with concerned commiseration, and uttered demure agreements.

Olwinn glanced around for a moment before returning his gaze to Clerin. "Lembin's... I don't know... sick or something. Midinarre, who, of course, knows about the marriage thing and approves of it, has been talking to Lembin almost once a week. There is so much traffic there it's... weird. Midinarre won't tell me exactly what is going on. No, wait, scratch that. Midinarre won't tell me anything that is going on. In fact, when I asked her what Lembin wished to commune with you about, she said that *you* would know. Ha! Right? So I asked her again and she threatened to fire me and make sure I never worked for another family again. So, technically, you are supposed to know more about what I should fill you in on than I do."

"You are just going to blame this on my mother?" Clerin finished her glass.

"If you were able to, wouldn't you?" They both laughed and the mood lightened slightly.

"So, they are really going to make her marry?" It was Escha, not Rewista, who brought it back up. Torpalin was quietly staring forlornly into his cup, ignoring all.

"Now, in Weitno's defense, this is a specific type of marriage. No one cares who no-names marry. This is not a general Fluen issue. And, if your family is powerful enough, you can choose whoever you'd like to marry. Depending on the family. This would be a Familial Marriage—a bringing together of two families in the hopes of creating a dynasty. For that to work, there must be children, children of the two parents. Not adopted children, not children from a previous marriage, not children spawned from a different father, none of that. It is a new family line that is being created. It is, as Midinarre would say, quite an honor. It would solidify the Toswin name for generations. Clerin could even get a small town. Nothing like Vatlisi, of course, but maybe a small, but bustling, port town?" He raised an eyebrow to her.

"So, she does not have to marry? This is merely an opportunity?" Escha pressed forward.

"Yes and no. In theory, this is merely an opportunity. The issue is that by the time the participants are told about it, everyone else, or at least everyone above them, has already gotten excited about the idea." He turned from Escha to Clerin. "You must understand what this means to Midinarre. Especially now, with Aillel dead." He had the decency to cringe a little at himself as he said that.

"Yes. I will want to talk about that as well. Some other time, however. I feel like I need a little rest. It has actually been a long day." Clerin glanced one more time into her glass. Yep, still empty.

All the others agreed and stretched. Olwinn looked a little hesitant, as if they should chat some more after all the others had left, but Clerin did not feel like it. She really was tired.

It took until the next evening before she was able to be alone with Olwinn. Her day had been full of typical meetings and Weitno's group took up any spare time she might have had. They were quite willing to promise all sorts of help for the repairs, but much of it seemed to be just stalling. Certainly nothing more was going to happen until the Princess arrived. So, even though her day was full, she only got so much accomplished. She spent the last hour or so just getting books in order to hand over. She would probably have to do that for a good chunk of the next day as well.

It was after dinner and she invited him to her study. They drank a little wine and talked of nothing for an hour or so. He was quite charming. When she was younger, she may have had a crush on him. Then, as she grew into her rebellious years which, for her, were not actually that rebellious, she wondered if he had had an affair with her mother. She was never quite sure, and it was difficult to tell her mother's true moods or emotions, but there were signs. Glances, mildly flirtatious innuendo, meeting at odd hours and the like. More than anything, it was just a feeling that she had had. It had certainly been enough to kill her crush. Now, however? Now he was still charming, and she was unsure if she had just been being paranoid about the affair. She was caught between the realms, not really belonging to any specific camp. She did, however, wish that Vrric had gotten back from the peninsula already.

They were laughing and enjoying themselves, so she was not sure why she did it. It had been a nagging question in the back of her mind all day, scratching away at her brain. It finally boiled to the surface.

"So… How did he die?" Her eyes immediately dropped to her cup. "My father." The silence blanketed the room like fresh snow.

"Ah. I had thought you already heard?" He started to look at his cup, but his eyes snapped back up quickly. He might get nervous, but he was never really shy.

"I know he died, yes. I just was not sure what had actually happened." She took a big drink and met his gaze. "Who was there with him? Was he alone?"

"No, he wasn't alone. I was there. So was Midinarre." He took a deep breath. "He was talking about something, I can't remember what, but he was very animated about it, very passionate. He, ah… He was saying something about something and then just had this stricken look on his face. He stiffened and froze, like he was stabbed in the back with a spear. Then he clutched his chest and his eyes got bulgy. He dropped to his knees and then fell over. It was incredibly quick, Clerin, completely sudden, out of the blue. I don't think he suffered."

"What was he talking about? Before his, you know, accident." She remembered why he died and who killed him, but she was curious as to his last words. Did he know a Beleg was killing him in a desperate attempt to communicate with her? Or, as Olwinn alluded, did he just drop painlessly to the ground? Even he could not tell her that, however. That would always be a question unanswered.

"I just… I really… don't know." His brow scrunched and he rubbed it intensely for a moment. "It was so shocking afterwards and Midinarre was running over and shouting orders, my mind is just blank. Really."

She wanted to press him, but for what reason? She was not going to get the information she wanted, that was for sure. It may have been cruel, but she did plan on asking her mother when they next met. If any derlian could recall the substance of a banal conversation just before a crisis, it would be her mother. She never forgot anything.

Then it was upon them. Princess Inquella arrived. Clerin had everything ready. The rooms were prepared, the townsfolk were out in droves, the feast was to be spectacular. She had all her ledgers caught up and in an easy-to-read format. She had the repairs at a good stopping point, structurally stable but still architecturally unfinished, ready for the Princess's whim. Though Clerin was pretty sure the Princess would not personally enjoy it, they had a small route chosen for her to ride along that wound through the city a little—a bit of a parade. Clerin would have certainly hated it, she would always prefer a long hot bath after travel and before being on display, but it was expected by all, so it was arranged. Luckily Clerin did not need to meet her at the gates, waiting with the others. She was to meet the Princess at the palace entrance to hand over the crown she had never worn and the scepter she had never wielded. The crown was heavy gold with colored gemstones apparently chosen for their size rather than their smooth appearance. The scepter was skinny, unlike a war mace, but still heavy and clunky. Clerin assumed she could kill a derlian with it if she really needed to. There was to be a small ceremony in front of all the great families of Vatlisi, surrounded by the guards in their full regalia. Certainly nothing compared to a full coronation. Then they could shut the doors on the gawkers and the Princess could get cleaned up at her leisure. Then the feast!

Clerin had been a little too prepared. She had little to do but fidget and wander a couple of rooms in the palace while waiting. She was at the northern tower, the one above the main gates, so she could better hear the fanfare. The parade was short enough to only last an hour or so. She cursed herself for getting dressed in her finery before the Princess was actually at the gates. She could have used that hour to finalize her outfit or fix her hair. As it was, she was beginning to sweat from all the tight, heavy, clothing. She had on a light-blue gown, over a kirtle, over a chemise, over her undergarments. She had forgone the cloak for the time being, leaving that for once the Princess was near. Her hair was braided into ropes that wrapped her head, as a sort of miniature, natural tiara. She was not allowed to wear any jewelry, not while handing over the trappings of state. She paced barefoot, her slippers being the other item to don at the last moment.

It was into the afternoon when the quiet commotion of the Princess's arrival could be heard across the city. Clerin had gotten dressed approximately two hours too soon, but at least she was prepared, at least the Princess had finally arrived. She required help with her slippers and accepted the help with her cloak. Her hair was fussed over after her clothing was settled. Eventually she made it down to the palace gates. She had to wait about another half hour before the Princess's retinue became visible. They were going agonizingly slow.

The mounted guards entered first and then fanned out. The carriage with the Princess was large and ornate. It had rich colors of mahogany mixed with ebony, some colored enamel, and some golden gilt. The wheels were large and had red spokes and felloes, with a bronze, or some other brownish metal, hub. There were two horses pulling, both as white as the driven snow. There were two drivers at the front and a guard hanging onto the back. The windows in the carriage doors were too hard to see through at their distance, no matter how Clerin squinted. The carriage came to a slow rest, the only sounds that of various horse hooves on the flagstone courtyard.

The guard from the back of the carriage hopped off and ran around to the side door, opening it with a low bow punctuated by a flourish. The Princess exited the carriage slightly stooped, as required by the opening's geometry, but soon straightened her spine until it was perfectly plumb. She had long blonde hair that flowed unrestrained down her back, to end somewhere along her thigh. She was wearing pure white, even white gloves, which seemed a little excessive considering the season. Everyone immediately bowed as she exited, including Clerin. It was not until the Princess walked over to her and placed a light hand on Clerin's shoulder did she rise and stare into the Princess's eyes. They were a deep blue, like a deep lagoon. She smiled slightly to Clerin. Remembering her role, Clerin placed the crown upon the Princess's head—the Princess had to lean over a little for her to reach—and handed over the scepter. Then the Princess really smiled. Perfectly white teeth behind blood red lips.

"I thank you, Clerin Toswin, for securing and preserving my crown. Your efforts to support Vatlisi will not be soon forgotten." The others straightened as she started to speak, leaving their bow. The Princess turned away from Clerin, rotating in a slow circle to take in the new faces, the great families of Vatlisi, and those faces that she assumedly already knew, those in her retinue. "I thank all of you who have gathered here to witness my arrival. I promise to treat Vatlisi gently while she heals from the grievous wound inflicted upon her by the previous Prince. I promise to listen to your concerns and provide for your needs. I promise to treat you fairly and justly. I will not be opening court for a week's time, but look forward to meeting all of you during tonight's feast. Thank you!" She completed her circle and was back at Clerin. Her smile was a little weary. "Please, lead the way, I have got to get out of these clothes." She spoke through her teeth, somehow not moving her lips, but the words were clear to Clerin. Rather than responding, Clerin gave a quick head bob, spun a half circle, and marched back towards the gates. All those in front of her parted and flowed backwards, leaving plenty of room. It was one of those motions that appear rehearsed but was certainly not. Everyone just knew what to do and was paying close attention. The Princess's retinue followed slowly, leaving plenty of space.

Clerin did not turn around and did not pause, though she strained her ears to make sure that the Princess was still following behind. They wound through the main hall, up several flights of stairs, and down two more halls before reaching the Princess's suite of rooms. Clerin had not stayed in them, not even one night, so that she would not get a taste for what she could not enjoy. Her rooms were still quite opulent, she certainly did not feel slighted.

"This will be perfect, thank you." They were alone for a brief moment before the Princess's retinue showed up with her copious luggage. Clerin understood that she was being dismissed with the statement, so she bowed low. She again felt a light hand on her shoulder, so she straightened herself. "I do thank you. I cannot imagine how chaotic things have been. I understand you have handled things very competently, and I want you to know that I appreciate that. Starting tomorrow we can go over all of the bureaucracy. I have given myself a week to learn, but tonight I just want to get clean and try to enjoy the feast."

"Of course, your Highness." Clerin smiled and performed another small head bob.

"Please, if we are alone, you can call me Inquella. I am going to have to deal with a lot of pomp during the feast and I am just too tired to deal with it now." She smiled her perfect teeth again.

"Of course, Inquella." Clerin smiled back, her sincerity showing up in her dimples. The ruckus of the retinue was upon them, however, and so she made another small bow and left. She could hear the Princess directing them where to put her luggage as she walked away, the commotion getting softer the farther she got. She realized, as she was heading towards her own quarters, that she would be staying in Vatlisi a little longer than Weitno may have wished. She smiled a little to herself as she walked.

The feast was fantastic. It was huge and loud and crowded and filled with smiles and laughter. Inquella kept herself a little isolated and a little aloof, but all others were given free rein. She was at the head of the table, at one end of the giant hall, and surrounded herself with her own retinue. The families of Vatlisi had to approach slowly and in small groups to be introduced to her. They had to provide their information to Inquella's seneschal, who would then loudly state their names and ranks, if they had any. Then the Princess would wave them over and let them flatter her and promise fealty. She would say some quiet words of kindness to them, and they would head back to their seats to continue feasting and drinking. Clerin was probably the only one at the table that did not participate in the introductions. She figured that, one, they had already been introduced and, two, she would be leaving Vatlisi soon, possibly to never return.

This was, for all intents and purposes, her last publicly official act in Vatlisi. Therefore, more than anything, she just wanted the evening to be enjoyed by all. She wanted everyone to remember having a good time, especially Inquella. She did not even really care if the families thought the Princess had arranged the feast. Clerin did not need praise or even acknowledgment, but she wanted it to be successful. She had picked out most of the dishes, leaving enough choice to the chefs that they could still shine with their specialties. After all, they could be cooking for the Princess and her court for many decades to come. She picked out some of the wine as well, but leaned heavily on the steward's advice. Her palate was capable and certainly willing, but she worried it was not as refined as it should be for a feast such as this. She did not create a seating chart, however. Her mother would have been disappointed in her, but she knew very little about the families and nothing about Inquella's retinue. With the buffer that Inquella had built around herself, it did not matter much that the first guests to be seated chose the chairs closest to her. Clerin had even picked out the minstrels who were playing softly in a corner. She smiled to herself and, if she were able to do so comfortably, she would have patted herself on the back. She might have been a little tipsy but, yes, the feast was fantastic.

The next week flew by. Clerin enjoyed Inquella's company, and it appeared that Inquella enjoyed hers. They covered all the construction ledgers within the first couple of days, the morning after the feast being a little slow to start. They covered the rest of the ledgers, the actual running of the city, and whatever limited knowledge Clerin had about any of the prominent families over the next couple. It was amazing how little specifics Clerin knew. She had spent all of her time hunting the Cabal and working on the repairs that, unless the family was full of traitors or stone masons, she could barely recognize the family name. Inquella was smart and capable and wanted to make up her own mind about the derlians that would live their lives under her, so she did not make Clerin feel foolish or inadequate about her lack of knowledge. The last couple of days were spent discussing smaller items that had a larger impact, more personal items.

"Stall for as long as possible. Really." Inquella enjoyed a glass of wine in the middle of the day. Mostly, drinking during the day just made Clerin tired, but she could not really refuse a Princess. "Make them give you something before you agree."

"Who is they?" Maybe it was because Clerin was on her second glass, but she was not quite sure what Inquella was getting at.

"The Catajohls, of course. You think I do not know why Weitno is here? They are the harbingers of the bridegroom." She stopped for effect. Clerin assumed she was referring to "harbingers of doom," so she laughed. Whether or not that was the real joke, the laughter satisfied Inquella, and she continued. "They have tried to fix me up for almost two cycles now. They told me how much they wanted to elevate the Erintwala family, but they kept parading no-names in front of me. Sure, some were cute, some were smart, some were strong, some were funny, some had a smile to die for. But the families were just not useful. If you are going to be forced into marriage, you should make a powerful choice. Look at me, I have Vatlisi now, second only to Tureyn."

So, you did not fall in love with any of them? Clerin thought it, but did not speak it. It was a useless question on so many levels and one that Clerin doubted Inquella would appreciate. As indicated so many times the last week, a Familial Marriage was not about love. Besides, how could she love anyone as she loved Vrric? How could she give up on him and live a powerful life with another? She was definitely going to stall for as long as she could, just not for the same reason that Inquella had.

"Oh, do not look like that." Inquella smiled and moved her face into Clerin's view. Clerin had not realized she had been staring off towards the floor in the distance. "You have a powerful opportunity here, whether or not it is something you would have chosen for yourself. I am just saying not to waste it. It is okay to be picky. It is okay to take some time and make them sweat." She lifted Clerin's face with a finger on her chin. "You know, you do have a choice here. You can walk away from your family and be with the Fluen of your dreams. Just know that there are plenty of unhappy Fluens who have nothing. Everything grows old and stale, even love. May as well get the most out of it."

"So, your husband is on his way? You will be getting married here?" Clerin leaned back and, for want of much else to do, took another drink.

"Yes. He hates that I have made him wait. He wanted to arrive in Vatlisi together, to dazzle the locals with his smile, confuse them as to who kept their name." When Inquella laughed it was a musical sound, and yet, there was just a hint of cruelty behind the music, almost inaudible. "I would have none of that, however. He will not arrive for a moon's time, so that the families here get to know me before he even shows up. We are going to feast twice a week!"

It was only after Clerin had left to go to her own room, to begin packing for her own trip, that she realized she never got the name of Inquella's betrothed. Not even his family's name. At least she now had an angle with which to stall Weitno with. She only had to hint at her conversation with Inquella and he would know he was going to have an uphill battle. Of course, he may have realized that already.

She spent the rest of the day packing and most of her last day saying goodbye to those she had gotten to know. The cooks, stewards, maids, carriage drivers, woodworkers, and stone masons. There were so many she interacted with that she wanted a quick word with. She knew she should be placing her face in front of the powerful families of Vatlisi, to solidify her name in their minds, but she was not overly concerned with that game. Besides, she had to get the rest of Trela's coterie on the move as well. They would all meet up in Tureyn soon. Since she had to travel with several wagons of hidden Yaven items, they might even arrive there before she did. By all accounts, they had every known item of the Cabal's and had hunted all of the members down. Wesduin was excited to be back in charge of something, especially something as important as those wagons.

The trip to Tureyn was uneventful and boring. She was asked about a hundred times why they were not taking a ship by the citizens of Vatlisi, or at least it felt like a hundred times. Trela had been adamant about moving the Yaven items by land and she had the rest of the coterie agreeing with her. Her main argument was concern about the ship sinking, which seemed like a low probability in Clerin's view. She thought wagons were much more conspicuous than using a ship, with their own vulnerabilities, and if secrecy were the main goal, doing things as most Fluens would do them would have been the least suspicious. She had been outvoted, however, and was now back on her horse, Riverlightning, swaying in the sun.

As when she had entered Tureyn with her mother cycles ago, it was dusk as they neared the great walled town. The fires were being lit as they approached, outlining the tops of the towers with a flickering red. It took another hour to get to the town itself, owing to the slow pace that the wagons were being dragged. The massive arched gates were open and inviting, even in the dark. The iron gates were covered with filigreed gold, hiding their strength behind beauty. The filigree was shaped as starfish and seashells, with the top of the arched gates bent to look like crashing waves. She had only seen them a couple of times in her life, and they took her breath away each time. It was not long before they were behind the tall gray-stone walls, which appeared black at night. The main thoroughfare was well lit with lanterns and torches, while the side streets, if they were small enough, dropped back away into darkness.

They would be unable to stay at the Liar's Lyre as she had the last time she had stayed in Tureyn. No, Weitno had insisted they stay at the Catajohl villa. The amenities were probably nicer, to be sure, but there was a certain amount of anonymity at an inn that she desired at the moment. He had hinted that her mother would visit while they were staying there, as if the anticipation of her mother surprising her at some random time was to be considered a treat. But she was being unfair by reflex, she knew that. It had been quite a long time since she had seen her mother and it would be good to catch up.

They traveled much of the town, turning off the main avenue before reaching the citadel. They climbed up and up, the villa apparently being at the top of a hill. It did not matter to Clerin much, it was Riverlightning who had to cope with the slope, but it seemed to add time to the journey pulling the wagons uphill. The streets got darker and darker as they climbed, getting farther from the lighted avenues, and the new moon was of no help. They were headed towards a bright spot at the top of the hill, what she assumed was their destination. When they finally arrived at the villa, porters swarmed out to help them.

The villa was perched at the top of the hill and large enough to encompass the apex. A dark stone wall surrounded it, with a large open garden area beyond. A giant tree was centered in the garden. It looked like a willow from a distance. The building itself was well lit, creating the beacon-like atmosphere. Clerin felt good to be off Riverlightning, to be able to stand on her own wobbly legs. There was a quiet commotion behind her and she immediately turned to investigate.

Wesduin and Rewista were arguing with the porters, adamant that they would not hand over the wagons. Gyllhelon stood silently by, looking deadly and glaring unhappily. Torpalin and Escha were making their way over to the wagons, to add their assistance. Clerin hurried over to help, keeping an eye out for Weitno, since his word would be law to the porters. She had struggled with explaining the wagons to the Fluen contingent they were traveling with, but had never come up with a real solution. Instead, relying on the "none of your business" type of response. That was coming back to haunt her now.

She arrived at the porters at the same time that Weitno did. "Now it has already been explained how important the wagons are to us." She directed herself to Weitno, ignoring his servants who were staring a little wide-eyed at the aggressive response.

"You know, now that you mention it, I never really did get a good response about the wagons." He was smiling at her, also ignoring his servants.

"I am serious, Weitno. They will be guarded by us day and night, touched only by us. There is no arguing about this." Clerin leveled her gaze and stared as hard as she was able. She wondered how her mother had always stopped everyone in their tracks and tried to channel her now. To her great surprise, it worked. Weitno stopped and suddenly looked very serious, his smile slipping.

"Trylayn, show these good derlians where the stables are. And, if you're smart, you won't touch their wagons." He turned back to Clerin, one side of his mouth still attempting to smile. "You are definitely a Toswin."

Clerin followed Weitno and the others into the villa, while a group of her contingent followed the porter. As they were being led in, she tried to think of something to lighten the mood, to take their minds off the wagons just outside, but came up blank until she stepped into the villa's vast entrance.

The flagstone floor was of a similar dark stone as the exterior walls, and they were exposed to the elements. The door opened into a courtyard, with only a little ceiling for the first two rods of width or so. Then, the sky. There were two staircases in front of her, each curving up and around to the second floor's massive balcony. The courtyard was small, four benches and a central fountain surrounded by roundly shaped topiary, but beautiful. There were various doors heading in various directions, but Weitno immediately started taking one of the stairs.

"What a lovely little courtyard. This is gorgeous, Weitno, just stunning." As she gushed about his home, he paused a moment at the bottom steps and turned to her smiling, the wagons momentarily forgotten.

"Wait until you see it in the daylight. We'll open the plumbing for you so you can experience it in all of its splendor." He climbed the stairs and she followed.

There were pillars and paintings and niches with vases along the way. It was quite opulent, but not overly ostentatious. They eventually got to a far corner of the upstairs. There were several open doors, three on one side of the corner, and two on the other.

"These will be your rooms while you are my guests. I was worried that they would be a little cramped, but with part of your retinue sleeping with your wagons in the stables, it should not be too bad." He flourished his right arm toward the doorways, allowing her to take it all in.

Clerin had thought they would still probably be a little cramped, but that was before she saw the size of the rooms. "Thank you so much for your hospitality, you are too kind."

He nodded in agreement. "You may get cleaned up, take your time. We'll have food laid out for everyone to come and pick at what you like. Nothing formal. Then you should have a good rest. I believe Midinarre will be joining us tomorrow morning." He nodded again and turned it into a shallow bow.

The rooms were gigantic. They were mostly open, broken only by periodic skinny columns. There were beds scattered about the perimeter, pure white with a white gauze netting that hung around each one, giving the room, empty of derlians, a ghostly appearance. There were sofas and couches and ottomans scattered about the center of the room, also pure white with pillows scattered across them. In the direct center there was a circular oaken table, its dark stain appearing darker due to being surrounded by all that white, almost matching the dark wooden floorboards. There were a few chairs around it and, centered, there was a white vase of white lilies with bright green stems peeking out. The decorating scheme was almost absurd. It made Clerin wonder if the rooms were always this way, or if this was just for her and her retinue.

There was a communal bath area, with five tubs. Though she wanted nothing more than to bathe, she needed to talk with those choosing to sleep in the stables. They needed to post guards in shifts. She could not have a group of her retinue unwashed, tired, and grumpy by morning's light.

The stables were quite large and fairly clean, at least for stables. There was a loft above the corral where the wagons were stowed, full of disheveled hay bales. Gyllhelon and Rewista were up there, setting up sleeping areas. Wesduin had actually set himself up in one of the wagons. Dartsyle and Escha were releasing the remaining wagon from the horses. Torpalin approached her.

"I hope you brought food?" He smiled a little. It was typical Torpalin humor, his stomach always being fair game, but there was a sadness to his smile that Clerin did not understand. She realized that it had been there for a while. She would have to remember to ask Escha about it.

"Food is provided inside, as well as baths. I do not want anyone out here for more than three hours at a time, understood? We will take shifts guarding the wagons." She raised her voice enough to engage the others in the loft as well. There were nods all around, though a very reluctant one from Wesduin. She was sure he would sneak as many shifts as possible but, she figured, as long as he ate and bathed, he could stay out in the stables for as long as he cared.

Clerin had taken the last shift. She had wanted to be in the stables, awake up in the loft, when Weitno came looking for her. She wanted to show that Vatlisi had not softened her, but why? He would have not thought of her in any other way. She was from a prominent family, of one who communes with the Beleg Lembin, and a supreme bureaucrat. Weitno would have little clue of her travails since she left the Fluen realm, though there were surely rumors. She wondered what type of match Weitno would assume she would agree to? Maybe that was why she wanted him to find her in the loft, to give him the idea that she was no longer purely Fluen. But why would she want to help him at all?

To her slight disappointment, Weitno did not arrive. Escha came to relieve her. She did bring breakfast, which was considerate. They ate together and laughed about the vast opulence of the villa. Escha certainly had little-to-no Fluen within her. Clerin could not remember why, but the conversation eventually turned towards Torpalin.

"Is Torpalin… How is Torpalin doing?" Clerin had just been thinking about his smile last night.

"Do you really want to know?" Escha rubbed her forehead for a moment. "He's standoffish lately. At best."

"He seemed fine when we had dinner with the Fluens of Tureyn back in Vatlisi. He did not balk at the invitation or anything."

"That's because it came from you. He can't refuse you, you see. He can't refuse Trela or, or even Feyazki. It's me he can refuse, can shut down for. He's always around me." She rubbed her head again. "He needs to be taken from his shell. Like, actively, constantly. I just don't have the energy sometimes. You know?"

"Well, I…"

"It's been going on since the Tlana incident, way back in the Gaen villages. I don't know, he's just changed. He used to be happy all the time…"

"Is there anything I can do? Want me to force invite him to dinner?"

Suddenly Escha laughed. A tension that had been invisibly building eased.

"No, no, it's fine. Thank you though." She paused for a quick moment. "It's no rush, I brought food out, everyone knew that, but you're needed inside." She waved a hand towards the giant sliding door. "Your mother will be here a little later on."

"How much later?" Clerin suddenly wondered if she could bathe again. It was not really required, she had bathed and slept in a clean bed. She had been sitting in the loft for the last few hours, but had not been mucking out the stables or anything. It was just her instant reaction. To be able to put her best foot forward, as her mother would say.

Escha shrugged. Clerin thanked her and headed out of the stables. She crossed the beautiful garden on the way to the villa proper. The willow in the garden was large and weeping, its greenery draping to the ground in spots. The garden as a whole really did caress the senses in the daylight. She would have to remember to compliment Weitno.

She strode through the main doors, walked past the fountain in the small courtyard and entered the main lower room, beyond the stairs. There were many Fluens there, some she knew, some she had just met, and some were complete strangers. She had the briefest moment of panic as she wondered if Weitno was already bringing suitors by. Then she was hit by the whirlwind that was her mother.

"Clerin, my beautiful daughter, it is so great to see you after so long." Her mother smiled a warm smile and came at her with open arms, pulling her into a full hug. Clerin was a little shocked as her mother was typically not a hugger, but the feeling of her arms and the familiar smell of her hair was comforting. Clerin hugged her back with gusto. Then her mother stopped and held her at arms-length, a hand on each shoulder. "My, you have grown, travel suits you." Her pale blue eyes were misted with emotion. The smile on her face rounded out her typically thin cheeks.

"Thank you, mother. You look as lovely as ever." Clerin's smile came easily and naturally. All of her nervousness faded as the dew evaporates under the beaming sun.

"We have much to talk about, yes. I would like nothing more than to sit for an afternoon with you and a nice bottle of wine. However, we have errands first. I am under strict orders from Lembin to bring you as soon as you set foot in Tureyn. Luckily for you I was asleep when you arrived." Her wink told Clerin that she had certainly not been asleep. It was a nicely conspiratorial wink which made Clerin smile all the more. "I apologize, but you will have to bathe rather quickly. Here is an herbal satchel and a vial for the oils. Do not forget to put your boots back on before touching the floor with your feet." Though her mother was more friendly than she could recall, the brusque interruption and oddly specific instructions was a more normal attitude; it was oddly consoling.

She bathed as quickly as she could. It helped that she had had a nice long bath just hours earlier. Still, it is hard to rush oneself through a nice warm bath.

Clerin remembered that she was not supposed to touch anyone before the ceremony either, though she could not recall if she had observed that rule each time she had visited a different Temple. So she waved to those in the main room as her mother gave thanks and apologies to all around. There was a carriage waiting outside, so she did not have to saddle Riverlightning. They were soon heading down the hill, towards the citadel, towards the Temple. She suddenly got a little nervous, the messages within her vibrated with anticipation. She wondered if Lembin expected any responses, or if it even knew she had communed with Gorbanax as well as Linchon. Though she did not fully commune with Gorbanax, so maybe that did not even count. At least she did not have to speak with any suitors.

Clerin wanted to ask about her father, to say what Olwinn had told her, that they were all together when he died. She kept trying to bring up the courage to say something, staring out the carriage window, watching the streets go by. The voice in her head repeated itself, as if she just did not understand what was wanted, that if she only just knew she would say something. But she did know what she wanted to ask, she was merely unable to for some reason. They rode in silence for a while.

"You really have grown. You have grown into your features, lost some of that baby fat."

"Mother!"

"I just mean you have become a lady. A beautiful lady. Adventuring suits you." There was a small pause where Clerin almost thanked her mother, but she was quiet for too long. "What is the most exciting thing you saw while you were adventuring? You made it to the Pyran realm, I hear. You made a full circle, yes?"

Most exciting thing? thought Clerin. *Who can say what the most exciting thing was when it was all exciting? Well, except for the boring parts.*

"Um, yes. I was able to meet Queen Vanelia in the Luften realm. I saw the well in the center of the Northern Desert and was attacked by a Tlana in the Gaen realm. I was able to help the Pyran Queen get queened. We stayed in Agoge after the big battle at her behest, which is just a lovely city. I have communed with Linchon and, sort of, Gorbanax and, by proxy, even Gunzgak. But most of all, mother, I am in love with a Luften mage. That is probably the most exciting thing to happen to me. And, no matter what the Catajohls offer me, I will probably not get married to some boring Fluen fop just to become a princess and squeeze out babies for the rest of my life." It just poured out of her.

It was quiet for a while as her mother absorbed everything. "Is that what you think I did? That I chose status and to squeeze out babies instead of love?"

"What? Where did that come from? I was talking about myself, mother, not you. I have no idea what you did, what choices you made in your youth. You are a closed book to me, you always have been." Then it hit her. "So... You did not love dad?"

It was quiet for another while. This silence, however, felt more uncomfortable for her mother than for herself. So she was more willing to let it drag on. She stared out the window again.

"Of course I loved your father. You know that. But, yes, we had a Familial Marriage. It was arranged by others. My family was unknown, comparatively, and I had not begun my translating with Lembin back then. The Toswins were a very respectable family, Clerin. The Toswins *are* a very respectable family. You, you are a Toswin, and you should not forget it. You have done some very important work for Lembin. Respectable work that has elevated our name, just like I have. But do not let that fool you into thinking the rules do not apply to you. Do not let that make you think you are more special than you are."

It was quiet for another moment. Long enough for Clerin to realize that the attack was in self-defense. Her mother was sore about how much she loved, or did not love, Aillel. It was a reaction, maybe even unconscious. There was something there for Clerin to follow-up on later.

"Now listen, I apologize, that was rude of me. I am happy that you think you have fallen in love, really I am. I hope to someday meet this Luften mage you speak of. Just... You cannot make any decisions right now, not like that. We need to think everything through. We need to make thoughtful decisions." And then they were at the citadel.

Midinarre left the carriage first and Clerin followed soon after. There were several nice brass handles on the outside of the carriage for her to use to get down. A small cluster of guards formed around them as they began to walk through the large gates, wide enough to fit three warriors abreast, and into the citadel. One of the guards began to lead the way farther into the building. They did not have to state their name or business. There was no conversation whatsoever. They were known and expected and, it seemed, Lembin was impatient enough that they dispensed with the pomp. Many of the guards peeled off at the first room. As they got deeper into the bowels of the citadel, more and more peeled off. By the time they were at the temple entrance, they only had the one guard leading them.

They were at the bottom of a turret, the turret closest to the sea, Clerin could smell it. There were three mages in black robes with gold-thread writing on their hems and sleeves. All three bowed low as they entered.

"We welcome you to the temple. Lembin is waiting for you. Will you be breathing for yourself?" One of the black-robed Fluens approached as she spoke.

"No, please, if you would." Clerin nodded to the mage. "If you could make it long lasting as well, I would appreciate it. I do not know how long I will be down there."

"Of course." The mage made a quick bow. "Surtecfluarc!"

Clerin could feel the energy rush through her, into her lungs. She closed her eyes for a split second to steady herself. "Thank you." She made a small bow herself. Then it was through an open wooden door, opposite the one they had entered from. The round room was small and held only a spiral staircase centered within it. The stairs led to a pool, which was connected to the underwater temple. She disrobed and placed her clothing on the only furniture in the room, a small bench. For no reason other than habit, Clerin took a deep breath to steady herself and then descended the stairs. She let her breath out after realizing she was holding it, at little burst escaped at each step.

With no air in her lungs, she was not as buoyant, so it was fairly easy to walk down the steps, to step off the stairs at the bottom, and to stride along the stone floor. The wall was covered with a strange writing that looked like a cross between semi-shattered window glass and an angular spiderweb. There was an eerie green glow that seemed to emanate from the cracked writing. There was another small wooden door in that room, similar to the one above but on the opposite side. It was through that door that the Temple proper lay.

It was nice that she had done this all before, long, long ago. The massive spaces, the giant pillars, the underwater well that she headed towards before she could even see it in the distance. Everything was familiar enough that it did not induce the nervousness and, yes, even the fear that she had originally felt. Which was great because she felt a fearful nervousness rush through her veins for another reason. The messages within her vibrated so mightily that she thought she might vomit. There was a tiny part of her that wondered how that would work under water, but the rest of her held it down and carried onwards. As she neared the well it felt as if her stomach would burst.

There was a rumbling as she approached, a deep thrumming, she could feel it in her feet as she walked. The pain increased the closer she got. The rumbling vibrated through her entire body. The pain was excruciating. There was a burst of color, all colors, all shimmering and vibrating, that escaped from the well and quickly engulfed the room. She closed her eyes, attempting to avoid it, to mitigate it even just a little bit. But it did not lessen. The color was in her mind, not in the room. She dropped to her knees, half crawling towards the well, her stomach a screaming torment. It was as if she had eaten a ball of knives that, now that they were well into her stomach, had somehow gained sentience and decided to slice their way out from the inside. She crawled towards the well though she could no longer see it through the rainbow that scintillated through her mind. Her hand touched stone, she thought. Yes, that must be the wall of the well. Then her stomach burst. The knives had made their escape and they took her entrails with them.

Clerin screamed a thousand screams. They sounded muted to her ears, muffled by the water, but they were clear in her mind. As clear as the blinding rainbow. Then, suddenly, mercifully, the pain stopped, the color stopped, time stopped. She lay there at the base of the well, panting under water.

After some time had passed and her stomach wall felt solid once more, she opened her eyes. There, standing in front of her, was an image of her father. She had not seen him since the Luften Temple and knew what it meant. At least they had not killed another family member to converse with her. He was wearing the same white robes he was wearing during her Telling, with his long white hair pulled back in the same style. He smiled warmly at her for a second, his hands clasped comfortably in front of him. He mouthed something to her and, more than reading his lips, it made her recall what he had told her before.

"Losidtotarc!" The spell to commune with spirits.

"Oh, my poor little derling. What have they done to you?" He had an empathetic smile on his face, making his words encompass all of the time that had passed since they had last communed, all of the things that had happened, not just the current pain.

"Father..." She wanted to talk with him, to ask him questions, to tell him of her experiences, but he interrupted.

"I do not have time, I apologize." His face suddenly got firm. "You failed, you know? You were supposed to give Lembin's message to all the Belegs before returning. You have not given it to any besides Linchon. Why is that?"

"Well, Gorbanax communed at a distance. I do not know why. Now that we have destroyed the Cabal, Gorbanax will accept the message after we have resolved the items, the trapped Yavens. That was the agreement between us. It is just the timing."

"The timing?" Her father's face started to grow dark. "You understand that Linchon's return message to Lembin starts a clock. That is the new timing. You have started a new timing. You were not supposed to return until both Gorbanax and Gunzgak had been fully communed with. And what of Gunzgak?"

"Well, I... Gunzgak would not even commune with me. There was an intermediary, a Yaven that communed between us." Clerin stood though her legs still felt shaky. She did not like being looked down upon by the image of her dead father. "I was told Lembin wished to commune. I was told to come here."

"Do you think I care at all what Lembin wishes? You mistake me girl, I do not come from Lembin, I am from Linchon." Her father's face was filled with anger. She had never seen it like that while he had been alive. "And you have ruined the timing I directed you to keep!"

The colors behind her eyes started flashing again, the rumble came back. The world started to shake again. She dropped back to the ground, hoping to avoid falling. At least the pain within her had subsided. Fire erupted from the well and bent towards her father, engulfing him. Then, just as suddenly, it stopped.

"Ha! You have been spending too much time with your precious derlians, Lembin. You think fire causes damage? You think any element hurts us?" Her father strode to the well, standing just above Clerin. He seemed to have forgotten her, so she stayed curled up, waiting in nauseated apprehension. "You've already done your damage, not sure what you're complaining about now." His head cocked to one side.

Clerin watched from her position on the ground as images popped up over the side of the well and came before her. There was an air cloud shape, a water drop shape, and a derlian shape, the same that she had seen so long ago. The derlian shape representing her. A white cylinder left the water drop and sunk into the derlian's forehead. Then, almost immediately, it left her and moved towards the air cloud shape. The air cloud dodged and moved around, but seemed to be stuck within a small space, frantically travelling the confines, appearing to try to find a way out. The cylinder eventually entered into the air cloud. Nothing moved for some time until, quite suddenly, the cloud exploded and several cylinders struck the derlian shape. One bounced and struck the water drop, being absorbed instantly. The others, however, did not reemerge.

Her father's head cocked in the other direction. "You don't have to repeat it all for her, she's not daft, you know."

Then a fire shape floated out of the well to rest in front of her. It hovered there, doing nothing aggressive, when a cylinder shot from both the derlian and the water drop and they both got absorbed. The fire shape exploded, and several cylinders struck the derlian. Another bounced and struck the water drop, the same as for the air cloud. Then a stone shape floated out of the well. It seemed to notice Clerin and the water drop, and shot off into the distance. Then three other crude derlian shapes floated out of the well. They, along with hers, shot off into the distance, following the stone shape. There was a long silence as her father peered after the tiny images. Finally, though suddenly, the stone image dropped right in front of her, striking the ground with a vibratory thud. Then the water drop, then some cylinders, then the crude derlians. All right after each other, all adding to the vibrating thud. Clerin was not sure if they had exploded or sunk into the ground or what.

"Lembin feels confident the new timeline will work out. I, myself, am not so sure." He shook his head. Then he seemed to get lighter, more transparent.

"Wait, father!" She had so many questions to ask.

"Don't worry little derling, I will be around." He nodded. "I'll let you talk once you commune with Gorbanax. You must do that quickly, you understand. Whether or not Lembin is confident, you must hurry. Some imbalances need to be righted, no matter their cost. Some things may not be left undone." He was barely visible. "We will have a good long chat at the volcano, I promise. But hurry. You must hurry." Then he jumped into the well. Or maybe he disappeared before he made it over the lip, it was difficult for her to tell.

Then the rumbling started again, more aggressive this time. The ground shook and shivered. Clerin backed away from the well at first, then turned and ran. At least, ran as well as she could under water, arms attempting to swim in front of her while her feet pushed against the ground as well as they could. Her body was at a slant, with her arms winning the race. The rumbling got louder as she decided to just swim. There was an odd deepness to it, like most of it was below her hearing, subaudible. It felt like she was missing something, like a child not understanding their parent's argument through a closed door, the voices muffled more than the emotion. She did not want to stick around to figure out what she was missing, however, so she swam as fast as she could. She was ready to enjoy the Catajohl villa, to bathe for hours in a quiet room filled with the scent of lavender, even if it meant meeting random suitors afterwards.

She finally made it to the stairs. She swam up them as far as she could before, finally half crawling and half stepping out of the water. Her hands went from the stone steps in front of her to the walls so she could steady herself. The rumbling continued unabated. She finally popped out amongst the dark cloaked mages and her mother. Their eyes were round with surprise and concern.

"What have you done?" It was the mage that had cast the breathing spell upon her.

"Nothing more than was asked of me." Her reply seemed sharper than the question when she heard it aloud. Truth be told, she was just as confused as everyone else. She hastily got dressed as the other mages eyeballed her and seemed to be gathering courage to ask her similar useless questions.

"We are leaving. Now." Midinarre grabbed Clerin by the arm and began to steer her towards the exit. There was some slight stumbling, but the ground was not shaking too heavily. Nothing came crashing down at least. "You can put your boots on in the carriage."

They made it out of the citadel with only one fall between them, Clerin's of course. The rumbling seemed to be fading farther into the distance, but the ground was still moving underfoot. The carriage was waiting for them at the exit and they both slid in quickly. Clerin pulled her boots on as the horses dragged them away.

They rode in silence for a while, Clerin listening to her beating heart and watching all the Fluens leaning from windows and doorways to see where the rumbling was coming from. A few glanced at the carriage careening past, but most stayed looking towards the citadel. She glanced over at her mother and took a deep breath. "So, Olwinn said that you both were there when father died."

"You should not listen to Olwinn."

"So you were not there?"

There was a long sigh. "Yes, we were there."

"How did it happen?"

"What?" Her mother gave her a sidelong glance before returning her gaze out the carriage window. "Oh, that. Nothing happened. He just fell over."

"Were you arguing?"

"Of course we were arguing. What do you think married couples do?"

"What about?"

"Ask Olwinn."

"He told me to ask you. Besides, you just told me not to listen to him."

Another long sigh. "We were arguing about an old affair."

"What?! You and Olwinn?"

"No, not us."

There was another bout of silence as Clerin mulled it over. "Father and...?"

"Yes. Happy?"

"No."

"We had a Familial Marriage. There were things I could not do for your father. Besides, I just... It was easier. It was easier to ignore it all. It is not like I had a lot of spare time anyway, I just poured myself into my work."

Clerin was stunned into silence. Her father had always been so pristine in her mind, he could do no wrong. He was the one who made a poultice for her scratches, kissed her bruises, comforted her after a nightmare. He was the one who made the meals and made her laugh. He was always there; he was who had made their house a home.

"Listen, I loved your father as well as I could. It was certainly not all his fault. I can be a bit… distant. I know that. You will understand more later." She laughed for a brief second. "I almost said that you will understand when you grow up. Ha! But you have already grown, have you not?" She squinted into the distance for a moment. "Things that really anger you when you are younger do not always feel the same once you are old. Time is funny that way. You are always changing."

"You are not old." It was the only statement Clerin could hang on to. It was a nice neutral statement.

"Maybe not, but I am not young either." She squinted again. "You do what you want, Clerin. How about that? You have my blessing no matter what you choose. You can let the Catajohls work their charms or not. I… I trust you. I want you to know that, my dear. I trust that you being true to yourself will give you the happiness that eluded me. Do not worry about the Toswins, we will be just fine."

Clerin could not believe the conversation. She never would have guessed it. It did not seem that it was her mother speaking, at least not the mother she remembered. It was as if her mother had been taken over by the kindest Tlana that existed. She had never before heard her mother scatter duty or honor to the wind. Certainly not for something as ephemeral as happiness. But maybe she was being unfair to her mother. Maybe she had always been unfair to her mother.

The rumbling continued all the way to the villa, though it was faint by the time they arrived there. She looked back down the hill, half expecting some buildings to have fallen or at least cracked, but nothing looked damaged. At least not from this distance. *All that fury*, she thought, *for naught.*

Chapter 5

Vrric was excited to be sailing towards Tureyn. He had been assured that Clerin would be there by the time they arrived, probably with enough time to have already gained an audience with Lembin. They needed to collect any other Yaven-infused items that Tureyn had gathered up and head towards Ariellyna. There, hopefully, Vanelia was also gathering up any items to be found in the Luften realm. The Gaen realm had supposedly been cleared already and their items had been sent to Vatlisi before Clerin left. Gunzgak was actively behind the plan, as were Lembin and Gorbanax, which should have gone a long way towards success, but Vrric was still worried about the Blind One at a minimum. They had already gathered some items from the Pyran realm, but would meet with some select subjects of Trela's at the Valley of the Caves if more were discovered by Lishean. Then they needed to find the well. Croy was adamant that he had dreamt of the way to dispose of the items properly, and they certainly had no other plausible idea. He was hoping that the vague itch of nervousness that followed him would be scratched away once they found the well again. Since he was a little unsure as to what caused that feeling, however, he was a little unsure of the solution.

The trip was cold and a bit dreary, but passed quickly for Vrric. His sights were set on their future destination. He was surrounded by friends, which helped to pass the time, but he had difficulty recalling anything specific happening. Just like the mists they were sailing through, his memory was gray and amorphic. Lots of cards, good conversations, good wine, but nothing that really stood out. He could not wait to be with Clerin again.

They arrived at night, during high tide. The city was lit up with a thousand torches. He had been able to see it for leagues, slowly getting brighter and larger the closer they got. Vrric was from a large city, Ariellyna being, by far, the largest city in the Luften realm. But it was hidden. Since much of the city was up in the helioarc trees at varying elevations, there was a lot of additional area or, more correctly, volume in which to hide the denizens. The various trees themselves offered a lot of cover on the ground as well. There were certainly large avenues between the enormous trunks, but there were many other smaller trees obstructing one's view. A Luften home could be a mere twenty rods away and still remain unseen, nestled amongst the leaves like a baby bird in a nest. But not Tureyn, no. Tureyn was flat and broad. Not in the sense that there were no hills or tall buildings, but that no one lived underneath them and only so many lived above the ground floor. Not like the helioarcs reaching up to the stars. Vrric suddenly wondered about the caves of the Gaens. He had only seen the tiny village caves, certainly nothing like what Serif was supposed to be. He wondered if there were hundreds of levels cut through the stone, families living above other families. He had never properly discussed that with Croy before, though he had heard much about the city—did it run deep, or did it run wide? Tureyn definitely ran wide. The torches stretched to the right and left as far as he could see, glittering and flickering in the mild wind. There was so much light, it gave the impression that a quarter of the town was still awake. He knew the streetlamps were to provide a feeling of safety, but to Vrric it was eerie. Maybe it was due to his vantage point.

The first thing he noticed when he disembarked was the rumbling. It was a small vibration under his feet as well as the sound, like a roaring forge fire far away in the distance. That did nothing to lower the eerie sensation.

There were a string of carriages to gather them all up and head towards the villa that Clerin and the others were guests at, four in total. He had originally assumed they were arriving at night so as to keep a low profile, but a line of carriages heading from the dock into town did not seem very stealthy. It was as they were heading up a hill, the carriage slowly rocking back and forth, that he began to wonder why they would need to be keeping a low profile in Tureyn. Clerin was obviously not. Between running Vatlisi and communing with Lembin, he figured she was about as high profile as they come. It relaxed him a little to think that they did not have to obscure their aim here.

They finally arrived at the villa. It was quite large and, even in the night, appeared to be a very beautiful building, with very beautiful gardens. Everyone piled out and grunted in the midst of those already there, vying amongst each other to see who could enjoy a bath first. Clerin was there wearing a pale blue dress with simple embroidery curled along the sleeves. *She could make a potato sack look like an elegant gown*, he thought.

"You smell like the sea." Her smile brightened the room more than any torch.

"Is that a good thing?" His head shifted ever so slightly as he started to lean in for a kiss. She waved a hand slightly and took half a step back.

"My mother is here. And others. I will have to introduce you." Her brow was slightly furrowed, but her dimples were still smiling.

"Ah. Yes, there will have to be a large amount of introductions, I'm sure." He nodded back at her.

"You should bathe. I need to chat with Trela real quick." And she ducked away.

As he walked through the entrance, his mind was fumbling with what had just happened. Being orphaned, he did not think of familial ties all that much. There had always been Kaihlu to think about, his adoptive mentor, but he had been fairly permissive as long as Vrric kept up on his work. There were the sharp differences between Fluen and Luften cultures to also think about, though if Vrric had been born into a royal branch he was sure to have had more constraints placed upon him. Maybe he was reading too much into it. He was tired and foggy from the journey in any case.

He had his head down while he was thinking, staring at the beautiful stone floor. He wondered if he could catch sight of Clerin's mother, to see if she had been watching or wore a scowl. He wondered if she would be inside or outside and if he would even be able to recognize her. He could probably wait until morning before being introduced, then he could at least scrub up a little. His head popped up as others bottlenecked in front of him and there, as obvious as could be, was Clerin's mother. She was across the room, towards a poorly lit alcove, but it was definitely her. The resemblance was unmistakable. And she was staring back at him, as if she had been watching him before his head came up. She had a stern look on her face but, right as he glanced away because the bottleneck was clearing, he thought he detected a smile. At least he hoped that was what it was. Dartsyle was suddenly in front of him, clasping hands and laughing and shouting salutations. Vrric let himself be led away farther into the villa. At least there would be a bath at the end of it.

The bath itself was a little odd. He had been travelling with groups of varying sizes for so long that he had lost any shyness when it came to bathing. However, he had been hoping for a small room that he could steam up and wait for Clerin to arrive, not for five tubs to be scattered about a room. The room was of decent size, but half the tubs had someone else hanging around, chatting or flirting or both, so the room was fairly full. Vrric did not lounge around and soak, but cleaned himself off fairly quickly to give another travel-stained adventurer a chance to scrub up. He was about to get out and dry off when Clerin entered. She found him with her eyes and immediately headed over. She smiled and leaned in to kiss him on the cheek.

"Meet me at the stables. We have the next watch over the wagons tonight. It will give us a chance to talk." She smiled brightly and stood, leaving the room as quickly as she had entered.

"Sure thing." Of course, he said that to her retreating back. He kept his voice slightly muted, though that was a bit unconscious. He watched the water vibrate slightly to the low rumble. It was fainter out there, at the villa on a hill away from the sea, but it was still in the background.

It did not take Vrric long to get out to the stables. He had decided to shave after the bath, to be looking his best as it were. He was a little tired but could certainly manage another few hours. His sleep schedule had been erratic on the boat anyway, with more shorter naps than one long sleep at night. It was probably around midnight.

He was a little saddened to realize how many derlians were on guard duty. He had been hoping it would just be Clerin and him. Rewista and Wesduin were sitting on the half-empty wagon, playing cards of some sort, and he heard voices trickling down from above. He chatted briefly with Rewista and Wesduin, checking in with old comrades. Before he could head up the ladder, however, Zira and Silvadhin came down and motioned him to go up. When he got to the loft, only Clerin was up there.

"We will have to whisper." She spoke in a low conspiratorial voice.

"Okay." He kept his reply so quiet as to barely be audible. He smiled widely at her. He was not really sure what she wanted to talk about with him. It had been weeks since they had last been together. Honestly, he would have preferred to just go for a long walk with her, winding through a strange city, maybe holding hands.

She reached out and pulled his right hand into hers, as if she were reading his mind. She smiled sweetly at him, showing her dimples and white teeth. He smiled back at her.

"First, let me say that I have mentioned you to my mother. Well, not by name, but I did tell her that I loved a Luften." She was still whispering, so he just pantomimed the word "wow" for her. "But… but we cannot be together here. We cannot be alone here. I'm being offered a husband."

"What!" It popped out of his mouth at the same time his hand escaped hers.

"Shhh, wait."

"Don't shush me."

"Please, wait, let me explain."

He held his breath and gritted his teeth. He took a long slow inhale through his nose until his chest puffed with the air, then let it out through his mouth. He let the chaotic energy that had filled him in that moment of surprise leak out with his breath. He nodded to her.

"It is something being offered. I am certainly not going to take them up on it." She did look fairly pained, which was oddly comforting to Vrric. "But that is why we have this villa, that is why we have the cooperation of Tureyn."

"I thought we had the cooperation of Tureyn due to Lembin. I thought they were rewarding you for taking care of Vatlisi." He kept his voice at a whisper. "Doesn't the opinion of the Beleg override… the king? Override derlians?" He tried to recall who ruled Tureyn but realized he had no clue.

"How often was Linchon consulted by Hulgert? Or the previous king?"

"Just because Luftens don't ask their Beleg about everything doesn't mean Fluens don't. You've told me the stories, how important Lembin is to the Fluens, how your mother's political power came from her translating. You can't compare the two."

"Of course not, I am sorry. All I am trying to say is there are a lot of perks and assistance we are getting and could keep getting if I just meet with a couple of prospects. Do not worry, I will refuse them all. And soon, we will be back on the road, heading towards Ariellyna, and everything will be back to normal."

"And what if you meet a beautiful, rich, witty, and intriguing Fluen who sets your spirit ablaze?"

"Is that what you are worried about?" She somehow whisper-laughed. "No one compares to you, not in my eyes."

Altrond did. He almost said it. It took all his willpower to keep himself in check and to only think it instead. He realized it would have done serious damage to Clerin if he had spoken those two words. At that same moment, he realized he did not want to damage her. He did not want anything to be damaged, there was no reason for it. He was getting worked up for no reason. Besides, Altrond was dead and it was best if he was simply forgotten by Clerin. Or, at least, not brought up by Vrric.

"It's fine, it'll be fine. We should get all the free stuff and perks we can out of these Fluens before we escape."

"That is the spirit I was looking for." She leaned in and gave him a long kiss.

"And you really did tell your mother you were in love with a Luften?"

"Yes, truly. It was the scariest moment of my life." Her eyes got comically wide. They both laughed heartily and somewhat quietly.

It was odd being near Clerin, but not *with* her. They stole glances periodically, but that was about it. Since she seemed to be occupied all the time, he attempted to keep himself busy with little tasks. He assisted Wesduin in readying the equipment, wagons, and horses for the long trip to Ariellyna. He took as many guard-duty shifts as he could. He helped gather part of a wagon of items from the citadel of Tureyn. There really were not many items, especially compared to what they had found in Vatlisi. They performed that transfer at night and kept it well guarded with a wagon of warriors in front and one behind. They tried to camouflage it a little bit. The wagons looked like the typical pompous palace ones. Vrric was not sure if no one knew about it, or that no one was interested, or that no one wanted to take on the defenses, but the trip was completely uneventful. So much build-up and intrigue and it was mostly boring. So Vrric's time passed without Clerin.

It was the evening before they were to head to Ariellyna when Midinarre, Clerin's mother, cornered Vrric. He was leaving his shift guarding the wagons with Dartsyle when she strode up to him. He was not sure how she found him but, by all accounts, she was one who was thorough with her research.

"You are the Luften mage who destroys Tlana?" Her eyes flashed like polished steel.

"I've destroyed a couple." He had not really thought about it much. He had been referred to as the mage who bested a Tlana before, but hearing it in plural gave it a more grandiose ring. While he was certainly not shy and did not lack an ego, it still sounded a little weird to his ears. Which is why his reply was a little weak.

"We must talk. Walk with me."

Dartsyle nodded slightly as he walked back to the villa proper without really looking at them. Vrric gave a small wave towards his back and turned to face Midinarre.

"Sounds great. This is your city, lead the way." He had taken a couple of walks through the neighborhood without getting lost during the last couple of days, but he wanted to give her the control. He was unsure of what the conversation was going to be, but was sure she would feel more comfortable being in control.

They walked for a little bit in silence. He assumed that was to get away from any prying ears and towards the safety of anonymity, just another couple of derlians walking down the street. At the end of a random block, they turned a corner and she started talking as they walked uphill.

"So I hear you are an orphan, maybe even a bastard, and were taken in by a smith. After years of that you switched mentors and disciplines and became a mage. You worked briefly for the Royal Branch in Ariellyna and met Clerin there as she sought the Luften Temple. You traveled with her, killed your first Tlana, found the Well of Eternity, and joined up with a bunch of Pyrans. After she communed with Linchon in the Temple, you all went to join the Pyran revolution and make your friend a queen. After Clerin communed with Gorbanax, you joined the mission to destroy the Cabal of Lochom and personally destroyed more Tlana. Am I getting all this right?"

"You're leaving out a lot of details but, yes, that is the gist of it."

"When Clerin was young, well, old enough but still young, she had a lot of boys interested in her. She is very fetching, is she not?"

"Yes, she is very beautiful."

"Not just that. Beauty fades, trust me, but she is charming, enchanting, lustrous. She had boys coming from all the nearby villages to be near her. To take their chance with her. And do you know why I never worried?"

"No idea."

"She gets bored." Her hands flew up in front of her as she talked. They looked strong and skinny, like talons. "Some boy would charm her for a while and she would get bored and break his heart and move on to the next. She was not sleeping with them, or at least not that I know of, maybe a few of them, but each moon another one would be around, bringing me flowers, thinking I would help them. Ha! The stupidity of children. Anyway, what I am trying to say is that I do not think you have bored her yet."

"Has she said that she loves me?"

"Love? My dear, love waxes and wanes like the moon. You are young, you do not understand. Love is as fleeting as magic, as fleeting as hate. What I think she feels, is that... I think she *likes* you."

"That's... better?" He thought of his childhood when he was asked if he liked any girls. It seemed the first stage, not the goal. Love was always on a higher level than like.

"It is if you avoid messing it up. And not let her get too bored. But that is not really why I wanted to talk with you."

"It isn't?"

"No, of course not. You know my daughter has true political potential, do you not? You understand that she could end up a duchess or even princess fairly easily, do you not? You know— in your heart of hearts, the deepest darkest chamber down in there— you know that her 'love' for you will destroy her future? Do you not?" She made air quotes with her talons at the word love.

"Ah, so you want me to let some chosen idiot with a name marry her, someone she does not even know right now. Someone who will keep her bored, who will not 'love' her." He made the same air quotes around the same word. "You want me to step aside and let her be miserable."

"Honestly, I am still on the fence about that one. I am not a monster, truly." She placed her right hand over her heart, as if she were swearing that she was not a monster. "You do have to let her breathe about that one, though. I do believe that. Are you powerful enough to give her that space, I wonder?"

"I'm confused. Do you want me to step aside or not?" *Not that I would do what you asked,* he thought silently to himself.

"I already told you I am not sure." She stopped and put her hand on his chest, stopping him. "But I know what would make me sure."

"And what is that?"

"You are powerful, yes? You have killed many mighty beings, yes? What would you do if a warrior attacked Clerin? Or a mage, or even a Tlana?"

"I would destroy them. In fact, I already have. Even a corporeal Tlana."

"What would you do if I attacked her? Say I had this knife…" She pulled a knife from her belt, brandishing it in front of Vrric's confused face. "…I had this knife and I leapt across a table at her?" There was a weird glint in her eye that made him nervous. She twisted the knife around in front of him as if she did know how to use it.

"I would stop you in your tracks."

"And if you could not, if I was unable to be stopped?"

"Then I would be forced to destroy you as well. But that would do almost as much damage to Clerin as your knife, so I really would try to stop you first."

"Good. Better than good, perfect. She needs protection, Luften. That is what she needs until all this Beleg business is completed. This is getting uglier than I had imagined at the beginning. She is being forced to create very powerful enemies and she will need excessively competent protection. You have a reputation for being excessively competent, you know that? And I do not care who is threatening her, I do not care if it is even me, myself. You need to destroy everyone and everything that is a danger to her. You cannot think about it, you cannot hesitate, you just must do." She tapped the tip of her knife against his chest. "You want me to back you? You want me to fend off all the princes and dukes that will be lining up for a chance at the most fetching catch this side of the Clatsvol Sea? You want me to allow my favorite, most promising daughter to throw her political career away, to tarnish the name of Toswin? Then you protect her and you bring her back to me. Unharmed, unwounded, untainted. Understand?"

"Yes, of course."

"Good, then we are done here." She put her knife away and started walking farther in the city.

"The villa is back that way." He pointed behind his shoulder.

"Yes. You are a big boy; you can find your own way home." And she walked off into the night.

Vrric's mind reeled. Not much of the conversation made sense. He turned and started back towards the villa, lost in thought. *What did she mean by untainted?* he thought.

They traveled well-worn roads but tried to avoid any large villages or towns. They would try to pass through anything of size in the middle of the day, sleeping on either side of it. They were not secretive, just overly protective of their cargo. Sleeping outside meant every single warrior was available at all times and the sentries could be easily swapped out. Everything was accounted for at all times, and there was no chance of a thief sneaking up on them. Of course, a large overwhelming force could probably have overcome them, but in the Fluen realm that would have meant it either came from Tureyn or somehow slipped past it. No, they felt fairly safe from large direct attacks. And, best of all, they had not seen or even heard about a Tlana since leaving Vatlisi.

They were making good time through the Fluen realm. The roads were well maintained and clear, and many of the provincial villages knew of their passing and readily provided provisions or any minor wagon repairs required. As they were riding along, Clerin approached him. They had been typically traveling together since she was no longer concerned about being caught alone with him by some spy or other, though she still rode through the villages alone; but she had been at the front, helping to steer the scouts. She grinned as she rode up beside him and pointed over his right shoulder.

"See that lone mountain far off in the distance?"

"Um… sort of." He squinted hard. "Yes, yes I see it."

"That is Scout Mountain." She paused. When he did not reply, she let out a little sigh. "I am sure I have told you about that mountain. I grew up on the other side of it near the Yamhill River. Well, not exactly near, but those are the closest landmarks."

"Have you ever climbed the summit?" The mountain looked like a mountain you would see in a painting or a tapestry. It was nicely sloped, sharply peaked, and snow-capped.

"No, never. We used to picnic up in the foothills sometimes, but never got near the snow."

"Well, we'll have to do that sometime. When we're done with all this…" He waved his hand around indicating everything and nothing. "…we'll have to come back to the Fluen realm and you can show me where you grew up. We'll take a nice picnic and I'll fly you up to the peak of Scout Mountain. How does that sound?" He was rewarded with a big smile with deep dimples.

"That sounds great, really."

It was not until they started to encroach upon the Luften realm that the travelling became more difficult. They were trying to skirt the Vanpicke Range, which placed them brushing the cusp of the Northern Desert as they passed through the large mountains' shadows. The road was more of a track where they were, and it was fast approaching trail status. They were not near any dunes, the ground was hard enough to easily support the wagons, but Vrric was starting to feel the heat. He was already missing the ever-present cloud cover of the Fluen realm, if not the drenching rain. He knew, however, that once they passed the last of the mountains in the Vanpicke Range, they could swing back into the Luften realm proper and find shelter from the sun in its forests.

It did not take too long for them to skirt the range and head south towards the ocean. The trees came first, then the trail turned into a track and then back into a road. The road popped in and out of the trees as they headed towards the Ariel River, which would lead them quickly to Ariellyna. There was a large stand of ash trees that greeted them near a meandering feeder stream where they were able to stop for the night. They had yet to see any helioarcs, the giant trees that made up the town of Ariellyna and much of the populated portion of the Luften realm. Those were generally south of the Ariel River, cupped between the Vanpicke Range and the Yadel River. Vrric's heart silently cried out with joy at the thought of them. It had been way too long since he had last seen a helioarc. His excitement was mixed through with nostalgia and the yearning for home.

They set up the camp quickly, easily falling back into the rhythms of the road after the comforts of the Fluen realm. They were still some distance from anything that could be called a town, so they relied on Escha's bow to bring some deer to the campfire. It was delicious and added to the slow relaxing feel of the evening.

They went over the simple plan once again. Vrric and Clerin were to gain an audience with Vanelia. All of the Luften warriors, of course, would accompany them. It was to be a great reunion. It was in service with Vanelia that Vrric had first met Clerin and the warriors. He felt he had to find a way to thank her for that meeting. Something quick and quiet, but sincere. Trela was to be there as well, to meet queen-to-queen as it were.

There was supposed to be another half-wagon of Yaven-infused items that Vanelia had collected. They were to take those and head to the eshrams at the Valley of the Caves, meeting a Pyran contingent, if needed. Lishean was supposed to be looking for more items. Whether or not he found more, Trela was not sure. From there, with the full collection, they would head into the Northern Desert and attempt to find the well. Yes, quite the simple plan. They only stayed amongst the ash trees for one night.

The whole coterie slowed to appreciate the lone helioarc they were approaching. Most had never seen anything like that. Vrric recognized it from a distance, when it was so small that it looked like a single tree surrounded by grass, rather than a gigantic tree towering above the rest of the forest. The tree appeared to grow the closer they got, towering above them, too tall to see the top. The miniscule trees surrounding it turned into a regular forest. It dominated their vision for an entire day as they travelled. And they were not even to the Ariel River yet, where the helioarcs really started.

When they finally arrived at the base, they set up camp. Some of the coterie jogged around it, some just stared up at it. It was as wide as a small house was tall, about four to five rods. It was a small helioarc, probably only about a hundred rods tall or so. Vrric did not fly to the top to check. He smiled at the awe that this one helioarc instilled in his companions. He could not wait until they saw the real ones, the big ones, that made up the city of Ariellyna. Then they would be properly astonished.

Soon after they reached the Ariel River. The road turned to follow the river a while before they were able to find a robust enough bridge to bring the wagons across. After they were able to cross, they passed through a small village or two, not stopping at an inn. They camped outside of the villages, attempting to attract as little attention as possible with as many derlians as they had. Soon the road widened considerably. Though Vrric did not know the exact road they were on, he could tell they were getting close to the city. He felt a little elated at the thought of returning home. He knew he would stop by to see Revkin, his magic mentor. He was unsure, however, if he should see Kaihlu, his old smithing mentor. They had left on such uncertain terms. *But,* Vrric thought, *surely he has forgiven me by now.* Still, there was enough nervousness in his gut when he thought about it that it gave him pause.

He was thinking with his head down, lost in various reveries, when the column stopped. He looked up to see what was in the way. It was several guards who had the road blocked. Vrric could not think of a time when a road to Ariellyna was blocked off. The whole thing had an air of unusualness about it. He kicked his horse forwards. Trela was, of course, at the head of the column, already arguing with the guards. There were two in front. The other four were back out of the way, but watching intently.

"No, you may not search all of us, that is absurd." Trela stayed mounted and so was glaring down at the guards. "We are travelling to Ariellyna to meet with Queen Vanelia herself. You may escort us to her if you wish, to ensure we are not up to anything nefarious, but we are not letting you root through all of our belongings."

Vrric dismounted once he reached the guards. He thought that would put them more at ease. Plus, maybe they would rather argue with a Luften.

"The reason we are here is that Vanelia is no longer our queen." The guard glared back at Trela. The simple sentence stopped Vrric in his tracks, momentarily stunned.

"Vanelia died?" Vrric was too shocked to say anything more coherent. His right hand still gripped his reins, more out of habit than anything else.

"Oh, no, Vanelia is alive and well, but she has been usurped by the Branch of Largon. We are under strict orders from King Chiavel to search all foreigners attempting to gain entrance to Ariellyna." The one guard nodded to the other, who nodded back. "So, you see, we are going to have to insist."

"What are you looking for? Your search?" Vrric thought he would see how intrusive they planned on being. Maybe it was to be quick and inconsequential.

"For weapons, of course. The new king is worried about an insurgency this early in his rule." One of the guards spoke.

"Yes, and a large contingent of foreign warriors trying to enter less than a week after he ascended the throne appears a bit suspicious, does it not?" The other guard piped in.

"You know, there's not many of you." Trela somehow made her eyes glare harder.

"That sounded like a threat, didn't it?"

"Oh, yes, that definitely sounded like someone who needs to be searched."

"If you search us and find a bunch of weapons, what do you plan to do with them?" Vrric was worried that he already knew the answer. Trela was certainly sure of it, but he wanted to hear it from them.

"We'll confiscate them, of course. For the good of the realm and safety of the new King." One of the guards nodded to the other.

"Over my dead body." Trela looked as if she was about to unsheathe a weapon.

"So, what if a couple of us flew over to Ariellyna, unarmed, and spoke with the King. We could return with a signed and sealed letter from him that allowed us passage." Vrric butted in a little late.

"You had better come back with more than a letter. We're not falling for some mage's tricks."

"Hmmph, like the King would see one such as you."

"Good, good, we'll do that then." Vrric waved to Trela to have her back her horse up. Which she did with some obvious reluctance.

Vrric remounted his own horse and rode back the short distance to where all the others were waiting. They had, of course, been listening.

"We'll camp back there, just out of their sight." Trela pointed into the distance. The others turned and started off, grumbling quietly and without rancor. "Who are you taking with you? Malghain?"

"No, not for Chiavel. I'll just take Clerin. This is a diplomatic mission, not a fight." Vrric scanned the sea of mounted riders for a moment before he found Clerin. "Besides, it will be quicker with just two."

"Well, be careful. If you are unable to talk to the new King, find the old Queen. She may be of more assistance to us than he."

She shook her head and tapped her heels on her horse's flank. "Usurp is such an ugly word."

They flew fast enough that conversation was difficult. Vrric did not want to keep the rest of the coterie waiting for too long. In the back of his mind, however, he did have the audacious hope that they would somehow get stuck in Ariellyna together. Even if that hope had no basis in reality.

It took a little over an hour to reach the outskirts at the speeds they were travelling. The city itself was made up of a large cluster of helioarc trees, the largest in the entire realm. There were buildings built up in them, roofs canted over the sides of large branches. There were platforms spread about at different levels, with dark entrance holes burrowed into the trunks and ladders leading to other platforms. There were rope bridges strewn about connecting the trees like wispy spider webs. There were Luftens flying about their daily business, disappearing and reappearing amongst the foliage. The leaves themselves, though several times larger than a regular leaf, were not gigantic in proportion to the trunks and branches, but splayed out from limbs sticking off large branches, making it appear there were smaller trees growing on the giant helioarcs. It swelled Vrric's heart with pride and something akin to nostalgia. A version of homesickness that only cropped up in the midst of Ariellyna.

They headed for the largest helioarc, roughly centered in the city, the royal helioarc. That would be where Chiavel was, where Vanelia used to be. Vrric pondered for a while about whether or not to land at the base of the tree. That would be standard protocol, to provide his name to the guards at the main entrance. He wondered how long it would take for their names to wind themselves up the helioarc, how long before Chiavel would even know they were down there, in the mud, waiting. If he decided to alight on one of the platforms higher up, he might get the message to Chiavel sooner, but it would also be taking the chance that breaking protocol would anger him.

As they approached the royal helioarc, he noticed that there was a platform about halfway up with a large amount of Luftens on it. He decided they could land there to investigate. If he was surrounded by guards when he gave his message, how far off protocol could he really be?

They floated in slowly so as not to cause any alarm. Still, by the time they landed, there were several guards gathered to greet them. They were all very cordial and had their weapons tied down with peace knots, though Vrric assumed that was due more for the other guests than the two strangers flying in. Each guard had a patch sewn on the shoulder of their sleeves, that of a blue heraldic lion above a green field of grass, that of the Branch of Largon.

"Greetings, do you have an invitation?" The guard in the center spoke up.

"We are old friends of Chiavel."

"I'm sure you are. Which means you should have an invitation."

"We have just returned from the Fluen realm, you see." Vrric paused for a moment, pointing towards Clerin. He did not want to mention that they were originally supposed to meet with Vanelia. He was pretty sure that would not secure their trust.

"If you do not have an invitation, you will have to use the main entrance. The guards down there will relay your message for you."

Vrric stood there for a moment, trying to think of something. He had assumed there was a good chance they would have to do that anyway. He glanced at Clerin, wondering when she would jump in. At that moment he saw someone approaching. It was not Chiavel, which would have been great, but it was someone else he recognized. The straight black hair held proud on a stiff back and neck, the somewhat crooked nose, there was only one derlian it could be.

"Sempere!" He held his hand aloft even though Sempere was already headed over. Vrric was trying to gauge if he was coming over because he recognized them, or just because he was wondering what was going on.

"It's okay, Mespin. Chiavel does actually know them." Some of the guards nodded and moved away, but Mespin stood by, keeping a wary eye on them. "Though I am not positive if he will see you today." Sempere tilted his palm towards the crowd, indicating the importance of whatever it was they were gathered to do. He had the same patch on his sleeve as the guards did. "Please, come with me. We should talk in private."

They followed Sempere through the crowd until they reached a double-door sized hole in the trunk of the helioarc. They all slowed slightly as their eyes began to adjust to the darker interior. They walked down a hallway for a bit, took one or two quick turns, and then Sempere led them into a small room.

The room had six or seven chairs around a smallish round table. The table had some sheets of paper and a quill standing in an inkwell off to one side. There was a window hole in the exterior wall, which let the light stream through. The furnishings were quite stark. Sempere motioned for them to sit and then pulled out a chair for himself.

"You were working for Vanelia the last time we met, were you not?" Clerin started before Sempere had a chance. He looked sheepish for the briefest of seconds.

"I work for the Royal Branch. That was with Hulgert and Vanelia while they ruled, and it is with Chiavel for now." He nodded sharply once, possibly to himself. "In fact, I was a valet for the Branch of Largon before being hired by Vanelia. So you could say I am getting back to my roots."

"How soon after she gave birth did it happen?" Clerin's eyebrow shot up.

It was not like Vrric had forgotten she was pregnant, but he just had not thought about it much. He did not get much time to think about the Luften realm, his home, in general, let alone anything specific like the Queen's gravid status. Clerin's… edginess… made more sense now.

"Not too long after. The baby was quite fussy and Vanelia quite devoted. She was unable to allow others to look after the little one and was unable to keep her eyes on the realm at the same time. Honestly, she may be happier now. Chiavel was generous with her retirement stipend. That is not often the case. In fact, there are those that worry a child will complicate any succession. Vanelia has promised not to pursue it, in return for her safety and the stipend, but the future is murky." He glanced between the two of them. "Chiavel has been more restrained than I had first worried. Of course, he is just starting to consolidate power, gather the Branches together if you will. He may decide to be less generous when the public has forgotten about their former Queen. Though she was quite popular, Luftens have a short memory as far as that is concerned." He had on a wry smile.

"Is she still in Ariellyna?" Not all who were dethroned were allowed to stay in the capital. Vrric thought he would check.

"Yes, currently. Probably for a while at least." Sempere smiled wryly again. "At least while the public still remembers her."

"So, if we were here on a mission that Vanelia was assisting, would that be taken up by Chiavel?" Clerin skirted the subject.

"I know nothing of a mission for Fluens. No, that would have to be taken up with him." Sempere held his hands up in front of him.

"Well, then we need to ask two favors of you." Vrric put on his own wry smile. "We need you to get us an audience with Chiavel. And, in case that does not work the way we are hoping, we'll need to know where Vanelia is."

"I'll certainly show you where Vanelia is. In fact, she would probably enjoy a visit." He began to draw on a sheet of paper, making a map of the major helioarcs. "Did you bring the others back with you? The warriors?"

"Yes, we are all here, but the guards have closed off the roads. We need to chat with Chiavel about that as well." Vrric was reading the map upside-down. It looked like Vanelia was in the Medical Branch's helioarc. He was unsure why.

"As for Chiavel," Sempere spoke without looking up, "he will speak with you if he likes. There is little I can do there. I am, after all, merely a servant in his employ. I'm well known enough to talk you past some guards here, but I really have little influence over Chiavel himself." He stopped drawing and shifted the map over to Vrric. "I will certainly let him know you both are here. However, you may wish to try to get his attention at tonight's festivities. He should be in a good mood tonight. This is his first public appearance after the coronation. Now, I have much work to do and must beg your leave. He should be arriving in a couple of hours, and I doubt you will get your audience while he is preparing. You should grab some mead and make yourselves comfortable."

"Thank you, really. This is a great help." Vrric nodded and folded the map up.

"I am just doing my job. I could see Chiavel wanting to chat with you, so I am willing to assist. If, however, he flies into a rage due to whatever it is you ask of him, it would be appreciated if you did not mention my name." He looked completely serious. Vrric was about to laugh at the joke, but then thought better of it. Maybe it was not a joke.

"Of course, you have our discretion. If he approves, we will be sure to mention you." Clerin smiled warmly at him.

They followed him out and back to the platform. This time the guards paid them no heed. They wandered over to a line of small tables that had rows of goblets on them, all full of mead. He grabbed one for himself and one for Clerin.

"You are in for a treat."

"I have had mead before." Her smile was radiant, showing off her cute dimples.

"Of course, but this is royal mead."

"This is fifty goblets on a table mead."

"Well, we'll see then, won't we."

They wandered over to an edge of the platform where the throng was slightly less thick. It was a little difficult and they had to weave a bit through the crowd, but Vrric wanted a view. He leaned on a baluster and raised his goblet.

"To the most beautiful derlian in all of the realms."

"You should be more modest."

"I meant you. You know I meant you." He lost himself for a moment in her sparkling blue eyes. "To you." He took a sip before she could say anything else. "It *is* rather good tasting mead… But I built it up too much. It certainly doesn't match anything to be called 'royal mead,' my apologies."

Clerin also took a sip. "Well, it also does not match 'fifty goblets on a table mead' either. In fact, I will bet you a silver crown that the next goblet tastes even better."

"No, I will not take that bet. The only thing that tastes better than a free goblet of mead is the second free goblet." Vrric chuckled a little. "And it's 'heads' here, not 'crowns.' You sound like a Fluen."

"And why is that? All the usurping?" She lowered her voice and raised her hand, waving it around at the crowd slightly.

"Ha! No, not really. Hulgert's brothers were all short lived. The one right before him, Islen, only ruled for about two moons." He took a decent drink of mead. "We used to call coins by the ruler's name, back when they lived a long time. When I was young, they were called 'Ravials,' after Hulgert's father. No, to be honest, this usurping is quite new to us, or at least new to me."

He also kept his voice low when discussing "usurping." They were surrounded by Luftens celebrating Chiavel's rise. He wanted to talk about it with Clerin, to explain how steady their system was, that it was not like the constant upheaval of the Pyran realm, but he felt like his hands were tied. He could not really say certain things in that crowd. Almost everyone he saw had the Largon patch with the blue lion over the green savannah. He took another sip of mead and looked out at Ariellyna. They were quite high up and the city spread out before them in all directions, glimpsed between the leaves. Up, down, left, and right. As far as the eye could see. He preferred to fly rather than walk the various rope bridges between the helioarcs. The thought of walking for so long, swaying in the breeze and the vibrations of your own feet, with one slip between you and plummeting to your certain death, was simply terrifying. When he was younger, before he became a mage, he was not allowed up into the city proper, but scurried around at the base of the roots. He was not sure if the bridges would have induced vertigo in him if he had walked them his entire youth.

"What are you thinking about?" Clerin pierced his reverie.

"Just how I can be standing here on a quite solid platform, and staring at the Luften crossing that rope bridge in the distance, see them over there? And I can feel vertigo just by watching someone else. Isn't that odd?"

"Well, you say this platform is solid, but I swear I can feel it swaying slightly underneath me."

"Well, solid compared to that." Vrric gestured out to the swaying bridge with the Luften walking. "Look how it moves. And they are not even gripping the rope rails. It makes me grip my goblet tight just thinking about it." He laughed, then she laughed.

They finished their goblets and then seconds. The sun set, streaking the sky with dusky reds and oranges. Fires were lit in the various helioarcs, candles and lanterns could be seen through the myriad windows. It looked as if the stars had come down and surrounded them, flickering and ebbing and flowing in intensity. He told Clerin stories of his first mentor, Kaihlu, and of learning to be a smith. It took some time before Chiavel arrived, but at least he showed up before Vrric began speaking of Revkin, his magic mentor.

The crowd had been swarming about randomly, like lost and lazy bees, before he arrived. Then, almost as if they, collectively, sensed he was coming, the attention began to shift, to focus. Soon everyone was staring at the dark hole that was the entrance into the royal helioarc. A small tension formed. Voices quieted to urgent whispers. Then the moment they had all gathered for arrived. Chiavel walked out from the shadows and onto the platform.

He was just as tall and skinny as Vrric remembered. His black hair was snug against his skull, cropped up around his ears. And his oddly imposing eyes darted back and forth, drinking in all the derlians on the platform. They had an intensity that seared everything they gazed upon. Vrric and Clerin were well hidden at the far edge of the crowd, safe from being noticed.

A round of applause, the stamping of feet, a small roar of approval. The crowd gained its own intensity and cheered Chiavel in slow but increasing waves. He seemed to swell with it.

"Citizens, citizens, please." He raised his hands to lower the applause. "Thank you, thank you. Today we officially have a new Royal Branch. Today we are gathered here together to usher in a new era of leadership, a new way of thinking, a new golden age. Today the Branch of Largon has officially become the well of sovereigns, from which Ariellyna and the entire Luften realm shall be nurtured. Today is an auspicious day that would never have happened without each and every one of you. I thank you all!" Then they cheered again.

It went on like that for quite a while. He would quiet them down, say some platitudes, say something rousing, and they would applaud again. Vrric wished he had topped off his goblet before it all started, for it was empty about halfway through. Clerin seemed to pace herself better, taking small sips all the way to the end.

At the end of Chiavel's speech, at the other end of the platform, about thirty floating lanterns were lit and set aloft. The cubeish coverings of the flames glowed softly in the dark sky. They all slowly flowed away from the platform with the prevailing wind.

"Wow, that is beautiful. Is that done by magic?" Clerin's face was enraptured, watching the lights waft around.

"Actually, no. That's just the heat caught in the balloon, the bag on top. You should see the festival of Pinarch, we light thousands then. There really is nothing like it, it's like the stars have fallen from the sky."

"Is that... safe?"

"Oh, no, not at all. There are always little fires caused by the lanterns. Luckily they do not burn very long, so they are typically cold by the time they hit the ground, but that is where some magic might come into play, actually. For something this small, a little private celebration, there might be one or two mages who make sure the lanterns don't do any damage. But at Pinarch there's a small army of them."

While many of the derlians were watching the lanterns, Chiavel was shaking all the hands that were crowded up near him. Then he waded into the throng and slapped shoulders and laughed and winked at each of them. He really did seem to want to get a quick introduction with everyone on the platform. Vrric waited his turn, flowing with the crowd, gaining ground ever so slowly, watching Chiavel get nearer, until finally they were face to face.

There appeared to be a moment of recognition followed by a genuine smile, a smile that lit up his darkly intense eyes. Vrric immediately smiled back. Not because he had been waiting to talk to Chiavel about the coterie and had finally gained the meeting, but because he actually liked Chiavel. He always had, ever since their first meeting at that very helioarc, both waiting for an audience with Queen Vanelia. He knew he should be angry about the usurpation, and he was, he truly like Vanelia as well, but in that moment he was merely face to face with an old friend.

"Feyazki, it is so great to see you again. It has been too long, and I am sure you have many stories to fill me in on. Sempere had mentioned you were here to talk to the throne about past promises. Today is, obviously, too busy to accommodate you, but how about we get together tomorrow before noon?" He was shaking Vrric's hand and staring intently into Vrric's eyes and gave an expectant pause after the word "noon."

"Yes. Yes, of course." Vrric did not quite stammer, but he was a little taken aback by the swiftness of the conversation.

"Perfect, I will have Sempere provide you with the details."

Then he moved down to Clerin. He stopped and drank her in, from tip to toe to tip again. She was smiling warmly at him, her right hand held slightly in front of her. He lifted that hand with both of his, slowly bringing it up to his lips and kissed the back of her hand gently.

"Clerin Toswin. You look even more ravishing than my memory of you, and that is saying a lot."

"We have been travelling…" She had a half-embarrassed smile on her face and almost imperceptibly bit her lip, her eyes dropped for the briefest moment and then popped back up, staring into his, her pale blue eyes flashing like lightning. Her hand slipped from his and waved downwards, indicating her disheveled clothes.

"You must accompany my old friend Feyazki when we meet. I wish to hear your stories as well." He made a tiny, quick bow to her, then rotated slightly and performed the same bow to Vrric. "Until the morrow."

Vrric took a stunned moment looking forward before glancing over to Clerin. She turned to him, smiling, and fanned herself comically. She mouthed the word "whew" or maybe "wow" before stepping into the small space between them. Chiavel was already a couple of derlians down, but she still leaned in to whisper in his ear.

"You should check him for a magic aura. No one should be that charismatic naturally."

Vrric had forgotten how Clerin had liked Chiavel previously. How he had paid for her stay at an inn, how he had taken her out and had shown her Ariellyna. They had even talked alone for a while above the Luften temple before Hulgert died. Vrric had never really asked her about him, had not even thought about it much. The past was the past in his mind. Except when the past resurfaces. He felt an odd pang where his jaw connected to his skull.

Clerin suddenly wrapped her arms around his neck. "Jealous?"

"Actually... maybe a little." He furrowed his brow, thinking for a moment. "I don't feel that very often."

"Well, maybe you should. Just a little bit, mind you. Just as a little reminder for how good you have it. Nothing full blown that makes you stupid, okay." She gave him a small kiss, they were still in the middle of a public function, and her soft lips created a warmth that erased the pain in his jaw. "Now let us find an inn and I will show you that you have nothing to be jealous about. I know of a great one not far from here, the Cloak and Stagger."

Did Vrric remember they were supposed to talk with Sempere before they left? No, he did not. They left for the inn immediately, flying up and over the edge of the baluster and out into the warm air. The lights from the myriad windows flickered as they flew by, reminding him of the floating lanterns.

✳✳✳

The next morning came quickly. They were up and had already broken their fast when Sempere *whispered* to Vrric. They were to meet at noon, in about three hours, at the royal helioarc. Same platform for simplicity's sake.

"Do you want to visit Vanelia before or after Chiavel?" He posed the question to Clerin after his *whisper*.

"Before, of course. We should really know what we need before talking with Chiavel. Besides, I would like to know how angry I should be beforehand. Maybe Sempere is right and she is happier not being queen, but I somehow doubt it."

They got dressed fit to meet royalty and they left. Clerin was wearing a pale blue dress with elegant white embroidery up the sleeves and along the collar. The upper portion of the dress was quite form-fitting with a plunging neckline. Vrric had on a green tunic over a somewhat grayish undershirt, heavily embroidered as well. His trousers were a little tight but fit nicely into his knee-length leather boots. He did not enjoy dressing up, but it was not necessarily horrible either. He was ambivalent to it. Mostly, it just seemed like a time-consuming exercise. Whether or not Chiavel actually cared if he was dressed up, he knew that Chiavel would notice if he had not. And if it were noticed, it would be marked down on the ledger that lived inside Chiavel's head. He never forgot a slight, no matter how miniscule. It was better to put in the time than to get some unspoken demerit.

They arrived at the helioarc's platform that led to the passageway that led to Vanelia's quarters. There were no guards, no courtiers, no servants, no one. They landed quietly and headed straight in. There were several side doors, but they walked straight to the door at the end of the passage. It was a stout looking door with a tiny, covered portal at head height.

Vrric knocked three times and waited. Soon footsteps arrived and the tiny portal opened. Vanelia glanced out for a moment and then opened the stout door. She stepped back and waved them in. Her curly shoulder length chestnut hair bounced as she turned. She had a small quiet infant in her left arm.

"Vrric, Clerin, please come in. This is quite the pleasant surprise."

It was shocking to hear the name "Vrric" out of anyone's mouth besides Clerin's. And she only did that while they were alone.

Even Chiavel had used Feyazki. He did not correct her, however. It seemed natural.

"Thank you, my Queen." It popped out of his mouth as he entered. Vanelia paused for a moment.

"Do not be silly. Please." She looked slightly hurt for a moment before smiling again. "I am just Vanelia now."

"I apologize. I meant no offence."

"Of course not. No, it is sweet. We just do not want to give Chiavel anything to worry about, do we? We must not start any rumors." She glanced down the passageway before shutting the door. "Please, come in, sit. Welcome to my humble abode."

They were in a large and lush parlor. There were several couches and low tables, with dressers or buffets against some walls, and mirrors and paintings covering much of the rest. There was a lot of red, which was odd since Vanelia always wore white. Though she could hardly wear the same color of her furniture. They both sat, while she went into the other room for a moment to put the baby down before returning.

"We will have to speak softly please. Hynara only rests periodically, and you never know what will set her off." Vanelia's smile looked more tired than her previous one. She sat down opposite them in a high-backed chair with red velvet covers and cushioned arms.

"Of course." Clerin tilted her head and gave a sympathetic look. "You have a lovely home."

"Yes, it is a beautiful cage, is it not?"

"You are not allowed to leave?"

"I am just being dramatic." Her hand waved downwards. "I am allowed to leave and go to the market and the like. I just cannot socialize with powerful Luftens. What was the word in the contract...? Ah, yes, fraternize. I am not allowed to fraternize. Unfortunately for me, most of my friends are powerful, so I do not get to see a lot of them." Her smile turned a little wistful. "I should probably use the word 'were,' not 'are.' Not that they are not still powerful, they most definitely are, but more that they used to be my friends." She gave out a short barking laugh.

"You have a contract?" Clerin sounded incredulous.

"Oh, yes. It was that or watch them kill Hynara and then, of course, they would have to torture and kill me. Or some such nonsense. Chiavel has a flair for the dramatic. It was a simple choice when it came down to it. Certainly not one I cared to make, but there are only so many options available at certain times in one's life." Her smile was sardonic. "To be honest, the bloodless coup was—is—appreciated. Historically speaking, not many families that have fallen from power were treated as well. But you did not come here to listen to me complain, now did you? I assume you have found out that I refused to allow Chiavel access to the weapons and are here to pick them up."

"Oh, actually no, we have not spoken with Chiavel yet. We are to be at the royal helioarc at noon." Vrric spoke up.

"Well, in that case, try to act surprised." Her smile increased in vigor. "I think I know Chiavel fairly well. He would have been too tempted to keep one, well at least one, just so he would be the only derlian to have the only Yaven-infused item in all of the realms. I am not even convinced he would use it, though he certainly would if he felt his rule was threatened. But he would have it stashed somewhere hidden away, and he would visit it. He would bask in its glory, the glory of its uniqueness, a glory only he could enjoy. And then he would put it back and rule over his subjects and, while they were complaining about something, his mind would wander back to that glory and he would grin at his own magnificence and half ignore the derlian in front of him. No, I do not trust him enough to test him."

"How did you get him to agree to that?" It was Vrric's turn to sound incredulous. His mind cast back to the letters that Wreyvaine had. Had some of those truly been signed by Chiavel? "Are you sure he gave everything over?"

"As sure as I can be. I have many loyal subjects and a bloodless coup was desired by all. Chiavel did not wish to murder his way through to the city center. When we worked on the contract it was just something I insisted upon. Honestly, I think he just wants to consolidate power over the next moon or so. Your timing is quite fortuitus. Once he has everything nailed down, who knows what he will be like. I have several plans on how to leave Ariellyna if it comes down to that, but right now he is quite distracted." She glanced, maybe unconsciously, towards the room that Hynara was sleeping in.

"So... I'm assuming you don't actually have the items here." He was still a little shocked about the whole situation.

"I have them well hidden nearby. You need not worry about that." She grinned at him.

"We are hoping to get Chiavel to provide our caravan protection through the city so we can get some rest before moving on. We could try to pick them up then." Vrric was already getting nervous about it, right after he said it.

"Or we could go around Ariellyna with the main group and take what you have out of the city at night with a smaller group." Clerin gave voice to Vrric's sudden nervousness. "If you really think Chiavel is that untrustworthy."

"That is up to you, but I certainly would not trust him."

"In his defense, you trust him with your life." Vrric was unsure of why he would say anything in Chiavel's defense, it just sort of popped out.

"Well, on that I have no choice and have plenty of contingency plans. Your point is well taken though. He does appear to have a certain amount of honor if you squint just right. If you do wish to trust him, I suggest a contract. That is what Hynara and I did." She laughed louder than she had been talking and then quickly quieted down, glancing to the other room nervously, but no crying ensued.

Vanelia looked nervous for a moment. "Vrric, I must apologize, but if you have just arrived here, you may not have heard." He merely cocked his head. "Revkin has died." She paused for a moment. Vrric paused for a moment, so did Clerin.

"How?"

"Completely natural causes, I hear."

Vrric was stunned. It was not that Revkin was the picture of health the last time he saw him, he certainly drank too much, but he had not been overly unhealthy either.

"He was training another apprentice, one called Pashkaun, I believe."

What was Vrric to say to that? Did this apprentice confirm that Revkin had died of natural causes? Luckily, Clerin came to his rescue.

"I hate to ask this, and feel free to not tell me, it is only my curiosity, but it appears as if you live alone." Clerin had a pained smiled on her face. "Is Hynara's father not around?"

"Ha! No. He is not."

"Again, feel free not to tell me, but who is Hynara's father?"

Vanelia breathed a large sigh. "Not Hulgert. How about that?" Clerin's face did not shift, but kept the smile. "He is just… gone. That is really all I am prepared to say."

"Of course, of course. I apologize for prying." The pained smiled was overwhelmed by a relieved one. "Is there any way I could take a quick peek at little Hynara? I promise not to wake her."

"Yes, of course." Vanelia slowly stood and glanced around for a moment, as if she was looking for something she had misplaced. "Vrric, would you like join?"

"Ah, yeah, I'll just peek around the corner a bit." He stood slowly as well. Clerin was already halfway to the room.

They flew directly from Vanelia's to the royal helioarc. They went through several layers of guards but arrived soon at the second throne room. The smaller, more intimate throne room. Sempere was standing back and away, not quite in a corner, but almost out of sight. The room was lushly tapestried, providing Sempere with some minor camouflage. There was a small dais in the center of room with two thrones on it. Chiavel stepped down from the one on their right and motioned them to a small table off to the side. There were three chairs there already, waiting for them. They all sat.

"You simply must tell me of your adventures." Chiavel uncorked a bottle of mead and poured three goblets.

It seemed a little odd that Sempere was not drinking either, as if they were to forget him. They all drank. *Now that*, thought Vrric, *is royal mead.*

Vrric did his best to skim everything that had happened since they had last seen Chiavel at the Luften temple. Clerin joined in quite often, embellishing or adding jokes. It took at least an hour and by the time they were done, they were on their second bottle of mead. There was not too much detail involved, or at least not too much as far as their missions were concerned. They spoke of Tlana, the Cabal, and Vatlisi, but did not mention following the Blind One across the Clatsvol Sea. They were fairly in synch with what to gloss over.

"Please, we have told you ours, now you must tell us how you came to depose Vanelia." Clerin laughed behind her goblet.

"Only if you promise not to hate me." Chiavel laughed behind his own goblet. Their eyes did not have the same level of mirth their voices did.

"Is it that bad?"

"No, of course not, but I know you have already spoken with Vanelia. I am sure you have already heard this story."

"Funny enough, she did not talk about it really. Not beyond that it had happened."

"Though she did want to impress upon us how grateful she is that it was a bloodless coup." Vrric interrupted their banter. Did he need to bring that up now? No, not really, but he had wanted to bring it up at some point.

"Right?" Chiavel made the word sound like a question. Like a full paragraph of question wrapped in one syllable. "It did not have to be, truly. There are those who say I usurped the throne, but that brings to mind illegal and violent overtones. There was no violence whatsoever. And there were those who clamored for it, believe me." He paused for a moment and turned to Vrric. "I am glad she appreciates the restraint I have shown."

"But, really, how did it happen? Did the opportunity just arise?" Clerin was not backing down. At this point, Vrric figured they would have to have to coterie skirt Ariellyna.

"In a way, yes." Chiavel put up his hand to deflect her response. "Please, let me explain. You see, nothing was working. The city was shutting down. You see, Ariellyna was hit with several crises at once. First, there was the insect attacks on the crops outside the city, devastating our grain production. Vanelia did try to lend mages out to farmers in an attempt to kill the insects, but that led to arguments about who got what aid and who would ultimately pay the mages. There were those in the city who did not want to help the farmers, even though that is where their food comes from. The insects were incredibly difficult to kill as well. Every time one farmer's crop was focused upon, they would hop to a neighbor's, which would set up more arguments between the farmers. Some folks in the city looked at the work to hand-harvest as more bountiful than the jobs they were doing here. At least there were always free meals. So they started to leave in droves, which left the grunt work of the city unfinished or at least finished slowly and badly. It went on and on, with every fix that Vanelia could come up with ruining something else." He held up his hands again.

"Not that anything could really be done, I am certainly not blaming her. But the thing is, she was heavily distracted at the time. She was just about to give birth when the insects arrived, and then the birth itself was long and arduous and the baby was colicky and it was just too much. Too much distraction. Even if she was unable to really solve the grain issue, she needed to be present, to show a brave face, to convince others she was working on the problem." He took a deep breath and managed to look a little sheepish. "Part of ruling is showing your subjects empathy, that their struggle is yours. But Vanelia was nowhere to be found."

"Where did the discontent come from? Was it the Groundborn who vocalized their complaints against Vanelia, or the Airborn?" Vrric guessed where Chiavel was headed with his story, so he thought he would clarify it a bit before it became bogged down in the details.

"Ah, yes, to the point. That is why I like you, Feyazki. You do prefer Feyazki over Vrric, yes?" His smile was a little crooked as he raised his goblet. "It was the Airborn. The crop issues had not been felt yet, certainly not in the city. There were not derlians starving the streets, creating a down-up revolution. But a revolution *was* brewing. It was just that those at the top noticed first, felt the pain first. The looming loss of those crops was going to decimate the merchants. Vanelia did not help with her altruistic ultimatums of 'free food for the Groundborn' either. Who was going to pay for that food? The farmers? No, the same that were already paying the mages to try to kill the insects. The merchants. Us."

"So… the Branch of Largon started the revolution?" Clerin added her own incredulousness.

"Well, not only the branch of Largon, there were certainly others as well, but yes, Largon was heavily involved. That was how I got tangled up in all of this." His dark eyes widened, exuding innocence. "I have a group of cousins that are quite… passionate. They get a head full of mead and who knows what can happen? They, and a couple of groups from other family Branches, came by to round me up, to make me go with them. They knew that I knew Vanelia well. They were just going to talk, they said. They wanted to reason with her, to figure out what to do together, how to spread out these costs. I… I really should not have used the word 'revolution.' That was not how it was supposed to happen, not what it was supposed to be. We were just going to have a discussion, a conversation."

"You and a large group of your drunk, possibly violent, cousins? Along with other groups of drunk, possibly violent, Luftens?" Now she sounded annoyed.

"How did you get past the guards?" Vrric interjected into the small pause.

"Well, that is part of it as well. The Branch of Shiloan has many guard members and, honestly, several of my passionate cousins were also guards. And guards know and respect other guards. So, you see, gaining entrance to the royal helioarc, gaining entrance to the throne room, was not the difficult part." He put his goblet down and looked seriously between them, spreading his hands on the top of the table. "The difficult part was controlling the multitudes of passions. It was like trying to steer a tornado. There were several moments, separate discrete moments, where I was afraid violence would erupt. There was a group of about six very loyal guards surrounding Vanelia. There was yelling and weapons were drawn. Poor Hynara wailed the entire time. I did my best to calm all parties. And, in my recollection, it was Vanelia who offered to step down. She behaved admirably under all that duress."

"And you ended up picking up the crown?" Clerin's right eyebrow shot up.

"It was quite difficult to keep the temperatures in check, to steer the tornado. Several times I had to situate myself between Vanelia's loyal guards and the rest of us, just to keep blood from being shed. I did not suggest that I become the next king, that came from another. One of the Shiloans, I believe. At the time, however, it did seem that I was the only one in the room capable of satisfying all parties." He looked almost plaintively at Clerin.

Vrric pondered for a quick moment. In his mind, what was done was done. It was certainly unfair to Vanelia. More than that, Chiavel most certainly planned much of the so-called "revolution." He probably even chose who would suggest that he take the crown. But what would venting his own growing frustration do? Anger Chiavel? He was merely passing through Ariellyna. He could not even call the city his home anymore. At least it had been a bloodless coup. He could feel Clerin's frustration from where he sat. It was palpable. So, before anything else could happen, he raised his goblet.

"To King Chiavel!"

"To King Chiavel!" To his surprise, Clerin immediately followed.

"Thank you, thank you." The grin on Chiavel's face looked genuine.

Vrric drank down the rest of his goblet. Since it was about half full at that moment, it was quite the draught. He could feel it in his face. Chiavel poured more and they talked for a while longer. He spoke of the enjoyable difficulties of being a king. Clerin spoke of how she had run Vatlisi briefly and the difficulties in doing that. They spoke of nothing else difficult. They certainly did not mention the items that Vanelia had stashed, nor their own carts stuck at the outside of the city. Sempere was quiet through it all.

It was not until they had arrived at the Cloak and Stagger and went up to their room, locking the door and dropping into the mildly comfortable wooden chairs, that Vrric felt safe enough to say what had been troubling him.

"The real question, in my mind, is who instigated the insects?" Could Chiavel have done that? Would he have done that? How far back did his planning go? Or was nature just being nature?

Chapter 6

They had decided to move the coterie away from the guards in the road while waiting for Clerin and Feyazki. That meant they went back a bit and off the road a little. Trela kept the campfires to a minimum, but it was not like they were hiding, just letting the guards forget they existed if that were possible. It took three days before Clerin and Feyazki got back, which was certainly better than it could have been, but far longer than she had hoped.

It was decided to avoid running the entire coterie through the city. Trela was a little disappointed, she had been looking forward to wandering the branches of the giant helioarc trees, but she had to trust her ambassadors. If they did not trust the new Luften king, she could not endanger the mission. Certainly not for some sightseeing. She promised herself that she would try to return one day, though she was not sure when she would be back in the Luften realm.

Though Trela herself was unable to go, she did need several members to get the wagon that Vanelia had, thankfully, gathered up for them. She thought long and hard about it, but was unable to feel comfortable with sending any non-Luftens besides Clerin into Ariellyna. In the end, she let all the Luftens go. They had been incredibly loyal to her, being the first to join her warpack. Before any Pyrans even. She wished she could have given them a couple of days in Ariellyna to visit family and friends, but she was unable to. They could ride in and arrive in the evening, spend the night, and at dawn they would need to get the cart from Vanelia and head out. There was no time to waste.

That meant the main coterie would travel well into the night and start again before dawn. They needed to get to the road that swung around Ariellyna, which traveled almost twice the distance as going through the city. So they headed out soon after Clerin and Feyazki had arrived.

It was a hard march, but they made an incredible amount of distance. By the time noon rolled around, they had arrived at the junction in the road where they were to meet up with the others. They were a little early, so Trela was not overly concerned. She did have Serghno *whisper* to Feyazki just to make sure everything was going smoothly. She did not want any surprises. She could not imagine how to resolve the situation if the new king decided to take the cart by force. Luckily that was not what was going on. She was a little early, they were a little late. No one was worse for the wear.

They set up a small camp and prepared a large lunch. It took about two more hours before the others showed up. When they arrived, they had one additional Luften with them, Pashkaun. Apparently, he was Feyazki's old mentor's new apprentice. She had heard the mentor, Revkin, had recently died, but had not known the apprentice was to be travelling with them. Feyazki vouched for him but, of course, did not really know him.

They let the Luftens eat and relax a little before heading out again. Wesduin took in the new items and redistributed the wagons, tying canvas tarps over them all to keep the casual observer from seeing anything. Once they were on the road, they moved quickly to gain some distance. But since it had been a long day, they set up an early camp. After a long night's rest, she woke everyone early and made a hard march. She hoped to make the trip to the Valley of the Caves take as little time as possible since they had to enter the Northern Desert after that. She was hopeful that as long as Croy was correct about where to destroy the items, they would be able to find the well without too much trouble. It was often difficult to find, and she felt they needed to pay the desert the respect it deserved. Then there was the question of how many of her coterie to take into the desert and how many to leave in the valley. And, finally, how to get the wagons through the desert itself.

Clerin had suggested taking a riverboat to the Iltrolin Pools as they had done previously, cutting their travel time down considerably. Trela was nervous about the chance of the boat capsizing, but felt they would be able to retrieve all the items from a river—it was not like traveling over the sea, where things could get lost irretrievably. And since they were out of Ariellyna already, the next available village with a dock was only another day's journey. As they were heading along the road, Trela started her other plan. She needed Serghno to fly to the edge of the Pyran realm as the rest of the coterie wound their way towards the Valley of the Caves. There he would meet up with a contingent from Lishean that had gathered up any remaining items from the Pyran realm and fly them back. Trela had wanted to send Ryshial with him, to assist with the flying, but he insisted that Arnasta be the one to help. Trela was not really sure if Arnasta was a great flyer, but she did not argue the point. It would certainly keep them happier than splitting them up.

It took them the day to get to a boat and almost another four to get to Plyraxus Falls. They disembarked at the top of the falls and the ferry was hauled back upstream by a team of donkeys and a couple of mages. The falls themselves were quite amazing and the vista at the top was impressive. Trela could see the pools down in the distance, below the thundering roar, and could see the forest stretch off into the vista, with the Ariel River winding through it. There were a couple of helioarcs, but most of the trees were typical. At the top of the falls, near the road before it switch-backed its way down the side of the cliff, there was a stand of hawthorns. They had a small picnic there while the wagons were getting readied. It was beautifully idyllic.

They took a leisurely day to get to the pools. They were going to hire another ferry to go from the pools to the confluence of the Ariel and Yadel rivers which, from what she was told, only left in the mornings. They would need to spend the night near the pools no matter what. They still had some coins from Tureyn or Clerin's matchmakers, or whatever those Fluens were called, so she felt keeping the travel as simple and pleasant for as long as possible was worth the cost. Once they got to the outskirts of the desert, things would no longer be easy. It was a concern of Trela's. Another item of concern that she had not resolved was just how to get the wagons through the desert. The only real solution was to load up the horses and walk beside them. She had tried her hardest to come up with something different, but nothing presented itself beyond forcing her mages to do everything.

Luckily the inn at the ferry was quite empty and happy to accommodate the travelers. Still, it was quite cramped with all of them in there. If there had been many other guests, her coterie would have had to camp outside.

Most of her coterie spent the last hour before dusk exploring the pools themselves. She spent her hour keeping guard over the wagons. It was not that she did not wish to explore, but more that she did not want to have to choose who had to stay behind. It was just simpler to do that herself. Which meant a concerted effort could have overpowered her to burgle their belongings, but they did not seem to have been followed and the stables were mostly within earshot of the inn itself. Eventually, Estfale and Wesduin came out to keep her company.

The meals in the great room of the inn were staggered, due to space and security. Trela went with the first group, figuring she would return to help with guard duty later in the evening. There she ended up sitting with several of the Luftens. They were chatting about their brief time in Ariellyna. Even Torpalin, who had, since at least Vatlisi, been oddly quiet and morose, appeared to be enjoying himself. Apparently they had visited his sister's bakery while they had been in the city.

"The scones were fantastic, and your sister was incredibly nice." Escha had her hand in Torpalin's, smiling warmly at him.

"What is the name of her bakery? I'll have to visit when I get back there." Pashkaun was grinning sincerely. Trela had yet to speak with him, which was part of the reason she chose to sit down with them.

"The Lofty Flour. She did not name it, that was the previous owner, her mentor." Torpalin leaned back in his chair, as if the others would give him a hard time about the name. "It is one of the few bakeries allowed up in the helioarcs. Her ovens are fully contained in thick layers of clay brick, perfectly safe."

Trela let them chatter on for a little bit while she ate her food and smiled at their stories. Eventually Escha, Torpalin, and Gyllhelon left, leaving only herself, Haswyxe, and Pashkaun. Trela promptly ordered three goblets of mead. No one ever left a table that had a free drink coming. Pashkaun looked quite young, with dark disheveled hair and a quiet, nervous smile. Trela wanted to know more about him, especially since he suddenly showed up towards the end of a sensitive mission. It was not as if she did not trust Feyazki's judgement, but it seemed as if he was added just because no one knew what else to do with him.

"So, tell me a little about yourself. How did you get into magic?" It was a terrible segue, but what she had thought was, *So, you were Revkin's last apprentice.* At least that had not popped out of her mouth.

"I had always been interested, ever since I can recall. It was difficult to learn as a child, my parents were not mages themselves, but I did well enough in the Trivaste tests that Revkin offered to be my mentor. For no charge even, only the promise to try to get grey mages established. I think Feyazki made the same bargain." The goblets arrived and Pashkaun took a large swig. "But that's not what you really want to hear about, is it?"

"Hey, Pashkaun, she's..." Haswyxe tried to interject but was cut off.

"No, it's fine. You want to hear how he died, don't you? You want to know if I found his body, if I'm somehow to blame for his death, all the grisly details." His smile was gone, and he took another swig.

Trela wondered how he could be triggered so quickly. She had not even said anything yet, was only making small talk. She felt a little attacked, which got her defenses up. But she did not respond to him, she did not interrupt.

"Yes, I found him. He was half on his bed with his sheets all twisted around. There was vomit and probably feces, it stunk horribly. I almost vomited myself. There were empty jugs of mead laying around, but there were often empty jugs around. I ran until I couldn't, not really sure who I finally got ahold of, but others showed up. Eventually the mage's guild representatives arrived. It is something that I'll never forget, something that will haunt me until the end of my days. Is that what you wanted to hear?" He stood and left the table.

Trela was stunned. Utterly. She thought back over her words and could find nothing that would have instigated that response.

"He's very sensitive about that." Haswyxe looked at the door that Pashkaun had left through. "I wouldn't bring it up again."

"Yeah—oddly sensitive." Trela frowned. "And I didn't bring it up in the first place. I merely asked him how he got into magic."

Her statement seemed to slow Haswyxe a little. He frowned in concentration for a moment before standing. "You're correct." He nodded to her once, then turned away, then walked away.

The whole incident was so bizarre that she sat there sipping on her mead for a while before deciding to see Knill before heading back out for a round of guard duty. Far from making her feel better, the exchange bothered her quite a bit. She did not walk away feeling sympathy for Pashkaun. Quite the contrary, she felt more wary about him than she had previously.

They purchased as many provisions as possible at the inn. Since that cleared out most of their stores, it was not cheap, but they would get another shipment soon and so were able to part with a fair amount.

∗∗∗

The next day they were back on the river. It took them another few days to reach the confluence of the Ariel and Yadel rivers. After a while they had to disembark for what was left of the combined river split through the maze that made up Ruyogn Canyon. There it multiplied and floundered, eventually being swallowed up by the desert or meandering into the Pyran realm. There were supposedly some swelling and ebbing lakes hidden there as well. They would head to the Valley of the Caves on horseback where they were to meet up with Serghno and Arnasta returning from the Pyran realm. And once they left that valley there would be no more water. No additional provisions. Trela needed to figure out how many others she wanted to bring into the Northern Desert, to the well. She had to stop putting that decision off.

It took over four days to wind their way through Ruyogn Canyon, to find the Valley of the Caves. The last location of life before the Northern Desert clung on in the form of the eshrams, where mages driven mad by their search through chaos gathered to live away from polite society. Some, supposedly, were able to return, but Trela assumed most just died there as semi-hermits. She had been hoping to see Serghno and Arnasta before they investigated the eshrams, but that had not happened. Worst case, they would have to stay in the eshram called Algathia until they were able to locate them, maybe sending out Feyazki and Ryshial if unable to make contact through a *whisper*. Algathia was the eshram with Feyazki's, and she supposed Pashkaun's mentor's mentor, one Elange. She had heard tales of him from Feyazki and Clerin. They had met with him as they trekked the same path previously.

The first eshram they reached was called Tlimpid. It reminded Trela somewhat of an open-air Serif. The rock walls stretched up towards the sky, providing much needed shade, and were pocked with many black entrances, some covered with blankets. These were the caves of the namesake valley that the denizens lived in. There were wide pathways up the sides and terraces along the way, making an almost pleasant imagery of a cooperative society. However, they were not cooperative with strangers. They shied away from strangers, and anyone from Trela's coterie was certainly a stranger. They stayed the night on the valley floor, somewhat in the middle of the eshram but tucked away from the trickle of a stream.

That bit of water seemed to be the only thing the eshram denizens left their caves for, at least while the coterie was around. They certainly did not want to disrupt the rhythms of life there, or at least to disrupt them as little as possible. Their mere presence appeared to pain the denizens.

They left for Algathia early the next day. Feyazki had tried to *whisper* to Serghno before they left but heard no reply. It took another two days of hard travel northwards to reach Algathia. The compasses that they had brought with them began to diverge from one another slightly. Trela knew they would end up useless but had been hoping to get into the actual dunes before that happened.

It was in the evening when they arrived, so they decided to camp in a similar situation as in Tlimpid, in the middle of the eshram but tucked out of the way. Algathia was much smaller than Tlimpid. There were no terraces, only small footpaths that spiderwebbed up to the various cave entrances. Rather than a trickling stream, there was a dry bed and a tiny well. They stayed far enough away from the well that the eshram denizens could visit it without fear of getting talked to. Since it was evening, Feyazki decided to wait to visit Elange until the next day.

Once they were all awake and eating on one of the last campfires they would be able to have, Trela had Feyazki *whisper* to Serghno and Arnasta again. Nothing. She was starting to get a little nervous about it; it should not have taken them this long.

"You and Ryshial should go to look for them. At least to get within *whispering* range. Once you've made contact you can head back." They were still in shadow on the valley floor, making it oddly cool. She knew it would warm up quickly, making travel more difficult.

"Well, I was hoping to spend a couple of days with Elange while we were waiting." Feyazki smiled a hopeful smile at her.

"And I was hoping to send two derlians out, you know, just in case." Trela raised an eyebrow at his reluctance.

"Yes, you should definitely go. Two would be much safer. I can speak with Elange for you if you like, just point out his cave." Trela had not even realized Pashkaun was behind her. It was slightly startling when he spoke up.

"Well, I did not have anything in particular I wanted to speak with him about. Nothing really. Just wanted to spend a little more time with him, to pick his brain if you will." Feyazki's smile lost a bit of its hope, but was still there.

"Well, there will be plenty of time once you get back. I won't pick it clean, I promise." Pashkaun laughed a weird little laugh. Trela was getting her hackles up but was unsure of why.

"I could always send Croy with Ryshial if you like? That way you could spend some time with Elange." She spoke to Feyazki, but was watching Pashkaun out of the corner of her eye. It seemed that he flinched for the tiniest of seconds.

"Wouldn't you want the most powerful mages you have at your disposal to look for the others? You know, just in case." Pashkaun nodded to Trela while he spoke, as if he was trying to get her to nod as well.

"He's right. It should not take too long to find them. I'll have plenty of time to chat with Elange afterwards." Feyazki was nodding to Pashkaun.

"Well, why don't you all visit him now? You could say hello, make introductions and the like." She was not sure if she was being paranoid, but something about Pashkaun did not sit well with her. She figured if she went along, she could linger behind and warn Elange about her... what? About her paranoia? Her nervousness?

"Well, he wouldn't be expecting us, now would he?" Pashkaun added another obstacle to the path. It just made Trela more wary. "I would hate to be a bother."

"We'll never know unless we check." Trela started to move towards the well since she had no idea where Elange's cave lay. "Come on, we can all say a quick hello."

She did not have a plan, was not even sure there was a reason for one. She was only deciding things because they seemed the opposite of what Pashkaun wanted. That was certainly no strategy and not even a very good tactic.

Feyazki started walking after her and Pashkaun after him. Soon, Feyazki was in the lead. They wound up a steep footpath towards a blanket-covered entrance. Feyazki stopped in front of it.

"I think this is the one." He took in a deep breath. "Elange! It is I, Vrric, Revkin's apprentice. We met some time ago."

"Come in, come in. You are expected." The voice sounded muffled behind the blanket.

They all entered and had to crouch a little, even Trela. It was a fairly small cave that had a nook in the corner for sleeping. There was a rug on the floor with several pillows scattered about. There was a stone wall that had kitchen utensils and another that had crates stacked against it. There was barely room for the four of them in there.

Elange himself was small for a Luften but still taller than Trela. He had gray wispy hair and wore brown robes with various shades of leather patches scattered about. He was sitting on a pillow nodding to himself.

"Ah, you've brought another cat and… something else." He squinted at Pashkaun. "The cat waits outside." He shook his hand towards Trela, waving her off.

Trela did not speak, but nodded as deeply as she could, attempting to make a bow to the venerable old mage. The mage, as grimy and squalid as he was, was quite deserving of respect. It emanated from him. She paused while Feyazki and Pashkaun sat on their respective pillows, memorizing their shapes and locations. Then she flipped the blanket back and left.

She stood outside of the cave entrance for a little while, trying to listen in. The blanket did a great job at muffling the sounds so that they were hard to make into words. So she just listened to the tones for a while. The sun beat down on her fairly relentlessly. But it felt good. It had been a while since she had been in a proper desert. The sun thrummed with power, warming her face with its love. She smiled to herself.

The tone began to shift a little, bringing her mind back into focus. Then, suddenly, the tone changed entirely. Trela pulled her favorite dagger from its sheath, the one that was weighted perfectly. The tone changed into yelling, someone screamed "murder!" and another cried "help!" A burst of flame shot from behind the blanket, setting it alight. She threw back the flaming blanket and tried to peer within the cave. There, in a mangled mass of pure light, were three mages trying to kill each other. Flames flickered in all directions, burning her face with hate. Lighting crackled throughout the cave, blinding her to anything beyond outlines. There was screaming all around. Trela did not know what to do, could not tell who was who or what was what. So she did what she was good at. She acted. She threw her dagger at the shape closest to where Pashkaun had been sitting. It had certainly seemed like the correct shape. Then everything exploded and she was flung off the cliff.

✳✳✳

When she came to, it was Clerin who was attending to her. It made Trela feel good to see Clerin since she assumed her wounds were not overwhelming. If she had seen Nochiel over her, she would have known it was bad. Of course, that all depended on how long she had been out.

"What happened, where's Feyazki?" She did not feel too out of it, so she hoped she had only been passed out for a little while.

"He's fine, Nochiel is looking after him." Clerin's face seemed to glow above Trela like the sun. "Elange, however… Well, Elange did not make it." A cloud passed over Clerin's face, but quickly left. "Are you able to stand?"

They walked over to the tent that housed Feyazki and Nochiel. She left as they entered. His smile was weak but it perked up when he saw Clerin.

"What happened?" Trela spoke before considering his health or wishes. She was about to backtrack before he spoke up.

"Pashkaun was well-trained and vicious. A black mage sent to assassinate the grey mages before we got a large enough guild to compete with them. Or any guild." He coughed a little, briefly. "That's what I think at least. He said he would have destroyed the white mages as well, but they were already too well established."

"Why do you have a black mages' guild at all? That sounds foolish."

"They live in secret. They are not really a guild, just a way of life." He paused and then narrowed his eyes at her. "I was trying to neutralize him so we could question him later. Not kill him." She almost spoke up in her defense, but he raised a hand to cut her off. "I'm glad you were there and knew you were just trying to help. You did help. Just explaining why I did not destroy him immediately after he attacked Elange."

He coughed again, making Trela realize how much she was intruding. It did not really matter what had happened, at least not right now. They could talk about it all later. Trela nodded to Feyazki and took her headache and left. She needed to find Ryshial and Croy to send them after Serghno and Arnasta. Too much time kept slipping between her fingers.

✳✳✳

It took another two days for Ryshial and Croy to come back with Serghno, Arnasta, and the rest of the Pyran Yaven-infused items. There were not many, which was nice. Trela had assumed there had been a lot and the delay was due to carrying all that weight that distance. The delay, however, was on the Pyran side. They were late getting to the arrival point. Serghno had thought about trying to get word back to the coterie, but he did not want to leave the post and did not want to split himself from Arnasta. Though Trela would have liked the status update, she also understood the danger of wandering about alone.

It took them several more days to reach the last eshram. They filled up on water and left who they could. Those left behind could move from eshram to eshram if need be, so when they came back through, they would have to look for them. They only needed to bring enough derlians to walk the horses that carried the items. Trela ended up choosing everyone who had found the well previously, in case that helped at all. Therefore, all of the Luftens were coming as well as Croy, Knill and Clerin. She also brough Ryshial for additional magic. But she left what warriors she could. Estfale would not be left behind, but Dartsyle, Rewista, Jalin, and the other Pyrans would stay. Silvadhin, Verin, and the Dylsun twins would also stay. She did want some who had seen Vijen before, so she brought Aedon but not Nyhan. She also, and this was with a heavy heart, included Mika and Hupdor. She was unsure of what to do with her semi-prisoners and worried she would need to make a decision at the well. In the end, there were fifteen derlians chosen to travel through the inhospitable Northern Desert, mostly because they needed fifteen horses to carry the items.

They stayed one more night as a group, then all said their goodbyes the next morning. Trela looked out over the vista. They were still at a small elevation. There was literally a hard path before them, but once they reached the lowest elevation it turned to sand. Pure sand stood in front of them, as far as the eye could see. Just dune after dune, undulating in the sunlight. The Northern Desert proper.

Trela checked her compass and then looked down at where the path disappeared. She was hopeful that when she reached that spot, the compass needle would still be pointing the same direction. They needed to have some sort of direction before everything fell apart.

It took them three days of travelling "north" before their compasses completely disagreed. Trela's would show north while Estfale's would show west. It was a mess. They traveled another couple of days before Trela began to worry. The sun was relentless and it was no longer enjoyable. It seemed to stay directly above them the entire day, never moving. Having to walk their horses did not help either. The hot sand shifted underfoot making her feel as if she slid backwards every step, lessening her stride.

The nights were pitch black. No stars, no moon, nothing. They wished to walk at night, to avoid the heat of the day, but could not see anything. A strange feeling of foreboding accompanied the nights, and it built up. By the third night, they were unable to sleep it was so bad. Not any of them. They lit a fire, thinking that would help, but they did not have much firewood with them. They just could not afford the weight. The campfire lit a small area which did help, but there was a dome of pitch black that surrounded them at its meager edge.

Another day passed. It was maddening. Trela was getting annoyed. That was how she dealt with despair, by getting angry. The Belegs did want them to succeed, did they not? Then, when her anger was heating her more than the sun, they saw it on the horizon. A storm. A lightning storm. It headed their way with alarming speed, unnaturally so. Trela cursed herself for leaving any mages behind. Why would she have done that? What aid could someone like Knill provide compared to Serghno? She had brought him just because he had seen the well before? Her anger turned inward. All she had really done was to expose him to danger and endanger the rest of the group at the same time.

They hobbled their horses and waited for the storm to arrive. What else could they do? Feyazki, Ryshial, and Croy were at the front, ready to take the brunt. The others were to try to keep the horses together and to distract the coming Tlana. It had been a while since they fought anything at all, and certainly a while since they had to fight a Tlana. Since the Gaen realm, really; at least for her. Somewhere in the back of Trela's mind there was the absurd hope that this was just a regular storm. That the lightning was just lightning. Even though that hope existed, a tiny candle-flicker in the corner of her mind, the rest of her understood the truth.

The day turned to night when the storm arrived. The black roiling clouds found them, covered them, enveloped them. There was no rain, nothing to soothe them, just the black clouds. Trela could not see her hand in front of her face.

Lightning struck in front of them, and everything lit up as if it were noon. There, in the distance in front of them, was the silhouette of a figure. Then the world went black again. Lightning struck to Trela's right and there was another silhouette. Lightning struck to her left and there was another silhouette. Lightning struck all around; they were surrounded. There was a hollow horror stuck in Trela's throat.

Then came the attack. Lightning shot all around. A bolt struck near Trela's horse and flung her back. Some of the lighting that lit up the sky was, hopefully, coming from Feyazki. There was certainly a giant pillar of fire coming from somewhere along the front—Trela assumed that was emanating from Serghno since Ryshial had been practicing using wind to attack Tlana.

She got to her feet and, for the lack of something productive to do, unsheathed her shortsword. There was movement near the front, so she ran in that direction. More lightning lit up her surroundings. It appeared that there were several silhouettes over there, taller but not wider than a derlian.

Trela was knocked to the side by another bolt striking near a horse. She had lost her grip on her sword, but was able to find it again during the next flash. She picked it up and again tried to reach the front where the mages were. Her legs felt heavy, as if she were wearing lead pants and shoes.

A bolt struck in front of her and, for a split second, it looked as if there was a figure there. She swung with all her might, gripping the hilt with both of her hands. Her shortsword slid through the empty air and the shape in front of her appeared to be in two pieces. One piece, the torso, arms and head, was above her flashing blade, floating, levitating, while the legs and hips stood below. A small swirl of golden leaves followed her sword out of the Tlana's body, like smoke following an incense burner.

She staggered forwards, trying to reach the mages, trying to be of some assistance. Another bolt struck in front of her, another figure appeared. She again swung with all her might, thinking that she was at least distracting the Tlana. And it hit something solid. Thunk! She struggled with the shortsword for a moment, trying to loosen it, when another bolt lit up the sky. The sight in front of her sickened her to her core. She felt the same full horror she had felt when she watched Nolt die in front of her, because of her. Her sword was stuck in Aedon. There was a moment of recognition, a realization of what had happened, then the light left Aedon's eyes, then the light left the sky. Trela screamed until she was hoarse. She did not feel the crippling sadness she felt when Ilana berated her about causing Nolt's death, she would never feel that again, but she felt an anger that swallowed her up and a frustration that chewed her to pieces. She wanted, more than anything, to strike her enemies with her sword. To cut them into little pieces, to crush them under her blade, to swing and hit and swing and hit. She wanted to be doing something with her rage, to be physically solving something. She understood, however, that it was that same desire that led her to strike Aedon. The frustration of being unable to anything to absolve herself just kept chewing. She could not even get her shortsword out of Aedon's side. All she could do was to scream her rage out. A wild, wide-throated, head thrown back, clenched fists, clenched eyes, arms outstretched and quivering, howl of utter rage was torn from her for who knew how long. Certainly not Trela. At the end of that howl, for nothing can last forever, a different type of light filled the sky. A large draping tree with golden leaves was in front of her, shimmering and shaking. A Vijen had finally arrived.

Feyazki began shooting lightning in all directions. The Tlana around them burst into showers of leaves like slow motion explosions. The golden leaves on the Vijen reflected the lightning in scintillating patterns. The golden leaves from the Tlana shimmered the same. It would have been stunningly beautiful if it had happened at any other time.

"You're too late!" Trela was shocked to realize that those words came from Clerin, not herself. Clerin was crouched beside a crumpled body but her head, and her anger, was directed at the Vijen.

"She died protecting me. She placed herself between the Tlana and me. She pushed me back." It was hard to understand Clerin through the tears. It was hard to see who the figure was. Then Trela saw the jet-black hair pulled back into a ponytail lying motionless on the sand. It was Gyllhelon. It had to be.

"We arrived when we received the signal, not before. Though we are quick, we are unable to follow every bird everywhere. We had not known you were in the desert, we had not realized the birds were flocking." The great tree shook and shivered as it spoke. "It was the intensity of the Pyran that called to us."

"But the clouds... Surely you noticed the storm approaching." This came from Haswyxe. The clouds were already fading, the light was getting stronger by the moment, the merciless sun began to beat down upon them again.

"We were far away when we received the signal. This argument is for naught. Are you not grateful you did not all succumb to the birds? What if we had arrived later?" Trela thought they could not anger a Vijen, but she was unsure of why she thought that.

"Then we would have failed the mission given to us by the Belegs." Malghain spoke up in a flat voice.

"Failed? Maybe, maybe not. We do wish the Belegs well, they gave us our purpose, but we are not privy to their quests." The tree shook for another moment. "You wish to find the Well of Eternity, do you not?"

"Yes, of course. Any assistance would be appreciated." Trela answered before anyone else could chime in.

"Then look away and we shall appear on the horizon. When you have readied yourselves, walk towards us. If you reach us, look away again. The well wishes to be found. It should not take long." It shimmered some more.

They all looked away and the Vijen disappeared and reappeared way off in the distance. Trela looked around at the carnage. There was another body crumpled up that she had not noticed earlier. To her great relief it turned out to be Hupdor, who had shielded Mika. She felt a pang of shame about her relief, but that was short lived. The deaths of Aedon and Gyllhelon shook everyone to the core. They all stood around in a daze for a little while, quiet and stunned. Croy tried to heal them both of course, and Hupdor as well, but there was nothing to be done. Trela was grateful that no one mentioned that it was her sword stuck in Aedon. They were attacked by Tlana. They lost three of their members, two great friends. It was that simple, it was that horrible.

Most of the horses had survived. They took some time rearranging all their belongings while the Vijen waited in the distance. Maybe it waited patiently.

They decided to bring the bodies with them to the shantytown at the well. With the Vijen leading, they did not think it would take too long. The walk was done in silence. As if in commiseration, the world around them was silent as well.

They reached the Vijen twice. It shot off into the distance again and Trela started to wonder if they should stop and make camp. But before they reached the Vijen a third time, they could barely make out some buildings in the distance. They had finally found the well.

As they approached the gray shanty town, Trela noticed that the denizens appeared to be waiting for them. There was a group of them in a bit of a shallow V-shape, funneling them towards the center, towards the well. Somehow, she had not been watching very closely so she was unsure of when it had happened, but somehow the Vijen had slid farther into the village and was now positioned behind the well. It all appeared very odd, very staged.

The end was in sight, they had reached the well, she should be happy. But all she could think of was poor dead Aedon and the impending feeling that there was more doom to come.

"Looks like a gauntlet." Feyazki was beside her, plodding along. He nodded up at the lined-up denizens.

"Pretend it's a parade." She was also plodding. It seemed to be her coterie's only speed.

"Sounds like a joke, 'what's the difference between a gauntlet and a parade?' Or, maybe, it would be better to ask what's the same between them." He smiled a little while he plodded.

"Shut up and keep walking." She did not want to be cheered up, though part of her was grateful that he was trying.

"Exactly! *That's* what they both have in common." He laughed while he plodded. It was infectious and, despite her mood, Trela found herself smiling a little bit as well.

The denizens that made up the parade route did not make a sound as her coterie silently plodded past them. No one spoke or waved, cheered, or jeered; it was eerie. There, in front of the well, outlined by the shimmering Vijen behind, was Lemniscate, the ancient guardian of the well. The only derlian to have lived since the realms were first populated, the only derlian to have been a Yaven, at least if his tale was to be believed. The well, granting an odd mixture of eternal life and trapped existence, may have been created at his behest. Again, if his tales were to be believed. At his side was Ilana, Croy's wife who had accidently drank from the well the last time they were there, thereby chaining herself to the shanty town for eternity.

She had not realized at first, but as they got closer, she noticed that the ancient Fluen and young Gaen were holding hands. She wondered if it would have an effect on Croy. Since he had spent several moons with Baltuz, she assumed not. With Ilana trapped in the Northern Desert, the two were as separated as any handfasted couple could be.

"You have finally arrived. We have waited long and faithfully for your return. Do you understand what needs to be done?" Lemniscate bowed to them while speaking and had turned towards Croy at his question.

"Yes, I was shown in a dream to throw the items into the well." Croy bowed in return.

"We are here to act as a shield. Once you begin, you must continue until it is all resolved. Ignore all else around you, it will be mere distraction." Lemniscate bowed again and moved out from in front of the well, towards Trela's left. A silent Ilana bowed and moved towards her right. There was a clear path to the well. They led their laden horses as close to the well as they could, taking Lemniscate's warning seriously.

Feyazki stepped forwards. "We can't just dump them all in at once?"

"No. And no magic." This came from Croy. Trela would have been more comfortable with the rules coming from Lemniscate, but all in attendance were nodding, as if everyone already knew, as if it were common sense.

Every one of her coterie grabbed up an item from their horses and waited. They all looked at Trela. She looked at Croy and said, "Begin."

Croy dropped a scrying mirror into the well. Trela pricked her ears up, hoping to hear the Yaven escape, to hear something, anything. All was calm for a moment, then there was a strange whooshing sound that came from behind them. Trela turned to look and there was a small black cloud of smoke hurtling towards them. It was somewhat elongated, as if it were being pulled towards the well. Then it humped over the edge and got sucked down out of sight. There was a small sizzling sound, like water being thrown on a fire, but much higher pitched.

Clerin was next, tossing a dagger that had a weird sickly green hue to it down into the well. It was quiet for a moment, then a similar cloud of black smoke hurtled itself across the desert and down into the well. The same high-pitched sizzling sound occurred.

Then Feyazki, then Trela, it became a faster endeavor once it was understood what was happening. The Vijen shook itself behind the well with something akin to joy. Then the clouds rolled in out of nowhere again, darkening the skies. Escha tossed in a sword, Torpalin tossed in a shield. Trela had just happened to have been looking up when he did and, before the sky completely blackened with the roiling storm clouds, she thought she saw just a little smoke pour out of Torpalin's mouth as the small cloud of black smoke went down into the well. She wished she had been paying attention when Knill had tossed his item in, but she had been gathering a bow from her horse and had her back turned.

The storm clouds overhead were now so thick that it was difficult to see. It was like before, they bubbled with an animated animosity. The winds were gaining in volume. They continued to toss items in, going as fast as they could now, still one at a time but not waiting in between for the accompanying small cloud of smoke to get sucked down into the well.

Then there was a loud cry. It was definitely a derlian sound, a derlian scream. Trela turned to see what it was out of an ancient instinct, not due to any conscious thought. One of the shanty town denizens was fighting with another, hands gripping the other's face. Lightning struck outside of the village, providing some light to reorient to the well. The Vijen tree was whipping around, she was not sure if it was due to the wind or its own animated quivering. It almost seemed like there was a humming sound coming from the Vijen, but it was difficult to tell with all the other activity going on around them.

They tossed more items in the well. The storm's winds picked up even more speed and ferocity. There were lightning strikes all around, still outside of the village but getting closer. What was disturbing, however, was the yelling and fighting denizens. There were some truly awful blood-curdling screams emanating around them. Some were on the ground wrestling and biting. Some were upright, punching, kicking, gouging, swinging, yelling. Constant yelling. As Trela tried to concentrate on tossing in her next object, then getting another from her horse, then waiting to toss that one, et cetera, she began to feel a tug on her mind. It was minor at first but became more insistent. She started her chant in her head, *I am the Krüshan, I am the Krüshan.* It was the only defense she had. As she tossed another item in, she glanced at the Vijen. It seemed to stop shaking for a moment and stare into her without any eyes. The shallow background hum grew louder. Everything was outlined and silhouetted in lightning flashes. She thought she heard a powerful "Ha!" from the Vijen. The tug on her mind waned slightly. The violence around her raged on, grew louder.

They were getting close to the end of their items. They were getting close to the end of their denizens as well. There was a pile of writhing, struggling derlians all around them. Unable to die due to the tainted well water that they lived on, they continually fought and murdered each other. The tug on her mind was coming back, quicker and more insistent. They were almost there, she held her last item in her hand, Strife. Qizern's sword that, so long ago, seemed to have spawned the entire quest. She gripped it overly tight, concentrating on holding it, concentrating on waiting her final turn, concentrating on the well. Her head felt as if it were being crushed in a vice, it was excruciating. *I am the Kriishan, I am the Kriishan,* she thought, over and over. Seconds stretched into hours. She was finally able to toss the sword in and soon after, how soon she was unable to say, a gigantic bolt of lightning came crashing down from the sky directly onto Vijen tree. They were all blown back, and there on the ground looking through the tiny slits of her eyelids, it appeared that the tree was on fire and the clouds were lifting.

Trela lay there for several moments. She watched the sky turn blue and listened to the others shifting around. Some of them, the shanty denizens, scuffled up and wandered back to their gray weatherworn huts. Some of the sounds were her own warriors helping each other up. The horses had, from what she could gather from the ground, scattered at the last lightning strike, so some went to go gather them up.

She was tired. Utterly tired. It felt good to have the sun baking her face. So she rested for just a few moments. Nothing greedy, nothing shirking.

Trela rolled over and then stood. She dusted herself off and looked around. The Vijen was not on fire. In fact, it looked no worse for the wear. Most of her coterie were standing about, she was not sure who was looking for the horses. Maybe Croy and Knill. She glanced over at the well, and Lemniscate and Ilana were still standing there. He was smiling a large grin.

"You have one more item and one more action." He looked enigmatic.

"What? What item are we missing?" Trela suddenly became concerned that one of the horses had run off with something. She glanced around with a brow furrowed with worry. What if a horse escaped the village itself, would it never be able to find the well again? Did that sort of thing work for animals, or just derlians?

"The messenger has it. She has used it repeatedly. However, it is the most subtle, the most quiet, the most cunning, the most cloaked ancient item. We will not begrudge if it is thrown now." Lemniscate nodded towards Clerin.

"That cannot be. Do you mean Elange's stone?" There was a look of surprise mixed with horror on her face. "I never..."

There was a moment of silence while they all looked at her. Then, as if startled awake from a trance, her head jerked and she walked up to the well, fishing around for a pouch she had hanging around her neck. She upended the pouch, not touching the stone as it slipped out of the pouch and into the well. There was the same whooshing sound, but quieter, and there did not seem to be much smoke pulled down with it, but Trela was still feeling a little dazed and was watching Lemniscate more than the well.

"I never..." Clerin repeated it quietly with her head somewhat bowed, looking at Lemniscate through her hair.

"Now. The action." Lemniscate glanced over to Mika. Mika, for her part, was staring back at Lemniscate with large eyes and taut muscles but she did not twitch. Her fists may have clenched slightly at his glance, but otherwise she gave no indication that she had noticed anything.

Trela had forgotten about her, if she were honest. She did not want to admit it, certainly not at that moment, but she liked Mika. There was something unabashed about her. And there was Trela's blood oath to Rumhulga, her promise to Mika, to herself. That she would argue for Mika's safety to the Beleg's. That she would do her best to save Mika. Trela glanced over at Lemniscate, but his eyes were hard and sure.

Best not to think about it. There was a job to do and Trela could not shirk. She turned away, pulling a knife from her wrist sheath, keeping it close to her body. She kept turning, keeping her feet close together so that it could look like she was just turning to walk away. Then, as she came back around full circle, she swung her arm and thrust her leg forwards, flinging the knife in a controlled twirl. It struck Mika in the throat, then passed completely through her and kept spinning.

"Wrong one!" Suddenly there were five or six Mikas in the area and they all started running in different directions.

Malghain thrust his arm out to catch one of the Mikas by the neck, but that was also an illusion. Estfale jumped on a different illusion, attempting to tackle it. Trela began to chase after another one. Lemniscate raised both arms and yelled something incoherent. At that, all the denizens opened their doors, half of them even stepped out.

"I will allow whoever catches the renegade Cabal member, the Fluen illusionist, triple rations for three moons. Every meal. Triple the well water. Bring her to me dead or alive." He lowered his arms and there was a flurry of motion. Before they "slaughtered" themselves during the Tlana attack, Trela had never seen them move with such vigor and intent.

"Stop!" The real Mika stepped out from a nearby shanty. "Stop. I do not wish to be hunted. But I do not wish to die either. There must be some middle ground. Can I not join your village and drink from the well? Won't that keep me from starting another Cabal? Isn't that what you are afraid of, that another Cabal will be created? If I am with you until the end of my days, there will be no danger."

"I had not really thought about that. Come here." Lemniscate had a half-frown on his face.

Mika started to walk over to him but kept glancing around at what was left of the coterie as well. When she glanced at Trela, Trela happened to be looking at Lemniscate. To Trela's horror, Lemniscate very clearly mouthed "kill her." He overemphasized both words, leaving nothing in question. There was no doubt. There would be no argument. When Mika turned back to him, his face warmed into a smile.

"You are very clever, and I can see that you wish, more than anything, to keep on living." His smile looked utterly sincere. It stunned Trela for a moment, freezing her in place. Mika stopped in front of him.

"Trela." He snapped his fingers several times. "Come here and apologize to the young Fluen."

Trela walked slowly over, getting a dagger in her right hand, blade held flat against the inside of her forearm. Mika did not turn around, just stood in front of Lemniscate with her head slightly bowed.

"I have been the guardian of this well since it came into existence. I dole out the rations and warn strangers from the dangers of the well. You understand, don't you, that once you have tasted the waters you can never leave?"

"Yes. I have been told the story of the well by these others who have seen it and chosen not to drink." Mika had her hands clasped before her demurely.

"The waters poison you, you understand. It is only because they also keep you from dying that the poison is not effective. Once you stop drinking the water, you will only survive the poison for a couple of days. There is no realm within a few days journey of here. There is no way to escape the Northern Desert.

"I understand. Fully. I accept the burden gladly, of my own free will."

"Good, good. I can only provide the waters to those who understand the effects." His benevolent smile beamed down as he nodded while he spoke. "Now, Trela, apologize."

Trela wanted to hesitate, to make sure, to ask Lemniscate to be more clear, to try to argue for Mika's life, but she could not. Her arm flashed out from her side. Her dagger slashed Mika's neck. Deeply. She could not afford to give warning again, could not afford to hesitate.

Mika did not look completely surprised, only saddened. But then, as quickly as that crossed her face, it faded. Her body slumped to the ground. Several of the denizens scurried over and dragged her body off.

"Thank you. She was the last who actively worked with the Cabal and had to die. Now, only now, can we explain who we are and why you are here." Lemniscate motioned to Ilana and turned towards the largest shack. "Bring Croy, the mage, and the messenger, oh Queen of the Pyrans. We have much to discuss."

The Vijen tree shivered and shook as Lemniscate passed by the well. It did not speak, not that Trela could hear, but Lemniscate paused and half turned towards it. "You are correct." It was a soft whisper and then he continued to the shack.

The shack was barely large enough for all of them to sit in, because a low ramshackle bed took up an entire corner. They sat on the floor since, besides the bed and a chest, there was no furniture to speak of. The slatted walls had enough gaps between the boards that wavy bands of light shot through onto the ground. It was an interesting space of light and shadow, being dim and brightly lit at the same time. Lemniscate and Ilana sat close together, near the corner with the bed.

"What would you like to know?" Lemniscate nodded around the room, but seemed to be looking at Trela when he asked his question.

"What are the Tlana?" She knew the question was too broad and so tried to narrow it. "It seemed they were directly tied to the items of Yavencide, were they not? But they have been around longer than Yavencide, correct? They are the oldest legends I know of."

"Yes, in a way. They are both tied to the items and have been around longer than the items." Lemniscate waited for a moment, probably trying to gauge if she was going to add a more clarifying statement. He did not get one. "They are regulators, in a way. They regulate derlians or, more specifically, they react to derlians' actions. And I mean derlians as a whole, not necessarily specific derlians, though sometimes that as well. They become more rampant as derlians do damage to the world. When some of that damage is undone, as when you destroyed the items of Yavencide, their energy wanes though it does not fully dissipate." He paused and crinkled his brow for a moment. "But they are not cognizant of their role. They are pure instinct. They desire to coalesce and thrive. They desire mayhem. They are attracted to evil. They could, in a sense, be called evil. But evil requires cognition, does it not? Do we consider the ravaging bear an evil creature?"

"So, if there was no evil in the world, then they would disappear?" Feyazki had his brow crinkled as well. He put up a hand to stop Lemniscate from answering. "Wait, that's not my question. Is their existence directly tied to derlians' actions? I mean, if all the derlians did absolutely nothing for a day, or a week, no evil at all, would there be no Tlana, or would they be hidden, or would there just be less of them?"

"Ah. I will assume your question is very astute. What regulates the regulators? That is your question." Feyazki merely nodded to Lemniscate in response. "Your actual question has no answer since it is impossible that all derlians do nothing for any length of time. But your astute question, that strikes at the heart of the matter. The Vijen is the judge. It is through the Vijen that coalescence occurs. It is through the leaves that the Tlana gain their true power."

"We were told that the leaves just fall," Croy interrupted quietly.

"You were told that the Tlana believed they caused the leaves to fall by way of their dances, and that the belief was false. You were told that the leaves fall through natural processes, not by the whim of the Vijen and certainly not by the compulsion of the Tlana. That is true."

"So, wait, is there only one Vijen?" Clerin popped out her own question.

"Yes. But it can be in several places at one time."

"That doesn't make any sense."

"Only because you do not understand space and distance." Lemniscate smiled warmly at Clerin. "Or time, for that matter."

"But there are many Tlana, correct? You said that Tlana desire to coalesce earlier." Trela still did not fully understand the roles both species or entities played.

"Yes. Maybe it can be explained thusly. The Tlana are, in essence, tiny unthinking beads of evil. When you get enough of these beads close enough to each other, they begin to coalesce, to pool together. The larger the amount of beads in any pool, the more sophisticated the Tlana. It is still not cognizant, but can cause more havoc, begin to control derlians, inflict more pain and damage. In the smoke form, it cannot be killed, but can be dispersed and can be held at bay. The final evolutionary leap is when a sophisticated Tlana gains Vijen leaves. The leaves are a form of energizing armor. With this a Tlana becomes a physical being, it can control many derlians at once, it gains its lightning strike. It is still not necessarily cognizant of anything. When you defeat a corporeal Tlana, you are dispersing the beads. Dispersing it does not necessarily kill it, but it destroys the pool holding the leaves. The tiny beads are invincible, indestructible. The best derlians can hope for is that the beads do not coalesce."

"You said the Vijen controls the coalescing as well as the gathering of the leaves, is that correct?" Clerin cocked her head slightly at Lemniscate.

"Not quite, the word 'control' is overly confusing. What if there was a bead for every derlian? When a derlian does something good, the bead raises up into the air away from others. When a derlian does something bad, the bead lowers and they get closer together. If the beads get too close together, they are naturally attracted to each other like magnets. So, if the word 'control' is used, it is not meant that the actions of the derlian are controlled by the Vijen. The Vijen cannot affect any individual bead. What is meant is that the Vijen decides what is good and bad, in a general sense. It is the judge. It sets the field of magnetism. It is a catalyst that sets the acceleration of the reaction, faster or slower, depending on… well, depending on whatever it depends upon. Though I communicate with the Vijen, I do not pretend to understand its choices." Lemniscate was nodding to himself, lost in his thoughts for a brief moment.

"Wait, wait. That sounds like different things can be good or bad at different times. Like in a general sense. Murder is murder, is it not?" Croy looked to be getting slightly frustrated.

"You have killed, have you not?"

"Well, yes, but the circumstances…"

"Correct. The circumstances. You wish these things such as 'circumstances' to be immutable? Some things, many things, one may even say most things that are evil in one circumstance are evil in all. You are correct that murder is murder. What do you think happened when the first Yaven-infused item was made, however? Do you think the Vijen immediately created Tlana? Or do you think it was an evil that increased as more items were made? Maybe not even increasing linearly, but exponentially. Is the evil not worse when there is a group performing this task for money, a factory of evil if you will? At what point does the Vijen increase the magnetism of coalescence? I do not understand these things myself. I only know, in a general sense, of their occurrence. My explanations are hampered by my interpretation, your capacities, the natural limitations of spoken language, et cetera. You may ask the Vijen why things are weighted differently during different times, you may ask what circumstances are immutable, but you will probably be given the same non-answers that I have."

"Wait, I think I see my confusion. Are you saying that it is the collective choices of derlians that the Vijen is regulating through the Tlana? Not the individual actions?" Croy squinted a little.

"Exactly, well put. Individual actions are of little concern to the Vijen. It is the overall derlian direction that is of concern. In fact, if enough derlians of just one race were to instigate the Vijen, other races could be beset upon by Tlana through no fault of their own. Not even know why the Tlana were increasing. Individuals who are attacked by Tlana may have nothing to do with why the Vijen has increased the magnetism of coalescence."

"But Tlana are attracted to evil, aren't they?" There were a couple of things that bothered Trela about this explanation, but that was the first she was able to articulate.

"In general, yes. But they attacked you, did they not? And, even if they are attracted to evil, they are indiscriminate as to who they harm along the way. They come from the Northern Desert, meaning they ravage nearby villages first. And they are attracted to evil much like the Vijen is concerned about the collective direction of derlians. They may be attracted to a location or a group but will still attack everything in their path." Lemniscate's explanation brought Trela's mind to what else had bothered her.

"Wait—if the Tlana were increased due to the Yaven-infused items, why would they try to stop us? We were trying to fulfill the Vijen's wishes. Shouldn't we have been protected?"

"The Tlana, though not cognizant, have the same impulse to survive and thrive as all life. They tried to stop you for their own survival." Lemniscate squinted for a moment. "But that is not your real question, is it? Why were you not helped along the way? Or not helped more than you were? That is your question?" He was nodding to himself. Trela was not positive about that, however. She had not been implying they had wanted more aid, it sounded petty the way that Lemniscate put it, but just the dichotomy of why something was created versus why it existed. But he did not pause long enough for her to articulate anything. "First, the Vijen is trapped here, in the desert. It may not travel as far as the Tlana. Second, the Vijen really has only the one skill, the regulation of Tlana. Third, the Vijen does not have 'wishes' as you state. It, in itself, is not good or evil, it merely observes the collective actions of derlians and passes judgement. It will help when it can, especially if it senses you are an ally, but if it is unable to help it does not feel bad about it, does not think about it at all. It does not 'wish' anything, it merely has a job to do, a function to perform. And it does that to the best of its ability. Always."

"Do the Belegs get a say? I mean, it seems odd that the Vijen decides when derlians are collectively dangerous. Would the Belegs not be better judges of their own world, of their own creation?" Clerin looked quite earnest in her question.

"Who do you think created the Vijen? The Tlana? The entire regulating system? Remember what I said earlier. *One* race could create enough disruption to plague all of them. *One* Beleg may disagree with another. You, of all the derlians in the world, understand that. The Belegs needed a neutral party, one that could not be controlled by a particular Beleg. One who did not favor anything, was not biased in any way. The only way to do that was to create a system they could not control, for the good of them all, for the good of *all*." He smiled and beamed that around the room, at each of them individually.

"So, to sum up, the Tlana are regulators of overarching derlian behavior, becoming more rampant as derlians do damage to their world. The Vijen is the judge, allowing more Tlana to coalesce as things get worse in the derlian world. The Belegs created both so they would not need to regulate amongst themselves. Any further questions?" He looked a little smug to Trela, so she asked what she could.

"Then what are you?"

"I'm the guardian of the well."

"I saw you speak with the Vijen as we walked over here. You know all of this. You know more than this I would wager. You are not a mere guardian."

"It is worse than that. Honestly, I am not even that good of a guardian. What I am, young warrior queen, is *old*. That is it, that is all." His head was slightly bowed when he gave a little self-deprecating laugh. "I'm so unimaginably old that I know what was here when here did not exist. I was a Yaven, a *Yaven*! I lived in a realm full of water, only water. For eons, for aeons, for an amount of time that has no concept to the likes of you. I knew everything about water, I understood water, I *was* water. I knew so much about such a small subject, the only subject that existed as far as I was concerned, that I grew complacent. I grew bored with eternity and I chose… this." His arms flailed for a brief moment. "Well, not this, I did not choose this. I begged for this. What I chose was out there, near the Clatsvol Sea. The sky and wind, the sun and fire, the stony ground. It was incredibly beautiful for the flash of a moment. If you had never known of them, could you imagine animals? Trees? Clouds? I can tell you that you could not, I know from experience. I *know*. The shock of so many unknown things at once was the most incredible experience… of all. Ever. It is unexplainable. Most beings would give their life for just such an experience. Could you imagine being hungry for the first time? Could you imagine watching a friend stumble off a cliff and die, when before they would have stood up unharmed? The shock of the fragility of this diverse life was just as incredible. The fear almost overshadowed the beauty. We had much to learn from the animals that had already populated the world—they understood instinctively how to navigate the fragility of life. More than anything, more than everything, I…"

Lemniscate paused for a moment. He looked distraught for a second. His eyes became misty and then grew clear. He took a deep breath.

"The regret was almost instantaneous. Which, for as fast as time here flows, is a bit of an exaggeration. But it was swift and complete, at least for myself. All I wanted was to be a Yaven again, back in my own realm, surrounded by the comfort of my beloved, known, water. I would never have visited here again, never created a Menel, never met a mage. I would have given it all up forever, just to be back to the way I was. This…" He flailed his arm around once more and became a little choked up. "This is no life. It is no death, true, but it is no life.

"You ask why I have so much knowledge of the Vijen and Tlana. My answer is that there is nothing else here, in the Northern Desert. Whenever a newcomer arrives, I will pick them for all the information they have, to better understand the world beyond this tiny gray existence. But it is, overall, a gray existence. There is little here to do. I got my wish, I regained my eternal nature, but I was cursed as well. So I have delved as deeply as I am able into the questions of the Vijen. There are still many unknowns, there is still much to learn. If I were younger, I would be quite interested to hear from you, Clerin, about the Belegs and their communications." He turned to Clerin, and her head popped up a little.

"I know very little of the actual communications but would be glad to discuss my experiences with you." She had a wide, bright smile on.

"You surely know more than you think you do. But I also assume you are sworn to secrecy about certain things as well." He was smiling as well but shaking his head. "But that is neither here nor there. I have made up my mind. I am handing my duties, such as they are, over to Ilana. She will be the new guardian of the well."

There were gasps all around. Trela was completely dumbfounded. She had no clue that was what Lemniscate had been leading up to. It took her completely by surprise.

"That is why I wished to explain it all to you, what I have gleaned. I have told Ilana as many stories as I could in the short time allotted to us. I have let her DreamWatch over me. I have let her ask as many delving questions as she desired. But I wanted to have a chance to speak with all of you before I go. For you to hear it from me in case you asked a question that Ilana was unable to answer." He nodded to all of them, or maybe just himself. He paused long enough for someone to interrupt, but no one did.

"More than that, however, I wanted to watch you destroy the Yaven-infused items. I knew that the Tlana would create a storm to stop you. A storm that would turn derlians against each other, murdering each other, as the Tlana in their desperation infested everyone around. The only way I could think to help was to provide the immortal bodies of our denizens as a buffer. To allow them to murder each other over and over and over until you were able to destroy the items. This has all come to pass, and I am proud for any small part that I may have played." His chest inflated as he took a large breath. "When I leave here, after we have discussed all you wish to discuss, I shall leave with the Vijen. It has promised to show me even more knowledge and insight. It is an opportunity that I am unable to pass up. Whether or not I wither after leaving the well, I know not, but I will spend those last days doing what I enjoy most. Learning."

Chapter 7

Croy was unable to tell if he was falling or flying. The sun warmed his back softly. He was moving through a beautiful blue sky, heading towards a thick, white and fluffy cloud. He shot through the cloud, into an ocean, through the ground, surrounded by magma, surrounded by the sun, shot down through a cloud, into an ocean, et cetera. This happened slowly at first, but it gained in speed each iteration. The odd thing was, however, that Croy enjoyed it more each time as well. He giggled and laughed uncontrollably, rolling around, spinning in space clutching his tummy. It became a blur with its repetition. He was becoming ecstatic.

Then he stopped and hovered over a barren, rocky landscape. Green mosses and lichen appeared, and he felt a ripple of joy course through him. Grasses appeared. Then shrubs, then trees. He grew more ecstatic with each new plant. Then he dropped through the ground, surrounded by magma, surrounded by the sun, et cetera.

Then he stopped and hovered over a verdant landscape. Insects of all kinds began to appear. Then small lizards, then rodents, then birds, and soon there were deer running through the forest. He felt more ripples of joy run through him at each new being. Then he dropped through the ground, surrounded by magma, et cetera.

Then he stopped over a lush landscape teeming with life. Suddenly, derlians began to appear. A diamond shaped flash of light would grow out of a random spot and increase rapidly in size and then disappear, leaving a derlian standing there, dusting itself off rather comically. He felt more ribbons of ecstasy run through him at each new derlian. Then he through dropped through the ground and woke.

The sunlight streamed through the gaps in the boards of the shanty walls. That was what made the entire village a little creepy to Croy. That feeling of otherworldliness that comes from waking, after fitful slumber at best, amidst the heat and thick unmoving air, and seeing the slashes of light streaming between the slats pierce the deep blackness of the interior. They created shards that warped vision through lensing, making a mockery of his depth perception, creating the illusion that the illuminated portions of the room were closer to him than the dark portions. The juxtaposition unnerved him slightly.

That was not the only creepy aspect of the shantytown, but it started off the day. It set an unsettling mood. It was not this one morning that unnerved him, but the remembrance of the last time he lived there with Ilana—the first time they found the well. Waking up in the slashed light brought the entire mood back, as if he had never left.

The denizens themselves were incredibly shy, rarely leaving their own shanty walls while those who had not tasted from the well were around. When one did appear, it was typically to make the short trip to the well and back, head down, refusing any sort of eye contact.

Croy had wanted to thank them for the help they provided during the Tlana attack. Though they could not die or be permanently maimed, it appeared that they felt pain. It had certainly seemed that way during the attack, as their screams overpowered the sound of the storm, if not the thunder. He wanted to thank them for enduring the pain as they repeatedly "died" during the attack, for distracting the Tlana enough during the orgy of violence for the coterie to be able to get all the items down the well. But Ilana was steadfast about their privacy.

"You do not understand what it is to live like this." She swung an arm around to indicate the entire village. "It is fine when we are alone, alone with each other. We have games and parties like any other derlians. But we've lived through similar games and parties thousands of times. At least some of them have. It brings a dullness to it. The bitterness of joy is redundancy. However, we get along well enough, we can ignore it well enough, we can spend days, weeks, alone in our shacks, feeling the wonderous effects of the well water, just enjoying the euphoria, and not feel any shame. Lying in the shaded heat, sweating and breathing, just feeling the blood pump through our veins, just feeling the well water pump through our veins, shamelessly. We can just *be* when we are alone.

"It is less fine when we have to see you walking around." She swung her arm around again, indicating all of those who were still mortal. "You are a reminder of what we've given up. You are a reminder that there is life beyond the village, a life we can no longer participate in. You bring shame with you." She held up a hand as he was about to protest. "Not on purpose. I am not chastising you or telling you there is a certain way to behave. There is no set of manners that would alleviate that shame. It is your mere existence. You are a visitor, a tourist, to our world. If you do not gawk, if you do not even glance, we still feel the gaze of the other. Those that are other than us, those who are not bound to the well."

"What can we do then? Should we stay inside the whole time so the others can walk around, un-gazed at?"

"You can leave." Ilana looked down at the ground for a moment. "That is all you can do, my love. You can leave."

"But I just found you again. We're handfasted, we should be together."

"No. This is like before, only we both have much greater responsibilities. You do not understand what is happening, Croy. The Belegs are at war. Well, maybe not at war, but they are arguing again. Arguing even more forcefully than at any other time, if what Lemniscate has told me is true. More than after they created derlians, more than when they decided to enter their temples. Something terrible is afoot. Or something wonderful, Lemniscate was not sure and, honestly, he had given up already. It is the strangest thing, but he does not wish to know the end of the argument. Maybe he already knows and did not wish to tell me, but it did not seem that way. All I know, truly know, is that you are integral to this argument. You will sway it. Whether or not you want to, whether or not you know which side you will be on, you will sway it. You are too important to waste away here with me." Again, he was about to interrupt and she stopped him with a gesture.

"I am important too. I miss you too. I love you too. I wish that we could spend the rest of our lives together, just talking and holding hands, just kissing and loving, just being together." She paused and took in a deep breath. "I tell you what. I will give you a promise that I hope I can keep. When this is all over. When the Belegs have resolved their argument, when you are no longer needed by destiny, come back to the Northern Desert. Come back and I promise I will do everything in my power to allow you to find the well. Come back and we can both drink from it and be together for as long as you like. Forever if you like. How does that sound?"

"That sounds nice."

"Good. Then take care, you understand, be careful. I need you to get back to me in one piece, okay?" She patted his cheek delicately. "I may need you to leave, but I really want you to come back."

A commotion outside diverted their attention. Some of the voices were clear and recognizable. Trela had a very stern "command" voice she used which carried quite well. Clerin was obviously on the other side of the argument. Other voices were involved, but not immediately recognizable. Croy and Ilana left her shack to investigate.

"This is foolish and, quite frankly, dangerous." Trela was standing stiff-spined and arms crossed staring hard at Clerin.

They were close to the well, with Feyazki and Estfale. There were two denizens looking meek standing next to the well, with their eyes downcast staring at a shrouded body lying on the ground. There was a peek of black hair that had escaped the shroud. *The body must be Gyllhelon's*, Croy thought. He knew Clerin was distraught over her death but had not realized she had been planning anything.

"I am just asking to try. If it does not work, then it does not work." Clerin crossed her own arms in front of her. "Why would this even matter to you? It is not like I asked for your help or anything."

Ilana strode over to the group, making her short legs appear longer. "And just what is it you are attempting to try?"

Clerin turned towards Ilana, and Croy realized she had been crying. Not too recently, but recently enough to show the dingy tracks on her face. She was typically quite fastidious about keeping her face clean, but travel in the desert had a way of making everyone look dingy. There was just no way to waste water on keeping clean.

"I merely wish to put a couple of drops of the well water in Gyllhelon's mouth. Just to see, just in case it works." She looked, more than anything, tired. Just completely fatigued.

"She's been dead for a while now." Trela uncrossed her arms and took one step towards Clerin, but then stopped. "I miss her too, Clerin. I miss Aedon as well. You do not know the pain I go through thinking of how it was my blade that killed her, she was a dear friend. I even miss Mika." She gave a small laugh at herself. "But that is what happens when fighting Tlana. Derlians die."

"Do you mind?" She had not turned to Trela but had kept her gaze intently focused on Ilana. "You are the guardian of the well now, are you not?"

"What is your plan?"

"I was going to have these two pull up some water and then have Feyazki cast some telekinesis to take just a miniscule amount of the water and drop it in Gyllhelon's mouth." She gave a somewhat ingratiating grin. "No one touches it that has not already. Worst case it just wastes a little. Lemniscate filled a vial for Hulgert the last time we were here. Surely the well will not miss a few drops."

"Poila, Erataq, have you already had your draught?" Ilana turned and glanced over at the denizens, whose heads barely shifted from staring at the dead body in front of them in tiny nods.

They seemed stunned or enraptured or something, but Croy had a hard time telling the denizens' emotions typically, even though he had spent over a moon in the shantytown previously with Ilana, before he was lured away by Clerin's quest for the Luften Temple. The stood for another long moment, staring at the shrouded body, before turning and slowly walking away. The denizens of the shantytown rarely did anything fast or with gusto.

"Do you care to watch this experiment? If not, you should just leave, Trela." There was an odd mixture in Ilana's voice as she talked to Trela, part fire and part ice.

Croy had forgotten that Ilana blamed Trela for Nolt's death, something that he had never quite felt himself. Having spent so much more time lately with Trela than Ilana, he had forgotten the issue entirely. Not the news of Nolt's death itself, Nolt had been one of his oldest friends, but that Trela bore the responsibility for it in Ilana's mind. Was that the reason for the fire and ice? Was that truly animosity in Ilana's voice? One could never be sure, unless one asked of course, but if Croy were a gambler, that would have been his bet.

"Yes." It was a simple and curt reply. Trela's arms were crossed in front of her again. She had not moved, had not twitched, but even if there was no animosity at Ilana's end, Trela exuded something akin to it at the moment.

Ilana turned and walked over to the well. She tossed a tiny bucket tied to a rope into the well and pulled up a draught. She poured most if it back into the well and brought it over Gyllhelon's body. She nodded solemnly to Clerin.

"Please, uncover her face."

Clerin knelt next to the shrouded body and paused for a moment, looking at the shrouded face. Then she gingerly pulled apart the wrappings. She ended up uncovering Gyllhelon's entire head, laying and straightening the hair out in an attempt to keep the corpse from looking disheveled. She gently stroked the face a couple of times, keeping the hair behind Gyllhelon's ears.

Croy had seen a lot of corpses in his life. Many, many, many more than he had ever wanted to. The battlefields he had unfortunately witnessed were littered with them. Mostly they were grotesque, faces contorted in agony, decay setting in, visible gashes and wounds, the horrible smell. Some, however, a small percentage to be sure, looked peaceful, at rest. Especially if they had died in the medic tent, with all the energy spent on saving them. But Gyllhelon's looked the most serene. She had been beautiful in life, Croy could say that, but she was also beautiful in death. There was a calm eeriness to it all.

"Okay." Clerin did not move from her position, shins against the sand, her butt on her heels.

"Open her mouth."

Clerin carefully did so, and Ilana carefully poured a quick tiny stream into her mouth. Not enough to fill the small vial provided to Hulgert, but certainly more than a couple of drops. Then Ilana stood.

They waited for a moment. Nothing happened. Clerin stroked Gyllhelon's hair for a little while. Ilana put the tiny bucket back. The rest of them stood around, not speaking or moving, as if any disturbance would ruin the effects. Nothing happened.

Croy was not really sure what he had been expecting. There had not been enough time for him to really think about it. But he had been hopeful during it. Hopeful for Gyllhelon a little bit, which would then make him hopeful for Aedon, whom he considered a dear friend as well, but mostly hopeful for Clerin. She was not crying at the moment, just looking sad and pensive, but he knew it was affecting her deeply. She had seen as much carnage as Croy, but had always been in the medic tent, away from the combat itself. She was as capable as anyone in the coterie but, unlike everyone else, she carried an aura of innocence around her. Everyone felt an urge to protect her, or at least Croy did. The silence lasted minutes, very long minutes.

"I wish that had worked Clerin, truly. I apologize if I added any pain and am sorry for your loss, for all of our loss. Let me know if there is anything I can do." Trela broke the silence.

"I just... I would like to be alone. Is that okay?"

Trela bowed to Clerin, which was slightly odd because she rarely bowed to anyone, then turned and walked away. Estfale, dutiful as always, also bowed and then followed Trela.

Croy was unsure of what to do, so he bowed as well. As he was walking away, he faintly overheard Clerin speaking to Feyazki.
"Alone. Please."

They left that evening, just after the sun had set, so they could get some distance behind them before the sweltering heat slowed them down. Everyone was eager. The tourists were a little unnerved by the shantytown and the denizens were tired of the obligatory shame. Everyone was happy that they left.

They left their dead at the shantytown. Ilana said she wanted to investigate a little more and it was impossible to say how much time it would take to find a place of solid ground. No one was overly eager to toss the bodies down and merely push sand over them.

It only took three days to find the Valley of the Caves again. The whole time Croy was trying to look over his shoulder or peer around dunes, just hoping to catch a glimpse of the Vijen. He had this image in his mind of the great tree on a hilltop, off a little bit in the distance, with the silhouette of Lemniscate shaded by the golden boughs. Lemniscate would raise a hand tentatively and wave goodbye, the tree would shimmer and shake. It was a nice image, but one what that did not happen. Though they were surely guided out of the Northern Desert by something, he never saw anyone or anything. Nothing but sand dunes the entire time.

They reached the eshram of Algathia, where the others were waiting for them, in the evening. They had walked for a while during the day once they had seen a rocky hill in the distance. There was the typical elation of reconnecting, everyone was excited that all the items had been destroyed. There was also a great sadness when they heard about Gyllhelon and Aedon, they had been good friends to everyone. The emotions were mixed and tense that first night, and Trela allowed a fair amount of mead to flow.

Croy felt a little odd about them staying in an eshram. They were obviously a disturbance in the rhythms of those who lived there. He did not think it was as bad as at the shantytown that followed the well, he did not think they brought shame with them, but they were still an obvious disruption. The plan was to stay one day there in Algathia to regroup and repack. So Croy was hopeful that whatever disruption they were causing would be brief. Most of the coterie had been waiting outside the eshram while they were at the well, trying to keep any disturbance to a minimum.

The next morning came late to Croy even though he drank very little mead the night before. The strains of travel, the fight at the well, leaving Ilana again, all had been building up and it was nice to sleep in a little. He had set up his little tent off to the side of the group, as out of the way as possible, but still within the coterie's chosen boundary at the edge of the eshram. He tidied up the tent before heading out for breakfast. He hoped he was not too late for some hot food, but figured others were sleeping in as well.

He ate tucked away, alone. Though not necessarily on purpose, he did not seek any others out. He wanted to think a little, to try to figure out the implications of Ilana's words. He ate slowly and deliberately, wondering what the Belegs had to argue about. Especially now that the Yaven-infused items had been destroyed. As he was sitting, relaxing, his mind wandering away from the Belegs, Feyazki meandered over.

"Croy, just the derlian I was looking for." He smiled with big teeth and sat down next to Croy.

"Oh, hello." He was going to continue with something about Gyllhelon, a platitude for Clerin or something, but thought better of it. It was not the time, and Croy doubted he had the words. So, instead, he just stopped talking, which created about half a second of awkward pause.

"I was thinking of going through what is left of Elange's cave. Just, you know, to see if there is anything of interest left." He smiled again. "And since you can sense magic being cast quicker than anyone I know, I thought I'd ask you to come along. You know, just in case."

Croy immediately felt tickled by the prospect. Very rarely did someone ask for his assistance for anything to do with magic, especially for anything beyond healing. And if someone really needed something new or powerful concerning healing, they asked Nochiel, not Croy. Also, it was quite a personal thing Feyazki was about to do, rummaging through the remnants of his mentor's mentor's abode. He was flattered that Feyazki would ask him to come along and share the experience. Certainly the odds of some attack or some delayed trap spell were quite low. It almost felt like Feyazki was asking Croy to accompany him for reasons of companionship, rather than magical support.

He sometimes had a hard time gauging Feyazki's feelings towards… well, towards anything, but certainly towards him. There were plenty of times that he would proclaim to everyone Croy's skill and have him cast something. And, though rarely, there were times that he tried to help Croy progress magically, suggesting spell thoughtforms or meditations. But there were also entire moons that Feyazki ignored him, though maybe not consciously avoided him. No matter how much learning he had gleaned from Feyazki, it never truly felt that he had been taken on as an apprentice. All in all, however, Croy was tickled that Feyazki had asked him to accompany him now. These thoughts were not pure thoughts, as in words, but almost merely feelings, meaning they all came in one bundle and would need to be sorted out later.

"Oh, yes, that sounds fine." Croy answered with nary a pause. "I'm not doing anything else this morning."

"Great, thanks." Feyazki then leaned back, looking relaxed. As though he could wait for hours.

Croy realized he was sitting there with his empty plate in his hands and that Feyazki did not wish to interrupt him if he planned to sit like that for a while. In fact, he had already been sitting like that for a while, which is probably why Feyazki timed his interruption as he did.

"Well, no time like the present. Let me hand my plate off." Croy got up to head back to the "kitchen" and Feyazki followed him. Sometimes they rubbed the plates with dry sand, sometimes they used magic, sometimes breakfast was hard jerky and stale biscuits. Though there was a small well at the eshram, the coterie tried to avoid taking water as much as possible.

Croy followed Feyazki up the various cliff trails towards Elange's cave. It felt good to be leisurely walking along the rocky path. They did not get high enough and the path was too dry to completely remind Croy of hiking in the Gaen realm, but a sliver of nostalgia still wormed its way into him. It was pleasant even though it was short.

There was a curtain at the entrance that Feyazki pushed aside. It looked new. As they entered, Croy noticed the smell of burnt hair. It would have certainly faded since Feyazki had last been there, but it lingered in the nostrils. In the back of the scent, underlying the obvious stench, there was the slight smell of cave which tugged lightly on Croy's nostalgia. More than the smell was standing in the small room. Croy did not crouch as Feyazki did, but stood there drinking it in. He had noticed that most non-Gaens crouched when there was a low ceiling, whether or not they needed to. As if something was going to reach out and knock them on the head. Living in a cave gave you a great understanding of your height and the lift of your step. He was able to enter just about any enclosed area and instinctively know how much room he had above his head, it was innate. That feeling, and the feeling of being surrounded by stone, gave him a rush of nostalgia. It had been quite a while since they had explored the safety caves of the Gaen villages at the edges of the Northern Desert, chasing or being chased by Tlana. And it seemed a lifetime ago since he had last walked the halls of Serif.

The rug was burned and the floor pillows were either immolated or stolen by a neighbor. Random scorch marks were scattered about the cave—the walls, floor, and ceiling. There were some metal kitchen items that had survived, some crates, and some small, scorched chests stacked on each other, but not much else. Croy, not sure how to help except to yell if he sensed any magic, picked an out of the way spot to sit while Feyazki started to go through the crates.

"Tell me about Elange." Croy spoke more out of boredom than for any particular reason.

"Oh, not much to tell. I only spoke with him briefly. He was my mentor's mentor, not mine." Feyazki was starting at the top crate and seemed to be shuffling contents back and forth. "I did have a small book written by him, given to me by Revkin, which I thought was interesting. Honestly, while talking with Elange, it seemed that he did not feel Revkin was his best apprentice. Pretty sure he thought he drank too much." He stopped rummaging for a moment to turn a smile to Croy.

"Well, then, tell me about Revkin." They had already talked about Revkin before, so Croy assumed he would not be learning anything new, just filling in the time.

"He probably drank too much." Feyazki's quick laugh was infectious. "He is the only mentor I had, and I feel fairly confident in my own capabilities, so I guess he was a decent mentor." He removed the top crate and started on the one below. "It was pretty crazy for the first half cycle or so. He kept me locked in this tiny room, it had bars over the window and everything. I had some books and a desk, but the furnishings were pretty sparse. He made me do the same things over and over, a whole lot of meditation and energy work at first. Just very... time consuming."

"I suppose I should not complain about how the Blind One treated me then." Croy gave a quick self-deprecating laugh.

"Oh no, don't say that. I was never held in a prison like you were. It was more just isolating, I guess. Learning magic takes an incredible amount of concentration and I think the isolation helped. Was necessary even. Plus, the food was fantastic. No matter what anyone might say about Revkin, he was an amazing cook. He could even make porridge taste good." Feyazki switched from the crates to the chests. "How... Was there ever anything good about being the Blind One's apprentice? We've never really talked much about that. I understand if you're hesitant."

Croy thought for a moment. They had had so many different conversations. He had certainly heard about Revkin multiple times, though not always in depth, sometimes just in passing. But he avoided talking about the Blind One. He tried to think of their conversations before he was imprisoned, before Trela became queen. He was sure they had chatted about the Blind One being a mentor, they had to have, but it all seemed so far away now. All he could think of was his anger at being stuck in Rycher, having his dreams spied upon.

"No, not hesitant. But it was still a weird relationship. I think it was the fact that I was happy herding sheep. I never wanted to be a mage." Croy paused for a second, thinking that Feyazki would explain how he had not wanted to be a mage either. That he had been happy banging metal at his forge and only took the mage test by accident. But he kept his head down and carried on with his quiet rummaging, leaving Croy to continue.

"He was always just so massively more powerful than me. Still is." Croy laughed a little. "And there is something creepy about him. And not just his eyes, it's more complicated than that. It's his personality. It's like he's always hiding something, some huge secret that no one knows about. And that he enjoys having this secret, it gives him an additional power over you. I don't know, it's hard to explain. It's easier just to hate him now, after the imprisonment, I don't have to think about it. But when he was teaching me magic, when I was his apprentice, there was just something..."

Croy thought long and hard about it. What was it, really? It was not like he was beaten or tortured, not even in Rycher. And, honestly, he did enjoy being a mage. He liked healing mostly, which meant that Nochiel should really be considered his mentor, not the Blind One. But, of course, she may not have been able to teach him if he had not already learned so much from the Blind One. And, sort of, had gleaned some knowledge from Feyazki as well. He realized it had been quiet for a while. Feyazki was rooting through another chest.

"I guess the problem was me. I was afraid of him. Completely. When I first met him, I was brought to him and some other 'jin just after finding Trela. I thought I was in trouble, they were just so imposing. Then he was trying to get me to do things I was nervous about, or worried about. Magic is difficult and I'm not very good at it." He was staring at the ground but could feel Feyazki's face start to turn. "Maybe I am okay now, but at the time I was not good at it at all. At all. The frustration of trying to do something that I knew I couldn't do was just overwhelming. And so, it seemed that he was always disappointed in me. My progress was so slow and painful. I just never felt comfortable around him or around magic. You know, I was once so stymied that he let me just go home. He said I couldn't learn anymore, at least not from him. Ilana helped me trance and we ended up going to the desert searching for Vijen with Aedon."

At the word "Aedon" they both stopped. Croy stopped talking and Feyazki stopped rummaging. He still could not believe she was dead.

"I still cannot believe she's dead." Feyazki spoke softly and then turned back to his crates.

"Me neither. Nor Gyllhelon." He peeked at Feyazki as he said her name, trying to gage some sort of reaction, but Feyazki kept his face turned towards the chests and barely twitched.

"Yes, she'd been there since the beginning, almost as long as Clerin." It was the most that Croy would ever get out of Feyazki concerning Gyllhelon.

Croy's mind raced to change the subject. Not because he did not hope to hear more, but to ameliorate the silence. The thick, heavy, suffocating silence.

"What are you looking for anyway?" It was all he could come up with.

"Elange had a pebble he gave me for a vision quest, and I was thinking he might have some more. But really, I don't think there's anything useful here."

"What did you do with the one he gave you?"

"What? Oh. No idea. I was attacked by a Tlana, figured out my Minora syllable for lightning, and found my magical name, Feyazki. The pebble was lost somewhere along the way."

"Wow. You've told me that story before, but I guess I forgot about the pebble. That was quite a vision quest."

"Yes. And even though it made me who I am today, I wouldn't wish it upon anyone. I thought I had died during that fight." He paused, staring down into the last chest. "Not even a book. I was kind of hoping he had some writings at least." His voice was quiet.

Croy looked around, not wanting to interrupt. There was nothing else in the tiny abode. If Feyazki did not find something of interest in the crates or chests, they would not find anything at all.

"I suppose this was a waste of time. Sorry to bring you up here."

"Not at all. I had nothing on my agenda for today."

The coterie left Algathia and arrived in Tlimpid. They were all gathered together and ready to leave. Most were ready to head to the Pyran realm. That was where they needed to go next, so that Clerin could commune with Gorbanax and Trela could check in with her kingdom. Or was it queendom? Croy would need to go through the Pyran realm before heading to the Gaen realm, if that was where he was headed, but not everyone needed to accompany them.

Croy was eating with Feyazki, Clerin, and Trela when Escha and Torpalin arrived. They were both grinning from ear to ear, chatting to others and then pausing to whisper to each other. It was cute. It was more than that. Torpalin had been quite morose for a while, not his typical old talkative self, but he had been all smiles since the Northern Desert. They had plates of food and plopped down next to Croy, opposite of Trela.

"You're looking awfully chipper this morning." Croy smiled over at Torpalin.

"Oh, yes. Very much so. I've been cured."

"Cured?"

"Of the Tlana taint." He laughed and swooped his right hand downwards, as if saying goodbye to the taint. "I didn't want to talk about it at the time, not even to Escha." He nodded to his better half. "But I'm sure you all noticed something. It was… dark." His eyes glanced down for a moment, almost losing his smile. "It was like a constant constriction. I could never breathe. Like a heavy thick wool blanket over me, wet and tight, with a thousand tiny weights attached with a thousand tiny fishhooks, making it difficult to keep my head up or to move my arms. And a whirring stick in my brain, knocking all stable thoughts off kilter, ricocheting around until I couldn't remember what I was originally trying to think of. And a constant stomachache, coupled with a nauseous feeling that never quite dissipated, just a feeling of being sick of feeling sick. And some things that did not make sense, like feeling sad and numb at the same time. It was like I forgot who I was, just a little, just in the ways that mattered. I still remembered I should like the taste of eggs, for example, but they no longer tasted good—like nothing really had a taste and all I could experience while eating was the feel of them in my mouth. Floppy but stiff whites, mushy gelatinous yellows, and covered in grease. And not just food. I could remember liking exercise, but all I felt while doing it was a draining sensation, as if my essence was melting away and sliding off to the floor. I could remember liking being around other derlians, talking, but that was draining as well. It was just a… taint. It affected everything I experienced.

"But not anymore!" He twirled his forefinger up into the air and his smile beamed back at full force. "Now I do not have to think, *'how would Torpalin react to this situation? what would he say?'* now I just do. I can just be me again. I am me again." His face got slightly more serious again. "I felt it tear away from me and get sucked into the well. I know when it changed, when I got better, the actual moment I was cured."

They all smiled and laughed and commiserated with him. It was good to have him back, the old Torpalin. Croy had missed it.

"And that is why we must leave you all." It was Escha. She had been speaking with Trela, and Croy had been chatting with Torpalin, so he had not been paying attention and would have missed it completely had the sentence not been followed by utter silence. Everyone paused for a long moment.

"Leave us? Where will you go?" Trela was the one who responded. The statement had been directed to her in the first place.

"Back home. Ariellyna." She raised a quick hand as several others opened their mouths at the same time, all attempting to speak at once. "We've thought long and hard about it. We know Clerin still has to commune with Gorbanax, that you are all headed to Agoge in the Pyran realm. But the main fight has occurred and we have been victorious. The Cabal has been defeated. The items are destroyed."

"It just feels like a good stopping point, you know? I've been given a second chance. My sister could use some help with her bakery. Chiavel may be in a hiring mood. We're not exactly sure what we're going back to, but we gave this our all. We gave you our best, Trela. And it has been great, don't get me wrong. We love you all. Just, now, we need to put our energies towards each other. Just the two of us. You know?" He was still smiling but his eyes were slightly tight, as if waiting for a blow.

"Of course, of course." Trela's sigh was almost inaudible, and her smile was bright. "We've enjoyed having you with us, you've been integral, essential. We'll certainly miss both of you, but only hope the best for you." She paused for a moment. "See me before you leave, and I'll see what we can send you back with."

Torpalin looked as if he was about to waive her off, but Escha lightly touched his knee. There was a small pause. "We understand that this is not the best timing, that there a not a lot of extra resources right now. But anything at all would be appreciated, truly." Escha nodded to Trela.

"Of course. I'll do my best." Trela was still looking pleased.

Croy was too stunned to speak. He had figured that eventually everyone would end up at a different location, cast far and wide into the various realms, but he had not really thought about it. That seemed like such a far distance into the future. He had barely left Ilana to delve deeper into the quest. He wondered for the briefest of moments if that had been a mistake, but knew deep down it had not. The adventure was nowhere near over. At least not for him. He was amazed that Trela appeared so elated. He, himself, was devasted to lose the company of Escha and Torpalin. Escha was probably the greatest hunter they had, she provided much of their food between villages. And Torpalin… well, he was finally back to his old self. He was such a gregarious derlian, he could make the most mundane conversation entertaining. For Trela, however, it must have been devastating. She was always trying to keep everyone happily moving along the path, even when she did not seem to know what path they were on.

He wondered briefly if this would cause others to leave. Would Haswyxe feel the same? Would he assume they had accomplished their goal and want to head back home? Croy could not imagine it, but he had not expected this either.

Everyone was smiling and nodding, and he quickly joined in. He loved them both dearly, they had been a part of his family. More than anything, he would miss them. It was as simple as that. He felt his eyes begin to fill with tears but was able to hold them back. As they stood, Escha held her hand out to him. He was sure his voice would betray his sadness, so he shifted in to get a big hug. They stood there for a moment, quietly embracing.

"Take care, Croy. Find your way back to Ilana when all is said and done." They peeled away from each other and Croy nodded to her. In his defense, her eyes looked misty as well.

"Hey, I've to get some of that as well." Torpalin gripped Croy and lifted him up off the ground in a massive bear hug. Croy's legs dangled above the ground for a while as he was being embraced. He could still breathe just fine, but the feeling of floating there in the giant Luften's arms was a little disconcerting. Then, almost as suddenly, he was back on the ground. Hugs were passed all around. He figured they would say goodbye again, but that would be something official, in front of the rest of the coterie. He was glad he had been around when they stopped by. It was both a sad and happy moment.

They traveled for some time through the Ruyogn Canyon. It was a bit of a maze, but they finally found the vestiges of the Ariel River and started to follow that back upstream. It was a bit arduous and Croy started to wonder when they would be able to find a ferry back. Which slowly morphed into wondering *if* they would be able to find a ferry back. It was much easier to float downstream and there was no waystation in the canyon. They would have to hope that the ferry was bringing others down to be able to catch it all the way down there. They might hope to find some assistance at the confluence of the Ariel and Yadel rivers, but they might have to wait until they had trekked up the Plyraxus Falls. At that point, from what he understood, they would be shifting away from the river and heading towards the Pyran realm anyway.

It was after an evening meal while he was taking a small digestive walk in the bright moonlight that he noticed Clerin was doing something similar. Croy cut diagonally to catch up with her at an angle that would not surprise her, though she was staring down as she strolled. He made himself crack a few twigs under heavy feet to get her attention.

"Oh, hello there." Her smile was fleeting and lacked luster, which was quite out of the ordinary. Clerin typically had the most infectious smile in the coterie.

"Hi. Just out for a stroll, trying to work off some dinner." He patted his stomach for comedic effect, but she did not bite. "Can't believe Escha got so many hares, it'll be different when she's gone."

"Yeah, she is pretty amazing. We still have a lot of good hunters though. Haswyxe got almost as many."

Croy stopped to get her to stop. "How are you doing? Really. I'm here if you need to talk."

"Need?"

"Want, then. I'm here if you would like to talk." He looked up at her with real concern in his eyes. Clerin was one of his favorite derlians. "You just seem a little listless."

"Hmm." She glanced around and spotted some large rocks with an advantageous height. "Well, I cannot talk to Vrric about it."

Croy had rarely heard Feyazki referred to in that way, maybe never in a casual conversation. He knew the name, of course, but had always known Feyazki as Feyazki. It took him a split second to recognize and realize; he hoped his face did not betray his thought process. He was certainly not going to mention it.

She slowly headed over to the rocks. Croy followed a step behind. They each sat, though Croy had one foot down on the ground to help with balance.

"I cannot think if this is... I do not know... necessary. There is no way you can help me, really. I do not need advice or... or consolation. At least not that I know of. I think I know what my problem is and, honestly, I do not need..." She paused for a moment, staring at the ground in front of her. "You have always been a good friend, Croy, always been a good listener. So I guess I should not keep on about what I do not need.

"It is Gyllhelon, obviously. She was a friend and she died right in front of me, died protecting me. The images are burned into my brain. It was so dark with the storm clouds that the images are all in brief motions, lit colorlessly by the lightning flashes. I can see the Tlana rushing towards me in a flash. I can see its right hand pulled back, a weird grin on its face, some sort of bizarre mixture of ecstasy and starvation. I know that Gyllhelon was near me, though I am not sure if I saw her earlier or just felt her presence. Then the strike came, and she leaped in front of me, sword diving into the Tlana as the Tlana's hand dove into her chest. I have this image of her flying sideways, somewhat diagonal, as she pierced and got pierced. In the image I could see the Tlana's face over her right shoulder as the sword entered its left side. There is a bizarre mixture of pain and excitement on it. The next flash image in my mind is Gyllhelon crashing into the ground, and the Tlana standing in front of me with her heart in its right hand and her sword sticking out of its side. The next image it takes a bite of her heart. And then the Vijen showed up and the Tlana exploded into a thousand leaves."

Croy was silent for a moment, remembering his own harrowing experience, though he was nowhere near the front lines and had not been individually sought out by a Tlana. Then he realized Clerin was waiting for him to speak.

"That would sadden anyone, shake anyone's foundations. You have nothing to be ashamed of, it will just… it will take some time to process, is all." He was going to continue, to tell her that her wish to walk alone was quite natural and that he should not have bothered her, and so on. But she interrupted.

"That is not even the weirdest part. At the end, when we were gathering the dead, I noticed that Gyllhelon's body was undamaged. There was no hole in her chest. Nothing that would imply her heart had been torn out of her body. She looked… pristine. Like that she was so beautiful in life, that she stayed beautiful in death."

There was another pause. Croy's mind spun uselessly. He was unsure of what to say at that point. His assurances were obviously not what was needed. So he stayed quiet and patted the top of her hand with his in what he hoped would be perceived as a fatherly commiseration and not some sort of condescending placation. Not that he was her father, not that he was anyone's father. She pulled her hand away.

"That is not the issue, however. That is not why I feel I need to wander away from the others every once in a while, not why I need to be surrounded by the quiet." She waved her hand slightly. "I have never told anyone this, but I used to hate Gyllhelon. Well, not hate, that is too strong of a word. We were always friends of a sort. You know how gorgeous she was, right?"

"You are the most beautiful…"

"No. Do not. That is not what I am looking for Croy. This is the truth, the ugly truth." She drew in a deep breath that, at the end, was slightly ragged. "She was incredibly gorgeous and everyone knew it. It does not matter how beautiful I may or may not be. The whole warpack lusted after Gyllhelon. To be honest, there were times I lusted after her. But she did not seem to want anyone. She was always about the business of the warpack. Oh, she had her occasional flings, of that I am sure, but she never really chased after anyone." There was a long pause and then another deep breath, ragged all the way. "Except for Vrric."

Croy tried to interrupt, wanting to say something soothing. But since he had no idea what he would say, it was easy to close his mouth as her hand shot up.

"No. Do not. This is the truth, Croy. She really liked Vrric. Really, *really* liked him. I could tell, and not just because I was paying attention. And, worse yet, he really liked her. They liked each other and they are both so beautiful. It would have been…" Her hand fluttered around in the air for a moment, not finding what it was looking for.

"Well, who knows what it would have been. *I* liked Vrric. Really, really liked him. Still do, he is the love of my life. But it was rough at the start. I do not know exactly what he was thinking. I do not know what *I* was thinking. We both danced around everything and everything was new. I was in a new realm around new friends, foreign friends, personalities that I never knew existed before. There were times when Vrric would make me so crazy, he can be incredibly annoying at times. There were times I did not want to be with him. I wanted anyone besides him. And not just to spite him, I just was not thinking about him at all. It was all so…" She stared up into the sky, her eyes wet even though she was not crying.

"There were plenty of times that I was thinking about him, however, and plenty of those times he was walking around with Gyllhelon. Riding next to her on a march, laughing, smiling, being beautiful. And she was smiling back at him, looking perfectly gorgeous. And I... I hated her. For no real reason other than she was trying to be happy. I hated her, Croy. At least in that moment, those brief moments." Another deep, ragged breath. "And I thought she hated me. Not always. In fact, hardly ever. Just like I hardly ever hated her. But she never said or did anything to me. I cannot recall a time when she yelled at me, or even scowled at me. She was just so perfect!" Her fist came down on the top of her thigh with a thump.

There was a long silence. Croy wanted, more than anything, to be able to think of something to say. Not to interrupt, not to distract, but to just give her something. Maybe an assurance, he was not sure, but something. But he could think of nothing, and so he stared at the same patch of ground that Clerin's wet, uncrying eyes stared at. Mute.

"Every time I saw her with someone else, I hoped that was the one for her. He would make her happy and she could forget about Vrric. But really, she was not much for stepping out. And then Vrric and I finally got together, like truly together, and I just avoided her. He avoided her. We avoided her." A small pause. "There used to be times, back in the warpack, where she and I would drink some grog together and were... friends. She was fun, you know? We had a great time when there was no tension, I really did like her."

Another long pause happened and Croy was still mute.

"Do you know what the worst part of it all is?"

He just shook his head.

"The worst part is that she loved me so much that she died for me. She protected me when no one else was there, when no help was around, when I was alone and vulnerable and under attack. She gave her life for me, Croy. She died so that I could stay alive. I... I do not know how to feel about that. I do not deserve that. All I feel is what a horrible derlian I am. How petty and mean spirited and foolish and stupid and... and how great she was. How could I ever have thought a bad thing about her? How could I have ever hated her, no matter how briefly?" She turned to Croy. There was a track of tears from each eye, like mirrored tiny waterfalls. "How could I have ever hated her?"

What could be said to that? What response could be appropriate? Croy hated himself for his muteness, but everything sounded so trite in his mind.

"You cannot tell me, can you? The answer is just that I should not have. Thanks, Croy, you have been a real help. Now you know why I like to walk alone. Alone, Croy, without anyone prying into me." She stood.

"Wait. Seriously, wait." She stopped and turned, arms crossed hard in front of her. "You're right, I can't answer that question. You can't answer that question. No one can answer that question because it is the wrong question. It's not even a question, really, not when you look at it. You can't ask 'how' about a feeling. It is just something that happens, like a seismic tremor, like the sky being blue."

"The sky is blue because the Belegs made it that way. There, see, I answered your impossible question." She interrupted him with a mean look.

"No, you're just being contrary." He raised his hand to lower her anger. "Please, listen, what I'm saying is, if you asked the Belegs, if you asked Lembin, why derlians have certain feelings, it could not answer. Not even Lembin knows and Lembin helped create the world. Feelings are chaos, Clerin. Uncontrollable chaos. Should you, in retrospect, have felt any ill feelings to Gyllhelon at the brief—your word—at the brief moments when you did? Maybe. Really, I'm being serious here. You both liked Feyazki and he liked each of you, and you two were not always together. Right? That is how you explained it. It is completely, thoroughly, derlian to feel threatened in that circumstance. To feel jealous. Is it correct? Maybe not. But asking if jealousy is correct is like asking how you could have hated someone being with the derlian you love." Croy paused for a moment, to let her interrupt if she wanted to, but she just stood there, glaring at him.

"Did you poison her?"

"No. Do not be stupid."

"Did you slap her? Did you yell at her? Did you throw anything at her? Did you tell lies about her behind her back? Did you tell Feyazki he couldn't be around her? Did you try to get anyone to hate her? Did you try to embarrass her? Did you try to get Trela to send her back to the Luften realm? Did you do anything, anything at all to her?"

There was a long pause. It appeared that Clerin was truly thinking about it, mulling it over, trying to dredge up dirt on herself.

"Not that I know of. I probably complained to others that he was spending so much time with her." Her eyes looked upwards as she thought, and her arms loosened slightly.

"I'm not going to worry about complaining, you certainly never complained to me in such a way that I remember it." He tried on a small smile, but she did not reciprocate. "Listen, what we do have control over is our actions. At no time during the long campaign did I think, 'Clerin really hates Gyllhelon.' Seriously. You could ask anyone in the coterie, those that know you best, and I think you would get the same response. You did nothing to hurt or sabotage Gyllhelon, and she did nothing to hurt or sabotage you. At least as far as I understand. So, here is a question for you. Do you think, at any time, for the briefest of moments, that Gyllhelon hated you?"

"She died to protect me."

"Yes, and that is the greatest sacrifice, and no one is saying anything less. All I'm saying is that we do not know what she thought at all times. There were probably moments, and I may be wrong here, I am quite often wrong, but I think there were probably moments when she was annoyed that you were spending so much time with Feyazki. Why? Because it is a feeling. It is a natural, chaotic, uncontrollable feeling. That does not mean she didn't think of you as a friend, want to protect you, love you enough to die for you. It just means she was derlian." Croy wondered, briefly and to his great shame, as to how much thought went into a derlian's actions during combat. Did Gyllhelon really think, "I love Clerin so much I'd die for her?" Or did she see a Tlana attacking a friend and react. In the final analysis, however, was there that much of a difference?

"Hmm. You have actually given me a lot to think about, Croy." Her arms were still in front of her, but they were no longer crossed, they were held low and loose, with her left hand over her right, holding it with a light grip. She had not wiped away her tears, but they were no longer flowing.

"And, even if you had done something small to Gyllhelon, I would not think less of you. You are a kind and thoughtful derlian, Clerin, I truly believe that, and we all make mistakes. Please don't beat yourself up over this."

"Well, now you are pouring it on a little too thick." Her smile was small but appeared genuine. "I do thank you for our little talk, you are also kind and thoughtful, but we should be getting back."

✳✳✳

It took them a couple more days to finally get to the Iltrolin Pools at the bottom of the Plyraxus Falls. They had not found a ferry, though they travelled along the path next to the small river on the way there. As they finally approached the Pools, Croy could see off in the distance the large wooden sign hanging off the side of the inn that just said "Inn" in giant letters. Others had complained about the generic name but Croy kind of liked it. There was nothing else around for leagues, certainly not another inn. Also visible in the distance was the ferry itself, sitting idle at the long dock. It looked kind of sad there, unused.

They arrived late in the afternoon. Torpalin and Escha were going to stay one night and leave for Ariellyna in the morning. The rest of the coterie were to stay at the inn for another night, to enjoy the amenities and relax before the long trek to Agoge through the Pyran realm. Croy hoped to travel through some of the same areas as Trela's warpack had. It would be nice to see something like Dun Oengen now that she was queen and they would be welcomed.

The inn was small enough that they were grouping derlians into rooms. Croy ended up being grouped with Tumu, which meant Knill would be there much of the time even though he would, technically, be staying with Trela. It was a fairly common grouping and one that he enjoyed. Knill and Tumu were his closest friends. But since they had been in tents for a while, he had gotten a little used to sleeping alone.

They unpacked in their room, setting everything up for the two-night stay. The bed, though small enough for one Luften, was large enough for Croy and Tumu to share. They had asked about a cot, just in case, but there were none to be had. It was evening by the time everything was settled, so they all headed down to the common room.

Almost everyone was already down there, sitting close together on benches, drinking mead and eating venison. It had a celebratory atmosphere. It had been almost a fortnight since they had destroyed the Yaven-infused items, but this was the first time they were really able to sit and enjoy the culmination of their labor. They could order more food if they wished, they could drink as much as they liked, and they could walk, or crawl, back to their rooms whenever they felt like it. And tomorrow would bring a warm breakfast and hot bath, no matter how late they slept in. They could truly let their guard down and just enjoy.

Croy, Knill, and Tumu all sat together at the end of a long table, requiring them to squish slightly closer together than typical. The food was amazing and the company even better. The mead was a little too sweet for Croy—well, it was a lot too sweet—but he enjoyed it all the same. The vast room was a little loud, voices echoed oddly amongst the rafters. The conversations were inconsequential but the feeling of it all was just fantastic. Croy enjoyed every moment.

At one point, after everyone had eaten but were all still sitting, Trela stood. It took a couple of moments of fists pounding on tables, but everyone soon quieted and turned their attention to her.

"My fellow warriors!" That simple statement got more fist pounding and some cheers. "We have accomplished what we came to do. We destroyed the Cabal and everything they created. Tonight is yours to do with as you please." More cheers filled the room. "Tomorrow is yours to do with as you please." More cheers. "And after that? Well, after that we are headed home to finish the rest. All here who wish to live in Agoge and enjoy being my warriors may do so. The worst, the absolute worst that I offer you is a little too much time on your hands, a little too much boredom. But if that is not something you desire, I am sure I can keep you busy with something of your choosing." There was some scattered laughter from the crowd. "For some of you, Agoge may be too far. For some of you, it may be too foreign, and you may miss whatever home you've left to accompany us on our mission. Now that we have accomplished what we came to do you may, of course, head home. If you come to Agoge first before leaving, I will offer you what treasures you can carry, so that you may live out the rest of your days in relative comfort. If you need to leave now, you may, but I can only offer you so much. I will do my best to send something more to you later, but we have a long trip back to any coffers of mine and longer still until we reach Agoge. Two amazing warriors have already chosen this route. Escha and Torpalin!"

Trela waved in an upward direction at Escha and Torpalin, encouraging them to stand. As they did so, the thumping of fists and cheers grew in rhythm and volume. There were hoots and hollers and scattered yelling which Croy was unable to discern words from.

They both stood, Escha looking a little embarrassed, Torpalin looking proud with his massive chest out.

"Now I know that I've sprung this upon you, but this decision has been known for at least a little while, so you've had plenty of time to prepare yourselves." Trela was grinning widely. She raised her goblet to the both of them. "Speech!"

A small chant arose as Trela sat down. "Speech, speech!" The word rang throughout the room.

"Please, please." Torpalin waved his left hand down to calm the others, while his right stayed steady with a goblet clutched in his fist. "We have made quite a journey with you. Through all the realms, seriously. I never thought I'd see the Luften or Pyran realms, and certainly never dreamt of seeing the Gaen realm. I never thought I would see a Pyran queen, let alone help her get her throne. I doubted I'd ever see a Yaven, never thought I would see a Vijen, never knew the Well of Eternity even existed. I had never, ever, *ever* wanted to see a Tlana." There was a large round of laughter that echoed through the room.

"But I did. I saw it all. We saw it all. And I made a lot of great friends along the way. Most of you may be a bunch of jerks, but you're the most beautiful and crazy and wonderful and likeable jerks I've ever had the pleasure to travel with. I wouldn't have wanted to almost die so many times with anyone else." A small round of laughter echoed around.

"But more than all that. More than experiencing the entire world. I met the love of my life on this journey. I met the derlian who perfectly complements me, challenges me, makes me want to be a better derlian. Trela understood her destiny from the beginning and chased it down until she achieved it, through amazing and daunting odds. I had no idea what mine was, wasn't even looking for it. I was just strolling along, enjoying life where I could, without a thought to the future. And then I met Escha. It took me a little bit, I must admit. I felt lust before love, I'm not ashamed to say that. But finding Escha was finding my destiny. I found pieces of myself that I had not known were missing, I found pieces of myself that I had not known were there. I am complete. I am healed. I have experienced the world and am now ready to settle down and live a boring and blissful existence with my love. And I tell all of you, all of you out there listening to this, that there is nothing greater in all the realms. Search or don't search. Understand or not. But when it comes, when it hits you like a hammer, act. Act! You must reach out and grab it, do not let it pass you by. I cannot imagine if I had let destiny slip through my fingers. For a while there I had little will to live, but Escha pulled me through. A warrior with little will to live does not live long." It was quiet during the pause. Torpalin turned to look at Escha, a big stupid grin on his face.

"You are the essence of my love." He took a big drink and cheers rang out again. He turned back to the crowd, his empty goblet dangling in his large hand.

"And that is why we must leave you now. I cannot wait to begin the rest of my life. We are sad to go, we will miss you all, but go we must. Thank you for being here, thank you for showing us the world, thank you for being the greatest of friends. I will never forget all that we accomplished."

They all cheered and drank and pounded tables. It was great. Croy felt good to have met Torpalin, been friends with him. There was the tiniest pain in his chest that all of his own destined loves had been torn away from him, but he felt great for Torpalin and Escha, and the pain faded with the joyous comradery that filled the room.

Soon two more chants started. "Escha, Escha." And, "Speech, speech." They overlapped and interweaved, at times intelligible. Finally she held up both hands, one with a goblet and one that was empty. The room quieted down.

She looked around the hushed room, smiling her quirky smile. Her shoulder gave a tiny characteristic twitch. "What he said." And she sat down.

There were some that were disappointed and tried to chant some more, but most broke into laughter and let her off the hook. Croy finished his own goblet and tried to talk to Knill about love and destiny, but Knill had a hard time hearing over the commotion in the room. Or at least that was how it appeared. Eventually the conversation, as was typical, turned to safe and banal subjects. It was a gloriously enjoyable evening that was cut short too soon by the imbibing of too much mead. Such was life on the road.

After a late lunch the next day, Croy, Knill, and Tumu went for a walk. It was often more comfortable to find a nice spot outside than try to fit everyone in a cramped room at an inn, and their room was quite cramped. They walked away from the river a little bit and into the trees where they found an oak tree. It was large and lush and had some clear area to sit under. They spread out and sat down, no one rested against the trunk. They chatted for a while about little things. They chatted for a while about Escha and Torpalin, swapping stories of the two that they mostly already knew. They talked for a little bit about the well and the Cabal and the Yaven-infused items. After a long time had passed, Tumu suddenly got silent. Croy wondered if it was time to start walking some more, his own legs were feeling a little stiff. He started stretching out a little when Tumu spoke up.

"I've… I've wanted to speak with you about something, Croy. I just haven't known how to bring it up." His voice was small but insistent.

"What?" He kept his legs stretched out straight, letting the blood flow more freely.

"I've had another vision. A couple of visions, really. And they are the most confusing I've ever had. I just… I don't fully understand them."

"And you want some help interpreting them?"

"Yes, but more than that. They involve you. And, well, I'm not sure how to tell you. They involve Clerin as well."

"Oh. Well, we just had a good talk, so maybe it has something to do with that."

"I doubt that."

"Well, I… I don't understand. What were the visions?"

"One was of a great cliff overlooking the ocean. The cliff was stony and strong. I watched it for a while, as wave after wave crashed into it, undermining it. It crumbled from the bottom, creating fissures that cracked up the surface, and then, all of a sudden, the entire cliff just fell into the ocean. It was astounding."

"And the other vision?"

"A great traitor flashing from one location to another. Gathering resources, plotting an attack. It was dark and almost impossible to make out, but as it flashed around it kept stopping around this boulder that looked like it had a crown. Then, as the boulder would roll towards it, it would vanish again."

"I think I'm going to need more descriptions. I have no idea what those could mean." Croy thought for a moment. "How did you know it was a traitor?"

"Well, it felt like it. More than anything, it just felt traitorous."

"Really, I have no idea. There has to be more." Croy thought for another moment. "What do these have to do with me or Clerin?"

"Oh. Well, the other day, while we were traveling along the river, I saw your silhouette as you turned towards me and, I swear, your face had the same outline as the cliff." He held up his hand to stave off Croy's immediate question. "And then today at lunch, Clerin's hair coiled and flowed in the wind in the same manner as that ocean."

"So, you think Clerin is undermining me and I'm… going to fall into the ocean?"

"I am only telling you what came to me. You must understand that these are very confusing to me as well. Usually my visions are much more clear and concise. I can feel things with certainty, like how I know that it was a traitor in my second vision. But this time, especially with the first vision, I felt nothing. No certainty, no understanding, nothing. Just the image of the cliff face and the ocean. Even when I saw that your silhouette looked somewhat like the cliff, it did not strike me as anything. It was only after seeing Clerin's hair this morning that I felt I had to say something. What does it mean? I have no idea. Is this how I typically see visions? No, it's not. When I saw Trela as the Kriishan, that was all I could see. It was blinding, it was total. When I saw you as the cliff face it was more like, 'That's an interesting coincidence.' There was nothing sure about it. Nothing definitive, or even circumspect. I didn't know how to tell you, didn't know if I even should, which is also not typical. All I can say is what came to me. All I can say is that you might want to be careful around Clerin. I have nothing else for you and for that I apologize. You are a great friend to me and if there is any way I could be helpful, trust me, I would. In fact, if you were not such a good friend, I would not even mention it. It took me all afternoon to decide to say anything. This information may make things worse, I have no idea. I have never felt anything bad from Clerin. Ever. But if something happened and I had not mentioned anything, I would not be able to live with myself."

"Well, then I thank you for telling me. I… I can only say that I've never felt anything bad from Clerin as well."

✳✳✳

That night, Croy lay in bed thinking. He mulled over Tumu's warning, over and over, and he got nothing from it. It did not make sense. If Clerin had wanted to hurt him, she surely could have at any point in the time that he had known her. It also felt bizarre that Tumu felt so unsure about his visions. No matter how Croy twisted it in his mind, he could not understand it. All it really did was keep him awake much longer than he desired, but he did finally fall asleep.

Croy was definitely dreaming and he was definitely falling in his dream. He could feel it in the pit of his stomach, a kind of nauseous vertigo. He was falling backwards, watching the sky pull away from him as he plummeted. Try as he might, he was unable to turn around to see what was coming. The sun burned his eyes, the wind chapped his skin, he slammed into a lake or some large body of water. The impact knocked the air out of him, making it seem like he was choking. He waited to strike the hard ground at the bottom of the lake, but it never happened. He gasped for some bit of air but found none. It was not like he was drowning, his lungs did not fill with fluid. It was more like he was unable to expand his chest, like it was strapped down in a leather suit of armor two sizes too small. His diaphragm heaved with urgency, he clawed at his own throat, his eyes bulged into the fresh water.

Suddenly, without warning, he popped through and the sun was in his eyes, blinding him again. The wind chapped his skin, his back slammed into a lake, he suffocated for a while, et cetera. This happened slowly at first, but it gained in speed with each iteration. He felt more and more nauseated each time, clutching his stomach reflexively. It became a blur with its repetition. He felt sick.

Then he stopped, hovering just below the hot and blinding sun. He began to sweat and there was a strange buzzing sound in his ears, like insects in the distance or if he had fallen and smacked his skull. A derlian shape shot out of the sun towards him. He had to squint to watch it approach. Once it got close enough for him to make it out, it was not a derlian at all. It was certainly the shape, but it was made out of large stones and small cobbles. They moved as it fell, looking like they were held together with wire, like a bizarre stone marionette. At first, Croy had thought it was going to fly past him, but he finally realized with horror that it was headed straight for him.

He curled up and flung his hands in front of his face, trying to protect himself. Then, crash!

The pain was excruciating. It felt like he had broken some bones. The collision shoved him so that he was falling again. He glanced around, trying to find the bulbous marionette, but could not see behind him. He crashed into the lake again and began suffocating.

This happened over and over. He would stop and be blinded, then get crashed into, breaking bones and knocking out teeth, then he would suffocate. All the while ribbons of nausea ran through him each time.

It was terrible, it was horrible, it kept happening over and over. He did not know how he had more bones to break, teeth to get shattered. He tried to scream, but nothing came out. He just wanted it to end. He would have done anything, anything at all, to make it stop. No matter how base, or vile, or cruel, or against his inherent character. It was an eternity of excruciating pain. Until he finally woke, drenched in sweat, snot, and tears. Tumu was nowhere to be seen.

Chapter 8

Clerin woke with the sun, even though they were allowed to sleep in a little bit. Trela was being generous, it being the first day of the long journey to the Pyran realm. The previous day had been a whole day off and she had wanted everyone to fully enjoy it. Clerin had decided to take it easy and rest rather than go explore. She had wanted to be as refreshed as possible. Vrric had decided to enjoy his time with the warriors and was snoring away next to her. It was a cute, light snore, the kind that she usually slept through, so she decided to keep her blame on the sun for waking her. She got dressed as quietly as she could and left the room to search out some breakfast. She would let him sleep a while longer before putting the finishing touches on their packing. They had done the bulk of it the evening before. Well, she had done the bulk of it, but in his defense, he was quite tidy and rarely unpacked much to begin with. She enjoyed spreading her things out on the rare occasions they were at an inn. It was best to take advantage of the opportunities when they occurred, in her opinion. They were few and far between.

The common room was sparsely populated and quite open. They had moved all the tables against one wall to have room for dancing the previous night and the innkeepers had not gotten everything pulled back together yet.

She got her food and went to an unoccupied corner to quietly eat and think. They were going to be headed to the Pyran realm where she, supposedly, would be able to commune with Gorbanax. Not just exchange crude information as she had last time, but to truly commune. She wanted to explain how Taglo had sacrificed itself to destroy the Cabal. There should be a monument to Taglo somewhere in the Yaven realm. Though she was unsure of how much communication happened between the Belegs and the Yavens anymore, assumedly not much, there had to have been a tie between Taglo and Gorbanax. She felt it to be true and not just because of the way Taglo discussed it. It was like an intuition.

She finished her plate and waited, just sitting there in the corner, enjoying herself. Eventually, the soft sounds of the inn coming to life wafted down. Others were waking up and starting their packing. It was a soothing pitter-patter. Before too many came down to eat, she decided to go for a walk.

She stood and headed out to the foyer when she realized the noises were becoming more insistent. Rather than go outside, she went upstairs to investigate. There was a commotion forming by the time she reached the landing. There were several warriors leaning on the railing, chatting. Croy came around the corner, asking anyone and everyone if they had seen Tumu. Then, when he realized she was there, he got quiet and passed her with his head down, heading downstairs in a hurried walk. She thought it odd but forgot about it as she headed back to her room. She had decided to see if Vrric was up instead of going on her walk. The hallways were certainly starting to get more clamorous.

Vrric was slowly getting up when she arrived at the room, so she finished her portion of the packing. He would float everything down to their horses after he had eaten. When they finally arrived at the newly crowded common room, the place was in an uproar. Tumu was missing and no one had seen him leave. Some were leaving to search outside, and others were asking the innkeepers questions, while most were simply exclaiming their surprise and worry to each other. It was a chaotic scene. Clerin decided to hunt Trela down to try to get some real information while Vrric was eating. She knew she would only be adding to the chaos, but found it difficult to watch him eat with all the commotion.

Trela was outside, directing small groups of search parties. As a group of three left her with their instructions, she was alone for a moment. Knill must have been out searching since he was nowhere to be seen.

"Wow, this is crazy, how can I help?" Clerin walked over and offered her services.

Trela looked at her askance. "You can stay away from Knill and Croy."

"What?"

Trela paused and looked at her more thoroughly. Then her face relaxed and a small smile appeared.

"Well, how would you be expected to know?" She glanced around, making sure another group of volunteers was not walking up on them. She leaned over conspiratorially and loud-whispered to Clerin. "Tumu warned Croy about you."

"What?"

"Yes.   Apparently, you are planning something… nefarious… for Croy. Or something. Knill was emphatic but vague and, honestly, I was only half paying attention at first."

"That is absurd!"

"Yes, I think I said something similar. He mentioned it last night and I was going to discuss it more thoroughly with him today but… you know." She waved an arm at the chaos.

"So… Croy thinks I have done something to Tumu because he warned Croy that I was going to do something to him?"

"I don't think it's gotten that far yet. But it may if we're unable to find him. Just… just stay here with me and help organize the searches. Everyone who isn't eating or harassing the poor innkeepers is already out looking anyway."

"It really is absurd, you must know that. I would never do anything to Croy or Tumu or… well, anyone. I am probably the least dangerous derlian from your warpack, certainly the least dangerous here. I do not… I love Croy. Really. I swear to you I am not planning anything nefarious towards him. And I swear I have nothing to do with whatever is going on with Tumu."

"I believe you, I do. Truly. But they've gotten really worked up about this."

"Maybe Tumu just wandered off?"

"I sure hope so. And I hope he wanders back quickly."

They were unable to find Tumu anywhere. They ended up staying another night at the inn. No one wanted to leave without him. It was a little scary in that he completely vanished without any of his belongings, but no one else went missing or got hurt or felt like they were being watched. It did not seem to be an ongoing or repeating problem.

The innkeepers were quite helpful. They joined in the search and allowed Trela's coterie full rein of all the buildings, pointing out little closets and hidey-holes. The biggest disappointment was when Arnasta could find no trace.

There had been several of them in Tumu and Croy's room. Serghno, Vrric, Trela, Croy, Knill, herself. She was not even sure why she was there, probably because Vrric was there. Arnasta had combed through Tumu's clothing and meager possessions, finally settling on a sweat-stained shirt of his. She sat in a corner for a while casting spells and mumbling to herself. After a while she tried different articles of clothing—some trousers, his boots. It was all for naught.

"I can find no trace from beyond the bed. It does not even seem like his feet touched the floor. He was just here, and then… vanished." Arnasta looked a little sheepish, a look that Clerin was unaccustomed to seeing on her face.

"Maybe it was a Yaven?" Serghno spoke to no one in particular.

They stayed three whole days after Tumu had vanished, hoping against hope. Luckily for Clerin, even though the story of Tumu warning Croy about her circulated, no one seemed to consider it real. At least no one confronted her about it. A few made some jokes, as in the "please don't hurt me" kind, but no one meant it. Even Croy seemed to forget about it. Certainly no one ever accused her of stealing Tumu away.

Eventually, they had to leave. The innkeepers had given them a discount the last few nights, but they did not have enough "heads," the Luften slang for coins, to stay forever, and they were told there would be a group coming for the ferry soon. It felt odd to be leaving without him, but there was nothing more to be done, not really.

They left early in the morning to get as much distance as they could that first day. It was not like they were reveling or carousing, though not everyone got a great night's sleep. Though they were close to the Pyran realm, it would take a while to get to a decent sized village.

It took about a week before the Unaqa cliffs were visible in the distance. They were not headed there exactly, nor toward the Delphin forest which was farther to the south, but somewhat in-between. The cliffs were too dry and the forest too far away, so they were heading to the spot in the middle. There should be water there and some decent hunting. And more importantly, it was a straight shot to the Yaniqua forest and Dun Oengen. Trela wanted to reach the fort as quickly as possible since they would be able to get full provisions and to fill their coffers there. And from there the Dekhan

Plateau. And from there Agoge. And from there, for Clerin at least, the temple and Gorbanax.

She knew she would have to continue from there. She would have to try to commune with Gunzgak and would have to return to Tureyn, but there was a path home. The end was nowhere in sight, but there was a horizon to watch.

The messages still vibrated within her, still clamored for her attention, in case she forgot her purpose. They still made her nauseated if she sat still and concentrated on them, but it was easier with Vrric there. She did not have to be alone, she did not have to sit still, did not have to pay attention to their vibrations. She could bring up just about any conversation topic and he would give it a go. She could give him a smile, a laugh, a joke, and he would give it back. And if she was at a loss to think of something, she could even give him a prod, a barb, a growl, and he would do his best to soothe her. He was amazing. Sure, he could be incredibly dense and did not always understand when he hurt someone's feelings, but he always tried, at least with her. In that way, she was able to travel on her path and ignore the vibrations within her at the same time.

They found a small village before they got to the Yaniqua forest. Trela decided to camp just outside the village to avoid taxing its resources. They visited in small groups, spending the last of their coin on the first grog they had seen in ages. Trela even spent some at the butcher so they could enjoy a small feast. She had Estfale go in for her since she was worried the butcher would have insisted on giving her the meat for free. Clerin doubted she would have been recognized, but the sentiment was in the right place. They pretended to be adventurers split from a warpack on their way to Dun Oengen to pledge fealty to the Queen and no one in the village cared otherwise.

They decided to stay back in the camp rather than head into the village. Vrric decided to use up the last of the mead he had from Ariellyna. Dartsyle and Lophina, one of the Dylsun twins, joined in. It was interesting, during combat and even just in the field, the twins were inseparable. Whenever the coterie had some time to relax, however, they almost seemed to avoid each other.

"Ugh, it's just so hot, we are heading back into the forests, yes?" The Fluen seemed to enjoy complaining about the heat. And the sisters had not even headed into the Northern Desert proper, but had stayed behind in the eshrams. Her blonde hair was pulled back into a ponytail, bouncing slightly as her head moved.

"I'm assuming you've never been to the Pyran realm?" Dartsyle had a wide smile on his face. She frowned slightly, but not grumpily, and shook her head. "Well, Yaniqua is the last forest you'll see for a while. There's nothing but desert the rest of the way to Agoge." He gave a small laugh and smiled his crooked smile. "But it's mostly a rocky desert. We don't have the pure dunes that the Northern Desert has. At least, not where we're headed."

"I say 'ugh' again." Her smile was not crooked but held something mischievous in it. Both of the twins always struck Clerin as looking mischievous. It was worse when they were together, always casting sly eyes at each other, sharing some unspoken thought, but the aura still surrounded them when they were without their coconspirator.

"Where's your sister, aren't you usually together?" Dartsyle kept his smile.

Clerin cringed a little unconsciously. She had spent enough time with the twins to know that they did not always like to talk about each other. Or talk about why they were not always together. But Lophina kept her smile as well.

"You're lucky you're cute." She gave Dartsyle a small wink. "We are not always together, warrior. Alphino went into the village to check that out. I thought I'd stay behind and check out Clerin's mead." She grabbed the bottle that Clerin quickly handed over.

"Sorry, I wasn't trying to insinuate anything."

"No, not at all. We get that all the time. It's just… well it's our mother's fault." She took a good drink and passed it on to Dartsyle. "She used to dress us the same. Anytime we went anywhere, even at home, she would make us wear the exact same outfits. She was quite the seamstress, really. She made everything we owned. Maybe it was just easier for her to make two of each item, but you think we could have had different colors at least. But no. She loved us, thought we were adorable, wanted to show us off to the entire town every time we left the house, but she treated us as if we were the same derlian." She laughed for a moment.

"When we first left to start our warrior training, I cut my hair. Just about shaved it. Whereas Alphino left hers long. We could finally look different, or at least as different as we could. We still trained together, and due to some horrible quirk of fate, our mentor made all her novices where the same outfits. It was a way to bring us all down to the same level, I think. But at least she let my sister keep her hair long."

"So, what happened?" Vrric spoke up while passing the mead over to Clerin. He waved his hand around his own short hair.

"Oh, right. Well, we worked various jobs together for some time with different hair, but you would be amazed at how many guards have to wear the same uniform. About four sun cycles ago we were hired by the Prince of Vatlisi. He was worse than our mother about our individuality. We had to always be together, always dress the same, wear our hair the same." She waved her hand briefly towards her ponytail. "He was a bit obsessed with vanity, mostly his own, but we were paid an exorbitant amount to 'make him look good,' as he put it." She turned to Clerin. "You met him."

"Ah, yes, well I cannot say that I enjoyed it much. Even when I was not being held prisoner." She thought for a brief moment. "I would say he was somewhere between unsavory and sordid."

Lophina laughed long and hard. "You come from a family of politicians, don't you?" She caught her breath after a moment. "I would have said sleazy. Just a good old-fashioned dirtbag. But a rich enough dirtbag that no one would mention it to his face. A powerful enough dirtbag that others would turn a blind eye." She took the bottle from Clerin. "Oh, he had his charms. He was quite charismatic when he wanted to be. I'm sure he had many admirers, both near and far. He had certainly pulled the wool over Tureyn's eyes. But for those who knew him, those who worked for him, he was just a sleazy dirtbag."

"So why haven't you cut your hair again?" Dartsyle twitched his right eyebrow up slightly. "Now that you're not getting paid to keep it how it is?"

"Well, I'm a little older now, and a little less distressed about looking like my sister." She took a pretty big drink. "But maybe, maybe. The night is still young." Her eyes regained their mischievous glimmer. "So, what about you, Dartsyle? I haven't heard much about you."

"Well, I was an only child." They all laughed at that. "No, where to start?" He took the bottle from Lophina. "I met Trela when she joined Iventorn's warpack, a long, long time ago. It was her first warpack, right after she and Knill had escaped the Gaen realm.

Although, I'm not sure if 'escaped' is the correct word. I was ordered to embed her with Lishean, who you've never met, but is currently acting as regent for Trela. Iventorn really wanted to attack a city called Parthia and Lishean was a holdout. Trela, being Trela, convinced Lishean to join in on the attack." He paused for a quick moment. "I'm sure you've heard how she was the hero of Parthia."

"Of course, though oddly enough, not from her."

"Well, it was in Parthia, before the fighting began while we were scouting it out, that I got to know the love of my life. Yarsurle. It was amazing, just amazing. And then, at the beginning of our search for the Cabal, in the Gaen realm, a Tlana took my love away from me. I've… I haven't been the same since. Haven't been able to get back into the game."

"So sorry to hear that. She must have been great."

"He. And yes, Yarsurle was great. He could make any moment… magical."

"Hmm. That must be why I think you're so cute." They all stopped and stared at Lophina. "You're doubly unavailable. You're pining for a lost gay lover."

They all laughed aloud, even Dartsyle who had become a little misty-eyed speaking about Yarsurle. It was a good evening for Clerin. It was fun and simple, sharing stories with some she knew well and others less so. Even Dartsyle, who she had been travelling with for over a cycle, told several stories of Yarsurle she had not heard before. He did so with an air of wistful nostalgia, but kept most of the stories light. Lophina, for her part, kept all her stories quick and humorous, following each up with a contagious smile.

They were finally in Yaquina forest, heading towards Dun Oengen. It would be the last time in the shade of trees, last time near any sort of river, for an incredibly long time. Even Agoge did not have a huge amount of trees.

The last time Clerin had come up the main road she was with Dartsyle and Serghno, in a wagon carrying casks of grog. She could almost hear the wagon wheels creaking. Since she had not been driving the wagon, she had just stared at the trees going by, worried about the task ahead. It felt a bit surreal to be riding back, surrounded by the same trees, riding up the same hills. It was not as if she recognized any individual tree, but it was a strong echo of her memory; it was the feeling in the air. A similar nervousness filled her, though she was surrounded by friends and heading to a fort that served Trela.

They finally reached the fort, and it seemed a little smaller than she remembered it. The gates were still massive, the towers still towered, but it seemed a little less imposing than the first time she had arrived. There were several Guards in their purple cloaks waiting outside and the portcullis was raised. Though she was pretty sure Vrric had not *whispered* to anyone in the fort, they were certainly ready for the coterie. Maybe Serghno had done it. Maybe they had recognized enough members of the approaching group to realize who they had to be.

Trela took the lead, riding at the tip of the column. The Guards bowed low as she passed and stayed low as the coterie entered the open gates. Clerin was towards the back, staring at the walls and trees, but she could clearly hear the jubilant response of the warriors and regular guards inside. It was a refreshing welcome that kept its enthusiasm throughout their entire entrance.

The courtyard was vast and open, with the barracks against the back wall, then the rows of gardens, then the taller building for the officers and the final third was lush grass. It seemed more verdant than the image Clerin held within her memory. Her mind's eye recalled the ring of hard-packed soil that Trela and the acting commander of the fort, one Lieutenant Uriels, had fought in. Not the soft grass.

The central building, somewhat defenseless but surrounded by the fortified walls of the fort, was where many of them would be sleeping. Clerin decided to unpack a little first and foremost. Trela had given them permission to stay a couple of days. Not everyone would be given a room but everyone would be free to roam and relax, with the full hospitality afforded to Pyran warriors and subjects.

The downstairs had several somewhat open rooms, a dining room, and a kitchen. She followed a guard up the stairs while Vrric followed her. She had some small bags picked up from one of Wesduin's wagons while he carried his saddlebags over his shoulder. He would have to go back to get hers a little later.

As they walked to their room, she had a sudden remembrance of Lieutenant Uriels showing her around. An odd feeling accompanied the memory. It was not déjà vu. She knew she had been there previously. And it was certainly not nostalgia. It was more like the opposite of nostalgia. She had a creepy feeling walking the halls upstairs, as if the ghost of Uriels was watching her.

They reached their room, and the guard opened the door and stood aside. Clerin also shifted aside, letting Vrric wander in first, which he did without hesitation. She thanked the guard and followed Vrric in, leaving the door slightly ajar. It was a small room with a small bed, though it was certainly large enough for the both of them. *Small enough to enforce some cuddling*, she thought.

Vrric dropped the saddlebag and stood there for a second, breathing deep. His muscles rippled under his shirt. He no longer had the blacksmith muscles of his youth, she had probably never seen him at his largest, but he stayed incredibly active and fit, especially for a mage. It gave her a naughty thought.

"You, ah... you should lose the shirt." She grinned a devious grin.

"I'm disgusting." He splayed his hands out in front of him, as if she was disgusted by a little dirt or sweat.

"I did not ask you to touch me or anything, just... you know... give me a little somethin' somethin'." She rolled her hand in front of her to move him along.

To her delight, he did remove his shirt. In addition to his muscular chest and well-defined abs, he had those diagonal muscles coming up along his hips, on either side of his pelvis. She had no idea what those muscles were called but enjoyed seeing them. On pretty well anyone. He then started to flex and move around. Sometimes it worked, it was nice to see his biceps bulging, but mostly his performance was too comical. She thought it was some sort of defense mechanism of his, to ruin her voyeuristic enjoyment by being goofy. Like being intentionally goofy reduced his embarrassment somehow. She gave him a quiet whistle and he looked sheepish, placing his shirt back on.

"Oh, come on. You know I have seen you countless hours without your shirt on."

"Yeah, but not so... directly." He was grinning, though. "Besides, I'm disgusting."

"Well, maybe, after unpacking, we can each take a nice bath. Then you can kiss me. You know, all over." It was her turn to look a little sheepish. He was smart and willing, but guys like him sometimes needed a little prodding. She sometimes had to ask for stuff that she thought should be spontaneous. It was worth the minor embarrassment, however, to be able to get what she desired.

Later that evening she wandered alone into the courtyard, feeling great. There were little groups of warriors scattered about, sitting, standing, drinking grog. She wandered until she saw someone she recognized—Jalin. As she got closer, she realized that Lophina was with the group as well. Her hair was cut quite short, which made it harder for Clerin to recognize her immediately. She sauntered over and received a cup of grog from a Pyran guard sitting with the group.

"Well, you look like you're glowing." Jalin had a big grin on. She took a small drag on a rolled-up joint.

"It has been a good evening." Clerin smiled and took a sip of her grog.

"I'll say. It's great to have Queen Trela back in Dun Oengen." The guard that handed Clerin her grog spoke up. He also had a big grin on and was quick with a wink.

"You were here when Trela took the keep?"

"Oh, yes, and I remember you and your wagon of grog. I can't say that I had ever seen so much drinking going on. We must have cracked ten barrels that night. Ha!"

"So, you are not… angry? Did you know anyone who died?"

"Warriors die in a warpack, that's what happens. And I'll tell you true, if it had been Qizern that had breached our walls, I wouldn't be drinking with you now. He was not one for taking prisoners, let alone leaving an entire keep intact. At least not during his conquering days. No, she came in, broke stuff, then fought that useless Uriels. That was it. No other reprisals."

"Oh. You did not get along with Uriels?"

"Few did. He was only here 'cause his father swung an axe for Qizern. Now old Ulriech was a warrior! I know she's the Kriishan and all, but Trela would have had a real fight if Ulriech had been around. Personally, I was amazed that Uriels even fought her. Would've thought he'd have jumped the wall and been halfway to Agoge by the time she called him out."

"You seem to have a very forgiving culture." Lophina smiled and took a drink of grog. She did not wince or clench her teeth, but it did not seem like she was overly thrilled with the taste. Though Clerin was certainly used to grog after living in the Pyran realm for so long, she missed her wine immensely. Even mead was not that far off.

"Oh, we believe in vengeance and punishment, don't get me wrong. But we have short memories. Once things are resolved, they're resolved." Jalin laughed a little.

"Nochiel sure rode Croy for a long time about his healing of Haswyxe." Clerin glanced around right as she said the name, hoping Nochiel was not standing right behind her or something.

"I'm not talking individuals. Qizern could nurse a grudge like none other, but, you know, in general."

"We're professional warriors, is what we are." The guard spoke up again. "Over our lives we can serve in various warpacks, for various commanders. We may fight against someone in one battle and then, a couple of cycles later, they're your best friend, saving your life. Then, who knows, maybe your paths split again. You just can't hold a grudge like that, not if you hope to live to a ripe old age."

"Well, how often does something like Dun Oengen get attacked, though?" Lophina waived her hand around the tall stone walls. "You can't always be attacking each other, not with these defenses. Can you?"

"No, no, not really. The forts are usually left alone unless there's a Kriishan in the making. Or an antoshan." He grinned some more. "Nobody attacks Dun Oengen who has nothing to prove."

"So, not to seem dense here, but why is there a fort way out here anyway? We are still quite a way from Agoge, yes? Are you just a target for aspiring Kriishans?" Lophina's eyebrow shot up, which brought attention to her close-cropped hair. She really did look different.

"Ha! I'll have to tell my brothers-in-arms that. No, no. We are on a trade route. Some of that is from the Luftens, though not much. But we have forests and rivers here. Now, you may not know this, since you have never been to the Dekhan Plateau before, but the trees near there are quite small and stunted. A lot of wood travels out of the Yaniqua and heads down south. We keep the roads open and make sure the traders make it out of the forest in one piece. We do patrols. We protect caravans at times. We do very important work here, though it is often quite dull. Which is why..." He held a hand to fend off being interrupted. Which was odd since no one appeared ready to interrupt. "Which is why it was fantastic that you showed up with an entire wagon of grog and we got to watch Uriels get cleaved in two. It really did shake up the tedium."

Lophina and Jalin immediately laughed aloud at that. Clerin laughed as well, though more with comradery than mirth. She finished her remaining grog with one gulp.

Clerin enjoyed the relaxing atmosphere of Dun Oengen. She walked through the trees when she wanted, slept in a bed, examined the fort, ate hot food, et cetera. Serghno even flew her up to the tops of the towers, just to reminisce about when she was there last, trying to entice the guards on duty to drink their fill.

There was a lot of reminiscing going on. And from all sides. Like the guard she had spoken with that first evening, many of those who were on the losing side looked back fondly on the fight. She thought that maybe it was due to the fact that so few had died that night since single combat had been declared so quickly, or that amnesty had been granted immediately and generously, letting even the loyalists escape. But the Pyrans, in general, really seemed to just enjoy talking about past battles. No matter the outcome or the amount of bloodshed, they would speak with fervent gusto about acts of amazement. Some they had seen, some they had just heard about. Some of the acts were heroic, that was true, but sometimes it was just something impressive or unexpected, like a warrior falling off a catwalk and landing on her feet or ducking under a sword and getting the plume of his helmet cleaved clean off. And they would laugh, heartily and often, slapping each other on the back or their own knee. Clerin began to wonder if the reason the warpacks all shifted around so much was that, after a while, all the stories had been bandied about and fresh ones were required.

They stayed in Dun Oengen for the better part of a week. It started out great for Clerin, but she became more and more agitated the longer they stayed. Her stomach got queasy after the third night. The fourth night she could feel the messages within her vibrating. She was nauseated on the fifth, enough so that she had difficulty sleeping. Luckily, they left the next day, and everything cleared up before noon.

It was a long and, especially according to Lophina, hot trek through the Pyran realm on their way to the Dekhan plateau. They were well provisioned and there were various friendly towns and villages along the way, making the journey mostly pleasant. They never stayed in a village for more than one night, keeping their momentum up and their burden on the villagers down. But sometimes, if they reached a place a little after noon, they would set up a camp nearby, or if the town was large enough, take over an inn. Then they, and their horses, would all enjoy some rest for the evening.

Trela would use those stops to talk with the locals and her representatives embedded there, getting to know them and hear their desires and grievances. She took extensive notes during her meetings, and if there was someone who was unable to attend due to the short notice, she would gather notes from others as her coterie left the next morning. Clerin had asked about it at one stop.

"The time spent through my realm should not be wasted." She and Clerin were heading towards an inn. "It is an opportunity that is being offered to me and I would disappoint destiny if I did not take it."

Clerin was not sure how disappointed destiny would really be if Trela were not to speak to these specific Pyrans, but she had no reason to argue against it. Those were certainly things Trela was good at, not wasting time and keeping destiny happy. Clerin, for her part, planned on spending a simple evening with Vrric and some grog. Was that a waste of time? Maybe. Would that disappoint destiny? She doubted it.

They eventually reached the plateau. They took the main road, which was a roomy width. It was a long uphill hike, grueling in the sun. Clerin was happy to be riding Riverlightning. As they reached the top of the plateau, they were greeted by two large towers straddling the main path. They were tall and skinny with many arrow slits scattered across their front faces. They were also greeted by Guards and guards. The evening was spent leisurely, and the next morning started slowly.

So it went between the various towers along the long, flat road to Agoge. They would stop at a tower and be greeted with pomp and food and drink. They all still slept outside, but each stop was more comfortable than the last, and each step brought them closer to the comfort of Agoge. In the far distance the volcano that towered over Agoge was visible. Its craggy crown was outlined starkly, hiding the lava within.

Then they could eventually see Agoge itself, nestled at the bottom of the volcano. It had been an amazingly long time since Clerin had seen the city, and so much had happened since she had left there, that she felt a pang of nostalgia as it came into view. It was certainly a different feeling than seeing Vatlisi, which had represented a return to the Fluen realm even though she had never visited it before. It was a different feeling than the sight of Tureyn, which she had visited several times though she had never lived there. It was the image of respite, of an oasis. She had relaxed there, in the Blaze of Agoge. Finally relaxed after a long and tedious struggle. And now, here she was, after another long and tedious struggle, returning to her oasis. It was a very narrow and specific type of nostalgia, if that was even the right word. She had no other.

The large exterior walls of the Blaze, with the somewhat haphazard towers, were visible first, in various shades of gray. Soon after the buildings that were clustered outside of the walls, the New City, came into view. It was low and dusty and full of vibrant life, with its own maze of small walls separating the eight boroughs. Clerin had spent much of her time in the Blaze, but had fond memories of the colorful bazaars of the New City, especially when everything spilled out even farther during the many festivals. The thought of the festivals made her think of Yihrum. A small smile crept unconsciously onto her lips. He was certainly not Vrric. He was a juggler and acrobat with catlike grace. She had not loved him, not in the strong everlasting sense of the word, but he was a fun lover and knew everything about every Pyran festival. She hoped that he had found the love of his life, as she had found hers. Or at least that he was happy in his search.

Clerin was a little shocked that their entrance was not made into a parade. The Pyrans seemed to celebrate absolutely everything, and their progress along the plateau was certainly watched, so it was a little anticlimactic to shuffle through the lines of guards and the small gate of the New City. If they were in the Fluen realm, the parade would happen the next day, after everyone was cleansed and refreshed. The Pyrans, however, never seemed to mind parading around dusty and sweaty. It was the effort that was the badge of honor, not the pomp.

As they wound their way to the Blaze, an impromptu crowd of citizens appeared. There were some whistles, clapping, random shouts, but they dispersed quickly once Trela and the coterie had passed, returning to the business of their day.

Once they entered the main gate of the Blaze, the atmosphere changed slightly. The tall stone walls gave a bit of respite from the heat, even though about half of the complex was not roofed. The main entrance courtyard was open and clear, without the makeshift stalls that peppered the New City portion of Agoge.

They were met by a group of Guards, proudly wearing their purple cloaks in the sun. Everyone dismounted and did some small stretching as they wandered in small circles. It felt fantastic to be off her horse, finished with the long march. Vrric came over smiling and put his hand on her back. She instinctively pulled away from his hot hand matting her sweaty blouse against her skin.

"I cannot wait to have a bath." She beamed a smile at him, explaining away the reaction. He smiled back and lifted both of his hands in the air slightly.

"It has been a long day, I know."

"It has been a long moon."

"It has been a long cycle."

They both laughed at that. She liked that he never held onto anything, certainly not to anything trivial. And she was really, *really* looking forward to a bath. If she knew where they were being stationed and knew it was waiting for her, she would have run the entire way there.

A Guard came for each horse even though Wesduin was driving the wagons farther into the Blaze. She knew that all their items would eventually find their way to their rooms. One offered to take the saddlebags for her, but Vrric waved him away. He folded both of their bags neatly on top of each other and cast a telekinesis spell. "Narkinheparc!" The Guard just shrugged and turned.

"Follow me." He spoke over his shoulder at them, barely turning his head.

They followed. It felt odd to walk by Trela, who was surrounded by a gaggle of Guards, and the others. No one was given any instructions, and she and Vrric were the first to be peeled off. She was sure there would be some meal or something planned that they would be invited to later, some sort of debriefing, but it was odd not to say goodbye to anyone. She turned and waved as they left, but no one was really paying attention.

The Blaze was like a giant maze, with many intersecting public passageways and many more private ones. Some were like hallways, surrounded by walls and covered overhead, but many were just walkways and paths that wove through open air courtyards, parks, and gardens, both private and public. The buildings were mostly built during different eras but melded together by time and weather. Some had been melded for so long that it was impossible to tell if they were intended to be that way originally. Though the walls were all of a similar stone where the only difference was age, the roofs kept up the haphazard look of the New City, jumbled about with varying slopes and materials.

Clerin recognized some of it, especially at the beginning, but eventually she was just walking behind the Guard. She was looking around, taking in the constantly varying scenery, but she was no longer paying attention to where they were going. She chastised herself once in the middle of the trek and made an effort for a little while, but eventually she was just lost again. She would get the lay of the land later. It had been a long day, moon, cycle.

Then they arrived at a small dwelling, melded in with its neighbors. The Guard showed them in and then left. Vrric floated the saddlebags down, kind of in a corner to keep the dust from the main room. She barely noticed, however, for there were two rooms and, to her great delight, steam was wafting in from the other room. There was a private indoor bath there, and it was already filled and hot. Vrric was saying something, but she ignored him and entered the other room as if in a trance. It did not take long before she was naked and soaking. It was fantastic. Vrric was in the other room, making muffled noise doing… something… but it did not bother her in the slightest. Nothing could have bothered her at that moment. She had scrubbed herself clean and was just sitting there, basking in her basting.

She eventually had to leave the tub, it would have been unfair to stay longer. Well, it was probably already unfair, it would have been almost cruel for her to soak until it was time for dinner. The trunk from the wagons had arrived and she pulled out the cleanest dress she could find. She put the rest of the rarely used items away while Vrric cleaned himself. She enjoyed deciding where the best location for everything was. She kept a catalog of all their belongings in her head, so even if there were things left aside to be cleaned, she still left the perfect spot for them open. They, of course, would need to spend the next several days washing everything they owned. It was impossible to fully get the dirt and dust off everything while on the road.

Soon after Vrric was fully dressed, there was a knock on the door. An invitation to the anticipated dinner arrived. It helpfully had a handwritten map on the back of it. By this time Clerin had gotten quite hungry, so she was happy that the dinner was to be at dusk, less than an hour away.

The dinner itself was pleasant and uneventful. Everyone was tired, clean, and full. Trela promised there would be more celebration over the next couple of days, which kept everyone a bit subdued. The one thing Clerin had not necessarily been expecting was that Trela wanted her to commune with Gorbanax the next day. It was not an inconvenience, but she had been expecting a day or two of recuperation before getting back up on her horse, both literally and figuratively. All in all, it was a very pleasant evening.

Clerin and Vrric walked back to their quarters alone. Even a relaxing word like "walk" was probably incorrect. They strolled. They moseyed. They meandered. They stopped and sat on a garden bench for a while. There was holly bush behind them, cut back enough that even though it reached out for them, it never quite touched.

"It's good to be back here." Vrric snuck an arm around her shoulders, pulling her in a little bit.

"Back at Agoge, or back off the road?"

"Ha, yes, it is good to be off the road. But I meant back at Agoge. It was relaxing last time. Almost too relaxing. And I walked and wandered the streets and passageways, I enjoyed the Mage's Guild and being one of Trela's inner circle. But I had all that time earlier and didn't get to enjoy it with you. Now, here we are, the both of us, and we can relax together. We can walk and wander and have fun together. I think I'm going to really enjoy the time here. I can feel it." He gave her shoulder a small squeeze. "It's good to be with you. Here, now. I love you, Clerin."

Clerin had been staring up at the moon. It was full and bright, shining down on them with its cool blue light. It was peeking around some roofs, to the side of a chimney. It was still a little low, which is why it looked so large. She had not been paying full attention to what he had been saying. She had just been enjoying the warmth of his body, the grip of his hand on her shoulder, the clean smell wafting up from him, the vibration of his chest as he spoke. She had just been blissful. He had told her he loved her before, it was not something he kept from her, but the moment was just right when he spoke those four words. She would never forget the look of that full moon, the feeling of the bench, the feeling of his arm. It was one of those moments that could have lasted forever. She did not want to twitch in fear of ruining it, but knew the moment could only stretch for so long. She stared at the moon intently and drew a slow breath.

"I love you too." It was not much, but it was enough. He squeezed her again, and they sat that way in silence for what seemed like a long time. It was as if neither of them wanted to twitch and end it. They both silently agreed not to talk about it, not to shake the moment with words or motion. It was beautiful.

The next morning came early. Both Trela and Vrric were to ride up with Clerin. Trela, of course, because she was required to get to the temple. And Vrric simply insisted. Clerin bathed again, steeping in the same herbs she had used the last time—some lavender, cedar, and sage. She ate salad and some fruit while Vrric had a large breakfast in the other room. Luckily she could not smell it until she left the bathing room.

They met Trela at the main castle gate. She had wanted to take horses up the path, as they had done before, "To keep the proper respect." Vrric was quite adamant about it the previous night at dinner, however. He would fly them up to the entrance. "What is the use of a mage if you don't use him?" he had said. It was a bit convoluted, but Clerin was fine either way. She did not think the Belegs disliked magic—each one practically required it to even meet with them. Water breathing, protection from lava, and the like. She had wondered if Trela merely wanted to ride past all the checkpoints populated with her Guards, but that seemed beneath her. Clerin had been worried that Vrric would tire himself out before they got to the lava protection, but he insisted he would be fine. In any case, Vrric was the more stubborn. They would fly.

"Lumkinderclo!" They shot upwards into the air. Clerin watched the Blaze, and then all of Agoge, shrink below her. It was amazing just how spread out the city really was. It seemed gigantic by the time they reached the large clear ledge at the entrance to the temple.

There were four Guards waiting for them, standing at attention. They bowed low as the three of them came into view and alighted on the ledge. There was a low rumble that passed through the ledge under her feet, though it was a much smaller rumble than at Tureyn.

"My Queen, we are so pleased to have you here with us today." The Guard rattled on with effusive language for a moment. He was scarred and wiry, reminding Clerin of the Guard that guided them the last time they were there.

The cave entrance was quite large and dark; its top was a smooth arch. There were no doors or gates, only Guards to guard it. She could not imagine anyone trying to sneak into the volcanic temple and if they did, she assumed Gorbanax could take care of itself.

Trela started to move towards the entrance and Clerin naturally followed. Vrric fell in line behind her. The light from the opening faded behind them as they turned corners, the sunlight eventually being replaced by scattered torches. As they walked along the tunnels, there were occasional offshoot hallways, but they did not deviate from their course.

It got quite warm as they delved farther into the cave complex, closer to the molten rock. Clerin was already sweating and they had not reached the main cave yet, though she thought they had to be getting close.

They turned another corner and there, at the end of a short hallway, was a pair of doors guarded by a pair of cloakless Guards. They were at attention, waiting for the group, short pikes gripped in their hands. Clerin wondered briefly about the wisdom of a pike in a tunnel, but figured it was mostly ceremonial.

"The Queen and her companions wish to commune with Gorbanax. Step aside." The Guard that guided them projected his voice down the tunnel.

The cloakless Guards turned sideways, facing each other. The other Guard strode forward and thrust open the double doors. He then backed up out of the way and bowed to Trela. As they all passed through the doors, he closed them behind them.

Clerin's eye was immediately drawn to the left, to the far end of the long room they were in. The room itself was rounded at the top and bottom, making it more of a tube than a room. The tube opened up at the end as it reached the lake of lava. Above the lake, unseen from the end of the long tube they were standing in, the roof opened up to the sky. She only knew because she had been there before. She could feel the rumbling from the stone under her feet. It was increasing slightly.

Unlike the previous time Clerin was there, there were no more Guards in the tube, just one mage. She had on a long dark robe and bowed deeply as they entered, staying horizontal until Trela addressed her.

"Rise." The word echoed slightly. The mage straightened her back. "We have brought our own mage for the protection spells. You may leave."

"Of course, my Queen. I shall just be on the other side of the doors if you have need of me." Her voice was high and lilting. She bowed again, turned, and exited.

Clerin waited a moment while the doors were being shut. Vrric and Trela were silent, just staring at her. Waiting. She did not know what to say, so instead, she disrobed.

"Lumtecpito!" Vrric's hand lightly touched her shoulder and several pulses of coolness washed over her. It removed the heat of the room from her as well, leaving her quite comfortable. "Narteclufto!" That spell was for her breathing, she knew. "Be safe."

"Thank you." She kissed him quickly and then walked towards the lake of lava.

It was a long walk down the tube to the lake. She took her time, breathing smoothly to calm herself. The messages within her were vibrating slightly. They were not obnoxious, she did not feel sick to her stomach, but they were certainly making themselves known. Waking up, as it were. They vibrated along with the low rumbling that permeated the tube.

Clerin stood at the edge of the lake for a moment, collecting herself. She breathed in deep and took a step. Her foot made an impression in the molten rock. She took several more, and her feet were sinking into the lava. She took a few more, and she dropped down to where her head was barely above the lava. It felt like slipping into a giant mud pit. To get farther in, she swam a little, then she dived down.

She reached a spot where she was fully immersed in lava, stopped, and righted herself. Even when she was floating and breathing normally, she felt more comfortable with her head up, facing the direction she had entered the lava pool. Even though she was floating, she could feel which way was down. The rumble was getting more insistent.

An image of crossed pikes appeared before her, the same as before, barring her way. She waited patiently, not wishing to do anything Gorbanax did not want. The messages within her started to vibrate a little more aggressively, completely in rhythm with the rumbling.

A flat black silhouette appeared behind the pikes, the same as before. To make sure it represented her, Clerin lifted her left hand. The silhouette mirrored the hand lifting. She then lifted her right hand and they each had both their hands raised. She dropped her hands and the crude fire image appeared. The flat black image of a bonfire was the same one she had seen the last time she was at the Temple. It should represent Gorbanax itself. She waited for the two silhouettes to shake "hands," as they had done before, but they both stood behind the crossed pikes, passive and still.

"We have destroyed the Cabal. We have gathered every Yaven-infused item in all the realms and we have destroyed them also. We threw them into the Well of Eternity. We have done what you asked." Clerin was unsure of what else there was to say. The messages inside her were starting to make her nauseated.

The silhouettes turned toward each other, shook around like they were dancing, but then the one that represented Clerin backed away from the other one. The bonfire one got closer, or larger, or a little of both. Then a silhouette of a wave appeared, looking like a crude cutout from a puppet show. It was large, like the bonfire, but was situated near Clerin's silhouette. Then a crude silhouette of a cloud appeared, and then one of a boulder. All the Belegs were represented. The pikes were still crossed in front of her. The rumblings and her messages still kept time with each other.

The cloud and bonfire were together, and the boulder and wave were opposite them. They danced around a bit. The word dance was overly descriptive for what was going on—they shook up and down, and rotated sideways, back and forth. At first the groups kept to their own sides, but eventually they were all dancing together, then all dancing separately. Then the groups switched over. The bonfire and the boulder were dancing together while the cloud and the wave danced over near the silhouette of Clerin.

The wave danced close to the silhouette of Clerin and then, suddenly, the wave touched her silhouette and swung it violently into the cloud, shattering it. At that moment, Clerin stopped being able to breathe. As she was suffocating, the messages spun and roiled within her. The rumbling grew louder, it felt louder, the lava that surrounded her seemed to vibrate with the rumbling.

She stayed calm for as long as she could with what felt like a steel band around her chest, constricting. It took a while before she really began to panic. She had felt no animosity during it, so she assumed it would only last a few moments. She started to see spots, she started to writhe around. She tried to scream but, of course, could not. She clawed at the lava around her, kicking and flailing. Strange rainbow colors, mostly in the green-yellow range, glowed and flashed eerily through her eyes. She passed out. For how long, she did not know. She would have thought she was dead, but her consciousness returned surrounded by lava. The pikes were still crossed in front of her. The silhouettes, now just four of them, were still in front of her, beyond the pikes.

Clerin was curled up and had difficulty straightening herself out. She slowly did so as the silhouettes began to move again. Her silhouette moved over towards the bonfire, but the crude pair of crossed pikes interrupted it. Then it wandered back, and various silhouettes of items appeared. A crude sword cutout, one of a shield, one of an axe, one of a crystal ball, et cetera. Each time an item appeared, her silhouette would touch it and it would shatter. After a while, no more items appeared. Her silhouette then floated over to the bonfire. No pikes appeared and they each reached out a crude hand and they touched. The bonfire shattered.

The rumbling increased even further, her messages vibrated even more violently, and once more she was unable to breathe. This time the panic came earlier. She was sure to suffocate until passing out again, but was less sure that she would wake up. Was this how Gorbanax planned to avoid the messages, by killing her? Would that save Gorbanax? But the panic did not help. She could not exhale to pass out faster, to speed up the inevitable process, whatever the end of that process happened to be. She kicked and flailed and clawed uselessly.

She woke back up. She was unsure if she was pleased with that outcome or not. The rumbling was deafening. Her stomach felt like there were knives inside, vibrating and slashing around. It made it so she could not straighten herself out. She extended her arms to swim them around and get her to face the right direction. Through the crossed pikes.

There were just three silhouettes left. Her silhouette approached the boulder, but it backed away. The silhouette followed it and chased it, but it always dodged her. Then, suddenly, another silhouette appeared behind the boulder. It looked like a derlian silhouette, but due to the crudeness, it was impossible to tell what race. The boulder backed into the silhouette and got stuck. Then her silhouette touched it and it exploded. Then the wave rushed over and touched her and exploded. Then she suffocated and flailed and, in repetitious agonizing pain, passed out.

When she regained consciousness, Gorbanax was before her. It looked like a giant pulsating Yaven. Even amidst the bright yellow lava, its form was readily discernable. Flames spit off of it in various directions, diving into the molten rock. It was a deep yellow with an orange outline. Like Taglo, it attempted a vague derlian shape, though she was unsure if that was just for her benefit. And it was huge. It took up most of the space in front of her. The crossed pikes were gone. The rumbling continued, but the vibrating knives that had been held within her were no longer noticeable.

"You confound me, derlian. Truly." The "face" of the Beleg was somewhat crude but had white hot eyes that stared directly into Clerin with an intensity she had never experienced before in her life. "You understand you bring death, do you not? You must understand you are the assassin's blade being thrust between my ribs. You must." The voice was loud and deep and came from nowhere. Or, more aptly, seemed to come from the center of her own skull.

"I... I only know that I was told to provide messages." She spoke the words, not knowing how else to convey them.

"When you killed Linchon, did you not know?"

"I had no idea that the messages were weapons."

"Maybe not before. I understand that. But afterwards. Did you not understand what you were doing?"

"I was given no further instructions by Lembin. I... I was told by Linchon that I had to give my messages to you and then, only after I had communed with you, that I was to take its reply back to Lembin." She racked her brain. She had known something was wrong with the messages, of course, but it had not fully occurred to her that she was killing anyone. "Linchon did not mention anything about death. In fact, Linchon spoke to me through my own dead father in Lembin's temple just recently. I had thought they were just arguing. No one mentioned death."

Gorbanax did not move for some time. The pulsating continued and the eyes, somehow, grew more intense. "Forgive me."

The Beleg reached a fiery hand into her brain. It seared and burned. The pain was excruciating, far worse than being suffocated into unconsciousness. She hoped to—no, she wished to pass out. She screamed an animalistic howl. The hand stayed in there, shifting itself, scouring, sending pulsating waves of different types of pain up and down her spine. It was hot, then cold, then it was like lightning. There was no way to describe it. Eventually the hand left her skull. Eventually her screaming stopped. Her limbs kept twitching sporadically, spasmodically, against her will. She was having a hard time focusing on the gigantic flame before her.

"Linchon did want its revenge, which is why it misled you about your own deeds. I understand that now. Its revenge could only happen if the pendulum swung hard enough. If only Linchon was assassinated, then maybe there would be three Belegs. Maybe a balance—no, not balance—maybe a truce could have been struck." Gorbanax stopped for a moment, staring intently at Clerin as she floated and twitched. "Do you know why I have not killed you?"

"No." She drew in a ragged breath. Speaking hurt her lungs and she coughed for a moment as if she had inhaled campfire smoke. "I have no idea."

"I have not killed you for the same reason Linchon misled you. No offence, but your life is inconsequential to me. When you first appeared, I felt a tingling of nemesis, but I controlled it. I assumed whatever trick Linchon was playing, whatever prank Lembin had performed, I could use you to solve a vexing problem of mine. Or that you would die in the process of trying. Whichever. The problem, of course, was the Cabal of Lochom. Which, amazingly enough, you resolved. I was a little shocked to feel the Yaven-infused items slide into the well. It was… delicious. When you came again, just now, I felt another tingling of nemesis. That is one of the differences between Yavens and Belegs, however. We can control ourselves, even in the face of impending doom." It paused again, tilting its head in a derlian-like manner. "Are you able to control yourself in the face of impending doom."

"No." Her left leg twitched quickly. It was as if someone were tickling the sole of her foot, in the soft spot under the arch, but with a sharp fork. "I cannot even control myself now." She tried to laugh but could not muster it up.

"I knew that if I communed with you, if I accepted the messages from my fellow Belegs, that I would die." It paused for another moment. Clerin was sure she was supposed to say something, but her brain was still too foggy. Foggy with lightning strikes of inanity. "I have not killed you since I am already dead, though not quite literally yet. I would be curious to commune with Linchon, to see what already, but not literally, really *is* after a certain amount of time. But I digress. I have not killed you because there is an imbalance now that must be righted. The other Belegs must die so that the world can be brought back into the harmony of equality. There cannot be only two Belegs. No, that would not do."

"So... Not because of revenge?"

"Ha!" A strange sound emerged from the Beleg. It kind of sounded like the hissing of steam through a smallish opening, though nothing like a whistle. Clerin thought it must have been something like laughter, though she was not sure. She was not sure if she had ever heard a Yaven truly laugh, but she was positive she had never heard a Beleg express that emotion. "Ha! Yes. Revenge. Of course there is that too. No one who has ever been assassinated has not felt the desire for revenge, either before or after death, at least for a moment. But truly, your mission will not be fueled by my desires in this regard. If you are to be my vessel of revenge, you need a cause. I will not mislead you like poor Linchon."

"I do not know if I can be a vessel..." She was interrupted.

"Oh yes you can. You must! You are the only option. You are the only assassin's blade in all the realms, in all of existence. You are unique, Clerin. You, alone of all our creations, are capable of keeping the balance. You have the weapons within you, and I will provide you with more." It paused again, staring at her with those infinitely bright white eyes. "How did poor doomed Taglochprefwaskintruld put it? You realize that you are necessary, do you not?"

She thought long and hard, but really, was just stalling like a frightened or petulant child. She would have to think that one over later. Was she frightened or petulant? In any case, she knew she could not refuse. To do so would mean a horribly painful death, at the least. It would also mean that only two Belegs existed. She could understand how unbalanced that was, even if she did not want to do it. That was it. That was the issue. She just did not want to do it. Period. Nothing in her wanted it, she had not wanted any of the damage she had already done. She had never wanted to kill anything, let alone her, and the entire world's, creators. She had never wanted to damage anything, not even a fly. Well, maybe a fly, but not…

"Do you require further convincing of the unbalanced nature of having only two of four Belegs?"

"No, I understand, I just… I do not want to. I do not want to kill anything. I do not want to be the cause of your death, or of Linchon's, or of anyone's!" She started crying. She did not want to. It surely was not helpful. But it happened anyway. Her right arm twitched a little.

No comforting hug came. No words of condolences. Nothing to soothe her.

"Would you like me to remove the pain?"

"No. I would rather feel pain than be numb." She thought for a moment. "Maybe the physical pain. When you reached into my mind…"

A soothing wave overcame her like being dunked into a cool lake. Her limbs no longer felt the ticklish urge to twitch and her mind felt more clear. She was able to relax a little.

"What other aid may I impart?"

"How? How am I to commune with the other Belegs?"

"Gunzgak will be difficult. Put your focus there. Linchon's message to me states that it will be working on Lembin. Indeed, your earlier statements appear to corroborate that. Besides, Lembin is its own issue, since it is the instigator. For Gunzgak, you will need assistance. There is already a plan in motion by one who sees further than most. You will need to resist nemesis when you feel it coming on. And you will need the help of all your friends. Now is not the time to skimp or shirk. Now is not the time to split up and go home and enjoy your lives. Now is the time for action." Another pause. "Are you ready?"

She was not. She thought about extolling the greatness of Taglo, which she had promised to herself to bring up. She thought about asking more pointed questions, especially about how to commune with Gunzgak. She thought about asking Gorbanax if there was more she could do to assist it, to ease any of its burdens. She thought about asking which ones of her friends were actually necessary. She thought about many things, many questions, but they all boiled down to one thing. Stalling. Which would not please Gorbanax, would not please anyone. She should not stall the inevitable, not when buying time did not provide her with any advantage. She knew that, deep down. So she did not.

"Yes. I am ready."

Gunzgak punched her in the stomach. Its fist penetrated in a burst of fiery agony. It dropped a message, or some messages, or returned some it had previously received while she was passed out, who really knew? The cycle was completed. The fist removed itself. The rumbling around her rapidly gained in intensity.

"You must flee now. Flee to your lover. Only he can save you now. I will hold off the inevitable for as long as I am able, but it will not be long. I will spare as many lives as I am able but cannot spare them all. The dissolution has begun!"

The rumbling was quickly becoming deafening. She turned and swam through the lava, swam with all her might. The molten rock was shimmying and vibrating along with the rumbling, making it difficult to swim. She was near the edge however, still near her entry point, and soon was able to find more firm purchase. She half swam, half climbed, up out of the lava pool. The whole world was shaking. The pool was bubbling. She was beginning to panic.

She ran away from the pool, towards Vrric and Trela, shaking her limbs as she did so in an attempt to slough off all the lava as she ran. The image would have been comical if she had not been so scared.

"We need to escape! Now!" Even as she screamed, she doubted it was audible.

Both Vrric and Trela were running towards her. It was obvious something terrible was about to happen. The rumbling and shaking made running difficult and communication impossible. Trela was waving her arms around and Clerin had absolutely no idea of what she was trying to convey. They all met about halfway between the lava pool and the doors they had entered through.

Vrric cast a spell and they all flew upwards, back to where she had come from, over the bubbling pool of lava. They were flying as fast as she had ever flown before. They were heading up and out of the volcano, directly over the boiling and rumbling lava. Vrric handed her a bundle of her clothes which she merely clung to, not being able to do anything about them at the moment.

She dared not look down, so she kept her face turned to the blue sky. The sound from below was deafening now. The sides of the rock were a blur. She clutched her clothing to her and squinted against the wind. They zipped quickly out of the narrow area and began shooting diagonally at a breakneck pace.

"Head north, over Agoge," Clerin yelled into Vrric's ear. She knew the safest direction was towards the population center. Gorbanax would do everything it could to keep the lava from reaching its Pyrans.

As they were heading there, the deafening rumble exploded into a roar. They were moving quickly enough, and the ash was going upwards while the lava and rock exploded southwards, towards the sea, that they were not caught in the devastation.

Though they were in the air, far from the shaking ground, she still felt like the world was vibrating. She clenched her eyes shut as they flew. She thought she could feel the messages within her trying to break free. She thought she could feel the agony of Gorbanax, hear its scream in her head. The wind whipping by as they flew made it seem like she could not breathe. The pain, agony, and suffocation made her think of bearing the brunt of Gorbanax's… what… wrath? It had not seemed angry, at least not at her, but she had been suffocated mercilessly several times.

Clerin felt like she was falling. She tried to open her eyes, but could not. The rumbling, the vibrations, flowed through her, melding with her pain, in rhythm with her pain. Gorbanax's death scream was not audible so much as it flowed through her with a specific rhythmically vibrating frequency. She *felt* it. That frequency, in harmonious counterpoint to the rhythm of her pain, is what she focused on as she passed out.

It was odd knowing that she was passed out. The sensation was other-worldly. Normally, she would just drop into darkness and wake up later, with zero cognition in between. This was almost like a dream. She briefly wondered if it was the same sensation that Croy got while he was Dreaming, with a capital "D." But then an image of her father floated before her, erasing everything else. In fact, when she would later think back on that moment, she could not recall any background images. It was like she was floating in a gray mist or something, but could not even recall the mist.

"My brave little derling." He used his pet name for her and walked over, grasping her in a big hug.

She held him in return, her cheek pressed against his firm and stolid chest. She did not weep, though she wanted to. Out of fear, frustration, weariness, or the bursting happiness she felt at his sudden presence, she was not sure. After a long moment, she pulled away. About a pace separated them. He was smiling down, surrounded by a soft glow. She knew he was not him, not really her father, not Aillel, but a way for Linchon to communicate with her. That Linchon had killed her father to be able to steal his likeness, his essence. She knew it deep down. But there was a part of her, maybe even the majority, that relished in ignoring the truth and embracing the illusion.

"You have done much that has been required of you, but you have much more to do. Did Gorbanax adequately explain your duties?"

"Gorbanax told me that, through Lembin's messages, I killed you." She used the word "you" to represent both Linchon and her father. She assumed, in a roundabout unconscious and unwilling way, that she had been the cause of her father's demise. "And, it appears, I have just killed Gorbanax as well. I was told that I must now commune with Gunzgak, delivering all the various messages to it, assumedly killing it as well. Then, lastly, I must return to Lembin and commune with it, assuming the same outcome." She sighed a little at the burden of it all, at the undesirability of it all. "Please understand that I did not want this, do not want this. Any of it."

"I apologize, but your desires mean absolutely nothing. Not just to us, the Belegs, but to everything. Your desires mean absolutely nothing to everything." It was the only statement that had steel behind it. It was still her father's voice, his stern "you've been being bad" voice, but Clerin felt something else behind it. During that statement she felt Linchon, and the illusion wavered slightly. "We understand that you did not choose this role, that Lembin chose for you, but you have no way of understanding what is really going on. You, and all derlians, were made inadequate for full comprehension. I do not mean that cruelly, if anything it is a failing on our part, but it is a statement of fact." Her father's voice softened and became fully his own again. "The word 'killed' has derlian connotations inexorably tied with it. What is happening to us is somewhat different, though explaining that would take a lifetime, so I will not do that here. There is not another derlian word that is closer to defining what is happening, but if it makes you feel any better, you are not quite, and not quite directly responsible for, 'killing' us." He had a warm smile on his face as he said that.

"You are correct that what is happening to me is now happening to Gorbanax and must, *MUST*, happen to Gunzgak and Lembin as well." He pushed his forefinger down in the air emphatically at the second "must" and his voice was stern, but it immediately softened again.

"How do I commune with either of them?"

"I believe Lembin is willing to accept my, and Gorbanax's, messages. We have communed in the Temple of Water and Lembin's desires have been explained, though not fully understood. Gunzgak will be difficult. Gorbanax would know more about that than I, for it has been planning while I have been 'dying.'" Her father used air-quotes with his fingers as he spoke the word. "Were you given any instructions concerning that?"

"What? No. I was told it would be difficult and that I had to gather everyone who helped destroy the Cabal of Lochom to be able to... commune with Gunzgak." She was a little unsure of how to put what she was to do. She did not want to use the word "kill," but was now tainting the word "commune."

"Hmm. Maybe the planning was not going well. I would state that Gunzgak must be tricked before it can be trapped. I will try to commune with Gorbanax but am not sure if that is possible. It is certainly not possible at this moment. Also understand that Gunzgak is now fully aware of what is happening, though it may have been so previously. The news of Gorbanax's 'death' is being flung to the corners of the realms through the volcanic eruption. There will be no surprising Gunzgak."

Clerin racked her brain trying to think of another question concerning the quest but was stymied since Linchon did not appear to know anything else. All she could really do was ask for open-ended advice, which just seemed like an excuse to drag the conversation out longer. Her thought process, however, was interrupted.

"I must be leaving, and you must return to the world."

She did not know what else to say, so she moved and grabbed another tight hug. Her father returned the hug and they stood there silently together for a long moment. It felt so incredibly real and true. Then she peeled back.

"Thank you. I love you. I will not fail."

"I know."

✳✳✳

Clerin awoke slowly. She felt the hard ground under her back, tempered by a thick cloth of some kind. She opened her eyes and blinked once, twice. The sky was dark with black clouds, blotting out the sun. She raised her head and looked over to the source of the clouds. The volcano, off in the distance, was between eruptions but the smoke and ash still appeared to funnel down towards the rocky top. Another Beleg was "dying." She closed her eyes and set her head back down on the cushioning cloth. She was tired and wanted some more rest. At least someone had grabbed the clothes she had been clutching when she had passed out.

Chapter 9

The escape was harrowing. The running, the flying, the deafening explosion of the volcano. Vrric was happy to be on the ground, away from Agoge, though they were only a couple of leagues away. Still close enough to hear the occasional group scream between the rumblings. The screams were barely audible and oddly eerie. The lava all flowed south, off the plateau and into the ocean, sparing the town. So the screams were not of pain, but of fear and confusion. Though there was a slow but consistent wind blowing towards the ocean that shifted the ash, it struggled against the monstrous clouds that continued to belch out of the volcano arrhythmically, keeping the sky somewhat dark and ominous.

Clerin was lying and resting while Trela paced furiously back and forth. She was far enough away to not disturb Clerin, but just barely. They would need to fly again soon. There was no way Trela would tolerate being away from Agoge for much longer. The entire city was in a panicked crisis if the eerie screams were any indication.

So Vrric decided to meditate and ground himself. To prepare himself for more spell casting. A type of forced rest and recuperation. The flight would probably be less draining than escaping the eruption, Vrric had never flown so fast in his life, but he could tell it was going to be a long day of spell casting. He needed to build up his endurance.

Vrric closed his eyes and breathed in through his nose, slowly and deeply. He blocked out the quiet but insistent sound of Trela's footsteps. His spine straightened as he inflated his chest. As he breathed in, he brought energy up from the ground. He held it in his chest for a moment as he paused. Then he exhaled slowly through mostly loose lips, letting the energy waft away from him. It branched out and floated down, like a weeping tree to be soaked up by the ground. Then pulled up by Vrric through his next inhale. It was a circular energy draw that, once repeated enough times, equalized his own energy levels. In his own opinion, it also moderated the small area he meditated in, like a spoon stirring a hot beverage.

He meditated for a while, enjoying the feeling of the energy flow, enjoying the conscious breathing. Clerin kept resting and Trela kept pacing, albeit at a slower, calmer tempo. He had decided to let Clerin dictate their timing. Unless, of course, Trela's patience gave out. He kept them both to the back of his mind while he breathed.

Clerin stirred a couple of times. Trela would pause her pacing and look over, but would let Clerin drop her head back down and close her eyes. Repeatedly. Vrric would watch through the tiny slits he let his eyes open to, attempting to keep his focus on his meditation. It was he who finally lost patience.

He quietly stood and walked over to Clerin and cast another healing spell. "Narliderto!" Once they got back to the Blaze, he would let her rest for the whole day, for a week if need be. His spell had the desired effects. Clerin sat up, somewhat bleary eyed, and Trela stopped her pacing. She flashed him a pained but grateful smile. He had cast a higher level than he probably needed to, but he wanted to make sure Clerin felt well enough to travel.

They flew the relatively short distance back to Agoge in one swoop. Trela wanted them to head straight for the castle proper, directly to the throne room in essence. She was ready to lead.

"So, just to make sure, Gorbanax is dead, correct?" Trela was facing Clerin as they flew along.

"Well, dying, but yes. It is irreversible, but I am unsure of how long it takes."

"Do you think I could commune with Gorbanax in the future? Could you?"

"No. Maybe. I think it would depend on how far into the future you are talking about."

"Okay. We will speak of the nuances at a later date. I just have to be sure of what I'm going to tell my subjects. And, you know…" She waved her hand at the truncated volcano still billowing and sputtering.

They arrived and alighted on a balcony. Trela had advisors and Guards waiting for her, visible through the window openings. She stopped Vrric before he left.

"Get her to somewhere out of the way. Maybe to Gyllhelon's old room. Somewhere she won't immediately be found, just in case there are those who assume she is the cause of what is happening. And get her a guard, someone like Malghain. Then come back to me. I will need your services." Trela glanced at the crowd inside and then back at him.

"And maybe someone like Serghno to guard her?" He smiled weakly at her.

"No. Sorry. I need all the mages I can muster." Her eyes were matter-of-fact. There would be no negotiating.

"I will be fine. I am feeling much better now anyway. I could even help here if…" Clerin was interrupted.

"No, not now. You just need to be invisible, out of everyone's minds." Trela glanced from Clerin to Vrric. "Not that she's in any danger but… just go." She glanced furtively through the open windows again.

Rather than argue, Vrric flew them off the balcony. He went straight up, the quickest way out of everyone's sight. Then he veered off to Gyllhelon's old quarters. He was not sure if that was the best idea. He understood that it was probably empty and would not be checked, but Clerin seemed like she was still shaken by Gyllhelon's death. Plus, what he really wanted was a mage to help guard her. He knew he was a little biased, but what would happen if someone like the Blind One blinked in and attacked her? Of course, the Blind One had abducted Croy right from under Vrric's own nose. So maybe having someone like Malghain was more effective than having a mage for a protector. In any case, Trela was obviously going to require every available mage to be with her.

"I doubt I am in any danger but, if I were, I would be much safer by Trela's side than hidden away somewhere. Running away just makes me look guilty." Clerin's face looked a little worried, whereas her voice just sounded annoyed.

"I think she is just trying to narrow any possibilities of distractions. She wants every mage out there trying to ascertain the amount of damage and to quickly repair anything important. I don't think she's overly concerned about a concerted attack on you, but more that she doesn't want to waste the hours to explain what happened to everyone's satisfaction. Some derlians, even in the best of times, argue for the sake of it rather than for any real confusion. Just as a way of inserting themselves as a distraction. I can see how, in her mind, this is for the best." He found himself nodding to himself.

"You know, you could just agree with me sometimes. Maybe just validate my concerns and move on." Her face was smiling, but something in the undercurrent of her voice sounded annoyed.

Vrric's mind raced for a moment. If he said something agreeable right away, would that be seen as pandering? She was sure to be annoyed if he tried to change the subject, however. That would be willfully ignoring her. And the silence that happened instead, as his mind circled uselessly? That seemed to be the worst of all the options.

"You certainly have a right to be concerned about how Agoge will view you once the dust has settled. There will be many who will gleefully blame the foreigner. And, you know, all signs do point to cause and effect. But letting them realize that the city has been spared the worst of it, that their daily lives are, in the long run, little affected by the eruption. Letting that sink in before thrusting yourself in front of them, even in a genuine interest to be helpful, might actually work to your advantage." Now he was nodding to her.

"Well, not exactly what I had in mind, but that was a good effort." Her face and her voice seemed relaxed and, if not overjoyed, at least contented. At least they matched up.

It did not take too much time before they arrived at Gyllhelon's old quarters. They gently wafted down into the small courtyard. The Luften warriors had been situated together. All the quarters appeared empty, however. Escha and Torpalin were in Ariellyna, of course. Clerin tried to open Gyllhelon's door, but it was locked tight.

Vrric went over to Malghain's closed door, hoping he was home. It would have resolved several issues at once but, unfortunately, no one answered. Vrric placed his ear to the door, knocking again, straining to hear anything from the interior but… nothing. He turned around to see Clerin knocking loudly on Haswyxe's door.

"I hate to point out any flaws in Trela's plans, but this one appears not to be fully thought out." Clerin laughed a little mirthlessly.

"Do you want to wait, or break in?" They both smiled.

"We can wait for a bit… and maybe find Jalin before breaking in." She squinted at the entrance area. "There does not seem to be an easy way in… You cannot pick a lock with magic?"

"Well, given enough time, probably. I've just never learned the intricacies of the inner workings of a lock, what's behind the iron shroud. Typically, if I'm in a hurry, I'll just ruin the lock." He felt a little sheepish about it, but there was usually a spy around to take care of things like that.

Clerin squatted down to peer into the lock of the front door. "Maybe we should just get Jalin. She is not too far from here, if I recall correctly."

Just then Malghain and Haswyxe came around the corner. The were chuckling amongst themselves, talking quietly, heads mostly pointed down. But right as they came into view, Malghain's head snapped up and he stared into Vrric for the briefest moment.

"Ah, just the derlians we were looking for." His face quickly relaxed into a grin.

"You were looking for us? We were looking for you." Clerin grinned back.

"We were with Serghno and Arnasta when they got called away. Trela has need of mages, not warriors. Or she has enough Pyran warriors or something." Haswyxe bobbed his head slightly. "The volcano has everyone in a tizzy even though, as far as I can tell, the only thing to rain on Agoge is a little ash."

"We hear you are the cause." Malghain stared into Clerin briefly.

"We are trying to keep the truth under wraps," Vrric broke in.

"Ha! Well, we certainly did not hear that from Trela. No. That is just the rumor." Malghain started walking towards his door. "And around here, rumors spread faster than the shaking ground."

"Yes, we were told to keep an eye on you, just in case." Haswyxe stayed standing where he was. "And you, oh great mage, are required back with the Queen. Us riffraff will keep ourselves out of the way."

"Do you have a key to…?" Clerin paused and poked her thumb back at Gyllhelon's door, rather than speak her name aloud.

Malghain unlocked his own door before turning his head back over to her. "No. But we know where Jalin lives, if it comes to that. You can stay over here for as long as you like if you'd rather not go over there." He shook his own thumb at Gyllhelon's.

Clerin smiled a little sheepishly, her eyes glancing around. Her delicate fingers were held lightly in front of her, motionless. But Vrric could feel her urge to fidget emanate from her. He walked over to her and lightly took her hands in his.

"You can *whisper* to me anytime you like. I may not be able to respond right away but will try to follow up as soon as I become available." He smiled warmly at her, but her eyes were downcast.

"I doubt I will want to bother you."

He almost argued with her but thought of something better. "I tell you what. I'll *whisper* to you just after the sun sets, before dusk ends. Then we can at least talk later and you won't be bothering me."

"Do not worry about it if you are busy." She looked up at the ash and dark clouds. The sky was still rumbling. Or maybe it was the ground. "You had better hurry. You should not keep the Queen waiting."

They both laughed a little. He held her face in his hands and kissed her tenderly. Then he stood back and remembered they were not alone. Malghain had entered his quarters slightly, somewhat hidden in the shadow of the door, while Haswyxe seemed intensely interested by something far off in an opposite direction.

"Keep her safe." He did not say it to either of them in particular, but to both of them in general. "Mekkinderpri!" He flew straight up before attempting to get his bearings. The sky was still incredibly ominous, forcing him to stay a little lower than he instinctually desired.

Vrric zipped along, just above the taller roofs. There were many derlians below, running in various directions. There were also many purple-cloaked Guards attempting to direct the flow and keep the panic to a minimum. Whoever Trela had placed in charge while she was away had been quick to respond. It was probably Lishean, but it may have been someone of lower rank since she was only supposed to have been gone less than a day.

He quickly arrived at the balcony. The room beyond the windows was full of animated derlians. He could hear in their muffled voices the tone of argument, even if he could not hear their words. He took a deep breath before opening the door.

"Gorbanax is dead!"

"Murdered!"

"Murdered by that Fluen!"

Then accusing eyes stared at him. It was as if they had been planning on his entrance at that moment. Sure, some of the snippets he had heard as he entered had been about the panic of the citizenry, what to do about the various small fires that had erupted, discussions about how best to deploy the Guards. But those were quiet conversations between friendly members of Trela's larger council and were drowned out by the angry accusers.

"Linloy! Seriously, keep control of your faction. This is not a theater." Trela's angry voice cut through all the others. It was as if a wet blanket had been tossed over the room and everyone quieted down within.

A thin, emaciated-looking Pyran with long brown hair stared hard back at her. He was surrounded by about five or six others that were definitely within his orbit. They all stared back at Trela as well, though their gazes were less intense. One even glanced down at her own feet as Trela focused upon her.

"No, this is not theater. This is the consequence of inviting vipers into our midst." Linloy's voice sounded a bit high and haughty, even though he was trying to make it into a low growl.

"I have asked Feyazki to join with us because he is a great mage. Are there any from the guild who would disagree?" The silence continued. "We are facing a crisis here and we need as much power and intelligence as we can muster. We must work together and attacking invited guests as they enter will not help at all."

"We are merely expressing displeasure at the company he keeps. At the cause of this crisis. We had not questioned his own capabilities which are, by all accounts, ample." The smile on Linloy's face was self-assured and smug. It made Vrric want to slap it.

"The cause of this crisis, as you call it, is greater than one Fluen. If you think Clerin desired this, or even more laughable, if you think that she caused this, then you are even more dense than you look. This is something that is way beyond one derlian, any derlian, all derlians, all Yavens. This is amongst the Belegs and only they may toss around blame. Only they understand causality. You, oh trusted advisor, know nothing." Vrric knew he should stay out of it, that Trela was dealing with her subjects in the way she felt best, but he could not help himself.

"So you are saying that the volcano just erupted by itself? If your Clerin was not there today, earlier, just before the explosion, that we would still be under a darkened sky of ash? You say that I am too dense to understand causality, but I know the sequence of events, and that is evidence enough for me." There was a chorus of approval from his adjacent cronies. "Maybe your understanding of evidence transcends mine, but…"

"Enough! Both of you!" Trela started to wade into the crowd of advisors, but they soon parted to leave her an ample path. "This is exactly the juvenile behavior I was hoping to avoid."

"But…" Linloy was looking to say more, to get one more barb in, or that was how it appeared to Vrric. He, on the other hand, had known Trela long enough to realize when it was best to just be quiet and take your talking to. It was typically over much quicker and easier that way. Trela could understand a mistake in the heat of an argument, even a stupid one, but she could not abide being defied.

"No." Trela raised her hand as she neared Linloy. "There is nothing you can say anymore. Nothing that will make this situation better." She looked around for a moment. "Hunvarb!" The name reverberated in the odd silence of the crowded room.

"My Queen." A short Pyran with long brown hair and chubby cheeks slid through the crowd as if it were water. "How may I be of service?"

"Linloy. You and all those under you are now taking orders from Hunvarb here." Linloy's face darkened as Trela spoke to him, but he did not respond. Trela then turned to Hunvarb. "Take yours and Linloy's and five Guards and head down to the grand market square. Gather any and all stragglers with you along the way, citizen or warrior. Make it a march, make it serious. I want others to leave their homes to join you, even if just for the curiosity of it. Then, when you reach the square, find Lishean. He should be easy to spot. Tell him to have Serghno *whisper* to Feyazki here for further instructions." She nodded to herself for a moment. "Understand?"

"Of course." Hunvarb nodded to Trela.

Linloy looked about to speak, but Trela raised her hand. "You follow her today. That is all. There will be no discussion." Before his facial expression changed, she turned on Vrric. "And you! You are supposed to be diligent and capable and not get sucked into these little squabbles. We have much to do." She grabbed his arm and started to lead him away. "All mages follow me!"

They left the main throne room and headed towards a second room. Various others left the crowd and fell in behind them. By the time they had entered the smaller chamber, they had quite a following. Many of whom Vrric did not recognize, though there were some familiar faces as well. Ryshial gave him a warm smile as he braced himself for Trela's barrage. But it did not come.

"I expected that from Linloy, Feyazki. He has been a thorn in my side for some time. But you have always been an ally. I'm a little disappointed that you took his bait." She gave him a pained look before stepping back to take in the entire crowd.

Honestly, he would have preferred being yelled at. He had all sorts of excuses in his head and would have enjoyed listing them out. He felt he had several that would have garnered some commiseration, but it was not to be. Trela was already done chastising him and was ready to move on. He was sure she felt she had let him off easy, but he felt that giving her the last word on the matter was part of his punishment.

"I *need* you. I need all of you. I may need the other mages that are currently with Lishean as well. This is a crisis of confidence. Yes, Gorbanax is dying, for lack of any better understanding. But Gorbanax made sure that the vast majority of the Pyrans remained unharmed, that Agoge itself remained unharmed. As far as I understand, the only deaths directly due to the volcano were the Guards stationed there. We are at the beginning of this, more tragedy may be on the horizon. We have certainly not checked the entire city for damage yet. However, I truly believe that many more Pyrans will be hurt, or worse, if panic is allowed to spread. If we can get the citizens to stay calm and carry on with their lives, we can avoid the bulk of that potential harm. And what keeps Pyrans calm?" She paused and glanced about the room, but carried on with her speech before anyone could attempt a guess.

"Perception. Perception breeds confidence. And that cloud—that giant black billowing cloud that hangs over our city—is forcing the perception of oppression upon us. The perception of danger, of calamity. That cloud must be removed before we can begin to repair any damage from the shaking ground. It must be removed before we can even assess the damage. And, for that, I will need all your help." She paused and looked around again.

"The cloud is still billowing out." A young mage that Vrric did not recognize spoke up.

"But, amazingly enough, there is already a breeze blowing out towards the ocean." Ryshial brought up what Vrric was thinking. He was glad she mentioned it since he did not want to bring anything up. It seemed like everything had a chance of being contentious.

"We are grateful for that stroke of luck, if that's what it is. It has not removed the cloud, however. And, as Invules has mentioned, the smoke continues to escape." Trela glanced around again, making sure no one had anything to interject. "We need to figure a way to assist the current breeze. We need to figure a way to stop more smoke from billowing out. We need to stop the tremors. We need to calm the citizens. And then we can assess the actual damage. Then we can begin the repairs."

"Give me Feyazki, Adzin, and Invules. We will find a way, my Queen." Ryshial looked very serious. *She must have thought of something,* thought Vrric.

"No." Trela stared straight at Ryshial with a strange intensity.

"Excuse me?" Ryshial's almond shaped eyes flashed with an intensity of their own.

"Take them all." Trela swept her hand around the room. "Solve it and return."

Ryshial nodded, and Trela left the small room. The commotion from the main throne room filtered in while the door was open, but softened once the door was closed.

"Why did you want so few?" Adzin spoke up. Vrric had met him before, but they were certainly not close. He was one of the masters at the Mage's Guild. Ryshial was the only master who had joined the hunt for the Cabal, so Vrric did not really know the rest of them. He knew the other masters only by reputation, an ersatz knowledge at best.

"I had thought we could just use an illusion. Invules would fly us into place and the three of us would create a 'mirror' of sorts." Ryshial made air-quotes with her fingers. "I figured if we could just make the smoke in the southern sky look like the bright blue of the northern, then the perception of safety would be there. And, since we are actually safe, the illusion would be more real than reality." The corner of her mouth smiled at her own little quip.

"And what about the very real smoke?" Another young mage Vrric did not recognize spoke up.

"That will eventually dissipate, will it not?"

"What if it doesn't?"

"What about the tremors?"

"What if the smoke billows wider than the mirror?"

"Or taller? How high is the smoke now?"

"We are wasting time. Let Ryshial try to make a mirror. Let some others beckon more wind. Let others attend to the tremors. Trela is correct—there are many of us here, we should be able to solve it. We have some of the greatest mages from the Pyran realm at our disposal, anything should be possible. At least until the smoke eases on its own." Adzin glanced over to Vrric. "And we have a Luften as well."

They all began nodding. As they decided who should spend their energies on flying the rest out there, as they decided who should be in which contingent, Vrric felt something. He felt an urge.

"I would like to be with the wind."

"Well, you are Luften, are you not?"

They flew out in waves, in different directions. Vrric was with three others, none of them masters. They had two focused on flying, to take turns keeping everyone aloft. Those were the younger mages, less skilled but strong and capable. The fourth mage was called Tritilan. She was older, or at least older than Vrric, and taught at the guild. Even though she was not considered a master, she was as close to one as could be. Vrric wondered if it was politics that kept her back, or if there was something she was lacking. Sometimes it was not even a skill or power that was lacking, but something as simple as ambition. She had shortish brown hair cut to flair a little at the shoulders and large brown eyes. She was apparently well-versed in air magic.

As they gained in altitude, Vrric marveled at the immensity of the problem. The cloud was wide, tall, black as pitch, and still billowing forth. The cloud was not over Agoge itself, per se, but was a gigantic backdrop to the entire city. If one of Trela's subjects were to look to the north, or even straight up, they might not see smoke directly over them, but there was no way the dark and ominous cloud could be missed. Ryshial and her team had their work cut out for them.

Vrric gauged the current breeze. It was not insignificant. And it seemed to increase in power and intensity the higher up they got. It seemed, as Vrric had hoped, that there were already forces at work.

Vrric's job, and Tritilan's, was to keep up the good fortune, not let it flag, and hopefully increase it. It was a cooperative quest. The sooner they could get rid of the smoke, the sooner everyone's job would successfully end.

They had stopped moving while he had been thinking. "Go ahead and get closer, maybe half our distance from the cloud, and get a little higher, maybe twenty rods or so." He realized that all of them, Tritilan included, would just wait for orders if he seemed preoccupied.

"Do you do better with pushing or pulling air?" He turned to Tritilan. They were all in a standing position, as if they were in a courtyard down on the ground, milling about on the grass and socializing.

"Pulling. Definitely."

"Hmm. Me too." He paused for a moment while thinking. "How about this? Do you feel better gathering wind around you, or would you rather call enticingly from a ways away?"

"That is a little more up in the air, so to speak." They all laughed politely at her little joke. "I would like to try to gather the wind from far away."

"Okay." That would have been his preference as well, but he was comfortable either way. Besides, they would probably be out there for hours. They could certainly switch back and forth.

They were still slowly floating to their staging location. Vrric was thinking of how best to pull wind in from a near source. He wanted a wide swath of intake so that he could keep his outflow as tall as possible. The blackest smoke was low, nearest to the volcano itself, closest to the source and before any dispersion affected it. He was tempted to aim down there and let the illusion hide the upper portions until the existing wind could push that out over the ocean. Before deciding where to aim, he decided to sense what was already going on, to sense the existing motion of the air.

"Nukinlufclo!" He set up a large but thin veil diaphragm of air and let the existing wind push upon it. He stood there with his eyes closed, attempting to block out everything but the sensation of the diaphragm. He raised and lowered it, shifting it from side to side, deciding where the greatest thrust was coming from.

"Ah, sensing the wind. Interesting. And where is it coming from? Or would it be better to ask where it is going?" Tritilan waited until he opened his eyes before speaking.

"It is fairly strong and broad, and heading towards the ocean. I think it is running at a high enough elevation that we could focus our efforts down near the top of the volcano. Of course, wind being the ficklest element, who knows if it will stay steady." He was staring at the mouth of the volcano. It was amazing how much smoke kept billowing out.

"You know, there are some who would argue that fire is more fickle than wind." She had an eyebrow raised as he turned around.

"I can understand the argument, but I'm not sure I agree with it."

"Then you've never seen a brush fire spread across a valley."

"And what is pushing that fire hither and yon? The wind, yes?"

They both laughed for a moment. The two very capable apprentices stayed silent. He tried to think of something to say to bring them into the conversation, but they were both staring hard into the distance. It was almost as if they were doing their best to ignore Vrric and Tritilan. Maybe they were concentrating heavily or conserving their energy. They all finally slowed to a stop.

"Maybe a little lower. I think we are going to aim for the top of the volcano. Well, a little above the volcano." One of the apprentices, the one not currently flying them, nodded. *They must be trying to concentrate*, thought Vrric. "Perfect. Great. Just hold us steady here."

"You want me to start from far away?" She was turned away from the volcano, staring into the distance. To where her wind would be coming from, he supposed.

"Yes. Go out as far as you can, and I'll bring what I can from around here." He looked around his own area for a moment. His eye was caught briefly at the view of Agoge from their height, but he quickly forced his mind back to the task at hand.

Vrric closed his eyes and spread his arms wide, facing towards the volcano, standing up on air. He breathed in through his nose slowly, deliberately. He filled his chest, letting it slowly inflate. He held it at the apex. He let his mind slowly expanded to encompass the lower area behind him and to each side. "Eqekinlufclo!"

He wanted to be able to cast many spells throughout the day, so he was pacing himself, not casting too high of a level. But he also wanted to cast fewer spells that lasted longer, so he did not want to cast too low of a level. Like dragging a large stone over wetted wood skids, the first push was the hardest—once the stone got moving, it was much easier to keep it moving. Such was the way with wind.

After the spell, he let his breath out slowly through his mouth. His lips were slightly pursed to increase the pressure, to increase the energy behind it. He pushed as much air out as he was able, his diaphragm collapsing into a tight band.

He breathed that way for a while, in through his nose, out through his mouth. His arms stayed outstretched, his spine as straight as an iron rod. He wanted to pull from the nearby air, from each side and inwards to funnel together with him as a focal point. Then it shot towards the volcano, towards the billowing smoke, pushing it out over the ocean.

Not that it was pushing much at the moment. Even with his eyes closed, Vrric knew that nothing was happening. It was just beginning. The pulling, the drawing, the pushing. The stone had not even shifted on the skids yet. It was a distance race, one of endurance not of speed. The pace was beginning slowly.

He breathed that way for some while before he started to bring his arms in. He would swivel them in, making the world's slowest clap, during his exhale. Then, as he breathed in again, he would open them back up. They were a symbolic bellows, but they were a bellows nonetheless.

He breathed for a while as the wind began to pick up. It was slow, but steady. It still was not pushing the smoke much, but it was strong enough to be felt through his hair, against his skin. He sensed that issue was not the level of the spell being cast, but of the volume of air being moved. He cast another spell, adding some more pressure, some more energy. "Eqekinlufclo!"

The wind became more obvious. He could feel it flow around him. He decided to wait a while before opening his eyes. He was hoping to see some visible change to the billowing smoke. So he stood, breathed, moved his arms, and kept a constant pressure of magic drawing the air to him, then past him.

He was close to opening his eyes when it happened. He had felt that enough time had passed, probably a half hour, to see what minor affects his spell was having on the massive plume of smoke. A huge rush of air buffeted him. It ripped at his clothing and tussled his hair.

He opened his eyes. He did check to see how his wind was affecting the billowing smoke first. It had not made much of a change, though it was slightly bent towards the ocean. Very quickly he turned and shifted his gaze to the magician behind him.

Tritilan was seated on the air, legs crossed. She had a serene look on her face and her eyes were closed. She was not breathing heavily or moving her arms. She was completely ignoring her hair flowing all about her. She seemed oblivious to her surroundings. Well, that was probably not the right word. She seemed so intent on what she was doing that her immediate environment did not seem to affect her. Maybe intent was not the correct word either—she looked so calm and relaxed. It had taken her nearly a half hour to summon the wind, which was not a short amount of time, but her results were hard to argue with. He wanted to give her words of encouragement but did not want to disturb her spell casting.

They continued for about another half hour. The smoke was still there but was bending noticeably towards the ocean. Vrric's eyes followed the column up, and it was bending even more than the lower portion. He marveled that the natural wind up there was doing such an excellent job of shifting the smoke. *Maybe that's why it's harder to get the wind down here,* he thought. It was all working out together, however, so it was impossible to complain.

"Would you like to switch?" Tritilan's voice broke through Vrric's thoughts.

"Sure."

"I was getting the best results calling to the northeast, at almost the edge of the plateau."

"Did you try any higher?" He pointed up to where the natural wind was flowing.

"No, no. I was a little worried about off-balancing anything." She smiled a bit and downcast her eyes, but they popped back up to meet his almost immediately.

"Well, I was just pulling from the north. Both east and west, just kind of a triangular shape."

She nodded and turned and stayed standing. He decided to sit with his back to the volcano as she had been doing. He closed his eyes and breathed for a while before switching his spell. He took the energy left over from the previous one to make the newer one easier, rather than trying to leave the other one going. "Eqekinlufclo!"

He cast his mind far to the northeast, as was suggested. He called and pulled, trying to keep the existing system going, rather than trying to create a new one. He felt it was somewhat seamless, though it was difficult to tell at that point. Once he got it going, however, he decided to shift his focus a little and began to investigate the natural upper wind currents. He did not want to modify anything, just do some simple investigation.

His mind wafted upwards. He paused it when it got to the upper stream pushing towards the ocean. He observed. He felt. He investigated. It was the most… natural… thing to him. He sensed no chaos around it, no magic. But it was more than just the absence of derlian meddling. It felt *right*, it felt *normal*, it felt *effortlessly true*. It felt natural—that was the best way he could describe it.

And then he felt touched by something. There was something there with him, something in the wind. It, too, felt natural. It, too, belonged. And then it spoke to him.

"It is pleasing that you are here. Now." The words were words, but they held no voice. They were dropped into his mind, rather than spoken.

Who are you? Vrric thought to himself.

"I am Linchon, or something less than Linchon. Or, maybe, in the right light and at the right angle, I am something more than Linchon." There was a small pause before more words came. "We have met once before. You and the Gaen Dreamer tried to enter my temple. To show the way for… What do we call her, do you think? One being's assassin is another's lover. Gorbanax called her the Communicator. Ha! That rings a little too benign for what she does, for either of us." There was an image before his closed eyes of an older Luften in white robes. His mind immediately went to Clerin's stories of communicating with Linchon.

And what do I call you? Linchon, or Aillel? Vrric thought it almost accidentally. It was more a question that vexed him, not one that he actually needed answered.

"I killed Aillel and took his memories. There is nothing of him left, no vestige. When I commune with… her… it is I who am speaking. If she thinks there is some of her father there to communicate with, well… is it my right to squash that hope? Is it yours? You are a holder of the truth here, now, are you going to tell her? That is always the big derlian question, isn't it? Is it better to tell a hurtful truth than a salving lie? I know my answer. I wonder what yours is?"

Vrric tried to pay attention to each word that was dropped into his head, to not let his mind wander, even during the pauses. He wondered if Linchon could hear his wandering thoughts with the same clarity as when he tried to think of something in specific. *We should call her Clerin,* he specifically thought.

"Do you not think it strange that derlians are named before their essence is known? Say what you will about the moniker Communicator, but at least it conveys something about her. What does Clerin convey?"

The name is the essence, it is like summoning a Yaven. It is just that the name is not defined until the essence takes form.

"So be it, we shall refer to her as Clerin. Even though you have taken my assassin as your lover, we are trying to accomplish the same goals and I would like to say that I would have enjoyed communing with you under different circumstances. You wish the safety and wellbeing of the Pyrans down below. So does Gorbanax; so do I. You wish Clerin to commune with Gunzgak and, finally, with Lembin again. So do I. You wish the derlian realm to be ruled by derlians. You may not believe it, but so do I. I was perfectly content to commune with a derlian once a generation. Once every other generation. I was perfectly content to ignore my derlian Luftens until the need was so dire that I was sought out. I, out of all the other Belegs, was content to be on the verge of where I am now heading. Maybe that was why I was chosen first, I do not know. It was a mistake on Lembin's part in any case. Lembin should have started with Gunzgak. It will be difficult to get Clerin to Gunzgak, you understand."

Where are you heading?

"I am dispersing. I am diluting into the world. How do you think I am able to come to the aid of Gorbanax on such a momentous occasion? Clerin will think that I came within her, since that is how it appears that I commune with her. Or maybe she will think that I was with Gorbanax. I came here because I was needed, I was asked for. I came here by dispersing here. She is incorrect on the whole. So, maybe, she can be thought of as correct in part. I am unsure if this matters. What matters is that you asked the wrong question. I asked you if you understood."

Vrric's mind raced back to what had been discussing previously. *The difficulty of getting Clerin to commune with Gunzgak?*

"Correct. You will need three things. You will need a name. You will need a trick. You will need an ally."

Please explain.

"No."

You want me to figure it out or it is impossible to explain?

"Yes."

Vrric racked his brain. He could probably figure out what was meant by the first and last things. *What is the trick? Or, at least, what is the nature of the trick?*

"A trick is a way to obfuscate intent. How does a derlian hide intent from a Beleg?"

By lying?

"Ha! You are barely trying. Think! How can a being of Chaos stay hidden from a being of Law that became, and then created, Chaos?"

By hiding the Chaos within Law? It was just a guess, almost a fleeting thought.

"Exactly!"

But how could that be possible?

"This, I do not know. I can only wish you the best of… luck? Inspiration? The diverse skill sets of all the derlians at your disposal working on the same problem? This word I would like to use does not exist for you, it is not within the derlian language. But I wish you much of it. And now I must concentrate on other things. I give you the wind stream at my disposal. Aim it where you will."

That was it. Vrric tried to think of other words and sentences. Tried to make them intriguing enough to elicit a response. But Linchon was no longer there, or no longer listening. It was certainly no longer responding. So Vrric did the only thing left for him to do. He diverted the natural wind stream such that it melded with the others, pushing the smoke towards the ocean, just over the mouth of the volcano.

It was amazing. It seemed to be more than just adding the streams together. It multiplied them. The wind moved with velocity and pressure, and all at a great volume. Smoke was still billowing out, but it was being fully diverted. The remaining smoke, that which was above the new stream, began to slowly disperse. To dilute.

Vrric wondered about how the other mages were doing. The grand illusion and getting the ground shaking under control. He was not overly spent, they had only cast so many spells, but he felt drained nonetheless. He lay down on his back, floating above Agoge, and closed his eyes again.

Tritilan oversaw the wind stream for about half an hour as he rested. Then he oversaw it. She had cast a spell to make sure everything continued seamlessly. When he took over, he did not cast anything. He kept a watchful eye on the wind, but it never flagged, wavered, or shifted. They both watched for a little while after that, but it seemed that it was flowing on its own.

Vrric explained his conversation with Linchon to Tritilan, though he did leave out many of the details. There was concern about trusting that the wind would flow perfectly for as long as the smoke billowed out of the volcano. The two apprentices even entered the conversation. It was Vrric's opinion that they did not need to worry about the wind, but he did not press his case. He understood the concern and, truly, it was better to be safe and sure. So they all took turns casting the flying spells and keeping an eye on the wind until nightfall. They did not need to summon any more wind.

They returned to the Blaze at nightfall. It was a simple flight back, especially since they were, on the whole, fairly well rested. They landed on the balcony and quickly entered the throne room. There were a lot of derlians there, though it was less packed than previously.

No one yelled at Vrric as he walked in. They were some of the last to arrive. Everyone seemed serious and thoughtful. A little tired from the day of exertion, but nothing too stressful. It was Ryshial's team that had the most difficult go of it. The illusion was not as effective as she had hoped.

"Friends, warriors, mages, everyone. We have accomplished much today, though it could be summed up in one sentence: We calmed the populace. My Pyrans' lives are, well maybe not back to normal, but back to being focused on their lives. Tonight will be a difficult one for sleep, I am sure. Tomorrow will bring more clarity about the mood, probably sour, to say the least. But today we have stopped a panic. A potentially dangerous and violent panic. And each of you assisted in that triumph in some way. We have accomplished this by working together instead of bickering amongst ourselves." Trela paused and looked over the room before continuing. "It is easy fall into patterns of argument and blame. It is easy to grumble and complain. What is difficult is to come together, make a plan of consensus, and act upon it. And what is most difficult, is when you can get the plan to work. You have all done that with your immense efforts. Thank you."

It was a classic Trela speech. Vrric smiled to himself as he half-listened. The only thing that would have made the moment better was if Clerin was with him to enjoy it.

When he returned to Gyllhelon's old quarters, Clerin was nowhere to be found. The door was still locked tight, as were Malghain's and Haswyxe's. He banged on the various doors a couple of times. Then he remembered he was supposed to *whisper* to Clerin at dusk. He hoped he would not be considered too late.

"Narfintotsfe! Clerin… Clerin… Clerin…" He repeated her name slowly, not overly insistently, until she answered. In truth, it did not take very long.

"We are at Jalin's, you should come over." She sounded like she had drunk a little grog. He headed straight over there.

Clerin and Jalin were there, so were Malghain and Haswyxe. They had hidden out during the day. It was almost a proper party, though a little somber. In fairness, however, Clerin was merely following Trela's orders. He entered and grabbed his own glass of grog.

"So, did you save the day?" Clerin's smile was a little off.

"What? No, hardly." He scrunched his brows together briefly. "I worked on calling the wind to keep the smoke from enveloping Agoge. And not just me, there were plenty of mages."

"Plenty of mages…" This came from Haswyxe.

Vrric drank the rest of his grog in an attempt to catch up with whatever was happening. "And Linchon. Linchon was there. Helping. With the wind." The burning grog was helping. He started to glance around for a refill.

"I thought Linchon was dead." Malghain spoke up.

"They… I'm not sure. They take a long time to die." Clerin looked a little pensive.

"Like, how long? A couple sun cycles? Ten? Thirty? A generation?" Jalin joined in. "If we are all dead by the time Gorbanax actually dies, then… what is the difference?"

"Well, you know, the volcano." Malghain waved his hand around at nothing in particular.

"No, really. I'm not trying to be obnoxious. But if nothing has really changed for us…" Jalin took a quick puff and blew it out slowly. "You know, for the vast majority of us Pyrans, we never knew what Gorbanax did. We never spoke to it, never heard edicts that derived from it. Qizern would go once a year, at best, and never speak of the experience. At least, not to the likes of me."

"Well, you've got us Luftens beat." Haswyxe gave a small laugh. "You had your Guard garrison up there and regular visits. You had the volcano to look up at each day. You had an obvious… presence." He motioned around to the others in the room. "We had nothing. Old Hulgert wouldn't even let anyone else near the temple. Linchon could have died an eon ago and I wouldn't have known."

"Lembin communes with various Fluens on an almost weekly basis. If Lembin died, there would be an obvious emptiness within our realm." Clerin poured some grog into Vrric's empty glass, and then some into her half-full one.

"So… Is that where this is going?" Malghain raised an eyebrow and his glass. He paused for the briefest moment before drinking.

"No one knows where this is going." Vrric replied immediately, as if to head something off.

"I wasn't asking you." There was the tiniest bit of steel in Malghain's eye. It was odd since Vrric was rarely on the receiving end of that look. He then cocked an eyebrow at Clerin, but she merely stared silently back at him. "But your point is well taken. My curiosity gets the better of me sometimes."

"And that is why I never ask questions." Haswyxe laughed loudly and finished his grog.

Jalin was looking intently at the side of Clerin's face. Not staring, not fully, but as if she was examining something from afar. Like a thief trying to ascertain a ring's worth from two tables over. But, of course, without any nefarious intent.

It made Vrric wonder. He assumed that Clerin did not want to discuss any of this, but did he really know that? She certainly did not chime in, and if she had wanted, she could have brought this up with them hours ago. But how long was all this to stay a secret? How long before others began to guess? One Beleg dying may be an accident. Half of them dying is not. And in such a spectacularly public way as Gorbanax. If they needed help, if Clerin wanted help, more honest discussions would have to happen. He had not really had the time to talk with her alone yet. It had been a long and grueling day for himself, and he could not really imagine what Clerin was going through.

They stayed and drank for a bit. The conversation wafted between mundane subjects. In the back of Vrric's mind he was wondering why they had not been out in Agoge, maybe with Lishean, helping to keep the peace by keeping the calm. He supposed they were protecting Clerin, which he should certainly not complain about. Eventually, however, the two of them decided to step out and head to back to Gyllhelon's old quarters. Which he should probably start thinking of as their new quarters.

The others were still enjoying themselves, so Vrric and Clerin walked home alone. They had replaced the lock on Gyllhelon's door, before everyone had started drinking. They had some minor belongings with them, but the rooms were a little stark. There was a small front room with one sofa and some cupboards, and then a bedroom behind a lockless door that held an armoire. Vrric thought he could detect a scent of Gyllhelon in the room but assumed that was just in his mind. Clerin grabbed a bottle of grog from a cupboard.

"I could not find any cups, so..." She smiled and took a small sip straight from the bottle.

"I doubt she would have taken anything like that on the road." He sat down on the sofa. She walked over with a little saunter. It was cute.

"Here, catch up." She handed him the bottle.

"Oh, I think I caught up over at Jalin's." Still, he took the bottle and a sip. "So, how are you doing? Really. It's just the two of us."

She sat down and he handed her the bottle back. The sofa was comfortable enough, and the day long enough, that he felt a weariness settle through him. He tossed an arm over the back of the couch. Clerin removed her boots with her left hand and then tucked her feet under her on the sofa.

"I feel... I am not sure. I do not want to be dramatic about it, really. But all I can think of is it is like a drowning derlian finally reaching air. Gasping and sputtering. And then the realization that you are in an underwater cavern, at an air pocket. Still trapped, still pressurized, but able to breathe for the moment. And always the thought in the back of your mind that you will have to hold your breath and duck down into the water again if you want to find a real way out. But it is not as if I truly feel like I am drowning, it is not that dire; like falling in slow motion is not dire as long as you never speed back up. So, if you could remove the overly dramatic portions of the rendition, that is what I feel like."

Vrric's mind reeled slightly. It was a little difficult to separate. To take the stated description and remove the emotionally charged reflexive response created by hearing it.

"I think I understand."

"I suppose I have known for a while that I am toxic to Belegs." She laughed for a brief moment, her eyes sparkling with the knowledge of a naughty secret. Without, of course, any actual secret, just that type of sparkle. "I sort of knew when Gorbanax would not directly commune with me the first time. It was made more obvious when communing with Lembin and, sort of, Linchon again. It should have been obvious after realizing what had happened to Linchon in the first place, really. But it was as if I did not wish to know what was going on. What the messages were inside of me. But this!" She laughed again with her sparkling eyes and waved a hand around the room. "This is impossible to ignore. Gorbanax's reaction to Lembin's message, once fully communed, is impossible to ignore. The entire volcano exploded! I am unable to think I am not toxic. I am poison, Vrric. I kill Belegs—our creators. That is sad, is it not?"

"Sad or not, this is completely Lembin's fault. Lembin created the poison and hid it within an innocent shell. It is not as if you are trying to be toxic, or even had an inkling, at least at first. You had absolutely no idea before Linchon, correct? Not even a suspicion?"

"No. None." She took a decent draught from the bottle of grog. "I thought it was a basic message, like, 'Hi, how are you doing?' or something like that. Nothing nefarious."

They both laughed at the imagined simplicity of the message. She offered the bottle and he took it. He held onto it before taking a sip.

"Then you have a clear conscience."

"But what about Gunzgak? Gunzgak does not want to be poisoned. It knows what is happening. It will have sensed the eruption." She looked somber. "Now I know, beyond any shadow of a doubt, just what I carry. How dangerous it is. And yet… I have been told by both Linchon and Gorbanax, the two I have already damaged, or killed, or whatever; I have been explicitly told to commune with Gunzgak and then Lembin. More than anything, more than the fear of their own mortality, more than the fear of dying, they did not want to die alone. They did not—do not, I should say— want any Belegs left. They do not want the realms to be unbalanced. So, now, if I go through with this, I will not be able to claim ignorance. I cannot claim innocence. I am as guilty as Lembin now, right?"

"No, certainly not." He raised a hand to ward off her protestations. It reminded him he was holding a bottle, and so he took a drink and handed it back. "You cannot claim ignorance or even innocence, certainly. However, you still did not start this, did not desire it, did not plan it, had nothing to do with it until you were in too deep to escape. Your main crime is that you were too innocent. You were chosen by Lembin because no one would suspect you. You don't have a cruel bone in your body, and believe me, I've looked." He chuckled a bit and then continued. "If it makes you feel any better, Linchon communicated the same things to me. Linchon was adamant about keeping the balance of power. You hit the nail on the head when you said the main motivating factor now is that none of the Belegs should be left. That now that this horrible thing has begun, it must be shown through."

"I am tired." She suddenly looked it as the smile slipped from her face. "I just… I want to be done. I want to run away with you. Hide somewhere where no one could find us. Live simply. Grow old together. Maybe have a couple of babies." She smiled a small hopeful smile at him, though her eyes were still sad.

"I want that too. The simple living." Did he though? It was easier to say than to think about. "But we both know that it will be a long time before we can rest. You've only poisoned half the Belegs so far." Luckily she laughed a little at that.

"Well, by all accounts, it is really only Gunzgak left. Lembin will either let itself go once Gunzgak has been poisoned, or Linchon will force the situation." She paused and Vrric took the opportunity to hand the bottle back over. "Now we just have to trick a Beleg. One who is already onto us and, probably rightfully so, a little paranoid. What do you call paranoia with just cause?"

"I don't know… vigilance?"

"Ha! Yes. Gunzgak is quite vigilant."

"Well, I'm not sure if it was my idea since Linchon led me there, quite directly in fact, but there was a statement that tricking Gunzgak would take hiding chaos within law. Not exactly sure what that means."

"How did Linchon commune with you?" She glanced up, then back down again.

"Linchon appeared to me, and spoke to me, as Aillel. You had mentioned that was how Linchon spoke to you, and I guessed… well, thought it. Aillel spoke to me, and I thought responses. It was quite efficient, really."

"So, you spoke with Aillel?"

And there it was. Linchon had mentioned it, had almost mocked him with it. He had decided he was going to think up his response before being asked the question. He had decided that would be the smartest move, to sit somewhere quiet and mull over the whole issue and all its ramifications. Linchon admitted it had killed Aillel, that there was no vestige left of Clerin's father, that only the likeness and memories had been taken, none of the spirit. And yet, if he did not mention it now, how would she ever know? If she never spoke to Linchon again, then him explaining that to her, right then, was just cruel. Even if they spoke again, if Linchon forgot or did not care to mention it, then Vrric explaining it was cruel. It was only if they did speak together again, and if Linchon did mention it at all and did mention that Vrric knew about it, it was only under those specific circumstances that he should tell her. Linchon's words echoed in his mind, "Is it better to tell a hurtful truth than to tell a salving lie?" He sat there in silence for a long moment.

"It is a simple question, I was just asking..." She seemed more confused at the pause than anything else.

"I know. I know." He reached out for the bottle though he did not drink from it after he received it. "You know what I think happened?" He paused while she stared at him in silence. "I think I just spoke with Linchon. Only Linchon. When I said Aillel earlier, I just... it was just the image... our only conversation topics were items of concern with Linchon. It was all about Gunzgak and needing a name, and about helping Gorbanax with the wind, and whether or not Linchon was dying or dispersing or whatever that should be called."

He said it, though he was not exactly positive why. It was the pressure to answer right away, really. He posited it as his opinion and as his personal conversation. He wanted to leave her able to think of her own conversations with Linchon however she liked. He did his best to avoid tainting her own experience while still stating what he was told was the truth. He took a swig to avoid speaking further.

"You are acting weird. There is no reason to be weird." She reached out for the bottle and he gladly handed it over. "So Linchon mentioned we would need a name? Like Gunzgak's full name? That seems nigh impossible, where are we supposed to get that?" She laughed a little and put the bottle down on the ground in front of the sofa.

Vrric was happy to change the subject. To have been given a reprieve. His mind thought back to his conversation with Linchon, but he could not recall anything useful.

"Well, we did not cover that beyond a name being required. It has to be Gunzgak's, I'm fairly sure you're correct." He thought for a second. "You don't think its name could somehow be within those ice caves up on the Eidyon Peninsula, do you?"

"Oh, I hope not. That is about as far away from here as possible. Could you imagine trying to get back up there?" She laughed and grimaced at the same time. It was a bit incongruous. "That would take moons."

"Several moons to get there and then several moons to search through all the caves for the specific name." They both laughed. "And that is the easy part?"

"The easy part?"

"Yes, of course. After that comes the tricking."

"Right. And what comes after tricking a Beleg?"

"Well, then we sic you on them."

They both laughed again. They chatted on for a while until they were tired, but not too tired. Then they left the small front room for the bedroom.

The next day Vrric was summoned to the throne. Like the previous day, he was to leave Clerin behind, alone. Well, not technically alone, not in danger. Malghain and Haswyxe stayed behind to protect her again.

He woke up slowly and got dressed. He had a leisurely breakfast and drank some water. Lots of water.

He then flew over to the same balcony he had been arriving at. The room was less crowded than it had been the last time he visited, but there were still some courtiers wandering about, being... courteous. As he walked in, he noticed Serghno standing near a corner, speaking with Trela in hushed tones. His portly frame and mustaches, like vibrating antennae bent upwards with wax, made him quite easy to pick out of any crowd. Less obvious, but also easily recognizable, was Arnasta standing almost behind Trela. At least from Vrric's current vantage point. Ryshial was even farther back, practically out of view. He walked his way over there, only having to weave slightly between the various courtiers.

"Ah, yes, there you are." Trela had been surreptitiously eyeballing him as he narrowed the gap but had kept her attention on her conversation with Serghno. At least as far as he could tell.

"Finally!" He decided to rib himself before Serghno could get something in. "What have I been doing this morning?"

Serghno laughed and clapped him on the shoulder. "You don't really want me answering that, do you? Because I can make a guess if you'd like."

"Now, now, I've asked you all here for serious business." Trela waved her hands downwards a couple of times. "I'm hoping that there are some Guards at the garrison near the entrance to Gorbanax's temple who survived." Vrric raised an eyebrow and turned to Serghno, whose own brow was raised. "Now, now," Trela continued, waving her hands again. "Gorbanax did its best to reduce injury and death. Agoge is almost completely unscathed. There really might be some warriors trapped up there."

"Of course, my Queen." Arnasta took a small step towards the group, enlarging the circle. "If there is anyone up there, we'll find them."

"Good. I knew I could count on you." Trela paused for a brief moment, looking directly at Arnasta, but then turned to Serghno and Vrric. "I know I can count on all of you."

They shuffled and weaved back to the balcony. The latticed glass door closed behind them, muting the background noise of multiple conversations. It was a little cool with a consistent breeze that still pushed south, towards the ocean. There were no clouds in the northern view they had, but Vrric knew there was still some minor smoke escaping from the volcano if they were able to look in the opposite direction. The actual rumblings were quite muted. All in all, Trela was right. Agoge had gotten away fairly unscathed, especially considering the magnitude of the disaster.

"If you fly us over there, I'll float us around while Arnasta searches for survivors." Serghno smiled and nodded to no one in particular, even though he was obviously talking to Vrric.

That was fine with Vrric. He was a little unsure of why he was tagging along. Trela must be concerned that they would find a lot of Guards up there, too many for just Serghno and Arnasta to rescue. Or maybe she was worried they would be buried, but still alive. In any case, Vrric would typically rather be doing something than doing nothing.

"Lumkinderclo!" They flew straight up, above the roofs and spires, then began moving with the wind towards the ocean.

Once they were high enough, they could see the tendrils of smoke still drifting up from the caldera. Vrric moved them along as fast as he dared, which made it difficult to chat while flying. As they got closer, he could see that the north face of the caldera, the side closest to Agoge, was mostly intact, though the top was truncated. It was the southern face that appeared misshapen. The ridge on that face dipped and waved, with a new slope of rock spilling and oozing through it. It did not appear to be actually moving, though it was difficult to tell from their distance, but the way it had solidified gave it the feeling of motion. Like a wave trapped in mid-roll.

It did not take them too long to reach the face. There was a well-worn trail angling up and winding along. It was quite finished, almost a road really. There were some straggly hazel trees that he brought them gently down beside. They stopped in the middle of the trail.

"Where did you want to begin the search?" Vrric kept the spell going in the background. He was sure they would be lifting off again shortly.

He glanced around at the ground looking for tracks of shoes or hooves or wagon wheels, anything really. The problem was that there were various tracks of a certain age. Some appeared to be going up even. It seemed there was not a stampede of Guards escaping the garrison, but that was about all he could say. Vrric had never hunted or tracked anything.

"Well, if anyone was down this far, they were probably able to make it back down to Agoge. So, maybe fly us slowly up the trail here and I'll cast my spells along the way. How much time do you have before Serghno will need to take over?"

"Probably another ten minutes. I cast it a little strong originally." He smiled and nodded to Serghno.

"Sounds good. Lift us up."

And so he did. They traveled slowly enough that they could examine the ground as they floated above. About halfway into his ten minutes, Arnasta had him land.

"Serghno knows the height and speed required for my most efficient tracking, if you don't mind." She cast her eyes down demurely. She always seemed a bit demure to Vrric. He hoped that it was just how she was and not as if she was afraid of insulting him or something.

"Sounds great, I'll enjoy the break."

They all nodded at each other. Serghno cast his flying spell and then she cast her tracking one. "Narfintotclo!" Her voice was strong and clear.

She must be searching for living Guards, Vrric thought. He wondered if he should cast something to look for bodies, that maybe the search could be shortened a little if they found either one. Then he wondered if that would be insulting to her. She was the master tracker. In fact, that was something Vrric did very little of since they already had an expert. Then he wondered if his concern of insulting her would be insulting in itself. It became confusing in his head, but then they started floating.

"Do you mind if I search for bodies?" He wanted to ask before they got moving too far, before Arnasta was so deep in her search that he would be interrupting her concentration.

"No, not at all. I was going to do that on the way back down but would always appreciate an additional set of senses." She turned and started concentrating.

"Narsidderclo!" He closed his eyes and started concentrating.

It took them much of the morning to travel up the trail. It was slow going which felt even slower due to the lack of results. They found a bunch of nothing. Not until they got close to the garrison at least. And the closer they got, the more large rocks and boulders began to clog the trail below.

They reached the gigantic ledge that held the entrance. The ledge itself was beset with rocks of all sizes, making it difficult for Serghno to set them down anywhere. The arched entrance was completely blocked. Vrric was not sure if it was blocked due to rocks from above or if the tunnel/cave had fallen in upon itself. If it was the former, they should be able to shift enough rocks to expose the entrance. If it was the latter… well, the amount of effort would certainly increase exponentially. Serghno floated them down next to where the entrance should have been, keeping them levitating slightly above the uneven surface.

"Do you need us to start clearing?" Serghno's voice sounded a little concerned, but also fully interested in helping Arnasta in any way she desired.

"No. Not yet at least." She smiled shyly for the briefest moment. "Let me see how far I can sense into the rubble. Eqefintotclo!"

They waited in silence for quite a while. At first, Vrric watched how Arnasta's eyes shifted back and forth under her closed lids, but he quickly sat down to face Serghno. Not that he sat down on the jumble of rocks. He was still levitating.

"Nothing. Well, no Guards at least." She was blinking as she spoke, as if coming out of a daze or from too bright of sun. "Let me try to sense bodies back in there. Eqesidderclo!"

They waited less time than before, but still in silence lest they disturb Arnasta. When her eyes popped open, they seemed slightly haunted and her breathing increased, but that faded quickly. She took a couple of deep breaths before speaking.

"There are a lot of bodies in there. Some died quickly, others more slowly, but I feel that they have all perished at this point. So, I am not really sure if digging our way through to them is very beneficial. If Trela wants to give them a hero's burial, she can come back with an army of mages. This will take some time to sift through." Her arm swept the scene.

Vrric was trying to think of when Serghno had last cast a flight spell. He was thinking of flying them back as quickly as he had shot them over there since there was little reason to scour the same trail they had examined on their way up. When his mind was wandering, however, it snagged on what Arnasta had first said after searching for Guards.

"Wait, you said you sensed no Guards. Was there something there you did sense?" His brow furrowed unconsciously.

"Well, maybe. I'm hesitant to even mention it, it was so faint." She looked down as she spoke. Demurely.

"Well?" Serghno prodded her lightly.

"I... I might have sensed the spoor of the Blind One." She raised her hands to silence the both of them. "It was so faint that I am unsure of it at all. Maybe not. Probably not. But, if so, then it was a light touch recently, or a heavier one just before the eruption. I only noticed because he has such a unique signature. It happens when he teleports—the specific signature. If he had walked through the area, I doubt I would have noticed." She looked down again. "But really, it was so faint that I may have imagined it."

"Oh, I doubt that." Serghno shook his head. "You would not have mentioned it if you thought it was an error. I know you that much, at least."

It was the most confusing news Vrric had heard all day. He frowned as he thought, biting his lip unconsciously. It made no sense. It made him think of the ice caves on the Eidyon Peninsula. Was the Blind One following them, or were they muddling along behind him? It just made no sense.

Chapter 10

Trela was shocked and saddened by what had happened. All of it. All of it was shocking. All of it was saddening. Gorbanax was dead. The volcano had erupted. Every one of her citizens were concerned and anxious. It was incredible that a full panic had been diverted. It was the worst disaster to ever befall the Pyran derlians. Or, at least, that was what her advisors told her. And that was just yesterday.

What made it worse was that it was Clerin who had caused it all. Her Fluen princess. She had brought Clerin to Agoge, had brought her to Gorbanax. It was Trela herself, personally, who had instigated their meeting. Of all the derlians of all the realms, she was the second most culpable for the death of Gorbanax, behind only Clerin herself. This, her advisors had not told her. Oh, she was sure they were saying it outside of her hearing. How could they not be? But no one was brazen enough to bring up her culpability to her face. Maybe they were being respectful, but maybe they were just afraid of being executed. Who knew? They did not have to say it, however. Trela knew it, could not deny it. It weighed heavily on her. Her only excuse was that she had not known, had had no idea of what had been brewing. This was the same excuse Clerin herself used, but Trela had the added advantage of not being the messenger herself. She truly had no idea.

Maybe she should have. There was what had happened at the Luften Temple. It was never stated that Linchon had died, however. Just that it had given additional messages, one in specific to Gorbanax. When Trela took Clerin to Gorbanax, she had assumed the main message was from Linchon, not Lembin. Gorbanax, however, refused to directly commune with Clerin. That was odd. That should have given Trela something to worry about. Then there were the rumblings in Tureyn. That was odd. The thought of those made her wonder if they were still occurring.

After Gorbanax refused to directly commune with Clerin, it sent them on the mission to destroy the Cabal of Lochom and all the items the Cabal had created through Yavencide. Which they did. Then, and only then, had Gorbanax allowed direct communication. Which meant that it knew what was going to happen and had let it happen anyway. It was also highly probable that Taglo knew and did nothing to stop Clerin. Of course, Taglo had died itself fighting the

Cabal. No, not just fighting. Taglo had died destroying the Cabal. That had a better ring to it.

So, Trela thought, *if Gorbanax and its Yaven adjutant had allowed it to happen, then it was accepted by them. And, if Gorbanax accepted it, then I should not feel horrible about it.* The thought assuaged her a little, it was a type of salve, but it was not a curative. It did not absolve her from her actions. Or, more correctly, it did not absolve her from not realizing what had been going on. A good leader should understand what is happening around them. Trela was queen and should have comprehended what had been building up just under the surface, like a volcano about to erupt. She had failed in that regard, no matter what Gorbanax had accepted.

So it was a new day, the day after the eruption. She started early with her advisors. Those bureaucratic advisors inherited from Qizern, not her privy council from the old warpack. She would speak with them afterwards. She felt she had to give the bureaucrats some deference. Though she certainly planned on ruling for many long cycles, they were the stability of the realm. They had overseen previous disasters and would probably oversee more. Besides, Trela had been traipsing across every realm but her own for almost a cycle now. Doing bidding for a Beleg that had just erupted.

Should she have invited Lishean to the early morning meeting? Sure. But he was in the main market, camped out with a large Guard contingent. She had planned to meet him out there for the second meeting. Maybe refine the plan with her less formal, more familial advisors.

Trela had the first meeting in the throne room. The setting added the required gravitas, even though it was a bit large for the amount of derlians invited. They all shuffled in a little after dawn.

There was Linloy and Hunvarb, of course, but many others as well. Linloy was thin, haughty, and a bit infuriating. Hunvarb was squat with chubby cheeks, and was more thoughtful than Linloy, making her easier to get along with than he was. They both gave good advice, however.

They started milling about since Trela had not wanted chairs set up. Once they were all inside, she walked out and down to mingle. She wanted to be on their level.

"This is not the time to cast blame. That was yesterday, and most of you spoke your piece. Let me say that I do understand your concerns and frustrations, I share many of them myself. I am not ignoring you or pushing you aside. In addition, in another week, we shall have a similar meeting in which you can all vent your complaints to me. Today, however, we have a different set of priorities. Today is only about how to move the Blaze, Agoge, and the entire Dekhan Plateau beyond the volcanic eruption. How do we reassure our citizens to continue with their daily lives after such a shock? How do we keep opportunists from taking unfair advantage of such a situation? How do we keep order without fear, to keep spirits up without glossing over the importance of what has occurred? We are not trying to get everyone to forget what happened. We wish to acknowledge the shock and pain we are all feeling, but we do not want those feelings to be overwhelming or crippling." She paused and no one spoke. She thought about filling the void with more speech, but felt she had already conveyed what she wanted. Talking more was not going to help. She felt that cajoling was not going to help either. So she stayed silent and waited, keeping her smile on her face. Letting the vacuum of emptiness suck the breath out of them in the form of words.

"Well, we definitely need more guard presence. And more *Guard* presence." The speaker was Nulveytra, an ancient Pyran with bushy white eyebrows. "We have to make sure everyone feels safe!" He jabbed his finger out at nothing in particular.

"Well, there is a fine line between feeling safe and feeling like you're being watched." A young, female, auburn-haired Pyran interjected her viewpoint. "We do not wish to be overbearing."

"More than anything, I think we need some days to decompress and recover." This was from Hunvarb. "Some days off from normal work. Maybe a period of mourning?"

"I'm afraid the word 'mourning' may send the wrong message. Certainly not a holiday, but I would avoid calling further attention to the fact that Gorbanax is dead or dying." Linloy spoke up. His advice was always concerned with the image of the issue, how Trela looked or was presented, not really about the actual policy being discussed.

"You will have to address your citizens. You must soothe and appease them, make them feel comfortable. You must shine your charm." Another old male advisor added his opinion. "This could be at the apex of some sort of non-holiday days off thing."

"We can't just give everyone the day off, who will bake the bread? Who will serve the grog? Do you want the guards doing the work of citizens? Do you want court mages doing it?" An angry young male said his piece. "No, of course not. Because that is dumb."

"You have all provided great advice. We should have a way to distribute free staples to the citizens. That should be through the guards, to increase their presence in a friendly acceptable manner. We could use some court mages for that as well." Trela smiled at no one in particular. "We will certainly not have the guards bake anything. I propose a day of work. A full hard workday for everyone, keep everyone's head down. The day after will be one of rest for all citizens. All the extra bread, food, grog, what-have-you, made during the first day will distributed during the second. We will pay market prices for all the staples—we meaning, of course, the treasury. That restful day will be spent in contemplation, not in mourning, not in celebration. At the end of the day, I will provide a speech at the edge of Agoge to all who wish to gather." She paused and looked at all their faces. There was some skepticism being exuded, but there was an air of something else as well.

"Is tomorrow good for the day of work? A different day? Should we have more than one day of work? More than one day of contemplation?" She could not have asked for a better, or quicker, session. They had brought up most of what she had hoped for and even a little more, which meant the plan was a group effort. They could not complain if they all had a part in it. Well, that was probably hoping for too much. Now she just needed a consensus about the details.

They decided on two days of work, starting later that day. Meaning it would probably be closer to one-and-a-half days. Then two days of contemplation. The volcano was already spewing much less smoke and the wind was still blowing favorably. She hoped that by the time she gave her speech there would be little trace of the eruption. Except, of course, the top of the volcano. Though most of the face of the volcano that had blown out fell towards the ocean, the silhouette above the city was still irrevocably altered. It was not horrendously obvious, but it was unmistakable if glanced at. Like a new scar on an old lover's face. The eye was just drawn there, unconsciously at times.

As the others began to leave, Trela felt great. She felt she had a good plan and had not even spoken with Lishean or any of her privy council yet. She wondered briefly if she could get a similar system set up with them but then discarded the idea. It would just be easier to tell them the plan and let them provide additional advice and suggestions. As she stood there staring at the floor and thinking, she realized Linloy was the last Pyran in the room with her. She looked up and blinked twice. He was obviously waiting for her attention now that they were alone.

"Yes?"

"This meeting was to discuss how to placate and assuage your citizens." He looked at her seriously, so she nodded her response in return. "It is not your citizens you need to worry about. It is us. It is your advisors, those who lead overly comfortable lives." He politely coughed behind a closed fist. "Your citizens love you. They lead difficult hardscrabble lives and will endure much for you. We work for you and refuse to endure anything that is not required to keep our accustomed level of comfort. You understand that Qizern made loyalty a requirement for the work? This is frustrating and cruel, and I am glad, for myself at least, that you are different in this regard. However, I feel I must caution you against having zero requirements for the work. The death or dying of Gorbanax has unnerved us. It, existentially, threatens our comfort. Your advisors need to be placated and assuaged, but not in a typical way. Not in a way that would satisfy a hardscrabble citizen. No, for us there must be a tougher love. Or, and I do not say this lightly, you should watch your back and keep a close eye on us."

"How would you suggest I manifest this tougher love?"

"You are you, and I am quite different. What I would do does not matter. I do not necessarily believe there is such a thing as the Kriishan, but your citizens do. Prove them right." He nodded to her. Then he bowed low with his frail frame. He walked backwards, half bent the entire time. It must have been excruciating for his back, but he made it appear effortlessly graceful. He did not look haughty during their exchange, not even for a moment.

Trela was suddenly very grateful that Linloy existed, that he was he. She had not always felt that they got along, was still unsure of it in fact, but felt that his advice, as vague as it was, was truly and deeply felt by him. He did not provide her the warning to scare her or contort her or manipulate her. He did so because he felt it was his job to do so.

There was something in there about the others, some way for them to feel compelled to do their best work. Voluntarily. With pride. But she could not think of the how of it and she needed to get to Lishean. She had a long day ahead of her and it had only just begun.

As she was trying to figure out how best to get down to the main square to meet with Lishean, courtiers began to filter in. She smiled and nodded and wondered where all of her advisors had gotten to. Surely a couple of them could have kept these others entertained. Before she could address that, Ryshial arrived with a group of mages and novices. It was great. Trela would leave a mage in charge and have Ryshial fly her down to Lishean. She squinted at the mages as they started to walk over, trying to pick one that she knew besides Ryshial. Finally, Adzin came into view. He was one of the guild masters, he would be a good choice. Not that he had to do anything besides keeping various arguments from getting heated.

Trela walked up to them to meet them halfway. "Adzin, great to see you again. I have a favor to ask." His face stayed stony and silent, without a muscle twitching. "I need you to make sure everyone plays nice and nothing gets broken while I am gone. Can you handle that?" She had not meant her last sentence to sound like that, but it did not seem to bother him at all.

"Of course, my Queen." He gave a small bow. "If I may be so bold, where are you headed?" Adzin had a habit of making sure he was not offending anyone, or at least anyone above his station. It was nice at first but got tedious quickly if Trela paid too much attention to it.

"I need to steal Ryshial away to attend a meeting with Lishean. Oh, and if the other invited mages arrive—Arnasta, Serghno, and Feyazki—make them comfortable as they await my return." She nodded to him and then to Ryshial. "Come with me, we have much work to do."

Ryshial dutifully followed as they went through the glass-paned door to the balcony. Trela wondered if she was going to get asked where Lishean was, or if she wanted to leave right away, or anything. But Ryshial merely cast a couple of spells and sent them soaring.

Lishean was, of course, in the main square, which was fairly well known. Their flight was quick but pleasant. Sometimes the wind, if traveling fast through still air could be called wind, was overbearing or bugs would strike her face, but Ryshial was always cognizant of their speed and would oftentimes cast a small shield spell in front of them for comfort. There were other mages more powerful than Ryshial, maybe, but there were few that were as conscientious. There were some retirements at the Mage's Guild that needed to happen first, but Trela was sure Ryshial would become the headmaster at some point.

It did not take long for them to alight in the center of the square. The square had open marquee tents in each corner and centered at each side—at each intersecting road in essence. These were set up as informational booths with regular guards in attendance, assisting all comers with small issues. The square itself had some citizens wandering around in it, using it for its intended purpose, but it was sparsely occupied. The center of the square was still the rock gardens and statuary, but adjacent to that stood Lishean's grand tent, surrounded by Royal Guards in their purple cloaks. It was at this central area that Ryshial landed them.

"Do you need my continued assistance?" Ryshial had sharp features and was quite tall and thin, which could make one look harsh in the wrong light. But her easy smile and quick laugh typically softened those angles.

Trela stared for a moment trying to figure out the question. Did Ryshial wish to head somewhere else, for some other obligation? Or was the question indicating something else?

"We are convening a privy council and I need your advice. Come with me." She decided she did want Ryshial with her.

As she walked to the main tent, the Guards parted before her. They did not bow and scrape, Trela had no patience for that amount of obsequiousness, but they lowered their heads slightly and shifted out of her way. It allowed her to stride about in a way she enjoyed.

The tent was mostly open but had ornate hanging curtains to delineate space. They were almost tapestries with their artistic weaving but were quite thin and fluttered about in the small breeze. She strode through the small maze before reaching Lishean. He was with many of her typical advisors. Estfale, Dartsyle, Rewista, Zira, and the like. But there were many omissions. Kryhir, Yarsurle, and Aedon were all dead. She paused mentally for a moment. She quite missed Aedon, the Gaen. And none of the Luftens from her coterie were represented. They were lying low due to their association with Clerin, unfairly or not. The mages were also underrepresented due to their being on separate missions. She realized, a little too late, that she should have had Serghno and Arnasta meet her at the square.

"Good, we are all here." Clerin looked around at the crowded curtained space. Whether or not there were to be some stragglers to the meeting, she felt they had a quorum and did not desire to wait. Lishean, for his part, merely nodded in deference.

Trela explained the overall plan to her council, adding details here and there as they came to her. It was fairly well received. The ideas were expounded upon and expanded. They were tweaked and modified. Mostly, they—and here Trela included the Guards that were nearby—knew many of the locals' names and vocations. Who could help with what, which bakeries were in what neighborhood, which grocers were nearby, what markets were open that day and the next. The details were fleshed out. Different strategies were discussed. The true planning happened.

Afterwards they sent the Guards out in every direction to spread the word. Trela had wanted to start as quickly as possible. She needed everyone working towards one goal. She needed everyone with their heads down so they did not notice the smoke.

Once the Guards had left, the rest of her council began to peel off, spreading out to various points of Agoge. The more prominent the recipient, the more prominent the messenger. The various guild halls would need a council member to deliver the instructions, not some simple guard. Eventually, it was just the three of them. Lishean, Ryshial, and Trela.

"Tell me truly, how are the citizens?" Trela watched Lishean's face intently, just in case there was some unconscious communication occurring. He squinted at her a little bit, but otherwise betrayed no emotion.

"For one, I've been trapped here, so have not been able to speak with them directly. Those who come here, looking at me as your representative, are obviously fearful or angry. But most appear to be continuing on with their lives." He paused for a moment, staring back at her. "I would say that most are concerned. Concerned about any current damage, any current loss of food or shelter, but also concerned about the future. Concerned that this means something greater than you or I, let alone them, is happening. I think most are concerned that there is a war amongst the Belegs, and Gorbanax has just lost. Our protector in this war, our creator—our Creator!—has just lost. What if Lembin rose up from the ocean and swallowed us whole? Hmm? What would stop that? What could stop that?"

His emotion at the end caught Trela a little by surprise. Lishean had always been stolid and eschewed thoughts that were considered fanciful. If this is what her First thought, her general, then what were her citizens thinking?

"You and I both know that is not going to happen." Trela did not want to sound condescending or flippant, but wanted to convey the absurdity of the idea.

"Do I? But, more importantly, do you? Do you really?" His cocked eyebrow began to slowly descend. "Maybe you do. Maybe you know what's going on, what the Fluens are doing, what this war is about. But I do not. And, more importantly, none of your citizens know either." He held up a hand to stop her from responding. "I'm not saying there's panic out there. The more time that passes, the less concern there will be, but right now there is concern. It is real and it is widespread. You would be wise to do something to assuage that. Sooner rather than later. Your plan is well laid, I see no issues, but as an advisor, as one who wishes you and the realm well, I would recommend you spend some real time amongst your subjects."

Trela's first reaction was a bit... reactionary. She wanted to argue, to point out things and win Lishean over. But that was not the point of his speech. Much like with Linloy, she was just struck by a feeling of gratitude, it just took a second of her own silence for it to bubble forth. She was grateful for Lishean's existence, for him being him. He had always had her best interests at heart, and the realm's. And he had always spoken freely when required.

"Thank you, Lishean, truly. You have always given me fantastic advice, and you have not faltered today. Please know that I value your input and will follow through as best I know how." She gave a deep nod, if not a bow, of appreciation. "We have much to do. Both of us. May your work go smoothly, and your efforts be productive."

"You as well." He was smiling as she turned to leave.

Ryshial, staying silent, turned and followed Trela out of the small, curtained maze. Trela racked her brain for the moment they were walking. She needed a way to travel if she was to visit groups of her subjects. She thought briefly about using horses and traveling with a group of Guards. They would be obvious then, and those who wished to speak with her could see the entourage and approach. It seemed like it would be best to be on foot and not surrounded by armed warriors. Then it seemed it would be best to be flown around. That it would be best to enlist Ryshial for the entire day. She would have to have Adzin notify the Mages' Guild of the overall plan then, in lieu of Ryshial. Trela had wanted to give her that honor, to elevate her standing in the guild, but maybe being the personal attendant of the queen would be better.

"I'm going to need you a while longer. I'm going to need you for the entire day. But first you must take me back to the throne room. I have some more business to attend there before attending to my subjects."

"Of course, my Queen." Ryshial bowed low and slowly.

Ryshial cast her spells and they flew off at a comfortable pace. On the way back, Trela watched the action below her intently. The vantage point was not the greatest for seeing details, but no one looked too hurried or chaotic. There were no bunches of groups roaming around like angry mobs. Nothing was on fire or flooded. The buildings all seemed to be intact, even with the low rumblings that had passed through the town. She thought about what Lishean had said. That the concerns were only partly about what had happened or what was currently happening, but those of the future. Of course, how would one go about preparing for an attack by a foreign Beleg? She needed to assuage the concerns about the past and present by showing that it had not been that bad, that they had been sheltered by Gorbanax. Then, once the simple foundation had been lain, she needed to assuage their concerns for the future. That would be the difficult part. She did not have a solution in mind by the time Ryshial landed them.

They spoke with Adzin, giving him an outline of the plan and some directions. He was trusted enough to be able to manage his own mages and novices. It was nice to have competent leaders. He flew off under his own power. Trela spoke with Serghno and Arnasta briefly. She had only gotten out the outline of the plan before Feyazki showed up. She then explained her concerns about any Guards that might be left alive in the rubble at the temple's garrison. They flew off under their own power. She spoke with some more of her court advisors, making sure that everything was moving in one direction, with singularity of purpose.

Finally, she was able to step away again. It was almost noon, and she was beginning to feel peckish. She could not delay any longer, however. She gathered up Ryshial and took to the skies once more. She thought she would start in the main square and check each direction, flying back to the square once they had spoken with enough of her subjects. She decided to go along the bakery street first. Maybe she would purchase some breads, meats, and cheeses along the way.

"I want a flag or something visible from a distance that indicates where I am. Then, if anyone desires, they can come and find me and talk with me." They were at an entrance to the square, the first one Trela thought about walking down, facing due south towards the Blaze. "But I don't want to make a Guard follow us around, carrying such a large and unwieldy item. There are so many awnings and balconies and whatnot, and I'll be entering many shops—it just seems difficult."

"Why don't I create an illusion of a flag? I can make it as tall or wide as you like. It would just distort when it went through an awning." Ryshial was looking up a little, as if watching the fake flag flap in the breeze. "I could make it colorful. I could even make the colors shift and shimmer to grab extra attention."

"Wow, that's fantastic, what a great idea." She thought for a brief moment about a shimmering flag. "But we should just have my typical bow with a lightning bolt as the arrow for the heraldic imagery. No need to make it shimmering."

"Suit yourself. How about this? Narfintotclo!"

And there it was. It was tall, beautiful, wafted in the breeze, everything. It looked like fabric. It moved like fabric. It even appeared to have a long staff that just kind of ended at waist height.

"Perfect." Trela grinned widely.

They marched for a while, and though plenty stared, no one stopped them. Trela was just going straight, not really sure what her own plan was. So, as she realized she was walking by a corner bakery, she decided to duck inside.

"Good morrow, good ma… My Queen. Apologies, I did not recognize you." A shortish muscular baker came around a long counter. She pulled her hat off and bowed low. Her hair was braided in a tight plait. "Or I did not really see you when you entered. I, of course, recognized you."

"Please, do not concern yourself with niceties or apologies. I gave no warning as I came in." Trela nodded to the baker. She noticed that the shop, though quite small, was empty of customers. She also noticed the flag was only half visible inside the shop and wondered if part of it was peeking outside, above the roof. That was a fleeting thought, however.

"I'm just out checking in on my citizens. How is your business lately?" Trela looked around the shop a little. "Is this... typical?"

"Yes and no. We are near noon, which is not my busiest time by far. I'm busiest in the morning. Then late in the afternoon, a little before closing, is my next busiest time. But there would be someone here, typically, at any particular moment. Your Guard, however, have already come through here, telling everyone to work with fervor until the end of tomorrow. So, those who were here skedaddled back to do whatever it is that they do. I'll probably have some more come by in the evening, which'll make up for the lost orders. Besides, I've got my own work to concern myself with. Will probably stay late tonight and start early tomorrow. I'd stay all night if it wasn't for my little one back home. My apprentices won't mind the brief respite either." She laughed a little to herself.

"So, not to pry, but are you not concerned about all that happened?" Trela waved vaguely in the direction of the volcano, even though they were indoors.

"Of course. But not overly, no." She was peering into Trela's eyes intently. It seemed she was trying to figure out what Trela's opinion was before she stated her own. Trela tried to keep her face impassive. She wanted to know this baker's own true opinion. "May I speak frankly?"

"Please do."

"Well, the times are changing, truly. We've lived with the Belegs our entire existence. All of us. Everywhere. It's hard to think of a time when that would not be true. But here we are." She pointed vaguely to the volcano outside. "Does it feel different today to you? Of course it does. But in a week? A moon? How often did you commune with Gorbanax?"

"Well, never, actually."

"The same as me. How often did Gorbanax do anything for us? Or against us? Or anything? How often did Gorbanax do anything?"

"I'm not sure."

"Same as me. Not sure. Could have been doing something, but maybe not. We'll find out now. We'll see if it all comes falling apart." She paused and straightened a little. "Don't get me wrong,

I've nothing against Gorbanax, never had a bad word and never will. I'm sad the era's over, truly. I would have been happy dying with Gorbanax still around, truly. I appreciate all that happened to bring life, to bring myself, to this point. Truly. But I'm betting that I don't notice the difference. Maybe you will, but my life is small and simple. I don't notice much beyond my neighborhood. Is that sad? Maybe it is sad. What do you think?"

"I don't think your life is sad."

"Ha! Then you don't know my life. But no, I'm asking if you think we'll notice a difference?"

"No. I don't." Trela needed that to be true, for her rule, for the peace of Agoge. But she also felt it to be true. Mostly because, like this baker, she had not noticed what Gorbanax actually did. Who knew, however? Maybe Gorbanax coaxed rain onto the crops, kept the locusts at bay, affected the birth rate. Maybe the volcano was going to erupt much more often now, maybe once a week. Truly, who knew?

"See? You know what the biggest fear I've heard all morning?"

"No. Please, tell me."

"Some are worried that some Belegs are gone, but others are still around. Like we'll be taken over by the Gaens or the Luftens because their Beleg is unmatched. Like the only reason we haven't been destroyed eons ago was because Gorbanax protected us from the other angry Belegs. Now, do I believe that?"

"No." The pause extended long enough that Trela thought the baker wanted a response.

"Of course not. But it still makes me angry. It's unfair now, isn't it? That we should be unprotected and beset by paranoia while the other half of the realms aren't? That doesn't seem right, now does it?"

"No. No, it doesn't."

"So, it feels odd. I don't feel that there will be a change. I feel safe in my familiar neighborhood. But I want a change for others, for the other half of the world. Is that right? I don't know. But if I'm honest, probably not. Does it change the way I feel? No. No, it doesn't. Is that sad? I don't know that either. I guess what I'm really saying is that I don't know anything. We'll find out, though, at least about what Gorbanax was doing. We'll find out if that was nothing or something, that's for sure."

It was an odd conversation, that was for sure. Trela had many such odd conversations that day, many much odder than that. Most Pyrans she spoke with were more concerned about the death of Gorbanax.

"Of course I'm worried!" That was from a leatherworker a couple of shops down from the baker. He was rotund and a little sweaty with somewhat wild eyes, though that may have been due to the subject at hand. "How could I not be worried? We lost our Beleg. Our Beleg! Without Gorbanax, we wouldn't be here now, would we? Nothing would be here. There'd be a void in the Void, now wrap your head around that! And, if I may be so bold, it was you who let the poison into the well. It was that Luften, that's what I heard. Her Beleg's attacking yours and you're still handing her grog! If that's not insult to injury, I don't know what is."

No, you may not be so bold, thought Trela. She bit her tongue hard enough that she had to concentrate to realize what else was being said. It was already getting ugly, and she did not want to respond before thinking about it.

"And what are you saying the solution is?" Trela did her best to not be shooting daggers from her eyes, but they must have looked like something because the leatherworker suddenly pulled his head back a little bit. But he pushed forward verbally.

"Well, punishment, of course. This must not be allowed to occur."

"Firstly, it has already occurred. The entire purpose of punishment is after something has occurred. Nothing can be done now to stop this from occurring."

"Part of punishment is vengeance."

"Do you think this was done on purpose? That this was what the Fluen came here to do?" Trela thought it was fine leaving Clerin nameless during most of these discussions. Most of those she spoke to that day, especially if they were angry, would refer to Clerin as "the Fluen" or "that Fluen." None of the regular citizens of Agoge seemed to know Clerin's name and that was just fine with Trela. She wanted the anger to stick on Lembin, not Clerin, which meant it was easier to leave the entire race being disparaged than correcting and directing some of that anger.

"Of course! Why else would that Fluen be here?"

There were so many reasons. One is very rarely in any particular place for any one reason. There is trail of inertia pulling you towards your past as you struggle forwards, altering your course as a rudder shifts the sailboat.

"I asked her to come."

"That was a mistake."

"Destiny is not a mistake."

"You feel Gorbanax was destined to die?"

"Yes." As she said it, she knew it to be true. "They chose this when they decided to inhabit the temples. They know what this realm does, they know what it means, more than anyone else. Only the Yavens might escape death here, and that is because they spend very little of their lives here."

Trela wanted to just yell that Clerin was off limits. That there would be no reprisals, no punishment. She was hesitant to come out and say that, however. She did not wish to rule in that manner. Though, if she had to, she certainly would.

"Still, murder must be punished, should it not? Assassination is punishable by death."

"What about an accident? If something were to happen that you did not intend, had no inkling of, then would you be willing to be put to death for your crime?"

"You are saying she was pure of intent?" His eyes narrowed. "That she was duped?"

"Yes. She was duped." Trela could not think of another way to explain things to that particular Pyran.

"Then the punishment should fall upon the Fluen Beleg." The leatherworker was nodding, squinting off at nothing in particular.

"Of course. And it will. A death for a death. But for that to work, it has to be planned in secret. We must not go shouting for vengeance in the streets. We must sharpen the assassin's blade quietly. We must be invisible as we move into position." Trela was not really sure what she was doing. She just wanted to convince this one Pyran not to try to make a ruckus. She had not really decided anything yet, she had not made any plans. She was merely sharpening her knives. But as she spoke, some small things seemed to fall into their proper places. The border of the puzzle was being constructed.

"Of course, my Queen." There was a brightness that backlit his eyes, a small smile that crept on to his lips. He nodded to himself. "Of course. That is your way. I should not have... well, I never doubted you, but, well... I am happy that you have explained yourself. Especially to one such as I. There has been some worry on the streets that nothing was to be done. That we were to just lie down and do nothing, that we were to take such monumental abuse and do nothing in return. We were worried that you were… excuse me… that you were less Pyran than before. That you had spent so much time with… the others, that you had lost your edge, your fire. I have never been happier to be so completely wrong. You are a planner. You have patience. You are working on your scheme, and we must join in on some of your patience. Yes, you have brightened my day indeed."

It was an odd conversation, surely. But each odd conversation steered her. Each one brought her a greater understanding of what her subjects were going through. She would let them say their piece, then keep herself from responding in a reactionary way. That was the most difficult part, to think of her response after they had spoken, not while they were speaking. What typically followed was another piece of the puzzle, another weft of the tapestry. As she was assuaging her subjects, she was working on her plans. Her schemes, as it were.

There was the blacksmith who was positive it was not Lembin, but Linchon. "That's what I'm curious about. I heard the Fluen's messages were only for Linchon. That it was Linchon who gave the Fluen the assassin's blade for Gorbanax. I bet Linchon is not even dead or dying or whatever. As horrible as the Fluens are, the Luftens are a thousand times worse. Always scheming against us Pyrans. They've always wanted to wrest the Oplet Lakes from us, our most lush farming region. They'd love to watch us starve. Oh, for sure, it was the Luftens. Have you investigated? I know things have just happened, but if you let too much time pass, they'll cover their tracks and it'll seem like there's no trail, no evidence. You must act quickly. You must investigate now. We must understand all the angles."

There were several who seemed to think Linchon was involved. There was only one who blamed Gunzgak, however. "The Gaens," as he had put it. It was much like the blacksmith. There were several items that brought these types of arguments under the same tent. They always complained about the race itself. They usually had some specific reason that the other race was jealous of what the Pyrans had, how they wanted to steal something from "us." And the grievances had very little to do with Gorbanax or the eruption. It was odd. The way the arguments were framed made ignoring them simple. *Though*, she thought to herself, *I really should understand all angles*. Linchon certainly did have something to do with what had happened.

Others were adamant that she do nothing at all, or at least not leave the realm looking for revenge. That the greatest thing would be to stay nearby and protect the realm. There were a fair amount in this camp, those uninterested in the broader implications.

"Does it really matter why? What's done is done. Our city, our realm, is damaged. Look there at the volcano. See how different it looks, how damaged it is? We must all work together to repair the city, to repair ourselves. We must prepare for more. What if we are attacked again? Should we remain as unguarded as we are now? We must spend our energies rebuilding and fortifying, truly." A pretty grocer with earnest eyes tried to convince Trela. "We need you here, all of us here, working together. What could be more Pyran than that?"

"We are under attack!" Others ran up to her flag as she walked between storefronts or near parks. "They are trying to kill us. You cannot seriously think this is over, can you? This is merely the first volley, the first strike. They are gathering their arsenal and preparing our downfall. All of us! Not just you, not just Agoge, but all of us. In a week's time, it'll all be over. We have less than a week, I wager. We should escape if there was somewhere to escape to. We should…"

And this was where it would get really odd. There were typically a list of things "we" should do. Much of it anarchistic or hedonistic, violent or sexual. Things that the speaker had thought about often, but never done. Old grudges rectified, old desires indulged, old flames fanned. It was as if the only thing keeping these Pyrans sane, as a functioning member of the society, was the thought that there was a tomorrow. That it was only the worry of the consequences that kept them in check. It was not the action itself that kept them subdued, no matter if it was abhorrent or stupid or dangerous. This was what had concerned Trela originally. These were the Pyrans that would riot and destroy. There was a darker nature in them, without any Tlana influence, that was held at bay by a veneer of respectability. It amazed Trela how thin that veneer was for some. She would do her best to assuage these Pyrans' fears, to assure them that not only there would be a tomorrow, but that the Guards were on high alert.

The "We should…" was not always violent. She was unconcerned about the hedonistic fantasies, as long as everyone involved was having a good time. Some of the "We should…" statements included professing love to a friend or previous lover. Would these be requited, or would Delubayn show up instead? Not all these confessions would work out, but some good might come of them. In which case, the death or dying of Gorbanax could seen as a good thing for a select few.

Others were not sure about what everything meant exactly. "Just because the volcano exploded, doesn't mean Gorbanax is dead. Maybe it was just angry. Or maybe, like someone partially poisoned, it was just vomiting out the noxiousness," an old wiry Pyran told her. "We all see what we want to see, that's what I've learned after the many cycles I've spent here. When some see a volcano explode, they see death and destruction. They see an ending. But what is an island but a volcano in the ocean? Some may see an explosion and see a beginning. Others, others may just see it as an explosion. These things happen. Now, they've happened at a temple, and when the Fluen was communing with Gorbanax. I'm certainly not saying there isn't a correlation. I'm certainly not saying that Gorbanax isn't dying. But… you should probably be sure, don't you think? You—" he pointed his finger directly at Trela "—you should probably make sure. You should go to the temple and speak with Gorbanax yourself. After all, Qizern used to do that. Every once in a while. You aren't afraid of anything Qizern wasn't afraid of, are you?" There was a bit of a twinkle in his eye. It made his words more cheeky than argumentative. Like he was just trying to pique her curiosity, not actually trying to harangue her.

It did pique her curiosity. Why had she not communed with Gorbanax? Was it just because Clerin always did? If she wanted to do it, and if it were still possible, then she should do it soon. For, no matter what different things her subjects told her, what theories they espoused, she knew that Gorbanax had been poisoned. That it was currently dying.

The vast majority of the Pyrans she spoke to, however, were angry. Her subjects wanted revenge. They wanted bloodshed. They wanted all the other Belegs to die, whether or not they were involved in killing Gorbanax. They wanted Trela to take an army of warpacks into the other realms and lay waste. The majority did not necessarily want a "no stone stacked atop another stone" type of waste, where salt would be poured on the fields, but most wanted her to march somewhere and kill someone. Or many someones. To leave a path of destruction through another realm, like a river of lava. These were not well thought out plans, they were just expressions of emotions. Yes, the Pyrans could be quick to anger. But considering their Beleg had just died, most probably murdered, it was an easily understandable emotion. One that Trela would need to redirect, but perfectly understandable.

So Trela spent that first day of work wandering amongst her citizens, interrupting them. She enjoyed herself and it seemed to help them, so she felt good about the time spent trying to understand at least the main archetypes of her subjects. So she decided to do that again on the second day of work. Then, during the first day of contemplation, she decided she should visit Gorbanax. She felt that would comfort her citizens, maybe Gorbanax, and definitely herself. Then, sometime that day or the next, she would need to think of some form of "tough love" for her advisors. Then she would have to prepare her speech at the end of the second day of contemplation. It would be a full couple of days.

On her way back she had a thought. She had not spoken alone with Ryshial about the recent events, even though they had been together all day. She knew that once they reached the balcony of her throne room, they would be surrounded by her advisors.

"Stop. Stop here." They had been flying, on their way back. The sky was the deep blue of dusk.

"Of course, my Queen."

"Listen, you don't have to…" Trela waved her hand in a small circle. "We are friends, are we not? We have survived many precarious situations together, haven't we?"

"Yes. And you are definitely my friend. You are also my queen. You can be both, yes? Even when we are alone, floating above your other subjects."

"Then, as both my friend and my mage, let me ask you something. What do you think of all this?" Her hand, unconsciously or not, waved towards the volcano. "You have listened to the many Pyrans who have given me their opinions today. You have listened to my responses. You have accompanied me on secret quests. You have an understanding of Belegs and Yavens, Vijen and Tlana, that is beyond most. You are, I believe, friends with Clerin, the one most blamed in this overarching conversation. With all that in mind, with everything, what do you think?"

"Hmmm. To be honest, I would have had an easier time answering that before this day, before hearing so many other opinions and responses." Ryshial laughed a little. She had a melodic laugh. "First, let me say that I do not blame Clerin. You are correct. I feel I know her, but even if I did not, it would not change anything. This—whatever this really is—is between the Belegs. She is a vessel, a tool. Not in a cruel way, as if she were empty, but it just means she is being steered, or pushed, or controlled, by beings beyond our understanding. We all are. We just went to the Fluen realm—I saw the Clatsvol Sea!—because of what the Belegs want of us lowly derlians. So, even if I did not know Clerin, I would not hold her responsible for what is going on.

"Second, from what I can gather, these deaths may take derlian generations to complete. So, I am unsure of the true impact to my personal life. Third, Gorbanax let this happen. Maybe it was unable to stop it, but it let it happen. So, in my opinion, there is a plan. Maybe the plan has already been completed, maybe not. So, if you are able, you should commune with Gorbanax, to figure out this plan." She looked pointedly at Trela. "Then you will need to follow the plan, which will, most likely, take you away from Agoge again.

"This brings me to the idea of vengeance. That was brought up by many of your subjects. I am perfectly happy with destroying Lembin. Lembin appears to be the root cause of all of this. But what of Gunzgak? Is that vengeance? I think not. Is that necessary?" Ryshial paused for a long time, staring over at the volcano. Trela let her take all the time she needed. Trela was not about to interrupt. "I do not think I have the power to say. Balance is desired, but it seems awfully unfair. As far as I understand, Gunzgak has done nothing against any of the other Belegs. I think that would be another reason to visit Gorbanax. To see if it has a plan, and whether or not that plan involves the answer to the Gunzgak puzzle. To hear it from Gorbanax itself, not through an intermediary or through some guess. And that is about it, really. I certainly do not think you should attack another realm of derlians. That would be even more foolish than blaming Clerin."

"And what about vengeance on Linchon? Do you think Linchon had something to do with this?"

"Those are two different questions. Vengeance on Linchon is like stabbing a corpse. I have seen warriors do it, and some of them appear to feel better afterwards, but it just seems useless to me. As for Linchon's involvement, I am not sure. I would have to speak with Clerin about it for a while, pick her brain about it, if you will. She is the only derlian to have an inkling as to what is truly going on here. And it is a very small inkle." Ryshial held her thumb and forefinger slightly apart and peered through the gap. Trela was not positive "inkle" was a word, but figured Ryshial would know more than she would. Besides, "inkling" had to come from somewhere.

"So, it all leads back to me communing with Gorbanax."

"In my opinion, yes."

"Would you take me up there and cast the required spells when I go? I'm worried that the garrison mages didn't make it out alive."

"You do not want Feyazki for that? Your Luften mage?" The emphasis of her voice turned the second sentence into a question. A belated continuation of the first.

"No, not really. I'd prefer my Pyran mage." Trela realized she leaned on Feyazki a lot. She already knew that but had thought of it from his point of view, that he was always being asked to do things. She had not really thought about how it would affect others. It was just that he was the first mage to join her, and he was incredibly competent. The Luften warriors were the first warriors to join her. She did not start coalescing her warpack until after the well. Her first Pyran warriors, mages, anything, really started when she found Lishean waiting for her. He had found the faithful for her, she had just needed to show up. And Ryshial, well she had come with the Mages' Guild after Trela had defeated Qizern. Ryshial was a master, one of the heads of the guild, one of the most powerful Pyran mages alive. And yet she had been made to feel secondary to a foreigner as far as her queen was concerned. Trela needed to fix that. Leaning on Ryshial more, and remembering to thank her, would go a long way towards helping.

It was in the same vein of her subjects thinking she did not want to rule since she kept running off to foreign realms. How could she be the Kriishan if she was never around? She needed to fix that as well. First things first, however. She needed to commune with Gorbanax. She knew she could not make plans until that had happened. Who knew what Gorbanax would want of her?

✳✳✳

The second day of work unfolded much like the first. Trela wandered the streets with her illusionary flag and spoke to all who came up to her. It was not as crowded around her as she had anticipated. Her citizens took the command to work quite seriously. It seemed they enjoyed having their heads down for the day, concentrating on what was immediately before them. On their work, on what they were good at. The day was long and though not overly physically demanding, felt a little arduous. Ryshial flew her from neighborhood to neighborhood, never complaining.

The first day of contemplation started simply. Trela knew the garrison had been destroyed after her meeting with Arnasta, Serghno, and Feyazki. So she had Ryshial fly them around the lava pit looking for the perfect place to land. Perfect was too strong of a word. They settled for "not bad." It was a flat-ish spot on the south side of the volcano, only about a hundred yards up in elevation from the lava. The smoke, though it was thinning up above, was noxious this close to the source. Ryshial had already cast some minor breathing and shield spells on them, just to get them there. Trela trusted Ryshial completely, but suddenly wished for a second mage. Just in case. What if the communing took a long time? What if Ryshial got tired casting breathing spells on herself while she waited on the ledge? What if she did not notice Trela drag herself out of the lava? What if Trela was unable to drag herself out? She shook her head to clear it. They were much too far down the path to turn back now.

"Okay, I'm ready." She was standing there in front of Ryshial, naked. She had not discussed this meeting with Clerin beforehand. She knew Clerin bathed in various stuff before she communed, but she felt quite certain that Qizern had not, though she had heard he had communed naked. So she had bathed in the morning, just to be safe, but that was it. Hopefully that was enough.

"Just breach the surface and think of me when you are done. I will find you and fly you out."

"That's what I'm counting on. In fact, if you think it is taking too long, just fly me out of there."

"How long do these things typically take?"

"Hmm. Maybe fifteen minutes?" Trela tried to think back when she would be waiting for Clerin. Impatiently waiting. Her sense of time when she was slightly bored was not the best.

"Okay. I will try to pull you out after fifteen minutes."

Trela was not sure if the word "try" was an ability thing, or a timing thing. She ignored it. She nodded that she was ready. Ryshial cast her spells. Trela took a leap into the lava pool.

The fall seemed longer than she had hoped, and the lava was incredibly thick as she struck it. The shield spell protecting her from the heat worked great for the impact as well. She slid into the viscous liquid, turning her world a bright yellow-orange.

Trela sank for a little bit, waiting for something to happen. She then swam a bit. Not really knowing where to go, she followed her nose. It felt like a good five minutes had passed, and yet nothing was happening. She started to worry that the fifteen minutes she had told Ryshial would be too short. Surely Clerin did not have to wait this long.

She began to wonder if Gorbanax was already fully dead. Was it no longer able to commune? She decided to send out thoughts. Maybe that would let it know she was there.

Gorbanax, this is Trela, she thought, over and over. She swam a little farther, peering into the brightness. There, off in the distance, was a black speck. She swam towards that. It may have been moving in her direction as well. In either case it increased in size until it was discernable.

It was a crude silhouette of a bonfire, as if it were carved out of wood. Trela had the advantage of having heard Clerin's descriptions of the way Gorbanax had shown her information. The silhouette bounced around in front of Trela for a moment, so she waved her hand in response.

Then, two other silhouettes appeared. They were flat black and were both roughly derlian shaped. They were close enough in appearance that Trela was unsure how to tell them apart. They shifted to each side of the bonfire. Not knowing what else to do, Trela waved again. The silhouette on her right waved when she did. The one on the left did not. Trela waved her left hand after that, then her left leg. The same silhouette made the same movements.

The bonfire moved forwards a little, or got larger, it was hard to say. Each of the derlian silhouettes rotated so they were facing the bonfire rather than her. They both bowed to the bonfire. The bonfire bowed to the one on the left, then to the one on the right. They all vibrated up and down a little, which made Trela think they were dancing.

Suddenly, the silhouette on the left touched the bonfire as they were dancing and it fell over. It looked like a flat line, as if the wood carving had fallen down and she was looking at its thickness, or rather its thinness. Trela gasped at the suddenness of it. Then, after a brief moment where all the silhouettes were still, the bonfire flipped back up and they all began dancing again.

They began to move while they danced, so that Trela had to rotate to keep them centered in her view. When they had moved enough that she had turned halfway around, she noticed another silhouette. This one was of a boulder. It noticed the dancing silhouettes approach and so it shifted a little, staying ahead of them. Trela rotated some more so that she kept her view between the boulder and the others.

The boulder sped up, the others sped up. After a moment, she realized the bonfire was nowhere to be seen. The other derlian silhouette, the trailing one, the one that did not represent her, had been too slow on the chase as well. She was now rotating quite quickly, keeping the boulder and her own silhouette in view. Her silhouette was gaining on the boulder. They were both still increasing in speed. She was having a hard time keeping herself rotating fast enough.

Suddenly the other derlian silhouette came back into view, as if it had stopped and waited for them to come back around again. The boulder touched the silhouette and fell over, becoming a flat line. When it popped back up, there were several silhouettes. A boulder, the bonfire, a cloud, and a wave. They, along with the derlian shaped silhouettes flanking them, all began to move like they were dancing. Even the boulder.

I understand, Trela thought. And she did. She had, kind of, wanted some ambiguity left to her. But Gorbanax's desires, whether or not they were anyone else's, appeared quite clear to Trela. She was going to have to leave her realm again. At least one last time.

A slow flow began in the lava, an upwards flow. Then the oddest thing happened. Though Trela could not feel the lava burning her, she could feel its density against her, like a soft mud. This was suddenly removed as an air bubble encompassed her. She could feel the lava being swept away as she became enveloped. Then lifted. She floated to the surface quickly. The bubble popped once she breached, but she floated into the air then, flying to a couple of rods above the lava surface. She was held there for a long minute, watching the smoke billow about and the yellow-orange lava bubbling beneath her. Half-spheres would reach the surface and then pop. It was like watching water boil with its time slowed down. Or with her own time sped up. How to tell the difference? She wiped herself down, making sure there was no lava stuck to her. The air bubble seemed to have taken care of that for her, however. It felt odd, not feeling the smoke in her lungs or stinging her eyes, not feeling the heat, but still able to feel her hands wiping her arms and legs, the pull of her fingers through her short hair.

Trela was then lifted to the height of the narrow shelf that Ryshial was on. Ryshial was mostly visible through the smoke, only periodically obscured. She made a gesture and pulled Trela towards her.

"Well?" Ryshial waited until Trela was mostly dressed before beginning the questioning.

"I don't know if there's a plan or not, but I certainly have my answer. Gorbanax wants Gunzgak dead." She decided to just say it. There was little use describing the antics of the imagery. Or, at least, she did not need any help with deciphering the imagery.

There was a hungry look in Ryshial's eye. She wanted more. More description, more information. It was palpable, but she held back.

"You will have to describe it to me some time." She nodded to Trela, and they began floating up with the smoke.

"Maybe after a meal. With some grog." She looked out towards the south, watching the world get smaller. "Maybe let's fly out over the ocean a little. I want to survey the damage."

Ryshial nodded, cast something quietly and shifted them horizontally. The side of the volcano contrasted somewhat with the cliff of the plateau. There was the inclined cone of new black rock gently sloping to the ocean, ending in plumes of white smoke. There was a portion of the caldera at the north, towards Agoge, that still pierced jaggedly into the sky. And farther out to either side, there was the unadulterated cliffs. They had a slight slope, but there were no beaches at the bottom, just ragged and jagged rock. Trela wondered what used to be there and when the last time an eruption had happened. Pyran history was a rich tapestry of wars and battles, but little time was spent on the natural happenings of the realm. Maybe whatever had happened occurred before there were Pyrans. Maybe nothing had happened and Gorbanax had just liked the look of it.

Trela was thinking of this and what it meant to run off on another Beleg errand when she thought of something to thank Ryshial for. "Thanks for pulling me out of the lava when you did, that was perfect timing. Or magma? How deep does lava extend?"

"What, no, that was not me." She shook her head slightly while continuing to stare at the scarred volcano. "I saw you pop to the surface. I just took over from there."

They flew back to Agoge, back to the balcony of her throne room. Trela found it interesting when, about a quarter into their way back, she suddenly felt the warm air against her skin. The protection spell must have worn off at that moment. She wondered if the energy of a long spell was spent at once, or if some energy was gotten back if the spell was canceled before fading. She did not ask while they were flying. It was probably common knowledge, just not common to her. They alighted softly on the balcony.

"Will you need me tomorrow? Or later today?" Ryshial glanced into the crowded throne room, then back again.

"No, I don't think so. I plan on using the amphitheater for my speech tomorrow and won't require your skills then. It can accommodate most of the citizens in the Blaze proper, not counting the rest of Agoge. But that should be enough. I'm assuming not everyone will attend, even if we made it mandatory."

"Well, I will certainly be there for the speech. But I do have some business at the guild to attend to."

"Good. Yes, go. I will let you know if I need something, but you should be clear until after the speech."

Ryshial bowed and then shot off into the air several times faster than when she flew with Trela. After glancing through the windows, a small sigh escaped from Trela's lips. It was the middle of the day, and her throne room was busy and bustling. *Being under lava and trying to communicate with a Beleg should be the last item of the day,* thought Trela. *Not the first.*

She opened the door with a flourish and strode in. Someone nearby closed the door behind her. There were some benefits to being a queen.

"I thought this was a day of contemplation?" She spoke with a grin on her face, soaking up the polite chuckles.

"We are contemplating how best to redistribute the food." This was from someone in the back of the room. Trela did not see who.

"I thought we were leaving half the food out today, outside the shops on carts, with Guards milling about making sure no one grabs too much." She had thought the plan was simple, yet still somewhat elegant.

"Well, yes, that is the plan. I think the issue is that the bakers are clumped together a little. They are not necessarily spread out throughout the city. They are especially sparse outside of the walls." Linloy spoke up.

"How do they typically eat? Surely they visit the bakers and grocers."

"Well, yes. But there is the idea that they should not have to go far from their houses, this being a day of contemplation and all." Linloy was nodding as he was speaking, which was odd since there was nothing to be nodding about.

"See? Even our queen thinks they are lazy. They should just walk to the shops!" Another advisor in the back raised his voice.

"No, now wait. No one thinks 'they' are lazy." Trela quieted the room with a quick wave of her hand. They had obviously been arguing about this long before she showed up. She needed to get up to speed with their previous unfinished arguments, and quickly. She realized Lishean was not there. Nor Estfale or Rewista or any of her trusted wartime advisors. Those before her were all wearing baggy clothes with things sticking out of them at odd angles, feathers and the like. There she was, in the heart of hearts of the Pyran realm, and she was surrounded by advisors who had never swung a sword. Had probably never slept outside for more than a week. She felt a twinge of nostalgia for the long campaign.

"Then we'll have the Guard move the food around. They can take some to the neighborhoods that do not have bakers or grocers." She glanced around her advisors, not quite glaring. "We can assume that those who live nearby, or do not mind a stroll on a day of contemplation, have already picked up what they need for the day. The carts can have various items on them—hard meats, dry cheeses, crusty bread—and they can be wheeled to where they need to be."

"Some are concerned about how long that will take, my Queen." Linloy raised a small finger as he spoke.

She wished he would just out with it. He had obviously been arguing something, and losing by the sounds of it. Maybe if she could speak with just him for a few moments, figure out what had been going on in her absence… But that would reek of favoritism, she supposed.

"We could have the Mages' Guild spearhead the mission. That would distribute the carts faster and easier." The thought came to her, and she spoke it. She was just trying to come up with a solution.

"Why would the mages give up their day of contemplation when no one else will?" That was from the back again. From the same voice that had mentioned her subjects being lazy. She felt good—she had figured out the thorn in Linloy's side.

"Who is that? Come forwards." Trela made a spreading gesture with her hands. "Part for him, make way. Come forwards." The second time she stated that was a little more heated than she had intended. It did, however, do the trick. Her advisors parted to allow the now somewhat reluctant speaker to have a path to walk up.

It was Shertzer, one of the leaders of the Mages' Guild. On par with Adzin and Ryshial. Trela had rarely interacted with him. It took her a moment to dredge his name from her memory.

"Shertzer, is it?"

"Yes, my Queen." He bowed his head shallowly.

"What is it that you do? Specifically."

"I am a guild master." He smiled and looked around. Some of those in the room smiled back at him. Some, those who could feel something coming on, kept their eyes low.

"And what does that entail? Are you a teacher?"

"Oh, no. No. That is for those lower in the hierarchy. You would not fill your day with teaching warriors how to swing a sword, would you?" He smiled around again. "I make decisions for the good of my guild. I represent them here. I provide advice to you, my Queen. I am here on this day of contemplation. I do not shirk. I am not lazy."

"So… you stand around and talk with your peers? When you are here, I mean. When you are not sitting and enjoying grog, I mean." She narrowed her eyes a little. "What do you do at the guild, then? What does this 'making decisions' entail?"

He glanced around a little nervously. Most of the others did not meet his eye. He was beginning to realize that something was amiss. It saddened Trela that he was that slow to pick up on things.

"We have many meetings discussing policies and duties. Myself, Adzin, Yenchak, Ryshial, and Ortunge. We discuss what the guild does and does not do, what—"

"Stop right there." Trela felt she had to interrupt. Then, to twist the knife a little, she paused for a long moment, letting his words fill the air. "You discuss what the guild does and does not do. So, you are saying that if I were to speak with Ryshial right now, she would explain how you discussed not using the entirety of the guild during this day of contemplation?"

They all knew that Trela had been with Ryshial almost exclusively for that last couple of days. They had no idea of what had been discussed between the two, what long conversations may have been had while no one else was around. They knew a trap was set; they were just not positive if Shertzer had already triggered it. Everyone kept their gazes either on Trela or the floor. No one glanced at Shertzer in that moment.

"No, not necessarily. I, uh, just wanted it to be fair. I mean, all the other guilds are using the day to contemplate." His eyes did not lift much beyond the floor as he spoke.

"That is an interesting word, 'fair.' Is it fair that you don't have to teach? That you get to sit around and make decisions? Is it fair that you get to stand around here and give me advice?" Her voice raised at the end of that last sentence.

"I have worked hard to reach my level in the hierarchy."

"No doubt." He may have been about to say more, but she interrupted again. "Do you know what angers me most about this?"

"No."

"It is that you have convinced yourself that you're helping. That you are a productive member of this advisory council. That you are a productive leader of your guild. We need help now!" She yelled the last sentence. He winced. They all winced. "I, your queen, just asked you for your help and what did you do? You projected your own laziness onto our citizens. Without discussion with the rest of the guild masters." She backed off a little but kept up her vehemence.

"I know that Ortunge…"

"No, you are not doing that." She interrupted him yet again. "You are not dragging anyone else down with you." She took a deep breath and spoke to everyone in the room. "You live lives that are not fair. All of you! You are allowed to parade around, thinking highly of yourselves, while you do nothing to solve real problems that are happening in the moment. That is your job! Your job, your quite cushy job at the top of the hierarchy, is to solve problems. And that is what I expect. Rightly so. If I ask what can you do, what can your guild do, I do NOT expect to be told 'nothing.' 'We're so sorry queen, our guild members are invalids who are unable to lift a finger in our realm's time of need.'" Her tone was mocking, maybe more so than she had intended, but her anger and annoyance were still rising. "Do you know what should happen to that response? Do you know what another ruler might choose as a consequence?" There was a moment of silence.

"No. Of course not. No one wants to make the suggestion." Trela calmed her voice down. "Well, I will tell you what I will do if you do not perform your actual job. I will take it from you." There was a scent of danger in the air, but Trela ignored it. No matter what she thought about him as a derlian, Schertzer was a grand master mage. He could surely be quite dangerous if cornered. "You will teach novices for the next three moons. I will then have a discussion with the other guild masters concerning your level in the hierarchy." She paused for a moment, lifted her chin, and spoke to the rest of her advisors.

"These are unprecedented times, I understand that. This has never happened before and it shall never happen again. But that is precisely why we must pull together. We must push ourselves, our subordinates, each other, to do better. To be better. We must reach for the stars now more than ever. And if the effort is put in, even if the outcome is not as desired, then the rewards will follow. It is this collective effort that I crave, that I demand. Now, those who are needed, go and perform your duties. Those that are not may rest and contemplate. You," she pointed at Shertzer, "will need to *whisper* to Ryshial and Adzin. Have them come here to speak with me about the guild's required involvement. And have one of them pick up Wesduin along the way. He will be invaluable."

"Of course, my Queen." Shertzer bowed his head humbly, but not overly submissive.

After everyone else had left, Shertzer included, Linloy came up to Trela. He had a small wry smile on. "You did well, my dear.

If you stick around, you might have a competent and obedient group of advisors."

Trela noticed the "stick around" part but ignored it. She thanked him for his advice and let him go as well. She had several moments of quiet in her large empty throne room. It was quiet enough to make her wonder about her chastisement of Shertzer. She had needed to make an example of someone, but was that the best choice? Was his hesitancy to help, and let's face it, his air of superiority, that egregious? He had been the only one to speak out, however. And Trela had responded naturally, without "malice aforethought" which, according to Knill, would mean that she was following her destiny. The thought of Knill made her smile a little. It had been a while since she had thought of him outside of his presence. She had just been so busy.

Trela's meeting with Ryshial, Adzin, and Wesduin was quick. She felt a little sheepish at bringing Ryshial back right after saying she was free, but what else was there to do? She needed swift competency. Adzin *whispered* to his guild and then they all flew to the main square where Trela explained to Lishean and Wesduin what needed to happen. Forty mages of various skill levels arrived shortly after they did. After careful calculations by Wesduin and some discussions amongst all gathered, the mages and their Guard counterparts spread out throughout the city to redistribute what was left of the provisions.

Trela stayed down in the main square with Lishean until the mages made it back. It only took about two hours. The swiftness of it all renewed her annoyance with Shertzer. It made her feel a little better about her earlier outburst.

Ryshial took her aside at the end of it all. "I have been doing a little research."

"About what?"

"About some help, some guidance. You say that Gorbanax wants to help Linchon and Lembin?"

"Yes." She glanced around warily for a quick moment, but there was no one else around. "Gorbanax wants death to come to them all."

"And you say that you are unsure if they can be trusted? The other Belegs."

"Yes. That is my main concern."

"Well, there is a mage in Ariellyna who may know a Yaven that knows Linchon. Or knew Linchon. Her name is Hyscarne. If we are headed in that direction, we may as well gather all the information we can."

"Thank you. I will surely keep that in mind." A direction to head was better than none. And at that moment she had no other direction in mind.

Trela decided to ride back up to the Blaze to avoid taxing the mages further, especially Ryshial—she had certainly gone above and beyond already. It was a pleasant ride. The streets were mostly empty, and the sky was clear as long as she did not look directly at the volcano. There was an apple tree casting comfortable shade to her right, a statue staring at a sundial frozen in time on her left. But she did not stop to enjoy, she had much to do. She tried to work on her speech in her head as she rode but did not get very far into it before she reached the open gates of the Blaze.

It was well into the afternoon by the time she finally got alone in her chambers and able to start on the speech. She was a little restless, however, and decided to have a quiet meal with Knill instead. It had been a while since they had spent much time alone together. Since all her chefs had the evening off, even Kolaf, they rummaged around the massive kitchen and threw together what they could find. They had a fantastic time.

Trela woke up late for the first time in a long time. She bathed slowly, got dressed slowly, got to her chambers slowly. She was well relaxed but was still having problems getting her speech written. She had nothing else to procrastinate with, however, so she stared at her blank parchment for a while. She wrote a couple of one sentence quips, hoping the rest would come. She paced for a while, stared out a window for a while, sat in different positions. Nothing really worked.

She was actually at the desk, quill in hand, when Knill knocked lightly at her door. She could tell it was Knill since no other derlian, certainly no Pyran, could knock that softly and still make it insistent. She was still in a good mood, even with her assignment going as poorly as it was.

"Enter." She kept her head down, scribbling nothing of worth.

"Hey. I hate to bother you, but Croy came by earlier and he would like to talk with you."

"Well, I really need to get this speech written. Is he with you?" She replaced her quill and peered around Knill's frame outlined by the doorway. Croy was not large, but Knill was a fair bit smaller. She did not think they could both be in the doorway and not be noticed, but the hallway was a little dim.

"No, no. I wasn't sure if you would be available. I wouldn't even be bothering you today, but he was quite insistent." Knill looked a little sheepish.

"Well, I… I am a little busy right now."

"That's what I told him. I did. But, you know, it kind of seems odd for you to be writing anything anyway. You know you can just stand up there and say the right things. You're the Kriishan." He looked hopeful at that. He typically looked a little hopeful, but it was the way it mixed with the sheepishness that almost changed her mind.

"Tell him I will meet with him tomorrow. Around noon. How does that sound?" She figured that would allow her morning to unfold organically and yet be early enough to indicate she was trying to be helpful

"Yeah, okay. I'll tell him that." He bobbed his head a little as he left. His smile did not seem *too* hurt. The door closed silently, with only the small click of the latch at the end.

Trela stared at her parchment. And stared. Maybe she should go talk with Croy? She decided that would be procrastinating and kind of wished she had responded that way immediately. But she had not. Nor did she write much, unfortunately. It was a frustrating day. She pushed lunch late, thinking she would write instead, but then became distracted by her hunger. By the time she had to get dressed for the speech, she only had a small outline. Which she ended up not bringing due to the size of the parchment and the amount of squiggles that covered it.

She wore a dress uniform. One that would certainly never be worn in battle, but still conveyed usefulness. The breeches were not baggy, and she carried a short sword and long dagger on her hips. Her top was of leather, but a supple leather. And it was all a rusted brown color, except for her black boots. She had her boots rubbed down with a little olive oil, giving them an unnatural shine. She felt comfortable in front of the mirror. Not too showy, but with an attire that understood the gravity of the situation.

✳✳✳

The amphitheater was full by the time she was flown in. There were four mages at the corner of the small stage, to re-sound her words back into the audience and behind her. There was more attendance than she had assumed, the seats were filled all the way around her and there were plenty standing in the aisles, right near the stage, way in the back. She had originally thought the amphitheater would only be half full, or slightly more than half, and she could just project her voice to those in front of her. The mages were chosen due to their skill and diligence, with special consideration of their standing. She thought it was partly an honor and partly a chore. She had not wanted the guild masters to be required, but they could certainly not be neophytes. The crowd quieted as she walked to the center of the stage. She took a deep breath.

"Friends." She liked addressing her subjects as friends. "We have witnessed a great shift. What was before will not be the same as what is after. There was a line in the sand, and we now stand on the other side. It is like a birth, in that everything changes after that moment. It is irreversible." She had though momentarily about likening the irreversibility to death but had discarded that idea for obvious reasons.

"Let me be clear, shifts like this, as great as this, can be unnerving. I do not wish to belittle or diminish anyone's experience of this. We are all digesting it, personally and collectively, and that will take time. However, I trust in my heart of hearts that we are not under any imminent threat from another Beleg. From another realm. I admit here, before all of you, that this is a tragedy that has struck us. But it is not an insurmountable one. It is not the beginning of a war, but the beginning of a truce. Gorbanax knew well what was happening—before, during, and after—and did not falter. Did not hesitate. Did not dodge or bargain or quibble. It did not strike out, in defense or offense, against any derlian, Yaven, or Beleg. We must trust Gorbanax to know what it was doing. That it was not taken by surprise, that it allowed things to happen willingly, that it had a plan. We must trust Gorbanax. Plainly and simply, no matter what else occurs, we must trust Gorbanax.

"Why do I say that Gorbanax was not taken by surprise? Because there were conditions placed on communing with it. Conditions you all know, if not specifically, at least generally. I was sent on a quest for Gorbanax. I, your queen, was unable to properly rule because I needed to do what Gorbanax requested of me. Soon after gaining my throne, before I could enjoy it, I was asked to leave the realm and conquer a foreign evil. What do you do when something is asked of you by your Beleg? You trust it. You comply. Gladly. I trusted Gorbanax completely and I accomplished what was requested of me. That is what a good Pyran does, is it not?" They were not expecting the pause, so there was a moment of silence before they responded. Trela needed them to feel invested, however, so she accepted the small stumble in her speech.

"I would also like to point out that, as derlians, we do things that the Belegs ask of us without question. The Belegs created us, created the world; who are we to question? I mention this because, maybe, if we understood what was being asked of us, if we had even posed the question, we might have argued. Not that we would have—if Gorbanax ever asks me to fall on my own sword I hope to have the courage to do so—but we might have. This is not the case, however. Since we do not ask the question, since our obedience to the Belegs is blind and instant, we do not even know what we are agreeing to. We merely perform. We accomplish or perish. Forgive me for this aside, but I think it is important to understand what has happened from the derlian perspective. From *all* derlians' perspective." She did not want to say Clerin's name aloud at any time during her speech. "When you are commanded a task by a Beleg, by multiple Belegs, you perform that task. That is what a good Pyran does, is it not?" She did not have to wait long for the response, but it was more muted than the previous one. She wondered if she had pushed the point too far. She certainly did not want her citizens obeying every order from any outranking Pyran without question.

"This is beyond just us. This is beyond our realm. This is beyond just one Beleg. This shift involves all of us. Every realm, every Beleg. The Belegs have a plan and they are implementing it. Gorbanax has a plan and is implanting it. Gorbanax is not gone, I communed with it myself just yesterday. There is a scheme brewing that we must engage in. We have more requirements from Gorbanax. I may have to leave you once more, for one more errand, for one more quest. To confront and defeat more evils in other realms. Trust in me, trust in Gorbanax. We are Pyrans and we will resolve this in the Pyran way." This pause received a quick and robust cheer.

"This shift involves all of us. Every one of you. We must be strong for what is to come. We must pull together and join with our neighbors. We must look out for one another. Now is not the time to cower in fear in some corner, hoping what has happened did not, or hoping it will go away and things will return to how they were. This is foolish. This is how children behave. Nor is this the time to take advantage of your neighbor; to rob, steal, or disparage. That would be bullying. This is also how children behave. We are what we make of ourselves through our actions. We must be cognizant of that in this time of flux. To be aware of our surroundings, including the history that shadows them. To be aware of our friends and strangers, including their choices that have colored them. To take the time to understand. To choose the better response. To not live reflexively, but with intent. This takes energy and effort. It is easier not to.

"But we do not have the luxury of a choice anymore. The labor pains have occurred and there will be plenty of pain to follow. The volcano has exploded. The shift has already begun. To face it and acknowledge it, to accept our reality whether or not we enjoy it, to cooperate and struggle together, this is what good Pyrans do, is it not? This is what we shall do." The applause was gratifying. She wished she had a longer speech. They had probably taken five times as long to assemble and would take another five to disperse. But she had not written much and had just spoken from her heart. She was a Pyran of action, not of words. And actions, positive actions, were what made a good Pyran, did they not?

Chapter 11

Croy was flying, which is how he knew he was dreaming. Anytime he found himself flying without remembering casting a spell, it was a dream. There were trees underneath him as well. Even though there were forests in the Pyran realm, there were not any on the Dekhan Plateau.

As he was flying along, a robed figure floated into view and floated alongside him, the brown cloak fluttering behind. As per usual, the cowl on the robe figure defied the wind and stayed up, hiding the face of the figure. The figure paced him for a little while.

Another figure slid into view and began flying on the other side of Croy. This one looked the same as the previous, the same brown robes, the same brown cloak and cowl. Croy was now flanked. The forest below was a sea of green, full of conifers that reminded him of the trees on the lower portion of the mountains around Serif. There was even a mountain barely visible through the overall haze.

Then another figure, and another. He was soon surrounded and more kept showing up. There may have been around twenty of them by the time they stopped arriving. They all seemed friendly, supportive. He was happy they were there. He felt he was lucky to have them around. He felt they were allies.

As they were flying along, they started heading towards the mountain. Visually, it seemed they were speeding up, but the wind did not appear to pick up. As they were getting closer, Croy noticed a dark spot on the mountain. It got bigger and seemed to get darker as they got closer. He realized they were headed for that spot. It swallowed his attention. He was eventually able to see that it was a giant cave entrance. His companions drew together, flying in a tight formation with him at the center. He was a little concerned at the speed they were traveling but they were not slowing down.

Croy was not looking around as they entered into the cave, but it did not appear that any of his companions were hurt or scraped off. The cave-tunnel was quite large and wound its way deep into the mountain, never narrowing or taking too sharp of a turn. Like many of his dreams, there was light from an unseen source making the underground visible.

Eventually they started slowing. Eventually they stopped. They stopped in a large round cavern, perfectly spherical. The figures spread out in a ring, outlining the perimeter. They all had their heads bowed, their faces still hidden by their cowls. Croy floated there in the center of the sphere.

A low chant started. It came from all around, so Croy assumed it came from the figures. The room created a small echo, making the continuous chanting multi-layered. It built up until it started sounding like a rumble. Then the rumble started in earnest. It came from directly below Croy, through the rock floor. He could feel it thrumming in the air.

Croy was looking down between his feet watching the static stone. Then, suddenly, the ground burst open and what looked like a Gaen Yaven floated out. It was gigantic, many times the size of Croy or one of the figures. It just kept floating out, half-filling the room. It stopped when its head was even with Croy. The head was taller than he was. The chiseled face looked more derlian than any Yaven he had ever seen, certainly more derlian than Phyna. There were lines on it, or cracks, Croy was unsure. The chiseled hair was curly and a little less than shoulder length. There was no beard, and the face was a bit androgenous, though Yavens generally looked that way. There was a sad expression to the giant face. That was what really hit him, made his breath catch in his throat. The sorrow that emanated from it.

"I have tried to communicate with you, through you, but it has been difficult for several reasons. Now that Gorbanax is dead, one of those reasons has been mitigated. It is quite unfortunate, Gorbanax was a great friend. They were all great friends. Now we have come down to this. I feel I need to speak plainly. We do not have much time left and there should be no confusion." The mouth did not move while it was speaking but the eyes betrayed great emotion. "You must stop Clerin Toswin. Do not hesitate at any cost. Kill her if you can. No matter the suffering, she must be stopped. Though she appears a harmless vessel, she carries within her the assassin's blade. I understand that you may have a fondness for her. You have traveled together and experienced much. I understand she has been kind to you and to others. You may love a mountain lion. They may love you back. In typical times, there may be no need for violence. But now the lioness is hungry, starving. Now she has lost her territory and is cornered. If she is able to strike at me, she will. And she will connect with the killing blow. I am doing my best to avoid such a strike. She is Lembin's only chance. Once she has been killed, I will be able to exact my revenge, but until then I must lie in wait.

"You are the only one I can commune with, Croy. The only one I can trust. I have tried others, but you are the only one who can listen and understand. You are my last and greatest hope. Through your dreams I have attempted to help you, to guide you in your life. Through your dreams I have given you glimpses into the future and shown you the correct response. I have been helpful to others of your group as well. It was I who shielded Trela and Knill as they escaped Serif. Tell her that. She needs to know that. She should, according to her own code, find that instigates a loyalty. She would have been trapped in Serif had I not sheltered her. She would not have achieved her destiny or, at least, not achieved it within the same timeframe without my interference on her behalf. You will need allies, Croy. You must cultivate these allies. You must gain their trust, which should be easy for you since you are always so kind. Trela should be your first attempt.

"The most difficult blockage will be Feyazki. He does not need to die, but I am afraid that will be the only way to stop Clerin. They are too close, they have been pair-bonded, and it may take death to break that bond. And it appears that he is not angered by the thought of his Beleg, his creator, being destroyed. I do not always understand derlians, certainly not Luftens, but his mind is utterly confusing to me. Maybe it is because Linchon did not interact with its derlians. Maybe that silence was confused with a feeling of abandonment. He is an orphan after all. I am unable to ascertain the issue, but he will be incredibly difficult to sway. As I stated earlier, begin with Trela. If she is able to be convinced, then there may be a way to convince Feyazki.

"Do not show your intentions too quickly. Your best asset is surprise. They will never suspect you. Which is why I am unable to explain my entire plan to you at this moment. The less you know, the better. If it is a surprise to you, it will be much more of a surprise to them. I did need to communicate this to you, however. I need you to understand what is going on, exactly what is at stake."

There was a small pause and Croy asked a question that had been bothering him for so long. "Where is Tumu?"

"That is an excellent question, one that I wish I knew the answer to. Tumu was not stolen in the Gaen realm and is not a Gaen. It does not seem like he has perished, but that can be difficult to tell.

Finding him may help your cause. Now that Gorbanax is dying, however, I am not positive. I do not know how his powers came to be, whether they were provided to him through Gorbanax or not. I assume that if Clerin reaches me with the assassin's blade, I will be unable to communicate to you through your dreams anymore. You will only know the chaotic random nonsense that permeates most sleeping derlians. Is that your desire?"

"No. No, of course not. My dreams are a part of my uniqueness. Part of me."

"And, knowing that I do not wish to die, do you wish it?"

"No, of course not. If you wish to live, you should be able to live."

"Good, good. Remember that when others wish to argue otherwise. It really is that simple. I will speak with you again, I am certain. Dawn is approaching, our time is almost up. Go. Find Trela and convince her that murder is not the way. If you are unable to convince her, we will have to find another way of persuasion."

Before Croy could respond, he woke up. He found himself sitting upright in bed, covered in sweat, heart pounding. He breathed in deeply several times to calm himself. There was nothing scary, specifically or individually within the dream, but it was all scary. All of it. He could not kill Clerin. He was incapable of that. He knew that. And even if he was able to, Feyazki would stop him before he spoke one syllable. All he could hope was to convince her that killing Gunzgak was wrong. Could he do that? He was not sure. Gunzgak was right about one thing, however. He would have to start with Trela. If he could convince her then there would be at least two voices against Clerin. And an entire realm's army. That could only be helpful.

He took his time getting ready. It was the second day of contemplation that Trela had declared and the odds that she would see him were slim. He would certainly make the effort, with the idea that he would set the meeting as soon after the volcanic explosion as possible.

Eventually he began his short journey from his quarters to the main castle of the Blaze. Or was it a citadel? Or a keep? He was never quite sure. Mostly because he never really referred to what building he was visiting, but who he was visiting. If he said he was visiting Knill, others would merely nod in agreement. That and the fact that the Blaze was a complete maze that made it difficult to know when one building ended and another began.

He was looking forwards to meeting with Knill even though it had not been too long since they had traveled together. They had barely gotten back to Agoge, had barely gotten their things in order, when the volcano exploded. *When Gorbanax was killed by Clerin,* Croy made himself think. He was unsure if he could find his way around Agoge again. But he figured, worst case, he could just ask a Pyran for directions.

He wandered a little lost at first, but the closer he got to the center of the Blaze, the more familiar things appeared. By the time he finally reached the Guards at the entrance to Trela's residence he felt comfortable with where he was going. Of course, from there to Knill he would be escorted. He could not get lost at that point even if he would have wanted to.

He followed the Guard through a maze of passageways, doors, and stairs. He was certainly glad for the guide. The Guards were a taciturn bunch and this one was no different. Besides being told to follow, the Guard said nothing to Croy. Until they got to the main chamber door.

"You may knock."

So Croy knocked. He wondered what would happen if Knill did not answer. Would he immediately be escorted back out? Would he be allowed to sit at the bench outside the door and wait? Would the Guard wait with him? He did not have to wait long, however. The door swung open to a smiling Knill.

"Croy, fantastic, come in."

Croy entered and the Guard closed the door for them. The room was quite large, it was the entrance room to the chambers, the waiting room or sitting room. Croy wondered for a moment what the main difference was, especially since they were already in the chambers. Surely, a waiting room should be outside of any chambers. Though, he thought, there could be some waiting before being allowed further in. And if he was allowed all the way through the chambers, he would end up in a throne room, back out into the public rooms.

"Please, sit." Knill sat himself down.

"What a wondrous sitting room." Croy was not corrected, so he sat down. "Did you ever imagine such opulence? Way back when you were an apprentice down in Serif?"

"No, not really. Things were never my motivation. I followed my heart here. To this dry, lifeless desert."

It was not completely dry on the plateau, but Croy understood what Knill meant. It was not really a comment about their surroundings, their environment. He had not wanted to start this way. Knill could get despondent easily if allowed.

"I just meant that I had never even imagined I'd travel to the Pyran realm, let alone know the queen." He had almost mentioned something about Knill but had been unsure of what to call him. The queen's consort? Was that the term if they were not handfasted? He was glad he had stopped himself.

"I have found myself wishing she had never become queen." Knill was looking down but raised his head. "But she is the Kriishan, and if it hadn't ended in her being queen, it would have ended with her being dead. So, all things considered…" Knill looked around the opulent sitting room and waved his right hand a small circle. There were four little tables with some chairs around them and a couple of low, long tables with sofas in front of them. All the fabric was exquisitely embroidered, all the wood some type of mahogany. One wall was glass, looking out to a balcony that looked out over the city. It let a lot of light in.

"But that is not why you came here." Knill brought his gaze back to Croy. "You are not here to chat, are you? We've been off the road for less than a week."

"No, sorry. I am here because I need to speak with Trela."

"Well, even though we had a lovely evening in last night, she is in her study today. Not to be disturbed."

"I assumed she would be busy. Last day of contemplation and all. I just needed to put in my request. The earlier the better. Though, if maybe you were able to convince her to speak with me later today, sometime this evening…" He should not have pushed it, but he did want to speak with her before Clerin could. He wanted to plead his case first.

"I'll ask. But, really, no promises."

"Of course not. No need to be pushy. Tomorrow would be great. If not then, then as soon as she is able." He sat there nodding for a moment. He should have thought of something to speak about before he came over. He tried at the moment, but his mind kept racing between Gunzgak, Clerin, and Tumu. Certainly not subjects to bring up with Knill. Maybe later. Maybe after he had discussed them with Trela. But he did not wish to plant any seeds in Knill's mind before he spoke with her. He wanted the subject to be brought up by himself. Not necessarily as a surprise, as a verbal ambush, but mostly to read her first reactions. To be there as her mind mulled it over for the first time. He would certainly enlist Knill at a later date if he had to.

"Are you going to the amphitheater? For the speech?" Knill broke the quick silence.

"Yes. Of course." He had not really thought about it, but in hearing the question he answered without thinking.

They spoke of little things after that, mostly about the Pyran realm. Croy's mind wandered to what Knill thought about what had happened to Gorbanax, but he kept the conversation on the mundane. He promised himself he would find out later.

Croy headed over to Trela's chambers the next day. Often the Guards would make one wait a while before taking them to meet with Trela, but they led him back to the chambers immediately. He had been unsure how informal their talk was going to be, if they were going to meet in an empty throne room or a study or her private chambers. They ended up sitting alone in the sitting room. It was comfortable, physically and otherwise.

"Knill said you wanted to talk with me." Trela spoke right as she sat down. Her smile was relaxed, making Croy think she was not trying to speed him up, just getting to business.

"Do you ever wonder how you and Knill escaped Serif?"

"Yes, sure. Why?"

"Because I know. I just found out."

Her face froze for a quick moment. If Croy did not know her, he may have assumed that her mind froze as well. He knew her mind sped up when she looked like that, however. It was her way to let various emotions wash over her and not betray anything. Her eyes focused back on Croy.

"I assume this came to you in a dream."

"Yes. And that mystery has been solved as well. Where my dreams come from."

"The suspense is killing me." Trela spoke into Croy's pause. "Gunzgak."

"Gunzgak sends you your dreams?"

"Yes. And it protected you. It kept the Gaen mages from tracking you down, it kept the 'jin from finding you. It knew of your destiny and approved of it, even if you and your destiny were Pyran. Now, I'm not saying you would have never left Serif without Gunzgak." He laughed and opened his hands. "All I'm saying is that when you left, when you escaped on your own, Gunzgak noticed and helped you from getting caught and sent back. You know the 'jin would have increased their surveillance of you."

"And how do you know all of this?" Her face, while not frozen, was certainly inscrutable.

"This last dream was had without a veil. Gunzgak spoke to me directly and explained everything. It wanted me to let you know that it helped you."

"Why?" Her eyes narrowed slightly, then relaxed. "I'm grateful, really. I don't want you to think I'm not grateful. I just… Why are you telling me now? Or why is Gunzgak telling you now?"

"Well, it alluded that that there was some sort of tacit agreement between the Belegs about direct interference, or maybe that Gorbanax had been blocking some of the communication, that part was a little vague." Croy knew where she was headed and, since he was headed there as well, he did not wait. "Do you wish to die?"

"Of course not."

"If someone came to kill you, they would be a murderer, would they not?"

"Only if they succeeded."

"And if they were sent by another? If someone else got them to attack you, they would be called an assassin, would they not?"

"Yes."

"And if they tried, you would try to stop them."

"Of course."

"Then why is Clerin allowed to do what she has been doing?"

That was the pause. They both knew where the argument was going. Or, at least, Croy had not tried to hide anything. But once it was said, it was met with silence and Trela's passive countenance. He wanted to keep arguing but was not sure how to say the same thing in a different way. He needed her response before he could provide his rebuttal. Trela took a deep breath.

"No one knew what was going on until it was too late, Croy. Nobody allowed anything to happen."

"Well, we know now, right? Now we know what is happening. Anything allowed beyond today will be a conscious decision. If you allow Clerin to commune with Gunzgak, you will be an accomplice. If you help Clerin to commune, you will be part of the murder. There is no more innocence. The veil has been lifted. After today, your argument pulls no weight."

"Croy, look, I understand your position here…"

"You understand my position?" He interrupted her. He probably should have let her finish her thought so he could provide a proper response, but the absurdity of her arguing against him was too much. "How are you not angry? How are you not calling for revenge? How can you sit here doing nothing?"

"Croy…"

"She killed your Beleg!" He stood, though he did not know why. There was too much energy running through him to leave him seated. It brought her to her feet as well. "She killed Feyazki's! She wants to kill mine! How are you calm through this?"

"Sit down!" She did not reach for a weapon, of which there was at least one on her person, Croy would have bet money on it, but she had steel in her voice.

Croy was a mage. He could have killed her before she got a blade in his throat. Maybe. She could be awfully quick on the battlefield, he had seen that. But that was not her concern, not really either of their concerns. Her voice was her weapon. Her authority was her blade. Croy, who had saved her life when she was an adolescent, sat down. His visage was dark and stormy, a frown plastered on his typically smiling face. She re-sat down across from him.

"There is a lot at stake here, Croy. These are not decisions to be made lightly or, I might add, heavy with emotion. Do I wish Gorbanax was not dying? Of course! Do I wish one of my greatest friends, my Fluen princess, had nothing to do with this… this assassination? Of course! But this is not the reality I'm living in. These wishes are useless, not worth the breath they are spoken with. Certainly not worth the time and energy I have already wasted on them." She did look a little sad, as if she really had spent some time with those thoughts.

"I wish the same things as you do. What has already been done to Gorbanax has not yet been done Gunzgak. These are not the same problems; they are completely different. These wishes of mine are not yet useless. Unless, of course, you wish them to be." Croy looked plaintively at Trela. "You are the key here. Which lock you wish to open is up to you."

Croy had wanted to stay and talk for a while. He had wanted to convince her that allowing a Beleg to be murdered was wrong. In his mind, before he had left his quarters, the entire conversation went differently. It was more cordial, more comfortable, friendlier. They would have laughed together about mutual experiences. She would have been reminded of how vulnerable she had been when they first met. His arguments would have built upon each other until there was only one logical conclusion. None of that had happened, however. He blurted out what he had come to say in the most prosaic way possible. There had not been enough time for… anything, really. But there it was.

Croy stood and wiped his moist palms on his trousers. Trela appeared to be deep in thought, which was probably the best he could hope for. He bowed to her; she nodded absently to him. He left feeling frustrated.

He wandered the grounds of the Blaze for a while. He was not really paying attention to where he was going, he was just enjoying being alone. He ended up in a small walled garden. There were little bushes, some benches around a simple fountain, and a vine creeping up the shady side of a wall. He stood there for a while, staring at the vine, hands clasped loosely behind his back.

What motivates you? he thought to the vine. *How can you cling to this lifeless stone for your entire life? Struggling to get higher, stretching towards the top of the wall, struggling to reach the direct rays of the sun? Especially since you know you will die before the struggle ends.* He was thinking about the futility of effort in the face of certain doom when he was interrupted.

"Hey, what are you doing here?" It was Feyazki. He was smiling and walking over. "I was just on my way to see Trela."

"That's funny, I was just leaving there." He had actually left a while ago, but that made no difference to their conversation.

"Oh, really? What did you talk about?"

"Just how completely wrong it is that Clerin is allowed to assassinate Belegs." It just popped out of his mouth, completely bypassing his brain. Feyazki's face froze but, unlike Trela's, it showed shifting emotions as he processed what Croy had said.

"I assume this is a subject that you brought up."

"Yes. Gunzgak came to me in a dream. Apparently, Gunzgak has been a source of my dreams."

"Well, you know my take on it, don't you?"

"No. Not really."

"Clerin is my lover and Linchon is already dead. I do not have a personal opinion on the matter, I certainly harbor no ill will towards Gunzgak, but I will protect Clerin with my life." He narrowed his eyes a little at Croy. "Seriously, Croy. I will not hesitate. I will even strike first if I feel the need to."

"Well, I..." He had not been on the receiving end of a warning from Feyazki before. He did not like it. There was something sparkling in Feyazki's eye as he spoke. Not necessarily of a desire, but something that spoke of the commitment to follow through. Not that he would enjoy the deed itself, but that he would enjoy the unfettering that committing the deed would allow. That rare freedom from society's norms that protecting a loved one entailed. The overreaction that would be sanctioned. Croy imagined that he would be obliterated without a second thought. The idea saddened him a bit. Not the actual obliteration, but that Feyazki would not be bothered by it. But then Feyazki interrupted him.

"Which is why you need to talk to Clerin."

"What?"

"My hands are tied on this issue. I will follow Clerin. Unless you feel you can stop me, you must deter Clerin."

"Do you think she would listen to me?"

"Clerin? Of course she would. At heart she is a diplomat's daughter. Sorry, that probably sounded condescending. I did not mean it that way, I was just trying to acknowledge where she came from. Let me start again. At heart she is a diplomat."

"Do you think I can sway her?"

"No idea. None. You have a good argument, you certainly have right on your side but, as I said, she is a diplomat, through and through." His smile was relaxed. Comfortable. "But you have a better chance at convincing her than the alternative. At least that's my take on it. She will at least consider your argument, whereas I cannot."

"Well... Thank you for your advice." Croy nodded to Feyazki, who nodded back.

"No problem. Oh, by the way, we are at Gyllhelon's old quarters, near Haswyxe. It would be appreciated if you didn't tell anyone where we are staying. At least for a little while."

Feyazki left with a smile. Assumedly on his way to speak with Trela. At this point, everyone would soon know that Croy was arguing against Clerin. He had thought it was a simple argument. Right really was on his side, as Feyazki had noted. But he seemed stymied by the periphery players. Feyazki was correct, he needed to speak with Clerin directly. He decided to head over right away. He left the vine in the garden to struggle on its own, as it had always done.

It did not take him too long to figure out where he was. Then it was a walk to where Haswyxe's quarters were. He knew how to get there, though he had visited Haswyxe less often than Haswyxe had visited him. Though he could fly, he had never really navigated that way the last time he lived there, so walking was much simpler.

It took less than an hour to get to Clerin's from the garden. All in all, it was an enjoyable walk. He enjoyed wandering and the weather was good and the sky was fairly clear. It was hardly noticeable that a volcano had recently erupted. At least not on the streets of Agoge. Apparently Trela's little holiday trick worked.

Croy knocked lightly on the door. He felt a little nervous. His previous conversations were mere warmups. And they had not gone smoothly. He needed to convince Clerin to stop doing what she was doing. To disobey her Beleg—to be able to obey his. The door opened and her face immediately broke into a warm smile, accenting her dimples.

"Croy, what a nice surprise. Please, come in." She backed up and swept her arm to the interior.

"Thank you, thank you." He hoped his smile did not look nervous. He headed over to the sofa that it appeared she had been lounging on. He sat in the chair adjacent to it.

"Would you like anything? Something to drink or eat? Some water?" He shook his head. She sat down on the sofa, turned to face him.

"I, uh... You know about my dreams."

"Of course. Quite prophetic." Her nose squinted up cutely. "Did you dream about the volcano?"

"Yes and no. Let me start at the beginning. You say my dreams are prophetic. They are, they really are. I've always had a hard time understanding them, but once I do, they have never been wrong."

"You famously dreamt of the location of the Luften temple. I will take your word for them never having been wrong."

"Well, some I never fully figured out. Some were very vague. I'm not trying to imply… Well, listen. I figured out where my dreams come from."

"What? Wow, that is fantastic. Where do they come from?"

"Gunzgak. My Beleg. Gunzgak has been communicating with me since before I found Trela."

"That is great to hear. Truly."

"Except… So, I had a dream yesterday morning. This time it was not vague. There were no symbols, no allegories, just Gunzgak talking with me."

"And so far from the temple."

"Yes… I had not really thought about that, but yes." Croy frowned a little for a brief moment. Were there implications with that? He could not take the time, however. "Gunzgak doesn't wish to die, Clerin. Please understand. That is acceptable, yes? To not wish to die. That is a natural response, yes? Gunzgak has asked me to entreat you directly, personally. I beg of you, Clerin. I beg you. Let Gunzgak live."

There was a short pause. Clerin's eyes were instantly empathetic. She nodded almost imperceptibly. She looked a little sad but her lips were held tight. She took a deep breath.

"Let me explain what has happened. Please understand that I had no idea of all of this until a couple of days ago. Maybe I should have known sooner but, honestly, I did not really think about it. I was told to go places by various Belegs, and I did. I did not question any of them." She took another deep breath and blinked a couple of times.

"So, I communed with Lembin. You have no idea what an honor that was for me. You also have to understand how common it was for Lembin to commune. At least once a moon with various Fluens. My mother had been communing for cycles, she was one of Lembin's favorites. I was told that I was picked by Lembin personally. So, it really… it was just such a great honor. So I went and I communed and I was told that I should go to the Luften temple and return. So I did.

"Vanelia tried to help me find the temple, but only Hulgert knew where it was. She wanted me to cure him from water from the well, and you know how that all turned out. You showed me the way to the temple. You say that Gunzgak showed you the way in your dreams. Gunzgak wanted me to go to the temple. You and Feyazki were terrified when you entered the temple and leapt blindly to the river below. Remember?"

"Yes. It really was terrifying." Croy chuckled slightly at his memory.

"I was not terrified. I was not chased out of the temple. I was let in by Linchon to commune."

"Because it had no idea what was going on."

"Maybe. Probably. But I am just saying that I had no idea as well. Once I had communed, Linchon told me to commune with Gorbanax before returning. This was different than Lembin's instructions, but I felt compelled to obey Linchon's orders. Linchon then wanted me to visit Lembin after Gorbanax, so I figured it was just an extra step.

"When I visited Gorbanax, I was not allowed to get too close. I was not allowed to truly commune. It required that we destroy the Cabal of Lochom before it would take any messages. You know how that all turned out.

"We returned, what is it now, a week ago? Not quite? It seems like forever." She shook her head slowly. "So, we returned triumphant. The items were destroyed. I communed with Gorbanax and… this." She put her fists together and then splayed them out, spreading her hands out and up, mimicking the eruption. "This all happened."

"Well, I understand you didn't want to kill the others. I believe you. But now we know what is happening. Now we know that if you commune with Gunzgak, you will kill it as well. We can end it here. No more assassinations." He was smiling because he could agree with her and still argue his point.

"But I have not finished with the story yet." His smile dropped as she spoke. "You see, part of the communication was an explanation from Linchon, which explains part of Gorbanax's response. Why do you think Gorbanax allowed me to commune with it after the fall of the Cabal? It had to have known, right? That is why it did not commune the first time. Because it knew. But it allowed the communication after we destroyed the Cabal. Why?"

Croy thought long and hard into the silence. There was not a good answer. Nothing that would help him, at least. Nothing that would help Gunzgak.

"I don't know. I cannot fathom." He finally had to provide a response.

"Because it accepted Linchon's premise. It might have agreed, it might have not. But it at least accepted it." She paused but he did not provide her with the prod she was looking for. So she continued anyway. "The premise is this. There cannot be an unbalanced number of Belegs. There cannot be a Gaen Beleg, providing the Gaens with assistance, attacking other realms, terraforming, rearranging everything. A lone Beleg, unchecked by any other comparable force, could do anything. They could destroy all the realms. They could take away the elements entirely. Do you not see? They would be an unmatched creator, all alone amongst all the derlians. That is what Linchon was most afraid of. That is why Gorbanax allowed me to commune after the Cabal was snuffed out. The fear of unbalanced Belegs." She shifted back a little. Croy had not even realized she had been leaning forwards. "Gorbanax allowed itself to be killed, Croy. You have to understand that is not an assassination."

"What if Gunzgak promised not to destroy anything? Not to unbalance anything?"

"Are you saying Gunzgak does not want revenge?"

The word "revenge" rung out in Croy's mind. He remembered it being mentioned by Gunzgak. Quietly though, almost in passing, as if it had not been a conscious thought. He could certainly not mention that to Clerin, however. That would just solidify her argument.

"What if I was able to get the promise?"

"It is not me that you have to convince." She sat back into the sofa with an inaudible thud. "You have to convince the two dying Belegs that a promise passed through a derlian is acceptable. That a promise at all is acceptable. I know I would have my doubts."

"So, the only way you will not try to chase Gunzgak is if Gorbanax and Linchon agree to accept the promise?"

"Correct."

Croy's heart sank. This was the type of diplomacy he was not great at. He could only hope that they were angry enough at Lembin to agree, but he doubted it. He would certainly try, but he was afraid Gunzgak was going to require him to kill Clerin. Which meant he would have to do it without Feyazki around. Which meant, if he was smart, he would do it right then. In the middle of their conversation, while she was thinking about something else. She did not have the reflexes of a viper that Trela had. She was probably unarmed to boot. He was unable to, however. He would have to exhaust every other avenue first. Or at least hear what the other Belegs had to say. Even then, he just did not know. He had never assassinated someone, and he worried he did not have it in him—though worried was probably not the correct word. He felt it had to be simpler if one was not aware of what they were doing.

"Then I will have to ask Trela if we can have a visit."

"Excellent. I will await the meeting with anticipation."

Sometimes she barely made sense.

When they headed out the next day, there was four of them. Croy and Clerin, of course. Trela was there as well. She had, apparently, recently communed with Gorbanax. Why she had not mentioned it during his earlier conversation with her, he was not positive. Then there was Feyazki, who was there purely as support, to fly them over and protect Croy from the burning lava. There was some chitchat on the way over, but nothing of note.

They arrived at a small shelf a little above the bubbling pool of lava. They did not take long before the spells were cast and Croy was being lowered to the lava. He did not necessarily want it to be a surprise, but he had made Clerin promise not to visit Gorbanax beforehand. He did not want the Beleg's opinion tainted by anything.

He watched his feet sink into the lava. He held his breath as the lava overcame his face, which was foolish he knew, but he could not help himself. His world was soon swallowed up by yellowish-orange as the lava melded together over his head.

He had a quick moment of panic as he sank deeper into the lava. All Feyazki had to do was release the shield and Croy would die instantly. Feyazki had even warned Croy that he would strike first if need be. It would be an effective crime as all the evidence would be consumed as well.

He waited for what seemed like forever. He started chanting Gorbanax's name in his head. He eventually chanted it out loud. He entreated the surrounding lava.

"Gorbanax? Where are you? Come and speak with me."

The word "please" was repeated often. As was the statement, "I come in peace." He begged and cajoled to no avail.

"Gunzgak wishes to know the process to alleviate its fears. Tell me of your ordeal so I can prepare Gunzgak." Croy tried everything he could think of.

Eventually Croy was brought back to the surface and floated over to the shelf. Feyazki was sitting and appeared to still be concentrating as Croy neared, while the other two were standing stiffly.

"Well, how did the communication go? I will need to verify anything that you indicate Gorbanax agreed to." Clerin was smiling like she had not just indicated she would not believe him.

"I was never able to commune. There was nothing. No response." Croy looked dejected. He felt dejected.

They all stared at him for a moment. It seemed to take them by surprise, which made him feel a little better. Well, not better, but less like he was being set up.

"I communed just a day ago and there was no indication of not being able to return, not being able to commune more. Maybe I should go check? How are you feeling Feyazki?" Trela turned towards the seated mage.

"Well enough."

Croy put his clothing back on and Trela took hers off. He kept his gaze on the rocky terrain. He was less worried about someone catching sight of him than of catching sight of anyone else. Clerin and Trela chatted amiably as she stripped down behind him, as if nothing odd were happening. Feyazki cast his spells. By the time Croy turned back around, Trela was out of sight.

"Can you promise me something?" He turned to Clerin, ignoring Feyazki.

"I can try, what is it?"

"I need to ask you something, and I need you to not lie about it."

"What are you going to ask me?"

"You need to promise first."

She was quiet for a moment. Several emotions quickly passed over her face, none of them readable. "I promise not to lie to you about your next question."

"Do you know where Tumu is?" Croy stared hard into her face, attempting to glean any passing reaction.

"No." She had not paused. It was a quick, natural, and for all appearances, earnest response. "Have you ever known me to harm a derlian? Or kidnap one? Or have I ever been cruel to Tumu? Ever even said anything unkind to him?"

Croy thought long and hard. He tried to come up with something, any memory, but he could not think of Clerin being cruel to anyone without it being defensive. He even tried to think of her being cruel defensively and, at that moment, was unable to come up with anything.

"I loved Tumu, truly. I do not know how anyone could not. He was so kind and gentle. I certainly never heard him say a bad word about anyone, not even to those who deserved it. Out of all the derlians in the warpack, it seemed that he deserved to be protected the most. I do not know where he is. I do not know who or what took him, if that is what happened." She just seemed so thoroughly earnest.

"I'm sorry, of course you had nothing to do with his disappearance. It is just… well… he warned me about you before he vanished. Now I'm thinking the warning had to do with all of this," he waved a hand towards the bubbling lava, "not that you were going to attack me. Or, I suppose, him."

"He warned you?"

"Yes. He had an image of waves crashing against a cliff face until it crumbled into the ocean. He said my profile seemed like the cliff and your hair matched the image of the waves. He told me all of that just before he disappeared so I… Well, I was unsure of how to process that." Croy frowned, attempting to bring a clearer memory to the surface, but was unable to.

"Wow. I wondered what had happened." There was a quick pause. "I assure you Croy, that I would never do anything to harm Tumu."

Croy believed her. And that was a problem. If he was unable to hate her, how was he going to be able to stop her?

Trela was brought up out of the lava. Croy turned away, waiting for the clothing switch. Trela had as little success as Croy.

Clerin was dunked next, in the hopes that she would jar Gorbanax loose from wherever it was hiding. It was that, or maybe it had already succumbed to death. Maybe the death happened quicker than they had been told.

"Nothing at all." Trela shook her head as they stood there, now facing each other.

"And you communed with Gorbanax when? The day before yesterday?"

"The day before that."

"Ah, yes." Croy thought for a moment. Each day seemed to be getting longer, more packed with required events. . "And you had no problem communicating?"

"None. Well, it is not like we talked. It was more like simple images and some concentrated thoughts. But I did not have a problem getting Gorbanax's attention. Gorbanax seemed eager or, I don't know how to explain, it seemed *healthy*. It did not seem like it would disappear or die or go dormant or whatever. I'm just shocked that none of us can seem to catch its attention today. Maybe Clerin will have better luck."

"What was the last thing you discussed?"

"I've been avoiding telling you."

"What?"

"You should find out from Gorbanax."

"What if we can never commune with Gorbanax again?"

"Listen…" She paused and stared into Croy. Her yellow eyes were not feral like they typically were. She looked a little sad. She took a deep breath. "Gorbanax wants Gunzgak to share its fate. I know this, Croy. I know this because it was shown to me, it was communed. Gorbanax even tried to imply that Gunzgak would be happy at the end of it all, just as Gorbanax was. Or at least, as Gorbanax indicated to me."

Croy's heart sank. He had already been concerned about that. The way she told it made him fairly certain she was not lying. That she was not exaggerating. She had been trying to spare his feelings, to let him try to convince Gorbanax to die without Gunzgak. To let the Beleg break its own news, its own druthers.

"That was the last thing you discussed?"

"Yes. That was the last of the images shown to me." She narrowed her eyes slightly, thinking, making sure there was nothing else. "Then an air bubble surrounded me and took me to the surface. Ryshial was casting the protection spells that day."

"An air bubble? Did Ryshial find you in the lava and pull you out?"

"No. I don't think so. Going in was like today—I could feel the weight, the thickness, of the lava around me, if not the heat. But coming out, it was like a protective sphere surrounded me. I did not feel any pressure from the surrounding lava."

"Well…   Are you sure it was Gorbanax you communed with?" The idea was forming in his head at the same time he was speaking it. "What if it was Linchon? What if Linchon tricked you and Gorbanax is already dead? I mean… Why would an air bubble lift you out of the lava?"

"I truly truly, doubt that. But for no other reason than a feeling. I have zero proof to argue otherwise, but it just seems so farfetched."

"So, you just felt like you were communing with Gorbanax? Have you ever spoken with it before? Do you have any other experience to compare it with?"

"Well, no. Which is why I'm telling you I have no proof."

"I will have to think this over."

"Honestly, me too. I will do my best to replay everything in my mind, every feeling, thought, emotion. If anything comes up different for me, if I find any doubt, I will let you know." Her face was soft and thoughtful. "The thought that it may not have been Gorbanax never crossed my mind, frankly."

Then Clerin was brought out and Croy turned around again. He was smiling to himself as he stared down the cliff. If there was a chance that Gorbanax had not wanted to die, if there was a chance that it did not wish Gunzgak to die, then there was a chance that Croy could convince Trela to help him. It was a small chance, for sure, but it was a chance nonetheless. It was a small glimmer of hope in the dark cave he was trapped in.

It made him think of something else as well. An idea too crazy to speak aloud. *What if Linchon was not even dying?* he thought. *What if it was not Lembin who was spreading the poison? What if it was Linchon?*

✳✳✳

Croy spent the rest of the day alone in his quarters. He had a certain amount of energy coursing through him. He did not classify it as nervous energy because he was not nervous at all, but it was chaotic, served no purpose, and would not dissipate no matter how he tried. He went to sleep that night, hoping to dream. He did not. Or, more likely, he was unable to recall his dreams since they were mild and mundane.

He awoke with the dawn. He still had a little energy and so cooked an omelet with many types of vegetables, just to give him something to chop. He sat on his sofa for a while, trying to think of what else he could do. He decided he needed to recruit more allies. He needed to recruit any allies.

Croy found himself outside of Haswyxe's quarters. He had not intended to go there, at least not consciously, though it was really the only place he could go. He refused to let himself think he had been heading there all along. He knocked on the door to quiet his mind.

The door opened quickly. "Ah, yes. I was wondering when you might show up." Haswyxe stepped outside and closed the door behind him. "You know, Malghain warned me not to talk to you." He smiled. "Right after he warned me that you would probably be looking for me."

"Well… Here I am."

"Yes. Here we are." He was still smiling. "We should probably talk at your quarters, however. Would that be acceptable?"

"Of course, of course."

They walked in silence all the way there. Haswyxe seemed relaxed, especially compared to how Croy was feeling. The energy he had was a little nervous. When they got to Croy's quarters, he went to the cupboard fairly quickly.

"Grog?"

"Yes, please."

Croy grabbed a bottle and two mismatched cups. He did not overpour, it was still the morning after all. He did bring the bottle over, however. He sat on his sofa and Haswyxe was in a nearby chair. The bottle and their cups were on the small table in between.

"So, I think I know why I'm here, but why don't you tell me. Just to make sure." Haswyxe picked up his cup and examined it.

"I am at odds with Clerin." Croy examined his own cup. "Through no fault of my own. I still think she's a great derlian. I guess I should say that Gunzgak is at odds with Lembin. Or maybe Linchon. Or maybe all the other Belegs, I'm not sure."

"So, she really is killing Belegs?"

"Yes." Croy took a sip.

"I was hoping that was a rumor, or at least a misunderstanding."

"Not that this has been fully corroborated, but it appears that Lembin made her toxic and she poisoned Linchon. Then Linchon added some toxicity and sent her to Gorbanax. However, we tried to commune with Gorbanax yesterday, and it was nowhere to be found. So, honestly, I am not sure if Linchon was poisoned or not. It certainly seems that Gorbanax was."

"Wait, what?" Hawyxe took a sip of his grog. "You know, on second thought, never mind. The issue is that you are at odds, but still on good terms, with Clerin. Correct?"

"Exactly."

"This means you are at odds with Feyazki. Which means you are at odds with Malghain."

"Well, when you put it like that..." Croy's brow scrunched a little as he thought through the ramifications.

"There is no other way to put it. I owe you my life, Croy. I will do what I can to help you. But you have to understand the quandary we are in. Gyllhelon is dead and Torpalin and Escha are in Ariellyna. Malghain is who I spend my time with. Besides, he is the one who got me working for Queen Vanelia. We go way back. Malghain has already spoken with Feyazki about this as well. But that is not the worst of it."

"What is the worst of it?"

"Malghain is better than I am, more dangerous than I am. At least with blades. I might be better at the bow, though I'm still behind Escha in that regard. And, no offence here, but I don't feel you are a match for Feyazki, magically speaking. We are not on the winning team, Croy. I just... I want you to understand that. Getting me to help you is, well, suicide."

"There has got to be something we can do."

"Of course there is. While we still have their goodwill, while we are all still friendly, we will need to sneak up on Malghain while he's sleeping—like passed out drunk, like so drunk that he's almost dead—then we both pounce on him, you with magic and me with my blades. Maybe we take him like that. Then, that same night, that same hour if able, we sneak up on Feyazki and pounce on him. Then, before an alarm can be raised, we kill Clerin. That is my best plan."

"You would do that for me?"

"Not for you. With you. And really, the word should be 'try.' Even naked, asleep, unarmed, and drunk, Malghain will be difficult. And Feyazki... Well, he's killed Tlana single-handedly now, hasn't he? I'm not too worried about Clerin. Unless, of course, she has some Beleg or Yaven protection or something. You don't think her toxicity would affect derlians if she was attacked, do you?"

"Why are you telling me all this?"

"This is what you want, isn't it? A way to kill Clerin. I'm just trying to get a plan together." He took another drink and then sucked air through his teeth. "Maybe we could drug their drinks. How quick do you think Feyazki could spot being poisoned?"

"Maybe we could talk Clerin out of it. That is what I have been trying to do."

"Nope, won't work. She's on a mission from Lembin. And from Linchon and Gorbanax if I understand correctly. Besides, once they get wary about us, we'll never be able to surprise them. Try getting Malghain pass-out drunk when he's nervous about something. Ha! And what about Trela? If we kill everyone, you know she'll have every Pyran alive hunting us down. That will be hard to dodge. Plus, honestly, she kind of scares me a little. I don't think she's as dangerous as Malghain, but she's killed some fairly skilled warriors in her day. Maybe we get her drunk as well? Where have I heard this strategy before?" He was grinning widely.

"I don't know if I can kill Clerin."

"I'm telling you she'll be the easiest."

"No. Not in that way. Just... she's my friend. I don't know if I can kill her."

"Oh. That. Well, we should probably answer that riddle first, now shouldn't we? If you don't have the stomach for murder, we probably shouldn't be aiming at some of the most dangerous derlians that walk these realms. Hesitation kills."

"Well, I... You don't understand what being given a directive from a Beleg is like."

"No, I don't. But you know who does, don't you? Clerin."

"I don't think I can talk to her about it like this." Croy waved his hand around the room, not indicating anything in specific. "If I tell her that Gunzgak wants me to kill her, then she'll be forewarned. Won't that affect our plan?"

"Only if our plan is to drug all of them and try to murder them in their sleep. Is that our plan?" Haswyxe finished his cup and set it on the low table. "Listen, Croy, I'll die for you. You understand that, don't you? I'll even kill my oldest friend for you. But if there is some other way... If there is any other option, you let me know. Because I have to admit, I am not particularly fond of the plan. I'd rather not have to do it. Really and truly. So!" He clapped his hands together. "First things first. You have one week to tell me if you are capable of murdering Clerin. Because if not, you are going to hesitate. And then all we are doing is committing suicide here and I have plenty of other ways I'd like to go out if given an option. Okay?" He clapped his hands on his knees, and then stood.

"One week?" Croy's mind was reeling a bit.

"Yes. One week. We probably shouldn't hang out during that week either. We don't want anyone to get suspicious." He winked and then he left.

Croy downed the rest of his grog and stared at the door. The quiet in the room was overwhelming. It just made Haswyxe's words echo in Croy's mind. *Was* he capable of murdering Clerin? He poured some more grog into his cup even though it was before noon. It was going to be a long week.

The day passed agonizingly slow. He kept himself busy by wandering the Blaze. He visited his struggling vine again. He sat in various park and garden settings. He tried to spend some of the day meditating in his quarters. It was all unfruitful.

Maybe that was not the right word, however. Maybe he was looking at it incorrectly. He kept coming back to the idea that he could not kill Clerin. That would be an answer. It was just one that Gunzgak did not want. But if it was the answer, then maybe his time had actually been fruitful.

He tried to imagine it, killing Clerin. Invariably it ended up with him choking her while she stared up at him with sad accusing eyes. The lightning blue of her eyes would dim as he strangled the life out of her. She would struggle, but not overly so. She would strike at his shoulders, attempt to get away and writhe around. But, in his head, she did not fight as if she were going to die. She did not scratch his face, gouge his eyes, try to knee him in the groin. It was a fake scenario in his head, he knew that. And maybe that was part of the problem, her imagined passivity. It was those accusing eyes that did it. Even in his own mind, even with complete control over what was being imagined, he could not go through with it. He always let go before she succumbed. Her head would move forwards as she gasped for air. There would be tears in her accusing eyes. She would never look at him the same again, that he knew. It was not even the thought of Feyazki killing him afterwards, even as he had been unable to kill Clerin. It was the thought that if he tried to do something that horrible, and he failed, he would have destroyed everything he enjoyed for nothing. Haswyxe was right. It was the hesitation that killed. And Croy could not convince himself that he could do it at all, let alone without hesitation.

He kept trying to figure out a way. He tried to imagine other scenarios, ones in which she attacked him first, where he was just defending himself. That helped a little, but somehow during the struggle they ended up on the floor again, with him on top choking her, and her staring at him with those accusing eyes.

Croy did not know if he could even think of those scenarios all week long. It was antithetical to his nature to even contemplate. It was eating him up inside. He could not perform the task his Beleg wanted to him to do. It was that simple. He had failed before he even began.

The evening was a little rough. He ended up drinking too much grog just after sundown and falling asleep on his couch. There was a bit of oblivion seeking in his drinking that night. Then he dreamt.

Croy was flying along, over a forest of evergreens. A robed figure slid into view besides him. Then another, and another. As a pack they hurtled along, Croy at their center. They headed towards the mouth of a cave. Soon they were flung into it. They snaked through the tunnel until they reached the large spherical room. The figures ringed the room and began a low chant. The chant turned into a rumble which crescendoed until Gunzgak floated through the floor. It stopped in front of Croy, its chiseled face on par with Croy.

"I have glimpsed your mind and am saddened. I had not realized your weakness. No matter, every tool has a purpose, and it is my own mistake if I use a tool incorrectly. I will give you a specific task and hope that you do not fail me. If this task falls within your capabilities, do you agree to it?" The same sadness as before emanated from Gunzgak, but there was something else as well. This time around there was some anger. Hidden deep.

"Of course."

"Good. You must accompany Clerin and the others. They will soon start their quest to find me. To trick me. To kill me. You must be helpful to them, to be kind to them. As you always are. You can do that, yes?"

"Yes. Of course."

"You will be my eyes and ears. They will not involve you for all the decisions, you have already tainted yourself in their eyes, but they will allow you to tag along and be helpful. Like a younger, less adept sibling. They will forget who you are, they will forget your taint, if you let them."

"Should I agree with their way of thinking? Should I tell them that your death would not be abhorrent to me?"

"No, never!" Everything shook, the entire room shook. "What is the truth, Croy? What is your truth?"

"I want you to live. I do. I will do anything..." Croy unconsciously swallowed as he stared into the massive features of the stone giant in front of him. "I will do almost anything to allow that for you."

"At least you understand your weakness. No, Croy, do not lie to them. They will not forget you if you lie. You re-stain yourself, you increase your taint to them, with each lie you give them. More than that, however, is that I still need a champion. Do not argue my survival to them but let them know I do not wish to die. They need to understand what they do is wrong. They wish to kill one of their creators. They wish to kill all of the creators! Is that not wrong?"

"Of course it is wrong. I want to help, truly."

"Good. That is good. You are good, Croy. Remember that. You are fighting for life, for what is right." The giant Beleg paused, in an almost derlian manner, closing its eyes for just a moment. When it reopened them, they were still sad, there was still some quietly deep anger in them, but there was something else in them. Something akin to how Trela would look before a battle. Grim determination mixed with hope.

"You are to be you, fully and completely. Be around them, more than you might normally do, but that is all. Listen intently, watch with understanding, but do nothing too intense, nothing to call attention to yourself. I may ask a favor of you during their quest. I may ask several favors, many favors. But I will not ask anything of you that you are unable to bear. I know your weaknesses and will steer clear of them. I will be cognizant of you and your abilities. You are a great boon to me, Croy. You are my champion. You are my only hope. And if this works, if Clerin dies before I do, I will provide you with everything you have ever desired. I know this is not your motivation, but I wish you to understand the depths of my gratitude. Go now. Awaken!"

It was the next morning. Croy was uncomfortable on his sofa and uncomfortable with his hangover. At least he no longer needed to make himself comfortable with murdering Clerin.

He spent most of the day recovering. He was not really sure what to do. He had his answer, or at least his answer to Haswyxe, but had several days before it was to be handed over. He was happy being lazy and useless for the day but wanted something planned for the rest of the week. He thought about contacting that family he had helped herd sheep the last time he was living in Agoge. What were their names? He could recall Vectuley, even recall the young lad's face. The father and his brother, the patriarchs, were Uldun and Ertyin, Croy was pretty sure. He was unable to come up with a family name, not that Pyrans used those very often, nor could he remember the daughter's names. That shamed him a little but, in his own defense, he spent very little time around them. He was amazed that he remembered anyone but Vectuley. *Yes*, he thought, *I should try to find them tomorrow. I could be helpful.*

In the late afternoon, however, he received a summons. It was to a banquet with Trela and who knew who else. The invitation made it sound lavish, so there was probably to be quite a few derlians there.

He was supposed to wear something appropriate. Luckily for him, he only had a couple of appropriate outfits. It was the struggle to make the right choice that bothered him, so he was glad for the limited options. They had been moldering in his armoire while he had been away chasing down the Cabal, so they were clean but dusty. He took both sets of clothing outside and beat them with his flat-faced laundry bat. It helped his mood more than he had anticipated.

He chose the reddish-brown one rather than the grayish one. It was a little more flashy, though still quite tame for Pyran standards. He then bathed and took a small nap. One could say that the day was not very productive, but Croy was feeling good about himself and life in general as he left for the banquet. The stables were farther away than the banquet, so he walked his way over there. He did not necessarily want to be early but gave himself enough time to walk leisurely. He was wearing his dress boots and did not want to feel rushed.

Croy arrived at the best moment. It was early enough that everyone was standing around, but late enough he did not have to wait long before being seated. The banquet guests were quite numerous, around twenty of them. There was not assigned seating and Croy ended up between Knill and Silvadhin. Sitting next to Knill made him wonder again about Tumu. He still found it odd that they had left the area before finding a body at least. It seemed that Haswyxe was avoiding him or, at least, did not seek him out. He did not seek out Haswyxe either, even though he felt he had a simple enough answer that he could say it in a crowded room and no one would notice.

The food was fantastic. Trela had several of her chefs working in the kitchen. The only one Croy knew was Kolaf, from their days in the warpack, but there were several specialists back there from what Knill had told him. One for appetizers, one for desserts. He nursed a grog for quite a while at first since he was still a little wary. By the end of the feast, however, he had drunk enough to feel a little tipsy.

The conversations were fairly light. No one was quite sure why they were summoned on such a short notice. Well, Knill surely knew, but he was not divulging. Eventually, at the end of the meal, Trela stood to give her speech. As she was so fond of doing.

"We have come a long way and certainly deserve some rest. I know I do." She paused for the polite chuckles. "But we have one last quest. Hopefully a small one, both in terms of time and effort. I would like each of you to join us. We are to head back to the Luften realm, to Ariellyna at first. But from there, I cannot promise. I am unsure. I must apologize for this. You deserve more solid answers, a more solid plan.

"Part of the vagueness of this has to do with where I got this quest from. It comes from Gorbanax, who I personally communed with a couple of days ago. It is the dying wish of my Beleg, and I cannot leave it unanswered.

"I have promised you all much over the cycles, but I have given you little respite. So it continues. You may refuse, if you must…" She paused and stared over to a grouping of Pyrans, including Estfale and Serghno. "Well, not you. Not those in my employ." Another chuckle rippled through the group. "But others here, our guests, you may refuse me. But, if you can find it in your heart to come along, you will be specifically rewarded. I will be in my smallest throne room for the rest of the evening. Come. Visit. Let me know what it is that you may want for your service. I am feeling generous tonight and, believe me, I understand the fatigue we are all under. We have barely been here a week, hardly time to rest and recuperate. But we will need to leave soon."

Trela stepped back and bowed to them all, turned, and left. She did not leave them any time to question her or provide opinions or discussions. The room was quiet for a time, but then slowly rose in volume as conversations began anew. Not all the conversations were about Trela's announcement, which made Croy wonder if it was not a surprise to all of them. He had certainly been kept in the dark about it. It did, however, resolve some things for him. Estfale was the first to get up from the table and head into the other room. It was a little odd since she had indicated non-Pyrans should do the visiting. It did, however, have the effect that everyone at the banquet chatted with Trela alone, for he set the precedent for the Pyrans.

Croy made small conversations with Knill and Silvadhin for a while, waiting his turn patiently. He did not want to push Knill too much for additional information, though he was a little curious. So they talked about nothing. Silvadhin was excited to join up. She had been sorely let down by not getting to see Ariellyna when they had passed by, and she was certainly not going to let the opportunity by her again. "A city in the trees," she said wistfully.

Knill and Croy had also missed Ariellyna but, at least for Croy, he was less enamored with it. He was not necessarily afraid of heights, he had done a lot of climbing through the caves of Serif, but there was no wind down there. There were not the swaying tree branches. Just good solid rock. He had seen the giant helioarc trees and they were truly massive. Maybe they did not sway in the wind as he imagined. He did not mind finding out, it did sound intriguing, but he was not as excited as Silvadhin appeared. He was not grinning and wide-eyed. He wondered what Baltuz would have said about it. She would have probably been excited. Then he wondered how Ilana would have reacted. She was less of a thrill seeker. Though, really, who knew? She had seemed quite changed the last he saw of her. Taking over Lemniscate's duties at the Well of Eternity. He then wondered if he was cursed to lose all his loves.

Eventually it was his turn with Trela. He had let Silvadhin go in before him. She was quick so he doubted there was much haggling that had gone on.

He entered the small throne room and marveled, yet again, at the opulence of it. The tapestries of hunts, the carpets, the thrones themselves. Who needed more than one throne room?

"Ah, Croy, I was hoping to see you tonight." Trela was sitting stiff-backed in the throne. He usually thought of her as standing or striding around. She looked a little small in the large throne. He felt it reduced her stature a little, when it was supposed to increase it.

"Yes."

"What?"

"Yes. I'll come. I'll be a part of this." He needed to make her think he was a little reluctant, but not too much. He had thought up the perfect excuse while chatting with Knill. "On one condition, however."

"What is that?"

"That we visit the Luften Temple. I want to see it again. I want to see if I feel the same terror as I did when I first entered it. And, more than anything, I wish to commune with Linchon. I wish to hear about all of this… this mess that we're in. I want to hear it straight from Linchon since I was unable to hear it from Gorbanax. If you grant me that, I'll be a part of this and help as much as I am able."

"Of course, Croy. Whatever you need."

Chapter 12

Clerin visited Trela in her small throne room. It was much less impressive than the large one, but still felt opulent. Rulers, especially those whose authority came from long-standing traditions, all seemed to have an eye to impress. Something that had started grand would have a little added by each passing king or queen. That would probably happen several times faster in the Pyran realm compared to the Fluen, where the rulers were killed long before they became too decrepit to swing a sword. Clerin had never really asked about the longest lived Kriishan. She wondered why she had never thought about it before. If a ruler was good and just, would the populace not wish to keep them on? Surely not every ruler was cut down.

"Clerin. I was not positive you would drop in for a separate visit." Trela was smiling, but it seemed slightly strained. Clerin had waited to be last, so maybe Trela was just ready to be done with that portion of the evening.

"Well, I noticed that Estfale entered first, even though you had indicated that those under your employ did not need to visit with you. I thought I would see how you are faring." Clerin had not even thought about it really. Everyone had seemed to be visiting and she had just waited her turn.

"Yes, I noticed he did that as well." Trela stared at the side door for a moment. "Are you the last?"

"Yes."

"Good, I need to stretch." She stood and performed some long stretches for a moment before walking over to Clerin. "Most of them are coming. In fact, I think only Nyhan has indicated that he wants to head back to his own realm. The loss of Aedon really affected him. For my own part, I had a hard time asking Rewista to join. If anything happens to Lishean while we are away, I would want her to take over. Along the same vein, however, is why I wanted her to come along. She is a great advisor."

"And she agreed?"

"Of course. If I asked her to walk across a bed of lava she would probably do it." Trela paused for a moment. "But do we have too many members? I keep going back to that thought. I'm not even sure where we are headed or how to resolve what Lembin wants."

"And Linchon and Gorbanax. They all want the same thing. You said you saw that clearly when you communed with Gorbanax." Clerin was not trying to be pushy, but she had been incredibly glad when she heard that Gorbanax had corroborated its desires to Trela. Or was it its requirements? "But you are correct. I do not know how to solve the quest. I do not know where to start. Which makes it difficult to say how long it will take, or how many derlians will be the proper number, or even what skill sets will be required. Let me say that I think you have chosen wisely with those you have assembled. It is quite the truncated coterie." Trela had not been the only one adding names to the list, but Clerin knew she liked to feel she was controlling the situation.

"We may have too many warriors. I don't know. Like I said, it seems impossible to guess at. We are only heading back to Ariellyna because Ryshial heard of someone who might know something peripheral."

"We did not know where we were going the last time either. We knew where to start, to try to find Aedon, but that was about all." Clerin would not have brought up Aedon's name, but Trela had done so earlier. "I am sure destiny will smile upon us again."

"Well, Croy knew the name of the Cabal and he knew Aedon. We will get no such help this time." There was a small frown forming on Trela's mouth.

"He has agreed to join us?" She had not attempted to phrase it as a question, but that was how it came out.

"Yes. On the condition that we go to the Luften Temple and attempt to commune with Linchon. He wants a Beleg to explain the majority's desires. He has already heard plenty from Gunzgak." Trela glanced at Clerin, her yellow eyes staring intensely for a brief moment. "So, if you have any persuasion over the Belegs, getting Linchon to commune with Croy would be a great boon for us."

"It was unfortunate that Gorbanax did not commune."

"Yes. Quite."

"Then that is where we shall go first. It should be easy to find the temple this time around."

"So... I've been meaning to ask. You warned me that Gorbanax may not be able to commune, that it may already be too far gone, yet I was able to commune with it. Then, when Croy showed up a couple of days later, there was nothing." Clerin was going to interrupt but Trela raised her hand. She was speaking slowly, picking her words carefully. "But I've also been told, I think by you, but certainly by Feyazki, that the dying a Beleg goes through may take a derlian lifetime. Or several. Or something. There's a contradiction there, I think, though maybe communication is the first ability lost. Then there's Feyazki communing with Linchon about the wind and smoke. I had not realized Linchon was here. 'Helping.' You didn't mention Linchon to me, however. Yet you've communed with Linchon recently. Haven't you?"

"Yes. After the volcano erupted. Did I not mention that?"

Trela only smiled back. "There's a curious theory that Croy brought up, while you were down in the lava attempting to commune with Gorbanax. Oh, and to be clear, you did not commune with either Gorbanax or Linchon down there in the lava, did you? Or anything or anyone? You did not commune with anything down there in the lava?"

"No. You have my word." Clerin was feeling a little nervous though she was not sure why. She knew Vrric had mentioned Linchon to several derlians and she had not thought of it as a secret. She mulled it over during the brief moment of silence and could not think of a reason why she would not have told Trela about it. It seemed more that it had just not come up. The last week had been incredibly busy for everyone.

"Aren't you curious?"

"About what?"

"Croy's theory."

"Oh. Yes. Of course." She had missed that during her musing.

"After I communed with Gorbanax, after I was shown that it wanted Gunzgak to die as well, I was pulled out of the lava in an air bubble." Trela's intense eyes were drilling into Clerin as she spoke, but she was still smiling. "I had thought nothing of it, really. At first, I thought it was Ryshial pulling me out, but she assured me it hadn't been her and I put it from my mind. Even when I mentioned it to Croy I thought nothing of it. But he has a theory about it."

"Yes?"

"He is concerned that Gorbanax was already dead when I went down to commune. He mentioned, mostly in passing, that maybe it was Linchon I had communed with down there in the lava. Wouldn't that be the oddest thing?"

Clerin felt a chill run down her spine. She was not sure why. She had nothing to hide, had told no lies. She had not even meant to neglect mentioning communing with Linchon. She was doing nothing nefarious. Yet there was something in the way that Trela was speaking that concerned her. There was something dangerous going on. She did not normally get that from Trela. Trela typically saved that for others, for adversaries. And that was what concerned Clerin the most. That Trela would begin to treat her in the same way she treated an adversary.

"That would be. I agree. But Gorbanax would not let me commune directly until we destroyed the Cabal. And once we did, it accepted the messages." She was going to continue but was quietly and softly interrupted.

"According to you." Trela's eyes were a little tight, just barely squinting, and her smile was still in place.

Clerin paused for a moment to think. She needed something simple, something logical. Everything that had convinced her of the truth had only happened to her. She knew what she knew, but if Trela was concerned that she was lying, those arguments would not hold water.

"I could tell you how Gorbanax communes and Linchon communes are completely different. But if you think I am lying, what is there to say? I could tell you that I am tired of running around these realms and want nothing more than to go live a peaceful life somewhere with Feyazki. I do NOT want to be doing this, Trela. Why would I lie about something that keeps me on the verge of death on some never-ending impossible quest? More than any of that, however, is that it does not matter. Gorbanax is dead, Trela. That is known, no one is lying about that. Your Beleg is dead, or dying, or whatever any of that means. Do you, personally, want Gunzgak to embolden its Gaens and take revenge on the other realms? Do you want to leave one Beleg alive?"

This pause was more comfortable. Trela was thinking. Her eyes were still intense, but they were not searing directly through Clerin.

"You know what I want?"

"No. Please, tell me."

"I want to make sure that Linchon is dying. I want to make sure Lembin dies as well. You are correct that I, personally, wish all the other Belegs to share the fate of Gorbanax. No mercy for any of them. I'm not sure what Croy thinks my concern is. But I'll tell you that my concern is being tricked. I do not wish to hunt down three Belegs only to find out that another is hiding in the shadows, healthy and well. That will not do." Her eyes pierced into Clerin again. "If you can somehow convince me of that, that all the Belegs will share the same fate, then I will take you to all the corners of the realms on the greatest hunt to ever occur. We will not fail. I will not allow it."

The intensity was the same, but it was no longer adversarial. Clerin would accept that as a win. Now she just had to figure out how to prove it all to Trela's satisfaction. Another impossible quest.

They were given a little bit of time. Trela allowed almost another week in Agoge as she got her logistics under control. Still, it felt like Clerin had barely unpacked and there they were, packing to leave again. Her clothes, those that she wished to continue using, had just finished getting washed. She had not lied to Trela, she was ready to be done. A small part of her wanted to let Gunzgak survive, just so she could go find a home and rest. She knew that was not an option, however.

"Weren't we just at Ariellyna?" Vrric was trying to be humorous. It had been funny the first time he had said it, but this was about the third. She gave him a polite smile in return.

He was packing his things in various piles on the bed, folding everything neatly and tightly. She was glad that he took care of his own packing. It allowed her more time and energy to pour into her own efforts. Which were not going nearly as smoothly as his.

"Luckily, I was too lazy to unpack any of my books, so… those are all ready to go." That was the first time he tried that one and she laughed more appreciatively.

"You do not have that many books. What are there, three, four?" She glanced over to the pile of saddlebags in the corner of the room. "Actually, you are lucky I did not get mad and make you unpack those." She pointed and he chuckled.

Since they were not together the last time they were at Agoge, they spent what little time they had this round visiting the places they enjoyed. It was entertaining and a bit filling. They apparently remembered a lot of places to eat. Sure, there were parks and scenic destinations, but when she was last in Agoge she was spending time with a younger Pyran called Yihrum. He was a performer and took her to all sorts of tiny performative stages and festivals. There were no festivals and she did not want to run into Yihrum, so they only visited a stage or two. Vrric had, at least it had seemed to her at the time, spent most of his hours with Gyllhelon or at the Mages' Guild. They did not spend much time at the guild. So, really, wandering around the town and eating was a simple and enjoyable way to spend what spare moments they had, at least in public. They spent a fair amount of enjoyable time in private as well.

The food in Agoge, and in the Pyran realm in general, was a little spicy for Clerin's taste. In the Fluen realm there are a lot of creams and cheeses, and certainly a lot of herbs and flavors. Of course, there was also a whole lot of fish. But Pyrans liked their food so hot with peppers that it was impossible to taste the actual dish. And, even compared with the rest of the Pyran realm, Agoge was known for its spicy cuisine. The dining was nice and the company was even better, so she enjoyed herself immensely.

Then the time came. They were heading back out. Through the dry hot desert. Taking the same path out as they had come in on. It was a bit surreal.

Travel through the desert was not Clerin's favorite, but at least the Pyran realm was not pure sand dunes like the Northern Desert. The roads through the realm attempted to skirt water or, at worst case, lead to oases. Survival was high in the minds of the original road builders, if not comfort. They finally reached the shade of the Yaniqua Forest and stopped by Dun Oengen. The warriors there were shocked, but pleased, to see them again. They stayed there for a couple of days before heading back out. It did not seem that Trela was in too much of a hurry. Clerin was not sure where they would eventually be going, or how to get there, but she was still a little surprised by Trela's lack of urgency.

Eventually they found their way into the Luften realm. The going had been pleasant enough for a while, but the trees and rivers of the Luften realm were more comforting to Clerin.

They headed straight for the Luften Temple, veering away from the larger roads that led directly to Ariellyna. Trela preferred not to see any Luften guards, or anyone at all, before they reached the temple. There were two different tasks in the Luften realm to her. There was convincing Croy of the quest and then there was trying to find a Luften mage in Ariellyna. First one, then the other. And, all agreed, convincing Croy should be the first. They finally made camp close enough to where they all agreed the temple should be. They would send out sorties the next morning to try to find it. Clerin was not positive if the illusion covering the cave's mouth would still be in place, but looking for it during the morning light after a refreshing sleep did sound like a good idea.

The next day started early. Clerin skipped breakfast and went to bathe by the river while Vrric ate. He was to fly both her and Croy around until the temple was found and wanted to be well fed for what might be a long day. They were the three that had seen what the entrance looked like. The only ones left alive who had been in the entrance before. The thought of it was a little bit humbling to Clerin. Of course, as far as she knew, she was the only derlian in all of time to have communed with three Belegs. And she had even spoken to Gunzgak through an intermediary, if that Yaven was to be believed.

They started by flying along the gorge until it appeared the right depth and verdant enough. Then they flew along the top, looking for the tree Croy had seen in his dream so long ago. They found that, then the orange formation, the scar on the cliff face. There was still certainly an illusion, as there was not a cave entrance visible where it should be. It was a little after noon by the time they had tossed a couple of rocks through the illusion.

They rested briefly, quietly, at the top of the cliff before attempting to enter. Everyone wanted to be at their best before entering. Clerin was not positive if it was going to work. Was not Linchon within her? Or fighting with Lembin in Tureyn? Or maybe helping with the smoke at Agoge? Though that had hopefully stopped smoking after they left. Why would Linchon be here, stuck in the temple? *Why would Linchon be waiting for us?* she thought. Of course, maybe it was waiting because it wanted to convince Croy to help with Gunzgak. Or maybe it was waiting to hurt Croy so that he could not hurt her. There was no way to tell, so Clerin was just wasting time worrying about something she could do nothing about.

"Well. Are we ready?" It was Croy. He was looking at Vrric who, honestly, was the only one who may have needed any rest.

"Yes, yes. Of course."

Everyone was up on their feet. Vrric flew them, and a small boulder and some smaller rocks, over the river, facing the illusion masking the temple entrance. Vrric was sitting cross-legged as he peered over at the cliff. Zing! He shot a rock that bounced off the cliff face. He tried several more times before one just disappeared— flying through the illusion. Then, after a couple more, he did the boulder. It arced and then disappeared. It was like the first time she was there. She only hoped he would not bounce her off the cliff face on his first try.

"All right. You first, Clerin?"

She merely nodded back. It was incredibly scary the first time and, though she had much more trust in Vrric than she did back then, it was still a little frightening. She sat herself down on the air in front of him, making herself as small as possible, half listening to the water rushing through the gorge below and half listening to the blood pumping furiously through her head.

Whoosh! She felt herself thrust forwards. She could not tell that she had sprung forth beyond the feeling of motion and the wind around her. She had her eyes held tightly closed. She could feel when the spell was negated by the way she started to arc downwards. She shifted slightly from sitting to a low crouch, but with her feet in front of her. She probably should not have moved, but the thought of slamming into the cliff face not feet first was too much to bear. She held her arms in front of her, in a minimal attempt to protect her skull.

Bam! She hit something with her feet and tumbled over. She rolled along the cave floor, her arms swinging out to slow herself down. She was a little scraped and fairly bruised, but nothing was broken. She crawled out of the way to avoid anyone else crashing through the illusion. The sound of the river, which had been so prominent moments ago, was gone. She could only hear her own breathing.

Croy came next. Watching him roll into the cave was almost more painful than the feeling of herself going through it. He crawled to a safe space, not talking to her, not really looking at her. Just trying to get out of the way.

Vrric arrived last. He rolled in and lay where he landed for a brief moment. Then he stood and tried to brush himself off. It appeared that he was smiling to himself, probably for a job well done if Clerin knew him at all. But then his smile slipped.

"Do you hear that rushing noise?"

"No." Both Clerin and Croy answered at the same time.

"It's… It's getting loud." His head jerked up suddenly. He glanced at Clerin and Croy, but then stared wild-eyed deep into the cave. He took a step back, then another, then he turned and ran back towards the entrance, the exit. He looked worried and concerned, it was not a look of sheer terror, but since he flung himself out of the cave at full speed, she was not sure what else to call the emotion.

"Well, I guess I'm accepted." Croy's smile was a little sheepish, a little timid.

They waited a little while just to make sure Vrric had fully gotten out of the way. Then they cleaned up the entrance, tossing the rocks back outside. Finally they rolled the boulder out. It was odd not hearing it bounce off the cliff face.

"Lead the way." Croy swept a hand towards the tunnel.

The walls gave off an eerie light, making navigation in the tunnels possible. It had been a while, but nothing had changed, and she was able to recall which forks she had taken the last time she was there. Eventually, the path began to brighten a little bit. As she got to a corner, she peeked around. There was the glowing pillar. She ducked back into the hallway.

"Here we are. Last chance to back out." She smiled warmly at Croy.

"I need to know."

Clerin just nodded in response. She had assumed he was not going to back out, not after coming this far. She started to undress. He coughed a little.

"You know, this seems like an odd tradition. This…" He pointed her stacking her boots on the ground. She figured the top of her boots were less dirty and would protect the rest of her clothing. At least a little bit.

"If it makes you feel any better, I'll promise not to peek." She smiled a little deviously as he stammered for a second.

"No, it's not that, it's just…"

She shook out of her jerkin, and he turned away, suddenly interested at some rock in the hallway. She finished getting undressed as he started taking off his clothes. Personally, she was fine being naked. Enjoyed it even. It was the most natural state. It was his response, his nervousness, that made it uncomfortable. She wondered if Linchon would care, similar to the bathing and not eating meat before communing, but why risk it now?

"We are unsure if Linchon is even here, if it even wishes to commune. I would rather not jeopardize anything by changing the traditions, as you put it. You did bathe this morning like I asked, yes?"

"Of course I did." He was continuing to remove layers of clothing. "I don't want to jeopardize anything either. I just... It's fine. We're almost ready."

Clerin was ready but waited for Croy. She figured it would be best if they both entered at the same time. She had never tried to commune with anyone additional before.

"All right. Then let us begin."

They both walked in, side by side, with heads held high and staring straight ahead. The room was circular with the pillar centered within it. It glowed a bright white with odd black lines all over it, like a bizarre angular writing style or like dark cracks in a light crystal. The black lines shifted as they neared the pillar, undulating slightly.

Suddenly a wind picked up. She remembered being buffeted before. She quickly cast a low-level flight spell, just to keep herself from getting scraped against the ground. "Lokinderpri!" She heard Croy quickly cast one as well.

They both began to float around the pillar. Not too fast, about ten seconds per rotation. Croy was somehow on the opposite side of the pillar from Clerin as they floated. She could barely glimpse him. The pillar's lines began to shift and flow at a rate similar to how fast they were spinning.

They sped up and the lines undulated faster. Clerin stayed facing the pillar as she spun around. Transfixed. They started to speed up again. Unsure of what to do, Clerin cried out.

"Linchon!" They did not slow, but did not speed up further. She yelled again, three times. "Linchon! Linchon! Linchon!" She was unsure of what else to yell out, what else to do.

The pillar began to pulsate its brightness in a slow wave. The lines turned into a fairly well-defined silhouette. It was not just an outline but gave some features as well, such as the eyes, nose, and mouth (when it opened) glowing from behind. It was obviously a silhouette of her father. She wondered if the same image was spinning on the other side of the pillar, facing Croy.

"I have been expecting the both of you." Only one voice emanated, and it was her father's voice. "I hear things through the air, through the ether, through the great communicator's mind. I have known you were headed here, and I know what you wish to ask of me. And yet… Yet, I still do not have a satisfactory response. How like a derlian I have become. You are here now. Ask your question. I will speak for Gorbanax as well as I."

"Why does Gunzgak have to die?" Croy started off.

"Why do you have to die? Why do I, why does Gorbanax? Your question is too general. Narrow it."

"If Clerin communes directly with Gunzgak, will Gunzgak die?"

"Yes."

"Do you wish Clerin to commune with Gunzgak?"

"Yes. We all wish it."

"Why?"

"There should not be only one Beleg. There should be four, or zero."

"That's unfair!"

"What? That is very fair. That is the definition of fair."

"Gunzgak does not wish to die."

"Do you? I could kill you now if you like."

"No. No, I don't want to die."

"Yet you will. Is that fair?"

There was a pause before Croy responded. They had slowed a little, but they were still being whipped around the circular room. It made concentrating on the conversation difficult.

"It is natural. Derlians die all the time. Fair or unfair does not enter into it."

"Yavens die."

"Not of old age."

"Correct. But they do die. Is that fair? What is a Beleg but a Yaven of four elements? In fact, unlike the Yavens, we have chaos within us, just like you do."

"Did you wish to die? Before Clerin arrived with her message from Lembin. Were you thinking that you would age and die?"

It was Linchon's turn to pause before responding. "I was not thinking I would age, regardless of the chaos within me. At the time, I was not thinking of death at all. But it is done. I have accepted it. Gunzgak shall have to do the same."

"You accepted it because you had no choice. It was, as you say, already 'done.' Even if you had not accepted it, you would still be dying. Gunzgak is not yet dying. Do you agree that your acceptance and Gunzgak's would be two different types of acceptance? One of the past, of merely acknowledging reality, and the other of the future. Of a future that is not part of reality yet, not true yet."

"I acknowledge that they are two different types of acceptance."

"Can you not see that Gunzgak's is much harder?"

"Harder than mine, yes. But not harder than Gorbanax's. Gorbanax had the same form of acceptance that Gunzgak has. The same decision, the same quandary. It came to the same conclusion as I did. There can be only four Belegs, or zero."

"How do we know?" Clerin interrupted. She could not pass up the opportunity.

"It is obvious that Gorbanax's form of acceptance is the same as Gunzgak's. There is no how."

"No. How do we know that Gorbanax accepted it? How do we know it came to the same conclusion that you did?"

"You communed with Gorbanax. You, of all derlians, should understand this."

"Yes. I understand. I understand that Gorbanax did not wish to commune with me until we destroyed the Cabal of Lochom. Then it allowed me to. Then it died, or began its death cycle, or however that works."

"Then your question makes no sense."

"Let me rephrase. How does Croy know what Gorbanax accepted?"

"Convince him."

"I have tried. But it has not worked."

Linchon paused again. Rather than giving it time to respond, Clerin waded ahead. More than Croy, she needed something to convince Trela. Anything.

"Does it not seem odd that we can commune with you, but not Gorbanax? You started your death cycle long before Gorbanax. At least in derlian time. We tried to commune with Gorbanax and were unable to. We then traveled great distance and some time to your temple, and we are still able to commune with you."

"Yes. And now you say that you speak for Gorbanax. Why is that? Why is Gorbanax unable to speak for itself?" Croy interrupted the pause as well.

"Gorbanax lost its voice first. I lost my ability to protect my Luftens first. Which is worse?"

"But that's... How could you prove that?" Croy sounded incredulous. They were still spinning on opposite sides, so Clerin could not see him.

"There is no proving. With Belegs, one must have faith. Yes, like your Trela. She has faith in destiny, and what has happened? Destiny has smiled upon her."

"Destiny is not the same as the Belegs. Surely you are not alluding to Gorbanax being the one who steered her towards being the Kriishan?" Croy sounded even more incredulous.

"Who can say? Not I. But, more importantly, it is the mechanism that is the same, even if there are different powers in play."

"I thought you said you spoke for Gorbanax." Croy sounded a bit smug at that statement.

"On the subject of other Belegs, yes. On the subjects that we have discussed. Not for every question you might ask of me." They started spinning faster again. The pulsating light from the pillar gained in intensity. It seemed that Linchon was getting aggravated. "How come you do not believe Clerin? Do you feel she is lying to you about the Cabal? About Gorbanax? Do you really feel that she would lie to everyone about that? Do you feel she *could* lie to everyone about that?"

There was another pause. Clerin was getting dizzy. She was worried that visiting Linchon had been a mistake. The idea that Linchon would somehow convince Croy that killing Gunzgak was necessary was a bit absurd. All he could be made to think was that it was inevitable. Maybe. And the conversation with Linchon did not appear to be helping anything at all.

"Can you prove that Gorbanax and you are different? That you and Lembin are different? How do we know who we are communing with? How do we know anything you say is true?" If Clerin had been able to see Croy's face she would have noticed his grim determination as he spoke. He needed to know that. That was the crux of the faith issue, at least for him. And for Trela.

"There is no proving! Clerin should have faith, at least of that. She has communed with Lembin, myself, and Gorbanax. Are we different? Do we commune the same? Did Gorbanax not require that the Cabal be destroyed before accepting your messages?" There was an anger building. They were spinning quite fast now. She needed to do something to assuage the situation, but still get something to convince Trela. She had given up on Croy for the moment.

"I know you are each different. I have that much faith, at least concerning that." She had an urge to mention the air bubble that lifted Trela out of the lava. If there was some way that Linchon could explain that away. She needed some way she could prove a negative, that she could prove that Linchon was not there when Trela communed with Gorbanax. The air bubble would not do it, that would just be explained away as something inconsequential. What she needed was a lie egregious enough to elicit a response. A response that might include an accidental confession—not that it would, but that the lack of a confession in the response would be indicative of proving the negative. So she hoped.

"Why did Gorbanax tell Trela that it was you who killed it, not Lembin?"

"When did Gorbanax commune with Trela?"

"Just after it communed with me."

"It is not true."

"Then why would Gorbanax say that?"

"It is not true that Gorbanax said that."

"How do you know that? Do you not have faith?"

"I know it because I can read your mind!"

The top of the cave exploded. They were flung up and out like ragdolls in a tornado. Clerin passed out and dreamt of nothing but a comforting velvety blackness.

When Clerin came to, she was dressed and lying on top of her bedding. There was no tent, she was just on a grassy knoll, and it was incredibly bright. She wondered how she had been able to sleep. She blinked a lot and rolled onto her side, half covering her eyes with an arm. Soon she could hear footsteps softly approaching. She guessed correctly that it was Vrric coming to check on her.

"Standing there silently is worse than just saying something." Her head was pounding.

"Only because you're awake. This is the fifth time I've walked by." There was a smile in his voice, she could tell even though she could not see him. It did very little to help her headache.

"Where are we? Did you fly me back to camp?" She moved her arm a little, letting more of the light brighten her lids.

"No. I *whispered* to Ryshial and had her bring clothes and some bedding. I wasn't sure if flying you around was a great idea. Figured recuperating in situ would be best. Croy is still out, by the way." She was not sure if he said that to keep her from waking Croy or what.

"How did you avoid the debris?"

"I had been off to the side. After the terror gripped me and I leapt out over the river, I decided to keep a little distance. I stayed over there, to have an angle on the entrance, just in case either of you came out that way, leaping into the river or flying. There was an incredibly loud rumble and then, whoosh! The ground erupted upwards. The two of you were tossed higher than the surrounding rock, so I was able to quickly cast a spell on both of you and floated you over here. Once you get to feeling better, you really should see what is left of the temple. There is a tiny valley. Well, not a valley, but a rift, or a gouge. Which is smaller? There is now a tiny dry gouge, an empty riverbed that leads from an inland circular portion out to the river's gorge. The circular part really is circular, almost perfectly so. It does not look natural." His voice was still smiling.

Clerin knew he was incredibly curious. He would want to know everything about their encounter with Linchon. It was probably painful holding back his questions, but he did. He let her rest with her arm half over her eyes and did not mention it at all. He could be nice like that.

It took her several minutes before she felt she could sit up. She drank an entire waterskin, hoping that would help with her headache. She was not positive it did, but it certainly did not hurt.

Croy started rousing soon after she sat up. He was also reticent to talk and complained of a headache. Vrric brought him some water as well and they all took it easy for a little while longer. Eventually, however, they would have to return to the camp. And they would then gather everyone around to hear the story of communing with Linchon. Clerin was not trying to delay the inevitable, but it was nice to lay on the grass and just not think.

They returned and Clerin let Croy tell most of the story, only adding little details if she felt they were pertinent. He had a good handle on it; she had not needed to add much. He was a little listless, or sad, or something, during his speech. He kept looking at the ground, even more than he was naturally prone to. She wondered if he was coming around to thinking Gunzgak would have to die. She would have to probe, lightly, at some later date. At the moment, she was feeling good that it was over with.

They decided to take a full day before starting the trek to Ariellyna. Clerin slept in and Vrric brought her breakfast to eat in their tent. It was pleasant. More importantly, she awoke with only a small headache.

Eventually she got a visitor. Trela had come to talk with her about Linchon. She wondered if Trela had already spoken with Croy.

"Could we chat somewhere?" It was still morning, or at least before noon. There were small groups of warriors about, some practicing with their weapons, some playing games. It was a tiny version of warpack life.

They wandered a bit, not speaking much, and when they did speak, it was about nothing of import. They got to some trees with ivy growing up their trunks, fully surrounding them. It was oddly beautiful; it was like the bark itself had leaves. She wondered if it was a healthy relationship.

"So, I've spoken with Croy already. He mentioned that he tried to get Linchon to prove that it was not pretending to be Gorbanax but failed. He then stated you asked something weird and then everything exploded. Can you explain all that?" She did not appear adversarial, which was nice.

"Well, as I tried to explain to you earlier, I do not think Linchon was pretending to be Gorbanax when I was communing. There were just too many differences. And the whole acceptance after we killed the Cabal issue. As for when you communed with Gorbanax, I, of course, have no idea of what happened. From your description of the communication, it does sound like it was Gorbanax. I am sure that Croy explained how Linchon communed, so you know how different it is." She raised her hand to stave off Trela's interruption. "But that is not really what you are asking. The weird thing that Croy is referring to was a lie I gave to Linchon to try to trip it up. I asked, 'Why did Gorbanax tell Trela that it was you who killed it, not Lembin?' And I did it to see what its first response was. What do think it was?"

"That you were lying. Croy stated that Linchon said it could read your mind and it knew you were lying and then everything erupted."

"Nope. Linchon said that later. Everything Croy said was true. But that was not Linchon's first response. That was, 'When did Gorbanax commune with Trela?' Get it?" Clerin smiled to herself about her own ingenuity.

"So… You feel it passed your test. That if it had been pretending to be Gorbanax it would not have asked that question. Either because it knew when we had communed or it would have just jumped straight to calling you a liar."

"Exactly." She had not thought it completely through, she had just been trying to rest, but after Trela spoke the words, she knew that was it. It had turned out better than she had hoped.

"Unless it knew you were testing it, since it could read your mind, and it came up with a response that would throw you off the scent." Trela knew how to suck the wind out of her sails.

"Linchon answered very quickly, not as if it were analyzing the situation. Of course, Linchon is a Beleg. No one can say for sure what it is really thinking or doing, or how long it takes to think or do. But I did my best." Clerin had no good response.

"And what a best it was! I would not have thought of that. I doubt anyone else in our little group would have thought of it. It is not your skill under pressure that I am concerned about. It is certainly not your moxie… chutzpah… whatever; I cannot believe you lied to a Beleg attempting to get a knee-jerk emotional response out if it. That's… brave. As much bravery as I have ever seen out of any of my greatest warriors. I applaud your efforts." Trela was smiling widely. "There is nothing you can do about me being worried that a Beleg cannot be fooled, cannot be lied to. There is nothing to say about my concern that Linchon's response was too perfect. I worry about these things, that is what I do. Our quest has gotten too large for me not to worry. We are attempting to trick Belegs, to kill Belegs. We are aiming for our creators, Clerin. There are no higher stakes than that. I take that responsibility very seriously. Let me assure you, however, that you have performed perfectly. You are my Fluen princess. You certainly did not disappoint."

With that, Trela started to walk out of the trees, towards the camp. Clerin did not follow. After a couple of steps Trela turned back, still smiling. Clerin waived her on. She wanted to be alone for a moment. She stared at the ivy ringing the tree. She knew mistletoe was parasitic, but was ivy? If the tree was robust and healthy, would the ivy steal enough nutrients to damage it? Were their roots even at the same elevation? She wanted them both to live, to thrive. They looked so beautiful together. She just could not figure out if the relationship was healthy, however. She was suddenly sad that Nyhan had not come with them. He probably would have known.

They woke the next morning at dawn and broke camp soon afterwards. Clerin felt like she lived on a horse now. They had been constantly traveling since Vatlisi really, with only short breaks at Tureyn and Agoge. She did not count their last visit to Ariellyna since that had been so short. She was worried that the next one would be short as well. If they had enough time, she was hoping to see Escha and Torpalin again. As well as Vanelia. She did not have to see Chiavel, but they would probably have to see him at some point. He could certainly be helpful when he wanted to be. She wondered if they would encounter his guards on the roads into the city. Days passed.

The closer they got, the thicker the forests got. Soon there were scattered helioarc trees, reaching for the stars, standing far above the other forest trees. At that point the coterie was on a nicely kept wide road. Eventually they reached the outskirts of Ariellyna, at the full helioarc forest. Eventually they encountered some guards at a roadblock.

Clerin rode up with Vrric to reach Trela. They had not been too far behind, but she had not realized how close the coterie had been getting to the city. Trela was already dismounted and striding up to the guards. She had dismounted to not be intimidating, Clerin was sure. Guards did not enjoy feeling like they were being intimidated. Trela's stride, however, counteracted that effect a little.

Clerin lengthened her own stride to get there quickly. Vrric was not far behind. There were five guards up front and another five or so that were hanging back. Trela's voice was diplomatic.

"…no wagons full of weapons or anything. It is just us travelers." Trela glanced back quickly. "Ah, and here are my diplomats. Both of them know King Chiavel. Feyazki, please, explain our mission to these fine guards."

"Yes, we are here to speak with King Chiavel. We will send a note back once we have reached Ariellyna, something with the King's seal." Vrric was nodding shallowly. Amazingly enough, the guard started nodding along with Vrric.

"Yes. Okay. Be quick about it though." All the guards were nodding and saying small words of encouragement.

After they had ridden past the guards, Clerin asked him what happened.

"Oh. I cast a spell as I dismounted my horse." He was smiling just a little.

"What happens when the spell wears off?"

"They'll feel confused about why they let us through, especially their leader. But they will remember that they did let us through. We are well outside of Ariellyna, and they might assume we will be another station's problem. And I will try to get them a sealed letter. There is no real reason for us to be kept out of Ariellyna."

"Well. That is just it, is it not? We could have talked our way through there and then they would not feel confused afterwards. What if they send a rider after us?"

"They will not send a rider after us." His smile was gone.

Clerin kind of wanted to say more. He had added an element of chaos, of potential danger, to the mission. And for what? To be expeditious? This was not entirely out of character, he was brash and overly confident in his abilities, but it was certainly something unexpected. He was already unhappy with her line of questions, however. She decided to drop it. She did her best, but a small sigh escaped her lips. Maybe it was lost amongst the sound of the horses.

They traveled a while in semi-annoyed silence. No rider ever caught up to them, so she supposed he was right. It still seemed like an unnecessary risk, however. After some time, it was getting late in the afternoon, they came upon another group of guards. Trela slowed the column down and waved her and Vrric up.

"They seemed to recognize you last time. Go ahead and just push us through, no need for them to talk to a Pyran." She smiled warmly at them.

They both dismounted and walked over to where the guards were waiting for them. There were more this time. Still about five at the front, but about fifteen or so in the back. Buildings could be seen off in the distance. They were at the edge of Ariellyna. As they walked up, Vrric smiled to Clerin and then to the central guard.

"Clerin here will explain our mission." He swept a hand towards her and gave a small bow.

Clerin was annoyed but did her best to hide it. Part of her annoyance was towards herself. She should have known something like this was going to happen. She should have been prepared with a good cover story. They had just ridden at least an hour with her thinking of what? Nothing beyond her mild annoyance at how Vrric had handled the last group of guards. Her mind raced for a solution.

"We are here to help King Chiavel with Vanelia." It was the only thing she could think of.

The statement froze all the guards, or at least all of them within easy hearing range. The one in the front, the one she had spoken to, blinked twice and then grinned widely.

"You know where she is?"

"No. Not yet. But we can track her. We have brought the finest hunters, mages, and warriors from the Pyran realm to bring her in." She smiled back, giving him a flash of her white teeth. "I am an old friend of Chiavel's and so is Feyazki. He would like to contact Sempere, Chiavel's mage, to let him know we have finally arrived."

"Sure. By all means." The guard smiled, nodded, and took a step back.

Vrric just looked at her with a raised eyebrow and then turned to walk away a few steps. He was muttering some spell. She hoped he would be able to get ahold of Sempere. She had not really thought about it before she said it.

She turned her attention to the guards and tried to overhear their conversation. She only caught audible glimpses: "…told you Chiavel was planning something…," "…couldn't hide forever…," "…is there a reward…," "…where do you think she is…," "…can't believe she just called him by his name…," "…you think they actually know King Chiavel…," "…and even a Gaen on a horse…," "…are you listening…"

The last came from Vrric. She was, in fact, not listening. At least not to him.

"Sorry, I was… Were you able to contact Sempere?"

"Yes. He will come here to escort us." Vrric stopped and stared straight into her eyes. "And he's excited. Well, not him, you know Sempere, but Chiavel is excited that we have shown up offering to hunt down Vanelia. She's been missing for a week. They don't think she's left the city, but… who knows. For her sake, I hope she has."

"And what about Hynara?"

"Who?"

"The baby. What about the baby?"

"Oh. Not sure. Suppose we'll have to track her down as well."

"That sounds like you are being accusatory." It was her turn to raise her eyebrow at him.

"This is all your idea."

"Do you think your little mind trick would have worked here, at the entrance to the city, with almost twenty foreigners?"

"Not as effectively as your trick."

"What is going on here?" Trela walked up to them. Her body radiated a strong but low-grade intensity.

They both turned to her and opened their mouths. She swiveled her hand on her wrist near her neck, cutting them off. She then snapped, pointed to the ground, and began slowly walking away. Clerin was a little annoyed since those all gestures seemed like they were used on pets or children. She might have been a little annoyed with Vrric as well, so it was hard to tell exactly how annoyed she was with each issue. Rather than worrying about it, she followed Trela. Vrric silently followed afterwards.

"I'll ask again. What is going on?" They were several rods away from the coterie as well as the guards. Vrric just swept his hand towards Clerin. More hand gestures.

"To get past the guards I told them that we would help with Vanelia." She paused but they both just stood there staring at her. "Well, unfortunately, she is missing and Chiavel would love getting some help to find her."

"Missing? I believe the term is 'she went into hiding.' That is, if I'm reading the response from Sempere correctly." Vrric had his arms crossed.

"Wait. Who is Sempere?" Trela turned her gaze away from Clerin to glance at Vrric.

"He is Chiavel's mage. You met him when we camped at the temple with Vanelia and Hulgert."

"Ah. Well. That was quite a while ago." She turned her gaze back to Clerin. "What did you tell them exactly? About helping with Vanelia."

"Just that. I thought I was being vague. But they responded that she was missing and Chiavel was looking for her. Then they asked if we knew where she was. I said no, but that we could find her."

"Hmm. You were okay there in the beginning. But offering to find her puts us in a bind."

"You said we brought the best hunters from the Pyran realm to track her down." Vrric helpfully added more specific information.

Trela paused and glanced between them. She looked a little exasperated but said nothing. Clerin was not positive if Trela knew about the spell at the previous checkpoint but decided against bringing it up. There was enough tension in the air.

"I'm not sure why you two aren't working together here." Trela rubbed her brow briefly. "All right. We will be allowed full access to Ariellyna if we pretend to track down the deposed queen, is that correct?" Vrric drew in a deep breath, but Trela interrupted. "Just a yes or no, please."

"Yes." His chest deflated slowly after he spoke.

"Good." She then glared at Clerin. "Not good as in great, but at least that's settled. We'll need an inn that is centrally located. And maybe not too high up in the trees. I've heard some grumbling already about sleeping up in swaying boughs."

"Check with Malghain or Haswyxe. They will probably know of more inns than we do." Vrric nodded back towards the group.

Clerin kind of wanted to mention the Cloak and Stagger, but she was a little unsure of why. It was the only inn she had been to in Ariellyna, the only one she knew of. Yet the urge to provide an answer to a question, even a poor answer, was ingrained in her. She thought it must have started during her schooling, but maybe even before that.

"Good idea." Trela turned and left.

Soon Sempere was seen floating over to them. The guards were excited to see him getting closer, Clerin less so. Most of the guards had, apparently, never seen someone so close to their king before. It boggled her mind a little. Trela made a point to visit all her warriors periodically. Chiavel did not seem to share that desire.

Sempere dropped down next to Vrric, Clerin, and Trela. He had a careful eye on the other members of the coterie. He gave a quick nod to Vrric.

"Chiavel had no news of your coming. We are grateful for your assistance, truly, but are unsure of what reward you are looking for. Or how you even came to know of our situation." His face was stoic. "Convince me this is what you say it is."

"We are here to speak with a Luften mage about subjects that do not concern you. We heard about Vanelia and your troubles through our spies embedded in your city. As for the reward, we assumed there was a ransom in gold being offered. Is that not so?" Trela took his attention away from Vrric.

"Who is the mage you wish to speak with?"

"That does not concern you."

"We merely wish to help you get in contact with them." Sempere paused for a moment, looking between them all. "Then who are your spies? I need something, you understand. Something that would help corroborate your incredibly vague story."

"They must not be harmed or harassed. They are not spying on you or your king, they just provide us with general information when asked." Trela narrowed her eyes at Sempere.

"I would say that the missing Vanelia is not necessarily common knowledge. Or, at least, the fact that we are looking for her is not what we would categorize as general information." He paused and she glared. "But it is not necessarily a secret either. You have our word that no harm shall come to your spies."

Trela silently stared at him. He stared back. Clerin and Vrric glanced at each other.

"The warriors that Vanelia sent with you, yes? Torpalin and Escha?" Sempere cocked his head slightly. "You will have to nod if you are not going to speak."

Trela nodded. He visibly relaxed. Then the rest of them did as well.

"We had assumed. They were being watched." He raised his hand to ward off Trela's response. "Not harassed or anything. It was just odd that they had returned during this time of upheaval. Believe me, it was a good thing that they had been watched. Otherwise, it might have been assumed that they had helped Vanelia. As it is, they are either tremendously good at spying, or they lead very boring lives. For the sake of moving this along, we will assume they are mundane." Sempere nodded to himself, then turned to Trela. "We will assume you are here to help and will not hinder your search for the mage you seek. You should assume that you are being watched. If we feel you are not assisting us to find Vanelia, you will be asked to leave Ariellyna. If we feel you are assisting her… well… you will not be warned. Understand?"

"Of course. We would not assume otherwise." Trela appeared to be slightly amused. Why she should look amused at a threat, Clerin could not fathom. Then again, there were plenty of things about Trela that confused her, why should this be any different? In any case, the reaction appeared to appease Sempere.

"Will you need any assistance with lodgings?"

"No. Thank you, but we will find our own way."

Sempere nodded to her, then to the others. A quick smile touched his lips and then he turned and walked over to the waiting guards. Clerin could not overhear the conversation, but the guards all nodded seriously whenever Sempere spoke.

When all the conversation died down, Sempere looked over at them. At her, at Clerin. There was something in his eye, something he was trying to communicate. For the life of her, she could not tell if it was a warning or a threat, a question or a statement, good or bad. His eyes were intense for that brief moment, then he mouthed some magic and flew off above the trees.

"You have free rein, welcome to Ariellyna." The guard walked over and swept his hand towards the city, not that the city was visible through the trees yet. The road snaked ahead of them, vanishing amidst the green.

They all nodded and smiled, the guards and the coterie. They rode down the winding road, farther into the woods. Eventually, it started to open up. There were large empty swaths around the giant bases of the helioarc trees. There were a couple of small buildings at the base of some of them.

The bases of helioarc trees were gigantic, and staring up into them was like looking at a dusty road in the desert—they just seemed to extend to the vanishing point, until she could see no more, like the trees were infinitely tall though she knew that not to be the case. And there were spiraling staircases that wound up some of the trees, with various large platforms at differing elevations along the way. As she looked up, she could see the dangerous-looking rope bridges that extended to different helioarcs like spiderwebs. But the scale from the ground could not convey the city. Ariellyna could only be truly experienced up in the boughs. Only from that vantage point, way up in elevation, could the city be understood.

Clerin watched her friends around her ooh and ahh at the sights. The entire tiny coterie stood transfixed at the first helioarc with a stairwell, staring up at the infinite height and spiderweb extensions, mesmerized. She wanted to tell them to just wait. Just wait until they had reached the center of the town. Just wait until they had reached the upper elevations. Just wait until they could see the magnificence spread below them, and still above them, a city of true three dimensions. But they would see soon enough, and her interrupting them at that moment would help no one.

Malghain and Haswyxe walked up to Vrric. They were the only three not staring upwards. Even Clerin had a hard time keeping her head from tilting back.

"So, are we going to the inn before we surprise Torpalin and Escha?" Haswyxe was grinning. No doubt thinking of the surprise on his friends' faces. "If we wait too long, they may hear that we are in town."

"Yes, we should go to the inn first." Vrric smiled back at Haswyxe. "We just need to unload everything and get set up. Then we can surprise them. Besides, you don't really want twenty derlians showing up at the tiny bakery, do you? We can leave some at the inn who want to relax and bathe."

"What? Who wants a bath when we have friends that need harassing?" Haswyxe pretended to smell his armpit. "Besides, there are no private baths at the inn. And most of the public ones are based on the ground."

"Which inn was chosen, anyway?" Clerin had wanted to ask that for a while.

"We decided on The Flying Mouse. It is an inn high up in a centralized helioarc. It should have fantastic views for the non-Luftens and be easy to get to and from the other main helioarcs."

"Flying Mouse?" Clerin had said it under her breath, more trying to think of where she had heard the phrase before than of asking Malghain a question.

"It's the Luften nickname for a bat." He hooked his thumbs together and spread his fingers out, waving them. It appeared more like a flailing spider than a bat, but she smiled and nodded just the same.

"Okay, we hit the inn real quick, then we go find the bakery." Haswyxe was keeping everyone on track.

About that same time, the non-Luftens were heading over as well. Some were still looking up, but most were looking serious. Ready for the next stage.

They got to the helioarc supporting the Flying Mouse in good time. They handed over their horses and climbed the stairs up to the first platform. There was a large entrance into the trunkway there, into its hollow center, then the stairs continued to wind upwards.

Clerin walked through the entrance, marveling at how massive the tree was. The wall of the tree left over was easily two rods thick, almost making a tunnel. Just inside there were mages sitting cross-legged on multiple sleds. There would have to be more than one trip, each sled could only hold about four derlians. Clerin stepped on one and moved to the far side. Even though it was levitating, it did not shift under her feet, it stayed firm and flat. Once the sled filled up it slowly started to float up through the hollowed out trunkway.

They went a long, long ways up. The feeling of flight was a bit paradoxical to Clerin. When Vrric would fly her around, she felt safe, almost cocooned. But if she were to stand on something, and then that something would fly, she would get flashes of vertigo. Like she could just lose her balance and fall off the sled. Watching the wood slide past as they raised higher did not help either. She would have preferred the open air, though certainly not the wind.

They got to the top of the trunkway and disembarked. The tunnel back out to the branches was about one rod thick at their elevation. She saw Vrric place a coin in the mage's hand, so she did not reach for her own purse. Then she walked out into the splendor.

The helioarc continued for quite a while, they were only about halfway up. The dwellings below the trunkway were buildings built in the crooks of branches and attached to the side of the tree. Those were more easily visible clinging to the adjacent helioarc. Clerin knew from experience that the dwellings at the top of the helioarc were hollowed out at various locations, as if an enormous woodpecker had carved them out. The ones at the transition and for some distance above were a little of both. Rooms carved into the tree and exiting into buildings. It rained a fair amount in Ariellyna, though not nearly as much as in the Fluen realm, up against the Clatsvol sea. But the rain was typically shielded by the expansive leaves covering the upper regions of the helioarcs. So, there were also lots of parks, open air spaces that would have been called terraces in the Fluen realm. She wanted to call them balconies here, but there were also plenty of those, platforms cantilevering off the helioarc at various locations. All these areas linked by paths and ladders and stairs. And all the helioarcs linked by three-dimensional spiderwebs of suspension bridges. *No wonder Luftens are such prolific mages, even the warriors,* thought Clerin. *You need to be able to fly to get anywhere around here.*

Clerin stood there on an enormous branch and surveyed the view. How the regular trees blanketed the forest floor in green. How the occasional helioarc burst up through, stretching for the sun. There were easily eight in her current view, beyond the one she was standing on. And she was only looking in one direction, and not counting the distant ones. It truly was breathtaking. She would surely get homesick for the Fluen realm, but maybe she should try to live in Ariellyna for a while. Once Vrric had asked for her hand. Once all the Beleg business was over. Once they had survived.

On an adjacent branch, there were scattered tables covered in dyed linen, mostly black. There was a small fence on either side of the branch, keeping the mead drinkers from stumbling too far to the edge. On the branch she was on, there was the clearing, the landing area, and then a wood building which took up the entire branch's width.

Clerin followed the others into the inn's lobby. There were many windows with lots of light. A long countertop split the room, keeping the workers on the opposite side from the guests. She noticed there were at least three spots of hinges, where the counter could lift up and over and a derlian could easily pass through. Trela and Haswyxe were discussing something with the clerks.

Clerin passed her eye around until she caught Vrric. She smiled and gave him a wink. He smiled back but was still half listening to the Gaen talking with him. *Silvadhin?* she thought. So she stood in place for a while, looking around, especially out the windows. Not quite bored, exactly. She found herself staring out the windows and wondering why they should all be in the lobby at the same time.

Once everything was finalized, some porters came from behind the counter to assist them. Even though there were quite a few mages in the coterie, the portage service was free. They were all flown to separate rooms. Vrric even allowed the young mage assigned to them to cast the spells.

Their room was one of those carved into the helioarc, though it had a small balcony at the entrance for a landing. The small room was not too dim, there was a large window on either side of the door. One large bed took up most of the space in the room, leaving their large saddlebags stuffed in a corner.

"Do you want to head down to see Torpalin and Escha?" Vrric gestured back to the still open door.

"No. Sorry. I really need to bathe." She snapped her jerkin. She had hoped a puff of dust would shoot out. It did not, but he laughed anyway.

"I figured you would say that. But listen, there is a nice public bath less than half a league from the bakery. We could stop by with all the others, say our hellos, then step out and head to the bath. It would really just be on the way." His smile was charming. "Then we could see them for earnest on our way back, after everyone else has gone."

"That sounds like a great idea." She started rummaging through her saddlebags to find something to change into after she got clean.

About half of the coterie headed down to the bakery immediately. They flew over as a group with Vrric, Ryshial, Serghno, and Croy helping with the spells. The bakery was on the ground, nestled at the base of a helioarc. The chimneys were smokeless and cold as the day was getting on.

They all piled in through the doors, Haswyxe first. There was a great commotion as Torpalin and Escha realized what was happening, who all was there. Everyone talked at once for a while. The room itself was probably large, but it was hard to tell with that many derlians in it. There was another long counter bisecting the room with similar hinged openings. There were three loaves of bread left in a basket on the counter, everything else was bare. In the back, there appeared to be a bunch of flour and utensils, in the way back were the cold brick ovens.

Introductions to Torpalin's sister were made all round in the midst of the chaos. Tundalia had shoulder length dark hair, pulled back out of her face. She was larger and more muscular than a typical female Luften, but nowhere near her brother's size.

"We're about to close up anyway, we should all go to a tavern!" Torpalin's booming voice broke free from the general commotion.

A chorus of "Yeses" erupted from the crowd. There was a round of cheering as Clerin's heart sank. There was little chance that she was going to end up at the baths that evening. On the upside, however, she was going to have a great time.

Chapter 13

They all enjoyed the tavern immensely. It was relaxing. Not that Vrric had been anxious, but it felt great to just enjoy an evening indoors without thinking about anything else. Just being in the comfortable moment.

He figured the morning would begin at the baths. Clerin had made them toss a blanket over the bed to sleep on top of that. Not the most comfortable arrangement, but he had fallen asleep quickly. And she did have a point. They were quite grubby from the road.

He was right, Clerin did not even want to eat until she had bathed. He flew them directly there, stomach slightly rumbling. They had not eaten much at the tavern.

Vrric took her to the largest and most impressive baths in Ariellyna. He felt he might as well show off his city. The baths were a large complex. There were smaller heated baths in the back, under the cover of tall barrel vaults, and larger baths in the front, some covered and some open. There were separate changing rooms for the sexes, but most mingled when they hit the water. The greater separation was front to back. The heated baths cost more, whereas those open to the sky were free.

They were there more to get clean than to relax, but Clerin enjoyed it enough that they stayed for most of the morning. Vrric paid for a decent bathhouse, mostly because he had only used the free baths before. The deck at the shallow side of the pool had tables scattered about with benches and wooden chairs, some with cushions. They had entered through a gate at that end. The sides each had a narrow stone path lining the pool, whereas the deep side of the pool was against a fence half hidden by a wall of green reeds. There was certainly another bathhouse beyond. There were several Luftens in the bathhouse with them. Since that section cost more, they were supposedly a higher class of citizen. Vrric was unsure about that, but they were quieter.

In fact, *they* were the noisy ones. Clerin giggled and splashed around for several hours. She was such a vibrant and graceful swimmer, it was beautiful to watch. He felt like a lumbering tree trunk compared to her, mostly walking around in the shallow end. He could swim as a matter of survival and utility, getting from one place to another, but she frolicked, zipping around underwater like an otter.

Her naked body sliced through the water, turning and rolling as she willed. He was mesmerized enough that he forgot he was hungry.

An old and wrinkled Luften walked by on his way out of the pool, heading across the deck to a bathhouse, and turned slightly to Vrric. "You are a lucky derlian. I hope you know that." He smiled and laughed to himself as he let the water drip off him.

"I am and I do." Vrric smiled back, his hands absently stroking the water surrounding his waist.

"Sure, you know now. But do not forget. When a decade has passed and she's yelling and your child is screaming and the whole world is crying out at you, against you, all of it antagonistic. Do not just snap back. Stop. Think. Remember. Happiness is fragile, don't be the one to shatter it. It is easy to forget these simple times of beauty and joy. Take it from one who knows." The old Luften had a look on his face that mixed happiness and sadness and nostalgia. Vrric could never explain that look.

"Thank you." Vrric turned fully towards him, looked hard at him. His body was a husk, a bent sagging dripping husk, but there was a vibrant glow in the center, deep in the center. "Your experiences have made you wise, and I appreciate you for sharing." Mostly, Vrric wanted the old Luften to feel good. He had obviously been through a lot.

"Well, I don't know about wise, but when I was young, I wished to be a being that bore much. Then I did. I do not overly regret it, but…" He looked like he was going to continue but then his eyes glanced over at something behind Vrric, probably at Clerin, frolicking. "But I have taken more of your time than is necessary. Please, enjoy the day. Enjoy your dolphin over there. Enjoy your life. Yes. That would be doing me a favor, a great kindness. Enjoy your life." He smiled that unexplainable look at Vrric again, turned, and walked away. Vrric never saw him again.

Vrric turned back around and saw… nothing. He glanced about frantically for a moment, starting to lumber towards the deep end, when Clerin suddenly popped up in front of him, bringing a geyser of water with her. She giggled and swept the hair out of her face.

"Who was that? Are you making friends without me?" Her smile was perfect, her dimples deep and symmetric, her eyes like sparkling lightning, her pert little nose just… pert.

"No, never." Vrric laughed. "He was just admiring your beauty." He was going to say more, but she interrupted him.

"Oh. Jealous?"

"Jealous of him? No, no."

"Maybe I like them old."

"I think I know what you like."

"Do you though? Really?" Her eyebrow cocked up comically.

"I know you like being chased."

He lunged at her, thinking she was an easy target. Somehow she twisted out of the way and was back in the water with nary a splash. Safe in her own habitat. He did his best to swim after her and she almost let him catch her a couple of times. Almost. At least she led him back to the shallow end before too long.

"I. Am. Starving." It was staccato enough to be individual sentences. He gripped his taut belly and rolled his eyes for effect.

"Me too, we can go."

They went back to the inn after a filling early lunch to meet up with the others, who were waiting for them on the branch outside of the lobby. Or some of the others, at least. It appeared to be most of the mages of their group and Trela. Vrric and Clerin were ambushed immediately after they landed.

"Where have you two been?" Trela looked somewhere between slightly amused and annoyed. Vrric took that as an indication that they had not been gathered up waiting for too long.

"Well, after the tavern we slept in a little, then we needed to bathe, and then someone got hungry." Clerin nodded slightly in Vrric's direction. Her mood was too buoyant to be affected. Luckily, Trela was nudged closer to the amused side.

"We have a lot of work to do today. We need to find this Hyscarne, so I want all the mages for this. The warriors will hover around the bakery and the inn. We are trying to put out the message that we would like to be contacted by Vanelia. To help, of course." Trela nodded to Vrric as she spoke.

"Well, that seems like a lose-lose plan." Clerin looked a little stunned. Her statement stunned Trela for a brief moment as well. "I mean, if I were Vanelia, I would assume we were let into Ariellyna by Chiavel if we are just staying out in the open. Which would mean we are working for Chiavel since he does not easily grant favors. So, I would certainly not want to come by to say hello. If I were her." She slowed down for a moment but continued on in a quieter vein when she was not interrupted. "On the other hand, if I were Chiavel, I would assume that by sending the word out so publicly we might be making a show of helping him while trying to communicate with Vanelia clandestinely. Like if we were in contact with her before we showed up."

"And what would you have done?" Trela appeared to shift to the annoyed side.

"I think nothing. At least as far as Vanelia is concerned. Assumedly, she would know we were here, and she would contact us if she wanted. Or she could stay in hiding. Or, and this is my hope, she has already escaped the city and we will never hear from her again."

"How does doing nothing help keep Chiavel convinced we are on his side?"

"Oh, it probably does not help. Chiavel is not necessarily paranoid, but he is incredibly pessimistic when it comes to his assumptions of other's motives."

"So one of those 'lose' columns was unavoidable and you have no advice for the other." Trela raised an eyebrow and Clerin slowly nodded. "I thank you for your insights. If you had been here this morning you might have shared them in a more timely fashion. As it is, I think I'll have you meet up with Estfale at the bakery and discuss this with him. We shall be trying to resolve the other issue." Trela had definitely shifted into her annoyed mode. She looked around for a moment. "Croy, could you take Clerin down to the bakery?"

"Why me?" It was a little shocking to hear such a contrarian rebuttal from Croy.

"Because I'm thinking we should have Pyran and Luften mages only when looking for Ryshial's friend." She glared at him.

Vrric was fairly sure that Hyscarne was not a good friend of Ryshial's, but he dared not step into the conversation. He was perfectly happy to let the others argue everything out. He would have stepped in to defend Clerin if he had been able to think of anything, but it had happened so quickly. Besides, Trela rarely stayed annoyed at Clerin for any real length of time.

Croy merely nodded and shuffled over towards the trunkway. Clerin followed him just as silently. That left Trela, Ryshial, Serghno, Arnasta, and Vrric standing around on the branch. He wondered why Croy did not fly Clerin directly from the branch. In fact, she could probably featherfall down to the ground under her own power. He was happy not to voice any opinions concerning that as well. He was also happy not to voice his concerns that their group was much too large to go looking for one mage. He felt the day was going to be spent quietly following orders, at least as far as he was concerned.

They flew to the Mages' Guild's helioarc first. The white guild, the sanctioned one. What better way to find a mage than to ask the guild? Though Vrric had not spent any length of time at the guild, being mentored as a grey mage and leaving Ariellyna just as he was leaving Revkin's tutelage, he did know where the helioarc was located. So he led the flying expedition.

It did not take them too long to reach the helioarc. They alighted on an obvious platform near the base of the tree. There were two mages on the platform, standing together near the entrance to the trunkway. They both had long robes with glyphs along the hems and their hoods were up. The small group landed in front of them lightly, with enough distance between them to keep everyone from feeling nervous. Vrric knew the perimeter of the city was being tightly controlled, but he was unsure if the gatekeepers of any of the guilds would be on high alert as well. The taverns and bathhouses were certainly not concerned about anything beyond accepting coin and providing services.

The two mages approached them after they landed. Their faces were hard to ascertain within the depths of their hoods. Their hands were held together in their sleeves, meaning almost no skin was showing anywhere. Just the tips of their noses as they spoke.

"We have been told of your arrival."

"Yes, you must be Feyazki."

"I am, thank you. So, Chiavel explained that we wish to find a mage?" Vrric was unsure of which one to face while speaking.

"Ha! No."

"No, it is Sempere who explained that to us."

"Though that part was confusing, certainly."

"Yes, confusing. Why would you not tell Sempere the mage's name?"

"You will tell us who you wish to find, won't you?"

"If you tell us, we will find them. But, of course, we will tell Sempere as well."

"Which makes your earlier silence not only confusing but foolish."

"We are less apt to help a fool, you know."

"It had to do with the timing of our conversation, not an attempt to keep a secret. We welcome you to tell Sempere who we are looking for. And we will truly appreciate your assistance." Vrric was not necessarily unnerved by their manner of speaking, but it was certainly odd.

"The name then."

"Yes, the name first. Then the entrance."

"Curious too, we are."

"We would know of what you seek from them."

"Ryshial, can you provide them with who we are looking for?" Vrric turned back to his own group.

"Her name is Hyscarne. Hyscarne from the Branch of Weschuin. We met some time ago, her and I." Ryshial's typically serious face suddenly held the shadow of a smile. "But you will have to stay curious. We are not telling you why we wish to converse with her."

"That makes us sad. But no matter. We will still help."

"We have heard of that name, but it has been some time. Time enough that we will need to enlist the aid of others."

"And space. We never personally knew Hyscarne and are unsure of where she might be."

"Yes. Too much time and space. We will need you to wait here while we find who will best assist."

"No peeking. No listening to our *whispers*. Good behavior transmits respect."

"Of course." Vrric and Ryshial turned their backs on the mages to face the others. Creating the illusion of a thin wall.

The mages retreated to the entrance to the helioarc trunkway and whispered and *whispered*. None of it was audible, not that he was trying to listen.

It did take some effort to not ask Ryshial more about her encounter with Hyscarne while they were waiting. It seemed like the last subject he should bring up at that moment. He had been given a brief synopsis a while ago. He remembered that Hyscarne had visited the Pyran realm but had no inkling of when the meeting occurred, how many cycles had passed.

The two mages took some time before coming back. They walked slowly out of the darkened entrance, still whispering to each other. They stopped in silence in front of the group.

"Were you able to locate Hyscarne?" Trela spoke up, breaking the quiet.

"No, of course not."

"Hyscarne has been missing for some time, you see."

"We were able to locate the mages who saw her last, however."

"We will allow you into the Guild Branch to speak with them, even though you do not have a guild representative with you."

"Yes, even though you only have a grey mage."

There was half a moment of awkward silence while Vrric tried to think up a response that expressed his feelings on the issue without annoying them enough to affect their assistance. He could not come up with anything before Trela filled the void.

"Good then, lead the way." She motioned towards the trunkway entrance.

"Oh, no, not all of you."

"No, there are just too many."

"We will take two mages. The one who knew Hyscarne and the grey mage."

"The rest may wait. Here or elsewhere."

Trela looked annoyed, but did not argue. The others decided to wait back at the inn. No one was sure how long the meeting, or meetings, might take.

Ryshial and Vrric entered the trunkway and stood on a sled. Vrric was a little shocked that they had mages controlling the sleds at the Mages' Guild, but his mind quickly thought up a couple reasons why it was a good idea. The sled floated upwards smoothly.

The sled stopped before the trunkway did. They stepped off onto the landing, which opened directly into a building situated on a large branch. They went from the mostly darkened trunkway, lit by shafts of light streaming through varied apertures, to a bright building, lit by a multitude of windows.

There was an acolyte standing at the landing, waiting for them. His robes matched the mages at the lower entrance and his hands were still hidden in the opposite sleeves, but his head was uncovered leaving his face visible. He had brown hair, slightly unkept, and had a serious look on his face. He glanced at both of them briefly, then nodded.

"Follow me." It was almost inaudible. If Vrric had not been looking at his lips, he might have missed it.

They walked along the main hallway for a while, parallel to the branch that supported it. They did not see, or even hear, anyone else as they followed the acolyte. Eventually he stopped, turned, and knocked at a closed door.

"Your guests have arrived." The acolyte turned to them, nodded deeply, then left back the way they had come.

There were some muffled noise as wooden chairs were slid and scraped across a wooden floor. There was the quiet sound of soft leather soles on the floorboards. The door opened to an old mage. He was gray haired, both on his head and on his chin, and stooped slightly. His robes were similar to the others but had heavily embroidered intricate designs sewn on with a golden thread. He smiled at them both and swept a hand, beckoning them past him.

"Please come in. Have a seat." His eyes belied his age with a strong twinkle.

There were two other mages in the room, but they both remained standing. *If they are guards*, thought Vrric, *why did they not open the door?* They stood staring straight ahead, as if attempting to look lifeless.

The old mage slowly walked over to the other side of the table, so Ryshial and Vrric sat down next to each other, opposite him. The table was bare, without even a water glass to fidget with or a candelabra to glance at. The wood was thick and well-stained, the grain stood out nicely.

"First let me say how sorry I am to hear of Elange's passing. He was a great mage and a great friend. Even though he was considered dead when he was exiled to the eshram, it is a terrible loss." The old mage looked softly at Vrric. "Also painful, of course, was the loss of Revkin. Revkin was your mentor, was he not?"

"Yes, he was. They were both a great loss." Vrric felt he was agreeing with the old mage. But the mage tilted his head a little and squinted an eye.

"For you. But Elange was a different breed. He was far and away a greater mage than Revkin ever was."

"He had stopped contributing, though. Correct? You stated he was already considered dead. Revkin had years left to work with other apprentices. To gain a foothold for the grey mages." Vrric was interrupted before he could continue.

"Revkin was not going to contribute more, trust me. But that is not the point." The old mage raised his hand to stave off Vrric's retort. "The point is that Elange should be given greater respect. You did not know him, not in his prime. He contributed greatly to the guild here. He contributed greatly to magic in general. He was incredibly skilled and generous with his insights. He was a legend. Revkin was not. Elange put many mages to shame, myself included." He stared hard into Vrric's eyes. "Myself included. If I were to die just after Elange, I could only hope to be mentioned as a footnote to the true tragedy of that great mage's death. Truly, I do not mean to disrespect Revkin, I only mean to pay my homage to one of the greatest masters this world has ever seen."

"And who do we have the pleasure of speaking with?" Ryshial inserted herself into the conversation, stopping Vrric from ranting, or apologizing, or mentioning the grey mages again—whatever it was he was going to follow up with.

"Ah, apologies, I have forgotten my manners. I am Fultrenion. I am the guildmaster here. And you are Ryshial, one of the guild leaders from Agoge. And you are Feyazki, famed apprentice of Revkin, who has already outstripped your mentor in reputation."

"Forgive me. I had not realized who I was speaking with." Vrric was going to say more but was politely interrupted.

"No, I will have none of that." He nodded to them both. "How much time do we have? How long before your side becomes annoyed?"

"For figuring out where Hyscarne might be? We have at least an hour before they become concerned. Maybe two?" Ryshial glanced over at Vrric while answering, as if checking her calculus.

"Good. I wish to hear of the world before we get to where Hyscarne might be." He looked expectantly at Vrric. "You've killed Tlana, yes? You've seen the well of eternity? You've witnessed the volcano at Agoge erupt? And, most importantly, you have an idea of what is happening with the Belegs? We hear there may have been an issue at the Luften Temple as well. Around the same time you and your Fluen friend were there. Yes?"

"Well, before we begin, with all due respect, what is your side? How long before Chiavel gets annoyed?" It was not as if Vrric did not trust Fultrenion, but… he had been caught in enough dangerous conversations to carry around a certain amount of healthy paranoia with him. Especially concerning anything to do with Clerin. He would avoid any discussion of that if he was able.

"As far as this guild is concerned, Chiavel will hear whatever Sempere tells him. He will not be annoyed. He will not even know how much time passes."

"You are saying he does not have spies watching our inn? He will most assuredly know how long we are away." Ryshial added her opinion.

"Ah, yes. What I meant to say was that Chiavel gets his guild information through Sempere. And I personally give Sempere that information. You see, there is a bit of a spat going on in Ariellyna currently. Just as there is something going on with the Belegs. I have chosen to speak with you under the guise of this Hyscarne issue. Trust me, if I did not wish to hear of your exploits myself, you would be talking to someone much lower in the guild."

"Then we should make it two hours. We will trade you information concerning our exploits for information concerning your spat." Ryshial was always one to make deals concerning information.

"Done." Fultrenion nodded to Ryshial. "But we start with you." He turned to Vrric. "I wish to hear how you destroyed a Tlana."

Vrric told him. He explained finding the Minora syllable for lightning. He explained how the secret may have been that it pushed each mote of smoke away from every other. He explained how Vuildan suggested using wind to separate the smoke. He told everything he could about fighting the Tlana. There could be no betrayal against a creature as dark as the Tlana. And he did it as quickly as possible. He knew that the subject was a bit of an aside for Fultrenion. The real questions would come afterwards, and he would have to be much more careful about what he divulged. He might accidentally betray Clerin if he was not deliberate with his words.

The conversation eventually arrived at the Belegs. Fultrenion looked directly at Vrric to ask his opening question. There was an intensity behind his eyes that belied his age. It was Ryshial, however, who answered.

"The Belegs are dying. Were they dying earlier? We are not positive. But they are dying now. Linchon, your Beleg, appears to have already crossed the threshold of no return. Gorbanax as well." Ryshial's eyes held a similar intensity.

"That is a very small part of the story, and one that I already knew. Or at least had guessed at. What I want to know is why the Belegs are dying. In specific, who is killing them." His smile was kind, like a doddering old grandfather. It was in stark contrast to his eyes.

"They are killing themselves."

"And who struck the first blow?" There was a long pause. Ryshial appeared to be trying to think of something clever. Vrric almost spoke, just to break the silence, before Fultrenion answered his own question. "It was Lembin, was it not?"

"That we know of. This is something that could have been brewing for some time. This could have started at beginning of our world for all we know." Ryshial was still attempting damage control.

"Maybe. But maybe not. We do not know if less lethal barbs had been tossed around through all the ages, as you infer, but we know the lethal ones have started recently. Correct?"

"They take a long time to die, the Belegs. An earlier strike is not outside the realm of reason."

"I have an idea. Let us speak to each other as if we are not fools. How does that sound?" There was an anger brewing in Fultrenion's voice. "You do not know my ultimate response and yet you are hedging your bets. My time is precious, as I assume yours is. Now is the moment for some simple truths. You!" He jabbed his finger at Vrric. "Tell me if I am correct."

For some reason, Vrric's first thought was, *Correct, we are not fools*. He knew that would just anger everyone in the room, however, even Ryshial. He shook his head to clear his own foolish thoughts.

"You are correct. It appears that the first lethal barb was hurled by Lembin."

"Through whom?"

"What?"

"Seriously, this again? Through whom did Lembin hurl its barb?"

"Through my lover. So, if it is revenge you are after, you had better start here and now!"

There was a pause. The brief silence held mass. Such a preponderance of nothingness that it pulled on Vrric. He could feel himself leaning forwards slightly. He wondered if Fultrenion was about to cast a spell, if this was the feeling that Croy got when he sensed magic. Then, slowly and lowly at first, Fultrenion began to laugh. It was short lived, but longer than the pause that preceded it.

"I finally understand the hesitation. I had not realized the Fluen was your lover. This is partly my fault. Let me be clear. I do not wish revenge, I wish understanding." The humor stayed in his voice for a moment after the laughter left. Then he was serious again.

"Let me tell you what I know. Linchon has been useless to us for some time, only speaking with the occasional ruler. Honestly, I was shocked that Hulgert even knew where the temple was. We Luftens are self-reliant, always have been. Losing Linchon is like losing a relative you never met, thrice removed—sad because it is supposed to be sad, not like losing a child or even a recently acquired friend. That being said, if we had known of the attack beforehand, we would have stopped it. We would have attacked you, your lover, and your entire group, to keep it from happening. But revenge? That will not help us in the slightest. Revenge is a purely emotional response.

"I also know that your lover came through here previously and spoke with Hulgert and, more importantly, Vanelia. I know your lover brought the poisonous well water with her that killed Hulgert. Honestly, that would also be a reason to desire revenge if whomever ruled Ariellyna made much of a difference to the guild. I also know she spoke with Gorbanax and that you destroyed the Cabal of Lochom and destroyed all the Yaven-infused items that could be found. Vanelia herself oversaw that part. She used up every favor she had to cover that. Which was unfortunate, since that left her ill-equipped to deal with Chiavel.

"I also know that there has been a great volcanic eruption in the Pyran realm, presumably Gorbanax's last gasps. And I know that the Temple of Air has been destroyed, long after Linchon had first been attacked. Just before you arrived here in fact. I had hoped you would be more forthcoming with what I already know. That way I would feel more confident in your responses to what I do not know. We are here, however, nowhere else. If I promise that no harm will come to you and your lover and your friends, will that help? Can we proceed with clarity for what I do not know?"

"Yes." Vrric nodded.

"And you of the silver tongue?" He turned to Ryshial.

"We will be candid and forthcoming with you, if you are with us." Her smile was disarming.

"Good. Fine. So, tell me what I do not know. Why are you here? In Ariellyna. Why did you not destroy the temple and move on?" He glanced between them, willing to take the response from either one.

"We are here to speak with Hyscarne." Ryshial responded. She might have continued, but Vrric interrupted.

"And to assist Vanelia if we can." Ryshial glared at Vrric sideways for the briefest of moments.

"Thank you, I only wish complete honesty." Fultrenion nodded to Vrric. "We will take each of these separately. How do you know Hyscarne?"

"That may take too much time." Ryshial's disarming smile came back quickly. "The Beleg situation is precarious. Half are dead or dying, and half are very much alive. Both Linchon and Gorbanax, before they began dying, indicated that this was an all or nothing game. That if they should die, then all the Belegs should die." She paused, but did not get interrupted. "So, to accomplish this, we need cooperation with powerful figures. One of which is my queen, Trela. Queen Trela communed with Gorbanax directly, just the once, where she had its desires shown to her. There was some confusion, no wait, some concern that a trick was involved. That maybe Linchon had communed with her, even though it had happened in the midst of the volcano. It is a long story and the 'evidence' for the concerns are scant. Suffice to say there are members of our group who do not wish to bring harm to Gunzgak and they have worked these originally small concerns quite heavily. So if I were allowed to skip the full explanation, it would be appreciated." Fultrenion waved his hand, indicating she was free to continue.

"Thank you. In essence, I had mentioned to Queen Trela that I knew Hyscarne, who used a Yaven that knew Linchon. My only thought was to have Hyscarne summon the Yaven and have the three of them talk about Queen Trela's experience, to see if there was anything at all that seemed out of the ordinary. Once she felt comfortable that she had not been tricked, we would just move on from Ariellyna for our true quest. To destroy Gunzgak and Lembin."

Vrric was not used to hearing "Queen Trela" that often outside of Agoge. They typically did not want to call attention to her station while they were traveling abroad. And when they were alone, Trela just seemed like Trela to him. She had not changed after becoming queen; she had always had a somewhat regal air about her. Regal as in doing whatever she wanted whenever she felt like it. Regal as in her absolute assuredness of her own decisions, not regal in the sense of the pomp and pageantry that often accompanied royalty. Not regal at all in that regard.

"That seems… Well, I suppose my opinion of all that is not necessary. That is the truth of it? Do you swear that the only reason you wish to find Hyscarne is to fulfill this meeting?" Fultrenion was studying Ryshial's face.

"That is the honest truth. That is the entire reason we set out for Ariellyna. Well, that and the fact that we have no idea of how to fulfil our mission, how to trap or trick a Beleg. Or two of them, for that matter." She laughed a little wryly at that.

"I cannot help you with that. That is simply a death wish. And you." Fultrenion looked over to Vrric. "You state that you are here to assist Vanelia? Is that true? It was my understanding that you were here to assist Chiavel track down Vanelia. Those are mutually exclusive goals, you understand."

He sat there for a moment, staring at Fultrenion, with his mind spinning. He knew he needed to state the truth. He had already done so and there was no turning back from that, but he needed to state it in a way that would help indicate how Fultrenion felt about the situation. Chiavel was his king after all.

"I notice that you have not said 'King Chiavel' during our conversation." He might not have noticed if he had not been thinking about how odd Queen Trela sounded. "I notice also that you mentioned that whoever ruled the realm had little consequence for the guild." Fultrenion narrowed his eyes at Vrric momentarily and appeared ready to interrupt. Vrric did not let him. "These are not accusations. I am a mage and understand the power of the Mages' Guild here in Ariellyna. You are correct. I stated that we would rather help Vanelia than Chiavel. This is not something we are fully decided upon as a group and certainly not why we came here—we had no idea that she was missing or that Chiavel was planning anything for her. In fact, we have no idea of what he is planning for her. We were not allowed into the city since it is locked down while

Chiavel searches for her. In pure self-interest, we stated we could help find her, just so we could enter the city. To be honest, I've met Chiavel several times. He is quite charming when he wishes to be. If we are not friends, we are certainly friendly to each other. The same with Clerin, my lover." Brutal honesty was his only real option.

"It is just that Vanelia has helped us greatly. All of us. She has been kind when she did not need to be, when we had little power. She lent us mercenaries that have become great friends. She helped us find the Luften Temple. She helped our quest for Gorbanax, to gather up the Yaven-infused items. At a great cost to herself, as you mention. She has a babe, Hynara, who should of course be protected. And, for unknown reasons, I just like Vanelia better. How can you say why you get along with some more than others? Sometimes there are reasons and other times there are just not."

"You know that you just implicated yourself in treason." Fultrenion's smile was back to the old grandfather style.

"You asked for the truth. No reprisals."

"I never said there would not be reprisals. You there, silver tongue, did you hear me say anything about reprisals?"

"No. I did not." Ryshial looked generally annoyed. Vrric could only help to think that at least she did not look specifically annoyed at him.

"Of course not. Which is why she would not say anything useful. Which, I must say, was a little aggravating." He paused with a thoughtful expression on. Both Vrric and Ryshial allowed him to fully prepare his statement before speaking. "Like you," he gestured to Ryshial, "I am unable to state any true desires. For the guild, or for myself. I cannot tell you that Vanelia is preferred over Chiavel, or vice versa. We find ourselves in a world not of our choosing. We are given what we are given, good or bad, desired or repulsed. We then perform what we are able during the task at hand. For my part, I am very grateful for your honesty. And I wish more of it. If you finish your tales, as detailed as time allows, I will tell you where to find Hyscarne. And, as an added bonus, I will not betray you to Chiavel. How does that sound?"

It sounded terrible to Vrric. It sounded like they were to divulge all their information and not get anything in return. But there was not much to be done about it either. They had nothing to bargain with. Fultrenion was right about one thing, you get what you get and you do your best with that.

Ryshial handled most of the talking after that. She was quite forthcoming, in her own shielded, diplomatic style. Fultrenion appeared pleased with the information. When he needed more, he would prod Vrric a little. At the end of it all, they were given an address and a time to arrive. It was two days from then, meaning they would have some time to try to find Vanelia before meeting up with Hyscarne. He hoped Clerin and Trela were having better luck.

"We were under the impression that Hyscarne had been missing for a while." It was not that Vrric was ungrateful for the location, but it just seemed odd.

"Yes, you were given that impression." Fultrenion's smile quickly appeared and then dropped. "In a way, she has been missing. She has been in an eshram for quite some time. We will fly her back here to meet with you, however. That is how important you are to me."

"Except that she may no longer be in possession of her faculties. Meaning it will be useless speaking with her." Ryshial narrowed her eyes at him.

"There is nothing to be done about that. I cannot cure her. Hopefully she is not too far gone. In addition to bringing her, we will allow you to speak with the mage that used to be her apprentice as well, Eugonla. She will most probably know the name of the Yaven you seek. That is who you really wish to commune with, correct? The Yaven."

"Correct." They both responded at the same time. It would have been comical if the day had been going better.

"Then, before we go, I must ask you a question." Vrric had kept forgetting about it and, whenever he had remembered, it had not been a good time to bring up. Now they were about to leave. "You spoke of the greatness of Elange. Your respect and admiration of him. His consummate skills and eagerness to share them."

"Correct. He was a great mage." Fultrenion looked wary.

"He created, or helped to create, a new section in the Mages' Guild. He was, as far as I understand, the first grey mage. I do not understand why that has not been sanctioned. Why you have not created a space for them?" He stared hard at Fultrenion, attempting to read his emotions before they were spoken.

"Honestly? There is no champion. Elange was sent to an eshram and is now dead. Several of Elange's apprentices also ended up in eshrams or died. Revkin was the grey mages' most vocal advocate, and though we may disagree on his power, he has also died. If someone like you were here to champion the idea… Then, maybe something would give way." Fultrenion looked sad, of all things. It somewhat confused Vrric.

"I am unable to do that at this juncture." Vrric shook his head slowly. "No, it would have to be someone else. Cannot the guild itself become the necessary champion?"

"That is not how it works. The guild leadership has many branches, and sticks, and twigs. There was not enough energy before Elange succumbed. There was not during Revkin's tries. How could there be now?"

Vrric had several answers, most of which involved telling Fultrenion to do it himself. None of the answers were helpful. Most would have harmed the cause. So he stayed silent and nodded. It had fallen to him, and he was unable to take the task on. He was not going to get any luck.

None of them had any luck. Trela had been waiting for the return at the inn for the two hours and so, of course, had not learned anything new. Clerin had been down at the bakery with Estfale, also learning nothing new.

Trela took the knowledge that Hyscarne was being brought back from an eshram fairly well, considering. Vrric had not been quite sure how the meeting was going to work anyway. He was of the opinion that Trela did not really care and was only holding the meeting to keep Croy happy. Clerin warned Vrric of being too optimistic. It was odd that. She was typically optimistic. He just considered himself a realist, which often encompassed a pessimistic view in her opinion. To him it was like reading a compass. You should not be annoyed if you were not facing north when you looked at the instrument, you just needed to shift your view until it aligned with the needle. And when he looked at Trela, he felt she was ready to destroy the remaining Belegs. Or to try to, anyway.

The days flew by with no further information. Vanelia did not contact them. None of her friends or anyone who might know where she was contacted them. Chiavel and Sempere did not contact them. Neither did Fultrenion. They were sort of coasting, waiting for the one meeting they had lined up before pursuing Vanelia with the sort of gusto they were going to need. And that was only if they really wanted to find her. Vrric could imagine a scenario where they got what they wanted from Hyscarne and then decided to leave. To not entangle themselves further. To convince Chiavel that she had already escaped.

Ariellyna was odd. Odder than Vrric had ever seen it, and he had grown up there. There were guards everywhere. And not just standing there, not just a silent presence to warn against doing anything foolish. They were walking up, or flying up, to Luftens and asking them probing questions. They were searching Luftens trying to enter the guild helioarcs and certain family Branches, especially the royal helioarc. There were even lines forming outside some of them. And the rumors! Vrric knew how difficult it had been to get into Ariellyna and had assumed it was much more difficult to leave, but the rumors made it sound almost impossible. Even worse were the rumors of private residences being searched. Of course, anyone who had been a good friend to Vanelia had already been searched, but now, supposedly, random searches were being conducted. If you had ever even met Vanelia before, you might be a target. If you had ever angered a guard before, you might be a target. If your name was on some secret list of malcontents, you might be a target. Each Luften who came into the bakery had a different tale, a different worry. The rumors ran wild.

Only a few of them headed to the location Fultrenion had provided for Hyscarne. Trela, Ryshial, and Vrric were all going, of course, and also Malghain. Estfale wanted to accompany, but it was decided that a Luften warrior would be more appropriate. Clerin wanted to come as well and, honestly, Vrric thought that was a good idea and argued heavily for it. She had spent more time in Ariellyna than any of the other non-Luftens in the coterie for one thing, and she knew the most about how each of the Belegs communicated for the other. But that was also the argument against her. Trela needed to be convinced, on her own, that she had communed with Gorbanax. Supposedly. And Clerin had already tried mightily to convince her of that. There was also some concern that one or another Beleg was piggybacking through Clerin, and if she were at the meeting, that they might attempt to influence it. Croy was left behind for similar reasons, even though he had argued he did not have the skill set or experience of Clerin. Trela did not want anything tainted by anyone else, especially those who were in regular contact with Belegs, through dreams or otherwise.

The helioarc that Hyscarne was to be at was at the northern edge of the city, barely within the limits. Meaning they would not have to talk with any of Chiavel's guards along the way. There were no rope bridges linking the helioarc to any other trees. It was the lone helioarc in the area extending above the green canopy of the surrounding forest. They flew straight to the uppermost entrance, as they had been instructed.

There was a small building on a large branch. There were two mages posted outside of the door that led into the building. Vrric assumed Hyscarne was already inside, but he was not sure. Maybe there were always mages guarding the door, or maybe they had arrived earlier. The four of them landed in front of the mages.

"You're early." One of the mages cocked her head at them.

"We're not *that* early." Trela raised an eyebrow. "We can fly around for a bit and come back if you like."

"Let me check. We were expecting Hyscarne before you." The other mage turned and entered the small building.

They waited in silence for a few moments while the Luften mage just stared at the ground in front of her. However, it was not long before the other mage returned. He held the door open for them.

"Welcome. Enter and turn to your left. Follow that hallway into the helioarc until you reach the first door to your right. You can enter there and wait." He smiled warmly as they walked by.

The room had only one window, making it a little dark. There was a long wooden table with high-backed chairs all around it. The chairs were fairly ornately carved, with different animal heads on the arm rests and a myriad of finial shapes on the backs. Vrric chose a chair with lion heads and sat down. His fingers absently stroked the stiff mane as he waited. The others sat near him since he was the first one down, except for Trela. She stayed standing. Not necessarily pacing, but slowly moving, like she was looking for something to look at.

They waited long enough that Vrric was itching to go check in with the guard mages, even though he knew there was no news. He held himself back and, finally, a commotion could be heard down the hall. A few brief moments later and several Luftens entered the room. One was the previous guard. The other had to have been

Hyscarne. She was certainly the eldest of the group. She had long white hair that was held together at the nape of her neck with a leather thong, she had some wrinkles, and her head stooped slightly. But that was not what gave it away. She had a far-off dazed look that slowly shifted around the room but never got up above the table and never landed on any one thing for too long. It was a look that Vrric had seen before at the eshrams he had visited. The other Luften to enter was younger than Hyscarne, but appeared a little older than Ryshial, who was a little older than Vrric. She had dark hair that was also held back at the nape of her neck, but it was much less frizzy, being held tightly. She had a warm smile, but her eyes kept focusing on Hyscarne with somewhat worried glances. It was a small juxtaposition between her features. He assumed, correctly, that she was Eugonla.

The three of them who had been sitting scooched their chairs back and stood. Vrric gave a small bow towards Hyscarne. It was a small gesture of respect. He doubted she noticed it. The younger mage led her to a chair that was offset a little, not quite across from everyone. Hyscarne sat and held Eugonla's hand for a moment before Eugonla could break away and make the introductions. Trela's small group introduced themselves afterwards. The mage who had been on guard duty did not say anything and appeared to try to shrink into the wall behind him. Everyone sat down.

"This is, if I may say, an odd request. Hyscarne has been away for more than several cycles now." Eugonla glanced between them all. She was about to say more but got interrupted.

"This is lovely, Eugonla, just lovely. It is nice to be amongst the trees again." Hyscarne's eyes lit up for a moment. They dimmed again, but did not quite reach the vacuous daze they had started with. Vrric wondered briefly who the eshrams were designed to help.

"We thank you very much for taking the time to speak with us." Trela spoke into the brief interlude. "I am not sure what you have been told about our concerns, but let me explain. I am the Queen of the Pyran realm. We have been communicating with the Belegs, several of them, mostly through a Fluen who is not with us at the moment. I communed with Gorbanax recently and felt very good about our communication. However, at the end of it, I was lifted from the lava field in an air bubble. The Fluen has been visited by Linchon in the Pyran realm, and after a volcanic eruption, we know that Linchon assisted with blowing the smoke and ash away from our population center. So we know that Linchon was around the Temple of Fire at the time. My question, posed rhetorically, was wondering if Linchon could have fooled me by pretending to be Gorbanax. Ryshial here knew of Hyscarne and the Yaven… what did you say the name was?"

"Stulna." Ryshial nodded to no one in particular.

"Yes, Stulna. Who supposedly knew Linchon from before it became a Beleg. Ryshial responded to my rhetorical question by suggesting we come to Ariellyna. We are hoping to find something to confirm or allay any suspicions. Maybe by explaining the communication I had to Hyscarne or Stulna and getting their reaction." Trela ended by looking Eugonla in the eye.

"Well… how very straightforward. That is refreshing." Eugonla stared back.

"All of our time is precious. Besides, the more clearly you understand the reason for our meeting, the better the chance we get to a positive outcome." Trela smiled warmly to Eugonla.

"I certainly had not been told about your concerns in such detail. It was more that Sempere wanted the same favor as Fultrenion, for us to come here to speak with you. Since a favor to either is not something that the likes of myself could refuse, let alone the both of them wanting the same thing, this was a rare gem indeed. An intriguing, and yet mandatory, request. I felt both excited and annoyed by it. Similar to the vagueness of being told to bring Hyscarne with me. I mention this since I am afraid you may feel a similar emotion soon. I truly doubt that explaining your communication to anyone will shed any light as to what Beleg you communicated with. This will most probably just be a fascinating waste of time." Eugonla smiled back.

"I know you!" Suddenly Hyscarne spoke up, staring at and, eventually, raising a shaking finger to Ryshial. "You're a Pyran!"

"Yes. Yes, I am. Do you remember when we met?" Ryshial had a kindly look on her face.

"I… We… we met at yours. What is it called? In the shadow of the volcano?" Hyscarne looked perplexed but genuinely pleased as well.

"Agoge. Correct, we met at my city. Do you remember why we met?"

"I was… It was an errand, yes. Some errand I needed. And you were perfect for it, weren't you?"

"You wanted the name of a Pyran Yaven to summon."

"Yes! Yes, now I remember the errand. And you were helpful. But you wanted Stulna in return."

"I wanted to speak with Stulna. I did not need any errands."

"What did you ask Stulna? I remember not being overly interested at the time. My apologies."

"No need for apologies. I was asking about the Northern Desert and Vijen leaves. The legends that pulled my father into the desert." Ryshial looked slightly sad for a brief moment, but then it passed. Like a swiftly moving cloud blocking the sun for a moment. "Stulna commented that not even Linchon would know what I was asking. That was when we started talking about Linchon. Do you remember that?"

"Oh yes, I remember that part. Who forgets when a Beleg is mentioned?" Hyscarne's eyes were bright. "But all that was useless as well, wasn't it? Did we learn anything about Linchon?"

"We learned they were lovers for a time. That they had been pair-bonded."

"Yes, prurient rumors. Salacious indeed, but nothing of use."

Ryshial laughed. Heartily. It took Vrric by surprise.

"Well, I suppose we did not learn anything of substance. However, we wish to speak with Stulna again. We wish to use Stulna's knowledge of Linchon to see if there was subterfuge with Trela's communication with Gorbanax." Ryshial reiterated the request to Hyscarne, now that she was appearing more lucid.

"Oh, that will never work."

"What do you mean? Stulna will be unable to tease out which Beleg Trela was communing with?"

"No. I mean you will not be able to summon Stulna. It was a victim of Yavencide. Stulna is no more."

That silenced the room. Everyone stared at Hyscarne while she looked kindly back at Ryshial. The room was frozen in place for a long moment.

"How do you know?" Ryshial asked quietly, almost as if she were afraid of the answer.

"Well, it is not as if I did that to Stulna myself. I would never do that to a Yaven I knew. But you would be amazed at how many mages at the eshrams were involved with the Cabal of Lochom. Committing Yavencide was the surest way to go mad in Ariellyna at the time. You have no idea the difficulty of such an undertaking." Hyscarne's warm smile was still in place.

"So. You participated in Yavencide?" Vrric decided it would simplest just to ask. He knew the others would want to know.

"Yes. Only the once. Then I lost my capacities, you see. You may think those of us at the eshrams are unable to realize why we were dumped there. And maybe some of them are that far gone. But not all of us. The madness, it comes and goes, you see. There are good days and bad days, good hours and bad hours, except that they are reversed. When I am feeling good—like now, speaking with others that are untainted seems to help—when I am feeling good, there at the eshram, it is terrible. I realize where I am and do not wish to be there. When I am doing poorly, however, it is merely a haze. The mindtrap rotates and spirals. Time speeds up and the empty days slip by." She looked around at them, searching their faces, looking quite lucid. "I do not wish to go back. You can certainly let an old lady live out her last few days amongst the trees, can you not?"

The room was silent again. Vrric knew that Hyscarne had just signed her own execution papers. He knew what was unfolding in Trela's mind. He knew they were going to have to search through the eshrams and kill a bunch of kindly invalids who would not even remember their crime, might not even remember their own name. His only real question was how they were supposed to separate the guilty from the innocent. Some of the guilty would have no idea of what they had done. Some would have no idea what they had done was punishable, was even a crime. Some would realize what was happening and lie to stay alive. Some would realize what was happening and lie about others so that they would be killed, for whatever petty, or otherwise, reasons. And, in Vrric's mind at least, the purpose of the purge was to keep the knowledge of how to perform Yavencide from leaking back out. He was less concerned about punishing those already caught in their own mindtraps, but he knew others in the group would feel differently. And, truly, how would he know if someone was mad enough that they would never be able to explain the Yavencide process if pressed about it later. They might be having a bad day while the coterie was around but be having a good day when a mage aspiring to revive the Cabal came knocking. It was a daunting task that had few palatable solutions.

"I'm sorry. I do not even know what 'Yavencide' is. You all seem to…" Eugonla was interrupted by Ryshial.

"Nor should you. This is a subject that should be discussed in private. Amongst those who understand the implications." Ryshial shot a warning glance to Eugonla. There was real steel behind it. It was partly a threat, but there was an odd pleading portion there as well. As if begging her to shut up.

Trela was whispering something to Malghain, who was nodding. Vrric glanced at the mage standing against the wall. He was looking nervous. He had been looking bored not too long ago.

Vrric wondered how many Luften mages knew of Yavencide and would never pursue it. Fultrenion certainly knew. Most of the upper guilds, regardless of which realm they were based in, probably knew of its existence, its basic premise. There was absolutely no way for them to destroy everyone who had ever heard of it. In Vrric's opinion, it was only those who knew the technicalities of it, the "how" of it, who needed to be eradicated. Everything else was pure foolishness.

"You have given us much to think about, Hyscarne. We would like to speak with you and Fultrenion next. Would that be acceptable to you? Would you like to join us on a trip? A flight around Ariellyna to see the trees?" Ryshial was taking the situation into her own hands and bringing in Fultrenion. Vrric was not sure if that was because she was member of the Pyran Mages' Guild elite and felt this was a guild issue, or because she was concerned about Trela's whispering, or what. In either case, she got a quick glare from Trela. But Trela said nothing.

"Yes. Please. I would like nothing more than to see the city again." Hyscarne bobbed her head happily.

"You're going to have to *whisper* to Fultrenion. We need to resolve this quickly. This is an issue that is going to reroute our path." Trela was looking intense.

Vrric nodded and stood to find the farthest corner. He was not positive if Fultrenion would drop whatever he was doing when he got the *whisper*, but he did not know of someone on a lower tier of the guild hierarchy that he could contact first.

"Eqefintotsfe!" He figured he was not going to be casting much beyond flight spells that day, so he cast a more draining power level of spell just so he did not have to worry about Fultrenion saying he did not hear the call.

"Feyazki. I trust you are with Hyscarne. I also trust something has happened for you to use telepathy to contact me directly." Fultrenion responded immediately.

"Yes, something additional has come up. We would like to meet with you directly. Would you be available?"

"If you come quickly and keep it brief. I have other meetings today that will be difficult to shift."

"We will leave here at once." Vrric paused for a moment as he tried to think things through. "We are bringing Hyscarne and Eugonla with us but would like to speak with you alone first. Can you keep them separated?"

"We will do so, yes. But just make sure the meeting is brief."

They all arrived at the Mages' Guild's helioarc. There were several mages waiting for them, and they seemed to know what was going on. At least, they separated Hyscarne and Eugonla and brought Vrric and the others to Fultrenion immediately. They did not have to argue back and forth. When they entered the room where Fultrenion was waiting, he immediately frowned.

"You did not warn me about the warriors." He glared for a moment before sitting.

There were two mages standing along the walls, staring straight at nothing. Vrric and the others sat as well. Trela and Malghain the farthest from Fultrenion.

"Let me apologize. We were in a hurry, and I did not think to mention them."

"Yes, well, we are still in a hurry. What is so important that you required Hyscarne to stay back, but brought your warriors with you?"

"You understand that we destroyed the Cabal of Lochom and Vanelia gathered all the Yaven-infused items here in Ariellyna for us. That we destroyed all the items as well."

"Yes, we have discussed this."

"Apparently the eshrams are rife with those who have participated in the Yavencide rituals."

"Ah! So the Beleg vengeance must be wrecked upon the feeble minded as well."

"The knowledge must be eradicated. We cannot risk someone getting information from those who are too feeble to cast the spells directly." Trela interrupted their conversation.

"How do you know others with this knowledge have not escaped your notice?" Fultrenion turned to her.

"We destroyed the Cabal itself, which had members from all the realms. We tracked all we could from those members. We have also checked with the various guild lords, yourself presumably included, to root out any others. We just did not think to check the eshrams. They are, as you say, feeble and we underestimated them as a whole." Trela took a deep breath. "Not to be disrespectful, but you did examine your guild for any members with this knowledge, did you not?"

"We did not allow the Cabal to fester itself in Ariellyna, no. We feel that any Luftens involved were with the Cabal when it fell." Fultrenion smiled at her.

"Besides those in the eshrams." She smiled back.

"Correct. Vanelia did not tell us to investigate the eshrams and, like you, we underestimated them. Ha! Why am I using the past tense? We still underestimate them. They are difficult to communicate with. Many are old and will die soon anyway. It seems like a waste to go destroying such pathetic creatures." He held up his hands as she prepared her retort. "The guild is not stopping you. We understand your orders come from the Belegs, not some derlian. But it is a shame, and we are hopeful that you are not asking for assistance in this manner. We would prefer to turn a blind eye to the whole unpleasant process. Then, once their relatives find out, we can blame some Pyran queen for the bloodshed. You will be long gone by then and, as an even greater favor, we will do our best to keep them from trying to infiltrate your realm with dreams of vengeance."

"Like much in life, that is less than hoped for, but also less than feared." Trela nodded to him.

"Well, let me sweeten the pot for you then. Or make it more bitter, I am not really sure." His grin was a bit odd, almost sardonic. "We have word of Vanelia. It is our understanding that she wished to escape to the eshrams."

"She is still in Ariellyna?" Vrric asked out of shock more than anything. He had been hoping she had already left.

"Yes. And Sempere and I are unable to come to an agreement. So I will leave it like the eshrams. I will let you decide her fate. Bring her to Chiavel, as you had promised, or try to sneak her out of the city with every guard looking for her. If you choose the latter and you escape… well, hopefully you will be long gone before we have to blame some Pyran queen for the escape." He turned back to Trela. "You have given us many difficult choices. Whether to seek reprisals for killing Linchon, whether to help you help Vanelia, whether to allow you to slaughter our mindtrapped mages. We have decided, however, to be neutral in all things. Or at least in these things."

"I notice you assume we will help Vanelia." Trela's smile was lopsided.

"I would not mind that, if I am being honest. But I am a faithful servant to my king as well and will loudly deny any assertion to the contrary. You have given us these difficult choices, but at the same time, you are resolving them for us. We are having difficulties telling if this is good or bad. I suppose we will all find out in the end. After the final analysis." He had a full smile on, but if Vrric looked close enough, it seemed like there was a touch of sadness to it.

"We thank you for the guild's neutrality in these matters. We understand these are difficult times." Ryshial glanced around, making sure Trela and Vrric were accepting her interruption. "We are eager to know of Vanelia's whereabouts."

They all met together at the Flying Mouse. Even Torpalin and Escha were there. Or maybe especially they were there. The decision of whether to help Vanelia or not would affect their lives more than anyone else's. There was no way they could stay in Ariellyna if Trela and the others helped Vanelia escape. Torpalin would have to give up being a baker, at least for a little while. And then probably only in another realm. As Fultrenion had stated, they were difficult choices indeed.

They were all crammed into Trela's room, which under normal circumstances appeared decent sized. The furniture, or at least the furniture one was unable to sit on, was all pushed to the walls. Trela stood in the center, addressing everyone. Explaining that they were going to have to figure out a way to find the guilty amongst the addled denizens of the eshrams. At least she was defining "guilty" as having direct knowledge of how to commit Yavencide, at least a portion of it. They were not on a mission of vengeance, as she put it;

they were just taking care of loose ends. Everyone nodded solemnly. They knew the difficulty of the task. They also knew there was no choice. Trela did not allow any argument for or against the mission. It was not a discussion; it was a parceling out of information. The discussion concerned Vanelia.

"I know what I would choose if the choice was only mine." Trela had just explained the meeting with Fultrenion. "But this will affect all of us. Especially you." Escha, Torpalin, and Torpalin's sister Tundalia, were all standing together in one of the corners. "Therefore, we should discuss the merits and the drawbacks of both choices. Then I propose a secret vote, by way of ballot. I do not want anyone shamed or pressured."

"Those of you who do not live here, those of you who are not Luftens, outnumber us. We who will be most affected should not be drowned out. Chiavel will exact revenge if we help Vanelia escape." Torpalin spoke up. "I am not saying how I will vote. I have not decided yet, but I think a secret ballot is unfair."

"Ah. Apologies. I had been thinking that there might be some here who would fear Chiavel's vengeance and was attempting to... I am not sure what I was attempting. What would be your preference?" Trela bowed her head to Torpalin, indicating he had the floor.

"I know my preference." It was Tundalia who spoke.

"Please, let us know how you would resolve the vote." Trela turned slightly to face Tundalia.

"Oh, not the vote, I just know my preference. I have only just met you. Most of you. Some I've had to put up with throughout my life." She punched Torpalin lightly in the arm. "So I know very little about you, and you about me. I own a shop here in Ariellyna, a bakery. It is doing quite well, even. My brother has returned with what I must say is the greatest partner he has ever had." She smiled to Escha, then continued. "This has been my dream for as long as I have lived, as long as I've known what dreams are. My dreams have come true.

"Now you are asking me to relinquish my dreams. To give them up for some strangers. To this I say no." The room was deathly quiet. "However, I have lived under several rulers. They really only last so long around here. And Vanelia was the best. The most prosperous, the kindest, the simplest. She was not a fool who spent the treasury on parties for the old family Branches. She just had the unfortunate luck to suffer widespread crop failure. How is the weather, or insects, her fault? Anyway, I felt she was my queen more than I felt Hulgert was my king. And a thousand times more than Chiavel. He is not allowing anyone to leave the city, to enter the city. He is stopping Luftens on the street, he is searching our houses. You who are new here do not understand what is happening. I barely do. But I understand enough. Chiavel is not fit to be king. Vanelia does not deserve to die, for he will surely have a public execution. I... I do not wish to give up my dreams. I truly don't. But I cannot do nothing while my city is under siege from within. I vote to save Vanelia. To this I say yes. Maybe I can start a bakery in another realm, far from here."

Several warriors started clapping, but Trela cut them off with a wave of her hand. She turned her gaze back to Torpalin and Escha.

"Before the decision is made, what of you? What of Haswyxe and Feyazki? What of the rest of the Luftens?" She glanced around the room.

"I go with my sister." Torpalin smiled at her. "And I am proud of her."

"I was ready to go earlier. Vanelia was my liege, not Chiavel." Haswyxe grinned and Malghain nodded in agreement.

"It will be weird not coming back to Ariellyna, but I was ready to go earlier as well. Besides, maybe we can return once Chiavel has fallen." Feyazki spoke the truth and did not feel he was dampening the sentiment. He had always been ready to rescue Vanelia, would do so no matter what the cost. But it was weird to sever ties with his home. Leaving home and never coming back was different than never being *able* to come back. It just was. It did not enter his mind at the time that if he never returned, the grey mages would not have a champion.

The applause started up immediately. No one checked on the non-Luftens. Did not ask if they minded an obsessive foreign king hating them for the rest of his days. Of course, they were also on a mission to kill the remaining Belegs. What was the anger of one mortal to them, even if he was a foreign king?

Chapter 14

Feyazki, Malghain, Haswyxe, Clerin, and Ryshial were on their way to find Vanelia. The Luften warriors and Feyazki were an obvious choice. Clerin went because she knew Vanelia and there was a babe involved. Plus, Chiavel seemed to like her, and one never knew when being a foreign diplomat could be beneficial. Ryshial went because they needed another great mage and she was one of the best.

The rest of them were planning their own escape. Trela needed those who lived there to find a way out for her warriors, so Torpalin, his sister Tundalia, and Escha were indispensable. While the first group had the difficult task of escaping with Vanelia, they had the advantage of being few enough in number to fly out of the city at night. They were also given a rendezvous point to meet up with her from the Mages' Guild, meaning they just had to get to her and escape. That was not to say it would be easy, no. The entire city was looking for Vanelia. But they had a clear direction. The second group, Trela's group, had much murkier waters to navigate.

After that, both groups were to meet up a good distance outside the city. As long as everything went well. Feyazki and Serghno would *whisper* between themselves if further coordination was required, if either group was unable to meet at the appointed time.

Trela's group had a lot of derlians and horses, and all of the gear. So they needed a path out of the city, if not a road. Looking at the city in the forest, one could think that there were more ways in and out than an underground Gaen city such as Serif. But once the Helioarcs began to spread out, the forest grew thick with underbrush and brambles. She knew there were only a couple of ways out of Serif and those were typically well guarded. But she was beginning to think there were only a couple of ways out of Ariellyna as well. Torpalin and his sister discussed the possibilities for some time. Mostly, one of them would mention a road or exit and another would explain how many guards were stationed there. A lot of guard shacks and barricades seemed to have been installed recently.

On the other side, Vanelia had apparently been hiding in a different place each week. Due to the timing of the Mages' Guild's knowledge, they had to have Feyazki's group meet up with her before she was set to move again. So, if Trela's group was unable to come up with a good escape route, the others would have to wait with Vanelia. And then travel with her while everyone was looking for her. There was just no good way to rendezvous with her again if she moved before Feyazki found her. Apparently the guild's contact with her was tenuous at best.

Trela did not like being forced to make decisions before she was ready. That was how mistakes were made. Rather than continue to listen to the siblings, she grabbed Escha and Arnasta for a private meeting.

"I'm hoping you can scout out possible routes and you can sense whether or not they are being guarded." Trela pointed to Escha and then Arnasta. "We need to get some actionable intelligence soon."

"I will probably need to follow Escha somewhat closely. To be honest, I am better at tracking a particular individual than I am at just sensing anyone nearby." Arnasta looked very serious for a moment. "But I am certainly willing to try. We have been cooped up here for too long."

"Then you and I shall follow at a safe distance. Escha, do you need anything else for this? I mean, do you have an idea of locations to check?" Trela tried to keep her gaze neutral. Escha nodded almost imperceptibly.

"Should we grab another Luften citizen that is sensitive to our cause?" Arnasta glanced between the other two.

"No. Not yet at least. Let me exhaust what I know of first before we bring anyone else on board. Secrecy is best, no matter how sympathetic someone may be." Escha nodded with more certainty.

They decided to head out immediately, just the three of them. The first path checked was at the southwest edge of the city. No one stopped them or even looked at them, really. The best way to go unnoticed in Ariellyna, Trela was beginning to realize, was to be tethered to the ground.

Escha was about thirty paces ahead of them, certainly within visual distance even with the underbrush. She was not moving cautiously, at least not noticeably. Her movements were fluid and sure. Of course, Escha was naturally quiet, even when she was not trying. And Trela was sure her senses were far out in front of her, keyed into any potential sign for danger. Trela, for her part, kept at least half of her attention behind them. She was letting Arnasta keep track of Escha.

Arnasta suddenly stopped. Her head snapped up and she peered into the forest. They were at the edge of the city, where the smaller trees and undergrowth started to grow thick and close. She turned and glanced at Trela. There was a worried look on her face and she glanced back towards Escha. Unsure of what else to do, without taking her eyes off Arnasta in case it was a bad idea, she whistled. Long-short-short. It may have sounded remotely like a Pyran bird, but she doubted it was fooling anyone. It did have the desired effect of stopping Escha in her tracks.

Everyone waited there, frozen for a moment. Trela strained her ears but could hear nothing. Arnasta stayed quiet and worried. Escha eventually, silently, wound her way back to them.

"What is it?" Escha's voice was barely audible.

"There is a large group up ahead. I think they might be moving perpendicular to us, but it is difficult to tell. Maybe some of them are moving and the others are still. Waiting. I need the walking ones to shift far enough before I can triangulate the waiting ones' location." Her voice was just above a whisper.

"But the ones on the move are not heading towards us, right? Should we shift off the path a little just in case?" Trela felt nervous huddled and whispering in the middle of a trail.

Arnasta nodded and Escha silently headed into the trees. Trela was not loud by any measure, certainly quieter than Arnasta, but compared to Escha she may as well have been hollering and waving her arms. There were several blackthorns that they stood by, since the large shrubs blocked any further movement. They waited a while in silence until Arnasta started whispering again.

"The others have passed but there are definitely some that are still stationary. At least four… maybe five. Probably an eighth of a league or so in the distance. Give or take." She nodded her head down the path.

"Should I investigate?" Escha looked over to Trela.

Trela did some quick math. A league was about how far a derlian could walk in an hour, if they were not worried about being quiet. She did want to know how accurate Arnasta was, both in the distance and the amount of Luftens at the end of it.

"Yes. I want a full accounting of who is ahead of us, at the end of the path. We want to make sure they are guard stations and not just some picnickers or what have you. We want to know how well they are armed, how vigilant they are being, if they look like they're going to camp there. Everything." She turned from Escha to Arnasta, still whispering. "Would you know if they had dogs or anything? I assume Escha won't spook any horses."

"I am not positive. I can try to cast something else, but I have never checked for different types of animals. I would hate to confuse a dog with a horse, or even just a wild animal nearby. I am not completely positive of how far they are, just a general sense, really. They may even be on an adjacent path rather than on this one." Arnasta looked a little less confident than she had a moment ago. It made Trela regret asking.

"Don't worry about that. You've been a great help so far. I'll just pop over there and back real quick, dogs or no." Escha nodded to them both, turned, and headed silently out before Arnasta could cast anything else.

"Should I try anyway?"

"She is my best scout. If you want to do some experiments, that's fine. But we will probably be out all day, so if you want to save your strength, that'll be fine as well." Trela found herself still whispering. Considering how far they were from the others according to Arnasta, she was not entirely sure why.

They waited for a while in relative silence. It felt to Trela like it was at least half an hour, but she knew she was just feeling impatient. She thought about picking some of the blackthorn's fruit but figured it would be too tart this early in the season.

Escha reappeared as quietly as she had left. She was jogging in the middle of the path, not hiding herself at all, so it was not a surprise. But if Trela's back had been to the path, it may have been.

"There were five Luften guards sitting around. No dogs but five horses were loosely tethered nearby. I did not see any tents but did not get around the group to check the other side. So, not sure if there was a parallel path farther out. Oh, and they had a log across the path as a sort of makeshift gate. Though I would estimate that the log was skinny enough to step over without too much difficulty." Escha smiled widely. She did not even sound out of breath. Trela wondered how long she had been jogging for, certainly not the whole way.

"Horses? Good, I was thinking there were some large nearby animals." Arnasta turned to Trela. "The forest is teeming with smaller life essences, however. I am not sure if I would be able to sense anything else very accurately, certainly nothing smaller than a dog."

"Good, we are setting some parameters. We'll see how many different paths we can check today. Who knows, maybe we'll get lucky and one will not be guarded." Trela was feeling hopeful. Not necessarily that they would find a clear path, but that they were finding an efficient way to check the paths.

They checked five other promising paths. None of them were unguarded. The minimum number of guards per checkpoint appeared to be five, and two of them had ten guards or greater. Those two were much larger paths, practically roads, so Trela did not let Escha examine those in person. She figured they had the additional guards due to the size of the paths rather than catching the guards exactly at shift change. At least those routes were quicker to check.

They made it back to the others before sundown. There was some consternation that they had been gone so long but Trela was not overly concerned. She figured the mages and Vanelia would escape during that night or the next. She did not want her warriors to be gone before the mages had made their move. Therefore, even if she had found the perfect path, they would not have made their escape right away. Estfale still seemed a little annoyed with her, no matter her logic.

Trela assumed they were to make their move the next night, barring any unforeseen issues with the others getting Vanelia out, so she allowed some of her warriors to sleep in. She got herself, Escha, and Arnasta up fairly early to try out some more paths.

They tried several in the morning and finally got lucky near noon. It was not much of a path, more of a deer trail, and it was at the south end of the city, placing them a fair distance from where they wanted to meet up with the mages. But it was there, it was something.

Escha took quite a while exploring it, making sure Arnasta had not missed anything. When she finally returned, she had a big grin on her face. She mounted her horse with a quick bound.

"No wagons will fit, but horses should be fine. So, unless you want to fly or create a scene on the way out, this is the one." Her horse held steady even though she held her reins loosely.

They headed back in good spirits. They took a circuitous route back, just to be seen coming back to the inn from a different direction. Trela was sure the inn was being watched and fairly certain about the bakery as well. With most of the guards performing roadblocks, house searches, actual guard duty, and trying to find Vanelia, she was unsure of how many were left over for watching them, but certainly some. Realizing how many guards were parked at the outskirts of the city watching each path had been a little shocking.

Trela let Escha and Arnasta take what naps they could and headed down to the bakery. She needed to converse with Torpalin's sister and the others. They had come up with a plan the previous night and she wanted to know how it was progressing.

The plan was simple, maybe too simple, but it was all they had been able to come up with. Maybe if they had had more time… Mainly they wanted to keep the bakery open after they had left, to keep customers coming and going. Tundalia mentioned that she had a previous employee who had tried to buy her way into the business. When Tundalia refused, she had left somewhat angrily to start her own. That one had recently gone out of business and Tundalia was not shy about why she thought that had happened. It was odd how she spoke about her old employee, Nufenwy. At times it was with the fondness of an old friend. At other times it was with bitterness, if not rancor. They had certainly known each other for a long time and had certainly had both good times and bad. It was to Nufenwy that Tundalia had suggested, with a heavy heart, to hand over her business to so that it appeared to be in continuous operation. "But not for long," she had laughed.

Those at the bakery had been supposed to come up with a note to leave for Nufenwy. Tundalia was afraid that if she spoke to Nufenwy for any length of time she would end up saying something regrettable. So many subjects could be construed as regrettable that Trela had not pursed the subject. When Trela arrived at the bakery, she asked to read the note.

"I know how long you have wanted my shop. You have offered me plenty of opportunities and plenty of heads, though never as much as I thought it was worth. Well, here is your chance. I need to leave town for a moon with my brother. I need you to keep the bakery running smoothly, without a snag or a stumble. If, when I return, everything is as it is right now, if every customer is well cared for, if every vendor is paid on time, if not a hair is out of place and no one is the wise, I will sell you my shop. I will sell it for the last price you offered me. Which was not the highest amount you have offered but, of course, not the least amount either. Everything is paid up through the week. Show me you can handle the responsibility."

They argued a little about the wording, especially whether or not to leave in the "wise" part, but a better phrase was not offered up. No one wanted to indicate secrecy should be involved, and due to Tundalia's rocky relationship with Nufenwy, no one really expected the ruse to last long, certainly not an entire moon. Once she was directly questioned by a guard, it was assumed the note would be handed over. But it was hopeful that since the guards were currently stretched so thin, it might take a couple of days for them to personally pay Nufenwy and the bakery a visit. In any case, it was the only delay option they could think of that was not traceable like a spell, or obvious like burning down the bakery. Torpalin himself still argued for that route, that they just needed a couple of similar sized bodies to place in the bakery before setting it ablaze. He had few other backers, however. The consensus was that the fire would be big enough to have to be put out and that someone from the Mages' Guild would be tasked with talking to the dead. How embarrassing that would be! Trela wished she felt more comfortable asking the guild for direct favors but was concerned that once Chiavel started truly investigating, everyone who had willingly helped would be severely punished. Which made even asking if anyone was willing quite difficult. Fultrenion had already given them what help he could. She could not ask for more. Tundalia folded the key to her shop up with the note.

Arrangements were made, packing was finalized, everything was done as surreptitiously as possible. Trela tried to nap, knowing it would help in the long run, but she was unable to sleep comfortably. She did not like leaving details up to others. Even those she entrusted with her life. So she got back up after lying there for a while and finished up what little of her own packing was left.

Unfortunately, there was not a whole lot for her to do. Everyone had been given their assignments already. She did not want to go back to the bakery early, out in public so to speak. So she walked around the inn, inspecting things that did not need inspecting, making sure everything was running smoothly. Which it was.

Trela paid the innkeeper for another three days for all the rooms. Was it worth it? Was there any chance all their efforts would buy them more than a couple of hours in the morning? She was not sure but was certainly willing to spend a little coin on the off chance they got lucky. They had enough to live off of for a while. Eventually, however, they might have to head back to Tureyn to get more funds. Her hopes of their last grand adventure ending quickly were fading fast.

They left the town in small groups of about four at varying intervals, starting near dusk. A small group of Pyrans left first. They had been wandering the grounds of Ariellyna for a while, taking care to stay clear of the bakery and the inn. The next group was to be those at the bakery, including the mad old mage, Hyscarne. Then another group of Pyrans that were wandering. Finally, Trela, Estfale, Jalin, and Silvadhin all left. She had thought about keeping Serghno for the last group, to have a competent mage, just in case, but had decided against it. She had sent him with the first group. Arnasta was near the path, where they had waited while Escha investigated earlier in the day. She was there to make sure there were no surprises. They would pick her up as they passed by.

It was about midnight when they left. It felt weird that the paths above, those homes in the trees, the round elevated platforms, the gossamer rope bridges scattered about leading from one node to another, were lit with twinkling fires like stars in the distance, while the ground was as dark as the mud. Individual travelers carried torches, and some of the low buildings had light glowing from the inside, but most of it was dark. It seemed that even the moonlight shied away from the muck.

Estfale insisted on going first, as per usual. She chose not to argue and followed behind him. She left Jalin in the rear position, making sure they were not being followed. Trela was a believer that each member's talents should be utilized, even if that meant she was stuck in the middle of the pack, unable to use any of her own.

They took a bit of a circuitous route but tried not to waste too much time. The sooner they were with the main group outside the town, the sooner they could all start gaining some distance. It would be another circuitous route away from Ariellyna, sweeping west before turning back towards the desert. Trela hoped that Chiavel would not realize they were headed to the eshrams. And that mostly depended on Fultrenion and the guild—and their silence. He had allowed them to take Hyscarne but had kept Eugonla back at the guild. He had insisted on her innocence and that she would not allow any of them to harm Hyscarne, so it was better for all involved to leave her behind. They needed his willing assistance to accomplish their mission, so Trela was prepared to give him anything he asked for.

They met up and gained distance. Each day was farther away. They were not attacked, hounded, or ambushed. It appeared that Fultrenion kept his word.

It took four days before they met up with Clerin, Feyazki, Vanelia and the others. That group had flown as far as they had dared, then walked to gain some distance away from the last location they used magic. It would take some time before Trela felt comfortable hiring a boat, but that was really the only fast option for them. So they were stuck on horses for a while. It was funny, they rode horses the entire way to Ariellyna and it did not bother Trela one bit. But when the option for faster travel was curtailed, suddenly she felt like they were moving too slowly.

They traveled as far as they could until nightfall, making camp when there was barely any light left in the sky. Trela did not want a celebration. She wanted the next several nights to feel clandestine and the days to be filled with as much travel as possible. But she did want to acknowledge the escape and to converse with Vanelia.

Several of them gathered around the low embers used to cook over. No one was told not to be there, but only a few were invited. Only those invited showed up, mostly Luftens. Vanelia was there with her little one, Hynara, who Clerin held the entire time. Feyazki was there, and also Ryshial. Malghain and Haswyxe were on the perimeter, watching the darkness. Torpalin, his sister, and Escha sat around the embers as well. It was only because the circle was large that it did not feel crowded.

"I will not ask if you know what this means. What sacrifice you are making. You must surely be aware. I will only attempt to convey my gratitude. My life, to me, is certainly precious. And I am sure that you have saved that. So, thank you, truly, from the bottom of my heart. I might have made it out on my own, through what was left of my retinue, maybe. But you were a great distraction, a great help, and you were how I actually escaped. That is not, however, what I truly need to thank you for. Though I love myself and fear death, I have lived a long and wondrous life. I have been a queen and a fugitive and everything in between. My daughter, however, cannot even speak her own name yet. She has tasted naught but mother's milk and hurt no one and nothing. She is as innocent as the blue sky. It is for her that I wished to escape in the first place. It is for her that I would continue living through any and all hardships fate has in store for me. It is for her that I must thank you. Thank you." Her hazel eyes shone in the dying firelight, wet with emotion. Her curly chestnut hair framed her earnest face and moved along with it, bouncing slightly.

"But what does that mean? 'Thanks.' What a short and stumpy word for such a broad and deep meaning. Probably second only to 'love' in the disparity between length and breadth. Does it merely mean I would reciprocate what you have done for me? That is not even required. Does it mean that I would reward you if I could? Does it mean that I will never talk bad about you in the future? That is not required either. Nothing from me to you is required for my thankfulness, my gratitude. Certainly nothing more from you to me is required. Is it purely selfish then, if it requires no interaction, if it is wholly within me? It is purely a statement. Is a statement selfish? How can it be? How can it not? It certainly makes me feel better. Or is it merely protocol? Is it required by society if it is not required by either of us? I cannot explain it, this feeling within me, I have no idea how. There needs to be another word, one less flippant. A serious grand word that can explain how I feel. I *want* to explain my gratitude; I am compelled, and certainly not by society, or how I think you will feel if I do or do not. I suppose it is a bit selfish. I want you to understand how thankful I am that you helped my little Hynara escape. My entire being, every part of me, is grateful. And all I can say is thanks."

Trela was unsure of what to make of the speech. At first, she was happy to accept Vanelia's gratitude, but the whole speech was a little drawn out for her. Everyone else seemed quite charmed by it, however. So Trela added her own, "You're welcome," along with the others. She did not want to seem ungrateful in accepting Vanelia's thanks, which made her head spin a little. She then thought about explaining how they did not need thanks for helping a babe in arms, that of course they would help, it was merely the honorable thing to do. But would that diminish Vanelia's thanks? Maybe the whole concept was a bit selfish. In the end, Trela stayed silent until the conversation turned, which was most probably the right thing to do.

They discussed many things that evening. The Luftens all swore fealty to Vanelia, consolidating their treason against Chiavel.

They explained where they were heading, and why, to Vanelia. She appeared unhappy at the prospect of killing some denizens of the eshrams, but did not argue against it. They even spoke briefly about what was to happen afterwards. Would they go to the Fluen realm? Returning to the Pyran realm felt like defeat and they could only travel the less populated regions of the Luften realm after betraying Chiavel. Vanelia added that she would probably prefer hiding out in the Fluen realm, just due to the weather. She was not thinking of how unbearably cold the Eidyon Peninsula was, obviously.

They took longer than Trela had hoped to get to the Valley of the Caves, where the eshrams were. It was deemed too risky to travel on the river or even along the paths near it. So they ended up taking a rather circuitous route that swept in a long arc to the west before heading north. Nor did they wish to fly or use magic of any kind. It was a long and mundane trip.

Once they arrived outside the eshrams, they paused. They had many members in their party, and it seemed like a lot to just enter an eshram and plop themselves down in the middle. But Trela was mostly concerned that not all her coterie had the stomach for what was to be required, mainly the likes of Knill and Clerin. She, herself, was unhappy with the task, but what must be done, must be done. Just because evil was old and feeble did not mean it had turned good. And even if time healed all wounds, the chance that a younger and more devious mage would come to the Valley of the Caves looking for the knowledge of the Cabal was too great. Trela had been given her mission. She would see it through.

She chose Estfale, Malghain, and Verin for her warriors. They all had stomachs of steel. Feyazki would have to come as her greatest mage. She also felt that Ryshial had a stronger stomach than Serghno, but she needed Arnasta in case they had to hunt someone down, so she left Ryshial with the others. She also needed to bring along Hyscarne with them, for various reasons. There were plenty of other candidates, but she wanted a small retinue. So everyone besides the chosen eight were left outside of the first eshram, Tlimpid. They would be able to enter after the others had left to get water if they needed. Trela was hoping the whole ordeal would take less than a week, but she was unsure of how many eshrams there really were in the valley. The best guess put the number at five, but there was certainly some distance between them. There would also be some recluses that lived outside of the eshrams, which might take some time to find.

They entered Tlimpid near the evening. They had not planned that, it was just how their travel timing had ended up. They did not wish to bother anyone while they were preparing for bed, at least not in their homes. They set up camp at the communal well and only bothered those who were out and about.

More than anything, Trela was shocked at how many of the denizens were younger. She had not taken notice of that previously. There was a general assumption that the denizens would all be ancient and feeble. They were feeble-minded maybe, and sunbaked and haggard, but a few appeared quite physically fit and able. She was the first to admit she had very little knowledge of what drove one to an eshram. She certainly did not cast spells and Pyran mages were often just known for throwing fire and healing. Not performing bizarre research or searching for Minora or whatever it was that drove mages mad.

They would speak to those who were brave enough to approach their well even though it was surrounded by strangers. Trela left Hyscarne at the well as a sort of bait. She would say hello and attempt to engage. They ended up only speaking with two of the more lucid denizens that evening, but it was telling work. There was no way to figure out if they understood Yavencide without bringing up the subject. And Trela did not wish to tip her hand just yet, there at the beginning of the operation. Besides, it would take forever to get most of the denizens to just speak aloud, let alone spill their darkest secrets. She took Feyazki aside.

"You are going to have to scan their minds or something, this is untenable." She thought for a moment. "Remember that time after we had left the Forgotten Junction when Qizern's great nephew, Mynthur the Eastborn, tried to assassinate me? Didn't you enter his mind to find out who backed the attempt?"

"It was not overly enjoyable, and he was willing." Feyazki's eyebrow shot up. "Or, at least, as willing as one facing torture can be."

"Well, these are feeble-minded mages. That should make it simpler, shouldn't it?"

"Elange could have killed me the first time we met, even if his mind was not as sharp as it used to be. He was confused and muddled, not feeble-minded. And honestly, I'm not even sure how confused he was. He was just done with… with society. Or done with putting in the effort of… life. I am not sure." His hand rotated lazily in the air.

"You don't need to search around for specific history. Just whether or not they have participated in Yavencide. That should be a sharp enough experience to pick up on fairly easily, shouldn't it? Didn't Hyscarne say that the Yavencide itself could drive mages mad? We need to at least get some sort of triage going. Something quick to gauge whether or not we should delve deeper."

"I did mention it was not enjoyable, didn't I?"

"Do you think I'm enjoying this?" Trela waved her hand around at all the tiny caves built into the hillsides. "This whole thing is not enjoyable. But it is necessary. Some of these mages look quite healthy. They may survive decades. Do you seriously want another Yavencide? To have done all this for naught? To have the Yavens decide they would be better off if our entire realm was obliterated? I certainly don't. And the sooner we can get this done, the sooner we can figure out how to finish the Belegs, and the sooner I can get back to ruling my realm and the sooner you can get Clerin to where she wants to be."

He did not bite, merely raised an eyebrow. Which was just as well. He either knew where he was headed or he did not. It was not her job to tell him.

"I suppose you are correct."

"Of course, I am. I appreciate you noticing." She smiled warmly at him. She understood he did not want did not want to sift through strangers' minds, and she certainly did not want him to be annoyed about it, but she did need him to do it. "Listen, what you are about to do is appreciated, truly. Thank you." It made her feel better and made him smile. Maybe Vanelia was onto something, whether or not it was a little bit selfish.

Feyazki practiced on Hyscarne first, using Trela as a control. Though she knew what Yavencide was and had even been present when the Cabal fought against their Yavens, she had certainly never participated in the casting of Yavencide. He cast a couple of different spells, peering into each of them, until he felt comfortable. Trela, for her part, did not feel anything when he scanned her. And Hyscarne showed no outward response when he scanned her. Then he checked how far away he could be from Hyscarne and still get a good read.

Then how fast he could be moving past her. They checked everything.

The next morning they arose at dawn. Feyazki scanned everyone who came down to the well. He indicated on two of them. At first, Trela wished they had Jalin with them, to follow them without being noticed, but the denizens just wandered back to their caves, making keeping track of them quite simple. She conferred with her warriors just to make sure they were all in agreement as to which caves the two entered. They did that all day, sitting near, but not too close to, the well and scanning the denizens who came down for water.

After nightfall came the real tests. They had not told Feyazki which caves the mages he had indicated went back to. After it was dark, true dark near the middle of the night, they decided to slowly fly Feyazki along the lines of cave entrances. If he could at least pick out the two that he had indicated earlier, Trela would consider the test a success. She then needed to interview the chosen mages so she could feel comfortable that his assessments were correct.

There was the issue of some slipping through the cracks. That was a distinct possibility, Trela knew that. But that was a possibility no matter what method they used to ferret out the guilty. She was willing to bet that this method would be more fruitful than trying to get them to talk about Yavencide, even if they were confused.

When Serghno and Feyazki returned, they had three caves that Feyazki had hit upon. Two of them matched the two who had come down to the well. The third was either someone Feyazki had missed, or it was someone who had not gone down to the well during the day. Trela wished that she knew which it was, but it would have been nigh impossible to mark every cave that someone who got water went back to. Besides, what if some of the caves had more than one occupant? Even recluses could get lonely sometimes.

For the interviews, she wanted enough derlians to be able to subdue the mages, but knew how small the caves could be—they were large niches more than small caves. And she could not forget they were mages, either. She immediately felt regret for not bringing Ryshial along. She had way too many warriors with her and not enough mages. She would have to rectify that tomorrow.

Trela felt that they could not bring more than four. So, it was herself and Estfale, and Feyazki and Serghno. They flew to the first cave and entered fairly silently. Estfale went in first, as was his typical desire. They gathered around the sleeping mage, practically engulfing the entire room. Trela was on one side and Estfale the other, each with a long dagger in their hands. Feyazki and Serghno were at the sleeping mage's feet, blocking the exit. The cave was cramped and sparse, with rotting cloth draped everywhere and moldering wood crates stacked to one side. It was all lit by a very dim spell of Feyazki's. Trela took a deep breath, placed the tip of her dagger to the side of the mage's neck, and placed her hand over the mage's mouth. She was willing to kill the mage without speaking to him if that was what it took to keep the silence. The worst thing, in her mind, would be to awaken the eshram. She wanted as little disturbance as possible.

The eyes immediately popped open wide and there was some muffled screaming before the mage realized what was going on. She was lucky he was as cognizant as he was. He settled down after a moment.

"We would like to talk with you, is that okay?" Trela's voice was slightly above a whisper. The mage nodded. "Good, good. We need you to be quiet while we are talking, understood? No yelling, no sudden movements. And this is the most important part. If you try to cast a spell, we'll kill you. Understood?"

His eyes flashed back and forth between the four of them. Quickly, furtively, silently. He nodded again while looking at Trela. She squinted at him and slowly removed her hand, ready to strike in an instant.

"Do you know why we are here?" Trela kept her face close to his as she spoke.

"Of course not."

"Do you know why you are here?"

"What? Like under attack?"

"No. Here. At the eshram."

"I reached too far. Too fast. Too young. Not entirely sure."

"What spell were you working on when you came here? What Minora were you attempting to find?"

"Well, nothing in specific really. I was with a group. No Minora. Or at least not one sought by myself."

"Then what drove you mad? Or are you mad?" Trela did not think he sounded very mad. "What drove you here?"

"We were striving against forces larger than us, than any of us. Though, it turns out, not larger than all of us." His eyes flashed between them again. "Am I mad? Not as much as I should be. Am I done? Done with it all, the striving, the struggle? Yes. I am done. Do I feel bad? Do I feel regret? Do I wish my path had been different? Of course. Of course." It was almost inaudible. "Of course." He looked at her. There was an odd mixture of fear and relief.

"I know why you are here now. I see it now. I was confused earlier." He had a tiny sardonic smile lingering in the corner of his mouth. "You are the nemesis, aren't you? You arrived later than I thought, yes. It took so long that I had forgotten to expect you. But go ahead. This is no life anyway, not really. I breathe out of habit more than anything else. I had forgotten there was another way."

"I need you to say it. To admit it." Trela felt herself stiffen. Her muscles were preparing themselves. "Unburden yourself."

He closed his eyes. "We trapped a Yaven. We summoned it, trapped it, killed it, whatever. I know you are here to kill me for this. I am ready."

"Is there anyone else here that you know has participated in Yavencide?"

"What?" His eyes reopened. "Ah, several died during the ritual. Not sure of the others, but I think Zagriel might be in Algathia. There is no one here that I recognize."

He waited for them to nod amongst themselves and then reclosed his eyes. He was more tense than he was a moment ago, but Trela had needed to ask. His comfort was less important than being able to gather as much information as they were able. She waited a brief moment to see if he would relax again. He did not. She thrust her dagger and clamped down on his mouth at the same time. She made it as quick and painless as she was able.

They were unable to get a confession out of the next mage, but they were unable to get anything intelligible out of her either. She seemed completely mad. Trela took a while trying to get something actionable out of her, not wanting to finalize the decision only on Feyazki's spell, but to no avail. After almost a half hour of frustrating nonsense, Trela killed the mage with a thrust of her dagger.

The third mage immediately woke and attempted to cast a spell. He was killed immediately. Trela was not sure who got the killing stroke in on that one, it was all such a blur. So, no confession out of him either.

They took the bodies with them to dispose of them properly and cleaned the caves as much as they were able. It was a long night for just three old Cabal members. Trela tried not to think of them as victims, but it was a little difficult. The first mage who confessed was easy, but it went downhill from there. No matter the difficulty, however, they were committed, Trela was committed, to ferreting out the rest of them. As she understood it, Tlimpid was the largest of the eshrams. Finding only three Yavencide participants there was encouraging. There was no way to know if they had missed one, or even more, but she was willing to continue on.

They went to Algathia next. The main group walked along, heading in the correct direction, while Trela and her small group flew over there. They waited for part of the day at the eshram's well, resting a little in what shade they could find, with Feyazki scanning the denizens as they came for water. Trela and Estfale kept track of the one mage he indicated, seeing which cave the mage called their own. At dusk, Serghno flew Feyazki around. He picked out two caves, one of them matching the one they had had tracked.

They visited him first. He was completely mad. They were unable to get a coherent confession. The second one, however, was less crazed. Even more than that, the second one was Zagriel. And he made a confession before dying. It made Trela feel much better about the screening process. She had known Feyazki was talented, but he seemed to conquer each new challenge with ease.

They visited each of the eshrams in the Valley of the Caves. They spent the day near whatever well the tiny enclaves always seemed to be centered on and they spent the night flying and preying on the ex-Cabal members like voracious owls. There were only a few in each eshram, sometimes one, sometimes two. At the end of it all, they had found less than ten. It was less taxing than she had feared, though it was certainly the greatest grouping of those who had participated in Yavencide outside of Vatlisi.

They began their trek towards the Fluen realm. They skirted along the Northern Desert, far enough into the Luften realm that they could use the occasional comfort of trees or small streams. Trela was not really sure where they were going to drop Vanelia off. It would have to be far enough from Ariellyna that Chiavel would not dare to reach. Guessing that distance was difficult. She assumed they would err enough on the side of caution that they would end up back in Tureyn or somewhere on the frozen wastes of the Eidyon Peninsula.

It was less than a week after the eshrams when Croy confronted Trela about them. Well, maybe confronted was not the right word, but he certainly brought it up out of nowhere. It did seem to Trela that he was playing the spoiler more often. She worried a little about it. If he was unhappy, he could just not be helpful, that would be acceptable. But if he was actively attempting to make things difficult, she would have to be more wary. She hoped not, but the thought of it was making her a little paranoid about his motives. Which colored the way he sounded to her. She knew she had to be wary of that in herself as well.

"Don't you feel bad about it? Killing all those old mages?" They were sitting around a fire. A meal had just been eaten. There were a few others around, but they stayed quiet.

"You mean all those Cabal members? All those who committed Yavencide?" She took a breath to think over her response rather than just react, but Croy pressed his point.

"I've been told that some were so addled they were unable to confess."

"You heard correctly." Her gaze drifted to the fire. "Personally, I feel a murderer is still a murderer even if they have dementia. Your point, if I understand it, is that the punishment is wasted since they may not understand what they have done. And if the punishment was meant to rehabilitate, you might have a point. And you might argue that punishment for the sake of revenge is pointless along the same lines. I doubt you could convince *me* of that, but I have heard that argument before. That is not what this is, however." She drew in a breath, eyes still locked on the fire. "This is about eradicating any knowledge of the specialized skill they either possessed or witnessed. This charge was given to us by the Belegs. The requirements and the reasoning were well spelled out by Taglo. We risked life and limb to send the Cabal, all of its practitioners, all of the items, all of the knowledge, all into oblivion. Erased from the entire world for as long as possible, hopefully forever."

"But if they could not confess, how could they explain to someone else their specialized knowledge, as you put it?"

"Who knows if they are always addled? But no, that does not even really matter. There are mages who can enter their minds, Croy. They could be so muddled up that they are unable to speak at all, and the knowledge would still be in there somewhere."

"But…"

"No buts, Croy." She felt herself getting agitated and turned her gaze back to the fire to keep from glaring. "I was given a directive by the Belegs, and I accomplished it. They were guilty of heinous crimes. We all agreed Yavencide was evil, did we not? But more than that, I had no idea who those derlians were. None. Nor did I care. They were loose ends to me, Croy. That was all. You know who was not? You know who I *do* feel bad about killing? Mika! I liked Mika, Croy. We could have been friends. We were friends. Of a sort, at least. But I killed her too. She promised to travel with the Well of Eternity and never tell another derlian of what she knew, and I still killed her. Because I do not shirk my duty. I am filled with dedication to my obligations."

Trela was going to continue. She felt the tirade building, bubbling up like lava. But standing and ranting would not have solved anything, and it would have only made her feel good for a couple of brief moments. At best. So she stopped herself and stared at the fire. Calming herself with its hypnotically chaotic dance.

Croy did not say anything for a while. The only sound was the crackling fire. It was nice.

"I had not wanted to make you think about Mika. Apologies." He stood to leave.

"Are you still with us Croy?" She stood up and stuck out her hand. "Are we all traveling together? Do we share a common goal, a common adventure?"

He looked at her hard, his pale gray eyes searching for something. They softened, he smiled a little, and he shook her hand. He did not say a word, however. He turned and walked away, off towards his own small tent. Though she was happy for the small smile she wondered what the silence meant. She stood there for a moment, watching him walk away. Then she sat back down and stared back into the fire, surrounded by her own aura of silence. It was an odd parting to say the least.

✳✳✳

Several days after that, Trela found herself at a campfire with Vanelia. Clerin was there as well, holding Hynara. Feyazki was there, sitting on the other side, chatting quietly with Knill. So, in effect, it was Trela and Vanelia that were conversing. At first, Trela was just trying to figure out where they were headed.

"Just how far away from Ariellyna do you think you'll need to be to feel safe?" She decided to ask outright. She, herself, was not overly concerned where they were going. They needed to find something extraordinary—some way to resolve it all. That meant someone in her coterie needed to find something. Feyazki, or Clerin, or Ryshial, or someone. She was not sure who and not sure how. Her job was to keep the pot being stirred, to keep the chaos moving enough to allow destiny to pop up whenever she needed to. Which meant Trela was just traveling to keep the energy in flux. Getting Vanelia to wherever she wanted to be was helpful in that regard.

"I have been mulling that over. Do I want to be far and hidden, or not as far but protected? I have thought about high up on the Eidyon Peninsula, where I would never be found. But would that work? If I did get found, Chiavel could certainly send someone over there and I would not even know until it was too late. So then I thought about Tureyn. He would certainly know where I was, there would be no hiding. But, perhaps, Clerin could introduce me to the king and I could plead my case. Get some protection." She glanced over to Clerin who, in response, made Hynara wave at Vanelia by moving her arm for her. "That got me thinking. Maybe Vatlisi. That would be far enough away to make it difficult to find me, and it would be large enough to offer a lot of ready protection."

"Wow. Vatlisi. That really is about as far from Ariellyna as you can get without entering the Gaen realm." Trela had not been thinking that far, not all the way back to Vatlisi. But she had asked the question and Vanelia had answered. She had not realized how concerned Vanelia really was.

"I have no delusions about what I am doing. I am not just escaping Ariellyna, I am deserting her. There is no other way, not for one such as I." She sighed a little. "It is unimaginable to think I will ever return. At least, not while Chiavel, or anyone from Largon for that matter, rules the realm. No, my escape, this escape that you helped me with, it is the last straw. The final betrayal. Chiavel will not forgive this, I assure you."

"We will certainly get you where you need to go. We owe you that much." Trela nodded absently.

"I appreciate it, truly. But whatever hand I played in sending Feyazki and the others to you has long been played out."

"Oh, I do not mean that. Though I am grateful for that, truly." She smiled over at Vanelia. "I was referring to the gathering of the Yaven-infused items, especially while you were losing your throne. I can only imagine how you would have rather spent your energies during that time. We placed an undue burden on you when you least needed it. We owe you your escape at least."

"Ah, that. I could say it was a welcome distraction from the inevitable fall. I really do not know what more I could have done to avoid Chiavel." She sighed quietly. "I should have had him murdered when I had the chance, but... assassination was never my first inclination." She gave a low chuckle. "You had to kill your way to the throne, did you not?"

"Of course. That is our way. We faced each other one-on-one, in a ring. Face to face. No tricks, no spells, no allies, no proxies. He even had the better sword."

"Well, we pretend otherwise. We like to say we are civilized, that the idea of single combat is somehow... I do not know... unintellectual. Yes, that is it. We like to think we are intellectuals. That it is our arguments of how to govern in a certain time that wins the day." She sighed again. "In the end, however, it is still just kill or be killed. Or flee. I guess I chose to flee."

Trela had always thought of single combat as a way of letting destiny guide who rules the realm. She believed in it utterly, she was the Kriishan. But what could she say to Vanelia? Was Vanelia not destined to be queen? Was Chiavel chosen? Or did he cheat destiny? Was he, in the parlance of the Pyrans, an antoshan? What was to be done if one felt they were being robbed of their destiny? It made Trela ponder for a moment.

"Our system has our fair share of antoshans as well. Those who cheat destiny. Nothing quite works as designed." She was mostly trying to make Vanelia feel better about fleeing.

"I have no idea if Chiavel cheated destiny or I did. But if we were put in a ring together, I am sure he would win, whether or not he was a very good warrior. And he is not. I doubt many of our rulers were." She gave a small laugh. "Our system is filled rulers who are skilled at convincing others to get in the ring for them. Yes, that is it. We convince others to do our work for us." She turned to Clerin. "And how is it in the Fluen realm?"

"Oh, we do not have to convince anyone. Our entire system is built around everyone doing what they are required to do according to their lineage. Sure, there might be some minor fluctuations between generations, but not much. And certainly not if you are in the lower portion of the society." Her voice became higher as she turned to Hynara. "Isn't that right? Yes, it is." Hynara's arm reached towards her lips.

"Still, assassination has such nasty connotations. You probably feel better fleeing than having Chiavel murdered." Trela spoke as she hoped Vanelia wanted to hear.

"Well, is that fleeing or is it abandonment?" Vanelia turned from Hynara to Trela. "Did I abandon my subjects? Was my life so dear to me that I let one such as Chiavel take the throne without a fight?"

"No, not just your life. If there was a true fight for the throne, more than just your blood would have been shed. You saved many more lives than your own by leaving. I would not call that abandonment. That was a great sacrifice. You gave up the throne to avoid the bloodshed. You should not condemn yourself for that, you should be commended." Trela nodded to Vanelia, looking her in the eye, not letting her escape. Trela wanted Vanelia to know that she understood.

Trela herself would not have made that sacrifice, could not have. She would have burned the entire world down to destroy Qizern. Whether or not Qizern was worse than Chiavel, and Trela thought he was, did not truly matter. What mattered at the current moment was that Vanelia had been able to let go for the greater good—and Trela would not have.

They were quiet for a while, staring off in different directions. All the random sentences that popped through Trela's head were more of the same. Vanelia had said her piece and Trela had tried to make her feel better about it, and they had finished that conversation. Bringing it back up would certainly not help anyone, even if she did think of something nicer to say.

Eventually they started to stare in the same direction. The direction of Hynara, of course. Trela's incessant curiosity got the better of her. She tried to think of a nice way to ask, a comfortable way to bring it up, but was unable to. A more civilized derlian may have left it unspoken, but that was not Trela's way.

"So… just who is the father?" She glanced over at Hynara. "From what I understand, it was not Hulgert." Vanelia's eyes got big for a moment, then narrowed. Trela worried that she had overestimated their camaraderie. "You don't have to tell if you are not comfortable. No worries. I'm sure I have no idea who it is. I'm just curious, is all."

"Ha! No, no I am not comfortable. But I suppose it is a secret that cannot last forever." Vanelia took a deep breath. There was a long pause.

Clerin stopped cooing to Hynara and turned towards them. Feyazki and Knill almost turned as well, but Clerin suddenly started bouncing Hynara on her knee again. She was still paying close attention to Vanelia's conversation, but she was also keeping the others from noticing the pause. She started cooing again softly.

"The father was Revkin." Everyone stopped.

"What?!" Trela was not sure who actually said the word, maybe all of them.

"And that is why I did not want to tell anyone." Vanelia glanced between all of their shocked faces. She paused at each one briefly, making a small calculation. Her smile did not slip.

No one said a word. Trela felt that her mouth was hanging open, but it was closed when she checked. When Vanelia's gaze rested on her, she could feel the weight of the calculation bearing down. It was palpable. She had to say something. Anything.

"Are you sure?" Trela could not believe her own question. It was all just so stunning that she had not been able to think of something more suitable.

"Ha! Not one hundred percent, not fully positive, but sure enough to say it out loud and silence the lot of you." Luckily for Trela, Vanelia laughed it off. It was the perfect amount of absurdity, and the others gave a grateful chuckle as well.

"So, did you know when you told us of his passing?" Feyazki shifted away from Knill to squarely face Vanelia. Knill turned himself as well.

"Yes, of course." A small shadow passed over her face.

"Why were you not living together? Surely there was no reason to keep the secret once you had been deposed, was there?" Clerin added her own question.

"He wanted another apprentice and, well… No, that was not the real issue. It was complicated. Things were moving so fast." Her eyes tightened as she thought of how to explain it all satisfactorily.

"Did he know?" Feyazki asked what Trela was thinking.

"These are all good questions, truly." She breathed in deeply, held it for a moment, then released a small slow sigh. "We did not talk directly about it. We did not plan a future together or anything. He never asked or made demands… It was more that we both understood that if we discussed it, it would suddenly become real. Then something would have to be done." She sighed again. "And really, Hulgert died, I gave birth, the crops started failing, Revkin was murdered by that Pashkaun—by his own apprentice! Not that I knew that at the time, of course. But everything just came crashing down, one after another with no respite in between. Honestly, we barely spoke during that time. We should have spoken more. That probably would have helped." She trailed off a bit wistfully.

"How did it happen?" Trela's curiosity was overwhelming but not dangerous, like a kitten stuck in attack mode. "I mean, how did you meet? How did you get together?" She tried to modify her questions to something a little more palatable.

"Ah, well now, that is a story." Vanelia smiled and visible relaxed.

Trela relaxed her own shoulders in response. She prepared to settle herself in for the story. She was glad to shift Vanelia's mood away from turning melancholic.

"This was before you arrived, back when it was just Revkin, no apprentices. In fact, I suppose I should start earlier." She smiled at Feyazki. "Hulgert's father was king for a long time, and he had three older brothers. He did not think he would ever become king and lived like it. He was the realm's most eligible bachelor for some time. Quite some time. He enjoyed lavish parties with all sorts of derlians. He enjoyed drinking and eating. He enjoyed spending his ample allowance the day he received it."

Trela was a bit shocked by the description. Not only because of the way Vanelia was painting her dead husband, but because it did not make a lot of sense to the Pyran way of thinking. A son or younger brother were not thought of as that powerful. Yes, they may have the ear of the king or be given a well-paying, low-labor type of job from their relative. But to be really excessive, to be the center of lavish parties and not just on the periphery, one had to actually be the king. This seemed to indicate two things to Trela. One, the relatives of a ruler lived well in a hereditary regency. And two, the ruler themselves appeared to be expected to behave. The first part was at least understandable in a general sense. The close relatives could, at some point, become rulers just because of their proximity of birth. But the second part seemed a little off. Trela decided to interrupt to check to see if she misunderstood.

"So, is that always that way, or was it just with Hulgert's family?" Everyone stared at her as if she was raving. "I mean, did Hulgert's father throw lavish parties as well? Is the king typically given less freedoms than their relatives?"

"I do not recall all of your lavish parties." Clerin turned carefully and smiled at her. Hynara kept her head on Clerin's shoulder, maybe in sleep. "At least, not any that the entire warpack, or town, or realm, was not invited to."

"Well, no, but I cared about running my realm."

"It seems you have answered your own question then." Feyazki smiled at her, eyes full of mirth.

"And how is your realm being run now?" The cruel words came from Knill. She had not expected them and was taken aback.

"And who begged me to leave my duties behind?" Her automatic response was to attack back. A riposte without the cleverness.

"Wait, woah, where did that come from?" Vanelia skewered Knill with her eyes. "We are all on the same team here. Correct? I have just recently been deposed, I have lost my right to be called queen, lost all my power. These are sensitive issues and should not be made light of."

Knill looked suddenly sheepish. Trela wanted to thank Vanelia, to commiserate, to delve deeper into how she felt about losing her crown, about being deposed. But Clerin jumped in and smoothed everything over.

"Please, continue, I would love to hear more about Hulgert the bachelor." She smiled and carefully turned back to Vanelia.

"Well, he did not stay a bachelor long after I came upon the scene." Her laugh was lyrical, erasing all the previous tension. "He was older than me, quite a bit older if I am being honest, but he was still in his prime and had copious amounts of roguish charm. At first, it was just a bit of fun. I can admit that. Fun is fun. But it soon morphed into something greater.

"We were together for several cycles, just enjoying life, before his father died. We lived in Ariellyna, but barely saw his family. Or my family for that matter. His father died of a heart attack, we heard. He was very old, and everything appeared quite natural.

"Hulgert's eldest brother, Obzehn, became king immediately with a large amount of pomp. There was a large festival and an involved coronation. His brother had been handfasted for many years, but they had no offspring. There was some concern about that as I recall. It was hoped that they would find themselves with an heir quickly.

"But, of course, it was not to be. And it was proved to be his issue, not Jetual's. Obzehn was encouraged to get an heir by any means possible. And, though he professed reluctance, he certainly tried his heart out. Jetual was quite gracious about it all. I told her that she should set out to solve the problem, but that was not her way."

"I assume that you were friends with Jetual?" Trela smiled a little.

"Well, more than with Obzehn, yes. But we did not know each other before she ascended her throne." Vanelia shook her head briefly. "Even afterwards, for the sun cycle they had, we enjoyed each other's company whenever it occurred. But it was not very often, if I am honest. Hulgert and I were still flitting about. It was not until Obzehn's untimely death that that we became more involved with the Royal Branch."

"Oh, an accident?" Clerin chimed in.

"Well, it just might have been, but probably not. Corbune, the next in line, had a little boy and his fantastic wife, Haldaband, was pregnant. It was exactly what the kingdom wanted, what we needed." She took a short breath, collecting her thoughts. "Honestly, I am unsure of who performed the deed. It may have been someone from Largon, but Chiavel himself had a solid alibi. It may have been any of the family Branches, or maybe one of the guilds. All I know is that everyone was incredibly relieved when Obzehn's carriage was found at the bottom of the ravine. No one asked any questions, even his allies.

"The stability of Corbune's family was a relief. It was only a couple of moons, maybe three, before tragedy struck. It was an illness, swift and deadly. That was the real mystery of Hulgert's family. It was not only an unanswered question, how they could have all succumbed so quickly, but it was one that everyone was invested in. There was a full week of mourning. Which, though it does not sound like a long time, was one of the longest stretches our realm has gone without a ruler. We just wafted along, stricken and inconsolable, all knowing who was going to be the next king, but no one wanting to believe it was happening, not even Pilhurd himself. You see, it was not just that Corbune had a full family, but he was well respected by all. He was fair and kind, generous but not excessive, quick of wit and with a laugh. Haldaband was fantastic as well. It was a blow to us all.

"Pilhurd was fine. Nobody hated him, at least not that I knew of. He was smart, for sure. He had probably read every book in Ariellyna. He was quiet and slow to anger. But he was single and always had been. He had rarely left the helioarc he had been born in. And I truly believe that his most beloved brother was Corbune. Pilhurd was crushed by his brother's death. It was just… sad. It was sad.

"We all tried to find Pilhurd a queen. There were certainly no shortage of volunteers. We felt that he needed someone strong, someone fun, someone who could drag him out of his shell. I fear that the pressure was too much for him, however. He fell. He fell when no one else was around, at night. He could cast spells. It was assumed he could fly. He was rarely outside at all, let alone wandering some of the thinner branches away from the trunk. Let us just say that many felt it was intentional. It was heartbreaking, especially so soon after Corbune and his family had passed. That was how Hulgert and I gained the throne."

There was a small pause, but Trela did not want to interrupt. Did not want to prod for the sake of prodding. No one else interrupted either.

"Elange and Hulgert had already been friends, so he was the easy choice to become the royal mage. They were similar in age, and though different in temperament, they had a healthy mutual respect for each other.

"I met Revkin while he was Elange's apprentice. We would run into each other periodically. We were of similar age and similar temperament, at least at the time. We would drink together, chat together, we became friends. Though, I must say, I was unable to keep up with him, even back then when I was less concerned about what others thought about me. But still, we only saw each other so often. He was busy learning the art of magic and I was learning the art of being a queen. He threw himself into his studies while I threw myself into mine."

"How would you describe your studies?" Trela, having recently thrown herself into her own study of queenship, was curious what Vanelia had to say. She always seemed so calm and thoughtful, so wise and measured. So regal.

"Well, it was mostly the study of the others at court. There were many meetings, councils, audiences, parties, and social gatherings. And everyone was vying for Hulgert's attention. It was almost as if I was invisible, even during the more social events. It gave me time to study their faces, their words, their manners. Some Luftens cajoled, others used thinly veiled threats, some were ingratiating, while others pretended to be emotionless logicians. All were trying to convince Hulgert of something, to sway his opinion. Honestly, the most successful were the friendliest. Hulgert listened most to those he enjoyed. He certainly did not respond well to aggravated confrontation."

"And you learned how to manipulate Hulgert from watching others?" Knill spoke up quietly, almost shyly.

"I would not say manipulate, that has different connotations. And besides, I already knew how to manipulate Hulgert. No, it was more of the social graces. Of how best to react to each type of situation. To pick the best route to my preferred destination, no matter who I was with, or what destination I wanted to head towards." She paused briefly again, gaining her bearings. "Watching the various courtiers gave me an understanding of how each of the personalities gained favor, yes. But it also gave me insight into how to, for the lack of a better word, manipulate them as well. Each personality had their own foibles and weaknesses as well, and Hulgert was actually good at his job."

"You will have to give me some pointers." Trela laughed, and then so did Vanelia.

"So, you did not have your affair with Revkin at this time?" Feyazki prodded Vanelia. When Trela thought about it, there had to be some overlap time when Feyazki was Revkin's apprentice. Her curiosity was piqued as well.

"No, not then, not right away. We did not cross paths that often back then, though when we did, there might have been a little flirting. That may be too strong of a word, really, but I knew that he liked me, I could tell, and I was intrigued by him. We saw each other a couple of times before Hulgert's accident, and there was certainly something there, a mutual spark if you will. After the accident I grew... frustrated. Quickly. And Revkin was there to commiserate with me." She paused briefly, swinging her gaze over to Feyazki. "And you. He had recently gained you as an apprentice. We were sworn to secrecy. He could not be seen with me outside of official business, and I could not meet his new apprentice. If I had known all that would transpire, Revkin would have been our royal mage, but Zafine was chosen by Hulgert instead. And honestly, at the time of Elange's madness, Revkin was not ready.

"It started slowly, our affair. Not in actual time, it was only a couple of weeks after the accident, but it was slow to build. At first it was just late-night meetings. I needed someone to discuss the day with, but it could not be any of the regular courtiers. I needed an outsider, one whom I trusted, one that already knew Hulgert and I and the court. Revkin was perfect for that. He understood my frustration, having lost Elange to the eshrams, and I understood his loneliness. Once it started, it was impossible to stop. I knew it was incredibly dangerous. That the smallest misstep on our part would endanger the throne. And not because of the affair, or at least, mostly not because of the affair. We were still pretending that Hulgert was uninjured. We were still hiding him from court, making excuses and stalling for time. We were the last, you see. The last of the dynasty. Who knows what would have happened if it became common knowledge that Hulgert was an invalid?"

"Chiavel would have usurped the throne?" Trela could not help herself. Vanelia had completely set up the joke, she had just spoken it. They all laughed for a few moments. After a moment of quiet, Vanelia spoke back up.

"Then the pregnancy happened." Vanelia paused and looked over at Hynara. Her face softened and a small smile crept onto her lips. "It was... amazing. It was perfect. It complicated so many things but simplified many others. No one could know that Hynara was not Hulgert's. That was the difficult part. But the courtiers stopped pressing to see him. Once the pregnancy was known, once the dynasty was again secure, an amazing amount of pressure was relieved. There were many who did not care at all who the father was, just that I was pregnant. Just that there was a transition, smooth or not, that they could work with. Scheme about. It was the not knowing that annoyed many of them. The possibility of outright revolt. Like many derlians, they just wanted to know the direction they were headed."

It was quiet again for a moment. They all wanted Vanelia to continue but were unsure of what direction to prod her. In the end, as was typical, it was Trela who came up short on patience.

"And the others?"

"What?"

"You said you were not sure that Revkin was the father. At least at first. The way you were just describing it; it seemed that he was the only contender." Trela's smile was a little too mischievous. She knew it, could feel it on her face, but could not stop it.

"Ah, well, that is a little embarrassing. There were two others at the time. As I said, I was quite frustrated. It seemed as if my entire world was being harassed and attacked, being defeated. I… I spent one night with an old friend. And I spent one night with someone I should not have. After that, it was only Revkin. Truly." She stopped and turned to Feyazki.

"He was a great mage. He was. Despite any of his foibles. But he was a great derlian, too. Kind and compassionate, intelligent and poignant, perceptive and earnest. He could make me laugh when I was sad, calm me down when I was angry, help me to find my own answers to my own problems. He did not deign to tell me what was what, he did not push me to react too soon. And his passion was laced with fervor. It felt good to be fawned over and catered to. He was great. And then, once there were true questions about the timing of my pregnancy, whether or not Hulgert could have been the father, that the dynasty might not be fully intact, he agreed to fade back. To not make claims, to not endanger my position, to not make me feel bad or ashamed." She let out a large sigh.

"I think that was my biggest mistake. It is certainly my biggest regret. I often wonder what would have happened if we had tried to make it work. Either in public, arguing that the throne should stay with me and my child, regardless of the father, or in private. Just the three of us. Moving to some tiny hamlet far away from Ariellyna." Her smile, and her eyes, grew wistful. "I spend far too much time wondering. A thousand different scenarios, a thousand different futures. All as counterfeit as the last."

Chapter 15

Croy was finally relaxing again. He did enjoy traveling, he did enjoy everyone's company. It had been a while since he had dreamt, truly dreamt. He was not sure if that was because they were so far from the Gaen realm or that he had been fulfilling Gunzgak's requirements so well and did not need additional guidance, but he was happy for the reprieve. He had been trying to keep around Clerin and Trela and the others as much as he could without calling undue attention to himself. They rarely spoke about anything of import, or of what might be considered of import to Gunzgak, but he was there just the same. Listening intently to all their small talk. They chatted about nothing most of the time. And not even new nothing, it was the same nothing that they always chatted about. It was as if they were not on a mission to destroy the Belegs. It was as if they were just camping in the wilderness with old friends. Not a worry amongst them.

It did not bother Croy that much. He did still like them all. It was just a little odd that they were not aware of the air of nefariousness that hung around them. It made him feel like he was a little removed. Just a little. Like there was a deep, but narrow, chasm between himself and the others. It made him want to speak up a little to get his voice over the chasm. It made him feel as if his face and hands were wrapped in gauze. That he was experiencing a slightly different reality than they were. But even though he felt like he was the one living "right," the one living the truth, it still felt like he was the one removed. The one who was muffled, who was wearing gauze. They seemed unencumbered by the truth that was happening around them. They were blissfully ignorant of the pain they were causing the world.

Croy felt he should keep such thoughts in check or else they might sense a weirdness from him. And, really, it did not bother him that much. They were all good derlians, deep down. Everyone was doing their best to navigate the difficulties that were thrust upon them. Mostly. He shook his head to clear his thoughts. He was thinking in circles and just needed to get his smile back on his face. But Knill noticed the head shake. There was a concerned look on his face for a moment. Croy smiled his best and gave Knill a quick nod.

"Are you all right?" His friend, his last good friend, asked the question quietly, with head thrust forwards to keep his voice low.

He did not want to call attention to them. It was a natural response for Knill and one that Croy appreciated. He did not want to call attention either.

"Of course, of course." How long had he been sitting there with a furrowed brow? Had there only been one quick head shake? He had been trying to pay attention to Trela but could not now think of what she had been talking about. "I could ask you a similar question. How are you feeling Knill?" Croy kept his voice low as well.

"That's fine, you don't have to tell me. I'd prefer not to talk either." Knill gave a weak smile.

There was more silence between them while the others chatted about something or other. Croy thought for a moment. Knill was an obvious ally. He could not always get Trela to listen to him, but he should be easily swayed to Gunzgak's cause.

"Do you ever wonder where Tumu is?" He thought he would start simple.

"All the time, yes."

"Do you think he's still alive?" Croy did for some reason, but he thought that if Knill thought Tumu was dead, it would sour his disposition further.

"Honestly, I think he was stolen. It's all I can think of." Knill looked thoughtful for a moment. "He would never just wander off. If he was killed, we would have been able to find blood, or something, at the inn. Or near the inn. I would think Arnasta would have been able to pick up on something like that. Wasn't she able to find Qizern for Trela with blood? I guess that is a little different." He looked thoughtful again, his gaze turning towards the ceiling. "Of course, he could have been stolen and then killed somewhere else, I suppose. Or maybe he died during the attempted abduction, like being choked or smothered. Then his body could have been removed."

Knill's disposition did not seem to sour during his macabre ruminations. It was almost as if he enjoyed dreaming up different ways their friend could have dematerialized. Croy thought about it for another moment. Tumu being stolen, while making some sense, would have had to have been done by someone outside of the immediate group. There was no way that Tumu was being hidden amongst themselves. Croy thought of, and then immediately discarded, the idea of Yaven involvement.

"I doubt he is hidden away somewhere." Croy waved his hand around in the air, trying to indicate beyond the immediate area. "I think you were on to something there. I bet there was an attempted abduction, or maybe just a threat or extortion to get him to state some false prophecy, that went horribly awry. He protested, tried to scream or something, and someone smothered him. Maybe even accidently. Yes, I think you are correct." Croy paused for a moment to allow it to sink in, but not too long. "But who do you think could have done such a thing? I mean, from around here, just hypothetically speaking."

"I don't know. Really. I cannot imagine anyone we know killing Tumu, accidentally or not. Even more, I cannot think of anyone around here trying to abduct him, or extort him. Not even one of the warriors I do not know well. Let alone a friend." His brow was knitted in a worried expression. He was trying to think of someone, Croy could tell, but the thought was too foreign.

Croy realized the whole conversation was a mistake. Knill was unable to come up with anyone to blame. It was doubly unfortunate, since Croy was unable to come up with anyone either. As much as he was annoyed about the direction of Clerin's mission, they were all still friends. No one would have harmed Tumu on purpose and, if it were an accident, no one could have remained silent. He let out a large unconscious sigh.

"We could have certainly stayed longer, looking for him. I thought leaving that soon was a bit rotten." Knill's brow was still knitted worriedly.

"Right? What if it had been Clerin missing?" He had almost said Trela, but then caught himself and shifted at the last moment. "We would have stayed a week, a moon, however long it took."

"Hey, what are you two conspiring about?" Trela had just barely glanced over, probably when Clerin's name got mentioned. He and Knill had started out talking quietly, but they had grown louder with each passing moment that the others ignored them.

"Nothing."

"Nothing."

"There is nothing more worrying than when someone states they are talking about nothing." She glanced between them with intense eyes but her mouth was smiling, counteracting the seriousness.

"We should probably be leaving anyway." Clerin hopped up, motioning to Feyazki, who had only been half paying attention. He smiled and nodded at everyone.

The others slowly peeled off soon afterwards, leaving Trela, Knill, and himself. It was oddly quiet for a moment. It was as if Trela was waiting for one of them to talk. To tell her what they had been whispering about. But then she stood.

"Did you want to come with me or stay here?" She was looking nonchalantly at Knill.

"Sure, I'll come." Knill popped up, gave Croy a quick pat on the shoulder, and then left.

Just like that, Croy was suddenly alone with his thoughts. He felt good. Not only had he been a passive spy, which is what he assumed Gunzgak needed him for, but he had, of his own volition, given Knill something to think about. Something to worry on. Nothing much, nothing noticeable from a distance, but maybe a seed had been planted. One small seed of discontent. Knill only wielded so much power in their group, but it was something. Croy smiled to himself as he got up to leave.

They were headed towards Vatlisi. Croy had hoped for Tureyn, though he was not exactly sure why. There was little chance of him meeting Lembin. Little chance of Clerin communing and then changing her mind about anything. He could not put his finger on it, but felt a visit to Tureyn would help the cause. He did not want to push anything, however. He did not want to call attention to any desire, however minor or obscure. He feared that if he did, they would automatically reject it. Or potentially worse, they would begin to view any suggestion of his with suspicion. That would ruin his only power: his ability to fade into the background.

The plan was to follow a river to the Clatsvol, then take a large boat to Vatlisi. That was the other reason he was not excited with the plan. He did not like boats. Not in the least. Certainly not on the sea. Not only that, but boats did not like him. It was a mutual animosity, one that scared him with its intensity.

Following the river was not bad. Croy enjoyed the forests of the Luften realm. Truly. He enjoyed not being worried about thirst or heat. There was always shade, there were always deer to hunt, berries to eat. Some of the best tasting berries, in Croy's opinion, were from the elder trees growing along the river.

It was not until they got closer to the Fluen realm that it began to get more muggy, more humid. The insects got bigger and the ground got softer. There was a particular evening, while they were still somewhere between the Luften and Fluen realms, that he complained about the closeness of the air.

"This is nothing. You have never really seen the depths of the Fluen realm, have you? We have mostly been on the coast of the Clatsvol Sea, or the cold reaches of the Eidyon Peninsula. Have you ever experienced a swamp?" Clerin was jovial, and her dimples punctuated her smile.

"No, never." He had heard the word before but had never been near one.

"Oh, you are missing out. Maybe we should try to find one on our way to the sea." Her eyebrows popped up briefly.

"What exactly is a swamp?" Trela entered the conversation.

"Imagine that a river slows and stops. It bleeds out in every direction. There are dry little hills, like tiny islands, but it is mostly just soggy soil. Grasses and plants that float on water cover the ground, with small misshapen trees dotted around. The ground is so wet and mucky that your feet get stuck in the thick mud. I have even lost a boot! And the humidity, it is like walking through a spray. And the swarms of bugs and flies. And the weird half-aquatic animals." Clerin looked like she could continue on like that forever but was interrupted by Trela.

"Nope. No thank you. Not ever. You can keep your swamp. I do not need to experience it." They all laughed.

It was a warm conversation full of camaraderie. It was like the random conversations Croy used to have with Knill and Tumu. He felt he needed more conversations like that. Easy, useless, and friendly.

Croy found himself flying over a river in a dream. There were trees to either side, but it was definitely the river he was following. He was flying against the current, upstream. Robed figures began to arrive, one by one, flying next to him. He recognized them, with their immobile cowls hiding their faces and their fluttering brown cloaks. As more and more arrived, he realized a giant waterfall was ahead of him. The source of the river. He was headed to the cliff face at breakneck speed, about halfway up the falls. He could not see behind the roaring cataract, but assumed there was a cave entrance somewhere back there. He had yet to ever splat against solid stone in a dream.

The water crushed down on him briefly, drenching him even though he was only in it for a moment. He slowed immensely after penetrating the cave. His robed and cloaked neighbors also appeared soggy. They all slowed, then stopped, in the roundish room. Croy was centered in the room. He wondered if he should start wringing out his clothes, but a chant started up. He had no time.

Gunzgak floated through the floor. Its gigantic stony face, as large as Croy, turned towards him. The body half filled the room, leaving a comfortable, but sparse, amount of space for Croy and the figures.

"I need to ask several things of you. Things I will be unable to fully explain. Will that be acceptable to you?" The derlianesque face regarded him intently.

"Of course. I will do whatever I am capable of."

"Good, good. I have set several things in motion and the timing will be crucial. I need you to get everyone to Johcal Island in one fortnight's time. Are you capable of that?"

"I… I certainly hope so. No one had been planning on going there. They will wonder why I am suggesting it."

"Tell Clerin that my name is hidden there. My full name. My summoning name. Tell them you know of a cave on the island." Gunzgak lifted a stony arm to fend off Croy's immediate protestations. "I will have another Gaen arrive at your party in a week. A mage. They will mention it. You must vouch for this Gaen. You must vouch for the cave. You must assist in all ways you are capable."

"Yes. Yes, I can do that."

"There is more. There is another name in that cave, not mine. You must find that name."

"Whose name is it?"

"It is Lembin's. I have worked tirelessly to find it. I do hope that it is not a mere legend, or not transcribed incorrectly. But that brings me to my other request. No, wait, not request—an edict. This edict is the most important of all. If I am unable to stop what is in motion, then I need to deflect one thing. Lembin must fall before I!"

The ground shook and rumbled. There was a thrumming in the air, a vibration that passed through Croy, bounced off the cave wall, and shot through him again. And again. It kept bouncing and flowing through him, bouncing and flowing. It lasted for too long, but eventually Gunzgak began to speak again.

"This edict should be your ultimate goal. You need to plant the seed in each and every one of your friends, your acquaintances, anyone within earshot. Do not call overt attention to it, but make sure everyone understands it. It is Lembin who wishes to die, that is what we have all been led to believe. Then it is only fair that it dies first."

"I understand." Croy was still shaken by the vibrations, by the intensity of Gunzgak. But it was certainly doable. There was nothing there that went against his character. He just needed to plant the seed. He just needed to keep himself easy, useless, and friendly. "I understand," he repeated.

"Good. Then go, champion. Awaken." The vibrations shook Croy into consciousness.

Croy did not typically take a long time to wake up and energize, but he woke feeling especially invigorated. He had his tent and bedroll fully packed on his horse, Buttercup, before breakfast. He ate alone and pondered. He felt could ignore the directive to Johcal Island for at least a couple of days, maybe the full week. He would certainly want to keep everyone moving on a good schedule, no allowance for shirking, but he did not think he had to do anything specific for that until the other Gaen showed up. Whoever that might be. No, it was the edict that Croy pondered. He thought long and hard about it. Who should he bring it up to first? Should he steer the conversation to that topic, or wait for an appropriate subject to organically sprout up? He actually thought he could just broach the subject with Clerin. If it worked with her, then it did not really matter what anyone else thought. Of course, what if the subject put her on guard? He was assisting with some of the early breakfast dishes, ruminating on it quietly to himself, when Feyazki arrived.

They chatted about nothing for a while. Feyazki helped with the dishes, using his hands to clean them like a mundane derlian. It was not until they were finished that Croy thought of something.

"In combat, who do you usually aim for first? Do you go for the most difficult opponent, the most powerful, or do you pick off the easy underlings, winnowing away the chaff?" He cringed slightly. It had sounded better in his head.

"Hmm. Interesting. Well, I guess it depends. Sometimes it is best to take care of the underlings, as you call them, first, so that no one can get behind you. But the problem is avoiding the blows from the powerful enemy while you are doing that. It takes time. I know if there is something truly horrific, like a Tlana, I will typically go for that first." He lowered his voice a little at the word "Tlana," but he had never shied away from using their name in conversation. "You cannot leave something like that unattended. They will destroy you and everything around you if you are not constantly distracting them."

That was not the answer that Croy had been hoping for. He had been hoping for the first part, to be able to argue that Gunzgak was the powerful target and should be held for last. But the second part—the second part made Croy angry with himself for bringing it up at all. A Tlana was powerful, but certainly not as powerful as a Beleg. He would have to attack the subject from another direction.

"Why do you ask?" Feyazki was smiling, drying the last dish. Croy had waited too long in silence.

"No real reason." Which, of course, was not a real answer. "I was just trying to think of priorities in general. What the best order to attack a problem is?"

"Ah, well that might be a little different. If I do not know how to start working on a problem, I will find the easiest corner to pick at, then move on from there. Getting started is half the battle for me, inertia can build up on itself pretty quickly." He laughed lightheartedly.

"Thanks, that is good advice." Croy felt he needed some more time alone to gather his arguments. It was not the beginnings of inertia, he told himself. It was just good preparation.

He spent the day traveling and enjoying other derlians' company. When asked if anyone needed a break, he argued for more travel time, more distance. But that was about it for assisting Gunzgak. He had hoped a big and powerful idea would come to him, but nothing did.

They stopped to camp at dusk. There was just enough light to easily set up camp and gather firewood. After eating, Croy found himself near Clerin and the others. Trela was usually around Clerin, and Knill had been trying to be near Trela, so it was easy for Croy to be around and not appear to be lurking.

"So, Clerin, when solving a problem, do you go for the most difficult part first, or start with the smaller issues." Feyazki brought it up with absolutely zero prodding. Croy could not believe his luck.

Feyazki had been a bit peripheral of late. Clerin was usually sitting near Vanelia, holding Hynara as much as possible, speaking of… queenly things. Or something. Which meant that he was often further out from the center when he was around. He was also with Ryshial and Serghno at times, engaged in a sort of tiny mages' guild. Croy had yet to attend one of those gatherings, even though he had been invited several times.

"Hmm. As a diplomat, I would say that I like to take care of the smaller issues first, keeping an eye on the bigger one. You do not want the smaller ones growing or merging." Clerin looked over Hynara's head to peer at Feyazki.

"As a warrior, I say go for the big one first." Trela spoke up before Clerin could continue. "You chop off the head and the body dies. Often, or at least half the time, when the leader dies the other warriors lose some of their intensity."

"And the other half of the time?" Knill laughed his question over to Trela.

"The other times the warriors get enraged and redouble their efforts to kill you." She smiled back over to him.

"So, that system works about half the time?"

"No, that's the beauty of it. When the young, inexperienced, leaderless warriors come charging passionately up the hill at you, that is when you spring your trap!" She clapped her hands together with glee. Hynara clapped along with her, most probably not following the conversation.

They all laughed for a bit. So, the group was all over the place for that particular question. That meant the question was the problem, in Croy's mind. It did not convey enough of what he was trying to steer.

"And you, Croy?" Trela shifted her gaze slightly from Knill over to him. "What do you think is the best method?"

"I think I agree with Clerin." He smiled over at her and she smiled back. "Yes, I think she has it right. You should soak up the little things first, leaving the big bad struggle for the end."

Whether or not the question needed to be reworked, he had to do his part to keep things moving in the right direction. Clerin gave him a small wink, then tipped her face back to Hynara. Was she sniffing the child's head? No matter, the wink was gratifying. It was a conspiratorial wink, a bridge of friendship. He only wished he had been able to wink back in time.

They made fantastic time over the week. Croy had not had to push *too* hard. They were all willing and capable travelers. When they had left Ariellyna, they had been concerned about being followed, being chased. Once that had faded, they did not replace their motivation. They were headed towards Vatlisi, sure, but what were they doing in the meantime? Where they merely traveling with Vanelia on her way into exile? Their actual quest, the best thing to get everyone energized, was not something that Croy wanted to bring attention to. He did not want to get them riled up about destroying all the Belegs. But they also had no way of knowing how to move forward with that quest. There is nothing worse than having a great obligation with nothing to aim for. It was kind of like trying to find a tiny entrance to a large cave. You could wander through the underbrush for days, years, trying to find something. But what if the entrance was sealed off? What if there was no entrance at all? No cave? They were trying to solve an impossible riddle, one that Croy did not want them to figure out. So, in that sense, his job was simple. The tricky part was to motivate without reminding them of their obligation. Of their quest. He did it through simple cajoling and helpfulness.

"Are we really stopping here? There's still light left."

"Race you to the next tree!"

"I don't feel hungry yet. We should probably reach the next rise before stopping for lunch."

"Do you need help with those dishes?" Or "…taking down your tent," or "…packing your horse?"

It was the little things, but just kept up over a span of time. He found that as long as he kept a smile on his face, even the grumpiest of warriors would follow uncomplainingly. No one wanted to feel like they were being the lazy one, the one holding the others back.

It was near the end of the day and they were traveling with a river called the Wyfrond presently in view, which was not always the case. It was a beautiful evening and Croy had been in good spirits all day. He thought he could see something in the distance, but was unable to tell what it was, when Escha came riding back to the main column. The sweat on her brow made it appear she had ridden back hard, but her face looked excited, not concerned. Her horse thundered to a halt at Trela. Escha always reported to Trela.

"There's a dock. And a boat. A big river boat, big enough to fit all of us." Escha nodded a little as her horse danced sideways slightly. "Due to the hour, I came back to you. If we ride hard, we could make it before sundown."

"Then let's ride hard." Trela grinned back at Escha, then stood in her stirrups and turned to yell behind her. "We pick up the pace tonight and rest on our backs tomorrow!"

Croy doubted that all behind her heard her, let alone understood her, but once the horses in the front started galloping, everyone did. It was almost a race. It must have looked like an attack to those on the boat. Croy wondered why a boat moored in the middle of nowhere would take passengers. Would they not be already full?

When they got there, however, the captain told a tale of dropping off a group of Fluens heading to some village. They would be back after a while, she said several weeks or so, for the return trip. Rather than heading home and coming back, she had decided to stay there and wait for their passengers. She could, of course, provide passage to the coterie for a fee. A reduced one at that since it would give her sailors something to do. It seemed too good to be true.

Then Croy realized what was happening. The captain gave quick introductions to her senior crew. Most were Fluens, like herself, but there was also a Gaen mage. He was short, even for a Gaen, and quite stout, making him somewhat roundish in appearance. He had brown hair and a long brown beard, sporting a braid down the center. He was quick with a smile and handshake for everyone. And just before he turned to leave, he gave Croy a conspiratorial wink. It was fast enough that Croy almost missed it, but its meaning was obvious. This was the Gaen that Gunzgak had sent. And generously enough, Gunzgak had sent an entire boat as well.

Croy was incredibly relieved that he had never met the mage before. He had grown concerned that the mage was going to be the

Blind One. He was not really sure why that had popped into his head, maybe just because there were so few Gaen mages, but it had been slowly building as they traveled into the Fluen realm. Just the thought of encountering the Blind One made Croy anxious.

The entire coterie set up camp adjacent to the boat. There was minimal contact with the crew that evening. The Gaen mage stayed aboard, but the captain came down to chat for a little bit. She brought a bottle of wine, which was not nearly enough, but it was a nice thought. Croy was not sure if she thought she was only going to be chatting with Clerin or Trela, but there was about eight of them around the campfire.

The captain was tall and blonde, with blue eyes that did not compare to Clerin's. Her hair was kept in a wide, loose braid at the back, with wisps of loose hairs floating around her face. She had on a white shirt, a leather vest, doeskin breeches, and some tall black leather boots. It seemed a bit like an ensemble, rather than just working clothes, but everything seemed well-worn and supple.

They talked about nothing for a while, complimenting the one sip of wine, commenting on the weather. Croy could talk about herding and crops for hours, but he did not have a lot to contribute to any seafaring conversations. He was barely paying attention until Clerin asked if the captain's outfit was based in Tureyn.

"No, we are based out on Johcal Island, though we often sail to Tureyn and sometimes even Vatlisi. We currently have our sea-worthy boat moored at Haliwell, where the river meets the sea. She's called Yifindur. We typically ferry passengers back and forth from the island to various towns and villages in good old reliable Yifindur. Sometimes we come up a river if we are paid for the trouble. But, of course, that requires a different vessel…" The captain trailed off and looked at the large riverboat that was outlined in the darkness. She did not provide its name. "So we have little satellite locations in some towns that surround the Clatsvol. Haliwell is not gigantic, but she is big enough to gain a lot of river traffic. It's mostly commerce up the river, but sometimes we load up passengers."

"And why would passengers want to come up the river this far?" Trela asked the question like she was joking, but she was certainly listening intently.

"Who knows? A good captain does not inquire as to *why* anyone wants to go anywhere, they just need to know the where." She paused again and a tiny smile crossed her lips. "Well, maybe not 'good captain,' but a smart captain. A captain who enjoys repeat customers."

"That is a smart policy, one that can be appreciated." Trela smiled back.

"How do you get the riverboat upstream? Donkeys?" Clerin changed the subject, slightly abruptly.

"No, no, though that is used sometimes. In fact, we have areas in our hold that your horses would fit since we are not using animals." The captain turned to Clerin. "No, we use mages when we can."

"Ah, yes, I think one of your mages is Gaen, if I am not mistaken. He mentioned that during our brief introduction." Feyazki interjected himself into the conversation. "That is certainly a rare bird, a Gaen mage. It would seem easier to find a Fluen one."

"I do not question how rare my employees are. Altinger Fyr'jin is a fantastic mage, knows his job, performs well, is cost effective and, most importantly, he gets along with everyone. I do not care that he is a Gaen and, frankly, neither should you." She narrowed her eyes at him a little. "Or would that be an issue for you?"

"Me? Oh, no, not at all. We have a Gaen mage with us as a matter of fact." Feyazki nodded to Croy.

The captain slowly turned to look at Croy. She had an odd half-smile on her face. It was impossible to tell what she was thinking, but she knew more than he had originally thought she would. Her smile seemed to indicate she was on Gunzgak's side of the argument and knew all about their mission—but was that true? How could he know without tipping his own hand? He would have to wait until he had spoken with Altinger. Though he was not sure how much, if any, time he should spend with Altinger. *No one could be allowed to get suspicious about this,* Croy thought. *That would end in the death of trust. At best.*

"It is just such a rare occurrence, especially here on this side of the Fluen realm. There is no judgement here, I am sure we will all get along great." Feyazki looked nervous at being called out for something he had not intended, so Croy decided to intervene.

"Feyazki has been teaching me some tricks. A mentor away from mentors, I suppose." Croy was going to continue, though he was not really sure where he was headed, but the captain interrupted him.

"Good, great. I am glad that is all settled. And who will be negotiating price?" The captain looked between Clerin and Trela. "I could show you around the boat tonight, or if preferred, we can speak tomorrow. I am not sure how exhausted you are from your travels. You certainly came in galloping."

"Yes, tomorrow would be great. I am sure we can come to an agreeable price." Trela nodded to the captain.

The captain looked a little disappointed, though Croy was not sure why. The looked faded immediately into a bright smile, making him wonder whether he had imagined it. She nodded to groups of them, right, left, then center.

"A pleasant night's sleep to you all. We will be at your service." Then she strode off into the dark, not looking back.

The next day was full of excitement. The air was abuzz. The sailors helped load everyone's belongings, including the horses. It happened fairly quickly. Croy was not involved in the price negotiations, but he was sure they got a good deal.

Croy was a little nervous about the boat. The river seemed very calm and quite wide where they were. More than that, it did not seem like there could be the rolling waves that were the bane of his existence when they crossed the Clatsvol to the Eidyon Peninsula. He was nervous, but hopeful.

The day started with no nausea. He did cast small healing spells on himself, just in case, but the ride was gratefully smooth.

Feyazki came and found him on the deck. He was near the prow. It helped him to face the motion and to see where they were headed. He had not expected to see Feyazki. He had assumed he would be with Clerin.

"How are you feeling?" Feyazki leaned on a rail. His tone was light and conversational.

"Good so far. Thanks for your concern." Croy smiled and nodded. The smile was a real one, not something forced.

"Good, good." His head nodded, maybe unconsciously. It was quiet for a while. They were both staring forwards, watching the peaceful scenery pass. "A Gaen mage on a Fluen ship near the Luften border. Crazy, huh?"

For a split second, Croy thought Feyazki was talking about him. He quickly realized what it was, however. Feyazki could not get over the odds. The probability was bothering him. He was looking for something.

"For a moment I thought you were talking about me. Ha!" Croy smiled even wider. "It does seem rare, but stranger things have happened."

"Yeah, I suppose." He stood straighter. "There is just something about it. I am unable to put my finger on it, but something feels odd."

"How about we go check? The quickest way for you to feel comfortable is to talk with him. We're both Gaen mages, it would seem weird if we didn't chat. Right?" Croy had to put his faith in Gunzgak's choice. Either Feyazki would be suspicious forever, or Altinger would assuage his concerns. Letting it fester was certainly not going to help.

"That's a great idea, Croy. Thanks!" He slapped Croy on the back jovially.

They set off immediately to find Altinger, but there were only so many crew members on the deck, while almost all the passengers were up there. Finally, Croy walked up to the captain to ask.

"We are wondering where Altinger is? I'm a Gaen mage and think it would be great to chat about our realm and get to know each other. Is he below deck somewhere? We don't want to make anyone uncomfortable just wandering around uninvited." He grinned at her, trying to make her feel comfortable.

"Croy, right?" She extended her hand for a shake. "Nice to meet you. Last night was so quick and informal it doesn't really count. And… could you remind me of your name?" She shifted her hand over to Feyazki once Croy had finished shaking it.

"Feyazki."

"Nice to meet you as well." When she pulled her hand back it ended back at her resting posture, arms across her chest. "I will go see if Altinger is awake. He was up last night with our navigator." She nodded, turned, and strode off, disappearing down some stairs in little time.

They stood around above deck for a little bit. It probably did not take long, but it felt long due to the waiting. Croy thought it was odd how waiting seemed to dilate time. Typically, he would be chatting with Feyazki about something concerning magic or spells, or maybe something small and innocuous, but they both just stood there silently staring at the stairs that the captain had used. Waiting.

Eventually the captain returned. Her hair bounced slightly with her stride. She smiled at them, maybe because they were standing in the same spot, maybe not.

"He will be up shortly." She then motioned to the side.

Croy and Feyazki quietly wandered off to the area she indicated, stopping only at the railing. Croy put his arms on the railing and glanced at the scenery sliding by at a decent clip. Feyazki turned his back to the railing, leaning on it and resting his elbows atop it. His fingers hung lazily.

"What do you think she told him?" Feyazki spoke up when they were "alone" at the edge of the boat.

"Uhm, that some passengers wanted to speak with him?" Croy did not want Feyazki being paranoid from the beginning.

"I doubt that would take that long. She was down there forever."

"I think it just felt like a long time."

"And what is taking him so long now?"

"Maybe he was asleep? We don't know."

Just then, mercifully, Altinger came up the ladder and walked over. The clop of his boots and Feyazki's silence confirmed it. Croy turned to make visual contact.

"Welcome! I am Altinger Fyr'jin and I hear you have need of my services. Who might you be?" He crossed his arms over his chest and kept his legs shoulder width apart. His sudden speech made Croy think he was going to thump his chest as Croy had seen some of the 'jin in Serif do. But he did not.

"I am Croy Sie'tin." It was all he could get out.

"No! That is impossible, I do not believe it." Everything he spoke seemed to come from deep within him, like someone used to yelling commands, or maybe a singer. "You are a great mage, are you not? How can you be called the lowliest of farmers?"

"Well, it is more that I have not returned to the Gaen realm and worked or applied through a guild. I've been… away." He waved his hand ineffectually. "I was thinking about petitioning for Beo'rem."

"Ah, a healer. That is noble. You should be proud." He nodded sharply to Croy, then turned to Feyazki. "And who are you?

What is your specialty? Probably not healing, I assume. You do not strike me as a healer."

"I am Feyazki. And though I can certainly cast healing spells, I am no healer. I fight when I must."

"Ah, yes. Fighting. That is why most mages in the Gaen realm are under the 'jin. But fighting sounds a bit neutral, does it not? You do not merely defend, do you? You attack! Yes."

"When I need to."

"There is always the need to attack somewhere. Always." Altinger looked odd belting out words while his arms stayed stationary across his wide chest. When he breathed in for another sentence, it was only his even wider belly that moved. "Which means also that there is always the need for the noble healer."

"Yes, we are both very necessary indeed. You, yourself, are 'jin, are you not?" Feyazki smiled and nodded. "I wonder why you are so far away from your realm. Just what are *you* fighting?"

"You have been very clever for such a long time, haven't you? You forget what it is like to just enjoy a conversation." Altinger's right eyebrow shot upwards. "Us Gaens have no mages' guild, you should know that. I am 'jin because I am not 'rem. It is that simple. You are correct about one thing though. I am a long way from home. And though I am not here to fight anything, I am here seeking something. Something that is only located amongst the Fluens."

"And what is that?" Feyazki's own eyebrow shot up in response.

"Wouldn't you like to know?"

"Yes. Very much."

"Maybe I do not trust one as clever as you. Maybe I prefer my company to be simple and nice, unclouded by subterfuge."

"I apologize for the 'jin comment. Truly. I only wished to… I was curious as to why a Gaen is on the Luften side of the Fluen realm is all. It is intriguing and something I could not pass by." Feyazki nodded slow and deep. It was almost a shallow bow.

"And how do you take this Luften? Is he trustworthy?" Altinger turned his head to Croy.

"He can certainly be obnoxious, yes. But I trust him with my life. In fact, I probably owe him my life." Croy nodded.

"And you have saved mine at least as many times."

"Okay, okay, save it." Altinger looked between them almost furtively, as if he really did have a secret. "How would the two of you like to have some genuine beer with me in my cabin tonight? Maybe we can each figure out why there's a Gaen mage on the Luften side of the Fluen realm."

"That sounds great."

As Altinger walked away, Croy released a breath he had not realized he had been holding. It was not until the meeting was arranged between the three of them that he could put the nervous thought into words. He had been concerned that Altinger wanted to speak with him alone before speaking with the group—that would have been the definition of a conspiracy looked at in the wrong light. He had accidently dodged an arrow he had not been consciously aware of. The feeling of relief was delicious.

"Thanks for vouching for me, Croy. There is something wrong with this Altinger fellow, I can feel it. We will have to ferret it out this evening, you and I."

"Of course. You can always count on me."

In the late afternoon, or maybe it was early evening, they were to have the oddest banquet Croy had participated in. The captain wanted to get to know everyone, but there was not near enough room in any one particular quarters, not even the galley. So they set up multiple tables on the deck, almost covering the entirety of it. All of the coterie was there, and much of the crew. There were some sailors required to keep the ship on course, some were asleep down below, and some were cooking the meal, but the rest were seated along with everyone else.

"We should be reaching the sea in two-and-a-half days, which means we will only have three dinners together. Unless, of course, you need a quick ride across the Clatsvol as well. So, I wanted this dinner, our first, to be one of consequence, one of enjoyment. I wanted to bring us all together to make some new friends on this journey. You are our guests." The captain raised her glass. "Even if you did pay for the privilege."

There was laughter all around. Most of the coterie, and all the crew, drank from their wine goblets at the toast, such as it was. That was followed by the sounds of eating and quiet conversation, as those next to strangers got to know each other, and old friends traded older jokes. It was a pleasant meal.

At the end of it, some lingered at the table and others got back to work. Croy, Feyazki, and Altinger all went below deck to chat. And hopefully to have a little beer.

Once they got down there, Croy realized why there were only three of them. Altinger's quarters were quite small. There was still some room on the bunk, but both Croy and Feyazki sat on the large rectangular chest that took up most of the rest of the room. There was a small jug that Altinger had removed from the chest before they sat. There was some stale and headless beer in there which Croy still tried. He did not drink much, but Feyazki passed without even trying it.

"Can I trust you?" Altinger took a deep swig from the jug. "Can you keep a secret?"

"Ooh, I like that beginning. Straight to the chase." Feyazki laughed a little but got serious quickly. "It depends, really. You can trust me if you tell me something that does not endanger my friends. But for an absurd example, if you say that someone is getting murdered in their sleep tonight, I'm sorry, but I am going to mention that to the others."

"And you, Croy?" Altinger shifted his gaze slightly. "Are you of a similar vein?"

"Yes, I believe so. I can be trusted until I feel threatened."

"But truly threatened, yes? Not just worried or concerned?"

"Yes. I am worried and concerned most of the time. That would not leave me very trustworthy."

"Ha! Yes, good. Well, I can assure you that no one is planning a murder tonight on this boat." Altinger smiled, paused, then took a deep breath. "I am in search of a cave. A special cave. The Fluens have certain habits that the other races never took up. One of these habits is carving the names of Yavens in caves." He took another breath. "Legend has it that they carved names of more than the Yavens. Legend has it that there are Beleg names inscribed in some of those caves."

"And which name are you searching for?" Feyazki had an intense look on his face.

"From what I understand, there are only two left. I seek both of their names; one should always be prepared. For in the times ahead of us, they may both be required."

"Yes!" Feyazki almost barked it out. "That… is… fantastic." His smile got bigger with each word. "I tell you right now that I personally, and probably many of our group, would like to help you with your search. As you say, one should always be prepared. Where is this cave you seek? Or is that part of the problem?"

"Partly. I know that it is on Johcal Island. That is the whole reason I have joined up with the captain. The whole reason I am here, working for little pay, hauling a boat up a river when required. A waste of my talents, I assure you. But a small price to pay. I have been doing steady research each time we debark on the island. I think I have the location narrowed down to just a couple of possible locations."

"Then I have to say that we are going to have to break your trust."

"What?!"

"We will all want to help you, every one of our group. I guarantee that once they hear about your quest, it will be taken up as our own." Feyazki smiled. "Which just means that I have to tell them."

"But you will not tell the captain, right? Or the crew? You must remain silent until we have disembarked." Altinger glared a little at Feyazki. "At least silent to them."

"Yes. Sure." Feyazki thought for a moment. "We will only speak with a few of our friends. We must at least get the captain to take us all the way to the island, not just Haliwell. We will need to speak with Clerin and Trela about this for that to happen."

"Good. The less who know, the better. Once we are on the island, we can start looking at the caves. There are only three possibilities left. They are, unfortunately, the largest cave systems on the island. I have already checked the smaller possibilities."

"How long have you been at this?" Croy was truly curious. The rest of the crew could at least corroborate how long he had been working with them.

"Two moons." Altinger gave a tiny bow from his waist. It looked odd from such a rotund Gaen sitting on a bunk.

"Wow, that long?" Croy was a bit shocked. When Gunzgak had contacted him a little over a week ago, he had assumed it was bringing friends over immediately. Not that it already had friends in the area. He wondered… Was it two moons since the Luften Temple exploded?

"And what if there are no names etched? What if it is just unfounded legend? Just rumors?" Feyazki spoke back up.

"Then you take a week or so to go through a couple of caves. You've surely spent more time performing more mundane tasks, have you not?"

Feyazki nodded to himself, then to Altinger. Then, oddly, he turned to Croy. "Agreed?"

"Yes, agreed." He then nodded to Altinger and Feyazki. He had not been expecting to have been brought into the decision. Not that there was much of a decision. He wondered briefly what would have happened if he had said "no." Would Feyazki have honored that? Would Altinger have?

"Excellent. Then we have a deal. I cannot believe someone is willing to help me with my quest. An entire group of someones. This is my lucky day indeed." He paused again, glancing between Croy and Feyazki. "I do not wish to sound ungrateful, truly. And I do not wish to jinx my fantastic luck. But I just have to know… Why would you help me? Why would you want to know the names of Belegs?"

There was a long pause. Croy was unsure of how to put it, and besides, he had been letting Feyazki talk them into the quest. Croy was certainly not going to answer.

"We are interested for the same reason that you are. There is a dangerous game afoot, and knowledge is power." He looked sideways at Altinger. "How many derlians do you think know that two of the Belegs are dead?"

"Well. At least three of us." Altinger laughed. "Not many, in truth. Which is why it is so lucky that we have found each other."

"Luck, yes. Unimaginably lucky." Feyazki sounded odd. But then, suddenly, his face broke into a large grin. "And who wishes to jinx such luck?" He sounded jovial. "We shall keep your secret from the crew. We shall go to Johcal Island. We shall search your caves. And who knows? Maybe we will all find what we are looking for."

Feyazki's laugh seemed sincere. Then again, so did Altinger's. Croy was the only one whose laugh sounded odd to him. It was weird, all three of them laughing. He could not tell if they were laughing at themselves or at each other. He supposed it did not really matter. All that really mattered was that a plan was in motion. Gunzgak's plan, by the sounds of it. He should have been happy.

✳✳✳

When Feyazki told the others about it, the close-knit privy council, they were certainly happy. They were cramped into Trela's quarters, which were only slightly smaller than Clerin's. They all sat around congratulating each other, which slightly confused Croy. Until he realized what it was really about. They had not really had a plan. They had no idea how to trap Gunzgak—apparently trying to find its name had not really occurred to them. Or, maybe, they had just no idea where to start, where to look for the name of a Beleg. Either way, the only reason they were even in the Fluen realm was to get Vanelia to Vatlisi. Everything else was a hope that destiny gave them a nudge. And here it was. Croy was certainly not going to be the one to let them know it was not destiny that was nudging them, but Gunzgak itself.

"That's great news."

"Fantastic!"

"I knew we were headed in the right direction."

And so on. It was not until the discussion started focusing on what to do if only one name was found that Croy started paying attention again.

"What if we find Gunzgak right away, do we leave?" Clerin posed the question. "Do we really need Lembin's name?"

"Well, we should try to find both, don't you think? When will we have another opportunity?" Trela, ever practical, gave her response.

"For how long do we search? Do we even know if both names are down there? What if we do not find anything?" Serghno added his worries.

"Well, what else are we doing?" Feyazki laughed. Maybe a bit too loud. "No, really, Altinger spoke as if the caves were not overly large. There are only three. Even if each cave takes us a couple of days, we are out a week, two weeks tops. I say we take our time and be as thorough as possible. As Trela noted, we may never get another opportunity. In any event, I would certainly hate to have to come back to the island after we have left. That would be frustrating."

"I agree with Feyazki. This is a great opportunity and should not be squandered. We should search each cave as thoroughly as possible." Croy wanted to solidify the thinking before any arguments could chip away at it. He was fairly positive that Gunzgak's name would not be in any of the caves, certainly not the ones that Altinger would take them through.

"And will Vanelia accept the delay?" Clerin glanced around the room. "What if Chiavel truly is tracking her?"

Croy had not even realized Vanelia was not with them. And that Clerin was not holding Hynara. It was obvious as he glanced around the tiny room that only held a few derlians, but he had not noticed until it was pointed out to him.

"She will be fine. Trust me." Trela was nodding to herself in that way she does when she has made up her mind about something. "If Chiavel were truly out for revenge, he would have attacked earlier. Closer to the Luften realm, or even better, before we had even left. If he is planning anything this far out, he would have had to have enlisted Altinger already. And if Chiavel has already gotten a Gaen mage to ambush Vanelia, we might be outmatched as it is."

"And that brings us to that." Clerin looked around with wide eyes. Nobody followed up her line of thought. "What if Altinger is planning an ambush? Not for Vanelia, obviously, but for us? Why do we trust him at all?"

"Because we have no choice." Trela hardened her eyes at Clerin. "We need a breakthrough, and we will have to take this chance. If it is not destiny assisting us, but an ambush being planned, we will just have to be on guard. We cannot let this opportunity pass us by. I wish I had something more soothing to say."

That idea had not crossed Croy's mind. He knew Gunzgak had wanted Clerin dead originally, but had thought it had given up on the idea. Trela saying the words aloud—well, actually, Clerin voicing her fears—made Croy rethink what Gunzgak was up to. What if it was a ruse? What if there was no name in any of the caves? What if it really was an ambush? What would Croy do? Would he stand by and watch it unfold, or would he reflexively protect his friends? Gunzgak may only wish Clerin dead, but how could that occur without killing Feyazki? Trela would certainly defend Clerin to the death, could he watch her die as well? Or Knill? Or, and Croy was unsure of why he suddenly thought of it, but what if it was simpler to just kill all of them? What if Gunzgak was unconcerned about his own demise? The thought wormed its way further into his brain.

Why would Gunzgak be concerned about his demise? He shook his head to clear it. Then he realized everyone was staring at him.

"Yes, we will just have to be on guard." He had no idea how long he had been quiet for, how long they had been staring at him. No one seemed fazed by it, however. "This is too great of an opportunity, only made more great because it is our only option." They all nodded in response.

Others were told of what they now referred to as "the opportunity." Everyone seemed excited even though about half of the coterie figured it was a trap. It was an odd mixture of emotions. They were discussing it so often that Croy was a little worried that word would get around to the crew that Altinger was going to quit once they reached Johcal Island. But no one seemed to notice. He wondered if that was purely due to the discretion of the coterie, or if the crew was mostly ignoring them.

It only took another two days down the river. The Wyfrond river was wide, with a placid surface even though the water was moving fairly swiftly. It was such a pleasant float for Croy that he decided to rethink his hatred of boats. At least on rivers. He was not looking forwards to the voyage after Haliwell, once they reached the sea.

The captain had readily agreed to take them to the island. Croy was not sure of the prices for any of the trips, but Trela did not seem to balk so he assumed they were low rates. The captain fed them and provided some wine during the evening meals as well, so they were not just purchasing the travel.

Haliwell itself was quite cozy. It was not tiny by any stretch of the imagination, but it was nowhere near the size of Tureyn or Vatlisi. It was a comfortable size and had some Luftens amongst the Fluen citizens. He did not notice any Pyrans and felt fairly sure there were only a couple of Gaens beyond those they brought with them. Of course, they only stayed a day and he did not even visit the market, so the town could have been more cosmopolitan than he thought.

There was no outer wall to the town, not with the giant iron gates of Tureyn nor the gleaming white stone of Vatlisi. It was open to all and sprawled about, full of single-story wooden homes and businesses. The Wyfrond deltaed out, leaving tiny islands and bridges everywhere, even though the town was mostly on the west side of the river. Croy wondered what happened when the river flooded.

They had the evening to do with as they pleased. Croy wanted to wander, but they were told to stay close. Even though the entire coterie crowded the inn's common room, he ended up grouped with the Gaen warriors, Verin and Silvadhin, and Altinger joined them. Altinger was from Hifrim and everyone else was from Serif, but they all seemed to enjoy each other's company. Well, it was sometimes difficult for Croy to figure out who Verin enjoyed, she seemed to always get along with everyone, but at the same time, did not really pal around with anyone. She just always seemed so serious. Silvadhin, however, seemed to enjoy chatting with Altinger very much. Which meant that one, he was unable to get much intriguing information from Altinger and two, he ended up talking with Verin most of the time. He would probably enjoy her company more if she did not remind him of the Blind One. Not that she acted like him, not in the least, but Croy had first met her during that initial investigation—searching through the burnt-out Pyran caravan where he had found Trela—before he became the Blind One's apprentice. Before he had been imprisoned.

They had chatted about their time together, the coterie, traveling from Vatlisi to Agoge and now headed back. She seemed quite pleased she had seen that much of the world, especially Ariellyna. She had never thought she would see the Luften realm, to sleep high up in the helioarcs. He had never thought he would either. He had never thought he would even leave Serif. And yet, there they were. It was not until later in the evening that their conversation extended beyond the typical campaign talk. And it was Verin who brought it up.

"Seems weird that we are now attempting to kill Gunzgak, no?" Her voice was held low, and she leaned her head in slightly to speak directly to Croy. He was a little shocked. She was a loyal warrior through and through. He had assumed she would just follow where Trela led, even if Trela was a Pyran. "I mean, destroying the Cabal of Lochom, that was honorable business. That was something to be proud of, helping the Yavens, helping the Belegs. But this? I don't know."

"I agree completely. I have even said the same to Trela and Feyazki. I have even tried to talk Clerin out of it." He spoke softly as well. It did not appear that Silvadhin was paying attention and

Altinger was fully ignoring them, though it was difficult to tell if that was purposeful.

"Yes, most know of your complaints. Though I was not really sure how thoroughly you have pursued this." She nodded almost imperceptibly. "Who is the greatest sticking point?"

"That is a little difficult." He paused and thought for a moment. "Reflexively I was going to say Clerin, since it is her quest. But really, I found Trela worrisome. She is convinced that since Gorbanax is dying, then Gunzgak should die as well. And as you know, once she gets something in her head, there is no stopping her."

"Typically, I would say that is what I admire about her. I can see that as an issue, however. I had hoped she was still on the fence concerning this. I assume that as long as Clerin is pushing for this, then Feyazki is undeterrable?"

"Yes. Exactly. Which is why I ended up talking directly to Clerin. I had gotten it into my head that she would be the easiest to convince to give up this madness." He shook his head, a bit despairingly. "She could not be swayed, however. At least not by me."

"Well, anything beyond what you have already tried is certainly not something to be discussed freely. And neither are my dreams. I have been having some strange dreams lately, Croy. Insistent dreams." She glanced quickly at the other Gaens, who continued to chat contentedly amongst themselves. "Just know that I am on your side. You let me know if you think of something and I will do the same."

Verin suddenly downed the last of her wine in an overt gesture. She placed the glass down a little heavily and let out a small, "Ahhh," at the same time. She scooched her chair back and nodded to Croy, then to Silvadhin and Altinger.

"That's it for me, I'm afraid. I should rest up for the sea voyage."

Rather than stay and try to worm his way into whatever conversation the others were currently involved in, he decided to leave as well. He hoped he would not get as seasick as he had previously. But that was what it was: hope. He knew he should get as much good rest as possible. So, he too finished his wine and loudly set himself off. He felt much better about his situation than he did that morning.

✳✳✳

The sea was much crueler than the mostly placid river. Croy cast spells on himself before boarding and then again after boarding, while the boat was sitting fairly still at the dock. But he could see the sea rolling towards them, infinitely. The waves lapped against the boat, the dock, the rocky shoreline. Even just hearing the rhythmic splash bothered him. He decided to grab a bucket and find his quarters.

It took a while before they cast off. Croy did not like the anticipation, but he knew he would like the motion less. Once the ship started moving, Feyazki came down to cast a healing spell on him. It helped. He cast another on himself, and that helped as well. But he did not think it would work forever, as it had not previously. They chatted for a while, but Croy could tell Feyazki would be getting bored eventually. Or at least, that was what he thought. He let Feyazki off the hook by saying he wanted to rest.

Croy sat in his bunk, trying to sway with the boat, which was oddly better than lying down. Then there was a knock on the door. It was quiet, not obtrusive, but a little insistent.

"Come in." He hoped he sounded more enthused than he felt.

"Hello there. I hear that the sea does not agree with you." It was Altinger.

"Yes. Nor I her."

"Good, good. That fighting spirit is necessary in today's times." He laughed for a moment. He had a softly deep laugh. It was less full of mirth than of happiness.

"If you are going to cast healing spells, I must warn you that they do not work for very long." He held up his hand. "Not that they're not appreciated."

"No, no, I did not come here for that. Besides, that is just treating the symptom, not the problem." He sat down opposite of Croy. "I would like to chat with you for a little bit. Completely alone. I figure since everyone knows you will be hurling into a bucket for the next couple of days, it is the perfect time. But first, we shall make your life less miserable. How does that sound?"

"Umm. Sounds great."

"You see, the healing has a difficult task since you are constantly wounding yourself again. We need you to be able to not be motion sick for long enough that the healing can work." He nodded as if he was making sense.

"Yes, sounds great."

"Good." He clapped his hands together, almost gleefully. "I will start with the levitation spell. Narkinderarc!"

Croy felt himself lift from the bunk. His body stayed perfectly still above the bunk while the room swayed around him. He grinned and closed his eyes.

"I'm not sure if I can watch the room while floating, but this feels a little better already." He took in a deep breath. "Narliderpri!" The queasiness poured out of him like wine from a goblet. It was fantastic, he actually felt good.

"That is good, Croy. Keep your eyes closed for as long as you need. We will work up to that later." Altinger's voice was soothing. Croy felt quite comfortable.

It was quiet for some time aside from sounds of paper rustling. Croy just enjoyed feeling good. He did not concern himself with what Altinger might be doing out of sight.

"I am providing you with some maps, Croy. In case anything happens to me, I need you to promise that all three caves will be searched. They need to be searched at least as far as I have drawn. Each of them. I may not have everything written down. You are free to search as much of the caves as you like. You can do the caves in any order, at any time. I am not hiding anything. All I ask is that you do the minimum. In there, somewhere, you will find what you seek." The paper sound continued as Altinger straightened them on a desk or shelf.

"Will we find all that we seek?" Croy felt himself smile a little. Just a twitch.

"I cannot vouch for every bit of information, no. But you will find what you are supposed to find, certainly. I trust that will be sufficient?"

"Yes, of course. Honestly, I had expected no more. I was a little shocked at the idea of finding both names."

"There are many names down there. I cannot say that the other is not somewhere. But, of course, I cannot say a lot of things." Altinger cleared his throat a little. "I hate to be a stickler for this, but I must. Do I have your promise? Will you ensure that all the caves are searched?"

"Yes. Of course. You have my promise." Croy paused for a moment, wondering if he should ask. He decided he had nothing to lose by it. "But why, may I ask, are you concerned that something might happen to you? You are surrounded by friends, and together, we make a formidable team."

"Yes. I am surrounded by your friends. And you certainly make a formidable team."

"But we are working together here. Even if only one name is found, there is no animosity. We are not at odds. You have nothing to fear."

"Then call me paranoid. You have my maps and I have your promise. That is all I need. I will help you with your seasickness periodically but will also have the Luften mage look after you. We should not be seen as spending an inordinate amount of time together."

"Of course. You are correct." Croy took in a deep satisfying breath, one without any nausea. "And thank you for the levitating trick. Truly. I had not thought of that previously. You have my undying gratitude."

"Oh, that. You are welcome, but it is truly the least I can do. We are nearing the final contest and we are sorely outnumbered. It is gratifying to know of your existence, Croy. You give me hope."

Chapter 16

They were on the ship Yifindur on their way to Johcal Island and Clerin was ecstatic. She loved the sea even though she was raised on a river. The smell of it invigorated her. The fish they had for their meals was as fresh as could be. She even enjoyed the rolling waves that shimmied the ship around. She almost felt bad about that last one, knowing what Croy was going through, but she was too happy to feel too bad. In fact, the only thing she wished was different was that the trip to the island was too short. They were there in just a couple of days.

Clerin had not spent much time with the captain, or even any of the crewmembers. It was a bit odd as she was typically quite gregarious, especially with other Fluens. Nor did she spend time with Altinger, going over the plan to find Gunzgak's and Lembin's names. No, she spent most of her time with Vrric, Trela, and the other members of the coterie. Part of it was that she did not want to call attention to Altinger's secret or accidentally give anything away. She was not positive what the other part was.

They disembarked at Umrhebo, the main town on Johcal Island and the closest to the mainland. It was certainly larger than Slasskord, located on the south side of the island, nearest to the Eidyon Peninsula. Clerin had never been to the island before, either side of it. It had always seemed so exotic when talked about during her youth. That made the idea of exploring Umrhebo exciting. Unfortunately, they would probably not stay long in the town. Maybe it could be explored after they found the names?

They had arrived late in the afternoon, almost in the evening, so they would be able to at least explore a tavern or two. By the time they were all settled at the inn, it was getting dark. They decided to find a tavern away from the inn, just to see more of the town. It was a large group, with the captain and many of the sailors with them. It was there, after only one glass of wine, that Altinger decided to announce his decision to leave the ship behind. Though he stated he could work for them again later, the captain still took the news a little hard. She had, apparently, been counting on him on their return trip, or else she would not have agreed to the additional excursion to the island. And she told him as much. The tavern was quiet for a while, all conversations held in hush tones as the group finished their second glasses. Even the locals seemed subdued. The captain and rest of the sailors left soon after, leaving even more silence behind for another couple of minutes. Then, once the tension had dissipated, the noise crept back up to typical tavern levels.

Altinger did not want to talk in front of the strangers, so even though most of the coterie knew of the plan, it was not to be fully discussed that night. They all knew there was something on the island, that they had come there for a reason. But for the moment, they were only there to enjoy themselves.

Clerin certainly enjoyed herself, but not too much. She did not want to start their exploration of the island while nursing a hangover. Trela did, however, let them all sleep in the next morning. She had apparently been discussing the maps with Altinger—if not that night, then previously. One of the caves was close to Umrhebo.

Trela and some of the others bought provisions while the rest of them packed up. They did not leave the town until noon, but they reached the entrance to the cave by nightfall. Everyone agreed that sleeping outside of the cave that night and entering early the next morning would be the best course of action. Clerin felt a little nervous, though she was not sure why. It took her some time to fall asleep even though she was tired. And when sleep finally did come, it came fitfully. She woke several times during the night, sometimes due to a noise, other times due to a dream she could not recall. Dawn came early for Clerin.

Breakfast was slow and pleasant. Trela did not bang any pots to waken anyone, but let the sun and surrounding conversation bring them all from their tents. The morning was quite chilly, creating little puffs of frost every time she exhaled. Once everyone was fed, Altinger spoke to them all.

"I understand that some of you have seen the great caves of the Eidyon Peninsula, where the names of Yavens are carved. Well, these are similar. Except that, supposedly, there are the names of the Belegs somewhere on the island." By then, everyone had been told why they were there, but there were still some appreciative responses. "I have been looking through many of the smaller caves while between jobs. But honestly, I have been afraid to tackle these last three by myself. They are, by far, the largest of the cave systems. The most treacherous to trek. The easiest to get lost in. From conversations with your mages—" Altinger nodded towards Feyazki "—we have narrowed down our exploration to two names. We are looking for Gunzgak and Lembin. Their full names. Their summoning names. We can only hope that the legends have not led us astray."

Clerin was amazed at how quickly Altinger absorbed their group. He said "we" constantly as if he were Trela. He made his quest theirs without any argument. It was an amazing stroke of luck that they ran into him. She could excuse some of his possessive language for that reason alone. She did her best to hold back a yawn. She was still tired from being unable to sleep well the previous night.

Trela, not to be outdone, stood up for her own speech. "We will stick together down there. I understand the desire to move through this stage of our quest quickly, the desire to comb through the caves as fast as possible. To split up and cover more ground. But that would not be prudent."

As Trela spoke, Clerin watched Altinger. A cloud appeared to pass over his countenance. A dark storm cloud. But then, as quickly as is appeared, it dissolved. It made her wonder if she had imagined it.

"We cannot afford to miss something. We cannot afford to come back. If, after the end of all these caves, if nothing is found, we cannot afford to second guess ourselves. We must be positive of our efforts, of our thoroughness. We will crawl through the caves if we have to. We will make every one of our group read every name if we have to. We will leave nothing to chance." Trela's feral yellow eyes narrowed quickly at Altinger, but then glanced around the group, happy and bright and vibrant.

Clein wondered if Trela and Altinger had already argued about this. It was such an odd but fleeting exchange. In any case, it was rare that anyone won an argument with Trela. She almost felt sorry for Altinger; she could imagine the logic of his side, if that was how the argument had played out. If there was an argument at all. But she did not really have time to think about it. Suddenly everyone was bustling about, breaking camp and preparing for the caves. The entire thought slid from her mind during the burst of activity.

A Luften contingent including Vanelia and Hynara, Torpalin, his sister, and Escha, all stayed up above with the horses and equipment. They were joined by Serghno and Arnasta, as well as Knill, Rewista and Zira. Enough had to be left to protect Vanelia and keep a lookout for thieves or bandits. They certainly wanted most of the coterie in the caves for as thorough a search as possible, but they could not fit everyone either. Which is why Clerin thought Torpalin and his sister were staying behind. They were fairly large derlians to be caving.

All the others grouped up to enter the depths. Ryshial joined Altinger at the front, so she could light the way. There were other Gaens up there, Verin and Silvadhin, but Croy was in the back near Clerin and Vrric. The Pyrans, Luften warriors, and the Dylsun twins were all somewhere in the middle.

The cave was narrow at first, a winding tunnel really, but it eventually opened up into a large cavern. It was different than the Gaen caves Clerin had been in, those were dry and craggy, and it was different than the frozen ice caves on the Eidyon Peninsula. It dripped water everywhere, had lichen growing throughout it, and perilously hanging stalactites. There were weird glowing mushrooms, and moss with a mild luminescence. The plants did not provide enough light to see clearly, but just enough to show pockets of an eerie glimmer in the distance. The real light was provided by torches and, of course, Ryshial and Vrric.

Their lineup shifted as they went further into the cavern. Everyone was milling about, looking for a way to continue. Altinger seemed to fumble around with some parchment for a bit before declaring he had found another tunnel.

They delved deeper into the cave. It took some time before the tunnel opened back up again. Then another tunnel was found. It was slow going, with the cave floor being slick and jumbled with various sizes of rocks. And it took quite a while before they found any carvings at all.

When they reached the first carved wall, Clerin was ecstatic. She was not sure why, but she had the hope that they could just find both names immediately. She was completely wrong. There were hundreds of names on that first wall, not one of them close to anything they were looking for.

Staring at all the names made her think for a moment. *What were the odds that more than one Yaven name started with the same first seven letters as Gunzgak? What if they found a name, but it was the wrong one?* She frowned to herself as she thought. As others read the wall searching for the specific names, she began to count how many began the same on that first wall. She counted a maximum of three names that began with the same three letters. None of them shared four letters. But of course, they had just begun to search the cave. And she could have easily missed some. It was difficult to keep track of all the permutations.

Clerin wondered briefly how many of the Yaven names were summonable. Those left alive and willing to answer the call. Of course, Gunzgak would not be willing, so she should probably have thought about it differently.

After some time, and some distance, they reached another wall. Then another. She knew the cave was one of the larger on the island, but she wondered how much farther down it went. There were plenty of spots that were narrow where one had to go single file, but the opening often went upwards as well, like being at the bottom of a narrow canyon. It made the caves seem larger than the Gaen ones she had traversed through.

They were at another wall of names, reading off another list of failures. To get farther into the caves, to get even deeper, they had to go through another narrow cavern. Clerin was not really paying attention to where she was, somewhere near the middle. She was not really paying attention to who was around for they were all old friends. They were sidling through the cavern, one by one, when she heard the commotion in front of her. There was yelling, followed quickly by the clanging of steel. Clerin was trapped between two cavern walls, almost scraping them as she inched along. The sounds gave her a sudden bout of claustrophobia. *What was happening?!*

She needed to push forwards, to escape her confines. She began to shimmy through the narrow opening as fast as possible, her body turned sideways just to fit. Then the screams came. There was definitely a fight going on. Derlians were wounded or dying. There was a flash of something bluish, maybe lightning. Was Vrric in front of her or behind her? She should certainly head towards him if there was a fight. But honestly, she had not been sure which direction the flash had come from. It had just appeared, then disappeared. She froze. Then, certainly from directly in front of her, a blast of flames shot through the narrow opening, almost singeing her. She had felt the heat on her flesh. It was only because it had been so short lived that she was unscathed. She decided to go the other direction, to head back. So she turned her head around.

There was little Verin, slipping between the narrow cavern walls towards her, towards the fighting behind her. She smiled. She had always liked Verin, though they had not been alone together much during their travels.

"You are a sight for sore eyes. I have no idea what is going up there, but it sounds awful." Clerin gave a small smile of relief.

Verin did not speak. And she was moving quite quickly. There was a grim determination in her eyes that suddenly scared Clerin. It was then that she saw the unsheathed blade in Verin's hand. Clerin tried to back away, but she just scraped herself on the cavern walls. It was that feeling of cutting herself on the walls that caused her to cast the spell, as much as the crazed Gaen in front of her with a knife. "Nutecgepri!"

It was a weak spell, but her skin was covered by a thin shield of stone. She began to crash through the cavern, attempting to escape Verin. Thump! She felt the thrust of the dagger, if not the bite of the blade. Thump! She tried to move faster between the rock walls. Thump! The dagger found a way in and cut her. Deeply. "Nutecgepri!"

Clerin needed to escape. She only cast low-level spells which, until that very moment, had never really bothered her. Typically, she was a healer and had time to think about what was going on. She had never charged into a fight spouting fire from her fingers. It was only because of her training in her youth with Olwinn that she even knew a protection spell. He had been adamant that she learn all the Majora, whether or not she felt like she needed them. But her mind was not on these thoughts. It was only on *escape!* The word ricocheted around her skull as she stumbled along. Thump! Thump! *Escape! Escape!*

"Nutecgepri!" She cast it again as the blade found a way through again. She had tears running down her cheeks. She was just so shocked and tired and scared. She could feel the couple of bites Verin's dagger had taken out of her. She could feel the blood dripping. What she could not feel, luckily, was the stone walls that she careened off as she fled. *Escape!*

Finally, she popped out of the narrow passageway into the cave beyond. She had fallen as she had burst forth and was crawling along when she felt something on her back. Verin had her legs around Clerin and was swinging her dagger wildly. Thump, thump thump! There was screaming all around. It looked like the entire cave was on fire. All Clerin could do was crawl forward. "Nartecgepri!" She cast what she could and crawled and screamed. All to the incessant thumping on her back.

Finally, before she felt another bite of the knife, someone crashed into Verin above her. Whether or not the crash was part of the general melee, or someone coming to her rescue, she was a little unsure. In either case, she stopped crawling and lay there. Just trying to remain conscious. She cast one more shield spell, "Mektecgepri!" She used to be able to cast low-level healing spells all day long but felt quite drained with the mid-level shield spells. She rested her head on the rough stone floor. It did not hurt because of the shield spell, but she could also not feel the coolness against her cheek that she wanted. *It is a bit of a double-edged sword*, she thought to herself. But she did not have the energy to smile and, if she were honest, it was not even accurate, let alone humorous. She was not even sure if the knife had been double-sided.

Clerin tried, for a moment or two, to figure out what type of fight was going on in the cavern. It had obviously started there. It was obviously some sort of ambush. But she did not have the strength to examine her surroundings. She did not have the strength to think. She did not have the energy to keep her eyes open. So she closed them. She took another deep breath. She slowly succumbed to the abyss.

Clerin did not feel that she had been passed out for too long. She had been moved, sure, but they were in the same cavern. Mostly she felt it had been quick because everyone was still yelling and arguing. Whatever had happened was over. Her side had obviously won or else she would be dead. But nothing had been resolved, no one had cooled back down. She gave a loud cough and that quieted the room.

"You're awake!"

She was pretty sure it was Vrric who rushed over and knelt beside her. It certainly sounded like him. Her other senses were still groggy. She could not tell if it smelled like him or looked like him.

"Mekliderto!" He cast a healing spell on her. She was sure it was not the first. She let the cold wave of feeling wash over her—it was a feeling of pure refreshment, pure rejuvenation. It was pleasantly shocking.

"You made it. We made it. You're safe now." It was definitely Vrric in front of her.

"Well, not everyone made it." Trela was somewhere in the background, shifting around. She liked pacing after a fight. Clerin wondered what it did to Trela to keep her cooped up in a small cave. To stifle her pacing, stunt her instincts.

"I assume Verin did not?" Clerin posed it as a question. If Verin could have been subdued so they could ask questions, she might have been.

"No. Nor did Altinger, or the captain, or any of the sailors that were with them." Trela stopped pacing in place. "But we lost Alphino and Silvadhin."

Clerin glanced around to find short-haired Lophina, Alphino's sister. Why? Were condolences really necessary at that exact moment? Was it derlian instinct that made her look around, or her sense of duty and protocol that was ingrained in her as a child? In either case, Lophina was in the back or at least out of sight. She had liked both of the sisters. They had so few Fluen companions with them, it seemed.

"Silvadhin is the one who saved you. Or at least, she's the one who leapt on Verin when you popped out through the narrow passageway. I was busy with Altinger at the time." Vrric glanced behind him. Clerin assumed that was where the bodies were situated.

"You see? It is not just a Gaen issue. If it were all of us Gaens in on the ambush, don't you think Silvadhin would have stabbed her too? Or at least not gotten involved?" It was Croy's voice she heard though it was hidden away behind everyone. She wondered if he was near the corpses. Then she wondered why he was not standing there in front of her like everyone else. Then she realized there was some panic in his voice.

"Like you?" Vrric turned in the opposite direction behind him. "Like you not involving yourself when Altinger attacked? Like you just standing there while flames engulfed Alphino?" There was a real anger in Vrric's voice all of a sudden. The tone was not something Clerin was used to.

"I was as surprised as everyone!"

"You sure seemed to be spending a lot of time with him, or he with you. Certainly more than anyone spent with Verin."

"He was helping me with my seasickness."

"You are just lucky Clerin lived. Trust me, I…"

"I cast the first healing spell on her, didn't I?"

"Stop. Stop! You both are giving me a headache." Trela raised her voice and quieted everything else.

"I'm the one tied up…"

"Seriously, Croy, that is best for everyone." Trela turned around to glare at him. He was still out of Clerin's view. "Could you imagine not being tied up and tripping or flailing your arms around suddenly or something? You would be instantly shot through with lighting, let alone steel. No, your physical incapacitation is protecting you as well right now. Being helpless is your only defense currently. So… Just watch it, or we'll have to incapacitate your voice as well. You are a mage, after all."

"Croy is tied up?" She knew it to be true, but it was all so confusing.

"The Gaens went crazy."

"Verin went crazy. I didn't do anything."

"Right. Even when Silvadhin and Verin fought, you did nothing." An angry looking Estfale joined in the conversation.

"That lasted seconds. What was I…"

"Seriously, enough!" Trela was glaring at Estfale even though she interrupted Croy. "We cannot solve this down here. We should have left for the surface a while ago." She paused. "Has anyone *whispered* to Serghno?"

"I was healing Clerin…" Vrric was the only one who spoke up.

"I will do it. The rest of you head up." Ryshial turned to head to a far corner as Vrric helped Clerin to stand.

As they were walking towards the surface, Ryshial called out from behind them. "They were attacked as well. Serghno says we should hurry, if able."

The attempt to hurry was made. Clerin was unable to move incredibly fast, however, and she and Vrric brought up the rear by the time they reached the surface.

There was carnage up there as well. They had been attacked at the same time as those below, but there had been no mages amongst the enemies. Still, the coterie had been outnumbered and Zira and Tundalia had been wounded. They were kept out of the way. Zira looked to be in bad shape, but she was still breathing.

When the surprise attack struck, Tundalia and Zira happened to be out in the open, chatting. They got struck first. Torpalin, apparently, then went crazy and slaughtered about half of them. Having mages helped, of course. And Zira, even outnumbered and surprised, had dispatched a few herself.

They gathered everyone around. Clerin sat with the wounded, even though she was feeling better by then. Croy was tied up off to the side, next to a silver fir tree. The others lit a fire, more to boil water for the wounded than anything else.

"Altinger sprang the trap. If it were not for him and the sailors, we could have dispatched Verin in a flash." Estfale had kept his anger. "It had to have been a trap from the beginning. Which means this whole island is a trap. It means the search for the names is a trap. I think it's the Gaens. They are striking out now that Gunzgak is cornered. I fear these traps will keep occurring until either Gunzgak, or Clerin, is dead."

"The names are real. There is a name written here, somewhere. Maybe not this cave system itself, but one of the three." Croy spoke up from his corner. His voice sounded defeated even as he spoke the words.

"No. There are just more traps. Have you not been listening?" Estfale kept his muscles taught as he spoke, ready to spring into action at a second's notice.

"Trust me, there is a name somewhere."

"Trust you? You could be a traitor!"

"Croy is not a traitor." Clerin spoke it softly, but everyone quieted down. "Or at least, he is not an assassin."

"How do you know? I mean, really know?" Estfale glared at her.

"He has had too many opportunities. I, myself, have given them to him. He could have attacked me at any time, many times of which I would have been wholly unprepared." She took a deep breath. She knew it would an unpopular sentiment.

"So had Verin."

"No. Not really. Not like Croy had." She held up a hand to stop Estfale from continuing his retort. "Seriously, he had ample time and tried to talk me out of it, tried to *talk* me out of communing with Gunzgak. All he really needed was a willingness to die right after me."

"So, Croy, tell me true, did you know Altinger was preparing an ambush?" Vrric stared directly at him. "No, wait, that is too easy. Did you know Altinger was scheming for Gunzgak?"

"I don't know if anyone knows that. We just know that we were ambushed. It is not like Altinger attacked Clerin or anything. He did not yell out, 'Death to Lembin,' or anything. It could have been over anything. Maybe the captain was trying to rob us and Altinger was the bait? I don't know." Croy looked despondent, more than anything.

"Really? That is your response to my question? That is your answer?" Vrric raised an eyebrow. "I just want you to be sure before finalizing your answer."

"I'm saying that no one knows. So how could I?"

"I know, Croy. I can feel it. I felt it as we chatted with him on the ship. And even if that was incorrect, for I was a little unsure at the time, I felt it when we were attacked." Vrric rarely talked about "feeling" anything. He enjoyed facts. He enjoyed logic. He enjoyed thinking things through. So the speech seemed a little odd to Clerin. Now, did she agree with him? Yes, completely. She too felt that Altinger was working for Gunzgak, as he put it. But she had always trusted her feelings. "The attack does not make sense as a robbery, Croy. You know that."

"But I don't…"

"You do. Everyone does." Vrric looked around. While only Estfale looked eager to agree verbally, no one looked like they disagreed. In the slightest. "That is not the worst part, however. You keep dodging. You keep quibbling and splitting hairs. This is not like you, Croy. It would have been better if you had just said, 'No,' and stopped there. But this ridiculous defense makes me question the entirety of it."

"Argh! Fine! Yes, I knew he wanted to help Gunzgak. He said he would lead us to Lembin's name first. He wanted us to find Lembin's name. I… I am not even sure if Gunzgak's name is on the island. That is all I knew. I had no idea he was going to attack us. I knew nothing of the ambush, I swear!" He looked distraught instead of despondent. It was as if he was finally realizing how dangerous his situation was.

"There, that is a much better answer." Vrric nodded approvingly. "And how about Verin? Did you know Verin was scheming for Gunzgak?"

"I did not think of it as scheming. She, like I, felt that trying to destroy a Beleg who does not wish to die is a form of murder. I have not been shy about that." Croy looked around at the others.

Not quite defiantly, but with more self-confidence than he had shown previously. "So, I knew she was annoyed and unhappy with our current mission. But I did not know she was going to attack Clerin. Truly." His head lowered slightly, and he got a little quieter. "She did say she was having strange dreams."

"What?" That got Clerin's attention. She doubted Croy would not have mentioned anything if he knew an assassination was brewing. And she was a little disheartened at him being tied up during the questioning. More than that, however, she did want to know what was going through Verin's head before the attack. Especially if it was something that could happen to others. Especially since she understood his dreams came from Gunzgak itself. "Did she describe the dreams? Are they similar to the ones you have?"

"I don't know, she only mentioned them in passing. She called them 'insistent,' I believe." He paused for a moment, looking around. He realized no one was going to insert themselves into his predicament, so he continued. "My dreams from Gunzgak are very clear. Gunzgak realizes that I am no assassin. It does not think I am much of a politician either but has given me this charge." He paused and took a deep breath. "I will tell you what Gunzgak wants out of me, simply because it seems I have no other choice. All I have left is honesty. Gunzgak does not wish to die and even if I am able to convince you of my charge, it will still struggle. It will still do everything it can to stay alive." He took another deep breath. All eyes, and ears, were focused on him. "I am to convince you to kill Lembin first."

"What? Does it think it will survive afterwards? That we will be unable to destroy it and so it can live forever as the world's sole Beleg?" Clerin was trying to think of the overarching motive with such a statement.

"No. Well, maybe. But Gunzgak is concerned that Lembin is trying to do exactly that. That Lembin is killing off the other Belegs and will sit back unscathed after Gunzgak perishes. That is the motivation I have been told of."

"But Lembin wants to die. That is the whole reason this plan was set into motion." Clerin was unsure if she was guessing about that or not. It is what she believed that Lembin wanted.

"What if that is what it wants you to think? What if, after all the other Belegs have died, it will not commune with you again? What if it seals off the citadel, the temple, Tureyn itself, keeping itself isolated? What if, and this is something I know worries Gunzgak, what if the assassin's blade that was given to you does not kill Lembin? What if you have no weapon where it is concerned?" Croy looked somewhat crazed, like a warrior in the heat of combat. "You have communed with Lembin after Linchon died, yes? Did your blade work then?"

"Gorbanax has given me something." Clerin was quiet, not quite sure how to respond. She did not believe that Lembin was attempting to kill the others just to go on living forever, all alone and uncontested. But she could see Croy's concerns, could see Gunzgak's. And, more importantly, she could see them on the faces of those surrounding her. There were a lot of concerned looks directed towards her.

"And what about Linchon? Did Linchon not give you something? Where is Linchon's revenge for its death?" He looked angry, with squinty eyes and trembling lips.

"That was something different." Vrric interrupted Croy. She was unsure of what he meant by that but was happy that he interjected. It gave her enough time to think.

"I do feel that they are arguing. That is the reason for the tremors that run through Tureyn now. Linchon is not giving Lembin a full pass." It was her turn to take a deep breath. "I hear your concerns, Croy. I may not embrace them as you do, but they are certainly valid. Would finding Lembin's name help?"

She needed to give him something. She believed that he did not know about the assassination attempt, whether from Altinger or Verin, and she believed he should not be left tied up. He needed a way to participate. More than that, she needed to deflect from the current line of query. It would, of course, come back up. But there was too much momentum to let it keep going at that moment—soon they would all be clamoring for her to do something about Lembin.

"Yes. I think it would." This came from Trela. She had a calculating look on her face. Clerin knew that look could lead to trouble if you were on the wrong end of the calculation. "There is no harm in it, and it may prove useful. It might even prove invaluable. If we are exceedingly lucky, maybe we will actually find both names here somewhere."

The others all chimed in. It was, on all accounts, a great idea. The more names they had, the more they had to bargain with. Soon everyone was nodding and smiling. Estfale eventually even untied Croy.

"I am not sure how to mention this, but Altinger left me some crude maps of the other two caves." Croy looked sheepish. Estfale looked like he wanted to tie Croy back up, but Trela interrupted.

"Great. We must assume there are traps. And there may be more attempts on Clerin's life, we shall have to guard her closely. We can take nothing for granted on this island. But having the maps are better than not. We will set up a strong perimeter tonight and sleep in shifts. Then, early tomorrow, we will set out. We still have much to endure." Trela nodded as much to herself as to the others.

Gaen warriors were often buried, as was their custom. Pyran bodies were burned, of course. Fluens were, as much as practicable, floated out into the ocean. Luftens were left on rocky crags to desiccate. Or much more likely in Clerin's opinion, get picked at by scavengers. It was the Fluen tradition that was most difficult, typically. They had not traveled with many Fluens, however, and the issue had not come up before. The coterie was mostly Pyran and, leading up to the fight with the Cabal, Gaen.

They buried Silvadhin with full honors, but also buried Verin. It was not as if she had been taken over by a Tlana, her level of innocence could not be checked, but she was following the command of her Beleg. That was a good enough excuse for the internment.

They took Alphino's body with them the next morning. The island was small enough and the cave had not been too far inland, so they were able find the coast before sundown. Lophina was oddly composed and did not appear to shed a tear. At least not while Clerin was around.

They gathered around several small fires in the evening in small groups. It was a somber meal, but afterwards the silence faded. Some, like Estfale, were angry. Clerin had always assumed that Estfale held a candle for Trela, and maybe he did, but he had seemed to warm up to Alphino recently. Some expressed exasperation. It seemed like the coterie was always getting attacked or stymied in some fashion. Jalin, however, grew thoughtful.

"So, what do you think is happening to Yifindur, the ship?" She glanced around with a look of genuine curiosity on her face. "I mean, the captain and at least half the crew are growing cold in the bottom of the cave back there. Do you think it was sold? Claimed by one of the sailors left behind?"

"It might not even have been owned by the captain. The profits of a boat often go to an owner who never sets foot over the sea." Clerin took Jalin's question at face value. "Boat ownership is looked at more as an investment. For a large one, at least. There are plenty of families that fish for a living on tiny boats."

"That is a little intriguing, Jalin." Lophina had a steely gleam in her eye. "I cannot think of a better revenge than of taking their ship. If they happen to have owned it, of course."

"Worst case, we could sell it to someone in Tureyn or Vatlisi." Trela was smiling.

"So how do we find that out? I mean, the caves are not going anywhere, are they? If we took a couple of extra days to investigate that, what would it hurt?" Jalin appeared to be getting excited about the prospect.

"Well... We should probably make sure the idea is acceptable to everyone. Even Croy." Trela nodded to Jalin. "Personally, I think a small break would be good. If there are traps in the other caves, they will get just a little older. But if there are further plans of ambush, making our enemies wait another couple of days could be helpful. Nothing sours a plan faster than uncertainty and boredom. And even if they have spies in Umrhebo and hear of our plan, it is always better to stymie the enemy than to be stymied yourself. You are correct. It is not as if the etchings of the names are going to lose their potency."

Clerin thought it was a good idea, but that was mainly because she was a little shaken up by the idea of crawling through more caves. She had to admit that the attack by Verin had unnerved her. It had just been so... unexpected. It reminded her of wandering through the Gaen caves before the Cabal, never knowing when an attack would happen. It was like constantly being on guard, constantly being on edge. She was not cut out for that. Typically, being in the middle of a traveling group, she did not have to be ready to slash at someone, or to cast the proper spell immediately. She was usually protected. When the fight was over, she would heal those of her friends who were wounded. But now it seemed that she was the target. She could not hide in the middle anymore.

Certainly, after Verin her sense of security was shattered. She did not think Croy or Knill would attack her if they were alone together but, and she hated to admit it, she did feel less safe around Gaens. She was glad they did not have any other Gaens with them currently, she could only imagine how she would feel about a stranger. Altinger had been the first strange Gaen she had been around for almost a full sun cycle, and he had been sent to assassinate her. But certainly not all Gaens would be assassins. She did not want to live the rest of her life concerned that every new Gaen she met was out to kill her. *It was merely because of Gunzgak,* she thought to herself, *not because of any individual Gaen.* The thought did not help. It merely made her concerned about Gaen dreams. It certainly did not make her feel safer, nor did it make her feel better concerning how she felt about Gaens, her paranoia. To counteract the feeling, she tried to think of Silvadhin, but that was depressing in its own right.

They headed into Umrhebo the next morning. They were not too far off, so it only took them until noon. There were too many of them to go charging the dock offices, so a small group split off. They could not steal the ship. They had no crew. Clerin wished they had been paying more attention during the brief sail over to the island but knew that would not have helped much either. They needed to have pitched in. To have been taught the ropes, literally. And for moons, not days. So what they needed to do was convince the dockmaster, or harbormaster, or some master, that they were the new owners of Yifindur. She was not really sure how that could be done, especially since the captain and crew were just "missing," and recently at that. But Jalin and Trela were very excited about the prospect. So, there they were.

Clerin went along, of course. Her name was becoming more renowned in Tureyn after Vatlisi, communing with Lembin, and even due to the Catajohls. The hope was that someone would have heard of her. Lophina went as well, being the only other Fluen. Trela insisted on being the bodyguard and Jalin wanted to go because... well, it was her idea. That left a mage, which was, of course, Vrric. Clerin did not really want to go anywhere without him. Luckily, he was so competent and skilled that he was the natural choice for all concerned.

They left all the others camping just outside of town. There had been talk about taking over an inn, but Trela was worried about the cost of that. Not that they were broke, but there was some concern that the ship would have to be purchased. Could Clerin bring the ship into Tureyn and get reimbursed? Could they still use it to get to Vatlisi afterwards? No one was really sure, and it was best not to take the risk of paying for it.

If everything went smoothly, or at least smooth enough, they would gather everyone up from the camp and bring them into town. They decided to leave their horses at the camp as well, just to make navigating the docks simpler.

Clerin walked in front and was flanked by Lophina and Trela. Vrric and Jalin followed behind. The roads were nice and wide. They walked through the town somewhat anonymously, or at least it seemed like no one was paying attention to them. Clerin would probably have to ask Jalin later if she wanted to know for sure.

The town was set up to lead to the docks. The main roads radiated out from that wide central point like spokes. The perpendicular roads were curved, like ripples flowing away from the dock.

They reached the docks without incident. They found the dockmaster's office, which looked a bit like quarters as well; there was a second floor that had various dingy windows looking out over the docks. The office was an offshoot from a warehouse. The warehouse portion was gigantic, extending off into the distance. With the roofs aligning, it appeared that the interior of the warehouse was tall and spacious. The bay doors were large, but their tops stopped near the upper floor of the office. The entire building was clad in grayish wood, with visible gaps between the slats of the walls.

Clerin walked up to the open office door with a straight back and confident smile. She was always amazed at how much confidence could sway strangers. As long as it was not tainted with arrogance.

She assessed the situation as she walked in through the door. With the windows, open door, and gapped wall slats, there was a fair amount of sunlight that penetrated the office. Though the lighting did provide an oddly surreal feel to the room. It was a large room, extending back into the building almost twenty rods. There was plenty of room on either side of the open door, with large bookcases along the side walls filled with all manner of books, rolled scrolls, and sheaves of paper. At the end of the office, opposite the door, was a gigantic desk made of what appeared to be thick planks, giving it an incredible mass. In any other room the desk would have swallowed the space, but there it just looked natural. On either side of the desk was a large leather chair, each filled with a bored looking guard. In front of the desk were three small and uncomfortable looking wooden chairs. On top of the desk was another large pile of books, scrolls, and sheaves of paper, along with ink wells, blotters, and quills. Behind the desk there was a chair, and it was probably comfortable, but in the chair was a Fluen that was larger than the bodyguards. He was not fat by any means, though he was not as muscular as they were. There were no cut lines for his muscles, though they were obviously there, underneath the surface. It was as if Torpalin spent an entire winter trapped inside eating fried dough and cream. He had long blond hair pulled back from his face with a thin leather thong.

The guards stood up at their arrival, suddenly brought to life by duty. They both had short blond hair and were exceptionally chiseled. They had jaws like anvils that lent an ominous air to their scowls. Their leather armor creaked as they crossed their massive arms in front of them. They were not twins, not at all, but the matching uniforms and coordinated motions reminded Clerin slightly of first seeing the Dylsun twins. The Fluen in the middle kept scratching his quill against parchment, not even looking up.

Clerin took her time walking to the desk, using a long slow stride. She allowed her bootheels to click on the wood flooring, as metered as a metronome. The guards did not twitch, so she assumed it was safe to go to the wooden chairs. Rather than shift them around to try to sit, she stood behind the middle one, resting her hands on the back of it. Her friends followed her lead, with Trela and Lophina standing behind the other chairs. Vrric and Jalin hovered behind.

They waited quietly for some time. Clerin felt it was some sort of test, but was a little of unsure of how it was measured. Would she be considered too meek if she waited to be acknowledged, or would she be considered rude and impatient if she interrupted his work? She decided to wait.

Eventually he stopped writing and placed his quill away. He carefully placed his writing aside and squared up some other items. He finally looked up and smiled. His teeth were ridiculously white.

"You're a sight for sore eyes, aren't you? It appears that you are from Tureyn, yes? And you there," he glanced over at Lophina, "appear to be from Vatlisi. The others are from everywhere else, I would say. Odd that you were unable to find a Gaen for your group." He laughed a little and clapped his hands, not allowing Clerin to explain she was not necessarily from Tureyn. "What wretched business brings you to a place like mine?"

"We wish to speak with the dockmaster about a ship." Clerin flashed him an earnest smile.

"Harbormaster. I'm the harbormaster, which means my domain spreads over every dock in the harbor."

"Oh, of course. How many docks are in the harbor?" Clerin silently chastised herself for not thinking that one entirely through.

"Just the one." He laughed again. Even his guards cracked a smile.

"Titles are certainly important." Clerin gave him a wry lopsided smile. It erased one dimple and accentuated the other.

"None more so than yours, I assume. What shall I call you and what ship did you wish to purchase?"

"I am Clerin Toswin, communer to Lembin. I have recently deposed the Prince of Vatlisi and placed Inquella Erintwala in his place. I have been given a mission of great importance and the ship I will be leaving this island with was given to me, it is not being purchased." She kept her back straight and breathed in, inflating her chest as she spoke.

"Ha, ho! Deposed, she says." He turned to each guard who glanced back at him. Though they did not have the large grin on that he had. "Even Johcal Island has heard of what happened at Vatlisi. Deposed means sitting somewhere without a crown. As far as I understand, the old Prince is lying somewhere without a head! Yes, Toswin, I have heard of you. Your name-dropping has had its desired effect." He nodded to himself for a moment. "Just how did he die, anyway? I would love to know the true story. We only hear shadows of rumors around here."

"Well, there may be time for that, depending on how fast my ship gets resolved." She gave him a quick wink.

"Oh, that, yes, of course. Which ship did you purchase?"

"Yifindur."

He stopped in mid-motion for a second. She could almost see him thinking. He certainly recognized the name and was certainly not happy about it.

"Ah, Yifindur." He breathed in slowly. "I would not doubt your sincerity, certainly not to your face, but that particular ship is owned by a particular individual." He breathed out slowly. "I assume you have the properly signed documents, yes?"

"We do, yes, we do. But unfortunately, they have been left behind with the rest of our group. There was some argument as to the safety and wisdom of carrying them around with us. I had, unfortunately, thought that my word and reputation would be enough to assuage you." Clerin had no idea of what to say. They were totally caught and she doubted she could ever come back to Umrhebo again. She was just trying to save enough face to leave the office at that point.

"Normally it would, yes. I do not wish to anger Tureyn in any way, or the new Princess of Vatlisi for that matter, but this is something that will need to be done under full review. There are those above me who are interested in that ship." He nodded again. "Now, there are those that would consider that you arrived here without the proper documents as suspicious. Not I, however. No. You are given the full benefit of the doubt. And I would appreciate, if asked, that you let Tureyn know that I am accommodating and sympathetic."

"Of course. And I do apologize for not bringing all the proper documentation with me. If you would let me know your name, I will keep you and your assistance in mind."

There was a pause. It was not overly long, but it was similar to when she had mentioned the ship's name. She could almost see him thinking.

"You know, I had not realized until now that I had not told you that already. But of course, there is no hiding the harbormaster of Umrhebo." He laughed a little quietly to himself. "My name is Telingard. No last name of note." He held up his palms and shrugged briefly.

"It has been a pleasure, Telingard. You will find that I am as sympathetic to your plight as you are to mine. I look forward to discussing more with you in the future." She nodded politely. He performed as much of a bow as he was able while sitting down. She turned and cursed herself, her plight, her unpreparedness, and Jalin. For it was Jalin that brought her to this embarrassment. The others followed her out. They had stayed silent the entire time, not helping or hindering. They were well out of the dock area before anyone dared to speak.

"Well, that was just terrible. I do not think I can show my face in this town again." Clerin was a little exasperated by the whole experience. Yes, it would have been great to get a ship, but did they even really need one? Had they not just been buying passage back and forth, was that not working out? She bit her tongue, however.

"It'll be great if we return with the proper documents." Jalin held her back firm, her arms crossed over her chest.

"Seriously?!" Clerin tried her best not to raise her voice. "Are you still trying to call this as a win?"

"Not if we skulk away with our tail between our legs. If we leave and never come back, that Telingard fellow will always know that you were lying. He will always have that story in him, that he was lied to by *the* Clerin Toswin and caught her at it. Stopped her dead in her tracks, that's what he'll say. She was no match for *me*, no sir. And he'll thrust that oddly oversized thumb back at his chest with a huge grin and a wink." Jalin thrust her own, much smaller thumb back at herself in an exaggerated pantomime.

Clerin was so annoyed that she could not think of anything to say. Well, she thought of plenty to say, but nothing that would have helped. Nothing that would take the sting out of Jalin's words.

"If you have a plan, you should get to it." Vrric squinted his eyes at Jalin. Clerin thought there was some animosity hidden in there somewhere. She would never admit that she liked that. Maybe the word "appreciated" was better than "liked."

"Of course I have a plan. The documents are all in that office, I would bet my life on it. The blank bill of sale, the current owner's signature, everything. We just need to break in, find out who owns the ship, fill out the paperwork, forge the signature, and bang! we are the proud new owners of one Yifindur. We just have to have everything filled out by tomorrow."

"You don't think there will be guards all over those docks tonight?" Trela did not look like she was overly concerned about the assumed guards, but she at least looked slightly skeptical.

"The current owner's signature may not be in that office, you know." Lophina interrupted before Jalin could counter Trela. "The Prince I worked for kept all ownership documents in the palace, not at the point of sale. He was incredibly nosy, prying into everyone's business. Nothing happened in Vatlisi without him knowing. And he kept everything pretty tightly locked up as well."

"Well, for one, Umrhebo is not Vatlisi, not by a long shot. And we do not need the main original document or anything, we just need a name and, hopefully, a signature to base the forgery off of. Maybe the signature is located elsewhere, I don't know. But we can find it. Even if the documents are hidden at the… well, not palace, but wherever the local ruler of Umrhebo lives… we can find them." Jalin raised her hands, fending off everyone's arguments. "And if we can't, if I personally fail, we can still slink off with our tail between our legs and Clerin can glare at me for an entire moon. What I'm trying to say is that we should try. The heavy lifting will be mine. I'll find the documents. I'll forge the signature. I just need some assistance, is all."

"Do you think Arnasta can find documents?" Vrric appeared to only be half-joking.

"Who do you need to come with you? This could still get worse if someone is caught, you know. We could just cut our losses and let Clerin glare at you all the way back to Vatlisi." Trela had a half smile on.

"Well, Telingard has a sweet spot for Clerin. I mean, who doesn't?" Jalin gave Clerin a slightly lascivious wink, but Clerin was still annoyed and just glared back. "So she should come in case he is one of the many Fluens guarding the office tonight. And Lophina, obviously. I want to say both of Telingard's guards snuck multiple glances at you." She turned to Lophina and gave another wink. Lophina rewarded her with a grin. "And Feyazki, just in case. And maybe Arnasta, just in double case."

"So, the only derlian you don't want on this mission is me? I don't get a wink?" Trela did actually look slightly offended.

"Well, we could really use a diversion…" Jalin trailed off briefly, looking up and away. "Would you consider a small fire to be too much collateral damage?"

"No, I like fires." Trela laughed.

"No, wait, we are not burning down the docks just so Telingard does not spend the rest of his life mocking me behind my back." Clerin glared at all of them. Just in case there was any confusion.

"There's a derelict boat at the end of one of the piers. I saw it as we came upon the docks." Lophina looked thoughtful. "It was definitely listing and definitely in the mid-to-late stages of decay. It might even cost more to repair than to build a new one."

"How would you know that?" Clerin could tell that she was the only one in a sour mood. That everyone else was attempting to find the positive in the bad situation, the glimmer of hope as it were. The realization did not help her mood any.

"I think it is a fantastic plan. And I know Estfale has been itching to set something on fire for a diversion. Parthia was a very long time ago." Trela was grinning irrepressibly.

"Good. Settled." Jalin dusted off her hands a little overexaggerated, but everyone was smiling.

Clerin still felt grumpy, but that did not mean she had to drag everyone else down with her. She could think of nothing beyond repeating what Jalin had just said, and she doubted she would have sounded very sincere. So she just nodded and smiled at them all. "Lead on."

That night everyone who was coming was prepared well beforehand. Trela, Estfale, Dartsyle, and Ryshial were all ready for the diversion. They had been in town since the afternoon, probably drinking at some tavern. Clerin had argued against that, thinking they should show their faces as little as possible before something like setting fire to a derelict boat, but she had been heavily outvoted. They wanted to circle back around and help put out the fire, thus solidifying their alibi and becoming heroes in the process. Clerin felt that the mission had grown past her. It was no longer a simple diplomatic mission but had turned into a full-blown clandestine spy affair. The decisions were being handled by Jalin and Trela, the voting was mainly for show. Her opinions were being politely ignored at best.

Honestly, most of the coterie planning was done by others. Clerin did not even care to vote much of the time. She wondered why this particular issue struck her as annoying. Was it because it was in the Fluen realm, and after Vatlisi, she had been used to running the show, as it were? She had truly enjoyed that. Her mind wandered over to the Catajohls' offer of power and prestige, but she squashed it before her afternoon turned into a daydreaming session. Thinking about her actual annoyance, it was not that she was being ignored, not really. No, she felt it was because she had started the first run-through and that had failed miserably. She wanted to salvage something from that for some reason, to somehow still turn that around. It was a foolish wish, she knew.

Clerin and Lophina were walking together through Umrhebo, wasting time. They were consciously avoiding taverns, so they walked slowly through the market and some stores—Clerin enjoyed the incredible variety of fabrics that the island had to offer.

It was a meeting point between the peninsula and the mainland and had specialties from both.

Jalin was supposed to contact them before breaking into the harbormaster's office. Clerin was not overly excited about her own proposed role either. She did not mind being a distraction, but she thought it would seem odd to Telingard. She thought he would, at a minimum, ask about the documents. She was sure of that. Too much time had passed since she had promised to fetch them. And then, after a bizarre dock fire, she would show up with them tomorrow? She calmed her fears again. She had lost the argument. There was no use worrying over it now.

Soon enough, dusk descended. The main streets were lit with lanterns. Leaving some cheery lanes as well as plenty of dark alleys. Though Lophina was an accomplished warrior, they stuck to the lighted paths. There was no reason to tempt fate.

Jalin and Arnasta came walking up while they were deciding where else to head. They had already woven through much of the area near the sea and did not want to just walk back and forth over the same ground. It was odd to see Arnasta without Serghno. It made Clerin wonder where he was. Which, for some reason, made her wonder where Vrric was as well.

"You are lucky I had Arnasta with me, you have weaved quite the chaotic trail through the town." Jalin smiled easily.

"Just enjoying the sights." There were a couple of Fluens wandering by, but they were mostly alone. In any case, Clerin did not wish to say anything overt. "Did you want to walk together?"

Jalin raised an eyebrow at the question, but her easy smile did not shift. "Of course. You really have to see a ship down by the dock. It has the masts we were discussing."

The walk to the dock was quick, Clerin and Lophina had been trying to stay close. Jalin was one of those derlians who did not look back while walking. Clerin watched her muscular shoulders sway and roll under her light shirt as they walked. It was like watching a prowling panther. Clerin was sure that Jalin still knew what was going on behind her, beside her, all around. Very little escaped her perception.

As they approached the offices, they appeared dark. Clerin felt a small burst of relief. She had argued that they should try much later in the night, but others had been worried that would mean any movement would have been considered suspicious. And there was hope it was early enough in the evening that no one would be sleeping in the loft above the office. That Telingard and his guards would be out at some tavern or other.

There were certainly others on the docks. There were occasional lanterns at the docks and some on ships, scattering the minimal light around. They slowed as they neared the offices.

"I'm going through the back. You wait here at the front for a while. If no one comes out, if no lights turn on, then you can leave or wander the docks. Just don't get too close to Trela's ship. She might light it up even if we don't need the distraction. She seemed pretty excited about the prospect." Jalin grinned, turned, and slipped into the darkness before Clerin could respond.

It was impressive how Jalin got swallowed by the shadows. Clerin was watching her directly, trying hard to keep any part of her body in view, but she just… vanished. It was an amazing skill. It seemed like magic. Arnasta wandered quietly over to the front doors. Waiting. Clerin and Lophina stayed where they were. They chatted quietly about nothing, not wanting to appear to be skulking. They wanted to appear like they belonged and boring enough not to entice investigation. It had been decided that Vrric would float around at the back, close enough to arrive at a moment's notice, but far enough to not be noticed by anyone. He was not even noticed by Clerin.

Eventually the door opened and Arnasta slipped inside. It appeared that everything was going smoothly, so Clerin and Lophina decided to slip away. Just when Clerin was thinking that Trela would not have to set fire to anything, they were called after by some approaching guards.

"Hey, hey. Toswin!" The guards were jogging slightly. The urgency in their voices did not seem to be due to their official jobs, however. They were not yelling, "Stop!" or anything. They were not loosening their weapons. It took a moment to realize that they were the same two guards from earlier.

"I did not realize I was so recognizable." Clerin stopped and let them catch up.

"Oh, you would be visible from the moon. But, ah, no offense, I was hoping to have a drink with your guard." He pulled up his ample frame and wiped his palm on his pants. "I was unable to be properly introduced earlier. Telingard can suck all the air from a room, especially when he is in the presence of his betters." The guard nodded to Clerin. "I am Suznedoon. And, well there is no other way to say it, and I hope you can forgive me my clumsiness, but you are quite exquisite. Is there any way I could learn your name?"

"I am Lophina." Her smile was just a little lopsided. She held her hand out for him to pick up and kiss the back of. "And I am flattered. Even if you are a little clumsy." She laughed lightly.

His smile slowly grew wider, as if he were unable to stop it. He let go of her hand and clasped his own in front of himself. He took in a breath.

"Then let me find the ways to compare your beauty. Which, for the likes of me, will take a little wine. Would you care to join me at a tavern?" He was nodding, as if trying to subtly get her to agree.

"Suznedoon, you will have to excuse me. I just need to pop into the office for a moment." The other guard was smiling almost as wide as Suznedoon. He nodded and began to turn down the dock. That must have been why they were down at the dock, to get whatever the other guard needed.

"Surely whatever you need can wait. That musty old office is not going anywhere. We, however, only have a little bit of time." Clerin touched his arm lightly, softly turning him. "Come on, be a good friend."

Suznedoon was nodding his head in the opposite direction, assumedly towards the tavern. Lophina laughed a little and patted Suznedoon's arm. She reached her other hand out to the reluctant guard, though he was too far away to reach her.

"A glass of wine never hurt anyone." She waved her hand to bring him in closer.

Clerin pushed a little on his arm, getting him over his inertia. Then she took a small step over to Lophina. His feet followed hers. And just like that, they were all headed to some dingy tavern.

Once they got inside and sat down, Clerin felt in the clear. Jalin would surely have enough time to sift through the paper and parchment at the office. They could all relax and enjoy some wine. Clerin tried hard to notice anything in Lophina's discourse or demeaner that would give away the game, but she truly appeared to enjoy flirting with Suznedoon.

Clerin chatted amiably with Defulsi. He had made sure that she understood he was not flirting with her. It seemed, maybe, that Telingard had said something to deter him, though she was not positive. Defulsi did not mention a girlfriend or anything of the like, so she did not think that was the issue. And that did not always stop a Fluen. They often looked at a chance to flirt as honing one's skills. But whatever the reason, he did not try any poetry at all.

Clerin was feeling good. It was not just the wine or the nostalgic feeling of a Fluen tavern. It seemed that everything was going to work out. They had not run into Telingard, they had not had to kill anyone, they had not been in any danger at all. Just a fun evening. There was a small group of musicians in the corner, adding to her warm and fuzzy feeling of comfort.

It was when they had just started a second glass that a small glow appeared outside through the window. At first it was the size of a lantern due to its distance, and so Clerin ignored it. But soon it was obvious for what it was. A ship was on fire somewhere in the docks. It was surely Trela who had set the blaze. Clerin was unsure of what she would have preferred. That Trela had needed to set the blaze as a diversion, or that she had done so out of boredom. In any case, everyone rushed out of the tavern and onto the docks.

They ran the entire way there. The guards cursed their luck loudly. Clerin and Lophina stayed silent. By the time they arrived, there was a crowd. The faces lit up by the giant flickering fire was slightly eerie. There were bucket lines, but they were not doing anything constructive for the boat, they were mainly trying to keep the dock from catching. The moorage ropes had been cut, but the ship was still dangerously close to the wood dock.

Out of the darkness, Trela and Ryshial suddenly appeared. They came running up the pier shouting something incoherent. Some of the Fluens standing around moved for them, but not many. Ryshial then made some overtly grand gestures and cast something. Water came rising up and poured over the ship like a giant garden fountain. There was a lot of hissing and steam, but eventually the fire was put out.

Soon afterwards some Fluen mages arrived. They took over and floated the charred remains out of the bay to sink it in deeper waters. The entire fire had not taken a large amount of time. Clerin was unsure of how helpful it was but would have to wait to hear about all that had happened.

The crowd slowly dispersed. Lophina and Suznedoon went back to the tavern. Defulsi would not be deterred after the fire and so Clerin accompanied him back to the office. She figured she could at least alert Jalin to their presence.

Defulsi took some time unlocking the door. She whistled aimlessly while he did that. Not loudly or obnoxiously, but a little something just in case. She held her breath when he opened the door, but nothing happened. He took his lantern and wandered into the depths of the office. Clerin did not notice anything out of place. He grabbed up some items from behind the large desk, parchments maybe, certainly a couple of scrolls, but she kept her gaze away from him, allowing him some discretion. When he was done, they left. Clerin went back to the camp outside of town.

The next morning Clerin woke up at dawn. She had been planning on sleeping in a little, but the sun was just too bright. She left Vrric resting noisily in the tent to grab some breakfast. Torpalin and Escha were up cooking early. Or at least, Torpalin was cooking while Escha was keeping him company. Clerin grabbed a plate and chatted briefly, but then wandered off to eat in the stillness of the chilly morning. When she was almost finished, who should come to join her? Lophina. She looked a little tired but was grinning as she sat down with her plate.

"And just where have you been?" Clerin grinned back.

"Well, let's just say that I really needed some time where I wasn't thinking about anything. I felt I had to lose myself for a while." She nodded to herself or to Clerin, it was not obvious to whom. "A long night with a big dumb ox, fully attentive and eager, is just what I needed." Her laugh was throaty but light.

"I am glad you enjoyed yourself."

"Oh, you have no idea." Her second laugh was more throaty and less light. "But that is not all. I was still doing reconnaissance work. You won't believe who owned that ship."

"Who?"

"Well, I forget his name, but anyway, it is the mayor of this little town." She waved her hand in front of herself for a moment. "And you won't guess who hates the mayor more than anyone."

"Telingard?"

"Ha, yes! Exactly. So, you see, Telingard figured we were stealing the ship and he didn't care." She was eating a little while talking, which was typically something that bothered Clerin, but Clerin figured she needed to replenish her strength, so she was forgiven. "But he needed all the proper paperwork, you see. He needed to have it shown that he was not helpful."

"But wait. What if the mayor shows up and disputes the signature?"

"I was worried about that for a little bit as well, but the mayor has not been seen for some time now. Suznedoon and I chatted about it, and I've come to my conclusion." She nibbled for another moment, ignoring Clerin's looks.

"And that is…?"

"That is that the mayor is a corpse down in a cave. I think he was one of the sailors or something. He was having money troubles, there was talk of embezzlement going on. There were those, Telingard amongst them, who were calling for an investigation. In Suznedoon's opinion, he needed to refill those coffers quick. Along came Altinger with a seemingly bottomless supply of crowns." She set her plate down. "We don't know for sure, of course. But it was thought that he was doing something with Altinger. Who knows, maybe he will show up and stop the transfer of the ship? But all we have to do is leave town before he shows up. Telingard will probably not even examine the signature too closely."

"If I know Jalin, the signature will be a perfect match anyway. That is all fantastic news. I am so happy that you sacrificed yourself for the reconnaissance."

"Anything for the coterie." They both laughed heartily.

The ship was received without issue. Telingard reiterated how pleased he was to be able to help Tureyn in general and Clerin in specific. She told him his assistance was appreciated and Tureyn would hear about it in due time. No one mentioned the mayor or the derelict ship that had been set ablaze.

They hired a full crew and set sail for Slasskord the next day. It was a quick jaunt around the island. The crew stayed in the town while the coterie went to the second largest cave on the island. They scoured it according to Altinger's map. They did their due diligence, spending a full two days down there. The last of the caves was a decent amount larger and they assumed they could need four days underground. It was a day's journey inland as well, up the side of one of the mountains, about a third of the way up. So the whole adventure would probably take a week. Unless they felt like they had to research that first cave.

Clerin doubted Gunzgak's name was in any of the caves. She also doubted that they needed Lembin's. Everyone else seemed set on the exploration, however, and she certainly did not mind. It added some direction to their quest, which was what was probably needed most. She only wished they had hired the crew after the cave exploration—it seemed a bit of a waste to park them at Slasskord for a week and a half. But everyone assumed they could sell the ship once they arrived at Vatlisi for Vanelia, or in Tureyn after that. They *had* received it for free, after all. Who was Clerin to argue with that?

Chapter 17

Vrric was getting sick of caves. Which was probably unfair since it had been an incredibly long time since they had scoured any until the island. And yet, there it was. The thing he hated most about it was the stale air. Just that thick, moist, cold air that left him gasping for breath. It did nothing to nourish, nothing to freshen his lungs. It just sat there like a boulder on his chest. Making it difficult to breathe. And it was only the first day they were in the large cave.

There were large caverns linked by little passageways up at the top of the system. Everything seemed to glow slightly—the lichen, the mushrooms, the walls themselves. It tried making light from magic unnecessary, but it was not quite bright enough to keep you from stubbing your toe. So Vrric kept casting light spells.

They set up camp in one of the larger caverns. They might as well enjoy the space before it got too cramped. With a small fire, it was almost like a real camp. He could almost imagine he could see the stars up against the top of the cave.

The next day was grueling. They found a cavern from Altinger's map that had many tiny tunnels branching out from it. Several of the tunnels were short, but most extended back quite a ways. It took half the day to cross all of them off the list. They had assumed the upper portions of the map were not going to be fruitful, but they had to be thorough. The latter part of the day was still obnoxious but was less grueling. They had several offshoots, but a couple of decent caverns as well. It was, however, just as fruitless.

The next day was where it got interesting. There was a river that ran through the caves. Or maybe, there were several rivers, it was impossible to tell. Much of the time they were more streams than rivers, something meandering around on the cavern floor. Some of the time there were ruts and gutters that the water sluiced through. The river they were at, however, flowed out of a hole in the wall, washed down a channel at a fairly fast pace, then funneled down through a whirlpool. The cave they were standing in was not huge and they filled it with just half the coterie standing packed together. Vrric would have turned and left. It was a complete dead end. But the map showed more caves underneath the whirlpool.

It did not, however, show the water at all. Not anywhere, not even the meandering streams above. Did the caves dry out beyond the whirlpool somewhere, or were they all completely inundated? There was no way to tell.

The map was quite rudimentary and so there were issues with the scale. It did show bigger caverns as being bigger, but sometimes they were only slightly bigger and other times there was a huge discrepancy—there was just no consistency. Even worse, most of the tunnels between the caverns were shown quite truncated on the map. There would be a short line between two caverns that, in reality, took almost an hour to traverse.

Vrric stood at the edge of the whirlpool and watched the water for a few moments. It swirled continuously. He could imagine it funneling infinitely. It was mesmerizing. Ryshial approached him while he stood there, staring.

"So the plan is to cast water breathing, flight, and go investigate? I hope one of us gets to stay up here as a safety rope." She was looking a little skeptical. "And I hope the safety rope is me."

"Yeah, sure." Vrric kept his eyes on the swirling water. "You know, I once cast a clairvoyance spell on a spyglass. I was just thinking if we should toss something down in there and watch it for a while."

"We could do that if you think you will be able to see anything."

"I don't know. Maybe it would be simpler if I just went down in there and took a quick peek." He glanced up at her, looking slightly hopeful. "Unless you think it's safer with two mages down there?"

"But what about the safety rope? If I am down there, who will pull you out in an emergency?" Her smile was a little crooked. She glanced behind them briefly. The water was making enough noise that Vrric doubted anyone could hear them, even if they were standing adjacent. "Would you trust Serghno to pull you out?"

"I'm sure he could pull one of us out. Just not sure about both." He chuckled for a moment. "How about Croy?"

"No, thanks. I am not sure where we landed on trusting Gaens, although I guess we are mainly looking for Lembin's name at this point—we are trusting Altinger's maps after all." She smiled and nodded to no one. "Arnasta could probably work with Serghno in getting us out. Listen, if it is an issue, I can go. I just want you up here to pull me out. I trust you and I trust your capabilities."

"And I trust you. No, I think it will have to be me. I'm just hoping that there will be a break in the water down there somewhere. It would be nice to walk around for a bit. And to be honest, I'm not really sure how I'll find a name etched in rock if I'm surrounded by rushing water the entire time." He took a deep breath. He did not necessarily want to go down through a whirlpool. At the same time, he knew he could not ask anyone else to do it either. He found it was always easier to force himself to do something unsavory than to try to push someone else into it.

Most shuffled out of the room. Ryshial, Croy, Serghno, and Arnasta were there, just in case. Trela was there because Trela was always there, wherever the action was. Clerin gave him a kiss and a wink.

"Come back in one piece."

She did not tell him to come back triumphant or give him a speech about how important what he was doing was. Of course, she also did not tell him to not go, to forgo the investigation. It was a bit of a middle of the road. She knew he would do his duty and she just wanted him to be safe.

"No need to prove anything stupid." Trela slapped him on the shoulder. "We are merely doing our due diligence. If there is no way to walk around down there, don't push it. We don't want Ryshial pulling you out of there blue in the face, choking and coughing up water."

Vrric nodded and took a deep breath. He had wanted to cast all the spells on himself so he could feel if they were slipping. But Ryshial assured him she would keep a *whisper* link open and give him fair warning. Any energy saved from not having to cast a water breathing spell on himself could be used to fly around under the water.

"Lumtecfluto!" Ryshial touched his throat. She had cast a strong spell, giving him some time. "Lumfintotto!" She cast the *whisper* link at the same level.

"Eqekinderpri!" He leapt into the swirling water without a second thought.

He entered in feet first because it felt safer. He groped around for a moment as he lowered himself with his flight spell. There was something glowing in the area, providing a low level of light, but it was still difficult to see with the water swirling the way it was.

"Nuteclufclo!" He cast a quick air bubble spell around his head, just so he could see easier. He would probably have to cast a light spell at some time, but he could see well enough at the moment that he felt he could save his strength. The hole he floated down was decent sized, at least two rods in diameter, he could have dropped down horizontally if he had chosen. He moved slowly, making sure there were not little side channels shooting off the main hole.

The hole went diagonally, then almost horizontal, then diagonal again. He flew through the water at a slow pace, examining everything as he went along. Keeping an eye out for something hidden. Then the hole went vertical again and so did he. Suddenly there was air again. He was not breathing it but could tell by the way the water crashed around him. It was no longer simply flowing about him in a laminar manner, it was now crashing turbulently about, white and frothy like a waterfall. He flew himself sideways out of the stream of falling water.

He was in a crevasse. The water tumbled away into the distance, audibly striking the rocks below, but the fissure extended in two directions as far as he could see. He whispered to Ryshial that she could cancel the rest of the water breathing spell. She may as well save her energy for something else.

"Are you sure you do not want company? Now that we know how long the underwater portion is?" Ryshial's voice was strong and confident through the *whisper*.

"Not yet. Let me investigate a little further. I like having you as a safety rope." He chuckled a little in his mind, though he was not positive if that translated well through the *whisper*.

"Okay. Just say when."

Vrric started floating downwards. He was going to investigate the bottom of the ravine. In his mind there might have been a path running adjacent to the river that he could follow. However, about a third of the way down or so, maybe fifteen rods or so, there was a ledge visible in the distance due to a massing of glowing flora. He flew himself over there. There was a small entrance in the cliff wall at the ledge. Small enough that he would have to crawl and squirm his way through. Small enough that he was a little frightened of getting stuck. He thought about turning away, of coming back to the tiny opening on his way back up to the others, whenever he had exhausted all his other options. But there was a strange symbol scratched into the glowing lichen above the opening.

It was a collection of scratches, almost random but obviously not. He had seen it somewhere before but could not think of where. He stared at it mesmerized for some time, trying to drag the memory back to the surface of his mind.

"What?!" It popped into his head hard. It was shock and awe. It was his own question yelled in his own mind about his own realization. He knew where he had seen the collection of scratches before. He remembered seeing them etched in stone. He had copied them with magic, then drawn them to study them. But nothing ever became of them, and he had finally tucked the drawing away in a book. He had seen that exact same symbol in the Gaen realm while they were looking for the Gaen mage, Vuildan, who had been traveling with Gyaer.

"Are you okay?" He must have accidently *whispered* his shock to Ryshial, and she was responding.

"No, I'm fine. Or yes, I'm okay. Nothing is wrong."

"If you make me too nervous, I will have to come down and check up on you."

"Seriously, everything is fine. I've just found an entrance to somewhere. I'll let you know if I need you."

Vrric screwed his eyes shut and took a deep breath. He opened them, peering as well as he could into the small hole, but could see nothing of note. There was only one thing left to do. He crawled on his belly over the sharp rocks and into the claustrophobic tunnel.

It took a while until it opened back up again. He was uncomfortable, but also grateful. It felt fantastic to be able to stand again. At first, he noticed the tall wall to his right. It was covered in writing and glowing moss. The ground under his feet was moist and slippery over the jumbled rocks. Then he noticed a figure in the distance. It was short. He was trying to figure out if it was truly derlian shaped, or if it was just a rock formation. Then it moved. It walked a pace or two but stayed a comfortable distance away from Vrric. It pulled off its hood. It was the Blind One!

"I thought it would be you. You know, you always seem to be the only mage that pays attention. Bravo." He clapped lightly for a moment. It could have seemed condescending, but he had sounded truly sincere.

There was nothing nefarious about how the Blind One looked. There was nothing alarming in his smile. But he made Vrric nervous. Just by being him. Part of it was because he always appearing and disappearing. That was surely nerve racking. The unpredictability of him. That was not all, however. No, whenever he showed up, something bad usually followed.

"You want me to trust you this time. That is why you are standing here so docilely, correct?" Vrric tried to keep his emotions out of his voice. He did not want to sound angry, or nervous, or even annoyed. He wanted some sort of upper hand in the conversation and that could only happen if he hid something.

"I typically want derlians to trust me. But yes, this time in particular. I need you to trust me because we are getting close now."

"Then you will have to answer some questions for me." Vrric did not take the bait about what the Blind One thought they were getting close to. He was sure that would come up again later in the conversation. "And if I think you are lying about anything, I'll never trust you again."

"Fine. We have some time. Ask away."

"Why did you betray us in Vatlisi?"

"That is an unfair question." The Blind One raised his hand to stave off Vrric's reflexive response. "It is unfair because I did not betray you in Vatlisi. But I can see how you could be confused. You understand, I had to make the Cabal think I was betraying you so that I could get the information I needed from them. You stumbled in while I was working on that, therefore you thought the same thing."

"They were waiting for us. We were ambushed!" Vrric took a deep breath. "How did they know when and where we were attacking?"

"How could they not? You were like elephants charging through the town! You had Pyrans at inns, you had Croy pretend he was some rich purchaser of evil equipment—Croy! Croy who could not appear even slightly cruel if he was dripping in babies' blood—in fact, that entire Stone Shield business was known to be a ruse from the start. Gyaer and Vuildan could not make that sound plausible, why did you think Croy could have? The Cabal thrived due to secrecy. Anyone looking for them, asking around for them, anyone who is not personally brought in by a trusted member, is suspect. Then Clerin and Trela walked straight up to the Prince and chatted with him. He was not the smartest Fluen I have ever met, not by a long shot, but he had an innate ability to smell a rat. And you brought Yavens! You had Phyna digging tunnels under their lair. Yes, in normal circumstances, Yavens are very hard to detect. But, and this is going to sound cruel so let me apologize here at the beginning, how could you think that a society that hunts and traps Yavens would have no way of sensing them? They can practically smell them. Or could—they could practically smell them. Past tense. For being utterly incompetent on some levels, Trela does know how to burn a thing to the ground." He took in a deep breath. He looked a little winded. "Oh, and a group of the half-Tlana-tainted Gaens betrayed you and were working for the Cabal. I never did find out for how long. Maybe since the beginning?" He turned the last sentence into a question.

"Then why did you not warn us? We could have been slaughtered. We lost a lot of valiant warriors that day."

"As I stated previously, I was trying to convince them that I was betraying you. Letting you tie your own noose was the simplest way to accomplish that." He raised a hand again as if he could sense a rebuttal. "I also had a strongly supported hunch that Taglo was working on something. I had not fully realized Baltuz's role, but that is beside the point. No matter what happened, there was going to be an incredible fight and many valiant warriors were going to die. Besides, I am working on something larger." He smiled a little, but Vrric still did not take the bait.

"Why were you at the ice cave on the Eidyon Peninsula? That seems like too much of a coincidence."

"The same reason you were there. The same reason we are both here. Names, Feyazki. I am searching for some very difficult to find names."

"Which names?"

"Gunzgak's and Lembin's. The only two names that still matter. You might not believe this, but I did find Linchon's a long time ago, before Clerin got to it. Never found Gorbanax's but, of course, all you needed for that Beleg was to destroy the Cabal." He chuckled to himself a little.

"Why would you be looking for Gunzgak's?"

"I think we are getting ahead of ourselves on that. What do you think that little symbol out there at the ledge means?"

"What? I just assumed whoever had left it in the caves outside of Pulthrim also left it here."

"Yes. Of course. But what do you think it means?"

"Oh, I don't know, it is a little chaotic, like a chiseled version of a water drop crashing on a rock?"

"Yes! Whew, you had me worried there for a moment, almost had me rethinking that you could pay attention. Yes, that symbol is Gunzgak's symbol for water. I placed it near Pulthrim so that whoever was attentive enough to find it would be able to recognize it here. You understand, I need some assistance to find Lembin's name here. And you are who fate has brought me."

"No, wait. I'm still not sure I can trust you."

"Oh, please. If I had wanted you dead, you would not have realized I was here. Whether or not I could have killed you in an ambush, we will never know, but I certainly would not have just walked out and started talking to you. Can we stop playing games now? Neither of us wants to fight to the death. Am I right?"

"Yes."

"And we both want to find Lembin's name, correct?"

"Yes."

"Then we should stop arguing and find it."

"One more thing. I, we, the coterie up above, want Gunzgak's name as well. I am a little concerned about finding Lembin's first. How do I know you actually want Gunzgak's name?"

"Because I have spent an enormous amount of resources tracking down how to get it." He sighed. "Fine. I agree. Everything should be out in the open. Do you know why I watched Croy's dreams?"

Vrric's reflexive answer was, "Because you are cruel," but he did not say it. He had enough willpower to rein his thoughts in and steer them into a different direction. *What was the secret of Croy's dreams?* he thought. "Because they come from Gunzgak."

"Exactly. I have known about this war between the Belegs for some time. It is fascinating beyond anything I have ever contemplated. I am unable to fathom Yavens, how am I to understand Belegs? How can you ever understand your Creator's mind, thoughts, emotions? And I, like you and, hopefully, most of the coterie above, feel it is all or nothing. If any of the Belegs die, they all have to. But, and this is what I figured out by watching Croy's dreams, Gunzgak thinks it can stay alive, be the last and only Beleg. I have no idea what Lembin thinks."

"You are telling me you accept that Gunzgak must die as well?"

"Of course. But Gunzgak cannot know that. The only reason I have been able to get the information I have gotten is because Gunzgak does not realize my intentions. In fairness, it has a lot of other things it is paying attention to, and I do my best to stay innocuous. And when that option is not available, then, much like with the Cabal, I make sure Gunzgak thinks I am betraying you." He held up both palms and gave a small shrug.

"All this fake betraying does make it difficult to trust you." Vrric thought for a moment. "Tell me how you plan on finding Gunzgak's name. Maybe then I will feel that I can trust you."

"If you do not already trust me, how is another story going to help?" He paused and shook his head slightly. His milky hued eyes "staring" at the ground in front of them. "Here is the truth of it. The only known location of Gunzgak's name is in the Yaven Gaen realm. The one who 'wrote' it down was one of Phyna's parents. Phyna, being, well, Phyna, had no idea what it was guarding. It was lost in plain sight, unnoticeable by being surrounded by so much other information. I had summoned a Yaven who could surreptitiously find the information, one called Alop. I then had Croy summon Phyna."

"Why haven't you resummoned Alop yet?" It all almost made perfect sense. It did not matter if Vrric really trusted the Blind One or not. They all needed to get Lembin's name anyway. But if he was honest with himself, he did want to trust the Blind One. It was certainly preferable.

"I have been busy of late. The amount of time that has passed for Alop will seem like a blink of an eye and I was hoping to perform that investigation last, just to give Alop a moment's breath. And not sure if you have noticed, but it has been difficult to get any Yavens summoned of late."

That gave Vrric a small pause. They had sent Wil back so quickly and had not even tried again. He wondered if mages everywhere were having issues. That was certainly what the Blind One seemed to be implying.

"So, will you want some assistance with the summoning spell?" Vrric wanted to get a promise out of the Blind One. Though if he did not trust him enough at the moment, what would another verbal promise really mean?

"Yes, exactly. Help me get Lembin's name and I will provide you with Gunzgak's. There is not better bargain to be had."

"Good, then. We have a deal."

"Excellent. We will need Clerin."

"What, no, that is not part of the deal."

"Do not be foolish. What type of help do you think I need? Do you think I want you to cast a spell or something? Do you think I need you to lightning the name out of the wall?" The Blind One's laugh was a bit harsh. Vrric recalled why dealing with him could be so vexing.

"I might trust you enough to put myself in danger, but she does not trust you at all." He thought for a moment about it and that just solidified his resolve. If the Gaens were trying to kill Clerin, this would be the perfect opportunity.

"I'll check, hold on." It was Ryshial's voice, speaking through the *whisper* link. He had completely forgotten about that, had just been speaking to the Blind One as if they were alone together. Rather than call attention to the link by responding, he turned his full attention to the Blind One.

"The only derlian that Lembin will allow in that chamber up above is Clerin Toswin. Trust me, I have already tried." The Blind One shook his head slightly.

"Well, maybe it is just you who are barred from entrance. Maybe it just needs to be a Fluen. Maybe it just needs to be someone Lembin trusts, or that Clerin trusts. Maybe it only needs to be someone who has communed with Lembin before. It appears that you are jumping to a large conclusion just because you, yourself, are being kept out."

"The legend states that 'only the Beleg's champion may enter.' I thought, legends being legends, that anyone could enter. That once I had figured out the sigil and made sure the name was not at any of the other rumored locations, that I could walk in, so to speak, and just read the name. Since I was unable to, I assumed that the legend had some kernel of truth to it." The Blind One looked a little annoyed. "But you are correct, I have not exhausted every trial and error. Be my guest." He pointed up the eerily glowing cliff face.

"How were you barred? Was it just sealed off?"

"I would hate to ruin the surprise." His smile was just barely on the cruel end of mischievous. "It did me no damage." He patted himself down. "Surely you, being so young and virile, will fare better than a decrepit old blind Gaen."

A hundred retorts bounced around in Vrric's mind. But they all seemed petty and dumb. They all came from the place of annoyance that the Blind One, apparently, liked to be observed from.

"Fine," was all he said.

Even though they had been chatting for a while, Vrric's flight spell was still working. He flew up the chasm a little in the direction that the Blind One had pointed, scanning for an alcove or something.

"A little to your left. Yes, like that, and up a little farther." The Blind One's limited directions were helpful and his voice had lost any bit of sarcasm, frustration, or annoyance. He sounded like he wanted to be helpful. Vrric could not fathom the Blind One at all. Nor did he have the time to contemplate him at that moment.

There was a tiny ledge surrounded by softly glowing lichen. Beyond the ledge was a tunnel that curved away into the distance. It was undeniably larger than the one Vrric had to crawl through to get to the chasm, but he would certainly have to stoop. Above the entrance was the etched symbol again, Gunzgak's symbol for water. He was obviously at the correct location.

Vrric took a couple of deep breaths and steeled himself. He held his left hand out in front of him, in case he encountered anything invisible. He stooped and slowly crept forwards. Nothing barred him. He crept along for a moment, wondering what the Blind One had been so concerned about, when it happened.

It started as a sound, a quiet rushing noise. It was a low moan, a deep chant. It gained in volume quickly. With it came a rising sense of panic. It started in his stomach but was soon in his chest, affecting his breathing and heart. He could feel the blood pumping in the arteries of his throat. The fear rose with the panic, turned to utter terror. The pulse in his throat seemed to scream, "Get out!" He turned and scrambled, kicking rocks and scraping at the tunnel walls with his hands, trying to move faster. Then he jumped into the chasm. The air on his face felt cool and refreshing, trying to dry the moist sweat that had appeared on his forehead.

Once he had escaped the tunnel, he realized he was plummeting. He slowed himself a little before the ground. He wondered briefly if the Blind One would have cast something before he hit the rocks. He was not positive either way.

"Do you see why I think Clerin is the only key to that lock?" There was a small smugness to the voice, but nothing overpowering.

"Yes, yes. I have only felt that once before. Or I guess twice, but at the same location."

"Really? Where?"

"The Luften Temple. And I must say that Clerin was the only one able to open that lock consistently." Vrric consciously brought his breathing and heart rate down. He did not like sounding out of breath while the Blind One was speaking calmly.

"Interesting." The Blind One looked thoughtful.

"So how many derlians' dreams have you spied upon?" Vrric was not positive he forgave the Blind One for stealing away Croy, but he was getting closer than ever before.

"Not as many as you think. I had really *really* wanted to see what went on in Trela's head as she slumbered. Especially when she was just rumored to be their Kriishan. When she was just Croy's charge. But try as I might, no matter the 'jin I had on her, she escaped before I could pry into her."

The Blind One stopped speaking. And Vrric, try as he might, could not think of anything clever to say. A blanket of quiet descended upon them.

"She will help on one condition." Ryshial *whispered* before the silence became unbearable. Which was not very long.

"What are the conditions?" Vrric was not positive if the Blind One had known that anyone been listening earlier or not, but he did not want to limit his responses at the moment. Even more, however, he did not want to stipulate only one condition. There were surely going to be an entire list of things they would need from the Blind One, to secure Clerin's safety at the least.

The Blind One narrowed his eyes at Vrric but seemed to keep his smile as well. It made it difficult for Vrric to figure out what he knew and when. Either way, the word "conditions" did not seem to bother him.

"She wants Gunzgak's name first. We summon the other Yaven before she does whatever the Blind One needs."

"We will need Gunzgak's name first. We will help if we summon Alop and get the name. As well as the same story. We would hate to just get a bunch of random letters thrust at us." Vrric was watching the Blind One's countenance closely. Trying to figure a reaction to anything. It was difficult to puzzle out, however. The Blind One had very good control of himself. Also, Vrric had not realized how much information he gleaned by watching other derlians' eyes. It was impossible to pierce through those cataracts and find any meaning. "And there will be a very rigorous security protocol when she arrives here to look for Lembin's name. You have to understand that she was attacked by Gaens. She is very nervous. You are not to harm her in any way. Understood?"

"Why would I want to do that?"

"Nope. No games. Promise me. It is just the two of us here. We both want the same things, correct? We are both just trying to find two names. This does not have to go sideways."

"Fine, yes. I promise I will not intentionally harm Clerin."

Vrric was not excited about the word "intentionally." Promises were only made against intentional actions, by definition. That same logic meant that his insertion of that caveat did not change his promise, so Vrric let it go.

"And that you will not teleport her at any time or to any place against her will. You are not sneaking her away to be harmed by another. You are not leaving her somewhere dangerous so she can be harmed unintentionally. You have stolen Croy from us before, you understand why we are nervous. You cannot teleport her without express verbal consent. Promise me." Vrric had his arms crossed but could not remember crossing them.

"I already explained that I needed to study Croy." He held up a hand. "Yes. I promise I will not take Clerin anywhere she does not wish to go. Happy?"

"I wouldn't call it happy, but I think we have a deal." Vrric nodded to himself.

"How do you want to get back to the others? If we teleport, will that make everyone jumpy?"

"Yes, probably. But the way back up is through a waterfall and underground river. I would rather not have to go through all of that." The odds that the Blind One would attempt to kill him, or kidnap him, or something else, were low but not zero. However, Vrric would much rather he show his true colors now than later. He would much rather be attacked than have Clerin attacked. He figured this first teleport was part of the trust building process. If he was going to be betrayed, he wanted it done sooner rather than later.

"Then teleport it is. You will have to think of where you left your friends, in all the vivid detail you are able. And you will have to let me tap into that." The Blind One's mouth twitched slightly into a small smile.

"Fine, yes. Let's do this. Ryshial, be prepared."

Vrric was concentrating so hard and the Blind One was so quiet casting his spell that Vrric missed the syllable the Blind One used for teleportation. Not that it would have helped him cast it later. Minora were individualized and only found through discovery. He was much too busy currently to be able to take the time required for something like that. He wondered what he would pursue when given the luxury of time. Probably not teleportation, but it was certainly intriguing. He wondered about the range that the Blind One could get.

Vrric did feel it happening, like being splashed with cold water but without the wet. It was so quick, however, that the feeling disappeared as soon as they appeared before the others. There was not a cheer of welcome when they arrived, but not everyone was scowling either. No one greeted them effusively, but all nodded in acknowledgement. Vrric was unable to tell if the Blind One was pleased with their quiet but polite reception or not.

"We understand you know of a Yaven who knows Gunzgak's full name." Ryshial broke the silence.

"I brokered the Yaven to research the name. I did not just find it, I sought it out and orchestrated its discovery. I want the same things you do. But I have had to perform all of my research in the shadows. Hidden even from my natural allies." The Blind One nodded towards her. "But this requires that the other name be researched as well. After this, Clerin will have to find Lembin's name."

"So you are willing to destroy Gunzgak?" There was an odd look on Croy's face. They had not gotten along ever since the Blind One had kidnapped Croy so long ago, maybe even before. But the look was not just one of annoyance or even animosity. It was one of betrayal.

"Oh, I had not realized." The Blind One suddenly appeared to actually look at Croy. Not towards him or near him, not at his feet, but directly at him. "This does make things more interesting, does it not? First, let me state that we are looking for two names today. Second, my motives are my own. They always have been."

"You just stated that you orchestrated finding Gunzgak's name." The feeling of betrayal that emanated from Croy was palpable. His lip curled into snarl. Vrric could not recall seeing him like that before. "This will not be forgotten."

"There is no reason for further delay. I think we should begin with the summoning, do you not?" The Blind One was no longer looking at Croy but nodding somewhat absently.

"Of course. Who would you like to assist?" Vrric was going to have to investigate what just happened. To begin with, he would probably just ask the Blind One later. Of course, that was not always the most effective method—the Blind One could be quite inscrutable when he wanted to.

"Just you and Ryshial, if that is acceptable to everyone." He was a little quieter it seemed. As if there was a slight reduction in his typically robust bravado.

Everyone else shuffled into an adjacent cavern. It took some time for everyone to filter out and it took some more for them to quiet down as they took various turns. The noise eventually faded to a low murmur but did not disappear altogether. They stood silent for a couple of moments before the Blind One spoke up.

"The Yaven's name is Alopnoughnreashunglyn. We shall each cast the summoning spell at the same time. We should each cast it at the Eqe level. We should be insistent, but do not wish to cause nemesis or anything untoward. If Alop does not wish to be summoned, we will have to discuss our options rather than forcing the issue. Agreed?"

"Agreed." Both Vrric and Ryshial answered at the same time. It seemed auspicious for the timing of the summoning.

"Okay. On three. One, two, three."

"Eqesidgearc! Alopnoughnreashunglyn!" They each cast the spell at the same moment.

There was a pause. It was a long one. Vrric wanted to ask if they should try again, but knew he was being impatient. Then a loud boom and a giant boulder rose up from the cave floor. A torso rose from the boulder, arms sprouted from the torso, and a head popped out the top. The torso looked as if it was wearing plate armor and the head had a helmet chiseled onto it. Vrric thought the helmet was easier to look at, and probably easier to produce, than an attempt at a derlian face. The facial features of Yavens were often vague and not well formed.

"Are you concerned over something, Narst?" It took Vrric a brief second to recall the Blind One's name. "Is something happening? The Cabal is destroyed, yes?" The lifeless-toned voice still betrayed a hint of emotion, of concern.

"Yes, I just… Listen, Alop, I need you to tell us Gunzgak's name right away and then start yelling about how you will never give it up. Struggle loudly, we will argue loudly, the others will come and then you strike me. Hard enough to be believed, but not too hard, of course. I do not need a concussion. Please, I apologize and will explain later if you like, but we need to do this with utmost urgency. Please, the name."

There was the tiniest pause. Vrric wondered how many different thoughts a Yaven could think in a moment. Their time was so much slower in their own realm, but he also assumed they were better in every way compared to derlians. He did not have any time to pursue his own thoughts, however.

"Gunzgakaphunchistiolanwendug." It was almost a whisper. Vrric repeated it in his head and would do his best, but he knew that Ryshial had a better memory and there was no way the Blind One would forget. But just as the yelling started, he thought of something. He *whispered* the name to himself, to be repeated in an hour or so.

"Mekfintotdelrefpri! Gunzgakaphunchistiolanwendug." He had never tried such a spell, that of referring the delay back to himself, and he was unsure if it would work correctly. He had a small moment of panic that the name would just be repeated in the room later and anyone who was around would hear it, ruining whatever game the Blind One was trying to play. The screaming had begun, however.

"Never! Foul wizard! I will die before giving up any name!" Alop had grown two more arms and was punching the ground and the ceiling. It sounded horrendous and made small craters, but nothing was crumbling around them, so Vrric assumed Alop was not actually damaging the stone around them.

"You must, I compel you!" The Blind One stood directly in front of Alop, though there was still some distance between them, and was screaming at the top of his lungs. "We compel you! Come, Feyazki! Come, Ryshial!"

"You must, we compel you!" Ryshial rushed to stand near the Blind One.

"Give us the name!" Vrric ran over there as well.

He was not really sure what to yell, but it was all just becoming a jumble of words. He had a hard time figuring out which words were coming from his own throat by the time the others burst into the cavern. The words "name" and "compel" were certainly repeated.

"No, never!" One of the arms flung the Blind One. Vrric found himself turning to watch it, but he never saw the body hit the wall because one of Alop's arms hit him directly after.

He did not quite pass out, but the wind was knocked out of him. He lay there for some time groaning to himself. There was a sort of high-pitched whine in his ears, half drowning out the yelling. Then it grew quiet and there was only the whine.

They were all healed. There was some dried blood on Ryshial's temple, so she must have been flung as well. The room was crowded again.

"Let's just go back to the larger chamber where there's more room. I'm starting to get claustrophobic." In truth, Vrric was still concerned that his delayed *whisper* would strike while they were all standing there, even though it was supposed to only be audible to himself.

In the other chamber the noise started back up again. Everyone began asking questions at the same time. Finally, the Ryshial spoke through the babble.

"Enough!" She frowned a little, her brown eyes glaring. Her brow was knitted behind the leather thong that kept her hair out of her face. "It took us a little time get the summoning to work. I was worried the Yaven was not even going to come. But we are powerful together." She motioned to all three of them.

"When it arrived, it was angry. Then the Blind One asked for the name and it got angrier still." She turned to him and frowned even further. "Which was odd since we were told you had brokered the name or some such nonsense. We were told no name would be given. No explanation, no discussion, just that it would not be given. We asked repeatedly. Got told no repeatedly. Then got attacked." She breathed out slowly. "To be honest, not exactly sure what happened after that, but it seemed like you all arrived immediately afterwards."

"I am just glad it was not full nemesis." Vrric shook his head. "That was the dumbest thing I have participated in in a long time."

"Admittedly, that did not go as planned. We will try again… later." The Blind One looked properly downtrodden.

"So, did you even broker anything? Was this just a ruse to get Lembin's name?" Croy, who had been so annoyed about the name in the first place, seemed just as annoyed now that he was told there was not a name.

"I did, truly. I am not sure what happened." The Blind One shook his head. "But I think we will need to gain these names out of order. I think we will have to get Lembin's name first."

"That was not the deal. I think I am with Croy on this one. How can I trust you?" Clerin glared at the Blind One.

"I don't know if he is lying or not, but until very recently we assumed we were just getting Lembin's name anyway. We are following Altinger's maps after all. At least... I don't know. At least we have a path here." Vrric put on his best determined smile. He needed to convince Clerin to come along but was hesitant to convince her that the Blind One was telling the truth. He was still unsure of what the Blind One's game was. But he did not want to give it up just yet.

"Really? You trust him after he got you flung against a wall?"

"I never said I trusted him. Just that we may as well accomplish what we can while we're here." He let out a long breath. "We are not trying to resummon that Yaven again right away. That much I know."

Several of them laughed, even those who had not been flung against a wall. It released some of the tension in the room. Though there were still a lot of glares focused on the Blind One.

"Okay, you are right. We should at least accomplish what we came here for." Clerin nodded to Vrric and then turned to the Blind One. "But you should know that I will not go anywhere alone with you. Feyazki, at the least, will always be between you and I."

"Of course. You may not think it, but your comfort is high on my list of things to keep. We may serve under different Belegs, but you are the great communicator to them all. That is an honor unlike any other." The Blind One nodded to her. "Would it be acceptable for all three of us to teleport there?"

Clerin nodded back. Then, from the side, Ryshial came up to Vrric. She whispered a *whisper* spell on him. "Lumfintotto!"

"I will keep the safety rope around you. Just say the word." She nodded to Vrric and then to Clerin. Even though he knew the Blind One had kept his word, he was still comforted by Ryshial's vigilance.

All three of them teleported back to where the Blind One had been waiting for Vrric. They were quiet for a little bit. Vrric was thinking about letting the Blind One tell Clerin, but he was obviously waiting for Vrric.

"We were given Gunzgak's name." Vrric whispered it, though he was not sure why.

"What?" She did not yell, but her voice was loud and she was certainly shocked.

"More than what is the why." Vrric looked over to the Blind One. "Why did all of that happen?"

"Croy is the ears of Gunzgak." The Blind One nodded to no one in particular.

"Wait. You mean Gunzgak hears everything Croy does? Constantly?" Clerin turned to him, looking even more shocked.

"I do not know about constantly, but Gunzgak heard through Croy while I spoke to him earlier. And I think Gunzgak responded through him as well." He was being quiet, almost as if he did not have his usual confidence. "I have never been more sure of anything in my life. That was why I had Alop argue with us to draw you in. That was why I had Alop throw me against a wall. I am not really sure why he did that to you and Ryshial, however."

"It certainly sold the story. I had no idea, none whatsoever. So we have Gunzgak's name? And no one knows we have it but us?" Clerin was still incredulous. She glanced at Vrric for another confirmation. He gave her a nod.

"And Ryshial, yes. Remember about Croy as well. Croy cannot know about the name, no matter what. Personally, I would not tell anyone who did not need to know. Just to heighten the odds that it does not get out. Each person you tell doubles the chances of failure."

Personally, Vrric thought of the saying that, "Three derlians can share a secret if two of them are dead," but he certainly did not mention it. The Blind One was trying to get his point across without being alarming. Vrric wondered how he would have put it if Clerin were not around. She had the tendency to make other derlians soften their language.

"So you have upheld your part of the bargain." Clerin nodded to the Blind One. "I supposed it is only fair that I uphold mine."

"That is true, of course. We are not necessarily in a hurry, but I am not one to stave off duty."

"Do you wish to fly me up?" She turned to Vrric.

"Of course, my love." He did not always say things like that around other derlians. Her head bowed slightly and her dimples pierced her cheeks in a sudden tight smile. "Mekkinderclo!"

They flew up to the ledge, which was not very far at all. She looked a little nervous, but did not hesitate. She gave him a small kiss and then stepped into the tunnel. Vrric waited for a moment, then drifted back down.

They waited for a while in silence. Vrric wanted, more than anything, to ask the Blind One to repeat Gunzgak's name. There had been a lot of trust built up between them recently and he sort of wanted to test it out. Sort of. Would the Blind One tell him something incorrect, even if he thought Vrric would not notice? Vrric doubted it. Whether or not he could be trusted in the long run. Once he convinced himself that the question would not gain anything, he stayed silent. The pause was starting to take some time.

"You said Clerin was attacked by Gaens. What does that mean, really? That seems vague and a bit like you are blaming more than the attackers themselves." The Blind One broke the silence.

"We joined the quest of a Gaen who was looking for Lembin's name. Well, he said he was looking for two names, but that did not seem to be the case. We have not found any evidence of Gunzgak's name anywhere near here." Did that mean anything? No, not really, but the Blind One did not seem to think Gunzgak's name was anywhere in the derlian realm, let alone anywhere on Johcal Island. "The Gaen's name was Altinger, and he made the maps we have been using. He had hired a Fluen vessel and found us in the middle of nowhere. He brought us to the caves and the first one, the very first one, we get attacked in a deep chamber by the sailors. Those left outside were also attacked. And in something that appeared quite coordinated, Verin attempted to kill Clerin in a narrow cleft. Clerin was, luckily, able to cast a shield spell and escape. Silvadhin, also a Gaen, attacked Verin and saved Clerin. She paid for that loyalty with her life."

"That sounds like a lot of Fluens to me. Or were the sailors all Gaen?"

"No, you are correct, most of the attackers were Fluen." Vrric thought for a moment, trying to sort it out in his head. "It is our understanding that Altinger hired them and they were mostly acting for profit, not ideologically. We considered them mercenaries. But really, it was Verin that shocked us. She had been an incredibly loyal warrior for a long time. We trusted her. And Croy mentioned that she had been having dreams before her betrayal. So we naturally assumed that Gunzgak had been communicating with her."

"And speaking of Gunzgak communicating through dreams, what did Croy do during the melee? Did he attack anyone?"

"No. He was not right next to Clerin when Verin attacked, but it did not seem like he was trying to do anything. To anyone."

"Hmmm. Do you think he would have protected Clerin if he had been closer? That he would have attacked Verin?"

"Personally? No. But I also don't think he would have attacked Clerin. We still trust him to that extent. Though, of course, we had no idea that Gunzgak was listening through him. But I do not think he would have attacked Verin either. And that is where my trust in him falters. He has been very vocal about letting Gunzgak be the only Beleg or, at least, of letting Gunzgak live. Honestly, I am not positive how he feels about letting Lembin live. That subject rarely comes up." Vrric paused for a split second, he was going to mull some of that in his head, but he realized the Blind One was about to interject. "I think Croy would have done nothing. Nothing to help, nothing to hurt. Whether that would have been through paralysis or timidity, or through a desire to let destiny take its course, I do not know."

"So, Gunzgak was able to turn Verin against you, to exact violence upon Clerin at the moment that the mercenaries attacked, but was unable to get the same reaction from Croy." An eyebrow shifted up as he spoke, even as his head was slightly bowed so that it appeared that he was staring at the ground. "That should prove something, yes?"

"It does. But Verin was a warrior through and through. She reacted to Gunzgak's urgings, or pleas, or demands, or whatever, in the same way she lived her life. Croy, by being Gunzgak's ears, may be reacting in his own way. His betrayal of us follows his personality, just as Verin's followed hers."

"I am just saying do not judge him too harshly. I have seen his dreams. I have felt the urges they instill, for the lack of a better description. Have you ever communicated with a Beleg? Or had one communicate to you?"

"No. Never. But Clerin has."

"I will not argue with you. But as someone who has faced the anger of the entire group I have traveled with, let me say how difficult that is. And I do not have the same dreams that Croy has. And neither do you. All I am saying is that if there is a moment where you could be kind to him or verbally attack him, you should try to be kind. That is all. He does not have a cruel bone in his body. And for that, I will give you something."

"What?" Vrric thought the Blind One was actually going to hand something over, but he did not.

"You have a mystery in your midst, do you not?" His smile had a little something behind it. Not cruelty by any means, but something cold. "I am the one who stole Tumu." He held up a hand yet again. "I needed his abilities more than the rest of you combined, and he is quite safe and comfortable. Just tell Croy that Clerin had nothing to do with it. Talk about another derlian without a cruel bone in her body. Not really sure how he got that into his head, but there you are. Let him know it was me. He already reviles me anyway."

Vrric wondered how the Blind One knew that Croy had originally blamed Clerin for Tumu. He thought about asking, but Clerin was suddenly yelling from above.

"Feyazki! Help me down, I have it." She sounded almost giddy.

He floated her down. She grinned to each of them, then handed the Blind One a piece of parchment.

"I brought some parchment, a quill, and powdered candleblack with me, since I knew I would never remember the name. We each have a copy of what was written on the wall through that tunnel now. At least, I copied the one that started with Lembin..." She nodded seriously. "I think I like things better when we are working together." Her bright smile returned.

"I as well. This has been most fruitful, thank you." He nodded and smiled as well. Vrric was not sure, but it may have been the largest smile he had ever seen on the Blind One's face. "We may need to cooperate once more. If you are unable to convince the powers that be, then you will have to find other powers. I will meet you there." Then, without another word, before they could even ask what he meant, he disappeared.

It was quiet for some time. Vrric was thinking about the Blind One and how much time they should allow to lapse before talking about him. Apparently, Clerin was doing the same. She broke the silence.

"So, do you think we actually have Gunzgak's name, or was that all just a ruse?"

"Did you provide him with the correct name?"

"Of course. Was I not supposed to?"

"No. Or yes. You did everything perfectly, as you always do. And yes, I sure hope it was not a ruse. If it was, it was quite elaborate and had to have been set up beforehand. The Yaven was not given any time. Or at least, not much time according to derlian standards. Of course, we are also assuming the Yaven was not lying to the Blind One either."

"Well, I suppose that is all that can be hoped for. Just, if it is wrong, we will all be destroyed."

"I was hoping that if it was wrong, we would just be unable to summon Gunzgak. Versus getting destroyed."

"It could go that way as well. Yes, that would be preferred." Clerin smiled through it all, even the destruction parts.

"What went on up there?" He pointed to the ledge above.

"I accomplished a task that was too great for the greatest magicians of the Luften and Gaen realms, that is what went on." Her smile somehow got larger. "And I bet Ryshial or Olwinn would not have been able to accomplish it either."

"Hey, I heard that." Ryshial's voice laughed in Vrric's head. He had forgotten she was listening.

"Ryshial says she challenges you to a duel of magic." He decided to remind Clerin that Ryshial could hear them.

"I think you already lost one of those to Olsfang, did you not?"

Olsfang was an old friend of Ryshial's who had died fighting the Cabal. Vrric was unsure of why he paused, the joke was on him, not the dead Pyran. So he tried to keep the momentum rather than dwell upon it.

"Oh, yes. Horribly so. I could not show my face in public for a week after that." He also did not mention that he thought the duel was faked to get him to convince Croy to speak with Ryshial.

Ryshial laughed in his head. Clerin laughed along with him. It was all glossed over quickly.

"Well, we are going to have to go back through the water since the Blind One has disappeared. Do you feel up for it?" Clerin changed the subject.

"Yes, I have been doing very little lately besides chatting." Vrric thought Clerin was right earlier. It was nice to work together with the Blind One. It dissipated a lot of tension. He only hoped that Gunzgak's name was provided without subterfuge.

It was after they had returned to the group and handed out Lembin's name that the word randomly flashed into Vrric's mind. "Gunzgakaphunchistiolanwendug." His spell had come back to him. He immediately asked Clerin for some parchment and her candleblack. He wanted that name written down as well.

They were finally above ground again. They had accomplished much, had gained both of the Beleg's names they had been searching for. Hopefully. There was no real way to test the authenticity of either one. Vrric had been fairly sure they were not going to get Gunzgak's name, even if they somehow found Lembin's. He could certainly not say it was worth the lives of Silvadhin and Alphino. But it was certainly worth something.

Zira had been recuperating near a giant gorse bush, which is where they set up their camp. If Vrric had his way, they would camp for a couple of days there, just to breathe fresh air and relax for a little bit. They were not positive where they were headed from the island. Most wanted Vatlisi, but there were some arguments for Tureyn as well. Vrric knew it was too soon to see if Lembin's name was correct. They would only be able to do that after having a good plan set for Gunzgak—at the earliest. No, he was leaning towards Vatlisi as well. It would be nice to see Vanelia situated and out of harm's way. He walked up to Zira, who was resting alone.

"What would it take for you to be too wounded to move for a couple of days?" He sat down next to her on the ground. He knew her, certainly. They had traveled together for over a cycle, but they had never become close confidants. He had orbited around the other Luftens and, of course, Clerin, during Trela's campaign. And even while they were hunting the Cabal, she seemed to prefer the company of warriors.

"Are you asking what the price of my pride is?" She laughed a little but stayed lying down. Her eyes glanced at him and then returned to staring at the stars above.

"Pride? You had many terrifying wounds when I first saw you after the fight. You appeared to be dancing with death at that point. I don't think anyone would begrudge you some recuperation time."

"Well, the quick boat ride to this side of the island *was* a little trying. But I've been up here recuperating for the last several days while you were suffocating through those caves." She laughed again. "If you want my opinion, no one would begrudge *you* a couple days of rest if you just asked. You don't need the likes of me to convince the group."

"Maybe not the group. But Trela is not the easiest to convince at times." He laughed and then heard footsteps approaching. Like the boots started making noise because their owner wanted him to hear them.

"And just what is Trela not easy to convince to do?" It was, of course, Trela who was walking up behind him. He cursed his luck.

"Anything, if we are being honest," Vrric quipped. They all laughed. Even Estfale, who had been right behind Trela. He had kept his boots quiet, however.

"Feyazki here wants a couple of days just lolling about the island. He's trying to convince me to play the invalid." Zira rolled to her side to better look at Trela. She barely winced.

"That could probably be arranged." Trela raised an eyebrow at Vrric. "If you are asking for yourself and not bothering Zira."

"All right, fine. Can we please just rest for two nights in one spot?" He thought about the statement for a moment. "Above ground." There, that explained his position better.

Trela agreed, and they sprawled the camp out. There was plenty of time for Vrric to explain to everyone that they could not speak in front of Croy. At least not about Gunzgak. He was able to get derlians alone or in small groups and quietly convey what the Blind One had told him. He was also able to get Gunzgak's name to a couple of derlians without raising suspicions. Only those who truly needed to know. Everyone else thought they were still searching for that.

Everyone already knew about Lembin's name. That had been a moment of celebration. One of their first acts outside of the caves.

Vrric told Croy, and everyone else for that matter, that the Blind One had stolen Tumu. It made a lot of sense when it was fully thought through—the sudden disappearance without a trace from a crowded inn. Arnasta recalled having thought she had sensed him at the time. It had been an overlooked possibility back then. No one had imagined the Blind One following them that far into the Luften realm. And he was easy to hate. An entire evening passed with various members of the coterie airing their grievances against him. Even those who did not know him very well. Vrric certainly did not stick up for him, even if his private opinions were slowly pivoting.

The last night their conversations turned to Vatlisi. Vanelia was certainly excited to be heading to their final destination. And she was not overly shy about saying so. She just wanted a peaceful place to raise Hynara, and who could blame her? But it was not only Vanelia who was excited. Torpalin and his sister were adamant about setting up a bakery. Even though it was not huge, there was a Luften Quarter there. Escha seemed happy about it as well, though it seemed she was mostly happy that Torpalin was happy. Vrric had a hard time imagining her stuck in a large foreign city. But he had an even harder time imagining her without Torpalin. They had one of the longest, and healthiest, relationships of anyone Vrric had traveled with. Probably of anyone he had ever met.

They returned to Slasskord where Yifindur was waiting. Even though they had stayed a couple of days near the cave, and it had taken a full day to make it back to the small town, they stayed another day in Slasskord. There was just not a huge impetus to go rushing back to sea. Most in the coterie did not know about Gunzgak's name still and so there was no reason to hurry. And Vrric himself, who was in the know, had a hard time mustering up any real ambition. What were they going to do? Just because they had a name did not mean they had a plan. How could you summon a Beleg who did not wish to be summoned? No one he spoke with had a guess to that question.

Most of the coterie spent their last evening on the island carousing around the town. He was sure the nearby taverns were full of foreigners downing bottles of sour wine. But he was not with them. Neither was Clerin, who had every reason to be enjoying the local hospitality. No, they stayed in their small private room at the inn. All alone together, with a fire blazing, the sheets moist with the sweat of their exertions. They did not typically get much time together. Even in a private room at an inn there were always others nearby. One could not help but hear the neighbors through the thin board walls. And the interruptions! Someone or other was always knocking on the door, asking about this or that, sharing a drink or trying to get one. It could be maddening at times.

The upper floors of the inn, the actual rooms well above the common areas, were fantastically quiet that evening. No one was staggering down the hallway. No one was yelling at anyone else. It was peaceful bliss outside of the room. Which gave them the ability to make a little noise, to not have to whisper, to create an assertively bold and audacious bliss inside the room. They were lying amongst the crumpled bedsheets, panting and giggling, when they heard the first of the warriors loudly return. Vrric slept well that night, deep and dreamless.

Yifindur was in capable hands. The crew they had hired seemed to know all the ins and outs of the ship. Which, to Vrric's mind, meant that Yifindur was generic enough that there was no secret to getting it to move steadily and speedily. It left a lot of time for the coterie to enjoy the decks. Except for the frequent storms. And the quick boredom. Vrric spent much of his time below deck with Croy. He felt a little bad that it took Altinger to find the secret to alleviating Croy's seasickness. So he spent some of the trip attempting to make up for times gone by.

Vrric cast the levitation spells and Croy healed himself. A lot of the time Croy would have his eyes closed, which made their conversations a little odd, but not too awkward. Most of the time they talked about nothing, or nothing of import. Vrric certainly did not mention anything about Gunzgak's name. He tried to not even think about it, just in case.

Their conversations rolled between topics, much like the ship on the sea, and Vrric could not help trying to argue a little. Would they really need Croy's help when the time came? Who could say? But he was the only derlian in the coterie who was dead set against their mission. The topic had somehow rolled over to Lembin's name.

"We already have Lembin's name. We need to use it." Croy's eyes were closed, but Vrric could see them twitching around under their lids. "We did not hesitate at Gorbanax, did we? Clerin certainly did not hesitate at Linchon. I just don't understand how we have this incredible tool in our hands and refuse to use it. You know if we had found Gunzgak's name down in that cave, we would have used it that same day."

"I am not sure we would have, but that's not the question. I do not want to sound annoying here, but you know that we will not use Lembin's name until we have Gunzgak's, right? We will probably not attempt anything at all concerning Lembin until we have finished with Gunzgak. That is just the way it is." Vrric did not want to sound cruel, but he felt he had to limit Croy's tendency towards wishful thinking.

"That is the worst excuse ever! Really, your answer to me is, 'That is just the way it is?' That is not an answer and isn't even an argument. It is something you say to placate a child. I am not a child, Feyazki."

"Of course not. I am not trying to demean you in any way. But the reality of it is that you're outvoted." He closed his own eyes for a moment. That was no better. In fact, it was the same statement, but just made meaner. "It is the fact that Gunzgak is fighting tooth and nail against this. We cannot use Lembin's name first in case Gunzgak actually does what it is intending to do—and that is to be the only Beleg left."

"Gunzgak was fine with four Belegs." Croy was quiet for a moment. "How do we know that Lembin does not wish to be the only Beleg left? I mean, think about it. Lembin started this war. How do you know that Lembin's plan all along was not to kill the other three. And not even itself, of course, but to use Clerin as an assassin."

"Clerin is the one who has communicated with the other Belegs. She feels Lembin is telling her the truth. And I trust Clerin."

"Well and good, I trust Clerin as well. But do I trust her to know when a Beleg is lying to her?" Croy's eyes were open, but he was staring at the ceiling. "A derlian, any derlian, cannot be trusted when it comes to a Beleg. Lembin could just be controlling her. Who knows? Lembin is one of the Creators of the world, Feyazki. Do you really think you can trust Clerin to see through the subterfuge of a Creator?"

"Yes, I do."

"Just because you have sex with someone does not mean you have to…"

Vrric did not want to hear what Croy was going to say, so he interrupted. "It is not just because we have sex, Croy. It just makes more sense to me."

"Fine. Then I'll use the word 'love.' Just because you love someone does not mean you have to take everything they think— their opinions, mind you—as truth."

"There is no doubt that Gunzgak will do everything it can to stay alive." Vrric was not performing well in the argument, he understood that. "The only doubt that exists, as you point out, is what Lembin wants, what Lembin will do."

"It is the murderer! How can you trust the Beleg that started the killing?"

Vrric realized that he could not win the argument, or more succinctly, he would never be able to convince Croy to any other way of thinking. However, he also understood that there was no way the coterie was going to go after Lembin first. Clerin and Trela were both convinced. And that was enough for him. Which meant that Croy could not win the overall argument, not against the whole of the coterie. It was, in its simplest terms, as he had stated earlier. Croy did not have, nor could he ever get, the votes.

Vrric needed a way for Croy to realize that there was no use arguing. That the decision was, by all intents and purposes, already forgone. And what he really needed was to make Croy somehow realize that on his own.

"What do you think the difference between wisdom and knowledge is?" Vrric needed to capture the idea in phrasing that Croy respected.

"You are just changing the subject."

"Maybe I am. But seriously, what is the difference? To you."

"Well, knowledge is knowledge. You read it, you hear it, you repeat it." He paused for a moment. Vrric did not dare interrupt. "Knowledge is something you have in your youth and wish to show it to others. Knowledge is loud. Wisdom is something that takes time to grow and flourish. It is old and quiet." He paused again.

"Knowledge is what you know. Wisdom is understanding what you don't know."

"Good, yes! Understanding what you don't know, that is interesting. Like a wise king asking a servant for advice." He cringed inwardly. He should not be attempting to interpret Croy's own words. But he was unsure if he would get a better opening, so he soldiered on. "I think it goes a little further as well. There are things that we can accomplish, which take courage to do. There are things we cannot, which takes courage to admit and accept. Wisdom is understanding which courage to reach for, Croy. Because one of them is futile and will steer you towards madness, or at least unhappiness."

"You can leave now." Croy had his eyes closed again. He looked peaceful. "I can work the levitation on my own at this point. Thanks for helping me with my seasickness. It is appreciated. Truly."

Vrric's heart sank a little. He had failed. He had hoped to plant a seed, but all he had been able to do was to tear up a garden. Why had he wanted to plant that seed anyway? He realized that he needed to work on his own wisdom in understanding futility. And courage.

Chapter 18

Trela enjoyed riding in the ship. She had never dreamt of such a thing in the Pyran realm, not even as queen. Sure, there were river boats. But they were rare and felt more like glorified ferries. Sailing on the ocean to the south of the Dekhan Plateau was unimaginable to a Pyran.

Yifindur was incredibly fast as it slid through the water. Certainly faster than a galloping horse. Trela enjoyed standing on the deck, watching the billowing sails strain against their ropes. She even enjoyed the rolling waves; they could feel like the slowest galloping horse that there ever was. She knew Croy was below deck and, if not laid out in sickness, he was certainly not enjoying the ship's movements. But that did not reduce her own pleasure. Trela reveled in new experiences, unimaginable experiences. She thrived on them. And the Fluen realm certainly supplied its fair share. The only downside she could think of was that she was getting a little tired of fish. It was a small price to pay.

It would take several more days to get to Vatlisi, longer if the winds slackened. She knew she should be spending her time with Knill, but somehow something always came up. This time it was to visit with Zira. She had almost died defending Vanelia and the others, and Trela had not given her the one-on-one time she liked to provide her warriors after a harrowing battle. She took another deep breath and watched the horizon. It was odd not being able to see land in any direction. Then she turned to the companionway to descend below deck.

Zira had her own room since she was still healing. Spells helped—they certainly saved lives in the short term—but time was the greatest healer of all in their realm of chaos. Trela knocked on the door and waited to be invited in.

Zira was lying in a hammock staring at the deck above. She turned her head and smiled briefly at Trela before returning her gaze to the overhead. Trela closed the door behind her and grabbed a chair to sit on.

"How are you feeling?" Trela added a smile to her face to bring the smile to her voice.

"I'll be up and about in no time. With a sword arm as quick as before. Don't you worry."

"I'm not worried. Not about you." Trela laughed a little. "I just wanted to say thanks. Officially. Repulsing a sneak attack while being outnumbered is certainly no fun. I just want you to know that I appreciate what you did for Vanelia and the others. What you've always done."

"I know what you're doing. And I'm flattered. Truly. But you don't need to do that, my Queen. I've followed you from the beginning. From when Lishean left Iventorn. And I'll follow you to the end, rest assured. I'm not faltering or flagging." Her gaze turned to Trela. "I'm a true believer. When all this is done and you are back being the Kriishan, I'll join the Guard and do my duty that way."

"I haven't stopped being the Kriishan."

"I don't know. Can you be the Kriishan in the Fluen realm?" She smiled briefly. "You are still you, I'm not saying that. And I certainly mean no disrespect. But it will be nice when you are back home as queen. Won't it?"

"I will enjoy that very much, yes."

"And no disrespect to Lishean, but he's no Kriishan. Correct? I mean, it is not just the place, but it is the right derlian in the right place at the right time. It is all of it wrapped up. And that's you, at home, as queen. Honestly, I'm just here to help speed it along. You know? To keep everything on an even keel, as the Fluens would say."

"So… You do not believe in the mission?" As soon as she said it, Trela felt it was the wrong way to frame it. But Zira took it in stride.

"My mission is to help yours. And I certainly like Vanelia. She's a hoot. I'd do anything in my power to keep her safe. But it's you that I would die for. You are my liege, my Queen. But it is even more than that. You know? It is a higher level. I love my family, my friends, my realm. You are destined to make the realm great, I truly believe that. You are the Kriishan. I want a great realm." She paused for a moment, staring upwards. "But you can't make the realm great from here. So here I am. My destiny is to help yours, so you can come back and help everyone else's."

"Well, I…" Trela was not sure what to say, so she was a little relieved that Zira interrupted.

"Not that I'm trying to rush you, or anything. Your destiny is yours, I've no inkling of it. You do what you need to. Everything you need to. I'm not ungrateful or impatient or making any sort of demands or suggestions. All I'm saying is that you don't have to worry about me. You don't have to say how much you appreciate my service, how grateful you are that I didn't let your foreign friends die. You don't have to say anything. Just use me. I am your loyal tool. Truly, I'd die for you. You could demand that I just stop breathing right now and I would."

"I would never do that!" Trela was aghast.

"And that is why serving the true Kriishan is such a pleasure." Her laugh had something odd in it. Trela could not quite put her finger on it.

Trela left feeling weird. She could not think of more conversation and so had just excused herself. Certainly Zira was one of her most trustworthy warriors, but she had already known that. What she had not realized was how trust worked to keep those loyal to her quiet. Their brief conversation was eye-opening, not just for the topic at hand, but that Zira had felt like that for a long time and had not said a word.

Trela was already feeling like she had not ruled her realm for long. Lishean had been in charge for longer than she had, that was true. Did it bother her? Yes, of course. She was so far away from her realm that she barely even felt Pyran sometimes. Her courtiers had probably forgotten what she looked like. One of the benefits of the Pyran system was that there was little-to-no interregnum. It switched from one ruler to another instantly, there was no waiting in between. It made her wonder what would happen if Lishean was challenged. Surely he would not accept it. But for how long? How long before the entire realm was up in arms?

Trela was back on deck, but she did not want to engage with anyone. Her mind was abuzz with chaotic and careening thoughts. So she just leaned on the rail of the ship and stared out at the water. The dark water reflected the cloudy sky, which was very appropriate for her dark thoughts.

She racked her brain trying to think of a time where a Pyran ruler was gone for as long as she had been. She could not think of one, and she had left at the beginning of her reign. She had not had enough time to endear herself to her subjects, her courtiers, her rivals. She had wandered off, returned briefly, then wandered off again. It was unprecedented. At least as far as she could recall—she wondered who from her group would have more knowledge of historical reigns. Maybe she could ask Ryshial? She seemed to know all sorts of things.

And, if it had happened before, how was it resolved? Was the ruler deposed while they were away? Right when they returned? Did nothing bad happen? Trela felt a small twinge of panic thinking about it.

She wasted some time wondering what everyone back in Agoge was thinking. Were they concerned she was abdicating? Were they scheming to take over without having to fight her? Did they still think she was the Kriishan? That one had stung a little. When Zira had asked if she could be the Kriishan from the Fluen realm—that stung. She had no response to that. She was not even sure how she felt about it, let alone how her subjects felt about it. It was like a riddle, or a conundrum. Could a Kriishan not rule and still be a Kriishan? The answer that immediately came to mind was not the one she was looking for. Another twinge of panic ran through her.

Trela also wondered if there were other Pyrans in her coterie that felt like Zira. She was sure that Estfale would follow her to the far corners of the realms. But would he just be doing it to speed her up, to get her back to the Pyran realm? And he was the most loyal. What about Knill? Knill did not like it when she was ruling since he felt ignored while she performed her duties. But Knill seemed distant here as well, even when they were traveling every day together, cramped in the same tent. Would he agree she was still the Kriishan? Being a Gaen, he had never had the same full understanding of what a Kriishan was, however. So, what about someone like Serghno? Was he just counting the hours until they could be done with whatever was going on and head back home? Or since Arnasta was with him, did he not mind? And whether or not he minded, did he think she could still call herself the Kriishan if she was stuck in the Fluen realm?

Of course, this conundrum could be answered by asking the right question. She wondered who to start with. Probably Estfale. He would be quick and blunt if she asked directly, if she asked for honesty. She would not have to pull the truth out of him. The thought of it made her panic a little more. Regardless of what he said, regardless of what any of them said, she needed to get back home and rule. The time was up. The time was past. She needed to speed up the quest. They needed to kill both Belegs and go home.

Trela knocked softly on Estfale's door below deck. She was fairly certain he was not napping, mostly because he never napped, but did not want to be banging on the door or anything. This was not that type of visit. It was a visit of tea and conversation, not of grog and loud tales.

"Enter." The voice was somewhat muffled by the door.

Trela walked in to see Estfale at a desk, writing. Well, not truly a desk, more like a plank that hung off the wall with small diagonal chains. The side at the wall had hinges, allowing it to fold away when not in use.

"Who are you writing?"

"My sister. I have a stack of letters to give her when we get back. It helps me think, more than anything." He smiled at her and then turned his head back to his work for a moment.

While campaigning in the Pyran realm, letters were moved around quite efficiently. The warpack system had many ancillary systems that existed mostly to support it. Unfortunately, that system broke down once they entered the adjacent realms. Trela briefly thought about trying to have chains of *whisperers* along routes to help with faster communication, but the idea of another derlian transcribing or communicating private correspondence was a non-starter. No one would feel comfortable with that. Which left only official business. But the concerns about interception and the logistical issues of having someone in a small shack in the middle of nowhere just to make communication quicker and easier, were unsurmountable. How would they get fed or watered in the desert? She often had thoughts that sounded good at first, but then fell apart under scrutiny.

Estfale finished off the ink in the quill before carefully setting everything aside. It gave her the time to release her thoughts and turn her attention to him. She took a tiny moment to recall what they had just been discussing.

"I want to discuss that very subject with you. And I will need you to be brutally honest with me. I need your advice, not your understanding."

"You want to have an honest discussion about letters?" His eyebrow shot up, indicating he knew his response was absurd. But she had not really spoken very clearly either.

"No. About getting back. About home." Trela took a deep breath. "Can I be the Kriishan from the Fluen realm?"

"Ah! Well. Now that is a question, isn't it?" He smiled widely. "Do you want some grog? I still have some stashed away somewhere."

"No, no. Please. I want a serious discussion."

"Yes. And some grog helps me have serious discussions." He held up his hands to ward off her reply. "You want my opinion, and I will provide it. You need to stop this adventure nonsense and head home. The sooner the better. Or else you will not have a realm to return to."

"How long have you felt this way?"

"Honestly… quite a while. Are you sure about the grog?" He looked a little wistful but did not give her enough time to respond. "You are not ruling Fluens, or anyone else. You are ruling Pyrans. And Pyrans have no patience, Trela. You know that. We need to be doing something all the time. So, if you are not around to tell your subjects what they should be doing, someone will soon be plotting to do that for you."

"That bad?"

"Yes. Listen. The Cabal was one thing. Gorbanax asked you to perform a quest and you went and did it. You're a hero. But this…" He waved his hand around a little bit. "Gorbanax died, Trela. The volcano blew its top. Then you left. Just when your subjects needed direction the most."

"Gorbanax asked me to perform this quest also."

"I know, I know. I'm here, aren't I? We're all here trying to be helpful. But what are we doing? Really. 'Go kill the Cabal.' That's a great command, a great quest. We can go and find it and kill them. But kill a Beleg? Kill a couple of them? Not just that, but try to trap one or trick one or whatever our plan is… Wait. What is our plan? Do we even have a plan?"

"We are at the greatest inflection point in all derlian history, Estfale. Life before the Belegs died will be different than after."

"Will it? I mean, the erupting volcano upended life. But who communed with Gorbanax? The king or queen. Maybe. Sometimes. But not a warrior out in a warpack. To them, nothing will have changed." He took another breath. "But that is not even the point. I agree this is a momentous occasion, this is a historical inflection point. If anyone even knew what we were doing, our names would be remembered in song for generations. Whether or not we would be loved or reviled for what we are doing, I'm not really sure. But we would not be easily forgotten. However… And this is a big one. However, no one knows what is going on. Not really. And it could take the rest of our lives to get this done. We have no plan,

Trela. We are just wandering around. I am so happy we have Vanelia with us just so we have a destination. Once we drop her off at Vatlisi, then what?"

Trela's mind was reeling. She had wanted brutal honesty. She had even asked for it. But she had not quite prepared herself for it.

"Destiny will guide us." It was the worst response in the world, but it was all she could come up with. It was as if her shield kept taking blows. She was too dazed to come up with the footwork that would get her out of the situation.

"Well, it had better hurry up. That's all I'm saying." He did not mock her response, but just kept hammering at her shield. "To answer your question: No, I do not think you can be the Kriishan while you are in the Fluen realm. I think those ideas, those geographies, are incompatible. And, if I may be so bold, if we are unable to accomplish this task, or quest, or whatever you want to call it, then we should get you back home now. You could be a great queen, Trela. You were a great queen. You should be the Kriishan. That is what destiny really wanted from you to begin with. Isn't that enough?"

"I agree with you partially. We need to get back as soon as possible. But I cannot abandon this last wish from Gorbanax. I won't. We will kill the last Belegs and then we will return. And then who knows, maybe we'll get the best bards in the realm to write the songs we want written." She really, really wanted to take him up on his grog after their conversation, but she had others to talk to.

"You asked for honesty."

"I did. And you delivered. Thank you, you have been very helpful. I mean that."

Trela walked away, reclosing the door behind her. Part of her wanted to get back to the deck. To breathe the fresh air, lean on the railing, and just stare out at the unforgiving sea. But part of her wanted another opinion. It would certainly not give her any more impetus to speed up the quest—Estfale had given her all she needed—but she wanted at least one more perspective. So she decided to go see Serghno and Arnasta. Then she could get two for the price of one.

They were similar to Estfale, but more circumspect. Serghno seemed to be mostly concerned with others vying for the throne while she was gone. That someone would be able to convince enough of her courtiers that Lishean would have to engage in single combat by proxy. He did not trust that her courtiers had been fully won over and felt she had not replaced enough of them with loyalists to cover her long absence. He was also concerned that Lishean, while an incredibly knowledgeable warrior, was just not as young as he used to be and could get worn down by the right opponent. He kept saying that it was not that he did not believe in her destiny or the importance of their current mission, but that he did not trust the schemers amongst her court.

Arnasta was a little more hopeful concerning the schemers but was quite concerned about Trela's subjects. That they would feel abandoned since she had left so soon after the volcanic eruption, the death of Gorbanax. That there would be grumblings amongst the poor in particular. Trela had not formed enough of an impression of her rule before she had left. That all the strides she had originally made against Qizern's style of overbearing control would be thought of as Lishean's. And when she did finally return, she would be compared against Lishean, not Qizern, minimizing how far she brought the realm. It was quite disheartening to hear. She had always thought of Arnasta as being loyal and a bit meek, making her bleak analysis of Trela's subjects that much harder to hear.

Trela did not want to hear any more. She would surely speak with Dartsyle and the remaining Pyrans later on during their voyage to Vatlisi, but she was done for the day. She had known she needed to resolve this last quest and return, had even understood that her being away for so long was starting to get detrimental. But she had not quite realized how strongly everyone else felt about it. And no one had said anything. They would have let her wander around in the Fluen realm for another sun cycle, wasting their time and her reign, and would have kept smiling in acquiescence. "Yes, my Queen. Of course, my Queen." It was a bit maddening. Did that mean she wanted to be second guessed at every turn? No, of course not. She was the queen, the Kriishan. She was in charge of her own destiny and was on a direct mission to accomplish Gorbanax's last wish. But it was maddening all the same.

The rest of the time spent on Yifindur seemed to drag and stretch. Trela was incensed with speeding up the process but unable to actually do anything to accomplish that. She could not yell at the wind to blow harder. She could get the mages to try to push the boat along faster, but they would have to be careful not to tear a sail or break a mast. She could get Feyazki to fly her to Vatlisi, maybe. There were options that she did not fully explore because of the most terrifying issue of all. What were they to do after Vatlisi? They had no inkling of how to confront Gunzgak. They had no real plan. That was the most maddening thought of all. That even though she wanted to speed things up, even after all her fellow Pyrans warned her she could lose her reign soon, there was still nothing she could do to help. She was unable to resolve the overarching issue. She was impotent. It made her want to scream at the wind.

They finally arrived at Vatlisi. Trela decided to wait until they were settled before lighting a fire under Clerin—figuratively, of course. She knew it was going to take some time and effort to get Vanelia situated. And there always seemed to be an inordinate amount of time spent on niceties and bureaucratic ritual in the city.

Trela like Vatlisi, she truly did. She enjoyed the way it was separated into sections even though it was the most cosmopolitan town she had come across. She felt that Agoge was quite eclectic but could not think of twenty Fluens who lived there permanently. Vatlisi prided itself on its variety. It went out of its way to keep the various races content. Plus, it really exemplified the Fluen way of life, at least to Trela. She enjoyed the open areas; the constant and random plays, juggling, singing, entertainment; the use of mercantile shops as paths; and especially the food. It was the only city she knew of where she could have grog, beer, mead, and wine all in the same day. Though she had never actually tried that. She certainly enjoyed Vatlisi more than Tureyn, but she had never really had the chance to explore Tureyn either.

The docks led them directly into the warm embrace of the blinding white stone perimeter walls. There was, of course, a welcoming committee of sorts to greet them. They had to state their names and business to the clerks that seemed to run the town. This time was much simpler since Clerin's business was to speak with the new Princess of Vatlisi, Inquella. She had some last name as well, all the great Fluen families did, but it escaped Trela at the moment.

Once it was established who Clerin was, they were ushered in with an incredible politeness. There were smiles and bows and flourishes. They were even given a small escort.

It did not take long to get to the palace. From there, they were given part of a floor in one of the small wings. Plenty of room for everyone. Each derlian could have had a separate room. Of course, there was some pairing up as well. Trela and Knill were given a large room to share. She had thought about asking him if she could call herself the Kriishan while in the Fluen realm but thought better of it. She did not want to give him a reason for concern or to argue.

"Won't this be nice? Lounging around in luxury for a bit?" She tried to butter him up instead.

"I'll certainly enjoy it if you will." His smile looked nice, natural, and relaxed. So she decided not to read anything else into his statement.

"Good. Because I think we'll have a couple of days, or a week, or whatever, to enjoy ourselves before running off." She let her smile relax onto her face.

"That's great. Maybe after we meet with the Princess and do all the required pomp, we could explore some of the other quarters again. You know, enjoy some of the local squalor." He laughed a little.

She thought the statement was weird, but he could sometimes be weird. She often enjoyed meeting the locals where they were at, to enjoy how they lived, even if it was quite simply. That was how she worked the warpack, attempting to fit in with the various groups that it was comprised of. But he made it sound like a bad thing, like they were better than that. She knew, however, that was the last thing on his mind. He truly liked simplicity. So, she could only think he was exaggerating for effect—you know, being weird.

"That is a fantastic idea. I would love to." She smiled and nodded. He grinned back.

They were to meet with the Princess the next evening. This gave everyone, even the Princess, some time to prepare. Everyone got clean and fed. Even though Knill was excited at the prospect of exploring the city again, Trela was unable to get out of her evening rounds. He took it in stride, which she appreciated.

Instead of a fun and frivolous evening with Knill, she had a small meeting with Clerin and a few others. They wanted to go over what the meeting with the Princess should entail. However, she was greeted by quite a large group when she arrived. Escha, Torpalin, and his sister were there even though they had not been on Trela's mind. Soon after Trela entered, Feyazki, with Vanelia and Hynara, arrived and spread out. Trela had wondered where he was. Clerin was not often without him as of late. Everyone sat around on the lush divans and couches and pillows that were strewn about. It was a decent sized room. It probably overshadowed Clerin's room. It certainly overshadowed Trela's.

"Before we begin, there is an announcement to be made." Clerin sat down after she spoke. Torpalin sat up at the same moment.

"As you are all well aware, Escha and I have been trying to remove ourselves from the warrior life. We had gone to Ariellyna and joined a bakery with my darling sister. For myself, I had never been happier." He paused, glancing at Vanelia, then Escha.

"Unfortunately, Chiavel was unable to enjoy merely taking over the realm. He could not very well leave Vanelia and Hynara alone." He stole another glance at Vanelia.

"We, and I mean all of us, collectively, we could never allow anything to happen to them. I am proud of that. Our trio of bakers gladly joined up with all of you to help her escape his grasp. And we have. We are as far away from Ariellyna as we can comfortably get. Where Vanelia can live in peace. Where our trio can live in peace." He paused again, looking at Clerin this time. He put on a large Torpalin smile.

"We are hoping to ask for the ability to start up a bakery here in the Luften quarter, of course. We have some money from the old bakery, so we are not asking the Princess for anything out of the ordinary. Just the ability to work in a foreign city. Which we hear can be filled with dizzying regulations in the Fluen realm. So, we are asking that if there is anything anyone can say to the Princess about helping our little bakery take hold, it would be greatly appreciated." Everyone chimed in and promised their assistance. Though, truly, it was only Clerin who would be able to help much.

Vanelia followed Torpalin. Her pitch was similar to his but on a much grander scale. Her discussion was the main reason for their meeting in the first place, at least in Trela's mind. She assumed it was for that reason Torpalin had spoken up first, to get his plea out of the way. They took some time trying to figure out what the Princess would ask, and how best to respond, to get Vanelia safely tucked away. Then they turned to other matters.

They had been relying on Trela's own largesse, and that of the Pyran realm in general, for the last several moons. It was a strain that Trela did not normally like bringing up. But of course, after they had defeated the Cabal, it was the Fluens who had been incredibly generous. So here they were, about to ask for further assistance. The idea of gifting Yifindur to the Princess once they were done with it was brought up and everyone was enthusiastic about it.

They discussed trying to gain some more warriors, but that was quickly voted out. Most thought that they already had enough mouths to feed, even with the loss of Torpalin and Escha. The clinching argument was that the upcoming struggles would benefit little from more swords. The fight was with a Beleg, or maybe two, and no amount of steel could help that.

They then tried to figure out if more mages should be asked for. There were a lot of arguments on that. Trela was not really sure which side won out, but they ended up thinking that if any mages were offered who had good summoning experience, they would be taken. They would not come out and ask for someone, however.

Trela wondered how often Clerin would be with the Princess alone. If something was outvoted currently, maybe Clerin could be convinced to bring it up in private later. Trela, personally, had wanted at least one more mage. She needed to speed up the quest and thought adding another expert could help that.

They tried to come to a consensus about how long to stay in Vatlisi, but even that did not get resolved. There were too many open questions, too many unknowns. No one wanted to set a hard date to leave. Trela had no idea of when they should leave either but did not like the open-endedness of their current situation.

Trela even brought up seating order. Everyone agreed that the Princess would choose where they all sat, but she was not so sure. Would there really be names spelled out by each chair? She had wanted to stay in the discussion and the derlians at the opposite side of the table from the Princess would not even be able to hear the conversation, let alone join in. Trela knew that Clerin would be adjacent to the Princess no matter what. So, her argument was that other rulers should be at that end as well—meaning herself and Vanelia.

In the end, little got accomplished or decided upon. The most direction gained was for Torpalin and Escha and their bakery.

And that was the part of the discussion which had been unplanned for.

    The next day went quickly. Trela did walk around with Knill for a bit, exploring a little more of the tiny Pyran Quarter. But they kept everything light and returned to the palace early. No one wanted to be out of sorts for the dinner with the Princess. Certainly not Trela.

    Trela refused to wear a dress but picked some very nice breeches and one of her least stained shirts with a leather vest. She did not have any traveling clothes that matched up with Fluen royalty. Pyran royalty rarely wore anything long or wispy, nothing that would hinder one in an impromptu fight. The races were on opposite sides of the fashion spectrum. It was not the styles that bothered her, but that she had to leave all her weapons back in the room. Not even a boot knife. She felt naked without any steel, felt too light without the weight of her weapons. Even though she knew there was no chance of any danger.

    The dining hall was gigantic. It was not as large as the one in Agoge, but almost. It was certainly more opulent, however. There were multiple chandeliers that hung from the ceiling, each with over thirty candles—or, at least, that was how many Trela estimated on one of them before she lost interest. There were tapestries covering the walls. Not the thick woolen ones that hung in Agoge, but wafty silken ones. The scenes were quite different as well. Landscapes with narrow trees and large moons rather than the hunting scenes preferred in the Pyran realm. The table that flowed down the center of the room was covered with delicate lacy linens, trying to hide the fact it was sectional, not one long slice of continuous wood. There were sconces on the walls and candelabras on the table. All in all, it was the most amount of indoor fire Trela had noticed outside of the Pyran realm.

    The evening started slowly, with everyone in the coterie and a bunch of Fluen courtiers standing around drinking wine. Introductions were made and stories were swapped. Even though she felt more comfortable around the burly guards, she knew the dangerous Fluens in the room would most likely be unable to lift a claymore. So she forced herself to chat with those in the largest dresses and the puffiest shirts. It took a while for the Princess to show up, along with the Prince. That may have been a show of power, but maybe she just took a long time to get ready. The dinner was not a negotiation really. She appeared to be draped in a dizzying array of fabrics, with copious golden jewelry, capped with a tasteful diamond studded tiara. The Prince was dressed in a simple white tunic and pants, though he did have multiple gold necklaces weighing down his clothing and a small golden tiara of his own. He immediately wandered over to a group of Fluen courtiers. Clerin started over to the Princess once she was alone and motioned for Trela to follow.

"Princess Inquella Erintwala, ruler of Vatlisi, may I introduce Trela, the Queen of the Pyran realm." The Princess had even longer blonde hair than Clerin did, and though her eyes were blue, they did not have the otherworldly luminosity that Clerin's did. Trela waited for the Princess to provide a small bow before she gave her deeper one. Though the evening was not a negotiation, there was still protocol.

"Charmed. I have heard much about you. Much about your prowess." The Princess nodded approvingly.

"As I have heard great things about your diplomatic skills, Princess. And coming from Clerin Toswin, the greatest diplomat I know, that is high praise indeed." Trela had, unfortunately, spent no time studying the Princess. She should have at least gotten a brief dossier on her but had not even brought the subject up. Both Inquella and Clerin looked pleased, however, so she did not lament her lack of preparation too much.

"We may enjoy a private conversation after the dinner, just the three of us. There are so many ears around us as we eat, making it difficult to speak plainly." She nodded slowly and Trela nodded in return. She was not positive if the Princess was referring to her own courtiers or to the coterie, but either way Trela was happy to keep the conversation light until later.

The dinner was exceptional. There were multiple courses, each with its own incredibly distinct flavor. Even more interesting, each course came with a specific flavored wine. Trela always thought grog was the most versatile drink due to the different amount of herbs and spices used in each blend, but there was an amazing amount of variety in the wine they had that night.

The conversations they had were easily shareable. They told stories and tales, mostly of how horrible the old Prince and the Cabal were. Stories of the battle that almost destroyed the palace. Stories of the reconstruction. Of rounding up all of the Yaven-infused items. The Cabal was the main subject they all had in common.

Torpalin shamelessly added his request of starting a bakery in the Luften Quarter. He was humored with promises, but Trela was unsure if they were just trying to skip to a new topic. Vanelia was not mentioned. Aid and favors were not mentioned. Everything was kept inconsequential.

Eventually the dinner ended. Some of the coterie went back to their rooms within the palace. Others stayed in the giant hall, drinking and chatting with the Fluen courtiers. Trela, Clerin, and the Princess slipped out into a narrow hallway. Though she doubted they left without everyone noticing, no one had the bad taste to call attention to their departure, not even the Prince. It was as if they had all agreed upon it beforehand.

The hallway was wide enough for the Princess in her dress and Clerin to walk side by side. Clerin's dress had layers and flowed behind her but was not as puffed out as the Princess's. She probably only took up a third of the width. Trela followed behind them. She did not mind being in the back as they walked, she did not even try to eavesdrop on their conversation. She held her hands behind her back and watched the torches in the sconces flow by as they walked. Her mind was not blank, but she was not thinking of anything in particular, certainly not of anything she could recall later. It was not a meditation, but it was still quite relaxing.

They entered into what could only be described as a sitting room. It had all sorts of couches and puffy chairs, even pillows splayed out in a corner. Some couches were straight and rectangular, others were of the fainting variety, and others were truly bizarrely shaped. The colors also clashed a little. All in all, it was much too busy to be a comfortable conversational room. At least for Trela. She preferred a couple of wooden backed chairs and a table with a nice map. She sat down dutifully when the others did.

"We will have plenty of time to chat later, I hope." Inquella was looking at Clerin as she spoke. "And we should certainly get to know each other as well. I meet so few Pyrans, and certainly none of your stature, of course. But we are here today to discuss a different realm. The Luftens. I need your honest opinion of Vanelia." She ended up staring at Trela.

"She's fantastic, really. Very reliable and mission driven. She was instrumental in assisting us with the Yaven-infused weapons in the Luften realm. Even as she was losing her throne."

"Well, yes, that is it, really." Inquella interrupted lightly. "I am sure she is a fine derlian, but what I really need to know is how dangerous it will be to have her here. Under my care. She is a fugitive, is she not? A deposed queen? I doubt we will be able to hide her identity for too long. But maybe I am being a little paranoid."

"Yes, she is a deposed queen." Clerin interjected before Trela could respond.

Which was fine with Trela since she had been taken a bit aback by the directness of the questioning. She had not really formed an opinion of the Princess yet but had assumed she would be a little more trivial, at least at the beginning of their conversation. She was pleasantly surprised.

"But she is not necessarily a fugitive," Clerin continued. "I have actually met with the new King, Chiavel Largon. I traveled with him briefly before he even became royalty. He is completely ruthless when he needs to be, of that I have no doubt. But I have not seen him need to be. He could have killed Vanelia long before. She has a child that could be considered to be in line for the throne. She is dangerous to his rule and so is her daughter. But he did not even strip her of privilege or monies, though she was ostracized and shunned from court. Even from some of her old friends. But the fact is that it was in his best interest to kill her and her daughter immediately, and he did not. In fact, as far as I understand, it was a completely bloodless coup. There was no fighting in the streets, not even between guards."

"Then why is she not sitting in Ariellyna? Or Tureyn? Why, if there is no ill will between the old queen and the new king, is she attempting to settle in the farthest corner of the Fluen realm?" She turned from Clerin to Trela as she asked her questions. There was a slight nod to her head as she finished speaking. Though her eyes were not as luminous as Clerin's, they held a strange intensity when she spoke directly.

"I think the decision came down to three things. First, out-of-sight, out-of-mind. Though there may be no immediate danger to Vanelia, there is no reason to risk it either. No reason to continually flaunt a potential heir. Hynara, Vanelia's daughter, is now just a babe. But what happens when she comes of age? It seems better to just remove the constant reminder that a queen was deposed at all. For everyone, friend and foe. Then there is the issue of intent. Vanelia understands she is no longer a queen and will never be one again. She accepts that. For herself, and her daughter. She does not have any ambitions beyond being a good mother. How does one prove that? How does one show they have given up ambition? By moving far away. By cutting all ties. By not even communicating with those who you used to conspire with—or, stated more properly, consult with. Thirdly, she performed an act of defiance when she gathered those Yaven-infused items and gave them to us. We destroyed them, just as we destroyed the Cabal. Chiavel? Who knows what he would have done? So, even though we feel there is no immediate bad blood between the two of them, there is not necessarily good blood either. He did depose her. She does have a claim to the throne through herself and, even more rightly, through her daughter. He is not the kindest derlian I have ever met, certainly not meek or humble. Certainly a schemer who understands the dark underbelly of politics, in my opinion. So, you are right to be wary. We are wary. We have come to the farthest reaches of the Fluen realm on purpose. With good reason." Trela took a small breath and looked Inquella directly in the eye.

"But we are not poisoning your well. We are not blowing embers into your forest. We do not bring a dangerous burden. Not in our eyes, at least. And more than that, we are not the type of derlians to do that. We would not do that to you, nor to her. If we felt she needed to be sheltered and hidden away, we would not be here. We would be in the Pyran realm if she needed protection, and in the Gaen realm if she needed to be hidden. Your only concern should be if we lack the judgement to make the correct decision, not that we would be setting you up for a trap."

"Oh, I had not been concerned that you were setting me up for a trap." Inquella laughed lightly but kept her intense gaze on Trela. "Good intentions have destroyed more than one royal household. I am just beginning my rule here. Vatlisi was given to me quite recently, as you well know, and I must show utmost competence. I would hate for my emotional response to a well-meaning friend's emotional request destroy everything my family has been building towards for generations. You, being a queen in your own right, understand the gravity of this decision, do you not?"

"I do. And we're not trying to get an immediate response from you. Think it over. Do some research. Ask us anything at all. We are here for a fortnight and do not expect anything from you now besides your wonderful hospitality. What I have found in my experience is that most bad decisions are made on a short timeline. We are not attempting to force your hand or make you feel rushed." Trela paused for a moment, debating in her mind whether or not to continue. Clerin spoke up into the silence.

"Would you consider speaking with Vanelia about this? I understand you do not wish to become emotionally attached at this stage, but talking with her may help your decision. I have found her to be incredibly honest and upfront with her situation, whatever that may be at the time. She would understand Chiavel and his intentions and proclivities better than either of us." Her smile was disarming.

"No. Apologies. But I know what would happen if I spoke with her. She would have her cute daughter with her, and I would melt at the sight of them and would just acquiesce to anything she asked." Inquella smiled back.

"You had it right to begin with, with no period: No apologies." Clerin waved away anything further. They all laughed.

More wine was imbibed, and they spoke about trivial things for a while. Eventually the conversation drifted sideways long enough that Trela could bring up something that had been nagging at her. It had been bothering her since the dinner.

"So, the Prince seems… oddly absent." Both Inquella and Clerin stopped and stared at her. Then Clerin took a sip and leaned back, removing herself from having to respond. "And he did not seem to talk much during dinner. Or before dinner. Or at least to the guests, the foreigners. He seemed fine chatting with the courtiers." She had been hoping to be more subtle about it but had decided to just ask. It was often simpler that way.

"Are you asking if he harbors fears or ill will towards Pyrans?" Inquella was smiling slightly, which seemed a little odd to Trela.

"No, not at all. That thought had not crossed my mind." And it had not. Until it was mentioned.

"Well, do not worry, he does not. As far as I know, he does not have any ill will towards anyone." Her smile grew larger and more relaxed. "No, it is just that he does not rule Vatlisi. Not in the least.

And so he enjoys being around his friends during large meals. He is quite handsome, is he not?"

"I suppose he is, but… So, he does not help rule at all? No advice, no consulting?"

"You are not handfasted. Do you need help ruling? When you are queen."

The last statement took Trela a bit by surprise. She ignored it for the moment, however, and thought about the question. Did she ask Knill's advice about everything? No, she did not.

"I have a privy council that I often consult."

"And that council only includes those you have sex with?"

"No. Of course not. Just…" She paused for a moment, trying to figure out what her actual question was. "You are correct. I am not handfasted. I will probably never get handfasted. But if I did, I would hope that I chose someone I could trust to offer me advice, to help me rule."

"Ah, yes. I think the main word there is 'chose.' I was unable to choose my mate. Well, I got to choose him, but only out of a select group chosen by others. Clerin will also face this decision. Will she allow the Catajohls to parade suitors in front of her until she can finally pick someone not completely nauseating? Someone who provides her with the political maneuvering she needs? Or will she decide to leave her family, her realm, her prospects and, dare I say, her destiny, and get handfasted to a no-name Luften?" Inquella turned to Clerin. "What do you say to that? You know they will figure out you are here soon and come asking."

"I really enjoy Feyazki. He is not only handsome and good at providing at advice, but he gives me that jolt of zing and zest, that feeling of comfort and security, that feeling of just… happiness… at something as simple as holding my hand. I doubt that my destiny does not include him." Clerin had a slightly wistful look on her face as she talked about him.

"Your secret is safe with me. I will not tell the Catajohls anything." She laughed a little. "But I really wanted Vatlisi. And there is only one way to get the second largest and, frankly, best city in all the Fluen realm under your control. And that is to get handfasted to someone brought to you by the Catajohls. And to start having babies. I envy you, really. How did you become Queen?" She turned to Trela at the end of her speech.

"I had to defeat the previous King in single combat. But that was not as difficult as getting him into the ring. I had to raise a formidable warpack before he would even consider fighting me. Even then, he refused me until the very end." Trela shook her head slightly, unconsciously. "We can make our own destiny in the Pyran realm, that is true, but many of us die before we can find it."

"Well, I might envy you a little less now. I doubt I could defeat very many warriors in combat. That is just not in my blood. Or anywhere near my skill set. I rarely even cut onions in the kitchen anymore." They laughed again.

Trela wondered about the "babies" comment. She wondered what would happen if the Inquella was unable to conceive. Would she lose Vatlisi? Trela could not imagine sacrificing so much for such a lofty goal, only to have it snatched away in the end through no fault of your own.

They stayed in Vatlisi for a week, waiting on the Princess's decision. Trela enjoyed it immensely. She spent some time with Knill, just wandering around the city. It had been a while since they had hung out like that, just the two of them, with nothing that needed doing, no agenda or requirements. It was nice. She had forgotten how much she used to enjoy being with him. She was always so busy that her time felt stretched and precious. There were always meetings and discussions. There were so many derlians that she felt responsibility for. And there she was, not doing anything that advanced any cause. It was delicious.

It seemed to have a calming effect on Knill as well. He was sometimes so wound up that she did not want to be around him. And hurt and sad. He was sometimes so wounded that she could not be around him. He was delightful, currently. And so was she.

The Princess did finally agree to take in Vanelia and Hynara. Trela had felt fairly confident in that outcome, but was fine letting it play out. She had not wanted to push the issue. Clerin spent much of her time in Vatlisi with the Princess, though. Who knew what they discussed?

The night they found out was the night they all gathered around Torpalin's new bakery. It had taken him, and Escha and his sister, and several rotating members of the coterie, a full week to get the building ready. Even Trela and Knill had pitched in a couple of times. Much of it was cleaning, scraping, and then whitewashing the walls. There had been some work done on the roof—the rains of Vatlisi were heavy and, in some seasons, constant. Trela had not helped with the roof work.

The festivities were fantastic. Everyone was in a good mood from relaxing in Vatlisi for days, everyone was primed to have fun. And the twin celebrations of Vanelia's acceptance and the bakery compounded on each other, making it a night to remember. Though, in all honesty, Trela's memory of the actual party was a little hazy.

One part of the evening stood out to her, however. It was a chance conversation she had with Ryshial and Feyazki. She could not recall where Knill was, or Clerin for that matter, but the three of them were at a tiny table outside of the bakery, testing the exterior ambiance as Ryshial had put it.

The bakeries in Vatlisi were different than the ones in the Pyran realm. In Agoge you would walk into a tiny front room with a counter in front of you covered with baskets that contained breads of various shapes, sizes, and flavors, and you would order something. If they did not have what you wanted, you might be lucky enough for them to have it in the back. But if not, you purchased what you could and vowed to arrive earlier next time. In Vatlisi there were tables everywhere. You might purchase a tiny piece of flakey bread called a croissant to eat there and bring a loaf back home. You might have some tea, or some wine depending on the time of day. All food in Vatlisi was to be lingered over, to be enjoyed, to be savored. It seemed that few ate at home. And the greatest pastime was to sit outside and watch the other derlians walk by, trying to find their own place to sit down and have a tiny piece of food and drink.

And so the three of them were sitting outside, in the dark, watching the night's stragglers walk by. Testing the ambiance. There was half a glass of wine in front of each of them and a small flickering candle in the center of the table. They were covered by a large cloth awning that jutted out from the side of the building, but Trela was happy that it was not raining.

"So. Where are we headed from here?" Trela mentioned it more as a dare than a real question. She was just thinking about finishing the quest and returning as Queen to Agoge. But they both stopped and thought about it.

"What was it that the Blind One said when we exchanged names?" It was Feyazki asking Ryshial. Trela knew that Ryshial had been listening in on a *whisper* during their conversations, but it was still odd to hear him ask her about it. Of course, Ryshial had one of the greatest memories in the coterie. And they were drinking and chatting and just having a good time.

"I believe it was something like 'if you are unable to convince the powers that be, find new powers.' And that he would 'meet us there.' Now, where that would be, what powers he was alluding to, I have no idea."

"So, wait, he said he would meet us somewhere?" Trela had not realized there had been much conversation beyond the exchange of names. "So, he knows where we would go, or wants us to figure out where he is waiting? Do you think Tumu foresaw something?"

"Well, I was trying to think of what he meant by powers. Obviously, the powers that be have to be the Belegs, right? Especially Gunzgak, if we are still thinking that Lembin wants to communicate. So what would new powers be? I mean, would they need to be as powerful as the Belegs?" Feyazki squinted up at the awning, trying to think of something on par with the Belegs. "Certainly not a Yaven, right?"

"What else is there?" Ryshial was looking at directly at Trela. As if she knew something and was trying to get Trela to speak it.

"There's the well, there's Lemniscate." It popped into her head, so she spoke it. "Of course, Lemniscate might be no more at this point. Did he not wander into the desert with a Vijen?" Trela took another drink; so did the others.

"There have got to be Yavens older than Lemniscate. Older than the Belegs. Do we know of the oldest Yavens? They are eternal, could there be any from the beginning?" Feyazki was still pondering.

"That is not a bad idea... I think Trela is correct, however. Where could the Blind One meet us? There is certainly no way derlians could ever visit the Yaven realms, is there?" Ryshial looked from Feyazki to Trela.

"That is not a bad idea either... What if, if we were unable to summon Gunzgak somewhere here, that we could summon it to a Yaven realm?" Trela tried hard to think. "But Gunzgak would be stronger there, correct? And us? There would be no way to survive without Chaos. No way to survive in a realm of one element, a realm of Law. We would be snuffed out, surely. Or at least, three-quarters of us would be snuffed out."

"I think we are getting ahead of ourselves. I don't think a derlian can survive in a Yaven realm, that just doesn't make sense. I think you were right about the well. There is nothing else on par with a temple here in the derlian realm. It is like the fifth temple. And it is a location that the Blind One *could* meet us at." Feyazki nodded to himself. "I still think we should try to summon some Yavens, however. I am really curious about the oldest Yavens, those who are older than the Belegs."

"We have been having difficulties summoning lately, but yes, that is certainly something we should explore." Ryshial sighed a little. "How difficult do you think it would be to find the well again?"

"It depends on whether or not it is our destiny." Trela laughed. She felt good about the decision. She wanted the quest to move along, to finish up. She hated inaction more than anything, that feeling of sluggish inertia. At least it was a direction. Feyazki and Ryshial joined in her laughter.

It felt terrible to be leaving Escha and Torpalin behind again, but if anyone deserved to be humble bakers far from danger, it was them. Trela was also sad that Vanelia was not coming, but that was just because she enjoyed her company. Vanelia was not a warrior or mage by any stretch of the imagination, and though she felt terrible thinking it, bringing her along would have had the effect of losing several warriors just to protect her and Hynara on a daily basis.

Everyone else was ready, willing, and capable. Trela had been worried that Lophina would want to stay in Vatlisi as well. But she was even more determined to see things through after the death of her twin sister. It worked well for Trela. Lophina was an incredibly dangerous warrior.

That left only sixteen of them left to venture into the Northern Desert. And some of them were less helpful than the others. Could she really count Croy? Was Knill helpful in a fight? They had been dwindled down indeed.

The Princess had provided them with provisions, equipment, and coin. They had left her the ship, Yifindur, in an attempt to reduce the imbalance. It was quite an impressive ship, so maybe the Princess broke even.

The first part of the journey, and hopefully the bulk of it, was to be on rivers, flowing upstream. A small riverboat, along with a small crew, was loaned to them. They would be able to flow up the Vatlisi river for a ways, hopefully even being able to skirt to the West of Hifrim. It was unknown how much farther they could get on the river, for the Fluens did not typically navigate into the Gaen realm. It would eventually be too difficult to portage, even with the amount of mages they had.

They would eventually have to return to horseback. Then they would have to endure the desert. Trela wondered about Tlana. Wondered about being able to find the well. Wondered if the Blind One would be waiting for them there and, if so, if he would be helpful. In her experience, he was not often helpful and could even be decidedly unhelpful. More than anything, she could not believe they were heading to the well again. At times, it felt as if they were just wandering in circles.

They had one more evening with Escha and Torpalin, one more evening of Vatlisi. Torpalin gushed about missing them all and gave great big crushing hugs to everyone. Escha was much harder to read, but Trela thought she caught her getting misty eyed during some of the goodbyes. They tried to summon a Yaven, to no avail. Vanelia was there for a little while but had to head back to her quarters after it had gotten dark. The Princess did not show up for the party, but she did see them off the next day. It was a cozy affair, limited to the shrinking coterie.

They did not leave too early the next day, but did get out before noon. Trela had allowed everyone to sleep in a bit, to shake off the wine from the night before. The time on the boat should fly by. A couple of hours would make little difference overall. It was traveling through the desert that she was most worried about.

The boat was fantastic. They ate up ground by leaps and bounds. The mages paired up and took turns propelling the boat upstream. Sometimes they would anchor to let everyone rest, but they did not have to leave the water for at least a week. The first portage was simply around some dangerous rocks. The second a small waterfall. The third was a tall waterfall and there was some discussion as to whether they should even continue with the boat. The captain had never been up the river that far before and it was becoming narrow and, at times, a little shallow.

Feyazki and Ryshial flew to the top to scout around. When they returned, it was not with good news. They reported that there was not much open river at the top of the falls, nothing easily navigable for as far as they could see. It was with a heavy heart that Trela allowed the ship to return to the river.

Part of the issue was that, even if they were able to "muscle" the boat up to the top of the falls with magic, the boat would not be able to return easily. The captain only had one mage with him and Trela did not want to lose a couple of days flying hers back and forth. No, it was simpler to leave the boat behind and begin the next leg of their journey.

The waterfall itself was difficult terrain. She ended up exhausting her mages getting the horses and equipment to the top of the falls. But she felt that they had made up a fair amount of time through the flights. There had not been a noticeable path nearby. The area at the top of the waterfall was more open, surrounded by heather. It was a beautiful splash of color before reaching the more rocky portions of the Gaen realm.

The camp was finally set up close to nightfall, so there was not much time for anything beyond a meal and some sleep. The mages had taken the brunt of the efforts of their travel up until then. Everyone else was fairly well rested. So Trela decided on a "mage appreciation day" where they were allowed to lie around and rest while everyone else made a feast. Massages were given, shade shelters were made, and the feast was bountiful. Trela opened some wine. Partly for the feast and morale, and partly because they needed the containers.

Later that day, towards evening, Trela decided to walk near the waterfall. Not right next to it, of course, but near it. The rocks were wet and slippery, which made her stroll a bit foolish. But the views were fantastic. She could see for leagues. The roar of the water drove all other thoughts from her mind. She was just enjoying the beauty before her, not really paying attention, staring between the clouds and the river far down below. And as she was walking near the cliff, she slipped. And fell. And barely caught herself.

Trela was hanging onto a tuft of a foreign grass or plant of some sort. It was a large tuft and it felt well rooted, but she could feel herself slipping. She screamed as she fell, of course. Her other arm reached up to grab more of the tuft, but it was difficult to get two hands on it. She screamed a little more for good measure, but all she could hear was the roaring of the waterfall. Her feet scrambled to get some purchase, to alleviate at least some of her weight from the tuft. She found something a little less slippery with her right boot, keeping herself hugging the cliffside. Her last scream was more for show than out of any hope.

Her mind flashed for a moment. What if she fell? She felt a little bad about Knill. She felt a lot bad about failing their current mission. She felt just horrible about squandering her opportunities as Queen. She had gotten everything she had ever dreamed of. She had been the ruler of an entire realm, the undisputed ruler. The Kriishan. And yet here she was, clinging to the side of a cliff. Alone. Worried to shift her feet should they slip. Worried her arms were getting tired. More than anything, worried about what falling would mean. That destiny had grown tired of her. That destiny felt she had not appreciated her gifts. That she had disappointed destiny. So much so, that she was going to die in the most ignominious way possible. Not defeated in single combat. Not destroyed by a Tlana or Yaven. Not cut down in the heat of battle. But by being clumsy at the edge of a cliff. Her. The Kriishan.

That is when she first thought it. *No!* She breathed in deep. *No, this is not how I die. I am the Kriishan,* she thought. She tried to shift her foot again, to get her left boot in a crevice. She breathed in deep again. *I am the Kriishan! I will not fall. I will not allow it to happen. I will dig my fingernails into the stone if I have to.* She gripped the tuft with two hands and pulled mightily. Her hands slipped a little, stopping her heart for a moment. She tried to bury her face in the stone, to keep herself centered over her feet rather than leaning out. She stopped and breathed for a few moments, re-gripping the tuft.

Keeping her face pressed against the wet stone she tried to look about. She needed to get one leg up. That was the only way to get back to the surface. To push from below rather than pull from above. She had felt more comfortable with her right foot at the beginning, but her left was well jammed into a crevice currently. There was a moist-looking outcropping to her right. She was unsure about it, but there was not another option. *I am the Kriishan. I am an agent of destiny. It is not my lot to die here today.*

She took another deep breath. There was nothing else to do but leave her comfortable foothold, step on the outcropping, push with all her might, and hope her foot did not slip. *I am the Kriishan.* She re-gripped the tuft with both hands. *I am the Kriishan.* She took a last breath. *I am the Kriishan.* She shifted, planted her foot, heaved with her thigh, and pulled with all her might with both of her arms. *I am the Kriishan!*

Her left leg scrambled for a moment, but her right did not slip. She reached with her left hand on to the flat surface above and found another tuft. Her right leg was stretched straight and taut. Her left foot found something. She heaved off of that. She scrambled for all she was worth until her right knee found the surface. She shuffle-crawled onto the ledge she had just been walking on. She laid on her back and almost laughed. Her stomach spasmed a little as she gulped in air. Her blood felt alive and tingling, as she assumed lightning would feel just before it killed you. She let out a small yell, a happy one, an ecstatic one, and rolled to her side. There was Croy.

"Were you going to watch me die?" Her body still felt amazing, her blood sluiced through her like a raging river, but her giddiness was quickly turning to anger.

"No. No! Of course not. I just got here, truly. I did not even know you were here until you hauled yourself up over the cliff." He did look horrified and distraught at the notion, which made her feel a little better. He would not really have let her fall if he had known she was there. He would have surely cast a flight spell. Wouldn't he have?

Trela rolled back onto her back. The solid ground beneath her felt fantastic. She even enjoyed the sharp pointy bits that dug into her. It felt incredible just to breathe.

"Okay. I believe you." She rotated her head slightly and peeked at him for a moment before staring back above her. "If I didn't, I would kill you in your sleep." She chuckled a little. Should she have said that? *Probably not,* she admitted to herself. But she was still feeling out of sorts.

"Did you… Do you cast spells?" He changed the subject, though she was not sure why.

"What? No. Never."

"Well, many derlians do. Even Clerin casts spells without being a mage."

"She's had training. She's royalty. I'm a warrior."

"Malghain casts healing spells and he's a warrior."

"He's a Luften."

"Well, what were you thinking as you pulled yourself up?"

"Just a chant I use when I'm stressed."

"I think you're using magic when you chant like that."

"What?" She sat up and looked at him. She had not really been paying attention to what they had been discussing, she had been listening to her blood sing in her ears and had only been responding reflexively. "I don't understand."

"I sensed magic as you pulled yourself up, that is all. I just thought you should know." He was nodding to her, or maybe to himself.

Unbidden in her mind came the image of Qizern as they were locked in single combat so long ago. The chant had been running through her mind at the time. She had always thought that she could feel his energy being sucked from his body and flowing into hers. She had thought it was her youth that made her feel that way, especially considering his age, but maybe it was magic. Maybe her feeling that destiny smiled on her was magic. That her desire to be the Kriishan, her complete belief in that, was manifested by magic. Nope, she decided she did not like that. She preferred to be destiny's chosen vessel than to just cast spells like everyone else.

"You must be mistaken."

"Maybe. Probably. It was just a feeling I had, that's all. I've certainly been wrong before." He laughed easily. "Anyway, I'm glad you're all right. I would have cast a flight spell on you if I had arrived a moment sooner."

"I know, Croy. I trust you." She felt a sudden urge of mischievousness. "I won't kill you in your sleep." They both laughed.

They traveled alongside the dwindling river for the next couple of days, enjoying every moment. It was getting warmer, rockier, and dustier, but the proximity of the water made everything else seem easy to bear. They traveled next to that for as long as possible and loaded up on water before leaving, replacing the wine they had been imbibing. She did not necessarily want to run out, but drinking wine in the dunes of the great Northern Desert was a bit self-defeating—she would much rather be carrying around water.

It took them a little while to enter the desert proper. Though more noticeable than from the Pyran realm, entering the Northern Desert from the Gaen realm was a gradual affair. The loss of green leafy vegetation happened soon after leaving the diminished river, but there was scrub brush for quite some time. The hard rock ground of an escarpment turned to smaller rocks once they reached the lowlands. And the rocks eventually turned to rough, pebbly sand.

Then, suddenly, they were in the shifting tiny grains that made up the dunes.

As they entered the dunes, Trela kept expecting the compasses to give out, to start spinning in slow circles. She kept expecting the sun to perform haphazardly, staying in the apex of the sky for longer. She was worried that they would be attacked by Tlana. But none of these things happened. They kept heading north, towards the center of the desert, and everything kept working the way it should.

Of course, that was of little help. Was the well at the direct center of the desert? That was always the assumption, but they never knew where they were when they found it. And, supposedly, it changed locations quite often, taking the surrounding shantytown with it. Would they be walking towards it for a while, get close, then have it shift away to some other distant corner of the desert? How would they even know? It was odd, but knowing they were heading north, heading to the center, made it seem less like they were following destiny. Less like they would just stumble upon it. Knowing where they were heading made it feel more like they were lost. It was an odd feeling.

They were lost for some time. Then, finally, the compasses started to hesitate, to slowly spin. The sun still seemed stable, they never did see a Tlana, but it did seem that the center of the desert still affected the compasses a little. At least that was something Trela was used to.

Finally, with no real reason why or how, it seemed they could see the small shantytown in the distance. The horses naturally started to walk faster. And the derlians, trodding along beside their steeds, walked faster as well. Whether it was for the same unconscious reason that the horses sped up or if they were just keeping up, Trela was unsure. She was certainly relieved to see the tiny gray buildings in the distance. Certainly relieved that they had found the well for an unprecedented third time.

It took the rest of the day to reach the shantytown. The other times they had found it, it had seemed to appear near them when they awoke. This was more like a distant mirage, shimmering in the oppressive heat. But it was a mirage they could arrive at.

It was a bluish twilight sky when they arrived. The denizens were safely hidden away in their shanties, but Ilana came out to greet them. She directed them to a location to set up camp but soon left with Croy, promising to have a full conversation in the morning. Trela could not argue, Ilana and Croy had been handfasted after all, and they were cruelly separated by space and time. But she did not necessarily like it. Croy was the one derlian in her coterie who did not want the mission to succeed. It seemed unfair that he would have the ear of the new guardian of the well. Trela could only hope that Ilana would not do anything to jeopardize the mission. She would have to wait and see.

The next day, much the like the previous ones, was incredibly hot and bright. Unlike previously, however, they awoke near the middle of the shantytown. Which was only odd because they had set up their tents near the edge of it, though certainly still within the perimeter of the shacks. Did the town shift a couple of hundred rods just to center them? It did not make sense, but little about the well and its surrounding structures did.

They had a small breakfast adjacent to the well, but not too close to it. It was of old crumbly stone. It looked disheveled, dilapidated. She wondered how something so powerful could be so unassuming. Everyone woke early. It was hard to sleep late in a desert. Trela scanned the surrounding area, unconsciously looking for Vijen. Nothing broke the horizon besides the dunes. Ilana and Croy walked up while the coterie was packing the rest of their things. Trela was not sure how long they were going to stay there, but she felt uneasy about leaving anything on the ground.

"I have someone you need to meet." Ilana was brisk. They had, sort of, remade their introductions the evening before, but it still seemed a little cold. She guessed at what Ilana and Croy had talked about while they were alone. But maybe she was just being paranoid.

"Great, thanks." Trela was going to add an "I would love that," but decided against it. There was no reason to be obsequious.

The two of them walked away alone. It completely shocked her that Croy stayed behind at the well. She could hear him starting up a conversation with Knill behind her. They walked to the edge of the shantytown, stopping at an old, weathered shack. The wood was a pale gray and looked brittle with small chips of it missing. It made her wonder at how it withstood the wind. Ilana knocked lightly on the door.

"She has finally arrived." Ilana yelled softly through a crack.

There was some noise from the interior of the shack for a moment. It was hard to tell exactly what was going on. The noises included a bed being vacated, that much was obvious, but there was some shuffling and light groaning going on as well. As if the owner of the shack were ancient and sickly. The door eventually opened inwards.

Trela did not recognize the hair right away, it was disheveled and dirty, making it hard to know how blonde it would typically be. Nor did she recognize the clothing, which were horrendous gray rags, loose and torn. But the face that stared at her, even though it was slack, and the blue eyes that looked out at her, even though they were meek, *were* recognizable. As was the jagged scar across her neck.

"Mika! You're alive?!" Trela threw her arms around Mika's neck and hugged her. It was too much, to be sure, but she did it instinctually, reflexively. A feeling of relief flowed through her. "I was sure I had killed you."

"And you had to be. You all did. No one can know about this, understand? Not even Croy. Especially Croy." Ilana's green eyes glanced back and forth between them. "In fact, I should probably return." She gave a small nod and left.

Mika's face tightened up a little, but her eyes were still dull. Her face was dirty and dusty, which made it hard to read her emotions. Or maybe those were dulled as well. All Trela could read, behind the neutral numbness, was a low despair.

"We should hide inside." Mika turned and shuffled back into her shack.

Trela followed, wondering. She had known she had felt bad about killing Mika, but her visceral response had taken her somewhat by surprise. She was not elated, by any sense of the word, but she was certainly relieved.

"I... I am so sorry." Trela could not think of any useful words.

"Oh, this? It's fine. I asked for this, if you recall. Asked to be exiled rather than murdered." As she sat on her ugly rope bed, her spine curved and her head shrank into her shoulders slightly, as if she were pretending to be a question mark. "I had not really understood what it meant at the time."

"Well, I am glad you are alive. Even if this is the most complete exile one could imagine."

"It's for a reason, you know? They saved me for a reason. I have been a bit listless. The well water is hard to explain. It feels fantastic right after you have some of it, but it does things to you. It hollows you out. You forget who you are—that you are even derlian, really. Does that make sense?" She stopped speaking for a moment but kept her head staring at Trela's feet. She probably did not notice the nod, but she continued anyway.

"But I have purpose now. You have returned and brought my purpose back with you." She raised her head and almost smiled. "You need me. You need knowledge of the Cabal. Well, not *of* them, but with them, what they understood, what they could do. You need the Cabal's knowledge, and I am their last surviving heir." Her eyes gained the smallest amount of fire. "You need me to help you trap a Beleg."

Chapter 19

Croy was amazed that they had found the well so quickly. Though the first time he had found it, he had not been looking for it at all. It had just appeared. And then had stolen Ilana from him.

He was certainly happy to be around her again. After Lemniscate had left, she had taken over being the guardian of the well. She had greeted them when they arrived, taking her role as ambassador seriously. Everyone else bedded down on the ground, while he was taken to her shack.

It was not a great shack, and he did not think anyone should be jealous of him. It was certainly one of the largest shacks in the shantytown. It had oddly gapped light-gray wood slats as walls and roof, just like all the others. It had an incredibly uncomfortable rope bed and a few other furnishings. It did little to protect from the heat. It did provide shade but also trapped air that stifled during the day. Even with the gaps in the slats. The main thing that the shack had going for it was the presence of Ilana.

Croy was handfasted to Ilana and they had spent part of their youth together. He knew more about her than anyone else, including Knill, even though they had been apart for cycles. He loved her green eyes and cute nose. He loved the way she laughed. The way she would look at him mischievously. The way she understood what he meant even when he misspoke.

They had grown apart as they had been apart, for sure. He was fairly certain she had taken Lemniscate as a lover, as he had taken Baltuz, but that was of little consequence. There was a certain nostalgic feeling of love. Of early love. Of the love of his youth. He did not care what had happened when they were apart. He only cared about the moments they were together.

"Will you stay?" It was a question she asked innocently about where he would be sleeping. But it could also be a question about the future, depending on how he decided to interpret it. It was complicated and powerful, that simple question.

"I will. At least for now." He decided to leave it at that.

The next morning arrived too soon. The outside was bright but not yet hot. He could not sleep but did not wish to wake. He pretended for as long as he could.

They talked about nothing for a while. Both lying there aggressively avoiding the new day. The thin blankets over the ropes finally made him rise and dress.

"So… How did Lemniscate choose you? I mean, you were the newest member here. Why did he pass up all the others to pick you as his successor?" It was something that had been swirling around in the back of his mind for a while. She was certainly worthy, he would never argue otherwise, but it did seem odd that someone who had been there longer was not given the opportunity.

"Well, he did allow everyone to be considered. There were few takers. You must understand that the well water has a draining effect. And not just energy, but it saps your ambition. The days run together and nothing happens and it just… weighs on you." She got dressed while talking. "So, my being the newest member was actually a benefit. I was still enthralled by his knowledge, by his stories. It was all new to me. The water and its effects, the learning, Lemniscate himself. It was all new and intriguing. So, when the others saw how much I poured myself into being his protégé, saw that they were up against someone who would fight them for the honor, most gave way. There were a couple that hung in there for a little bit, that listened in for a while, but eventually even the stragglers stopped coming around. He had been telling his story to everyone who cared to listen so often that the others had heard much of it before. It did not have the same power that hearing something for the first time has. More than anything, I suppose, was that I came along at the right time. I showed up when he decided he was ready to leave. Call it serendipity or destiny, I know not which, but I grabbed the opportunity with both hands and did not loosen my grip."

"So, what did you learn?"

"Everything. I learned everything." She stopped and looked at him, as if weighing what his real question was. "We only had a couple of cycles. So I only scratched the surface of his knowledge, truly. But he had a way of explaining complicated things simply. I learned more than I had ever thought possible. And, maybe, if you wanted to stay, I could explain everything that I know to you." Her smile was a little shy.

"I would like that. I would. But I am just not sure what the future holds for me. Gunzgak has been quite insistent with my dreams." Croy pinched his temples with one hand spread wide across his forehead. "I am alone amongst my friends. They will not listen to my arguments. They will not hear reason. They are set on destroying everything beautiful in this world."

"Seriously? It cannot be as bad as that."

"Well, I guess I am exaggerating. But everyone seems to be happy with destroying Gunzgak. I cannot get in a word edgewise. It feels like I am barely tolerated by the group. I am an outcast, shunned by anyone who does not wish to listen to me. It's… disheartening."

"So, you are giving up?"

"What? No." He sighed. "I don't know. I don't know!" He rubbed his temples again. "You know a lot, correct? You have sat at the feet of the great Lemniscate and heard his teachings? He who was a Yaven before, who knew Lembin in the Yaven realm? You understand truth?"

"I know what you are going to ask, and I am unable to help you with this."

"No. You don't and you can." He took in a deep breath. "What is it that gives life its authenticity? How can I be who I am— who I used to enjoy being, by the way—and still have the insistent dreams from Gunzgak, and still travel with my friends who disagree with my basic premise of existing? How?"

There was a long pause. Croy took that as a good sign. If she had known he was going to ask that, she would have dismissed him immediately. But she thought about it before responding.

"Are you asking how you can be true to yourself when you are pulled in two opposite directions, by those who you esteem as admirable?" She answered his question with one of her own. He considered that cheating but went along with it.

"No, not really. If I were to weigh the two, Gunzgak would win. They are not comparable in that sense. I do have some concerns about the admirability of Clerin at this point. But if I were not having the dreams, I would have found a way to ignore myself. I could have convinced myself that I was wrong and the others were right. My struggle is that I cannot ignore myself now. I feel that, to keep my decisions authentic to who I think I am, I am at odds with my friends. And there is no way to stop them without committing suicide. So I have nothing to grip on to. I cannot be me, cannot ignore Gunzgak, cannot fight the entire coterie. Does that mean I am inauthentic? How do I… how do I continue?"

Ilana placed a hand on either side of his face and kissed his forehead. She seemed especially dreamlike to him at that moment.

Almost as if he were underwater looking up at her on the bank. She had a beautiful smile.

"Lemniscate did not prepare me for such questions, my love. So, I will just tell you what I think. I think you have several options, that is the good news. You are not going to like any of them, and that is the bad." She pulled back slightly, but her smile was still in place, still looked ethereal. "You can attempt to sabotage your friends. You are correct in that you will most likely get killed. And it would probably not work. But you would die authentically, as you state. You can let Gunzgak know you are unable to keep assisting and ask for the dreams to stop. I doubt that they will. You can let Gunzgak know you are willing to help but unable to actually stop anything from happening. I think that is where you are now, and you state that is untenable. Or, and think about this one, you can let them leave here and stay behind with me. You can try not to drink the well water, but eventually you will get thirsty. But we would be together again. Wouldn't that be lovely?"

"I guess I do have to ask, even though I tried not to earlier. Do you think Gunzgak should live or die?"

"I told you I could not help you with that."

"It could help absolve me of this horrible choice."

"I cannot. The choice is yours, not mine." She looked at him with sad eyes for some time. He refused to respond. Refused to let her off the hook. She took in a breath. "Fine. I cannot tell you what you should do. But I will tell you what I think is going to happen. Gunzgak dies, Croy. Lembin dies. They all die. We all die. This whole world is death. They brought Chaos into themselves. Chaos does not exist without decay. They inserted decay into their being. Not you, not I. They did it to themselves. Will Gunzgak die sooner if you do nothing? Probably. But they created their own hourglass. They are no longer eternal. They gave that up, and it so disturbed them that they created this world. We, their children, were created so they could understand what was going to happen to them. I do believe that."

"How can you say that?"

"The truth is simple. At least, my truth, for me, my understanding and my opinion and my what-have-you, is simple for me to say. That is my authenticity. And if you recall, you asked me for this." Her eyes stayed sad. "If you, to keep authentic with who you are, need to sabotage your friends and risk your life, then do so.

Do it with a smile. But I do hope that you will think of me as a viable alternative."

"This did not make it any easier."

"I knew it would not. I would apologize, but I tried to tell you that at the beginning." Her eye glanced to the slat in the door, as if gauging the amount of sunlight, as if gauging the time. "There is something I must do. Something that you cannot accompany me for. You can stay here or go and out spend some time with your friends. If you feel they are still your friends."

"Yes, they are my friends. Even the ones who are destroying me." He tried to laugh a little, to show it was a joke, but Ilana's eyes narrowed when he said that.

"I would think they are in a similar trap as you are. The illusion that you are able to do as you please is what is destroying you. Your hope that there are more options than what I have listed, that there is some fantastical decision that satisfies your dilemma, is what is destroying you. And them. Do you think Clerin wished for any of this? For that matter, do you think I wished for this?" She waved her hand around the tiny, dilapidated room. "We must make the best with what we have. That is being authentic."

For you, maybe, he found himself thinking. *Complaining about my lot in life is being authentic to myself.* He did not quite believe that. He was not fully a complainer by habit or nature. But he did not like hearing "make the best with what you have." It grated on him. Even if it was sage advice.

"Of course. No one is happy with their lot in life." He did not mean to make it sound as pessimistic and hopeless as it came out. But there it was.

They left the tiny shack and emerged under the blazing sun. The desert was oppressive, and he was unsure if he wanted to live there, amongst the squalor, for the rest of his days, for the rest of eternity. But he would think about it. For Ilana at least.

Croy spotted Knill and decided to do a little prying. He was the last Gaen in the coterie besides Croy. He knew he could not convince Knill to betray Trela, but maybe they could commiserate a little. Ilana and Trela wandered off together, disappearing behind some shacks. He walked up to Knill.

"Hello."

"Hello."

"Would you like to chat?" Croy nodded his head in a random direction. He felt a little odd talking around the others. Or at least, in talking about Gunzgak around the others.

"Sure. Yeah." Knill turned to follow Croy.

They wandered off a little bit. Of course, there was only so far one could wander. Croy had never heard of the shantytown shifting while someone was just outside of its confines, leaving the hapless derlian behind, but everyone was a little nervous about it. The assumed consequences were dire enough that even with a low probability, few would risk it.

"How is Ilana?" Knill got the first question out when they stopped.

"Fine. Fine. Listen, I have a question I wanted to run by you."

"Is this about your doomed quest?" Knill sounded a little exasperated. It took Croy a little aback.

"Well. Yes, I suppose so."

"I agree with you Croy. In principle. But there is nothing to be done about it, not really. This whole… everything. Everything since I have left Serif, since we left Serif, has not wanted my input. I am but a leaf in a river. If you want me to talk to Trela with you, I will. But I've already talked with her alone and she will not be moved. You know how she is once she has made a decision. So, I will not convince her alone. And I will not be able to convince Clerin or Feyazki or anyone else." He had similarly sad eyes as Ilana had earlier. "I'm sorry, I did not allow you to ask what you wanted to ask."

"That's all right. I do not want you to feel sad or annoyed when I walk up to you. You should not have to feel defensive when we talk. I… was not trying to be like that." Like what? He was not sure. Like whatever he was being like.

"It's fine. I think it was just when you pulled me away, it felt like something big and dark, and I don't know." He sighed. "It's just depressing, Croy. It is like being in a prison. No one wants to be reminded where they are, even if it is all around them. Speaking about it just makes it worse. If there is something I can do, let me know. If there is a question I can answer that will help you, then ask. But if you plan to ask me how I feel about letting Trela and the others try to hunt down and kill Gunzgak, then don't. I'm helpless concerning this and I don't like feeling helpless. I don't like being reminded of it. We are on a path, one that could very well lead to all of our destruction, and I know we are doomed. Doomed in success and doomed in failure. And I don't want to think about it. I just want to try to enjoy ourselves for the last of it. The last of us."

"Do you think we will see Tumu again?" Croy decided to completely change the subject. He needed to cleanse his palate.

"Oh, I sure hope so. I miss him. I miss just talking, the three of us. We have been everywhere, you know? We have traveled so far and wide and to so many foreign cities and… whatever this is." His face had broken into a grin. He waved his arm out to indicate the dilapidated gray shacks. His mood noticeably shifted.

"I wonder what he would have made of Lemniscate?" Croy felt his own mood lift with the buoyancy of Knill's infectious one.

"Yes! Though he might not have even been able to stay in the same room as him. Tumu avoided Trela for a while, would not look at her directly, and she was merely the Kriishan. I could not imagine how he would have felt around someone older than our own world."

"I wonder where the Blind One has him. Is he in the Gaen realm, do you think?" Croy was still smiling, but realized his mistake as soon as he said it. He tried to think of a way to salvage it.

"He is probably where you were when you were stolen away. The Blind One imprisoned you in the Gaen realm to study your dreams, didn't he?" Knill was not grinning, but he was still smiling.

"Yes. The Blind One." Even though he had spoken the name earlier, he had not really thought about it. That was one derlian who could help. He worked for the Cabal, he stole Tumu, and Croy himself, he was unfathomable. Croy hated him more than any other derlian he could think of at the moment. But he was the one derlian powerful enough to help. If only Croy could figure out if he wanted to help. "What do you think his game is?"

"Oh, who can say?" Knill shook his head slightly. "He was looking into your dreams, yes? He was there to get Lembin's name, right?" He raised his eyebrows invitingly.

"Maybe the next time we see him, I will have to be nicer to him." Croy laughed.

"As long as he returns Tumu."

"Yes. As long as he returns Tumu, maybe I will be nicer to him."

"Did he ever say why he was looking into your dreams? Did he ever say what it was that he wanted?"

"No. Never. Though, if I am being honest, I am not sure I asked." Croy thought about it for a moment. "I am sure I yelled something at him in anger that may have been construed as a question concerning his motives. But I am not sure if I have really asked."

"You make it sound like you were dangerous."

"Oh, no. Not that I know of. Certainly not where the Blind One is concerned. There is something about the ability to show up out of nowhere that is disconcerting."

"And disappear at any moment."

"Yes, and disappear whenever you tried to counterstrike. Feyazki could kill me. Surely. But he does not unnerve me like the Blind One does."

They both looked around nervously for a moment. Croy did not feel magic being cast or anything, but he felt like he was being watched. It was probably just their conversation. He shivered for a quick moment in the hot desert air.

"Maybe we should stop talking about him." Knill was still smiling but glanced around nervously some more. Croy was not quite sure if he was being serious.

"Good idea."

They headed back to the group. Everyone was standing around chatting. Most were in the shadows of the shacks, keeping the direct sun off them.

The group did not avoid him. Everyone was cordial and chatty. But he felt like others felt nervous around him. That he was an unofficial outcast. It seemed to only be Knill and Haswyxe that emanated happiness when he appeared in front of them. So he let Knill wander off and found Haswyxe. Who was sitting with his back to a shack, chatting with Malghain.

"Tell me why we came to the hottest and most barren spot in all the realms again?" Croy sat down on Haswyxe's free side.

"We are just warriors here; they don't tell us anything." Haswyxe smiled a little lopsidedly.

"I thought we came here so you could visit Ilana." Malghain glanced beyond Haswyxe to look at Croy while he spoke. Checking the reaction, presumably.

"Yeah, right, why are you sitting with us when you could be with her?" Haswyxe gave him a light tap with his left fist.

"She went off with Trela, I think." He nodded in a vague direction.

"No, she's back here somewhere. I saw her a little bit ago." Malghain looked around a little, but Ilana was certainly not to be seen. "Not sure about Trela, however."

If Malghain said he had seen Ilana, then she was no longer with Trela. Croy was amazed at how Malghain always kept track of everyone. Everyone. All the time. Whether they were at peace or at war. Even in the middle of a party, if you wanted to know where someone was, you could typically ask Malghain. Of course, he just admitted to not knowing where his queen was.

"So you really don't know why we are here?" Croy tried once more.

"Really. We just go where the action is." Malghain swept his hand in front of them, taking in the boring landscape.

"Ilana should know. Especially if she was with Trela. Because you know that Trela knows everything, even if it has nothing to do with her." Haswyxe smiled. "But you know what? I try not to know anything."

Croy laughed quickly. The comment took him by surprise. Not that it was not something Haswyxe would say, but just that he had not been expecting it.

"No, really. Knowing things just get you in trouble. It's better to let things wash over you, to deal with what is at hand. That is why I like combat. You just need to concentrate on the moment. Knowing things makes you anticipate things. And you're typically wrong. And when what you anticipate doesn't happen, you get depressed or anxious." Haswyxe nodded seriously.

"Well, maybe that is why you lose to me while we are sparring so often. Anticipation, correct anticipation, is the essence of combat." Malghain squinted over at Haswyxe. Haswyxe cocked his eyebrow in response. "But I know what you mean."

"Maybe combat was not the best analogy. I just meant that expectation will let you down." The eyebrow stayed up.

"Agreed."

There was a long silence while Croy tried to think of what to say. Besides just repeating Malghain's, "agreed." It was a little awkward, which was a little sad. Croy thought about jumping up and yelling to everyone that he no longer cared if they were aiming to kill Gunzgak, just to please stop being awkward. But it probably would not have helped. Maybe he was the one being awkward.

"You're right. I should probably go seek out Ilana. Thanks for the chat." He patted Haswyxe's knee briefly and then stood.

"Anytime."

Croy wandered back to Ilana's shack. It was empty when he opened it, which was fine. He would have enjoyed being with her, of course, but he mostly wanted to be alone. He was feeling frustrated with everything when he tossed himself onto the uncomfortable bed. His mind was spinning, not really fixed on anything, which was typically not any way for him to fall asleep. But he did so quite quickly.

Croy could tell he was dreaming. It happened so fast that he could almost imagine that he was awake, but he was not near a desert. He was not near a forest either, or water, or anything really. There was a dim light, and he was floating. There might have been stone in the distance. Lately, when he had a dream, a true dream, he would be flying somewhere nice, a bunch of cloaked figures would fly near him, he would dive into a cave and meet up with Gunzgak. But no. He was floating lazily, alone, heading nowhere.

He spent some time there, floating in the haze. He looked around a lot. He tried to move, to propel himself somehow. Even tried to flap his arms a little. Tried to run a little. Tried to will himself to move. Then came the thought that maybe he could cast a flight spell in his dream. But he found he could make no noise, no matter how he tried. Being unable to speak, while odd and annoying, somewhat made sense in a dream. But when he clapped, he heard nothing as well. He snapped his fingers next to his ear. Nothing.

Another long time passed. Or at least it felt like a long time. Time passed oddly in his dreams. Sometimes he would have a really long and involved dream while he slept but a short time. It could have also been the fact that nothing was going on. That made time feel like it was going slowly, even while he was awake.

Eventually, though, he heard a rumble in the distance. He waited. It happened again. He tried to yell out, but still could not hear himself. At least he could hear something.

Eventually the rumbling got a little closer. Eventually it became something intelligible. Eventually it became a word. His name.

"Croy." There was a long pause. "Croy."

That went on for some time. With Croy trying to yell and his name slowly and quietly floating past in the haze. He had not been paying attention at first and so had not been counting how many times he heard his name. It was at least sixteen by the time he started counting. Then it changed slightly.

"Croy." A pause. Then, "You."

Those two happened a couple of times together. Then a third word was added. He was unhappy with the third word. It was, "Disappoint." The final word, when finally added, was, "Me."

"Croy... you... disappoint... me." It rang in his head for a while. Repeated much more than it should have been. Croy kept expecting another sentence. Or, at least, another word. But it was just those four, repeated over and over. It did start to speed up, which helped. Eventually it just rumbled along, "Croy, you disappoint me." An actual sentence. An actual sentiment. Not the one he wanted, no. He had enough of that nonsense running through his brain without any outside help.

Croy wanted, more than anything, to be able to yell something. He would have screamed, "Why!" but was unable to. He knew he was disappointing Gunzgak, could have probably guessed that before he fell asleep. He had not really accomplished anything. But what was it in specific that it wanted Croy to do?

He thought back to the last few times that he dreamed. It seemed that Gunzgak was not going to require him to try to kill anyone. Which was great since that was certain suicide. But he was supposed to be a conduit, an open *whisper* channel. He was supposed to allow Gunzgak to know of their plans as they were being made. Croy was trying to do that, he truly was. But it had been difficult of late. That could be the source of disappointment.

Croy thought harder. There had to be something else. During one of the repeated sentences chanting in his brain, it came to him. He thought Gunzgak wanted Lembin to die first. That was the other thing Croy was supposed to bring about. That could certainly be disappointing. But how to bring that about?

They had Lembin's name, and they did not have Gunzgak's. It was that simple. Of course they should kill Lembin first. That made sense. He would just have to think of a way to convince the others.

He did not wake up. Usually, if he could figure out what was being communicated, he would be set free. But he just floated there, lost in the haze, hearing how disappointed Gunzgak was. It was a bit maddening.

So, he put his mind to the only task he had. How could he convince the coterie to kill Lembin first? For a while, nothing came to him. Then, for a little bit, stupid things popped into his head, like trying to convince them that Lembin was going to cheat in the end. He had floated that previously, to no avail. He concentrated harder. It had to be something simple, something logical. Then it came to him.

What if, he thought to himself, *I could convince them that the only way to get Gunzgak's full name was through Lembin? What if I convinced them that Lembin knew Gunzgak's name?* It made sense. It seemed logical that it could be true. He smiled to himself in his dream. *Yes, that's it. If they needed to commune with Lembin to get the name, they could kill it afterwards. Couldn't they? Just how were they going to kill Lembin? For that matter, just how did they think they were going to kill Gunzgak?* It was during that round of thought that he woke.

Croy woke up with his hair plastered to his forehead. He was sweating profusely. The shack was oppressively hot. His muscles felt cramped and sore. It took him a moment to be able to shift himself up from the rope bed.

"Are you all right?" Ilana was across the way, staring worriedly at him. "You have been thrashing around and mumbling. Something about disappointment, I think. It was difficult to tell."

"Yes, I… whew… I do feel a little lightheaded." He sat on the side runner of the bed for a moment, collecting himself. "But I feel good. It was a good nap. I feel better now."

Should he tell Ilana? If he could not trust her, who could he trust? Maybe she would have some good advice. He had finally come to the decision to mention his dream when she interrupted.

"Good. Great. That is great news, Croy." She was smiling oddly at him. "Because I have some news for you. You have a visitor."

He looked around nervously, but there was no one there.

"Not right here. I did not want to spring anything on you. You see… I… I think it's important but am unsure of how you'll like it."

"What? Just tell me who is here."

"The Blind One." Her smile looked a little weak and pained, as if she expected him to start yelling or something. "He's brought Tumu with him." Her smile perked up.

Normally, Croy would have been annoyed. But he kind of wanted to talk with the Blind One. Alone. He needed a powerful ally and had already assumed that the only one he could convince would be the Blind One.

He put on his best grin. It was not that difficult. Obviously, fate, or destiny, or whatever was always helping Trela out, was smiling upon Croy at that moment. It was too much of a coincidence to be anything else. The Blind One here, at the well, while everyone else was there. It boggled the mind.

"Well, send him in. I would enjoy talking with him." His grin stayed in place effortlessly. Maybe something was going to go his way after all.

"Okay, I will tell him you are ready." She nodded deeply, or made a very shallow bow, he was not sure.

It took several minutes before the door opened back up. Croy had taken the time to get himself situated. Mainly to get upright and wipe the sweat from his brow. He did not wish to look like he had just had a nightmare.

The Blind One came in. He walked straight and with purpose. He was quickly followed by Tumu who immediately found a corner to shrink himself into. They both looked at Croy a bit expectantly. Ilana reached in and closed the door behind them all, leaving herself outside.

"Croy, my old friend." The Blind One's smile looked sincere. Which grated on Croy's nerves a bit.

"Tumu, are you all right? Did he hurt you after stealing you away?" Croy turned to the timid Tumu. Tumu, however, just sat there, staring at him.

"You will be able to speak with him after I have left. For as long as you like." The Blind One's smile had faded a little but was still there. "You and I have much to discuss."

"Okay. I agree. But first I have to know whose side you are on." Croy squinted at the Blind One in an attempt to show he meant business. The squint produced no measurable reaction.

"I am on your side, Croy. I always have been."

"No, not like that. Do you want Gunzgak to die?"

"I do not wish any of the Belegs death. Those alive, those dead, and those still in-between." The Blind One nodded.

"So you agree that we, this coterie, should not be attempting to destroy Gunzgak?" Croy ignored the wide response and honed in on the detail that interested him.

"I doubt that this coterie can destroy a Beleg." He gave a small laugh. "Do you really think Clerin is out there slaying Beleg after Beleg? No. She is but an instrument. The Belegs are destroying each other." He held up his hand to ward off Croy's sharp retort. "That does not mean they should be attempting to facilitate these deaths. I am merely pointing out that the war is happening, regardless of what any derlian happens to be doing. We are like insects to the Belegs. We are insignificant."

"Tell that to Linchon." He said it under his breath, but it was obviously audible.

"Listen, I am agreeing that the coterie should not be seeking out the death of Gunzgak. I am also agreeing, even though it is not defensible, that they should be trying to kill Lembin. And my reasoning is that Lembin started all of this. Live by the sword, die by the sword. Is that not some saying of the Pyrans?"

Croy was not sure if that was a real saying, but it sure sounded like them. He was trying to think of a clever response when a slow wave of euphoria washed over him. Though he was happy that the Blind One was on his side, he was not exactly sure why it was such an intense feeling.

"Yes, I think killing Lembin and sparing Gunzgak should be our exact goal." It popped out of his mouth unbidden.

"So, how do you think we kill Lembin?"

"Well, I... I have no idea." He smiled weakly. "I was hoping someone else would come up with the actual plan.

"The real answer is that we cannot, correct? That was what I was alluding to earlier. Clerin did not kill Linchon, Lembin did. Right?"

"Yes. Agreed." Croy's mind raced but could not alight on anything solid.

"Who is the last Beleg that could provide the assassin's dagger for Lembin?"

"The only other Beleg is Gunzgak."

"Exactly, exactly." The Blind One appeared to be peering at Croy through his cataracts. "So, how would we get this blade?"

Before Croy's own mind could follow the Blind One to the obvious conclusion, one that was simply being led to, he felt a sudden wave of loathing wash over him. It was just as intense and sudden as the euphoria earlier. Croy much preferred the euphoria.

"You cannot be serious."

"Correct, there is only one way to get the weapon that kills Lembin. And that is directly from Gunzgak. Someone, I assume Clerin since she has already proven herself to be a quite effective vessel and is probably the only derlian Lembin will let its guard down around, will need to commune with Gunzgak."

"No, never!" Croy did not think the words, they just appeared as they escaped his mouth.

"Croy. Listen. Think it through. Can you think of another way to kill Lembin?" The Blind One's eyebrow arched triumphantly. "If there is any other idea, we can certainly attempt it. But we have very little time and very few options. And, honestly, I am a little concerned that we will tip off Lembin if this is discussed with the rest of the coterie. Especially Clerin. She cannot know."

"Gunzgak will die if Clerin communes with it." Croy felt that to be true. "She holds several blades on her at this very moment."

"Maybe that is the only way to assure Lembin's death?"

"No." There had to be another way. Any other way. They had Lembin's name, after all. They could force it if desired. "Never."

"Well, think about it. Talk it over. I truly believe that is the only way to assure Lembin's death. If, on the other hand, the goal is to keep both Belegs alive, you can probably ignore me."

"I want Gunzgak alive more than anything. I would like Lembin's death. Maybe we compromise and let them both live."

"You will have to convince your friends of that. The last time I spoke with Trela, she seemed to think all of them should die. But who knows, maybe if you never find Gunzgak's name, you will be able to avoid that."

"I worry that they will be difficult to convince, yes. Especially Trela and Feyazki. It seems there is a lust for vengeance once their Beleg had been killed. Even for Belegs that had nothing to do with the assassination."

"I think it is a lust for equality." The Blind One looked thoughtful for a moment. "What if, and I am just throwing out ideas here, what if Gunzgak were to give you the message for Lembin, not

Clerin. Then, what if we could somehow get that message transferred to her from you. Maybe through some Yaven? Not sure, but that would be a way to have Clerin commune with Lembin, but not Gunzgak."

"I do not know if that would work, but... Maybe? Maybe that would be acceptable to everyone? I am a little worried that a Yaven would be unable to transfer the message."

"I as well. It was just a thought." The Blind One rubbed his hands together for a moment. "In any case, I have other messages of my own to distribute. As promised, I will allow you and Tumu to converse together for a while. I will be back later to pick him up. Goodbye, Croy." The Blind One bowed to him, albeit shallowly. "Goodbye, Tumu." He then nodded towards Tumu.

It was silent for some time. Croy had assumed that Tumu would start talking right away, but he did not. Croy also wondered if he should go grab Knill, but he did not.

"Come over here and sit down, Tumu. It has been an incredibly long time since I've seen you." Croy broke the silence first.

Tumu came over and sat down on the ground, not on the bed that Croy had patted with his hand. Rather than argue or have to look down on him, Croy got off the bed and sat on the ground as well. The ground may have even been a little more comfortable.

"You have to tell me everything. How did the Blind One steal you away?"

"He just appeared and grabbed me. Then we both appeared in a cave. The travel was over in an instant. I remember it was cold, damp, and dark. I remember being afraid. I remember feeling alone." Tumu's voice was even more quiet and demure than Croy had remembered it being. And Tumu would not look directly at Croy, but down towards the ground. At least he was facing Croy.

"Wow, that quick. That was similar to when he stole me away. Were you imprisoned?"

"Yes, but maybe not in a prison. It was just a cave that had no entrance or exit. So, I suppose it was technically a prison, but there was no one else there. No guards, no other prisoners. No one to talk to except him. No way to get food or water except through him. It was... disheartening." His brow was knit together in a furrow.

"I bet. My prison had locked doors and guards and everything else. I'll bet you were lonely."

"Yes. Terribly so."

"Tumu, why don't you look at me? We have so much in common, you and me. We were both kidnapped, both imprisoned by the Blind One." Croy felt odd talking without looking into someone's face.

"It is too bright. Everything is too bright." Tumu shook his head, still staring at the ground. "It is as if everything has a huge significance. I am unable to bear it."

"Well, if everything has the same brightness of significance, then nothing is significant, right?"

"Maybe. But it has just started here, at this shantytown. Maybe it is the place itself that is significant. Maybe it is the time. I do not know. But it is almost painful to keep my eyes open."

"If everything is bright, no object more so than the other, than why not look at me?"

"I do not know." He glanced up. Then glanced back down. "Maybe I am just used to speaking with my eyes downcast when things around me are bright." He then closed his eyes and kept them that way. The furrow in his brow lightened up. "How about this? I will keep my eyes closed and not look at anything. That way I will not be specifically not looking at you."

They both laughed for a moment. It was easy. It was nice. It reminded Croy of earlier times.

"So, did the Blind One hurt you as he kept you prisoner?" Croy was not sure why he brought the subject back around. It was more that he could not think of a new one.

"I do not wish to speak of my imprisonment. Nor of yours, no offense. I would like to put that behind me and pretend it did not happen."

"Of course, sorry. What would you like to talk about?"

"I would like to chat with Knill. He always knew what to say to relax others. He was never blindingly bright." A small smile crept onto Tumu's face. "But that will have to wait. I have news for you, Croy. Visions that I had while alone in the cave."

"What were they?" Croy hesitated to ask. They were obviously not great or else Tumu would have brought them up at the beginning.

"There is a road before you that splits into three. One split is short and brutal, ending in desolation. The other leads to a well and happiness. The third is long and winding, and I have difficulty seeing where it stops. Maybe back at the well."

"So you are saying the Blind One is right? I must abandon Gunzgak if I want to be happy? I must stay here and grow ancient. Doing nothing, forever? That is what you are compelled to tell me? That is your great secret, your great prophecy?" Croy grew suddenly angry. He was tired of being told he had no choice in the matter. That he must betray Gunzgak. Everyone said the same thing. Clerin, Trela, Feyazki, Haswyxe, Ilana, the Blind One, and now even Tumu. Defy and die, acquiesce and... what? Not be happy. Not really. How could he be happy betraying his Beleg?

"It is not really a prophecy and certainly not a secret. Everything is going clash. Everything that is left, at least. You just do not want to be in the middle of the clash. Not if I know you at all. Not if you are the same Croy I used to enjoy talking with."

"What about the winding road?" Croy was a little crestfallen. He did not want to argue with Tumu, but he did not want to agree with him either.

"It is difficult to say. It wavers a little. It fades a little. I am not sure if it changes or if my sight of it changes." He paused a moment. "I have to say, however, why risk it?" He looked sincere. Even with his eyes closed.

"Maybe I am unable to admit defeat."

"Are you? I mean, you always seemed pragmatic and easy going. We would typically be in the back of the warpack. You were a great healer, of course. Knill or I could not compare with your contributions. But you never seemed to be a champion of lost causes. You never seemed to charge headlong into the gaping maw of combat. That was more of Trela's style." He chuckled lightly to himself.

Croy did not admit defeat. Could not. Though he was not exactly sure why. Tumu was right about one thing. Croy did not typically enjoy struggle. He did not know why he got his back up about the subject. It was more that everyone kept telling him, "No." That everyone seemed against him, that no one would help him. That was what stuck in his craw the most. More than the reality of what was happening, it was the feeling of being dismissed and abandoned by his friends. He decided it was not worth contemplating anymore. Tumu had said what Tumu had come to say. Probably at the behest of the Blind One, but maybe not. He hoped not.

"Let's go find Knill. He has been hoping to see you again." Croy stood and wiped his hands on his dusty trousers.

"That sounds great. I have been hoping to see him again as well." Tumu opened his eyes as he stood, but kept them downcast. Croy did not mention it.

The last thought of his as they were leaving the tent was that the Blind One had said he would be back to pick up Tumu. Here they were, leaving their post and wandering about without permission. The tiny act of rebellion felt good to Croy.

Did he really want to leave with them? Of course not. There was the anger and frustration. The feeling of being alone in a room full of others. Of being ignored. Did he want to stay with Ilana? Of course. But did he want to stare at the same gray shacks, the same brown sand, the same emotionless faces, for the rest of his life? For the rest of eternity? It was a struggle. One that he could not fully define. It was a life of negatives no matter which road he took. He could escape one to end up in another. There was no real way out.

A small part of him, a tiny ball of angst and anger at his center, wanted to take the short road and be done with it. Maybe he could kill Clerin before anyone could stop him. Either way, he would soon be dead and no longer facing these types of choices. It seemed to him to be the only way out. Of course, that would mean that he would have to murder a friend. And potentially worse, if he were unable to kill himself quickly enough afterwards, he would become Feyazki's pet project of revenge. It might take him a while to die, if he were honest with himself. He had never really seen what Feyazki was capable of, and the thought was more than a little concerning.

A slightly bigger part of him, the squishy organs hidden in his middle, wanted to stay with Ilana and forget everything else. Everything. Else. They would live as one, surrounded by the void. They would be two elemental realms linked. As if the others had never been found.

The largest part, however, was made up of useless indecision. That shell that surrounded everything. This was a choice as well. The choice of choosing nothing, of floating along as he had been. There were two things going for the choice of nothing. For one thing, the future was more cloudy, at least according to Tumu. Maybe he would get lucky. For the other, he would not have to decide anything. He would just have to endure. Endure the others ignoring his wishes. Endure Gunzgak's increasing panic and frustrations. Endure his own disappointment at his inability to make a choice.

Croy knew he would have more aggressive dreams away from the well. He knew he would have to leave Ilana and might not ever find his way back. He knew he would be spending the foreseeable future surrounded by those who mostly tolerated him. But he could not give up and live out his life at the well, wondering what had happened to the others. Because of the others. Nor did he think he would be able to murder Clerin. It was just not in his nature.

So, he chose the nothing choice. Chose to continue on as he was. He had hopes that he would be able to find the well again. There did not seem to be any Tlana left in the desert, nor any Vijen for that matter. They had certainly found the well quickly this last time. And the guardian of the well would certainly want him to find it again. He also had hopes that Gunzgak would find a way out. There was not an easy way to trap Gunzgak. What could derlians really do to a Beleg? They did not even know its full name.

Croy told Ilana. Complete with his reasoning. She argued against it, but not too hard. Not with spite or venom. Mostly with a sad resignation. She said she would wait for him. Forever, if need be. But, of course, she would be at the well forever whether or not he returned.

He told the others of his decision to accompany them, even though he did not believe in their quest. They also tried to talk him out of it, without spite or venom. Clerin, in particular, tried to get him to think of Ilana. To stay at the well. He had a hard time figuring out her prime motivation. He ended up thinking she was a supporter of love and simply felt he should not leave Ilana behind. It felt mostly like the truth, and he preferred thinking that over thinking she just did not want him around, spoiling her quest.

The one who was most difficult to read, however, was the Blind One. Croy had not realized that he was going to accompany the coterie as well. Whether or not Croy came along. Croy still had difficulties figuring out the Blind One's true intentions. He certainly talked like he did not want Gunzgak to die. But he also kept mentioning that the message to kill Lembin with had to come from Gunzgak. Croy understood the logic but not the fatalistic view. He did not think there was no other way. He could not. In fact, that became his reasoning behind taking the long and winding road. To make that an actual choice. He would figure out a way to kill Lembin without communing with Gunzgak. There had to be a way. Even if the Blind One was sure there was not. Even if Ilana could not think of one. Even if Knill and Tumu and Haswyxe thought him mad. He would figure it out. And he would have to do it before they found Gunzgak's name.

Even though the Blind One was to accompany them on their quest, he was not traveling with them. It kind of saddened Croy. He wanted some more time to conspire with the Blind One, whether or not the Blind One wished to conspire with him. The Blind One was the last derlian who gave credence to Croy's arguments. He was also, arguably, one of the more powerful members of the coterie. But they left the well without him. He had given a promise to catch up with them at some point.

They headed through the Northern Desert towards Tureyn. There had been quite an argument about where to head. Many of the party thought heading straight into the Gaen realm was best. To get close to the Gaen Temple. To somehow ambush Gunzgak. Others thought that being as far away from Gunzgak was best, but no one really wanted to visit Chiavel again, so the Luften realm was quickly removed from the list. Some of the warriors wanted to head to the Pyran realm, but that was also nixed fairly quickly. Croy wanted them to head to the Fluen Temple. He figured it would help his arguments if they were already there. Derlians were often lazy when they had no clear option and proximity might help push opinion. So he argued that there was some rumor about Gunzgak's name being in a Fluen cave somewhere. If that was what they needed, if that was what their quest had become, then they needed to go to Tureyn to track down the cave's rumored location. He was not sure if his contribution to the argument is what pushed it to being resolved, but he felt good about the outcome.

They found their way out of the Northern Desert quickly. Less than three days. It was quite amazing, really. It gave Croy hope that he would be able to find Ilana easily again when it was all over. Although a small part of him worried that the Northern Desert was getting smaller with the deaths of the Belegs. A small part of him worried that the well would disappear altogether when the last one fell. Not all of him. Not even most of him. It was a regulatory system placed outside of the Belegs' control, why should it diminish with them? Maybe the size of the Northern Desert fluctuated with the amount of Tlana, and since they had destroyed the Cabal, the Tlana had been greatly reduced. They had not even seen one since the Yaven-infused items were all destroyed. And maybe the well had just been close to the Fluen realm when they left. Through coincidence or a desire to assist.

They were soon out of any remnants of desert. It was hard to tell where the Northern Desert turned into a desert, though much easier on the Fluen side than the Pyran. The Pyran realm was all desert, whereas the Fluen side had some hard scrub outside of the sand dunes, but soon turned lush. They stopped just at the beginning of the change, at a higher elevation where the rivers began, amongst a grove of aspens. Croy enjoyed the shade immensely. It was nice to be out of the sun. Trela was giving them a full day tomorrow to rest before trekking into the Fluen realm.

That night Croy was completely comfortable. The ground was soft where he was, the air was crisp and cool, but not too cold. He had a full belly and empty mind. He fell asleep quickly.

Croy's dream started with flying. He was going quite fast over a flat brown terrain. A desert, most likely, but he was quite far up in the air. He could tell he was wearing robes even without looking, just by the feel of the drag and fluttering in the wind. A robed figure slid into his view on his right. Then one appeared on his left. As he flew along, he gained fellow travelers. He knew this was a bit of a preamble, so just enjoyed the flight.

Suddenly, Croy and his fellow travelers plummeted from the sky. At first, it was not a change in speed so much as in direction. He had been going sideways, then he was heading down. But then he did pick up speed. It felt like he was falling to his death, gaining velocity every second. The wind whipped and grabbed at his clothes. The ground approaching him was certainly a desert floor. He was traveling fast enough when the impact came that he shut his eyes and covered his face with his arms.

It felt a bit like punching through parchment. Except for with his whole body. He slowed after penetrating the ground and his body reoriented to what felt like a standing position. He felt like he was sweating but a touch to his face came up dry.

They had stopped moving downwards and started to slowly float forwards. The cave was quite large and appeared to extend into the rock like a giant hallway. Croy levitated in the middle of that hallway.

The sound was quiet at first, almost like a whispered buzz. It was a repeating noise, somewhat rhythmic. Like a stream far off in the distance. It took a while to become truly audible, to hear it more than feel it. He realized it was coming from his companions. It sounded like a chant, slowly gaining in volume.

As he floated along, it became loud enough to make out the words. Well, the one word, repeated over and over. It sent a chill down Croy's spine.

"Kill, kill, kill." Over and over.

As he floated along, the chanting turned into shouting. Still in rhythm. Still from his companions to his left and right. Still the same chilling word, "Kill."

It seemed like they were floating towards a giant stone statue. Croy recognized it from his previous dreams. It was the image that Gunzgak preferred.

"Kill, kill, kill."

It struck Croy odd that he felt that the statue and hallway were giant. They were giant compared to his own relative size and the size of his robed peers. But what if the hallway and statue were normal sized, and Croy had shrunk down to the size of an insect? The odd and useless musings in his head tried to distract him from the chanting. That seemed impossible to drown out, however.

"Kill, kill, kill!"

The word now resounded in his head, reverberating in his skull. Trapped and malicious, like a badger trying to escape from the bony confines of his head. Ravaging and snarling, scraping and clawing. It tore at his mind to give itself more room.

"Kill, kill, kill!"

It was deafening. It was as if his head was the clapper of a bell, being clanged about incessantly by a lunatic. Still rhythmic, still chanting, just too loud to be endured. Croy tried to scream to drown it out, but he could not hear his own voice. He had his eyes scrunched shut. His fists clenched. His teeth gritted together.

The chanting suddenly stopped. Croy slowly opened his eyes to the giant statue that was Gunzgak. The sound of stone scraping on stone interrupted the silence as the statue opened its arms wide.

"The time is up. We are done with peaceful options. You must kill Clerin, Croy." The mouth did not move, no single feature on the giant stone face moved, but there was a small flicker of light behind the stone eyes that pulsated with the words.

"You said I would not have to. That I was not suited to that task. You said you would get others to do that, and I was to give you information by being near their conversations." Croy's joints felt like his limbs were being pulled on, even though his limbs did not feel anything. It was like the stretching sensation in one's shoulders one gets when hanging for too long. But without the hanging feeling. The sensation was in Croy's shoulders, elbows, hips, and knees, but also in his fingers, toes, and neck. It was disconcerting, to say the least.

"I do not care, Croy. You are not suited for the task, correct. Altinger was, and he failed. Verin was, and she also failed. Now you must try. You are the closest to Clerin. She will not suspect you. She will not shield herself. You must strike while you are alone. You must strike before she notices anything. You must kill with one blow. Do not leave her wounded, understood?"

"You said I just had to get them to kill Lembin first. Is that no longer desired? If I kill Clerin, Lembin will surely live." Croy's limbs were continually being pulled on by something invisible. It went from simply a bizarre sensation, to one that ached. He was concerned it would soon lead to real pain.

"You're hurting me." Croy said it out of desperation. The sensation stopped increasing, but did not cease.

"If Clerin lives, I may die."

"If Lembin lives, it will continue to attack you. Clerin is but a weapon being used. Just because you have ruined a weapon does not mean you are safe. Lembin will forge a new one." Croy did not want to kill Clerin. He kept making his mind up on that. The idea would get shaken, by himself or Gunzgak, but he always came back to the same conclusion. He could not be the one to kill Clerin. She was just too… Clerin. Too nice, too kind, too sweet, too fun, too harmless, too fragile, too innocent. Yes, innocent. Even though she was the being that Gunzgak feared most, she was too innocent for

Croy to muster up enough hatred to kill. This conversation with Gunzgak, this demand from Gunzgak, solidified his knowledge that he could not kill her. He needed to think of a way to deter Gunzgak, to make Gunzgak try another method. It made Croy think of his conversation with the Blind One, for he had tried mightily to shift Croy's mind to killing Lembin as the solution.

"I will never commune with another derlian. I will never let another weapon close to me."

"Then don't commune with Clerin, if it is that simple. Just stay deaf and mute to the world. What is wrong with that?"

"Kill her, Croy."

Croy's joints started separating again. This time there was urgency. This time there was pain.

"What about the Blind One? What about Narst? He would be able to kill her much easier than I." Croy decided to divert the task if he could not divert Gunzgak.

"Narst is difficult. He hides much of the time and I never created the link I have with you, Croy. You may enlist Narst in this endeavor if you think there is trust, but I am unsure exactly which side he is working on. I do not trust him."

"I do not trust him either, but I think he can be persuaded. If I try to kill Clerin alone, I do not think it will work and then you will have lost me as your spy. I am just not that great of an assassin. If I can convince Narst to help, we can accomplish your wish. He can teleport. He has the ultimate element of surprise on his side. Besides, he has killed plenty before. He is a much more accomplished assassin." Did Croy know that the Blind One had killed plenty? No, not really. Not at all. The Blind One certainly had the capabilities, but probably had others do his killing for him. It was the only stalling tactic Croy could think of, however. And the pain subsided instantly.

"You truly believe the odds of accomplishment are increased? You believe Narst will be able to assassinate Clerin?"

"Yes. Truly. He just needs to be convinced."

"I will search for him, yes. If I find him, I will convince him. If you are able to find him far from the well, then do so. The well is difficult for all Belegs. If you find him in Tureyn near Lembin, get him to travel away from there. Nearer to me, nearer to my Temple. At least nearer to the Gaen realm. When you find him, I will know. When you bring him near, I will pounce. I will convince him if you are unable to."

580

"Yes. Certainly."

"Do not warn him of his fate, Croy."

"And if I can convince them to kill Lembin first?" Croy was not sure when he was going to run into the Blind One again and wanted a more immediate goal. If the Blind One did not show up in time, he was fairly sure that Gunzgak would insist on him attacking Clerin. And there would be no more stalling.

"Then do so. I have not figured out a way to attack Lembin yet. It would be quite interesting to examine Clerin and her messages, quite interesting indeed. There are many secrets hidden within her. I cannot risk it, however. I will not. I must do my own research into the matter. So, yes, having the derlians perform that task would be advantageous."

"If we can do that, do I still need to track down Narst?" Croy was still fishing for an out.

"Do not think that Clerin will survive this. She dies or I do, regardless. Even if Lembin dies, she is dangerous."

"But surely you could avoid communing with derlians until after her death."

"What if she bears progeny? What if the messages are passed down?" The statue's eyes glowed brightly for a brief moment. "No, it is too risky. She dies, Croy, with or without your assistance."

"I understand. Truly. I will find Narst. I will get him to a place where you can convince him. And in the meantime, I will try to convince the others to kill Lembin first." Croy nodded. He doubted his abilities to accomplish the tasks, but it was better than murdering Clerin or being pulled apart in his dreams. So he swallowed his doubts and nodded as assuredly as possible.

"Good, Croy, good. I will be watching every moment."

Then Croy started to float backwards. The robed figures to his sides also floated backwards. There was a small quiet chant as he floated away.

"Kill… kill… kill…" It was audible, but not insistent. It was almost soothing when compared to the earlier chant. It repeated itself as he flowed out of the ground and into the sky. It repeated itself as he faded away from his dream back into consciousness. It repeated itself, as barely a whisper, almost unheard, for most of the day.

✳✳✳

When he awoke, it was morning the next day. Croy stretched and scratched his belly, thinking to himself. The dream could have been much, much worse. That was his main conclusion. He knew that he was under constant surveillance. He was not positive, but had to assume his thoughts might even be overheard. He needed to be as blank as possible. And he needed to convince the others to attack Lembin first, without explaining why. And he needed to find the one derlian who could not be found, the Blind One. It was going to be a long day/week/month. Who knew when it would all end? He found himself wishing he had stayed at the well with Ilana—which was apparently as close to a Beleg-free zone as existed—but quickly stashed the thought away. He had decided on the long winding road of his own volition. He had no one to blame besides himself.

At breakfast, Croy found Clerin and Feyazki eating alone. He could not believe his luck. He strode over to them purposefully, allowing them some furtive whispers to themselves before he arrived. They did not get up and walk away. They did not even frown. Clerin smiled warmly as he walked up, and Feyazki nodded towards a spot to sit.

"Does anyone know where the Blind One is?" Croy thought he would start out with the easy one. He pushed his food around his plate, not eating so much as having something to do with his hands. Having something to look at while they stared at him with confused faces.

"He could be anywhere." Clerin was short and to the point.

"You know as well as anyone that no one knows where he is. Or what he is doing. Or, most importantly, why he does anything he does. He appears and disappears according to his own whims." Feyazki put his plate on the log next to him. "I honestly cannot tell half the time if he is going to do something helpful or try to kill me. He is of the most inscrutable mind and morals that I have ever encountered. The very idea that anyone knows where he is at any given moment is so laughable that one has to wonder at the question itself. Why, Croy, would you think we could know where he is?" Feyazki's eyes were narrowed dangerously.

"Just making conversation." Croy began to wonder about his own assumptions of his station in the coterie. Maybe his position was even more precarious than he had thought.

"No, 'How's your day going?' is just making conversation." Feyazki did not let it drop.

"Feyazki, please." Clerin frowned at Feyazki for a moment. Then she turned at Croy and gave him a warm smile. "Did you want him for something specific? Something to ask him? He left Tumu with us. Unharmed, apparently."

"Well, it is just that we had left a conversation half-finished when he left. I just… thought that we could strike it back up. To explore it to its ends." Croy decided to segue into the next topic. He figured that would be distracting. "I am unable to figure it out alone, you see. We were sort of figuring it out together when he just up and left."

"Oh, see, that makes perfect sense." Clerin placed a hand on Feyazki's knee. "What was the conversation? Maybe we could talk it through with you?"

"Well, it was about how to know if we have the weapons for each of the Belegs. He was concerned that we did not have a weapon for Lembin. Nothing specific, at least. I mean, we all assume that to kill Gunzgak we just have to get it to commune with you. That the messages you are currently carrying will attack it without any effort on our part. But what about Lembin? You have communed with Lembin after communing with Linchon and Gorbanax, have you not?"

"Yes and no. I communed with Lembin after Linchon gave me its message, but I had not truly communed with Gorbanax at that time. I have not communed with Lembin since the volcano erupted." Her eyes searched skyward as she thought about the order of things.

"And is Lembin dying? Was it attacked by Linchon's message?" Croy had not fully realized that there was still a message for Lembin. From Gorbanax, just before it died. And Gorbanax knew it was going to die, they were all fairly sure about that. It had merely wanted the Cabal and the Yaven-infused items destroyed before it accepted Lembin's message.

It elated Croy to think of this. If this were true and there was a message in Clerin from Gorbanax that would kill Lembin, then Gunzgak was not required to provide the assassin's blade. That had been the Blind One's entire argument—that Gunzgak had to die first to be assured of Lembin's death. He now wanted to actually be able to talk with the Blind One. Not to just find him to have Gunzgak convince him to kill Clerin, but to actually bring up the argument with him. To see what he would say.

"I do not know. I do not think so, but it was an odd message. It was as if Linchon were there, arguing. Maybe they were fighting, I could not tell. But the streets have been rumbling with small tremblors ever since. At least, I have not heard of them quieting down. We have not been there for some time." Clerin was smiling and nodding, answering Croy's questions as best she could.

"So, even if Linchon was not currently trying to kill Lembin, Gorbanax gave you a message that may kill Lembin?" Feyazki added his own clarifying question.

"Yes. I am almost completely positive that I have been given something by Gorbanax that will kill Lembin."

"Are you completely positive that you have something that will kill Gunzgak?" Croy decided to turn the Blind One's argument against Lembin. "If not, then we should have you commune with Lembin first. That way, we are sure to get a weapon for Gunzgak. Lembin will provide that as it is dying, yes? We already have Lembin's name if it is reticent to commune."

"There is some logic to that. *Are* you sure that you have an assassin's blade for Gunzgak?" Feyazki added to Croy's argument. He could always be counted upon to point out anything logical. It was almost a fault of his.

"I am mostly sure that I have everything we need. Mostly." Her brow furrowed as she concentrated on the past. "I am completely sure that Gorbanax wanted Gunzgak killed before Lembin, however. The order of attack was shown to me clearly."

Croy's heart sank. Feyazki turned towards him and shrugged silently. Feyazki did not really care which Beleg died first. In fact, Croy wondered if he cared much about the entire ordeal. He cared about Clerin, about her safety and happiness, and not much else. At least not where Belegs were concerned. Besides, his Beleg was the first to die, which probably inured him to feelings of compassion for the others.

"Are you sure? I mean, we would not want to summon an unwilling Gunzgak to find out we were unable to attack it. Right?" Croy tried one last time, even though, deep down, he knew it was hopeless.

"I am sure about the order. At least, for Gorbanax's desired order." She looked almost pained to be disappointing Croy, for he was obviously disappointed. "I do not think Gorbanax would have led me astray about that. If I did not already have a weapon that worked on Gunzgak, I feel confident that Gorbanax added one." She nodded seriously to Croy. That was that, as far as she was concerned.

"Ah, of course, well... Still, if anyone hears about the Blind One's whereabouts, I would be interested." It was the least he could do for Gunzgak.

His other dreams on their way to Tureyn were simple. He was flying in a formation of other robed figures. There was a quiet, steady, chant. "Kill... kill... kill..." He always fell asleep immediately and felt fully refreshed in the mornings.

Chapter 20

Before they left the well, Clerin and Vrric met with the Blind One. He was adamant that they meet alone and unseen at the far end of the shantytown. They were inside one of the shacks, one that Ilana had emptied of its denizen. He appeared before them instantly, as was his wont.

"Thank you for meeting with me." He was not whispering by any means, but he was speaking quietly, in secret. "We may not meet again until the end, but I am not positive. Things have been hard to predict lately." He cleared his throat and took a deep breath. "Croy is key in this, absolutely crucial. Whatever Croy believes, Gunzgak will think is true. You must keep him close, but in the dark. He cannot know anything about our plans."

"Does Gunzgak directly experience what Croy senses?" Vrric was looking a little worried, though worried was maybe too strong of a word. Vrric looked concerned to Clerin.

"If it is paying attention and Croy is close enough, then yes." The Blind One smiled ruefully. "And you can bet it is paying attention right now."

"So we have to be careful of being overheard. Even accidentally?" Clerin was typically cognizant of those around her but would sometimes chat in her tent without being aware of who might be outside. Even if they were just innocently walking by.

"Yes, you will need to be extra cautious of your surroundings. Or better yet, just never talk about anything of consequence. Nobody wants to overhear inane gossip." The Blind One laughed.

"How close is 'close enough?' Should we be heading to the Luften realm?" Vrric glanced back and forth between both of them.

"No, no. Head to Tureyn. That will give you two things. One, it will give Croy, and Gunzgak, some hope. Which should distract them considerably. And two, it will allow Lembin to shield you. Once you are close to Tureyn, Gunzgak should have difficulties spying through Croy. How close? I have no idea. So do not ask."

"So, if we are to be spreading false hope, should we pretend to indulge Croy? Should we lie about our goals and agree with how he wishes to complete our quest?" Clerin did not feel completely comfortable about lying to Croy, but more than anything, she just wanted to complete the quest and go home with Vrric. To grow old somewhere, raise some children, live a simple life.

"No. Do not overtly lie, though I am not sure how you will accomplish that. Try not to state anything false. Your goals are known. Your methodology is certainly guessed at, if not outrightly known. You can lie by omission, but you do not wish to call attention to anything we are trying to keep hidden. You can certainly dangle some hope if it fits within the truth."

"And just what are we trying to keep hidden, then? If Croy already knows we are going to try to kill Gunzgak, then what else is there? Do we have an actual plan?" Vrric looked slightly frustrated.

"I do not. Do you?"

"Well, no. We were hoping you would." Clerin tried to smile disarmingly. It was lost on the Blind One.

"I have provided you with Gunzgak's name. I have provided you with the knowledge that Croy is a spy. I will bring you Mika when she is needed." It was the Blind One's turn to appear frustrated. "The actual plan is for you to decide." He paused for a moment. "I do wish that Aedon Dea'sol was still alive. She would have been able to figure something out. She had an exceptional mind." The last sentence was spoken quietly, almost remorsefully. Clerin suddenly had the thought that the Blind One had liked Aedon. It was an odd thought, since she had a hard time thinking that he liked anyone.

"Why are you helping us?" The question came unbidden to Clerin's mouth. "Should you not be helping Gunzgak? Do not get me wrong, I am quite thankful that you are here, on our side. You are incredibly resourceful. But it just seems against the Gaen character. And honestly, I had gotten quite used to the idea that you were out to get us. That you were an enemy of the coterie."

"If Gunzgak knew that I was helping you, it would ruin everything. If the Cabal had known I was helping you, it would have ruined everything. All that I do, for at least half of my adult life, has been done in secret. Secret thoughts, motivations, dealings. There are few who know my true nature." The Blind One was frowning, though at what, Clerin was unsure.

"You did not answer her actual question, however. Let us know this one secret thing. What motivates you to align yourself against your own Beleg?" Vrric raised an eyebrow with his question.

"Why did Gorbanax allow itself to be killed?" The Blind One turned to Clerin.

"It is difficult to say the motivations of the Belegs…"

"Your best guess."

"Well, it may have been tricked. It may have misunderstood the full scope of things." She knew that was not what the Blind One had asked for, however. She knew she was cheating with that answer. And truthfully, she did not think Gorbanax had actually been tricked. It was hard to say why she felt that way, exactly. Something hidden within their conversations. And that was what the Blind One was looking for. "But barring that, my best guess is that it was for the same reason it wants Gunzgak and Lembin to die. For symmetry, for balance. The world with only one or two Belegs would be lopsided. Gorbanax was quite clear about that."

"Good, yes, perfect. That is my reasoning as well. My secret motivation. When I saw what Gunzgak was showing Croy in his dreams, dreams that he said he could not recall even, I understood a great war was happening. It took me some time to comprehend what it was truly about. I did not immediately grasp the death of Belegs, but I knew of a struggle between them. I vowed to stay silent and out of reach until I could better understand what was happening. And when I did, well, I tried to think about it as logically as I could. To look at all aspects of the possibilities. Once that happened, I felt I had no choice. I needed to be the villain so that no one could guess at my reasoning, especially Gunzgak. And it worked, ha!" The Blind One gave a small rueful laugh.

"We know better now." Clerin tried to be comforting.

"Not Croy. Not Gunzgak." He sighed. "No, do not pity me. I have made my choices and stand by them. But you will need to come up with your own plan to trick Gunzgak. If you are having difficulties, might I suggest gaining the aid of another. One with much more wisdom. One who understands Belegs. A Yaven, perhaps."

The idea brightened Clerin. She knew of the perfect Yaven to summon. She had wanted to speak with Wil again for some time. Before she could say anything, however, Vrric interrupted.

"How did you get Ilana to go along with us and betray Croy?" He looked thoughtful with his question, not mean. "I can understand your motivation, which is similar to my own, but what about hers? The simple idea of balance does not make me think she would betray her husband. It just seems like… too much."

"You think spouses cannot disagree?" The Blind One smiled mirthfully.

"Of course they can, but… I mean, it just seems like a complete betrayal." Vrric gathered his thoughts. "She hid Mika from him. From all of us, really. She had some denizens whisk Mika away as she lay dying and give her well water. That was a prepared scheme, a coordinated one. And she lied to him about you, and… I don't know. It seems more like a betrayal than a disagreement." He held out his hands, waving them in front of himself. "Not that I mind. I'm happy she is on our side. I'm happy you're on our side. I just…" He trailed off and just stopped.

"Ilana made her decision long ago. She is of the same mind as Lemniscate was, I can tell you that. Was it he who convinced her? Only she knows. But her willingness to fight for what she believes in is not confused by who she loves. Just imagine: In her mind, it could be Croy who is betraying her." His smile, though it stayed in place, twitched slightly at that. "They are both doing what they believe to be the right thing. How can that be a betrayal?"

"But everyone knows what Croy believes. There is no subterfuge." Clerin weighed in on the argument. Just as quickly, however, she decided to weigh back out. It did not really matter to her why Ilana was doing what she was doing, her strength of convictions, what mattered was that she was helping *them*. The coterie. Clerin decided not to second guess why the fates were smiling upon them. "All I can say is that if you feel so strongly against me that you are willing to betray me, you had better keep lying. Keep me in the dark. For when I find out, I will drown you as assuredly as a leaky dinghy in rough seas." She turned her gaze to Vrric and squinted. Hard. Vrric looked shocked, but the Blind One laughed.

"I would heed her advice, mage." His smile somehow got bigger.

It was odd to see a smile on the Blind One's face, thought Clerin. She liked it. It made him derlian.

"I wish you both all the best. I will be staying here at the well until needed. You will have to signal me once your plan is in motion. Gunzgak will be searching for me, and I must stay hidden." It was not until they were long gone that Clerin wondered how they would signal him. She supposed that would be left to the mages.

✳✳✳

They were able to leave the Northern Desert easily. Clerin could not recall a faster time to escape the dunes. They were soon in the hinterlands of the Fluen realm. Still a long way from Tureyn, but at least they had water and were able to hunt for game. Though Haswyxe was decent with a bow, she missed Escha. Escha could find a deer every day, if need be. Or multiple small animals like rabbits, or marmots, or pheasants. She had been able to feed the whole coterie by herself. Clerin wondered absently if she would ever see Escha again.

Clerin was always cheerful and gregarious around Croy. This came naturally to her; she was typically cheerful. She would feed him whatever information he was looking for, besides their true aims, of course. He spent time with Knill and Tumu, as was typical, but he was not around everyone else as much as he used to be. He stayed in his tent most evenings. It was as if he shunned the camp. Or maybe that he felt they shunned him. Either way, it was a little sad. She certainly disagreed with him about the quest and about her role or choices in it, she obviously had no choice, but it pained her to see him so lonely. But it was also difficult to cajole him into participating.

Clerin spent time with some of the others as well. For a while she would get a member of the coterie alone and ask them about the group's next steps. Many of the warriors just joked and drank. Others would simply turn the tables and ask her what she wanted to do next. She was the one who needed to commune with Gunzgak, they would point out. They were not wrong. Ryshial, however, took the opportunity to examine the puzzle.

"So, what do we have, what do we know?" Ryshial had a twinkle in her eye as she spoke. As if it were an entertaining game. Clerin was a little amazed at how she made something as simple as a thin leather headband look elegant on her face.

"Everything? You want it all?"

"Yes, everything."

"Well, let us see, we have a reluctant Beleg that we need to commune with. We have its full name, its summoning name. We have been told we should summon a Yaven for advice. Also, something about Law wrapped in Chaos, or maybe the other way around. We have the Blind One and Mika hidden away back at the well. They should be helpful when the forced summoning does occur. Though, honestly, I am not sure how helpful anyone can be if a Beleg does not wish to be summoned."

"Nope. No detriments, no issues. Only assets." Ryshial interrupted, but then sat back and waited for Clerin to continue. It was a little disconcerting.

"Uhm. We have messages from several Belegs that should automatically do whatever it is they need to do once communication has been established. So, that is an asset. The last Beleg I spoke with, Gorbanax, told me the preferred communication order. That it should be Gunzgak, then Lembin. I assume I have the correct messages for Lembin…" She trailed off, thinking, but Ryshial's frown brought her back around quickly. She was only supposed to be listing assets.

"We have Croy as a spy for Gunzgak. Which, since we know he is a spy, we can use him to feed Gunzgak whatever information we want. We have all of us, the coterie. We have destroyed the Cabal… I think I am running out of assets." She gave out a small nervous laugh.

"Okay, those are good, those are all good. What are our parameters? What does Gunzgak want, for instance?"

"Not to die, ha!" Clerin could not help herself. Ryshial chuckled politely at the joke, but stayed quiet, staring at her with those large brown eyes. They were oddly engulfing.

"Gunzgak wants us to kill Lembin first. That is what Gunzgak wants." She could not think of anything else. Besides the not dying part, and that had already been glared at.

"Does Gunzgak want you dead?" Ryshial raised an eyebrow.

"Yes, of course. Gunzgak surely sent Altinger and even convinced Verin to attack me. We have been keeping Gaens to a minimum around here."

"Even though Silvadhin died saving you."

"We should not rehash this."

"Of course. I am not trying to rehash anything, certainly not about the attempts on your life. I would, however, like to point out that Croy has not made an attempt, correct? Croy, who is Gunzgak's spy. Who receives dreams sent straight from the Beleg."

"Well, yes. I have always liked Croy. Have always felt safe around him."

"Personally, I would not be alone around him if I were you. But that is your prerogative. I am just checking on what we know about Gunzgak's desires. It does not wish to die. It wants Lembin attacked first. And it wants you dead. Is that all?"

Clerin was going to answer quickly, but then thought about it. Was that all they understood of Gunzgak's desires? She tried hard to think of something else, anything else, but could not.

"So, you have mentioned Gorbanax's desired order of execution. Did it mention that it had given you messages for both the remaining Belegs, or just Gunzgak?"

"I am fairly certain it left messages for both. But no, it did not mention anything in specific. Not that I can recall now. I was under a lot of pain, a lot of duress, at the time. It was quite adamant that all the Belegs should die. I am sure about that." All the talk about the messages within Clerin seemed to awaken them. They were vibrating and jiggling around something fierce.

"Good. That covers Gorbanax's desires then. That all the Belegs should die. What about Linchon?"

"Linchon seemed more preoccupied with Lembin, I believe. But if pressed, I would say that both the dying Belegs want all them to share the same fate."

"Good. Then there is one left. What are Lembin's desires? As best as you can tell."

The question surprised Clerin a little. It should not have. Ryshial had been leading up to it. But she was still not quite ready for it when it came.

"Well, I think, and let me repeat that, I think that Lembin wants all the Belegs to die. Itself included. Whereas I doubt that Gorbanax and Linchon would have had that desire before they were poisoned, I think Lembin has held that desire for a long time."

"So, you think Lembin is suicidal?"

"Yes."

"I have always been interested in these types of musings. Do you think Lembin's suicidal thoughts led to its homicidal thoughts?"

"Well, I... What do you mean?"

"Do you think—I am purely asking for your opinion here— do you think that Lembin felt suicidal, but did not wish to leave the realm with only three Belegs? That the plan to kill the others was hatched within its own self-hatred and selfish desire to not be the only missing Beleg?"

"That is horrible!" The messages vibrated stronger within her. Angrily.

"Of course it is. This is all horrible! We are killing our creators. Or, I should say, *you* are killing our creators. What could be more horrible than that?"

Clerin wanted to change the subject. She was certainly not going to come up with a more horrible scenario to satisfy Ryshial. She cast her mind around but could only think on the most recent words.

"And I do not know if self-hatred is involved. Selfishness, sure."

"How can you be suicidal and not hate yourself?"

"I do not think that all death stems from hate."

"What do you think it stems from then?"

"All sorts of things. Maybe self-loathing?"

"That is pretty close to hate in my opinion."

"I do not think it is. But maybe Lembin got bogged down by the monotony of eternal existence?"

"Is that not why they created this entire realm? Created chaos? Just to remove the monotony of being the only Belegs? How can chaos and monotony be uttered in the same sentence?"

"Maybe it is the chaos that is killing them. Maybe they are already poisoned. Maybe Lembin merely wanted a quicker end."

"You..." Ryshial was about to respond reflexively, but she paused. Her brow furrowed and her eyes became less engulfing. "Why do you want what Lembin did to not be horrible?" Her eyes narrowed ever so slightly. "Is it so that what you are doing will feel less horrible?"

Oh, that angered Clerin. Immediately. She wanted to rage at Ryshial. Reflexively. Why, though? Clerin paused. She paused and she thought. Why did she want to rage at Ryshial? The messages within her were vibrating incessantly. They made her feel nauseas, which did not help her anger. She did her best to stifle her anger, to settle her sick stomach.

"You know I have no choice. Right? You know there is nothing I can do to stop any of this. That I did not want any of this. That I am caught off guard as much as Linchon was. You know all that, right?"

"I do. And for what it is worth, which is not much, I do feel bad for you." Ryshial's brown eyes looked empathetic, like a deer's. "It is all still horrible, however. There is no escaping that."

There was a long pause. Clerin supposed she was to agree with Ryshial. To say how horrible everything was. Or maybe she was supposed to have commiserated or said that she felt bad that Ryshial was trapped in this quest as well, or something. Something unknown. Clerin supposed that she was supposed to do something unknown. But she did not feel like it. She did not feel like doing anything. The pause would have lasted for hours if Ryshial had not broken it.

"So, it appears that we can summon a Yaven, or figure out what misdirection we can feed Gunzgak through Croy. Which would you prefer?" There was a small smile under her empathetic eyes.

"The Yaven. I would prefer to summon a Yaven."

"Good. Me too. How about tomorrow?"

"Yes. Tomorrow sounds much better than today."

Clerin was tired as she wandered back to her and Vrric's tent. It had not been too busy of a day, but it had been draining. When she got back to the tent and complained about it, Vrric just laughed and said, "Yeah, talking with Ryshial can really take it out of you." It was not helpful, but his smiling face helped a certain amount. She slept soundly that night, with nary a dream or disturbance.

The next day was early. They had a good warm breakfast in a group. Everyone chatted openly. It was not overly lively, many bleary eyes were looking around, but there was a close feeling of comradery. Trela knew how to push her coterie.

They traveled the entire day. It was a hard day and by the time they got to their resting place, Clerin did not feel like summoning Wil. Though, honestly, it was not as if it was her energy that was to be expended. She asked Trela for a slow day tomorrow, or at least a slow start, and Trela readily acquiesced. They did not have a true agenda really.

Clerin and Vrric set up their tent amongst some yew trees, a little bit away from the others, but not too far. It was impossible to get too far away from everyone. The trees were lovely, with some red berries visible. Of course, they did not eat anything from the yews, though she had heard parts of the berries were acceptable. She had seen too many livestock get sick to feel comfortable eating anything off a yew, however.

It was a relaxing evening as everyone was told the next day would be spent at camp. Wine was opened and imbibed. Stories were swapped. The fire burned low. Clerin even allowed herself to sleep in.

The next morning was spent in preparation. They had a location that allowed for many derlians to be about. They had most of the mages involved in the summoning. The last successful summoning took Vrric, Ryshial, and the Blind One working together. All very powerful mages in their own right. Clerin had been a little worried about using Croy but had been voted down. It was assumed that it would have been impossible to hide a summoning. Therefore, the omission would have been worse than having Gunzgak know immediately that a Fluen Yaven was going to be traveling with them.

Though the actual spell was being cast by all the mages, Clerin was allowed to be the one to call Wil. It took around ten minutes to get a response. It was exhausting to her—she could only imagine the toll it took on the mages. The previous summoning, there in the caves, had not taken that long. But maybe that Yaven had been at the ready.

They were not at a river or other water source, so watching the geyser erupt from the ground was a bit disorienting. The water quickly formed a rough derlian shape, though the legs were like wide robes, billowing about with flowing rivulets of water. There were actual arms and a head. Clerin had been around Wil enough times that she felt she knew its shape, its countenance, even through the constant motion of the shifting and shimmering "skin."

"Ah, great Communicator, it is a pleasure, though also a shock, to hear you across the Void." Wil bubbled and churned. "It has been quiet, very quiet, in mine own realm. As if we are all holding our breath. Waiting. Waiting."

"We have need of you one last time. One last journey. We head to Tureyn to communicate with Lembin." She wanted to keep Gunzgak out of the conversation until they were alone.

"Excellent. I have desired to commune with Lembin for some time. Though I am unsure if I am invited and do not wish to presume."

"You are certainly our guest. Honestly, however, I am not even sure if we are invited." She laughed briefly. "It is still our aim, and we will argue for your attendance."

"Good. I would be glad of that." Wil paused for a moment, turning its head around at all the derlians around it. The head spun in a full circle checking behind it was well. "But you did not summon me just for my company, did you?"

Clerin did not want to begin the full conversation yet. They were surrounded by everyone. Including Croy. Which meant Gunzgak. She had forgotten how direct Wil could be. Of course, it would be curious as to why it was being summoned. She wished they were at a river so that she could request help with travel, or something mundane. But they were not.

"We are concerned about Lembin. We are concerned it will not grant us audience or may even attempt to stymie our progress. We have summoned you to help us arrive safely in Tureyn." She silently cursed herself for not thinking of something more believable earlier. She mustered a smile. "We may have summoned you a little early in our concern."

"No matter that. I enjoy your realm and your company. I will gladly join up with you and assist in any way, even though we are not encouraged to answer summons at the moment." Wil gave a small bow. "Were you serious then, about asking Lembin to grant me audience?"

"Yes. Of course." Of course, now she would have to remember that when the time came. She could hardly forget while traveling with Wil. "You had mentioned, when we first traveled together, how much you had wanted to communicate with a Beleg. As long as you help us survive the journey, I will do my best to grant your wish."

She was making it sound dangerous. She almost hoped they got attacked on the way there, just to prove herself right.

"Might I ask, what is the reason you are not sure Lembin will grant you audience?"

"She is killing the Belegs and Lembin, though it started it all, may not wish to die due to its own weapon." Croy spoke up out of nowhere.

"You are killing Belegs?" Wil rotated to stare squarely at Clerin.

"I am taking messages to the Belegs for Lembin. Some of the messages may be poisonous." Clerin tried to glare at Croy sideways, but it felt like only a quick squint.

"And Lembin may be poisoned by its own messages?"

"No. Well, not that I know of. But Gorbanax gave me one that I think is tailored to hurt Lembin. And Linchon gave me one that allowed them to communicate. They are, as far as I know, still arguing in the Fluen Temple." She took a deep breath. She had been hoping to explain these things while there was less of an audience. "But the message that Lembin gave me to take to Linchon, back when we first met and you took me to the Luften realm, that message poisoned Linchon. That is how this whole thing got started."

"Then the rumors are true. It is even more auspicious that you have summoned me. My realm, the Fluen Yaven realm, has been abuzz with speculation about the Luftens. So, it is you. You have poisoned Linchon."

"And Gorbanax, though that may have come from, or through, Linchon. They are both in some state of dying. Half the Belegs are currently dying." She was unsure of how to phrase it. It was already out of the bag, so to speak. And it was, as Ryshial put it, all horrible. There was no way to make the idea palatable, especially to a Yaven.

"That is fascinating."

Clerin waited for the rant. Waited to get chastised, to get told how horrible it was, how horrible she was. They were all silent for at least a full minute. All the derlians staring in rapt attention at the Yaven in their midst. Probably all waiting for retribution, or nemesis, or whatever anger-based destruction was about to be wrought on them. Clerin was certainly waiting for it.

"Fascinating?" Clerin asked the word timidly. Merely as a prompt. She almost hoped that Croy would pipe up again, just to break the silence.

"Yes. Fascinating." Wil spun its head around again, presumably looking at all those around him. Clerin did not think it needed to actually do that—surely it could see in all directions—so she was not sure if it was for their benefit. To let them know that it was looking at them all. "There are many who were shocked at how long they had survived amongst all this chaos."

"They are not mourned?" Croy asked this, causing another face to appear on Wil's head. One looking at Clerin, and the other at him.

"I do not know what the other realms are doing. Though, as stated, there are rumors. And Lembin is still alive, so there is nothing to mourn in my realm. But I do take your meaning. It is like this. They are exiled. The Belegs are not allowed back in their home realms. It is known that they would die here. Alone amongst themselves and you. That is accepted by all. Even the Belegs, as far as the Yavens understand. What was not known was how. Many thought the chaos would eat away at them. And maybe it has. Some thought the chaos would drive them mad. And maybe it has. They are killing each other, after all. What could be more mad than that? Others thought other things. There were many theories. All that was known was that they were never to return home. They would have been destroyed by their brethren."

"So, there is no one in their home realms that will mourn their passing?" Croy spoke again. Clerin looked at his face more closely this time. His eyes were wet. Almost as if he were about to cry.

"I am sure there will be some. But in the Fluen realm, for Lembin, there will be very few tears added to the infinite water." Wil made an odd sound, sort of like a staccato bark. *It was trying to laugh,* thought Clerin. *Or maybe that was its laugh.* Or maybe it differentiated a laugh at another's expense with a regular laugh at humor. She could not tell. Though there were certainly many types of derlian laughter as well. "As stated previously, I know not what goes on in the other realms. Maybe Gunzgak will be mourned mightily."

Clerin was unsure if it mentioned Gunzgak merely since Croy was a Gaen. Maybe it sensed something in Croy. Maybe it knew that Gunzgak was using Croy as a spy, watching through his eyes, listening through his ears. She would have to try to remember to ask about that later.

"But Gunzgak is just as exiled as the others, right? None of the Belegs are allowed to return?" Vrric entered into the conversation.

"No. None." A third face appeared on Wil's head to look at Vrric. "The main issue, the true issue, is that they betrayed us Yavens and were exiled for it. If they return to the realms of Law, they will be attacked. That is my understanding."

"So there is no escape." Croy's voice sounded far away and a bit despondent.

"I do not wish them harm. I hold no animosity towards them. In my opinion, they may stay here in this realm for the rest of eternity. But the chaos has gotten to them. Something is happening. Not because of Yavens. But because of themselves. They are turning on themselves. I only say it is 'fascinating' because the rumor has been made true. I now have understanding of a situation that few had even heard about beyond the basest of rumors. When I return home, my knowledge will be sought out." Wil paused for a moment. "I will gladly assist you in any way I can. I am quite pleased that you have chosen me as your companion. I may be the only Yaven who is able to witness what is happening. You have made me unique. This makes me proud. I thank you."

They traveled on horseback for a while. It seemed that Croy was always around. Clerin even found him wandering outside of her tent once. He said he was foraging for berries. She asked if that was a euphemism, but he did not get the hint. She kept her private conversations with Wil to a minimum.

Wil, however, enjoyed publicly speaking with anyone who was around. The last time Wil was with the coterie, it kept to itself much of the time, but this time seemed different. On a random evening, while the entire coterie was noisily enjoying a large fire, Clerin pressed the question.

"When we were hunting the Cabal, you and the other Yavens traveling with us seemed shyer. Speaking with us in smaller groups or as individuals. You seem… more gregarious this time around."

"If one was to know their meal was their last, would they not relish it?" Wil appeared to be completely enjoying itself. For as much as Clerin could tell Yaven emotions. "I am not saying this is my last time in this realm. But it might be. Truly. Things are changing, I can feel it. I wish to memorize every detail of this realm. And I have already seen many of the plants and landscapes available to me. That leaves the most chaotic portion of the realm. You. All of you. You are all so unique and different. Not just from each other, but even from yourselves. You seem to feel time differently than Yavens do. We are who we are regardless of the day, the hour. You can be someone in the morning and someone else at night."

"Hey, we are true to ourselves." Of all the derlians to take umbrage with Wil's description of derlians, it was Jalin who spoke up.

"Yes. In your own way. Please, I meant no offense. It is just that your lives are so short that… No. That is no good either. I mean to say that Yavens are so long lived and stubborn that it is difficult for us to modify ourselves, to change our behavior. You could explain to me a better way to be, and I may even agree to it, but

I am so used to being the way I am, for I have been this way long since before your existence, that it is difficult for me to stay steady on the new path. Yavens have habits that span eons. These things cannot be diverted easily from their path. I meant to say that I admire your ability to constantly evolve. Yes."

Did Clerin believe Wil? Yes, she did not think it was lying. She thought Wil did admire that ability. But did she think that was what Wil had started out meaning with its speech? Would it have ended in that same place if Jalin had not spoken up? She had her doubts. It was a wonderful evening regardless.

Listening to Wil did make her wonder what would happen if Yavens were no longer summoned. What if, after the Belegs disappeared, the derlians and the Yavens just decided to go their separate ways? It saddened her a bit.

"Have you shown everyone your Menel?" She looked at Wil boldly as she asked her question. From her understanding, that was what kept bringing the Yavens back to the derlian realm. That tiny sliver of chaos they could collect.

"No, I do not think I have. Please, gather around. I am quite proud of my Menel." Wil grew a little. Maybe "swelled with pride" would have been a more apt description. It stood straight and made the center of its chest clear. It was like looking at a flowing river that suddenly transformed into a placid lake.

There, in the center of the "window," was the spinning medallion of Wil's Menel. It was thick and impressive. Wil's Menel was the first she had ever seen, and she had only seen one larger. That of Taglo's. But, of course, Taglo had been destroyed in their battle with the Cabal. Everyone oohed and aahed appreciatively at Wil's Menel. Wil swelled a little more.

They reached a stream soon after. They followed that for another day or two until it became more of a tiny river. Wil made itself into a large raft that could twist and turn with the banks. Soon they were on a larger river. Soon they were only having to exit the water at waterfalls and rapids. They made great time.

They did stop at the villages along the riverbank. They would get out of the river before the village came into view, for Wil could sense the derlians ahead. They would mount their horses and stroll into the village, purchasing all manner of supplies. It was not as if they were hiding Wil. Not necessarily. But it felt odd to float by a village, looking like their horses could step over the waves. They did not wish to call undo attention to themselves. At least, not more than a bunch of strangers would typically receive. Which typically depended on the size of the village.

Eventually they could see the walls of Tureyn in the distance. It was fantastic. Clerin could not wait to enjoy the city. The food, the taverns, the beds and tubs. She could not wait to enjoy the largess of the King. She knew she could not commune with Lembin yet. She would have to figure out a way to stall Croy's ambitions. But she was excited to be somewhere comfortable.

The massive gates of Tureyn were open and gleaming. They had gold gilding on them over much of the black iron skeleton, creating flashes of light as your vision moved around them. The tops of the gates looked like waves, eternally poised to crash down. There was plenty of filigree in the form of seashells, starfish, dolphins, and other underwater items. The filigree was tight enough that it was difficult to see the stone walls behind the open gates.

When they got to the gates, they were told to wait. There was a large group of guards at the gate, which was odd since there were typically only four or five at any particular entrance. Many in the coterie began to get nervous. Especially Croy. Soon, however, Clerin's mother came to meet them, Midinarre. She was resplendent in light blue robes. She smiled at Clerin warmly while whispering to the guards. It was not until she approached that Clerin saw the steel in her mother's eyes.

"Come, let us talk away from the others." Her head nodded towards the coterie on her long neck.

"Uhm. Okay."

Did they enter the gates? No. No, they walked along the exterior wall while the coterie stood nervously outside the gates. It was incredibly odd. They walked for quite a while in silence, one that Clerin did not dare broach. When they were far enough away from the guards and the coterie that her mother was satisfied, she stopped. She looked deeply into Clerin's eyes for a long moment, taking both of her hands in her own.

"What are you doing here, child?" There was empathy in her eyes, but the steel was still there.

"We have come to commune with Lembin." Clerin could feel her mother's bony talon-like fingers grip her hands in response.

They were not necessarily there to commune with Lembin. That had not been their goal. They were there to distract Croy. Which was a poor excuse for anything. Clerin was still hoping to figure out how they were going to summon Gunzgak. They had traveled so quickly through the Fluen realm that they had found themselves there, in Tureyn, without much forethought. She just wanted some comfort, some rest. And maybe communing with Lembin would knock something loose. *Maybe Lembin would have an idea of how to trap Gunzgak?* she thought. The more she thought about it, the more it sounded like a good idea. But that was mostly because Clerin did not have any other ideas.

"Whatever are you thinking, silly girl? You cannot commune with Lembin." Her mother scoffed. A bit derisively. It pulled Clerin from her own evolving thoughts. "No, no. You are not allowed near the temple, near the citadel. I am not even sure if they will let you in the city. No, I had to come down here myself just to keep the guards from arresting you."

"What? What do you mean? I have done everything Lembin has ever asked of me." Clerin's mind swam for a moment.

"There are still tremblors within the city, Clerin. These were caused by you, were they not?" Her mother's hands were like vises on her own. "The King is quite upset. It is one thing to visit Vatlisi. The damage you wrecked there was to destroy the Cabal. But it is quite another to cause offense here in Tureyn."

"Well, I… Wait, have you communed with Lembin? Is it Lembin's wish that I do not commune with it?" Clerin narrowed her own eyes at her mother.

"Lembin will not commune with anyone. Ever again. We did not understand what the tremblors were when you last left here. But let me assure you, you have caused quite a stir. The Catajohls have recently rescinded their offer. I am doing damage control here for our family, for your sister."

"Lembin indicated it would commune with me again."

"Why are you so insistent on that, child?" Her mother dropped her hands and rubbed her own face for a moment. "I know what you did. Did you think you would get away with that? Did you think you could bring the ghost of Linchon here and nothing would happen? They are fighting, Clerin. Fighting. Our Beleg is fighting for its life right now, and all you are worried about is if it specifically barred you from communing with it. You are barred! That is what matters. Not who or why."

"It does matter, mother. The King's desires are nothing compared to Lembin's. Nothing! Who do you think I follow? Who did you used to follow?"

"Your father is dead, Clerin. I was Lembin's favorite, but I have not communed with it since you left for Ariellyna. You were a great bargaining chip. I was even going to let you choose who you wanted. Did I get that choice? I would have even let you choose that mongrel if you had truly wanted to. I did want you to be happy. But did you just destroy your own image? Did you only destroy your future? No. When our family, when the Toswin name, was at its weakest, that was when you brought an enemy Beleg to our temple!"

"Mother, I... You have to know that I had no idea I was carrying anything of Linchon..."

"No! No excuses, child." Her mother pointed a bony finger at her. "Lembin cannot be distracted by you, or anyone. Your entire little group over there will be arrested if you step anywhere near the citadel. And you will be killed if you go near the temple. Do you understand?" Her mother's eyes were wet. Whether they held back tears of sadness or tears of rage, Clerin was unsure. "We have to pick up our lives. I have already lost my husband. I have already lost you. Do not make me lose anything else. Understand?"

No. Not really. Clerin was shocked to her core. What she did understand, however, was that her conversation with her mother was over.

"Of course, mother."

"Good. Good." Her mother took a deep breath. "I can see if they will let you stay at an inn at the outskirts of town. No promises."

"No. Thank you, but no. We will find somewhere to stay the night."

"Okay." She suddenly lunged forwards and hugged Clerin tight. "I do love you, you know? I want the best for you. You still have your handsome mage. You will do fine, just fine."

"My mongrel?" Clerin patted her mother's back a little. She was not in the mood for hugging. Not in the mood for forgiveness.

"I just meant that he came from nothing." She leaned back and held Clerin's shoulders, looking into her face. It appeared that she had been crying. "I do want you to be happy. You should go and be happy."

"Yes, I should go." There were so many things she wanted to say to her mother in that moment. The vast majority of them were rude. But not all. Later in her life she would look back at that moment and wish she had said something nice before leaving. Hindsight sure is cruel.

The coterie wandered off, away from the town, away from the amenities. They got out of direct vision from the towers before stopping to set up camp. Clerin explained that she was not allowed in the city, due to concerns about communing with Lembin. Croy did not take it incredibly well, vacillating between "I told you this would happen," to "We have to find a way to sneak you in there." He was right in a way. On both points.

It was decided that many of the coterie could slip in at another gate. It was Clerin they were looking for, mostly. Certainly Feyazki or Trela would be noticed. The Pyrans could have an issue as well. But Lophina and Haswyxe were probably fine, and they could take Croy with them. Which was what Clerin mainly wanted. Some time away from Croy, where they could speak freely without being concerned that he was lurking around. So she took Lophina aside and explained what she needed. They convinced Croy that they would be investigating a way to sneak Clerin in. A way to get to the citadel, the temple, to Lembin. Croy happily agreed.

Darkness arrived quickly. They ate a cold dinner, not wishing to call any attention to themselves. Clerin was chatting with Trela and Ryshial, venting about Croy mostly, when Vrric came trotting back up from their tent.

"We, ah, need to talk." He looked at Clerin and then nodded back towards the tent.

"Really? You two do not need to speak in code." Trela was grinning slightly, so it was difficult to say if she was annoyed.

"Really? Were we not going to use this time to converse with Wil? Who knows how long Croy will be gone for." Ryshial did look annoyed.

"It's not… Argh, fine, everyone can come." Vrric shook his head slightly.

"I'm flattered, but…" Trela was trying to make a joke, but realized everyone was getting up to head to the tent.

When Clerin peeked inside the tent, she realized what the issue was. It was the Blind One. And he had Mika with him.

"Come on out, there are too many of us for the tent." Clerin sighed inwardly. They were no closer to accomplishing anything, which was surely why the Blind One was there—to hurry them along. "Do not worry, Croy is not around."

"Of course not. That is why we are here." The Blind One and Mika left the tent. "I sensed that he was in Tureyn while you were here. I assume you wish to parley."

"Mika! How are you away from the well?" Trela clasped hands with Mika heartily.

"I have a vial of well water. Probably about a week's worth. He assures me that we will not be gone that long." Mika jerked her thumb towards the Blind One.

"No. We cannot." The Blind One scowled at her, though the scowl quickly faded. "We only have so much time. So... What have you learned." He turned back to Clerin.

"Nothing. Now, before you interrupt me, let me say we have been hounded by Croy constantly. It has been difficult to find time to speak to each other without being overheard." Clerin glanced around, but no one added anything in her defense.

"Then fly away somewhere. Or, if it cannot be helped, be overheard. We have no time. It is worse to have no plan than to have Gunzgak know of it." The scowl came back.

"We were going to speak with our Yaven tonight, Wil." Ryshial spoke up from behind Clerin. "Croy has been quite persistent. Clerin was finally able to convince him to separate from us. To infiltrate Tureyn and find a way to get Clerin to Lembin."

"So you were kept from Tureyn? I wondered what had happened."

"Yes. The guards would not let us pass the gates. My mother came out to explain how I have been banished from Tureyn. From communing with Lembin, in specific."

"Oh, that is interesting. Do we know if that order comes directly from Lembin? Maybe Gunzgak is right, maybe Lembin is trying to become the only Beleg."

"We can enter the Fluen Temple from the sea. Lembin cannot lock us out." At first, Clerin was unsure where the voice was coming from even though she recognized it. Then she noticed Wil, only the size of a large fist, come out of the tent and stop before them.

"I bow before your excellence." The Blind One bowed to Wil. "We have much to discuss."

"So, if you feel we can get Clerin to Lembin even if it does not wish to commune, then we can stay focused on the order that Gorbanax desires. First Gunzgak, then Lembin." Trela had a hand resting lightly on her short sword hilt. Not out of any aggression or annoyance, but just for comfort.

"Except we do not have a plan for that. At least we know what to do with Lembin." Vrric glanced between them all. "Maybe we do the simplest first?"

"No. We go in Gorbanax's order."

"What did you mention the other day? Before we had summoned Wil?" Ryshial turned her attention to Clerin, who had to turn to face her. "When we were listing our assets."

"I am not sure. We were just listing things." Clerin recalled many items but was unsure of what Ryshial was specifically thinking about. "Do you want to try listing them again?"

"It was..." Ryshial snapped her fingers a couple of times, thinking. "Something about wrapping Law with Chaos."

"Oh, yeah. I did hear that..." Clerin was trying to think of where she had heard it, and what exactly she had heard, when her thoughts were interrupted.

"I know what that is." Wil, still tiny, spoke up.

"What?" Several of them said the same word at the same time.

"I know what that is." Wil repeated itself, with the exact same intonation. But then it continued. "A great friend of mine has been collecting Chaos in the Fluen realm."

"No! That cannot be." The Blind One looked almost outraged. "You do mean the Fluen Yaven realm, do you not?"

"Yes. I have sensed it myself. My friend was quite pleased with itself. You see, my friend never made a Menel. It only brought water back to the Fluen realm, protected within itself. There, in the middle of my friend's abode, in the middle Law, there swirls an orb filled with water of your realm." Wil paused for a moment. Though it was too tiny to see expression, it seemed to be remembering something pleasant. "Oh, how it swirled."

"I cannot believe it." The Blind One was still skeptical.

Clerin herself was skeptical. It seemed to break every Yaven law. Every law of Law. It boggled her mind that such a thing could exist, even though she had never experienced the Yaven realms, even though it was pure water surrounded by pure water. She agreed it did not make sense. However, she knew that Wil would not lie about something like that. Or at least she thought she knew that. Did she really know what Wil was capable of? What any Yaven was capable of? Wil was the Yaven she had spoken the most with, spent the most time with. They had plenty of conversations all alone, just killing time, chatting as friends. No, no matter how crazy it sounded, she trusted Wil implicitly. If Wil stated it had a friend who had an orb of Chaotic water swirling around in the Yaven Fluen realm, then she believed it.

"Belief has very little to do with truth, derlian." Wil answered the Blind One. Clerin did not completely agree with that statement, but she let it slide.

"I still do not understand how that will help." Vrric spoke before she was able to. "Assuming it exists." He was smiling wide, indicating he was chiding the Blind One, not Wil.

"Nor I. I just know of its existence." Wil responded into the silence. There was another gap of silence before Ryshial spoke up.

"What if we summoned Gunzgak in the orb? It would be in Chaos, right? Magic could occur there. Then, if it escaped, it would be in the Fluen Yaven realm, not in our world, where its powers are boundless."

"How are its powers diminished in the Yaven realm? Is it not just as powerful?" Trela was looking at Ryshial thoughtfully, not argumentatively.

"Well, no, it has created this world. Its powers are much greater here." Clerin added her thoughts to the discussion.

"We could have the orb surrounded by some vengeful Fluen Yavens. That would slow it down, at the least." Wil sounded a little gleeful at that.

"Wait, our issue is not just whether or not Clerin's messages will kill Gunzgak, it is not just about escaping, but how do we summon Gunzgak at all. The Cabal is gone. How do we force a Beleg to do anything it does not wish to do?" Mika spoke quietly. To be honest, Clerin had almost forgotten Mika was there.

"We make it think it is a showdown. A final battle with Lembin. Winner survives alone." Ryshial smiled to herself. "Gunzgak understands we will not kill Lembin first, no matter Croy's current investigations. It understands we will not stop. I will bet that, faced with no other alternatives, it will accept a direct challenge. It will come prepared to destroy Lembin. It will be armed for the wrong conflict."

Everyone smiled, but no one spoke. It sounded decent. But would it work? There was no way to tell. At that point, however, they had no other ideas. Even something that sounds ridiculous will be examined in the absence of more viable options.

"Just to be sure, to be positive, you know you can get Clerin to Lembin afterwards. Right? After Gunzgak, you will make sure Clerin communes with Lembin. You will make sure Gorbanax's message is received." Trela looked down at Wil, somewhat aggressively. Her hand was clutching the hilt of her short sword a little tightly. "You promise you did not come up with this scheme to backstab us."

"I did not come up with this scheme." Wil paused for the briefest of moments. "But I do take your point. I promise I can get Clerin to Lembin afterwards. I promise I have no plans to betray you. I promise that I will assist in killing the last two Belegs." Wil grew to derlian height as it spoke. It bowed to Trela when it was done. Then it bowed to Clerin.

"That had better be true, Yaven." The Blind One was staring emptily at Wil. "That had better be true."

Mika was nodding along with the Blind One. Clerin wondered briefly how closely the Blind One had worked with the Cabal. She wondered how high up in the echelon Mika had truly been. Would it be enough? Enough to summon a reluctant, even if tricked, Gunzgak? Enough to punish Wil if it were to betray them at the last moment? Clerin did not believe Wil was planning on betraying them, but if it was, she would probably be the first to die. So, wondering if Wil would be punished afterwards was a bit moot if she was unable to be around to enjoy it.

"Then we should figure out what to say to Croy to convince Gunzgak." Ryshial looked at Clerin, then Vrric. "And you will have to prepare your friend for our visit." She smiled at Wil.

Croy returned around noon the next day. The Blind One and Mika were hidden far away. Clerin did not know where they teleported to, nor did she want to. They had not even mentioned to the rest of the coterie about the meeting that had occurred. The less who knew, the better.

Croy was despondent. Lophina and Haswyxe agreed that there was no way to reach the temple without going through the entire city's worth of guards, but they appeared less affected by the realization. Clerin was just happy Croy had not found some crazy way in.

They sat around eating lunch, discussing the impossibility of entering the citadel. It was decided that Clerin and Trela would talk with Croy. To plant the idea of the new plan. Clerin because she could be thought of as speaking for Lembin and Trela because she was considered more neutral and had to be there for the debriefing anyway. Haswyxe and Lophina were also there, as part of the debriefing. Croy had just finished explaining how they had been stymied in their research at every turn.

"So, you don't think there's a way in. Not without the guards noticing." Trela was nodding to Croy. Agreeing with his assessment, in a way.

"No. Nothing. Not unless there is a hidden entrance from the sea." He looked up at Clerin at that, with the tiniest amount of hope behind his eyes.

"Not that I have ever heard of. Every time I have communed with Lembin, I have entered through the citadel. Through gates and hordes of guards." She thought for a moment. Part of her wanted to warn Croy of using Wil to investigate the sea route. That if Lembin were to sense Wil, anything that might be open would surely be immediately secured. Instead, she chose not to mention Wil at all. It was best not to spark hope. And she would have an immediate response if he brought it up.

"Then I don't know what to do now." He stared at the ground in front of him again. "The Beleg we have a name for, the one we know we can kill, is impossible to get to. It seems we are stuck."

Clerin wondered at his despondency. She was sure he was sad they could not easily get to Lembin, but if it meant that both lived, would he be happy? Would Gunzgak be happy with two Belegs left?

"Well, you are correct, we have Lembin's name. And we know that Gorbanax has a message meant for Lembin alone. What if we tried to summon it against its will?" Trela brought the subject up that Croy had left lying in between them.

"The Cabal is dead. And even if they were alive, even if we had access to their secrets, would they be powerful enough to summon a Beleg that did not wish to be summoned? Could any amount of derlians summon a Beleg against its will?" Clerin set up the next stage of the argument.

"Well, I... I suppose you're right. It just seems we are so close." Croy sighed audibly.

"Wait. What if... What if we convinced Lembin it was for a fight. A fight between the Belegs. A fight to end the chase, the arguments. I mean, if Gunzgak were to kill Lembin, it would be safe, wouldn't it? It could just hide until we all died of old age." Trela's brow was knitted in wonderment.

"Wait, what? I thought you wanted Gunzgak to die." Croy's head snapped up.

"I did. I do. But I want Lembin to die as well. I want them all to die, Croy. They need to share Gorbanax's fate!" Trela looked annoyed as she stared straight into Croy's face. "But we need to end this. I would rather kill one than none. What is our other plan? We could always try to kill Gunzgak afterwards. Besides, I am quite fond of single combat."

"What if Lembin kills Gunzgak?" Croy looked intrigued. Almost unnaturally so.

"Well, they will both have to know about it. To allow themselves to be summoned. So, Gunzgak would not have an advantage." Trela kept her puzzled appearance.

"Wait, I know. What if... What if Clerin were there, at the fight? We know that Gorbanax has a message to kill Lembin within her, right? We know she carries an assassin's dagger within her specifically for Lembin." Croy looked positively excited. "Do we know for sure that she has one for Gunzgak?" He looked directly at her with wide eyes. "Do you know?"

"Well, I... I am not sure. I have the original message from Lembin. And I was given messages from Linchon for Lembin and, maybe, Gorbanax. There was some vagueness there. When I returned to Lembin, Linchon appeared and began to fight, or argue, or something, with Lembin. That is why there are tremblors. That is why my mother forbade me to enter the temple, to even enter the city. Lembin is quite weakened from Linchon, as far as I understand." Clerin kept a carefully studious look on her own face. They had already discussed that she thought Gorbanax had given her a weapon against Gunzgak—she did everything in her power not to think about it.

"But Gorbanax died, right? There was a message for Gorbanax in there somewhere." Croy still looked excited, but had his head cast a little to the side, showing a little wariness.

"Yes. But Gorbanax accepted it. Gorbanax merely wanted the Cabal destroyed first." Clerin nodded to Croy.

"Yes. Gorbanax accepted it. And Gorbanax gave you a message specifically for Lembin. And Linchon is fighting Lembin." Croy was almost talking to himself, his eyes were still wide, but they were directed back at the ground. "And if not single combat, with Clerin nearby, who may have messages for both of them, if not single combat, you still only have one name."

They had discussed this possibility. Clerin lamented that they had not already told Croy they had both names. She thought it would raise his suspicion, having that knowledge withheld from him. Besides, the names were not enough. It did not matter that they had the names if the Belegs were truly against being summoned. Or, at least, that was their current thinking. That was still their last resort.

"No. We have both names." Trela stared hard at Croy, waiting for him to raise his head again.

"Where? When?" His head slowly rose. "I thought we only had Lembin's."

"We did. But when Clerin's mother barred her from entering Tureyn, she also gave her Gunzgak's summoning name." Trela told the lie smoothly and forcefully. So much so that Clerin almost believed it. "The Fluens want Gunzgak to die, not Lembin."

That had not been discussed. Clerin thought Trela was going to say that the Blind One had given it to them, that had been the plan. Clerin turned her head to stare at the ground, as Croy had for half of their conversation. It took all her energy to keep her face passive.

"Why did you not mention this?" Croy looked at her, wide-eyed.

"You left so quickly to Tureyn and, well… it felt like a betrayal. I did not know how to mention it." It was the best she could come up with.

"It was a betrayal. The Fluens and their betrayals. So, if there is no single combat, things are even. Static. No one has the upper hand. But there are inherent advantages with combat." Croy looked directly at Clerin and took a deep breath. "Okay. Okay, single combat it is. With Clerin and I in the arena."

"No. Not you. Lembin will not come if there is a Gaen. Only Fluens." She said it resolutely. She could not have Croy there. There was no telling what Croy would do. He might even try to kill her.

"Fine. Fine, only Clerin. Clerin and her various assassin's blades." Croy looked truly wild.

They spent another day, preparing. Clerin told Croy she was using Lembin's name to communicate from a distance. Trying to convince Lembin to come to the meeting. The day felt exceptionally long to her. Throughout it she had to keep reminding herself it was not to be her last. But the seconds dragged, colors seemed brighter, food tasted amazing. It was as if her body was worried about the future and wanted to savor what was left. She started to wonder what she was trying to convince herself of.

They all went to bed. They waited. They needed Croy to be asleep, to not provide any foreshadowing or alarm. There was always the risk that Croy being asleep would be alarm enough, or that Croy would be woken and ordered to search the camp. But they did not want him to notice that Clerin would be with Wil, that the Blind One and Mika would be there as well. Vrric and Ryshial would be continuously casting a summoning spell for Wil, so that it could return at any time. Trela, Knill, the warriors, everyone else, were to keep Croy busy if they had to.

While they were lying in the darkness, Vrric gave his last-ditch effort. He wanted to accompany her. Badly. He had argued quite vociferously concerning it earlier. Now, in hushed tones, he was just as passionate.

"Who will protect you? Do you think the Blind One would lay down his life for you?"

"We have discussed this, darling. No one can protect me like you could—and no one would. But this is against a Beleg we are talking about. It is not a question of your honor or willingness or anything. It is a question of what skills are truly required. What can you cast against a Beleg?" She leaned over and kissed his forehead lightly. "Besides, what everyone will want is that, once this is done, that I can still get to Lembin. Everyone, including the Blind One and even Gunzgak, will want that. That is my protection. What protection would you have if you accompanied me? Of what concern is your life to Gunzgak?"

"Do you think the Blind One does not have a plan to escape?" He meant it that the Blind One obviously had a plan to escape, Clerin was sure. The Blind One always escaped somehow.

Clerin, however, knew that she had no understanding of the Blind One's motives and probably never would. The times she thought he was betraying them, those truly awful times, he turned out to be helpful. In the long run. But that was because there were so many times when his behavior was… She was not sure. Was he awful? Was he a betrayer? His personality was such that she found it easy to hate him. Sometimes even just talking with him. But they would not be here without him. And that was something great. Was he suicidal? Did he have a plan to escape? Was he willing to lay down his life for the cause? She had no idea. None. Yet, she also felt she did not have to understand to be able to trust. She did not feel as if she were walking into a trap. Not one of the Blind One's making, at least.

"Whether or not the Blind One has an escape plan does not concern me. I doubt his plan includes saving you. That is what concerns me, my love." She rolled onto her back, looking up at the dark tent canvas. "This fight is my destiny, not yours."

"Now you just sound like Trela." He laughed. She laughed. There was a long pause. "I won't end up like Knill, will I?"

"No, of course not." The question took Clerin by surprise. Before she could think on it, however, he spoke again.

"Good. Because that derlian is doomed."

Vrric rolled onto his side. Clerin laid there, staring at the dark tent. They were quiet but awake for another half-hour or so. It was hard to say in the dark.

They got up and flew over to meet with the Blind One and Mika. Vrric was quiet, but did not seem to be pouting or despondent. Clerin had a hard time thinking of anything to say as well. Everything seemed trite, to lighten the mood, or it seemed too heavy and emotional. There was no middle ground.

Wil was already there, with the others. It was giant, like an enormous pool. Clerin felt incredibly nervous. She did not know if what was about to happen would work. If it even could work. Her stomach knotted up a little. Maybe her body knew something that she did not. Maybe her body was prepared for the worst. Her mind was surely not.

"Ready?" It was the Blind One. He was grinning. As if this experiment were the highlight of his life.

"Yes." Mika nodded.

Clerin, unable to speak, also nodded. There was nothing else to do.

"Surtecfluclo!" Vrric cast a waterbreathing spell on them.

Though she did not hear it, the Blind One then teleported them. Into the orb of Chaos that was held in the middle of Wil. It was like swimming in the sea. In the depths, far from the surface. They were surrounded by water; their whole world was water. And it seemed to be vast. Though she did not feel brave enough to swim far.

Clerin could not feel any motion. She assumed they were traveling. Had assumed she would be able to feel it. To notice it. But they were just floating around, staring at each other. They could probably talk, but Clerin still did not know what to say.

Then there was something. Not the feeling of movement really, but the feeling of stretching. If felt like she was being pulled from both ends. It felt like she was elongating. Not that her joints were being pulled apart, it was not painful, but as if she were being drawn out, like a wire.

"Eqetecfluclo!" The Blind One cast a waterbreathing spell while they were in motion, breaking the silence. "No one is sure magic can cross the Void." He smiled and nodded in defense of himself.

"So why did we have Feyazki cast one as well?" Mika glanced over at him. It was odd to hear her so clearly, with her hair floating around in the water.

"He wanted to help, did he not? Sometimes someone must be given something to do, to help ease their worry. Besides, one can never have too many waterbreathing spells on one when traveling to the Fluen realm, now can one?" He smiled affectionately.

They continued in silence for a while. After some time, it was impossible to state how long, the stretching feeling stopped. After some more time, they heard the voice of Wil. It appeared to echo around them, it was impossible to state where it really came from.

"We are ready to begin. Cast the spell."

The Blind One and Mika were sitting cross-legged. They both had their eyes closed. They both appeared to be concentrating. Clerin merely stood there and, somewhat unconsciously, held her breath.

"Eqesidgearc!" It was spoken by both of them, in synchronization. "Gunzgakaphunchistiolanwendug!" There was a pause. "Eqesidgearc! Gunzgakaphunchistiolanwendug! Eqesidgearc! Gunzgakaphunchistiolanwendug!"

Then the most incredible sound flowed through Clerin. She was not even sure if she heard it, but she most certainly felt it. It was like a pure vibration. It set every finite part of her quivering along with it. She harmonized to it.

"What is this? More Fluen betrayal?" The voice vibrated with the same frequency that quivered through Clerin. "It does not matter that we are under water. I am a Beleg, fools. I *am* water." There was they tiniest of pauses. "Where is Lembin? Why are you all here? No matter, time to die, derlians."

"Kill me?" Mika opened her eyes and spoke, though she was still in a sitting position. "You're eternal, but not immortal. I'm immortal, but not eternal. How long do you think the well water will last in here?"

A sphere of water engulfed Mika. It appeared denser than the water around surrounding everything, but she was still visible in its center. It looked to be crushing her. Her body writhed and contorted, being pushed down into a ball. Was she dead? Was she actually immortal? Clerin could not tell.

"You cannot kill Clerin! You must give her your message to Lembin. Only she can make sure this all ends how you need it to." The Blind One stood tall as he floated there, looking confidently defiant.

"Betrayers!" A sphere of water engulfed the Blind One.

Clerin suddenly realized the folly of their plan. No, not the folly, but the pure stupidity. *Only a derlian could think of something this stupid*, she thought. *Only a derlian could think they could fight a Beleg.* Where were her messages? Did she not have messages to give to Gunzgak? She squinted and willed them to escape from her, to attack Gunzgak, to do something. Everything was happening so fast. She felt something tear from her but had no idea what.

"Betrayers!"

The orb shattered. Or something shattered. Or Gunzgak escaped the orb. Or the orb escaped Gunzgak. Clerin was instantly "swallowed" by Wil. Or was she still in the orb? The feeling of being surrounded by water, the feeling of being stretched, all occurred again. She held her breath and thought as hard as she could to Wil for it to travel quickly. The water felt different around her. It felt different on her skin. She was terrified to breathe now that the Blind One was dead. Did magic work like that? She was not even sure if it should have worked within the orb. Better to hold her breath and urge Wil on.

Then they were floating. She was floating in Wil, who was floating in the sea. Which was floating within the derlian realm. Wil opened up its surface and she felt the sun on her face and breathed deeply. It was glorious.

"The Fluen Yavens will have killed Gunzgak by now, if your messages did not. I should have stayed to make sure but needed to rescue you. Gunzgak had destroyed the orb and I had to react quickly. We had not anticipated that quick of a reaction. The thought was that Gunzgak would give you a message for Lembin."

"How… how many Yavens?" She was going to ask a different question. How had she survived, how had Wil engulfed her, how had they escaped? But it was easier to ask something simple.

"A hundred. I wanted no chances taken." They were quiet for a while. "We must finish this."

"What?"

"Lembin. We are near the temple. We must finish this. Then we may rest."

"Yes. Sure. Of course." Clerin felt tired. Which was odd, since she had done very little. "Let me… Let me check if Vrric's spell is still working." In her state, she had forgotten to state his name as Feyazki.

She plunged her head into the Clatsvol Sea and breathed in a little. Then breathed in deep. The spell was still working. Or had started working again once they had reentered the derlian realm. Clerin was not sure. Nor did she care. It would probably have taken half a day to get ahold of Vrric and have him recast something. Not something impossible, but Wil was correct, they needed to finish it before resting. Clerin disrobed as they traveled, not that she felt she had to. She was certainly not able to steep in her herbs. She had certainly not disrobed while meeting Gunzgak. It was more out of habit than anything else, really.

Wil flowed into the temple. There were no bars, no guards, nothing. It was completely open at the sea, though there seemed to be an underwater cavern that Wil was following, somewhat confining their path. She wondered if anyone had tried to get to the temple from underwater before, but then wondered why they would or how they would even know it was linked to the sea if they had not visited from the citadel side.

Pillars appeared in the distance. She could see two of them, and once she got close enough, she could see the bizarre archaic writing etched all over them. Then the old underwater well came into view. Then her father. Leaning nonchalantly against the stones that surrounded the well's open mouth. She knew it was not really her father, he was long dead, but the guise that Linchon took for her. She wondered briefly if Linchon appeared in that form when she was not around, when it was just Linchon and Lembin. She could not imagine why it would.

Once she got to the well, she could see the other two pillars on the opposite side. There was an eerie greenish glow that illuminated the area. Clerin was ejected from Wil and stood firmly grounded on the inundated flagstone floor. She did not experience the weightlessness of floating. The Fluen Temple was becoming almost familiar to her. All the things that had made it odd and otherworldly the first time she visited, now gave her a feeling of comfort.

"My little derling, you have finally arrived." He smiled. A tremblor flowed throughout the underwater cave. The shaking ground shook the water oddly. If she had not had her feet on the flagstone, she may have thought it was merely eddies within the water. "We have been waiting for you. Me, happily. Others, maybe not so much." His smile got wider.

Then a great voice boomed. Lembin did not normally speak with her, not in words. But these were as clear as day.

"I wished to speak first. I wished to commune. You come in with only murder on your mind." It had a similar vibrating boom as Gunzgak's voice had.

Clerin felt a message, Gorbanax's message she assumed, leave her midsection. It shot out like an arrow. It felt like she was being stabbed from the inside. She screamed. Oh, how she screamed.

The ground buckled violently, tossing her aside. The flagstones began to split and fissure. The pillars began to buckle. Large chunks of stone began to spall off and careen towards the ground. Wil encapsulated her once more. The entire Temple seemed to be collapsing around them. She screamed the entire time. The last thing she saw as she passed out in agonizing pain was the image of her father jumping down into the well. It was the end of the beginning.

Chapter 21 - Epilogue

After Wil returned Clerin to her friends, it decided to return to the Yaven realm. For good. It was done traveling between worlds. It had experienced enough Chaos for one existence.

Wil returned to the Yaven realm easily. There was no cargo. It was not running from anything. There was nothing tugging on it, prodding it, pushing it. It could just float across the Void at a leisurely pace. There were no time demands placed upon Wil by any other being. It was fantastic. Wil had experienced enough imposed time constraints for one existence.

Immediately after arriving, Wil traveled to visit Gluf, its friend. Gluf had provided the orb. Gluf had gathered the vengeful Fluens to attack Gunzgak. Wil had to make sure that Gluf was not harmed during that fight. Wil had not thought Gunzgak would destroy the orb. It probably did so in an attempt to escape, Wil was not sure.

When Wil arrived at Gluf's home, it paused in awe as it often did. Wil watched the spinning spirals, swirling whirlpools, graceful wavelike curls, and the multitude of splashing sprays that encompassed the front façade. Wil watched the rhythms play along the edges, the perimeters, and how those rhythms juxtaposed with those in the central areas. It was a complicated symphony of sights.

After an appropriate period of appreciation, Wil flowed through the simple maze to get to the foyer. There, waiting, was Gluf. Wil was overjoyed. It had not thought Gluf would have perished or been damaged by the raging Gunzgak, but it had not been positive.

"My joy at sensing you is boundless." Wil sent a prehensile tentacle out towards Gluf. Gluf wrapped that with one of its own. Then another and another. While they greeted each other in the foyer an interminable amount of time passed.

"Did any perish?" Wil eventually struck the conversation back up.

"Yes. A tenth. I was not prepared for that amount of struggle, though it should have been anticipated. It was, however, resolved quickly, as far as these things are measured." They stayed in the foyer, semi-entwined.

"And the orb? I assumed it was destroyed. I immediately engulfed the derlian and left the realm."

"Yes. Destroyed. Once the perimeter was modified too much, it instantly ruptured. The Chaos within it disintegrated. We were suddenly fighting with Gunzgak."

"Was there any stone that left the orb? Anything beyond the disintegrating Chaotic water?"

"No. Nothing. Nothing that was sensed." Gluf paused for a moment. "Why do you ask?"

"Gunzgak was constituted of so many elements. My curiosity stems from what might have remained."

"Ah. That does make sense." Gluf paused again, thinking for a moment. "There was absolutely nothing once the orb ruptured. Maybe we will communicate with the others who were there, to see if anyone witnessed any such an aberration."

"No. Or, not now. I assume it would have been mentioned if it had been sensed. Right now, I would rather spend my time with only you."

"I would enjoy that. Very much."

They stayed that way, in Gluf's foyer, intertwined, for a long, long time. They did not communicate with words or thoughts, merely touch and feelings. Wil found it very enjoyable.

It took Trela quite some time to return to her own realm. They could have gone through the Gaen realm, where a dead Beleg probably cursed them, or they could go through the Luften realm, where Chiavel was probably nursing a grudge. She was not overly concerned that Gunzgak itself would be able to damage them, for it was the only Beleg she was completely sure was completely destroyed. But she was concerned that the Gaens they would meet along the way might wish to do them harm. She chose the Luften realm, assuming that Chiavel had more important matters to attend to and, just maybe, he would be glad that they had ended all of the Belegs. Especially since his was the first to be poisoned. Of course, that assumed he had heard of that accomplishment. He was a king, after all, but some royalty paid more attention to foreign realms than others.

Trela did avoid all the large Luften towns, especially Ariellyna, and met no organized resistance. In fact, no resistance at all. No recognition. Either Chiavel did not care about Vanelia's escape, or he did not blame the Pyran warriors, or he had no idea they were traveling back through his realm. In any case, Trela was grateful that the journey, though long and somewhat arduous, was fairly uneventful.

When she finally arrived at Agoge, the fanfare was fantastic. She had been a little concerned she had been away so long that her subjects would have forgotten her or deemed Lishean to be their rightful ruler. The ones who greeted her along the way, and as she marched along the Dekhan Plateau, and especially the ones at the gates of Agoge, all seemed ecstatic at her return. She would have to check to see if Lishean had arranged the throngs or if they had gathered organically.

Lishean himself was quite happy to see her. He was sick of pretending to be a ruler and wanted to retire somewhere. He did not even want to stay on as part of the Royal Guard, even in just an honorary role. She gave him as much coin as he would accept and let him and Elzie ride off to some hamlet. She had really wanted him to stay, if for no other reason than to heap her gratitude upon him. He swore up and down that he had not arranged her subjects' enthusiastic response at her return.

Trela doled out as many favors as she could. She made Ryshial the guildmaster of the Mages' Guild. This was not only as a reward for Ryshial's incredible service, but it was a little selfish as well—she had complete trust in Ryshial. She would need that trust as she tried mightily to increase the guild's importance. If there was one thing she had learned during her travels, it was the importance of skilled mages.

In that same vein, Trela made Jalin her spymaster. That was a new title for a new guild. Trela trusted her subjects implicitly. She even trusted her advisors. Mostly. But she wanted to be able to keep an eye open and an ear to the ground. Jalin could do that with the nonchalant ease she did most everything.

Serghno and Arnasta were handfasted within a moon of their return. The festivities melded from those centered on the coterie's return, to a fortuitously timed planting festival, to their handfasting. It was as if the whole gigantic town of Agoge showed up. It was certainly the largest handfasting ceremony Trela had ever attended.

Rewista was elevated to leader of the Royal Guard. Trela wanted a true general, one with a mind for strategy, in that post. Dartsyle was in the running for the position, but he had wanted to train recruits. The physical exertion let him forget Yarsurle until, eventually, he ended up finding a husband for himself.

That left Trela with a struggle. She had been with Knill for so long that she could not imagine another. But Estfale had long been in love with her, and she enjoyed his company greatly. He became her most trusted advisor. Trela never did handfast, but her life between Knill and Estfale will have to be told at another time.

Croy was crushed by the events and fell to despondency and periodic melancholy. He felt abandoned by those he used to call his friends. He had been offered many places to go afterwards but could not imagine himself comfortable anywhere. Not even back at Serif. No, his only home had to be with Ilana.

Croy left for the well with Haswyxe, who promised to protect him until they found it. The journey was long, but they found the well soon after entering the Northern Desert. There were no tricks of the sun, no difficulties.

Haswyxe left soon after they arrived. He could not stand the gloom that surrounded the shantytown. He became a traveling warrior, spending his time in the various realms, staying in no particular place for too long.

It took Croy some time before he drank the well water. He eventually had to, as food and water were in such small quantities in the middle of the Northern Desert. He did not enjoy the gloom of the shantytown either, especially since it compounded his own gray mood that settled on him after he had failed Gunzgak. Ilana, however, was great. She taught him much about almost anything, almost everything. And what she did not know, they researched together. As much as they were able in a bookless shantytown.

Once Croy had joined their ranks, the denizens opened up to him. They still seemed to shuffle and walk with their heads down, but they all had amazing stories. Almost all should have died before he had been born. The collective knowledge in the shantytown was quite amazing.

When Clerin was brought back, Vrric was overjoyed. They could not live in Tureyn, nor in Ariellyna, but they were together. They had thought about going back to Vatlisi. They had plenty of friends there and Clerin felt that Inquella would offer them protection, but Vrric did not want to risk it. Not at first, at least. While they were deciding where to go, they visited Scout Mountain near Clerin's family home and camped for a week. It was beautiful and simple.

They decided to live at a tiny hamlet by the name of Ushwinsa on the western edge of the Fluen realm. Far enough north of the Eidyon Peninsula that it was not too cold and close enough to the Luften realm that they could visit if they chose. They never did.

Malghain went with them for a while but was too restless to stay in the hamlet for long. He decided to return to Ariellyna, to hopefully get hired by Chiavel. Vrric was concerned for him, of course, but he had made up his mind. Besides, Chiavel would have to have been a moron not to utilize Malghain's impressive skills. And for all of Chiavel's faults, being a moron was not one of them.

Lophina traveled with them for a while as well. She lasted longer than Malghain, but eventually became restless in Ushwinsa as well. She decided to go back to Vatlisi. Clerin and Vrric visited her periodically. Which meant they visited Escha and Torpalin, Vanelia and Hynara as well. It was always great fun to visit.

They got handfasted in a tiny ceremony. Vrric had a small, but highly regarded, school for young mages. He never charged for tutelage, but those with means were expected to donate to the school. Clerin became pregnant soon after their handfasting. They ended up having two daughters and a son. All were fantastic mages.

Clerin visited the sea often. She would stare off at the waves, if she was not swimming, and reminisce. She hoped to see Wil popping up out of the water, but that never happened. And she thought about Lembin as well. She never did decide on whether or not Lembin wished to die, there at the end. But, she supposed, not knowing did not really matter. What mattered were her children and her husband. She no longer cared about the world beyond them.

Appendix A (Races)

The general race descriptions given below are not absolute and are by no means considered exhaustive. Though rare, there are certainly blond Luftens and tall Gaens. Personality traits are even harder to pin exclusively to one race or another. These generalities are merely provided to assist in getting an overall flavor of the various derlian denizens of the world.

Race: Gaen
Element: Stone
Beleg: Gunzgak

The shortest of the races, the Gaens live in underground cave complexes and against rocky hillsides. They are simple and civilized, enjoying order and structure throughout their lives. They are skeptics and jinxers in general, and therefore are typically the weakest mages of all the races. Their hair is typically quite curly with mostly brown and red coloring. They are stocky bordering on pudgy. They love beer and are excellent miners, and colloquially refer to their coined money as "pebbles." They have a strict caste system based upon vocation. The last name of a Gaen consists of two syllables, the first denoting their rank and the second their guild:

Sie – Peasant	Tin – Farmer
Beo – Apprentice	Lak – Merchant
Ona – Member	Cha – Blacksmith
Mur – Overseer	Wir – Carpenter
Fyr – Teacher	Tul – Stoneworker
Cru – Guild Leader	Sol – Artist
Dea – Asembly Member	Rem - Physician
Ata – Assembly Leader	Jin – Warrior

Vyx – the Guild Lord

Race: Fluen
Element: Water
Beleg: Lembin

The blond, ship-building Fluens live around the Clatsvol Sea. Each royal family can trace their lineage back to the original Yaven they sprang from. Their family name carries much weight and responsibility. Bastards are shunned. They are strict adherents to tradition and even call their coined money "crowns" in deference to the monarchy. They are generally tall and thin, with long, straight hair to match. They are great cultivators of wine and masters of all manners of fishing. Magic is a skill much used in the Fluen realm by beggar and prince alike, though maybe not quite as specialized as in the Luften realm.

Race: Luften
Element: Air
Beleg: Linchon

There are two types of Luftens: those who live high in the cities amongst the helioarc trees, and those who shuffle along the ground. This demarcation means more than a family name or a chosen vocation, though those things may dictate where a Luften lives. They are somewhat thin with curly and mostly black hair, though there are also some browns. They are the tallest of the races, but are thicker than the Fluens, making for a more symmetric form. They harvest honey and ferment a deliciously sweet mead. They excel in woodcraft and magic. They are undoubtedly the most focused and engaged of the races when it comes to magic, as it is one of the most powerful guilds in the Luften society. There is a shaky monarchy, bound by a council of Branches, that has gone through so many kings of late that they have taken to referring to their coined money as "heads". There are both family Branches and guild Branches that make up the general council, balancing traditional aristocracy with meritocracy. In theory, at least.

Race: Pyran
Element: Fire
Beleg: Gorbanax

Pyrans are a nomadic race ruled by a caste of warriors. They are short and muscular and many of them travel in warpacks, fighting with each other and living off the land, sending what additional coins they can back to their families. The fighting is considered an art form, with warpacks growing and shrinking more from trading warriors than from actual death. A warpack is typically broken up into smaller units, a cohort having approximately forty warriors and a maniple comprised of two to four cohorts. They generally have straight, light brown hair. They drink grog by the barrelful, and there are more herders than there are farmers, though there are plenty of both. The king or queen rules with complete power, beholden to none. They have mages but they study, almost exclusively, destruction or healing magics.

Appendix B (Magic)

Magic is the art of sifting through Chaos to find a desired possibility, then willing that possibility into reality. A spell is comprised of one word, typically with four syllables: Power, Sphere, Element and Effect. This word defines the desired possibility in its simplest terms. The difficulty of the spell is estimated by adding the ranks of the syllables and then multiplying them by the Power's Multiplier. There are Majora syllables, those that are taught, and there are Minora syllables, those that are individually learned. The Majora syllables are listed below, separated into the four Pillars:

Power	Multiplier	Sphere	Rank	Element	Rank	Effect	Rank
Lo	3	Kin	2	Luf	2	Pri	1
Nu	5	Fin	2	Ge	1	Arc	2
Mek	8	De	3	Pi	3	Del	2
Nar	11	Tra	1	Flu	2	Sfe	3
Eqe	15	Tec	2	Der	3	Clo	3
Lum	19	Li	3	Hep	1	To	1
Sur	23	Sid	1	Pan	1	Kha	1
Tor	27	Mor	1	Tot	2	Ref	0

POWER:

Power designates a spell's effectiveness and duration. These are intertwined. A mage may make a spell shorter to increase its effectiveness, or they may decrease the effectiveness to increase the duration. This is known as "tilting the pillar." This list is simple since the Syllable is mainly defined by its Multiplier.

Lo:
Glyph: ●
Multiplier: 3

Nu: ● ●
Glyph:
Multiplier: 5

Mek:
Glyph: ● ● ●
Multiplier: 8

Nar:

Glyph:

Multiplier: 11

Eqe:

Glyph:

Multiplier: 15

Lum:

Glyph:

Multiplier: 19

Sur:

Glyph:

Multiplier: 23

Tor:

Glyph:

Multiplier: 27

SPHERE:

Sphere designates a spell's action, its sphere of influence. The following descriptions are from Elange's book, *Principles of Grey Magic*.

Kin: Sphere of movement. This Syllable brings your Mind to the Realm of Movement. This Sphere is dependent upon the Element to be moved. This Syllable may be used with any Effect of the Caster's choosing. Movement is defined as changing an object's location through adjacent space over a period of time, meaning the object must move through all intervening space between locations and must take a certain amount of time to do so. Objects cannot be made to disappear and reappear, nor can they be moved through solid objects.

Glyph:

Rank: 2

Fin: Sphere of the Mind. This Syllable brings your Mind to Itself and to Others. This Sphere is Elementally limited for Majora use. The vast main Element to be used is Tot, though Pan occasionally and Der rarely may also be used. This Syllable may be used with any Effect of the Caster's choosing. The Mind is defined as all mental activities including thought, analytics and perception. This Syllable may not be used to affect anything tangible.

Glyph:

Rank: 2

De: Sphere of destruction. This Syllable brings your Mind to the Path of Death, Damage, and Destruction. This Sphere is Polymorphic, but most often paired with Pi. This Syllable may be used with any Effect of the Caster's choosing. Destruction is defined by causing injury to the living and demolishing the inanimate. The type of injury depends upon the Element and Power level, up to and including Death.

Glyph:

Rank: 3

Tra: Sphere of transmutation. This Syllable brings your Mind to essence modifier of Transmutation. This Sphere is dependent upon the Elements to be transmuted. This Syllable may only be used with the Effect of Ref. This Sphere is used to create the only typical five Syllable Majora Words. Transmutation is defined as changing one Element into another. This Syllable may not affect shape, but may affect density and thereby mass.

Glyph:

Rank: 1

Tec: Sphere of protection. This Syllable brings your Mind to the Path of Protection. This Sphere is Polymorphic, so most Mages use lower ranking Elements in the Word. This Syllable may be used with any Effect of the Caster's choosing. Protection is defined as the stopping of physical harm/damage from immediately happening. This Syllable may not be used to Ameliorate or Heal.

Glyph:

Rank: 2

Li: Sphere of healing. This Syllable brings your Mind to the Way of Healing. This Sphere only affects living beings and is therefore Elementally limited for Majora use. The vast main Element to be used is Der, though Pan occasionally and Tot rarely may also be used. This Syllable may be used with any Effect of the Caster's choosing. Healing is defined as the temporary Amelioration of damaged tissue. Temporary Amelioration may close wounds, bind bones, reconnect severed arteries, numb pain, and even cure some diseases, but the spell will always wear off. Only time-based cellular reconstruction has long lasting effects on the derlian body, making this Sphere act more as a time accelerant than true Healing.

Glyph:

Rank: 3

Sid: Sphere of communication. This Syllable brings your Mind to the way of Communing with Spirits. This Sphere may not be used to commune with a living derlian and is rarely used with the syllables Hep or Pan. This Syllable may be used with any Effect of the Caster's choosing. Communing is defined as transferring thoughts with Spirits. This Syllable is used to summon Yavens and commune with the dead.

Glyph:

Rank: 1

Morf: Sphere of change. This Syllable brings your Mind to the way of Changing Shapes. This Sphere is dependent upon the Element to be modified. This Syllable may be used with any Effect of the Caster's choosing. Change, in this instance, is defined as modifying a purely physical form. This Syllable may not be used to change Elements or the Essence of the object.

Glyph:

Rank: 1

<u>ELEMENT</u>:
Element designates what type of object the spell is acting upon. Its basic constituents, its Essence. Due to the amount of different types of objects in the realms, some of these elemental categories are quite broad, though the first four come directly from the Yaven realms and are, therefore, specifically defined. These definitions are considered intuitive.

Luf: The element of Air.

Glyph:
Rank: 2

Ge: The element of Stone.

Glyph:
Rank: 1

Pi: The element of Fire.

Glyph:
Rank: 3

Flu: The element of Water.

Glyph:
Rank: 2

Der: The element of derlians, of flesh.

Glyph: 
Rank: 3

Hep: The element of metals, salts, and crystals.

Glyph:
Rank: 1

Pan: The element of nature: plants, animals and wood.

Glyph:
Rank: 1

Tot: The element of the mind.

Glyph:
Rank: 2

<u>EFFECT</u>:
Effect designates the target of the spell, the aim. This Pillar is highly affected by the Power level of the spell. The shapes of these Effects are intuitive and so are defined simply, below.

Pri: The target of yourself.

Glyph:
Rank: 1

Arc: A target in a line of sight.

Glyph:
Rank: 2

Del: The target of a sphere at a later time.

Glyph:

Rank: 2

Sfe: The target of a sphere centered around the caster.

Glyph:

Rank: 3

Clo: The target of a cube placed at the caster's choosing.

Glyph:

Rank: 3

To: The target of your direct contact.

Glyph:

Rank: 1

Kha: The targets are random living objects.

Glyph:

Rank: 1

Ref: The target refers back to itself.

Glyph:

Rank: 0

Appendix C (Map)

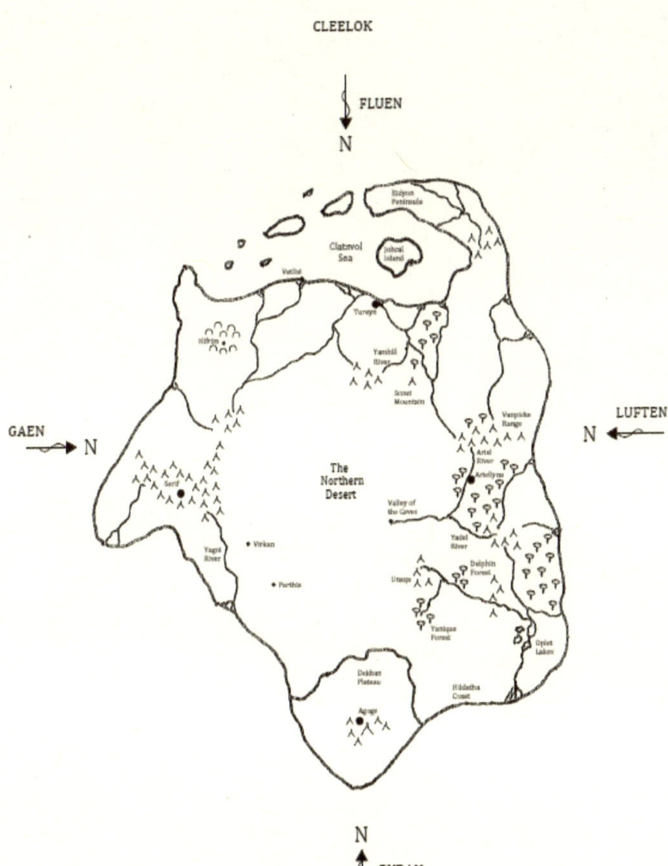